This book may be kept

FOURTEEN DAYS

A fine of TWO CENTS will be charged for each day
the book is kept over time.

Feb 19 '51			
Mar 5 '51			
Mar 20 '51			
Dec 10 '51			
Feb 1 '52			
Jun 18 '53			
Jun 30 '53			
Dec 9 '54 pd.			
Dec 12 '55			
Apr 26 '58			
Nov 19 '59			
Dec 8 '59			
Dec 6 '81			

The Rains Came

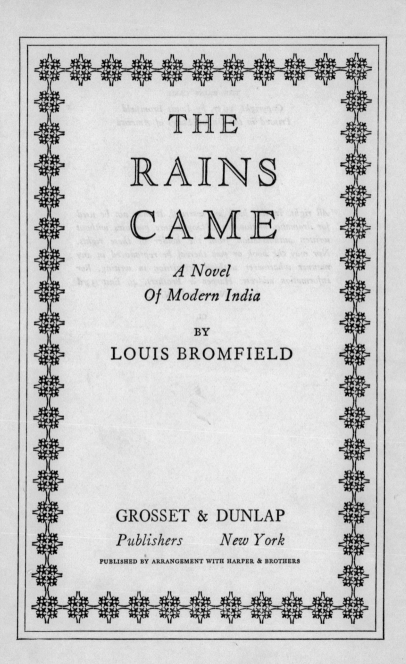

THE RAINS CAME

A Novel
Of Modern India

BY

LOUIS BROMFIELD

GROSSET & DUNLAP
Publishers *New York*

PUBLISHED BY ARRANGEMENT WITH HARPER & BROTHERS

THE RAINS CAME

For all my Indian friends—
the princes, the teachers, the politicians, the
hunters, the boatmen, the sweepers, and for
G. H. but for whom I should never have known
the wonder and beauty of India nor understood
the Indian dream.

Two men sat in a bar. One said to the other, "Do you like Americans?" and the second man answered vigorously, "No."

"Do you like Frenchmen?" asked the first.

"No," came the answer with equal vigor.

"Englishmen?"

"No."

"Russians?"

"No."

"Germans?"

"No."

There was a pause and the first man, raising his glass, asked, "Well, who do you like?"

Without hesitation the second man answered, "I like my friends."

For this story the author is indebted to his friend Erich Maria Remarque.

Part I

Part I

Between two worlds, one dead
One powerless to be born

—MATTHEW ARNOLD

IT was the hour of the day that Ransome loved best and he sat on the verandah now, drinking brandy and watching the golden light flood all the banyan trees and the yellow-gray house and the scarlet creeper for one brilliant moment before the sun, with a sudden plunge, dropped below the horizon and left the whole countryside in darkness. It was a magical business which for his northern blood, accustomed to long still blue twilights of Northern England, never lost its strangeness——as if suddenly the whole world stood still for a second and then slipped swiftly into an abyss of darkness. For Ransome there was always a shadow of primitive terror in the Indian sunset.

And here in Ranchipur there were other things besides the beauty of the golden light. It was the hour when the air grew still and laden with a heavy scent compounded of the smoke of burning wood and cow dung and of jasmine and marigold and the yellow dust raised by the cattle being driven home from the burnt pasture of the race course on the opposite side of the road, the hour too when distantly one heard the faint thumping of the drums from the burning ghats down by the river beyond the Maharajah's zoological gardens, when the screaming of the jackals began as they crept to the edge of the jungle waiting for the sudden darkness to bring to their cowardly yellow bodies the courage to start out and seek on the plains what had died during the day. At dawn the greedy vultures would succeed them, coming out of caverns and dung-covered thorn trees, for the beasts which had died during the night. And always at this hour too came the fine thread of sound from John the Baptist's flute, as he squatted at the gate welcoming the cool of the evening.

John the Baptist sat there now, under the vast greedy banyan which each year sent down branches that bit into the earth, struck root and claimed another square yard or two of garden. Up north, near Peshawar, there was an enormous banyan tree which covered acres, a whole forest which was at the same time a single living tree. "If the world went on long enough," thought Ransome, "that tree might take possession of all of it, like the evil and stupidity of man—slowly, relentlessly, thrusting down branch after branch with all the greediness and tough vigor of life in India."

Even the jackals and the vultures had to be out early to fall upon the dead, upon man and donkey, sacred cow and pariah dog alike, if they were to survive. If you rose early in the morning to ride out of the city into the open country you would see here and there, over the whole brown plain, small writhing quarreling black masses of life devouring the dead. They were vultures. If you set out even half an hour later they would be gone and in their places you would find only little piles of white bones picked clean, all that was left of a cow or a donkey or sometimes of a man.

Beyond the maze of his lazy thought he listened to John the Baptist's simple melody. It was an improvisation which went on endlessly, and to Ransome's Western ear it was always the same. So far as he could discover it was the sole means of release for John's soul—the music and the arranging of the marigolds and the blue lilies which were all that was left of the garden so late in the year. John had no girl, or if he had one he saw her in secret dubious ways. His whole life was his master's life— his master's tea when he wakened, his master's breakfast, luncheon and dinner, his master's shirts and socks, his jodhpurs and his shorts, his brandy and his cigars. He was a Christian boy, a Catholic from Pondicherry who spoke French more easily than Hindustani or the Gujerati native to Ranchipur—a curious French which, softened and rounded by his tongue, he made somehow into an Indian language, unfitting it for use in salons, dressmaking establishments and diplomacy. His proper name was Jean Batiste, but to Ransome he was always John the Baptist. The Prophet, he sometimes thought, with his skinny body nourished on wild locusts and honey, must have looked like this skinny miniature servant.

In the fading light, surrounding John, squatted three or four of his friends, one of whom accompanied him with malarial listlessness by thumping a drum. They were all, like himself, gentlemen's "boys"——

[2]

probably the Colonel's and Mr. Bannerjee's and Major Safti's and one or two perhaps from the Maharajah's guesthouse. It was very difficult to tell one from the other.

They would thump and play on the flute for a time and then the music would cease, but Ransome, on the verandah, knew they were not silent; they were simply gossiping. They knew everything which happened in Ranchipur. Not one of them could really read and none of them ever dreamed of looking at a newspaper, but they knew everything, not only about things like wars and earthquakes and calamities which happened in remote parts of the world, but thefts, adulteries, betrayals, and a great deal more in Ranchipur which never reached the papers in Bombay or Delhi or Calcutta or even the ears of those whom they served. John the Baptist had been with him ever since he had come to Ranchipur; he *knew* his master and now and then modestly he would bring forth a stupendous bit of news and lay it on the table at mealtime as if he were serving tea or putting down a bowl of rice. Mrs. Talmadge's scandalous elopement with Captain Sergeant, for example; John the Baptist had predicted it and so Ransome knew it three days before it happened. He could have warned Talmadge and prevented it, if it had been worth the effort of interfering.

The group beneath the banyan tree presently stopped playing altogether and, in silhouette against the fading light, Ransome saw their heads together. And then in the tree above them there broke out a fearful row—a wild cacophony of chattering and screaming, and along the dusty tops of the great mango trees raced a whole procession of monkeys, the sacred monkeys of Ranchipur—noisy gray black handsome insolent comic and confident in their age-old knowledge that no one dared to kill one of them, neither the Indians because long ago they had fought in battle by the side of Rama, nor the Europeans because of the awful row the assassination of a single monkey would raise. Ransome hated them and was amused by them all at once. He hated them now for shattering the stillness of the evening with their infernal row, and he hated them because they pulled the flowers off plants in the garden and stripped the tiles periodically from the roof of the potting shed. John the Baptist and his friends, deep in their gossip, never so much as glanced at the trees overhead.

The spell broken by the monkey's row, Ransome finished the last of his brandy, put down his fan and rose from his chair to walk to the back of the house and have a look at the weather.

The garden was a big square enclosure surrounded by a high wall made of yellow mud and wattle which gave it a soft mottled appearance wherever it was not covered by trailing bougainvillea and bignonia. It was dry now, the very earth bitten deep by the brazen heat of a sun which went on and on, day after day, unrelieved by any cloud. Here and there a tired marigold or a despairing hollyhock, its roots soaked by the gardener with water carried from the great bottomless well in the corner, still stood, raddled and spindling and exhausted by the glare. For days, for weeks, the whole countryside—the farmers, the shopkeepers, the army, the ministers of state—had waited for the weather to break and the rains to begin, those rich flooding rains which overnight turned the gardens, the fields, the jungle, from a parched and burning desert into a mass of green which seemed to live, to writhe, to devour the walls and trees and the houses. Even the old Maharajah had waited through long weeks of burning heat, unwilling to quit Ranchipur for the delights of Paris and Marienbad until he knew that the rains had come and his people were safe from famine.

And with the passing of each week the tension grew. It was not only the awful heat that wore nerves finer and finer, but terror as well, the terror of famine and disease and the horror of that burning sun which nerves could bear no longer; for no one pretended that even the good old Maharajah, with all his grain depots and his food reserves, could save twelve million people from misery and death if Rama and Vishnu and Krishna saw fit to send no rain. The terror spread through the whole people; one was aware of it even in the shaded gardens of the rich merchants and on the verandahs of the fortunate Europeans who could escape to the hill stations. It was like an infection which unknowingly one caught from one's neighbor. It touched even Ransome himself who need not stay in Ranchipur. For weeks now it had been an actual presence. You could feel it all about you. There were times when it seemed that you could almost touch it.

The flute and drum began again, a plaintive, almost wistful sound, drifting through the trees across the garden from the gate.

[4]

The house was big and plain, built long ago to shelter some British official in the days of the wicked Maharajah when there were two whole regiments stationed in Ranchipur—a house many times too big for Ransome, with vast high-ceilinged rooms beneath a roof made of tiles with a thick thatch of reeds and grass just beneath to keep out the heat. In the thatch the mongooses and lizards and mice rattled about all night and even disturbed dinner parties with their squeaks and rustlings. There was a quality of fantasy about a big square Georgian house which had a roof made of reeds that sheltered a whole menagerie of small beasts. On the outside it looked like any house in Belgravia, and inside it was full of mongooses and lizards. Ransome was equally fond of both—the shy, nervous mongooses for themselves and the lizards because they devoured mosquitoes. You would see them during dinner scuttling from behind one Mogul miniature to another, snapping up a mosquito or two on the way.

Then the sun sank suddenly and darkness closed over the garden as if a curtain had come down and the stars came out all at once, glittering like the famous diamonds of the fierce old Maharani. Quietly Ransome made his way along the garden path past the well surrounded by bamboo which was rustling now in the faint breeze that always came up for a moment when the sun fell. A mongoose slipped along the far path, scarcely more than a shadow, on his evening hunt for mice and snakes and snakes' eggs. Ransome hated snakes and it was beginning now to be the season for them. Already John the Baptist had killed a cobra in the Maharajah's park just beyond the gate. With the first splattering drop of rain they would come swarming out of old roots and crannies in the wall—the cobras, the Russell's vipers, the fierce little kraits, the giant pythons. The garden was walled, but mysteriously they always managed to invade it. Every season the servants killed a half dozen. Last year Togo, the pet wild pig, had died from the bite of a krait hardly longer than a foot rule.

In the windows of the house a light appeared and Ransome knew that John the Baptist had put away his flute and finished his gossip and was preparing supper. Ransome could see him moving about, clad only in a breech clout, softly, like a ghost. He was small, almost a miniature of

[5]

a man, not like a midget, but complete and perfectly formed like a bronze statue of an athlete under life size, lean with the leanness of a man who as a child has worked hard without ever having had enough to eat. During the heat Ransome gave him permission to go about the house naked to do his work. It was more reasonable and much cleaner, for John the Baptist naked was clean; the moment he put on white European clothes he became dirty. In five minutes the immaculate white was soiled with smudges of ashes and dust, with stains of soup and coffee. He had no gift for wearing European clothes. Naked he was clean, for somehow out of his Hindu past and ancestry had persisted the habit of bathing every day. Each morning he went to the well at the end of the garden and in the hot sun bathed from head to foot.

He only used a part of the big house—the dining room, a small sitting room and a bedroom on the ground floor. The drawing room, a vast empty room facing north for the cool, he used as a studio. Here he dabbled in painting. The rest was shut up and empty save for the lizards and mice.

When he had changed he came from his own room into the dining room. In the far corner of the room were electric fans which kept the air stirring, less picturesque than the old-fashioned *punkahs* but more efficient. Ransome thanked God that Ranchipur was a progressive state with an electric plant—an undependable and eccentric one to be sure— but better than none at all. After the waterworks it was the first thing that visitors were taken to see. Then came in order the narrow-gauge railway, the hospital, the zoo and the asylum for the insane.

The bare table had an enormous platter piled high with fruit—pomegranates, melons, mangoes, guavas and papaias. It was not only decorative but it looked delicious and cool and it pleased the painter sense in Ransome. The jackals had stopped screaming now. In the darkness they were silent on their nervous hunt for carrion. The breeze died suddenly and the night was still again and sprinkled with stars. Just before the monsoon arrived they seemed to come very close. Even the fans could give no illusion of cool.

When John the Baptist appeared with cold consommé he was no longer naked but dressed in a suit of white drill, fresh from the *dhobi*, but

[6]

already there was a smudge of ashes at the elbow and a spot of consommé on the front of the jacket. He put down the soup and waited and after a moment Ransome spoke:

"What gossip did you hear tonight, John?"

The boy wriggled a little before speaking, pleased that his master should show curiosity. Retailing gossip, telling the master things he did not know made him feel important and valuable and sure of his place. He said, "Not much, Sahib. Only about Miss MacDaid."

They had a queer way of conversation. Ransome addressed the boy in English and the boy replied in his strange soft Pondicherry French. Each understood the other's language but each preferred to speak his own.

"What about Miss MacDaid?"

"Anthony says she likes Major Safti."

"Oh! How likes?"

"Too much," said John, with a shy grin.

"Oh! And what else?"

"A big sahib is coming on a visit to His Highness. And his wife is coming with him."

"Who's that?"

"He's called Lord Esketh." John the Baptist called it "Eskitt" but Ransome knew what he meant. "Anthony said she is very beautiful. He saw her in Delhi. But he says she is a devil, sahib, a she-devil—a *sorcière*."

Ransome finished his consommé and John the Baptist carried away the dish without saying another word. He never spoke unless spoken to and never volunteered information which was not requested, so he went no further with the subject of Lord Esketh and the she-devil and left Ransome wondering why an English peeress, and a rich one at that, should be coming to Ranchipur by choice at a season when everyone who could escape would flee to the mountains. He knew who Lord Esketh was and frowned at the thought of his coming to disturb the peace of Ranchipur. The name "Lady Esketh" stirred something in his memory, but he could not quite remember who she was and he found the heat too great to make any great effort. The news about Miss MacDaid stirred him more profoundly because it seemed so unlikely and, in a comic fashion, so tragic.

He could have gone away. He was not kept here like the old Maharajah by a sense of duty to his people, nor like Major Safti and Miss MacDaid because to them had been entrusted the health of twelve million people, nor like the Smileys on whom the children of the Untouchables and the lower castes depended, nor like Mr. Bannerjee whose handsome wife chose to stay because she was an Indian and passionately nationalist and did not like the idea of hill stations. Ransome remained, almost, it might have been said, out of perversity. He had plenty of money and not a tie in the world, yet he stayed on and on through the burning heat, waiting for that day, if it ever came, when the skies would open and the floods descend and the fields and jungle would steam and writhe and grow in the incredible wet heat which was worse than the hot dusty dryness of the winter season. Something in the sight of the dead burnt earth springing into an incredible orgy of life stirred him as no other manifestation of nature had ever stirred him. With the coming of the monsoon a frenzy of energy would seize him and he would paint day after day as long as there was light, standing naked and dripping in the damp heat, sometimes in the vast empty drawing room with it's mildewed walls, sometimes on the verandah, tormented by insects, painting the garden which seemed to grow into life before his eyes, trying to capture the feeling of the miracle, until at last, knowing he had failed, he would destroy everything he had done and go back again to his brandy.

There was no temptation to leave for he had no desire to go to Simla or Darjeeling or Ootacamund to be with the small people with their small ambitions, the army officers and the civil servants with their wives and brats, their precedence and their snobbery, their clubs and their surburban British manners. He had tried that twice and found that it was intolerable—far more intolerable than the monsoon.

When he had finished his supper and had his coffee, well iced (thank God for the Maharajah's ice factory), he lighted his pipe, took a stick and went out for an evening walk. By the time he passed through his own gateway John the Baptist had returned to his friends beneath the banyan tree and was playing on his flute. As Ransome passed John and

[8]

the three other musician-gossips rose, salaamed in the thick darkness and murmured, "Good-evening, Sahib."

He turned toward the town, walking along the road from the race course toward the old wooden palace. Here beneath the mango trees it was a little cooler for the water sprinklers had passed just at sunset and the roadway was still damp. He passed the house of Raschid Ali Khan, the police minister, whom he looked upon as his friend, and then the house of Mr. Bannerjee. It was dark now and the eternal badminton which Mr. Bannerjee thought fashionable was at an end. There was a light in the drawing room but no sign of anyone in the house. Without thinking he paused for a moment at the gateway, in the indifferent hope that he might catch a glimpse of Mrs. Bannerjee, but there was no sign of her. She fascinated him, not so much as a woman but as a work of art—cold, classical, detached, like a figure out of one of the frescoes at Ajunta. The character of Mr. Bannerjee always aroused in Ransome a curious mixture of feelings—of liking, of amusement, of pity and of contempt. Mr. Bannerjee was like a feeble reed blown and battered by the winds which blew now from the East, now from the West.

Turning away from the gateway, he continued down the slope to the bridge over the river. It lay now, in the heat, an inert sleeping serpent, beneath the respectable cast-iron statue of Queen Victoria dubiously ornamenting the summit of the center buttress. It no longer had any current but was still, a long green canal clotted with algae and reflecting the brilliance of the stars. With the rains it would become a yellow torrent, flowing through the middle of the town, between temples and bazaars, hiding the great flights of flat steps which now led, naked and dusty, from the temple of Krishna down to the stagnant water.

Beyond the bridge he turned left along the dusty road which followed the river through the zoological gardens past the burning ghats. It was very dark here save for the faint light of the stars, and the unlighted path led away from all habitations, but Ransome felt no alarm, partly because in Ranchipur, unlike most Indian states, there was very little danger, and partly because he was a strong man, lean and tall, who, save in the war, had never found any necessity for physical fear. Besides, he was not really afraid of death. For a long time now it had been a matter of indifference to him whether he lived or died.

A little further along the dark path he became aware of a dim glow from the level ground just below him. As he drew nearer he made out the embers of three fires, two of them almost extinguished, the third, a little way off, still flaming. It was this one which illuminated the mango trees and painted the surface of the stagnant river with a phosphorescent glow. Gathered about it could be distinguished the silhouettes of three men, all of them naked in the heat save for breech clouts. At the barrier he stopped for a moment, watching.

One of the men, the nearest relative of the dead person, poked the pile of burning wood now and then and beat it impatiently. The corpse, only half-consumed, still had not yet lost its shape, but it was clear that all three mourners had had enough and were ready to go home. Amused, Ransome leaned against the barrier watching, and then one of the men noticed him and moved toward him. He was a thin middle-aged fellow and he addressed Ransome with a grin, inviting him to come in. Ransome declined saying in Hindustani that he found no novelty in the sight, and the man told him that they were burning up their grandmother and that she was taking an unconscionable time about it. He laughed and made a joke as Ransome, turning away, started up the path toward the town.

He came frequently along these paths to the ghats after nightfall. There was a kind of macabre beauty about the place, and in the spectacle of the cremation itself there was a kind of faith and certainty which gave him peace and pleasure. It seemed to him that by the very act of burning they denied the importance of the body. It was as if they said, "What is dead is dead," and hurriedly made off with the body to turn it back once more as quickly as possible before the sun set, into earth, simply, without show, without barbarism, without long speeches. The most they did was to go through a formal pattern of grief, sometimes sincere, more often simply conventional like the archaic dances from Tanjore. From the moment of death there was no longer left for them anything of that essence which they had loved, or possibly hated. The body was only a machine which sometimes gave them pleasure and quite as often brought them pain. In their detachment there was a kind of reality never attained by any Christian. Here they *believed* that the body was nothing and refused to

[10]

honor it. In the West they only pretended to believe that the body was dust. In the West the clodlike body held people forever in subjection.

He came at last to the square. It was enormous, bordered on the one side by the façade of the old wooden palace, long since abandoned and desolate, a structure with countless balconies and grilled windows which kept behind its walls the memory of dark and sinister stories of death by poison, by garroting, by the dagger. In the days before the mutiny the Maharajahs had lived there, but now for fifty years it had been a dead place, abandoned and haunted, kept as a kind of empty, dusty museum that was forever closed. The place always fascinated him as a monument to the darkness and evil which had been in Ranchipur before the old Maharajah came, sent by the gods and the English to change all that. There were no lights in the abandoned old palace but its white façade was illumined by the reflected glare of the cinema opposite where they were showing an ancient cracked film of Charlie Chaplin. It was the hour of the opening and a strident electric gong kept ringing above the noise of the crowd and the cries of vendors of eskimo pies and *pan* and vile-colored sweets. Now and then a man of low caste recognized him as he went past and salaamed a greeting. It pleased him that they had come to accept him as a fixture in Ranchipur.

On the far side of the square lay the tank, a great rectangular expanse of water entirely surrounded by steps, which for two thousand years had been the center of life in that dusty world burnt by the sun for eight months of the year. Here the poor came to bathe, the *dhobies* and washerwomen to beat their clothes, the old women to gossip and the children to play. Once the sacred cows and water buffaloes had wandered up and down spattering the wide shallow steps with dung, but now for a long time they had not been allowed to wander about, starving. It was part of the duties of the police to keep them from the square and the center of the town.

At this moment of the evening the whole surface of the tank reflected the lights of the square—the lights from the garish cinema, from the fires of the vendors who made rice cakes, from the kerosene lamps in the shops of the silversmiths who sat cross-legged tapping the metal into shape with little hammers.

As Ransome crossed the square the din of the cinema and the vendors grew less and he became aware of a new sound, equally confused and equally strident. This was the noise of the music school which stood on the far side of the tank, a great monstrous structure of brick built in the style of Bombay Albert Memorial Gothic. There were lights in every window and in every room there was a class at work. He knew how each room looked, with its rows of bare wooden benches lined with men of all ages, from ninety down to little boys of ten and twelve, all earnest, all enchanted, learning to make music because something in their souls demanded it and would not be satisfied without it. He went again and again to the music school, partly because the music and the students fascinated him, and partly because of the beauty of the spectacle itself.

For a long time he stood with his back to the incredible din, watching the lights of the distant square on the opposite side of the tank. Thousands of flying foxes, as large as falcons, drawn by the lights of the cinema, circled and wheeled above the polished surface of the water, only to turn back again, confused and baffled, in their aimless journey round and round above the tank.

Presently Ransome knocked the ashes from his pipe, turned and went into the music school. On the way he noticed that the whole of the maternity ward of the hospital just beyond was flooded with light. Inside, no doubt, another Indian was coming into the world, or perhaps two or three, to add the burden of their existence to the three hundred and seventy millions that spread over the vast mass of desert and jungle and city. Miss MacDaid would be there and perhaps, if the case were difficult, Major Safti. And then he remembered suddenly John the Baptist's bit of gossip—Miss MacDaid and Major Safti. And now, quite as quickly, he dismissed it. Miss MacDaid was sober, plain, efficient, tough—more of a man than a woman—and Safti was certainly ten years younger than she and could have what he wanted from the ladies. No, it was an absurd and impossible bit of gossip. Yet when he thought of it he knew that John the Baptist and his friends were never wrong.

Inside the music school, he went to the office of his friend, Mr. Das, the director. Mr. Das was in, going over a ledger in which he kept all sorts of figures in the European fashion and so remained forever hopelessly muddled as to his expenses and accounts. He was a shy sensitive little man with gray hair and a great many wrinkles, insignificant save

[12]

for the inward fire which now and then would rise and illumine his great dark eyes. He had but one passion in life, and that was Indian music, and no one in the world knew more of it than he—the stylized unworldly ancient music of the Temples in the South, the music of the Rajputs, of the Bengali, even of the Muslim descendants of Akbar which he held a little in contempt as "modern" and patternless, corrupted by Western jazz and forever changing. Save for the few hours when he slept Mr. Das lived in a perpetual din, since the school went on all day from early morning until midnight. The school was free, for the Maharani loved music and the Maharajah, like Akbar, sought to bring his people everything which could give them pleasure and make brighter their lives. They taught all kinds of music in the school. They had musicians from every part of India. As one passed through the great halls one heard the music of every caste and every people—Muslims and Bengalis, Rajputs, Mahrattas and Cingalese, and even that of the dark ancient peoples of the south, and of the strange wild Bhils who lived among their goats in the panther-infested foothills beyond Mount Abana.

At sight of Ransome Mr. Das sprang up and crossed the room to shake hands. He loved Ransome because Ransome loved music. He was the only European in all the state who was interested enough in the school to have come twice to visit it. It flattered the vanity of Mr. Das whose driving force in life was a constantly rebuffed desire to please. He expressed no surprise at the presence of Ransome in Ranchipur so late in the season and he knew that Ransome had come to hear music.

"What is it you want to hear tonight?" he asked with an actual air of anxiety.

Ransome said he would like to hear the Rajput singer.

"Ah, Jemnaz Singh!" and with many remarks about the heat and the weather and the delay of the monsoon he clapped his hands for a boy to summon Jemnaz Singh and then led the way along the big bare corridor to the little auditorium. But when he spoke of the weather even the voice of Mr. Das, absorbed perpetually by his passion for his school, took on a little the color of fear. The rains should have begun a month ago. It was an ancestral fear rising in the blood, born of ten thousand years of drought and famine.

The little auditorium was decorated in the style of a provincial British railroad station, but in the midst of it, on the tiny stage, there was already assembled a miniature of extraordinary beauty which caught the eye at once and somehow annihilated like a blaze of light the Victorian tastelessness of the room itself. In the center sat Jemnaz Singh himself, crosslegged, holding his lute, and on either side of him sat a boy, one with a large drum between his knees and the other holding a flute. The singer was a small man of delicate build with a lean face of extraordinary beauty. He wore an enormous Rajput turban in shades of poison green and violet and candy pink and an *atchcan* of brocaded silk in which the same colors were blended with silver and a deeper violet in a pattern of extravagant flowers. He was rachitic and beneath the pale golden skin of the cheekbones there were flushes of dull red. At the sight of Ransome he inclined his head and smiled, and when Ransome was seated and Mr. Das had gone back to his accounts the singer began.

The long pale fingers with the nails tinted and polished and lacquered felt their way along the strings of the lute, tentatively, for Jemnaz Singh was seeking an inspiration, a theme. On either side of him, their large dark eyes watching the movements of the beautiful hands, the boys waited. One phrase after another was tried and abandoned until at last the singer found the pattern he sought, and began to sing, establishing his theme. The boys still waited, listening and watching. It was a pure lovely pattern which he had found, an ordered filigree of sound. Once he sang it through, and then again with a slight variation, and then the boys, having understood, began to play, one on his drum and the other on his flute, each improvising an accompaniment. And so it went, on and on, over and over, like a Bach theme with variations, strangely pure, yet intricate and complicated, like the carvings of the white marble temples at Mount Abu. And Ransome, enchanted, closed his eyes to listen, for Jemnaz Singh was a great musician. Only now and then did he open them and then only because the beauty of the spectacle was as great as the beauty of the music; the body, the face, the pose of the singer made a design as exquisite as the music itself. For Ransome the world, the whole futility of his own past, the dull planlessness of his future, faded in the ecstasy of his appreciation. In his tired soul he was happy.

He had no idea of the passing of time but he was aware suddenly of a gigantic clap of thunder which roused him and blotted out the beauty of the music. The singer went on until he had finished the latest of his variations and then put down his lute and said a prayer of thanks to Kali. At last the rains had come!

The storm, accompanied by a sudden fierce wind from the Arabian Gulf, came up quickly, covering all the stars that were like the diamonds of the Maharani as if a thick curtain had been drawn across them, and the thunder and wild flashes of lightning drove the gigantic bats into new and wilder fluttering above the tanks. By the time Ransome had gone round the square, great drops had begun to splatter in the thick dust. The lights of the cinema went out suddenly, and with a great clatter and much screaming the vendors of rice cakes and eskimo pies began gathering their wares and scuttling like terrified chickens in all directions. The wind increased and the trees bent and swayed. There was no way for Ransome to reach his house save on foot, for even the bright little tongas which usually stood waiting outside the old palace had disappeared. He took the short way, across the bridge and along the road to the race course, but he did not hurry for the beauty of the music and the sudden violence of the storm had left him enchanted.

The lightning came brilliant and white, flash after flash, so that his whole way was illuminated as if by gigantic flares. Then the first big drops were followed, faster and faster, by others until the whole sky seemed to pour forth water in one enormous cataract.

By the time he reached Mr. Bannerjee's house he was as wet as if he had been swimming in the river with all his clothes on. A little farther on in a sudden flash of lightning he caught sight of a small figure on a bicycle, pedaling head down, into the full force of the storm. In a second flash of lightning he recognized the figure as that of his friend, Mr. Smiley, from the American Mission. On the handlebar of the bicycle was hanging a great basket of fruit. Out of the darkness Ransome shouted a greeting to the shabby little figure, but the sound of his words was lost in the storm. He wondered where he could be going at this hour of the night. It must be a good three miles to the Mission.

By the time he went through his own gate his linen clothes clung to him as if they had been molded to his lean body. Once inside the house he went through the long hallway to the verandah overlooking the garden and there he slipped off his clothes and stood naked, watching the violence of the storm. The branches of the mango trees whipped black against the wild glare of lightning, and the water fell in torrents on to the parched thirsty earth. Tomorrow it would be green again, miraculously green with the miracle of the monsoon. Presently he went down the steps into the garden and stood there, the warm rain beating against his bare skin.

It was like being reborn. The weariness went suddenly out of his soul.

In the maternity ward of the hospital Miss MacDaid kept running back and forth between the two wards. She was a big woman, not fat, but heavy, and in the dull burning heat she became slowly drenched with perspiration until it was as if she had just come in out of the storm. Vainly she sought to find a moment when she could return to the little office long enough to change and feel once more, not cool perhaps, but at least fresh as a good nurse should feel. It would have been easier if the women had all been in one ward, but since one of them was a sweeper, one of them a Bunya, the wife of a small merchant, and one the wife of a mason, they had to be separated, as the Maharajah, who was usually adamant in his attitude in behalf of the Untouchables, had made a concession here in the maternity ward and kept the Untouchables apart.

It was the Bunya woman and the mason's wife who were giving all the trouble, for the Untouchable woman went about her labor quickly and easily, like a healthy animal. The Bunya woman, as if she felt she owed it to the superiority of her caste, groaned and screamed and complained; and the case of the mason's wife was difficult since she had a deformed pelvis and the labor went on and on with little result save exhaustion. She was patient, with the hopeless resignation of the very poor. She belonged, Miss MacDaid knew, to the millions who were born and die in India without ever having had enough to eat. The pelvis was deformed because the woman had had rickets as a child. She was only sixteen years old and it was her first baby, but vaguely, in an animal way, she knew that something was wrong. She did not cry out but lay ash-colored and terrified, her great dark eyes sunk far back in her head.

Miss MacDaid might have trusted her two assistants at least with the Untouchable woman whose case was easy and natural. The two nurses were competent enough. One of them, a woman of twenty-six, was a niece of the Maharajah who had never married, and for five years she had worked side by side with Miss MacDaid. The other, Mrs. Gupta, was a widow, the sister of one of the Maharani's aides-de-camp. In both of them there was a sense of fate, a sense of dedication, which Miss MacDaid had discovered long ago existed in many Indians. They were patient, intelligent and thorough, but it was this very sense of resignation which Miss MacDaid mistrusted. In her Church of Scotland blood there remained few traces of a belief in predestination. She was bound to fight to the very end, to leave no stone unturned, and then if fate defeated her Scottish doggedness it deserved to win.

The two nurses did all that she permitted them to do and nothing more, for like all self-reliant people she dominated those near to her and destroyed their initiative. She cast a kind of blight over all those who worked with her, all save Major Safti to whose authority and intelligence she alone made obeisance. When things got beyond her she sent for Major Safti.

Presently, in the Untouchable ward, the baby was born and Miss MacDaid was there to see that all went well at the end. The woman lay back on her narrow iron bed, relieved and silent, watching Miss Mac-Daid with eyes which were bright with gratitude. She was, now that the labor was finished, like a wild gazelle which had been caught and become resigned to captivity. Miss MacDaid was struck, as she always was, by the wild, animal beauty of the Untouchables. They were a different race from the others, their origin lost in some remote unrecorded past. In Ranchipur they were well enough off and the old barriers were almost gone save among the benighted orthodox Hindus. Miss MacDaid liked them better than most who came to the hospital. Her Scottish heart liked their toughness and their defiance and their vitality. They had enough to eat; it was rare that they went hungry like the people of the poor castes. For five thousand years they had been simple scavengers, unhampered by the rites and ceremonies and taboos of a decaying faith, and so they were never starved and deformed like the mason's wife or even like the Bunya woman whose diet was all one thing. The Untouchable women ate meat too, and one saw it in the fire in their eyes and the tough strength of their bodies.

The baby was bathed now and lay beside the mother, a small purple-black monkey of a creature, wrinkled but plump, squalling so lustily that it managed to drown out even the bedlam of the distant noise from the music school. It was the Princess, the niece of the Maharajah, who had bathed the Untouchable baby. That was something which Miss Mac-Daid never ceased to find unbelievable—that in one generation this young woman of the proud warrior caste had quietly put aside all the prejudices of five thousand years to work calmly among the pariahs.

She smiled at the Princess, for she really loved her, and said, "It's a fine baby," and then spoke to the mother in Gujerati, praising her infant. And then she had a queer flash of Gaelic intuition which was like a vision. She saw this niece of a warrior Maharajah and this new-born little monkey of an Untouchable as symbols of the future of all vast India. From them would come help and salvation. Out of them was rising that strange current of hope, of confidence and faith which Miss MacDaid felt all about her in this country which she loved and which somehow, strangely, had become her own. It was out of the intelligence and tolerance of this young nurse and out of the vigor of this pariah babe that a great nation might rise again, that a whole civilization might be reborn.

Miss MacDaid, not through intelligence but through the canny instinct of her people, *knew*—perhaps better than philosophers and economists and historians who sat in locked rooms on the other side of the world and spun theories.

But the cries of the Bunya woman summoned her and she went back again into the other ward where Mrs. Gupta, the aide-de-camp's sister, told her that the child was being born. Energetically Miss MacDaid brushed her aside to see that all was going as it should. There were no complications here, but a moan from the iron bed where the mason's wife lay told her that the extremity had been reached. There was no hope of the child being born normally and the woman was sinking. That awful thing happened which Miss MacDaid always dreaded with Hindu patients—the woman had given up and lay now resigned, unwilling to make the faintest effort. She meant to die; but Miss MacDaid meant that she should live despite herself.

She turned to the nurse and said, "One of you will have to fetch Major

Safti. The other can prepare the operating room. Which ever one goes will have to take one of the boys with you. You can't go alone."

It was the Maharajah's niece who volunteered, because she had her bicycle at the hospital and because she would have less to fear from the fierce old Maharani. Besides she knew the vast rambling palace and could find her way straight to the Maharani without delay. So she threw on a cloak and called the porter and the two set out on their bicycles. It was about the same moment that the colossal crash of thunder shattered the fine thread of music spun out for Ransome by the Rajput singer.

Miss MacDaid had waited before sending for Major Safti until all hope was gone, because this was the one evening of the week which she tried to keep inviolate for him. It was the only time he had rest from work which was enough for three men, and he spent it nearly always at the palace. It was a kind of sacred engagement, a royal command. On Friday nights he played poker with the Maharani. He did it through no sense of duty nor even in deference to the will of the arrogant and handsome old lady but because like her, of all things in life, he liked gambling best.

Accompanied by the porter the nurse pedaled through the fast scattering drops of rain as far as the engineering school, and there the storm began in earnest. Soaked to the skin within two or three minutes, sometimes blinded by the flood of water and the wild flashes of lightning, the two turned in at the side gate of the grounds and rode beneath the tossing trees along the winding drive until the palace with all its turrets and spires and balconies showed black against the sky. They went to a back entrance, for she had been there before to summon the surgeon on Friday nights and she knew how to go about it. The old Maharani played poker in secret without the Maharajah's knowledge. He made no objection to her gambling in Monte Carlo or Deauville or Baden-Baden but at home here in her own palace among her own people he forbade it. But he had forbade her many things in their long life together only to have her follow her own will.

At that moment she sat in her own sitting room at the mahogany table, surrounded by Major Safti, two nephews, an aide-de-camp and

Major General Agate. The nephews had learned poker at Cambridge and played rather a stolid conservative game. General Agate played according to his temperament, which was explosive, and so he always lost. What he lost he would put down to the expense of his journey, for he counted this visit one of diplomacy. It was not an official visit, arranged by the Viceroy, but an informal one and therefore all the more important and valuable. He had simply broken his journey to Poona by stopping off for a few days to see his old friends, the rulers of Ranchipur.

He was a stocky gentleman of about sixty, with a red turkeycock face and a large white mustache. He had been in India half his life and was in a way a case of nature imitating art, for he was a perfect Kipling general not alone in appearance but in temperament as well. On his own solid shoulders he still carried the burden of all the dark races and he could outshout all comers on the subject of The Realm. It was a kind of game he was playing now with the rulers of Ranchipur, a game far more important and far more difficult than poker, which irritated him because his wits were slow and his temper choleric. Beneath his temper he remained smug in the belief that he was serving the British Empire in the grand tradition; that is to say, not only by force of arms (as indicated by his countless medals) but by the guile of foreign policy as well.

These Indians were important because they were rich, they were powerful, and they knew the game of politics in Europe as well as they knew it in India. This was no obscure state ruled by a doddering depraved prince. Ranchipur, even the General was able to understand, was important—and not only important but dangerous—because it had exploded the whole theory of the White Man's burden. In the fifty years that the old gentleman, asleep a good quarter of a mile away in another part of the palace, had been reigning, it had lifted itself out of the malarial apathy and superstition of ancient India into the position of a modern state, admirably staffed and administered. It had proved that Indians could be good administrators, that they could be good economists, that they could solve such complicated problems as that of the Depressed Classes. It was a state more civilized and more advanced than many parts of England and America—the Midlands or Pittsburgh (although to the General nothing in America mattered or even existed).

He would have preferred entering Ranchipur on an elephant at the head of a column of troops, with the populace flat on their faces lining both sides of the avenue from the old palace to the race course. That was how a British general should make an entrance, not like any bloody civil servant in a railway coach, to be met with condescension (of this he could never quite be sure and it troubled him) by a Rolls-Royce and a nephew of the Maharajah who explained that his uncle sent profound regrets but was kept at home by gout. (Why should a Maharajah have gout, which was a disease of retired generals?) If he had had the say he would have treated all India differently. If he had had the say there would be no Indian problem. He'd soon fix that. But the India Office was always getting in his way. Those civilian louts back in Whitehall thought they knew more of the situation than he himself, Major-General Agate, who had spent half his life on the Northwest Frontier.

He even fancied himself as a diplomat, convinced that the handsome black-eyed old lady opposite him believed him to be as gentle as a lamb and the most devoted of her friends. He had no suspicion that behind her poker hand she knew exactly what he was thinking and exactly how much he was her friend. To her he was simply a rather tiresome old boaster whom she on her account must entertain because it was all a game anyway, an interminable game of waiting which must be played with a poker face until Europe destroyed itself or fell into decay. It was easier to entertain him by playing poker than by listening to him talk about the necessity of enclosing British wives and mothers on the Northwest Frontier behind defenses of barbed wire in order to save them from rape at the hands of those wild handsome Muslim tribesmen (an experience, the old Maharani thought, which might have its own richness).

The room was a modern copy of a room the Maharani had seen at Malmaison, complete down to the smallest detail. The Aubusson carpet was covered now with white cotton that was taken up each morning before Her Highness arose and replaced by cotton which had been freshly washed. Beneath the table there were no shoes save the boots of the General. Nephews, aide-de-camp and Major Safti wore only socks and the Maharani and her companions wore nothing to cover the lacquered nails of their naked toes ornamented with emeralds and diamonds and rubies.

At sixty-seven she was handsome, for her beauty was of that indestructible sort which lies in the bones of the face and not in the flesh or the coloring. The large fierce black eyes were set in a perfectly lineless face the soft color of pale *café au lait*. Her lips were painted scarlet like the tiny mark of royalty that she wore just above the proud arch of her fiercely sculptured nose. It was a vivid mobile face, not only beautiful but extraordinary. It was the face of a woman who at thirteen had been a half-savage hill princess who could neither read nor write. Ransome always thought of her as "The Last Queen."

At the very moment that her niece, the nurse, came in through a back corridor of the palace, stepping over the guards who lay sleeping there, the Maharani had picked up her five cards. Four of them were spades, the two, the three, five and six. At sight of them her expression did not change. It was Major Safti, the surgeon, who dealt, sitting big and handsome and pleasant with a cigar in one corner of his mouth. The General picked up his hand and saw three aces. The two nephews found nothing and Major Safti discovered two pairs, kings and eights.

The Maharani's hand was one after her own heart, for her wild nature asked nothing so tame as three of a kind or even a flush, dealt and ready to play without drawing. It was in her temperament to welcome obstacles.

The two nephews dropped their hands, and their aunt with a face of stone opened. The General, puffing a little and very red, raised and in turn was raised by Major Safti. Her Highness was content to draw one card. The General drew two and Major Safti one. Before they looked at their hands both the Maharani and the General regarded the Major, the one still with an expression of stone, the other with agitation and fury. The General was the first to look at his hand and when he found there his fourth ace his face grew perceptibly pinker. When the Maharani looked she found in its place, as if it had been sent there by fate, the four of spades. For an instant the black eyes lighted up but not long enough for the General to notice. But Major Safti saw it as he saw almost everything. She loved playing with the Major because he was a match for her. The General was too easy.

And so the betting began, tentatively at first, with Safti staying in for two rounds to discover if the others were bluffing. When he *knew* that they were not he dropped his cards, and with a glint in his blue eyes waited for the struggle. They raised each other again and again and again and the Major, watching, knew that this was not simply a struggle over a winning hand at poker. It went far deeper than that. It was an Indian Maharani, the proudest and most beautiful of them all, pitted against the whole British army. Beneath the betting there was an electric current of hatred, of pride pitted against arrogance. The expression of the old lady changed not at all save that the black eyes grew a trifle harder. It was the General with his four aces who showed the first signs of weakening. At the fourth raise his face went from pink to red; at the fifth it grew purple and he compromised his honor by hesitating for a second. Then a glance of mockery from the Maharani goaded him on. Again they raised each other and again, and then graciously, but with condescension, she said, "General, I don't want to bankrupt you. I have a straight flush," and laid her hand on the table.

It was a bitter moment, as if the General had been defeated in the field by a force outrageously smaller than his own. Angrily he threw down his cards. For a moment he came very near to doing what she had meant him to do—lose his temper and show himself a bad sport. But in time he remembered cricket and the playing fields of Eton and saved himself from the worst. Nevertheless the gesture with which he flung down his cards was enough. She did not ask for more. She was satisfied. And she knew that his expense account would be enormous this month.

At that moment her niece appeared in the doorway, the water dripping from her clothing onto the clean white cotton. It was Major Safti, the surgeon, who saw her first and rose from his chair. Then the Maharani turned, all her jewels flashing against the black and silver of her sari. The girl bowed to her and talked rapidly, first in Mahratta to the Maharani and then in Hindustani to the Major.

"Excuse me, Your Highness," he said in English. "I'll come back." He bowed to the General and accompanied the Princess through the doorway.

In the moment while the nurse stood dripping on the threshold, the emotion of the General had transferred itself, conveniently, from one cause to another. It is possible that her arrival prevented him from making an ass of himself, and so took the edge off the full triumph of the regal old lady. And now suddenly he was no longer irritated by the defeat of his four aces but by the interruption of the game.

To the Maharani he said, "Why does he have to go away?" He did not say "Major Safti" but simply "he," for thus he accomplished two things; he avoided using the title of "Major" conferred not by the British Government but by a Maharajah, and he managed to imply his feeling that as a person the surgeon was utterly insignificant. The Maharani understood him.

With an impassive face she answered, "He has gone to make an operation. There is a low-caste woman at the hospital having a baby and she cannot have it."

The General snorted and said, "Well, whose deal is it? Let's be on with it."

The Bunya woman had her baby safely, in spite of all the disturbance she made. It was a boy and thin and undernourished, a shriveled little thing. While the nurse bathed it Miss MacDaid looked on in scorn. "Another good Hindu," she said, "who will grow up and marry and produce a lot more skinny children who will never have a proper diet."

That was what ailed India more than anything else, this "Hindu sickness." She knew it was not because its mother could not afford proper food that the child was skinny and feeble. The woman was a Bunya and her husband, like all merchants, had managed to wring money enough, honestly and probably dishonestly, to feed his family properly. The trouble was the religion and the priests and their silly superstitions. She had seen children and even grown men and women who, when rescued and fed properly, turn from rickety, spindle-legged, malarial creatures with swollen abdomens into healthy ones filled with vigor. There were moments when Miss MacDaid, in exasperation, would have liked to slay all the priests and rip their religion from suffering India as if it were a diseased organ which must be removed.

To the nurse she said, "You never see Muslim or Untouchable babies as sickly as that. These caste Hindus never have a chance from the start. That's what is the matter with Gandhi—besides being a Gujerati by race and a Bunya by caste. He's puny and tricky."

But, as always, she was unable to stay and make a speech. There were

[24]

too many other things on her mind. There was the mason's wife, already half-conscious in her bed, and the worry of whether Major Safti would arrive in time to save both mother and child. If the mother died she knew that very likely it would make little difference to the husband, but if the baby was a son and was lost there would be hysterical wailing. Alone in her ward the sweeper woman had gone quietly to sleep with the child at her side.

Outside, the storm still howled and the rain came down in floods. The din of the music school was drowned out now and, perversely, with the coming of the storm, it seemed to have grown hotter rather than cooler. A rich damp steaming heat enveloped all the world of Ranchipur.

And inside the prim efficient bosom of Miss MacDaid there was another storm, scarcely less violent than the one outside. For she was going to see the Major, a bit of luck she had not hoped for on a Friday night. For that she had to thank the deformed pelvis of the mason's wife.

It was like an illness. She did not know when it had begun. It had come imperceptibly, without symptoms, unless you could call symptoms the joking that had gone on between them from the very first. In a way it had happened the moment she saw him four years before when he arrived straight from a London hospital to become surgeon-in-chief of Ranchipur. She always remembered him as he arrived at the hospital in His Highness' own Rolls-Royce with His Highness beside him looking pleased, in his simplicity, at having picked a young man who was so clever and intelligent and vigorous. Miss MacDaid always thought of the Major as he stepped from the car and came up the steps, with a friendly grin, to greet her. He was dressed all in white—tall, muscular, with a pale skin and blue eyes. "He must be a Poona Brahmin," she thought, and she was terribly pleased when she found that she was right. It always annoyed her when Europeans said that all Indians were alike, because they were far less alike than Europeans, far less mongrelized. The remark always implied stupidity. How was it possible to say that the fierce maleness of a Northwest Frontier tribesman resembled in any way the delicate, chiseled beauty of a man from Rajputana, or that the volatile faintly mongoloid Bengali looked like a warlike Mahratta who was a tough muscular little terrier.

[25]

In the beginning, at that first glance, Miss MacDaid had fallen in love, not with the man himself, but with the idea of him. As he stepped from the Maharajah's Rolls she thought, without thinking, "This is what India might be"—her India which was a part of her very soul.

And then she had discovered as the weeks went on that he was as clever, indeed as brilliant, a surgeon as the Maharajah had said, that his big muscular hands were as delicate as a woman's and in their work as sure as the progress of a cat. Bit by bit, usually in those moments when they had a snack together at night at the hospital, when she made tea and they talked intimately, she learned other things about him—that his mother had been a leader in the movement to purge the Hindu faith of its superstitions, its degeneracy, its defeatism, and bring it back to its original purity; that he had gone to Cambridge where he had rowed in his college boat, that he had been a famous cricketer. And in letters from England she learned that what the old Maharajah had said was true. He was a fine surgeon, which she already knew. Even as an Indian he could have made a great career for himself, but he had chosen to come back here to Ranchipur because this was his country and these were his people, and in Ranchipur he could have what he liked with the old Maharajah to help them.

In the beginning she had thought of him as a boy, although he was already thirty-three when he arrived that day in the Rolls. She had never thought of men as men because all her life had been so full—there were never enough hours in the day; and because she was, in her way, a great woman, few men had ever come her way to whom she did not feel superior, not only as a woman but even at times as a man. In the beginning he had seemed more like the embodiment, a very attractive embodiment to be sure, of an idea, something to which she herself had devoted her whole life and her immense energies.

Her own story had begun long ago as the child of an eccentric Scotch doctor who chose to settle in Sourabaya, practicing his profession when someone needed him, but far more interested in his laboratory, in tropical fevers, in curious diseases. He had journeyed far and wide, peering into the lives and bodies of the whole swarming East, for he had in him that strange urge some Scotsmen have to wander, to settle in some far-off place, to colonize, to create for himself a whole new world rather than to take his old world with him like the Englishman. Something in the East had claimed his soul and he never went back to Europe until he died at last of one of the strange diseases which he was always striving to understand.

And so his daughter had been brought up in the East, not like the child of a merchant or a civil servant, raised in a compound or in the foreign settlement and sent to England to school. She had lived at times almost like a native, knowing the sons and daughters of the local merchants and the half-caste children of Dutch planters. She could speak Dutch and Malay perfectly by the time she was ten and by the age of thirty she had learned Hindustani and Gujerati as well. When she was twenty she went to England.

It was the first time in her life she had ever been out of the Orient, and although she loved the misty beauty of the Scottish hills and the quiet green of English gardens, they were always strange to her. And everything she saw seemed small and rather drab, for in her heart and in her soul were all the violence, the magnificence and the squalor of the East. Even the climate of England and Scotland seemed to her dull, and its foggy coldness infinitely more uncomfortable than the burning heat of the East. In England there were no magnificent sunrises, no violent floods, no earthquakes, no great burgeoning into life, none of that savage splendor which filled the whole world in which she had spent her childhood. And the squalor which she saw in the Midlands and the suburbs of London during her years of training as a nurse, was no better, no less horrible, than the squalor she knew during her wanderings through the Orient with that eccentric man, Doctor MacDaid. In Sourabaya itself there had been no squalor approaching it. And the Eastern squalor seemed better to her because it was not shut up, inside damp overcrowded houses, in dark narrow streets, but flooded outward into the air and the light. And she was puzzled too by the prejudices of the people she met, even intelligent doctors, on the subject of race and color, and by their belief in their own physical and economic superiority; for in her heart, out of her strange life, she had no prejudices. Miss MacDaid was one of The Blessed to whom human creatures were human creatures, without regard to nationality or creed, color or race, and so her life had always had a richness which most others had never known.

Then after four years she had come back without regrets to the East where she felt at home, happy in the grandeur and violence and the color which Europe never knew. She got as far as Bombay, and after she had been there a little less than a year there came an opportunity such as warmed the heart of a woman like Miss MacDaid. In all Bombay there was not another woman who would consider it, but Miss MacDaid had said yes immediately on one late December afternoon when she found herself in the office of the hospital superintendent, talking to the rather stocky little Indian in European clothes who was the great Maharajah of Ranchipur.

He wanted to found a hospital and a training school for nurses. He wanted to educate his people in the care of children. He wanted to stamp out plague and cholera and the terrible malaria which dissipated the energies of his people. A kind of makeshift hospital already existed, but he wanted to establish one of the very best and most modern of hospitals, like the ones he had seen in Germany. If he could find a nurse who was willing to face a hard life for a time, to find herself blocked and sometimes baffled by the intrigues of ministers and officers of state, to battle with ignorance and prejudice, not only of the Indians but of the Europeans in Ranchipur, with filth and disease, he would see that she had all the money she needed, half from the state, half from his own private purse.

For a moment she stood completely overcome by the extraordinary chance which had come her way, so bewildered that she could not speak at all. To be able to give orders and not take them, to escape from the backbiting, the gossip, the prejudices of that narrow world in which she found herself, a little fragment of provincial Europe engulfed in the East; to have all that power and authority! To be able to work, to build, to organize, to create! There was in her something that was David Livingstone and Mungo Park, which was in thousands of Scottish colonists the world over—a passion for adventure and a stern Calvinist desire to help the poor human race.

While she stood listening to the stocky little Indian all that was Gaelic and Scottish in her was appraising him. She saw that he was a simple man and a good man, because all that was written in his face. She knew that he was rich, fabulously rich, one of the richest men in the world; but of the rest she knew nothing. She did not know then that he was one of the great men in the East, one of the greatest men of his time (although she had already divined his simplicity and his goodness), for he had no genius for attracting notice and the great things which he achieved remained somehow muffled and veiled and unknown, either by accident or by design. What he did was dangerous. He was fighting to bring respect and dignity to a conquered people. He was one of those thousands only just beginning to awaken over all of India and all the Orient, to stir with faith and pride and valor.

They looked at each other for a full minute——the squat little Maharajah and plain vigorous young Miss MacDaid——and in that moment there passed between them an understanding and a sympathy which from then on was never to be broken either by intrigue or prejudice or despair.

The Scotswoman said simply, "Yes, Your Highness, I'll go."

The Maharajah said, "It won't be easy, you know, Miss MacDaid."

"I've lived in the East all my life, Your Highness. I know the difficulties. All I ask is this opportunity."

"I'd prefer it if you could find another sister to bring with you."

"I'll try, sir. Perhaps I can persuade Miss Eldridge."

In the end she persuaded Miss Eldridge, who was the daughter of an importer in the Madras Presidency, a pale tall thin girl who adored Miss MacDaid and would have followed her anywhere.

So the two of them set out for Ranchipur. It was in April, a little while before the monsoon.

In those days the work of the Maharajah was only just begun and the town presented a strange spectacle of chaos, not alone the physical chaos of roads and streets under construction, of new buildings going up, of old rookeries being torn down, but what was much more important, of the spiritual and psychological confusion of a whole people in the process of having their lives remade by their ruler and a handful of educated subjects. The parasite priests had been forced to work or to leave the state, so that there were only priests enough left to serve the temples adequately. The Maharani had just finished her book urging the women to come out of purdah, to learn to read and to write, to undertake professions. Her high school for girls had just been opened

and the daughters of ministers and princes and Brahmins had been ordered to attend it willy-nilly, side by side with any Untouchable girl
who wanted to learn. It was only a year or two since the banquet and
festival given by the Maharajah for the Untouchables of the City of
Ranchipur, at which he himself sat down with them to give an example
to other Hindus. His own servants in the vast palace were Untouchables.
And in Ranchipur all these things made for riots and assassinations,
intrigues and plots.

Into the midst of this came Miss MacDaid and her thin pale satellite,
Miss Eldridge, to find a hospital with earthen floors, a leaking roof, and
a native pharmacopœia, staffed by a half-educated surgeon more concerned with the cut of his European clothes than with the welfare of
his patients, and a couple of doctors whose equipment was a strange
mixture of midwife's superstitions and old-fashioned science. There was
puerperal fever and recurrent typhus, the ever-present smallpox and
malaria and the last traces of an outbreak of plague. There were no at-
tendants save low-caste servant girls. Miss MacDaid with her own hands
went to work with yellow soap and carbolic acid, and at the end of the
first week even her tough body and spirit were discouraged.

But something in her was undefeatable; it had always been so and it
always would be, to the very end; and so she went on. But worse than
the filth and ignorance and inefficiency which lay before her was the
quiet stubborn resistance of half the population of Ranchipur, the lying
and intrigue of the Orthodox Hindus, the resentment of the officials
at the presence of a European and of the authority given her. The Maharajah was on her side, with all his wealth and all his power, but there
were times when it was impossible to call on him for help, times when
an appeal only reached him distorted and made trivial by Oriental lies
and intrigues. There were moments when, in despair, Miss MacDaid
would ask herself what could motivate these devils who lied and intrigued and blocked every effort to bring the people education and health
and decency, and always the answer was religion, or superstition, which
passed under the name of religion. The worst enemies of herself and
the Maharajah were always the most religious. He was patient with them.
The fierce and beautiful Maharani had no patience. She had officers
of state dismissed. She ordered men to keep to their houses as if they

were prisoners. At last, through the influence of the Maharani and Miss MacDaid, the Dewan himself, an Orthodox Hindu with a pigtail and a wife in blackest purdah, was dismissed; and fresh troubles began because the Dewan, a capable if superstitious man, appealed to the Viceroy and there was an investigation of all the rumors of disorder in Ranchipur which for a long time had disturbed the peace of the Government in Calcutta.

It was all rather a farce and nothing much was accomplished, because Ranchipur was a rich and powerful state and the Viceroy was content to let well enough alone. Nevertheless the clash accomplished two things. It humiliated the proud Maharani and made her forever an enemy of British officialdom, and it made Miss MacDaid's position with the British in Ranchipur perfectly clear, once and for all. From that moment on she looked no longer to the people who were hers by race for help and understanding. During the investigation she came to suspect that Government House and all the vast machine connected with it were cold toward this mission to which she was giving her whole life. She suspected that they did not want either the Maharajah or herself to succeed and that they even disapproved of her association with Indians in such a movement of enlightenment and reform.

Until the Maharajah had come to power, with his passion for the dignity and pride of his people, Ranchipur had been a peaceful state, plunged in filth and ignorance, and it had been an excellent market for cotton goods from Manchester and hardware from Leeds and Hull, and now there was talk of the Maharajah establishing mills in his own state where his people might manufacture their own cloth. And somehow Ranchipur seemed to attract radicals and reformers and agitators. When life became difficult elsewhere they fled to Ranchipur.

It was all very disturbing and unpleasant, this feeble attempt of the East to waken and find faith and hope in the future. During the investigation there were one or two small government clerks who treated Miss MacDaid as if she were a mixture of charwoman and traitress, and one impotent little man from Clapham, who was insolent to the Maharani, received for his pains a dismissal from the Civil Service for having made an "incident." And when Miss MacDaid returned to Ranchipur after a loss of ten precious days from her work, she learned what it was to feel like an Untouchable among her own people. After that she went her way alone, fighting, determined and undefeatable. She meant to make her mission a success. No longer had she any doubts. Her rôle had been chosen for her. When she returned typhus broke out again and Miss Eldridge was one of the first victims. She did not try to find a new companion to replace her.

Year after year, without even a holiday, through the hot dusty winter and the monsoon summer she worked, through famine and plague, intrigue and despair; and miraculously the hospital slowly became a reality. Building after building arose, made of brick, neat, bright and sanitary. Of the servant girls she managed to make crude nurses. The surgeon and the doctors were dismissed one by one and new men came to take their place, not experts or geniuses but better than the men before them. There were rarely days when Miss MacDaid could find an hour or two for herself which she did not have to use for sleeping. And presently a better class of women, led by the few who belonged to the educated group, came to be trained as nurses——widows and women who through choice or by accident were not married. The hospital came to heal not only damaged bodies but hurt and wounded souls as well. That was how the Princess and the aide-de-camp's sister had come to her.

By the time young Major Safti arrived the hospital was a reality, a fine reality which Miss MacDaid knew was better by far than many hospitals in Europe. Alone, aided by Indians, she had created it, but it had cost her something, and at forty-nine her tough body was worn by the long battle against heat and superstition and intrigue; her hair was thin and brittle and dry, and the plain, good face, with skin the texture of leather, was lined. But she had won, and in her heart she knew a secret which few from the West ever suspected—it was that her East, with its splendor and violence and vitality, was not crushed and dead, slain by the shopkeepers of the West. It had only been sleeping.

She waited for the Major in the little hallway overlooking the garden and presently through the flood of rain she saw his Ford turn in at the gate. Watching the lights sweep along the drive, picking out the hedge of hibiscus stripped bare of every flower only that afternoon by a wandering troop of monkeys, she thought, "If only I were young and handsome. If only everything had not been wrong." And for a moment she almost divined what it would be like to be reckless, chucking everything for someone you loved.

Then the car drew up and he sprang out, followed by the Maharajah's niece and the porter. And after him came a drenched and miserable figure whom Miss MacDaid recognized as Mr. Smiley, the American missionary. He dragged out after him a great basket of melons and plantains.

"Is she ready?" the Major asked.

"Yes, Major. Your overall and gloves are laid out."

Forgetting Mr. Smiley, Major Safti hurried off to the operating room and Miss MacDaid, with the Princess, went to the ward with the wheeled table to fetch the mason's wife. It all worked quickly, efficiently and well, and in twelve minutes the first son of the mason was born as Caesar is said to have been. In half an hour his wife had slipped from anæsthesia into sleep and the baby was bathed. Major Safti, Miss MacDaid and Mr. Smiley were gathered round a table in Miss MacDaid's office having tea and biscuits. The Major had already eaten one of the Maharani's vast dinners and swallowed one or two of the sandwiches which always stood beside the poker table, but he pretended that he was hungry and stayed to eat because he knew that Miss MacDaid would feel hurt and disappointed if he went away directly.

Mr. Smiley was a small man who wore very large spectacles which made him seem even smaller and thinner than he was. He was only forty-two but he had the air of a tired man ten years older. It was the sun which had done that, the sun and the heat and occasional bouts with malaria, and his own devotion to the cause which the Major and Miss MacDaid had espoused. He rarely left Ranchipur even during the rainy season. In the mornings he taught until one o'clock at his school for Untouchables and low-caste boys in the middle of the town, and in the afternoon he taught at the girls' orphanage near the Mission. But that did not end his duties for he had an immense and complicated amount of bookkeeping to do in order to satisfy his Mission Board in the States; and he knew the families of all the boys who came to his school and there was always something going wrong with them, deaths or births, or illnesses or trouble with the police, so that he was always having to make visits at all hours of the night; and now and then he had to help Miss MacDaid because some of the Untouchables, in their ignorance, were terrified of the hospital and would not allow themselves to be treated until he had reassured them. And in addition to all this he had his troubles with the Reverend Elmer Simon who was in charge of the spiritual side of the Mission and complained that Mr. Smiley did not have enough faith and did not strive hard enough to convert his pupils to the Baptist variety of Christianity.

It was true that Mr. Smiley in his heart did not care two figs whether his pupils were Christians or Hindus or Mohammedans or just plain heathens like the wild Bhils who inhabited the rocky hills, nor that the Reverend Mr. Simon was an Evangelist by upbringing and an imitator of the Anglican missionaries through snobbery. Mr. Simon thought only of souls while Mr. Smiley leaned more toward hygiene, mathematics, the history of India and the rules for decent behavior toward one's fellow men. Like Miss MacDaid and the Major he knew that neither India nor her people were to be saved by conversion to Christianity or any other religion, but through education and the healing of all the terrible hatreds which separated them. But Mr. Smiley had learned long ago to dissimulate because that was the only way by which he could accomplish good for these people he loved, and so for the sake of the missionary board at home and the sake of the Reverend Mr. Simon, who he had discovered was sending home pious and insinuating reports behind his back, Mr. Smiley had to turn Jesuitical and pretend that he was a devout Baptist.

In his heart, when he reviewed the progress, history and actual state of Christianity in the West he was not convinced that conversion would do anyone much good, not even a low-caste Hindu. But he had never spoken of this save to his wife, who agreed with him, and to Miss MacDaid and the Major. It was as if they had all been in a plot together, striving to do good despite the superstitions of the Hindu faith in India and those of the Fundamentalists in the far-off Middle West. If you could have gotten the truth from Mr. Smiley concerning his faith he would probably have told you that, if he was anything at all, he was a good Mussulman.

And now Mr. Smiley was here in the hospital with his basket of fruit and a couple of jars of cold jelly on account of the Untouchable woman. She was the mother of one of his pupils, a boy of sixteen in whom he was interested. If the boy kept up his good record at the school the Maharajah would send him all the way to America to Columbia University. Mrs. Smiley herself had made the jelly.

"Three in one night," observed Mr. Smiley. "That's pretty good. It must be almost a record."

"Oh, no," said Miss MacDaid. "We've had as many as seven. You remember, Major?"

The Major remembered. The two of them had not had a wink of sleep all that night. They had had to leave in the very middle of one of Mr. Bannerjee's fashionable dinners.

Watching Mr. Smiley drink his tea, Miss MacDaid thought, "He is like a mouse. I don't see where he gets the vitality," never thinking that, like herself, he had an inner strength.

While the Bunya woman's child was being born Mr. Smiley had changed his dripping clothes for a white hospital suit of the Major's in which he looked completely lost. The clothes in which the Major looked so smart hung on Mr. Smiley like a tent, the sleeves and trousers rolled up, the jacket unbuttoned. They made jokes about it and Miss MacDaid went for a fresh pot of tea, thinking that thus she might hold the Major a little longer.

When she returned he was telling the story of the General's defeat at the hands of the Maharani in the poker game.

"The old gentleman nearly blew up," he said. "I wish you could have seen him. Poker is no game for an Englishman. He's always too simple when it comes to a thing like that." Then he looked at his watch and Miss MacDaid's heart sank.

"I have to be back," he said. "Her Highness will be in a bad humor if I stay longer than she thinks necessary to deliver a child. She is probably watching the clock now, and pulling the General's game leg." He turned to the missionary, "What about you, Smiley? You're not planning to cycle back in this flood?"

"I'd swim home willingly," said Mr. Smiley, "if only the flood would keep up. I don't want to see another lean year like we had eleven years ago."

"That was nothing," said Miss MacDaid. "You should have been here twenty-five years ago. Then we had a real first-class famine with plague thrown in for good measure. Now the railroad is working all right and that can never happen again. You should have seen them dying of cholera like flies, lying in rows on a mud floor. That was the year Miss Eldridge died."

"Well, I suppose those years will never come back."

The Major stirred and Miss MacDaid's heart sank again. He started to speak but a wild clap of thunder cut him short and he waited for it to pass. Then he stood up, looking very handsome in his white jodphurs with the black *atchcan* buttoned with diamond buttons and the neat smart red Ranchipur turban. It was the most beautiful of costumes for a man like him. It showed the breadth of his wrestler's shoulders, the narrowness of the hips, the muscles of his arms. Miss MacDaid thought again, "Indians are the most beautiful of races." There was something fine about them. When one had lived long among them even the most beautiful Western face seemed like a boneless anemic pudding.

"I'll drive you and your bike home, Smiley," he said, "and then go back to the palace." Smiley protested politely but the Major said, "It's only three or four miles out of the way. I wouldn't ask a pie dog to go out on a night like this."

Despite anything Miss MacDaid might do, they were off. She went as far as the door with them and there Mr. Smiley, his small figure enveloped in the big doctor's white linens, turned and raised his arms and winked. The sleeves hung from his thin arms like the wings of a strange bird.

"Mebbe I'd better call on the Reverend Simon like this," he said. "That would give him something more to write home about."

Then they climbed into the motor and waved to her and were off into a wall of water. They were friends, these three, Miss MacDaid, the Scotswoman born in Sourabaya, Mr. Smiley, the son of a clergyman in a small Iowa town, and Major Safti who came of the proudest of all Brahmins.

When they had gone Miss MacDaid went and looked at herself in the mirror of the washroom, but the image, even with the rouge which she thought no one would notice and the wash that killed the gray in her hair, gave her no encouragement. She said, half aloud, "I'm a fool. I'm a middle-aged woman who should know better. But I can't help it." And in her heart she was glad because it made her feel warm inside, and even young. Turning, she picked up Mr. Smiley's basket, put the jelly in the icebox and the fruit where the daughter of the aide-de-camp could find it so that the Untouchable woman might have melons when she wakened in the morning.

The Major dropped Mr. Smiley at the vast barrack of a house which he and Mrs. Smiley occupied opposite that of the Reverend Simon, his wife and their daughters, Fern and Hazel. Then he drove back to the palace and stepped over the bodies of the guards all in scarlet and gold who lay asleep in the back hall, and made his way to the Maharani's sitting room. Her lady-in-waiting, the old Princess of Bewanagar, was sound asleep sitting upright in all her jewels, but the game went on furiously. It was already two o'clock in the morning and it was dawn when the Maharani rose and dismissed them, seven hundred and eighty rupees richer than when she sat down. Nearly six hundred of them came from the General.

The first storm to break the drought in Ranchipur did not reach as far east as Delhi and Agra. In spite of its violence and the floods of water which fell, in spite of the fact that it covered an area almost as big as France and would have drowned Holland and Belgium, it was lost in the vastness of India and ended in a spatter of drops in the red dust somewhere on the borders of Udaipur. And so on the Bombay Mail there was not even the faint psychological relief from the dry burning heat which comes with the sight and sound of water.

In their private car Lord and Lady Esketh, in separate compartments, lay sleepless, for one might as well have tried sleeping in an oven. Even the cakes of ice which lay wrapped in towels in front of each electric fan made no difference, and at moments the dampness which the melting ice created seemed only to make it worse. When you touched metal it was still hot, even in the middle of the night. The yellow-red dust swept beneath and over the train, blowing about it in great blinding

[37]

clouds. It crept in even through the special fine copper screening which Lord Esketh himself had ordered for the car. It lay over everything, turning the towel-wrapped blocks of ice into cakes of mud, covering the floor in a fine layer which stirred and rose again whenever the current from the electric fan touched it.

In his compartment Lord Esketh smoked cigars and drank whisky and rang for his valet, now to open a window and now to close one, now to change the adjustment of the fan or to send in another cake of ice. Sleepless, he tried in vain to work—to compose telegrams or to bring order out of the chaos of figures on the sheet of paper before him.

He was a big man of forty-eight, big of frame and heavy with weight despite riding and massage and exercise. He had a large, rather round face, which was an anomaly, an ill-natured fat face. It was the thrust of the jaw and the almost lipless mouth which made it so, for they gave him a look of brutality and ruthlessness. On his nose and on the cheekbones there was a network of fine purple veins, for Lord Esketh was a great drinker and for a long time now his brain only functioned at all when he was filled with brandy or whisky.

The drinking had begun long ago in the East when as plain Mr. Albert Simpson, selling cutlery from Leeds and Hull, he drank to fight off the heat. And then afterward at home in England he had drunk to fight off the damp cold and to push his brain when it grew tired and confused, and finally, as he grew rich and his future became complicated, he drank because that was the only way he could save himself from the feeling that he was being crushed by the very monster of success which he had created. And so alcohol had become a part of his very blood; he was so used to it that now it sharpened instead of blurring his brain. He could not work without it. It was not whisky which confused his brain now; it was the suffocating heat.

He was one of the lords of the West, not a great warrior and ruler as Akbar or Napoleon had been, nor a great philosopher like Plato or Mohammed, but simply a shopkeeper with all the shrewdness and craft of a small shopkeeper magnified a thousand times. Instead of dealing in peas or nuts and bolts he had rubber plantations in the Indies, jute plantations in India, cotton in Egypt, newspapers in London and the Midlands, steamship lines which plied between the East and the West, steel and iron (not too profitable now) in England, oil (over which there was trouble in these times) in Persia and Afghanistan, and factories, perhaps the best investment of all, which made cannon and shells. Long ago he had sold out of cotton in England because that was finished forever. It belonged to the Japanese and the Indians (damn their low standard of living!). All those things had to do with the confused jumble of figures from which, in the heat, he could make nothing. The foundations of all this he had laid long ago as plain Mr. Simpson, the son of a building contractor in Liverpool, for he was no hereditary peer; he had bought the peerage shrewdly at a time, not many years before, when it was made cheap and easy by a cynical and demagogic prime minister.

He hated heat for it sent up his blood pressure and made his head feel as if it were bursting, and now although there was little else he could have done he cursed the very idea of ever having come to this hellish country. When people had warned him of the folly of going out to India in April he had laughed, saying, "Listen, my fellow, Esketh has been to Somaliland and Java and New Guinea. Heat isn't anything new to me."

But the man who had gone to Somaliland was a young fellow in his twenties called Albert Simpson, with the strength of an ox and the nerves of an athlete, and not the great Lord Esketh, a swollen, prematurely aged man who was being destroyed by the complicated precarious fortune he had built up shrewdly and not too scrupulously. He had come to India because the Government had requested it and because if he wanted further honors and recognition of services (which he did want) he could not well refuse; but the trip coincided too with his own needs and plans, for it was true that he needed to study the question of jute at the very source, and he knew there was a chance, a quite good chance, of snatching cotton mills in Bombay from their Indian owners for a price that was next to nothing. Cotton was finished in England but in India there was still a chance, even against the Japanese. In his heart he did not care about the East or the West, or Europe or England. He cared only about Lord Esketh and the power which shrewdness and money brought him——and perhaps a little bit about his wife and about horses.

If the Indian Government could be induced to put the tariffs high enough to keep out Japanese goods there would be money again in cotton mills, not in England but in India itself. Now he knew was the moment to buy. He had planned his schedule closely. A week in Ranchipur, which would at least be cooler than Bombay, twenty-four hours in Bombay, with everything planned by telegram beforehand so that there would be no delay, and then the Lloyd-Triestino boat to Genoa and ten days or two weeks on the Mediterranean on the yacht, if he did not have to go direct to London because of the trouble the bloody Bolsheviks were making over oil. He did not travel by the line in which he owned a great interest because the boats were slower than the Italian boats and Lord Esketh had a mania for speed. The damned "dagoes" had been cutting into his business lately! The Government, he said to himself, owed it to him to blackmail the Italians, by controlling port privileges, into running their boats on a slower schedule.

The Government, he thought, had no guts any more since these labor party bastards had had a hand in it. It no longer dared to threaten other nations and bully subject peoples. There were moments when the great Lord Esketh regretted not having been born fifty years earlier when the Empire *was* an empire. It would have made his career in many ways much easier. During one of his eternal moments of "juggling figures" he estimated that during the eighteenth and nineteenth centuries British capital had taken out of India five hundred thousand pounds for every pound invested. Colossal! Why, a man of his ability would have cornered the world in a time like that!

It was his strange passion for horses which led him to Ranchipur. In Simla, talking after dinner with a couple of cavalry officers, he learned about a breed of which he had heard but never seen—the tough little Kathiawar horses, bred in the dry wild peninsula on the edge of the Indian Ocean. They were, he heard, rather like Arabs but more heavily built and tougher. They not only had speed but they were weight carriers (which he always had to consider). They had always been the favorite mounts of the warlike Mahrattas and Rajputs. Esketh, having heard of them, had to have them, and he had to have no ordinary stock but the best. The best, the cavalry officers said, were to be found in the fabulous stables of the Maharajah of Ranchipur. So the Viceroy arranged it. He would go to Ranchipur and be received by the

Maharajah; he would be housed, not in the guesthouse, but in one of the smaller palaces, as befitted a great lord of the West. And at the same time he could see, persuade and perhaps bribe the shrewd old Dewan of Ranchipur to help in the deal for the Bombay Mills. The old Dewan was a power in Indian politics. Thus he might kill two birds with one stone, and he was a great one for doing that.

The Viceroy was certain that his friend the Maharajah would sell him a stallion and a half-dozen mares to ship back to England. That was the only bright spot before him, because even the prospect of putting over a sharp deal in Bombay on the Khojas and Parsees who needed money did not excite him much. If he had been a man given to examining himself he would have known that this was the first sign of failing strength.

Suddenly he felt hot again and rang the bell at the side of his bed. No one came and he rang again angrily, and then a third time in fury, and then the door opened and Bates, his man, came in, looking sleepy-eyed and pale with the heat.

Lord Esketh raised himself ponderously on one elbow and shouted, "God-damn it! What have you been doing? I've been ringing for ten minutes."

The valet was a lean cold man but detached and extremely efficient, the kind of person Esketh liked to have around him. Bates never asked favors and never gave any outward sign of affection or devotion. He did not tremble now. He simply said, "Sorry, sir. I must have fallen asleep."

This appeared to enrage His Lordship further. "I don't see why in hell you should sleep if I can't. Tell that black bastard to bring in some ice. There's nothing left of what's here."

"Very good, sir," and Bates retired, still outwardly unmoved. Nor was he much moved inwardly. He had put up with this sort of thing for twelve years and it did not disturb him very profoundly. The one emotion he felt toward His Lordship was that of a cold dispassionate hatred which never varied. But it was a good post with excellent wages, a great deal of prestige, quite a lot of time off and all sorts of perquisites most of which Lord Esketh knew nothing about. When he felt that he had enough in the bank he would simply quit, like that, one night. The time, he knew, was not far off, and then to hell with His Lordship. He would retire then to a semi-detached villa in his native town of Manchester, join the Communist Party for good and put at its disposal all the knowledge he had of the chicanery and treason and ruthlessness of Esketh and men like him.

The odd thing was that Bates had succeeded where far more clever and successful and brilliant men than he had failed. By his very indifference he had managed to keep a rich post for twelve years, and during that time he had seen partners, secretaries and clerks, chauffeurs and butlers, come and go, sometimes dismissed, sometimes driven away because life had been made unendurable for them, but always broken and humiliated. There were two people, Bates knew, whom His Lordship had never succeeded in breaking or even in humiliating. One was himself and the other was Lady Esketh. That was why they were both still with him. If the day ever came when either of them showed signs of weakening, they too would go the way of all the others.

In the next compartment Lady Esketh heard her husband's shouts. The sound of his voice, rising even above the monotonous beat of the wheels over the uneven track, roused her out of the stupor into which she had fallen, and she thought, "If he can't sleep, he'll be coming in here to annoy me," but almost at once she knew that it really did not matter. She had grown used to all that long ago. One more time could not matter. She would think of something else, pretend that it was not Albert but another man, almost any man, a train guard or even a coolie. That at least would be exciting. Anyway she could not be more miserable than she already was.

Languidly she sat up, holding her pink crêpe-de-Chine pillow over the edge of the bed, to shake from it the coating of yellow dust. That hellish dust was in her mouth, in her hair. She switched on the light and looked at herself in the mirror. Her face was yellow with dust and on the temples the perspiration had mixed with it and turned it to mud, which ran in a little stream down the famous complexion which had cost a fortune in beauty specialists. She gave a little cry of horror and then lay back again languidly among the lace and silk, thinking that the misery was only begun. At four in the morning they would have

[42]

to rise and dress and wait on a platform to change to the narrow-gauge train for Ranchipur. So far as she could see Indian trains never left or arrived at any hour save between midnight and dawn. For weeks now, it seemed to her, she had been sitting up to take a train which left at two in the morning or rising to change from one to another at four. The private car was all very well on the main line but it was of no use on the narrow gauge railways.

She took more sleeping medicine, thinking, "Then I won't notice it so much," and she had nearly fallen into a stupor again when the door opened and Lord Esketh came in.

In the morning when John the Baptist brought Ransome his tea the storm was over and the sun was shining once more as if there had been no rain and the drought had never been broken. That, Ransome knew, was the worst of signs. When the monsoon began thus, coquettishly, it sometimes meant that the rains would be violent but spasmodic and insufficient, no more than enough to startle the whole earth into a forward rush of green, leaving it tender and fresh, to be cooked almost at once by the vicious, hateful sun. Its rays brought anxiety to every eye which opened that morning in Ranchipur, but Ransome's ill ease had in it the special quality of one who had spent most of his life between wet green England and the fertile rolling green country of Middle Western America. His body, his whole soul, ached for the rain, not because it meant food but because it ended the terrible drought. For him the spectacle of a burnt dusty land had always the quality of unreality.

When he had had his tea and a shower of tepid water he went out on to the verandah to have his fruit and his first drink of the day.

The garden had been transformed by the rain. In the few hours of the night fresh shoots had sprung from the withered plants and the vines that covered the ancient walls, and underneath them the earth, instead of being burnt and dusty, was a rich dark color; but he knew that by evening it would be yellow again, baked hard by the sun. Nevertheless, when he had finished his drink he went down and, taking a hoe from the summer house, set to work to break up the soil. That, at least, would help it to hold the moisture for a few hours longer in case there was no more rain.

[43]

At the far end of the garden near the well he set to work with his hoe, but he had only worked for a little time when he heard his *pie* dog barking and found that the end of the garden near the house had been invaded by an army of monkeys. He called off the dog, retired into the shade of the trees and watched.

He knew the whole troupe, for they lived in the trees in the palace gardens on the opposite side of the river. Usually they stayed there, feeding on the bananas and mangoes and the stray bits of food put out for them in the evening by the servants of the palace. But sometimes they went wandering, not in search of food but bent upon mischief, adventure and destruction. Usually Ransome made relentless war on them and left orders with John the Baptist to drive them out if they arrived while he was absent, and John, being a converted Christian, had no scruples about putting the sacred monkeys to rout. Once or twice when there had been no one in the house save the Hindu servants they had arrived without warning and, as if aware of Ransome's enmity, had stripped the garden of every flower. Systematically they would go from plant to plant and vine to vine, tearing off every bright-colored object which caught their attention. They did not eat the blossoms but only threw them in the dust, looking over their shoulder from time to time to make certain that vengeance was not at hand. They were, thought Ransome, exactly like an invading army of men in wartime. The spectacle of desolation which they left behind reminded him of whole villages he had seen in the war, each house with windows and doors broken open and half the contents scattered in the mud of the road outside.

Now they impudently took no notice of his presence. They climbed over the verandah and swarmed up the waterspout. There must have been thirty or forty of them, all female save for the big monkey who sat solemnly on top of the high wall watching for danger. And there were a dozen baby monkeys of all sizes from half-grown ones to babies just born and still clinging to their mothers' necks. One, perhaps five or six days old, was being taught to walk. Its mother sat on her haunches while another female monkey, perhaps an aunt, squatted a couple of yards away holding out her arms. Then the mother shook the baby from herself and gave him a push. He returned to her at once, and a second time she pushed him from her. He returned to her again and this time, irritated, she gave him a sharp slap. He squealed and managed somehow to totter a few steps. Again she slapped him and again he managed a few tottering steps until now he was nearer the aunt than the mother. Halting, the baby turned from one to the other with a comical, terrified expression on his tiny face and then, in perhaps his first moment of decision, he perceived that the aunt was the nearer of the two and tottered uncertainly toward her. Here on her breast he was permitted a moment's rest, and then she too, with firmness, set him on his feet and gave him a push. When he returned for reassurance she too slapped him, and he was forced toward his mother, until presently she was comforting him with caresses and a fine flow of monkey chatter.

From the shade Ransome watched the lesson in silence, his whole face warmed by an unconscious grin, but after the third adventure he became aware of a hubbub on the verandah above the baby and turned to find a raid in progress. His breakfast table was covered with monkeys, chattering and eating the bread, the mangoes, the bananas. One of them, holding his teacup, turned it from side to side speculatively as if trying to make out its use. A third, a mother with a baby clinging to her, sat in the window investigating the stuff of the curtains.

The spectacle made him laugh but at the same time he felt that the moment for decision had come and he drew from his pocket a catapult made from a fork of mango tree and strips cut from an old tire. Cautiously he picked up a round pebble and fitted it into the pocket of the sling and took careful aim. It was the only way to keep sacred monkeys in check. Driving them off did no good, for they only came back when your back was turned and began tearing the tiles from the roof to hurl them at you. He knew that by now he had succeeded in establishing in their clever brains the fact of a hidden special menace that lingered inside the enclosure of his garden—a sudden burning painful sensation in the behind caused by something which came mysteriously out of the air itself.

At last he let fly the pebble. It struck the rump of one of the females clustered on the table. She gave a wild scream and fell on her nearest neighbor, scratching and screaming and biting like a fury. And then pandemonium broke loose. The food was scattered over the verandah, the teacup fell with a crash. Suddenly there was a stream of monkeys flying up the jasmine vine to the top of the wall and then by the lower branches into the mango tree. The last of them carried with her a bright cotton napkin which caught her fancy. Only the big male stood his ground on top of the wall, jabbering and swearing. Once more Ransome selected a pebble, but he was not quick enough. The old male was no fool, and before Ransome could hit him he was gone, still screeching, into the trees. The last he saw of them was in a wild procession along the tops of the mangoes, making their way in jabbering excitement back to the security of the Maharajah's park.

"I suppose," he thought, "Jehovah must sometimes feel as I do now." For a little while more he worked, but this morning his mind, instead of becoming absorbed and lost in the very earth, conjuring up new wonders of flowers and vegetables which would spring from every stroke of his hoe, wandered away into strange paths of speculation. He wondered why it was that America, a new, a young, a rich country should have fallen into the same decadence as Europe, why it was there were no longer any men great enough to lead the way, no leaders but only mediocrities and political opportunists and dictators who ruled by brutality and hysteria.

"Perhaps," he thought, "the times, the age, economics, the very passions of mankind have grown beyond the control of man in the West. Perhaps the tottering structure has become so great, so complex, so unmanageable that there could be no one man great enough to cope with it or even a part of it. Perhaps that was what happened when the Roman world tottered and fell. Perhaps that was how some universal law operated, a law as exact, as immutable as the Mendelian theory. Perhaps man was allowed to build and build until at last, in his pride, he was crushed by the very thing he had built."

The thought brought to him a sudden humbling sense of his own insignificance and at the same time a feeling of contempt and pity for the arrogance of man himself—that he should be so presumptuous, that a few men should conquer and control disease and pestilence while a few others, like Esketh and his sort, could arrange a wholesale slaughter in which not germs or pestilence killed men by millions but men themselves. Nature, it seemed, was not to be gotten round. She simply found, through the agency of man himself, new means of killing him off, of bringing him once more to his knees, as she had done long ago with Egypt, with Rome, indeed with the very Indians living all about him who had fallen from their state of magnificence to that of subject people, preyed upon by ignorance, defeatism, superstition and disease.

It seemed to him that he had never seen his own world clearly until he had come to India. Now he saw it in all its parts.

And presently he began to think again of Esketh, wondering why he should be coming to Ranchipur to disturb its peace with his boisterous pitiless brutal presence. Vaguely he remembered him in the days after the War when he had crossed his path in Whitehall, and he had no liking or admiration for the man, neither for his shrewdness nor his ill-spent energy, nor for his talk of empire. If Esketh were coming to Ranchipur it would mean no good to anyone there, least of all the old Maharajah who in his goodness and simplicity could only be a victim. The thought of Lady Esketh troubled him because the name was so familiar to him and yet so lost. For a long time now, for nearly fifteen years, he had been out of the important, worldly life of London. It had been lost to him, like most of the other once bright important names which no longer meant very much even when he saw them with faces attached in the "Sketch" and the "Tatler" and the "Bystander."

He knew that he was not the only man who was sick nor the only one who sought escape and peace. There were millions of others like him, in factories and offices, in schools and shops, who could not escape like himself because their grandfathers had not dug a vast fortune from the mountains of Nevada. As he hoed more and more vigorously, it struck him that it was only in the earth that men could find peace and hope in these times, for there was little peace to be found in the world which man had made, a world which in his own sickness, appeared to him dull and tired and apathetic, going from makeshift to makeshift and compromise to compromise, and arriving in the end at the same old evils which had destroyed peoples and nations and civilizations since the beginning of time.

In the East he had found nothing save perhaps a druglike peace, and that was not what he had come searching for because he knew that in that very peace lay the seeds of death. He had run away, he thought, from the spectacle of his own world, faithless and without hope, slowly and wearily destroying itself.

Hoeing and thinking he became excited so that he forgot the hour and even the boiling heat until John the Baptist appeared looking alarmed and comic in his breech clout, to ask whether after all he meant to lunch at home. It was one o'clock and the day was Saturday and he should have been, long before now, on his way to the Mission to lunch with the Smileys. Throwing down his hoe, he hurried into the house to bathe and change his clothes. Then he went to the potting shed to take out his motor, one of the seven motors in Ranchipur, not counting the Rolls-and-Packard-filled garage of the Maharajah. He rarely used it save during the monsoon, for there were only two roads in all Ranchipur outside the town, one to the vast artificial lake above the town that served as a reservoir and the other built three hundred years ago by the Moguls to the ruined city of El-Kautara at the foot of Mount Abana.

He found the old Buick standing in the shed, naked and open to the burning sun, for the monkeys had been there before him, perhaps early in the morning before they paid him a visit in the back garden. They had entertained themselves by throwing all the tiles off the roof on to the ground. He grinned, thinking that in the end it was the monkeys who had won.

The American Mission occupied two big barracklike houses a mile or two beyond the race course. In the beginning, long ago, just after the mutiny, they had served as buildings to house the officers of the British troops stationed in Ranchipur. Square ugly buildings, age had given them character and time had provided beauty in climbing vines and creepers—clematis and trumpet vines and bougainvillea. They stood, shaded by mango and eucalyptus and pepper trees, a little way from the dusty road. In one lived the Reverend Mr. Elmer Simon, with his wife and two daughters, Fern and Hazel. In the other dwelt Mr. Smiley with his wife and Mrs. Smiley's great-aunt Phoebe.

In the care and the appearance of the two gardens one could read the characters of the two families. Mr. Simon's garden had no flowers at all save those hardy shrubs and vines which in India needed no care and were impossible to kill, either by drought, flood or blight. Alone, apart, it would have looked like a garden moderately well furnished and well tended, but beside the Smiley house it had a barren, rather shaggy look, for the Smiley garden was filled with flowers which even during the long drought seemed more vigorous than any flowers in all Ranchipur. There were salvias and petunias and geraniums and marigolds and zinnias, mostly sturdy old-fashioned flowers such as Aunt Phoebe had grown in her garden back in Iowa fifty years before. Begonias and pansies stood in pots along the edge of the verandah, and suspended here and there from the lower limbs of the trees hung receptacles of one sort or another—tin cans painted green, cracked bowls held together with wire, bamboo baskets. These too were the work of Aunt Phoebe who from nostalgia had decorated the branches of the mango trees in Ranchipur exactly as she had done the branches of Iowa's cottonwoods as a farmer's wife, half a century earlier. The suspended receptacles held ferns and petunia plants and lilies, but Aunt Phoebe's greatest pride were the orchids which grew in the bamboo receptacles. They were a tribute to her from the Untouchable boys of Mr. Smiley's school. They brought them to her out of the jungle and in their workshop they made her the little bamboo baskets in which they grew. It was one of the reasons (she wrote to the folks back in Iowa) why she liked India. You could have orchids growing all the year round, right in the front yard.

The effort which, with the Smileys, had gone into this garden was expended by their neighbors, the Simons, on a double tennis court and a large arbor covered with trumpet vines which stood at one end of it. This was the work of Mrs. Simon, a powerful, pretty and tenacious woman on the verge of middle age. To look at her you would never have suspected her power. She was forty-one, small and plump, with curly blond hair which had faded only a little. At the age of twenty she had met Mr. Simon at the Baptist college at Cordova, Indiana, and married him while still in the throes of adolescent experience, under the misapprehension that her feelings for Mr. Simon were spiritual and unassociated with the body. Later, because in spite of everything she was a shrewd woman, she recognized the difference but admitted it to none but herself. By that time Fern and Hazel were born, and although she knew that she had made a bad bargain she knew too that she would have to make the best of it for the rest of her life, and so she did, and sometimes "the best of it" was extremely trying for the Reverend Mr. Simon and her daughters, Fern and Hazel.

The fault had been her upbringing and background, for she came from a Baptist family in a small Mississippi town and so her ideas of life in the great world had been somewhat false and warped from the very start. At twenty she was filled with zeal for the faith and regarded the prospect of life as a missionary with enthusiasm. It was only slowly, after she had left forever the backwoods Mississippi family and the hysterical atmosphere of the little sectarian university, that she began to see life in terms of the character with which nature had endowed her. She realized presently that in spite of all the calls she had had from God, she was not meant to be a missionary but for greater things. But it was too late and so she had to compromise. At heart she had been from the beginning an ambitious Southern belle with a will of iron concealed beneath a coy mid-Victorian façade.

Without ever suspecting it Mrs. Simon was at times heroic and, like many American women, undefeatable, because the world about her—her husband, her two daughters, Mr. and Mrs. Smiley and Aunt Phoebe, even the Maharajah and Maharani themselves—existed only in relation to her own ego. All her existence was concentrated into a struggle against the world in which she found herself, to raise it somehow, to alter it, to transmute it into something which it was not. She was the wife of a missionary, but neither those early vapors which had deceived her into throwing herself away upon Mr. Simon, nor the miserable state of the people among whom she found herself, nor even the words of Christ himself, made any difference to her. She was determined to be a person of importance and of distinction, a creature much more than the mere wife of a missionary; and to accomplish this she found it necessary to dominate her husband and her daughters, to assume strange affectations, to spend all of the little income she had inherited from the hotel block back in the small Mississippi town as well as all of her husband's meager salary. There were moments when she succeeded, moments of triumph when some acquaintance or new friend made during the summer months in Poona would say, "The last thing I would have thought you were was a missionary's wife."

She disliked very nearly everyone—the Smileys most of all because they were always there before her, just across the drive, a living reproach, a nasty irritant to her own conscience, remaining in Ranchipur all through the terrible months of the monsoon while she was enjoying the cool high air of Poona, working night and day, spending their money not on automobiles and tennis courts but on the people they had come to help. They were always there, recalling to her the disappointment of her own now distant dreams when for an instant she had known an intimation of the delights of self-sacrifice.

In moments of wild exasperation she would sometimes say to her husband, "They don't make all those sacrifices just because they're good. They do it to spite you and me and make us feel miserable." Mr. Simon would reply, "No, my dear. You mustn't exaggerate. They're good hardworking people, even if they are not quite up to date." For Mr. Simon had the great gift of self-deceivers——he managed to transmute his weakness and even his petty vices into virtues. He persuaded himself that with his automobile and tennis courts he was a "modern" missionary and that he was better able to do the work of the Lord if he did not wear himself out riding a bicycle and if he kept up his health by having regular exercise at tennis. He was the only person in the world before whom Mrs. Simon did not put on airs, and sometimes the spectacle of her nakedness was terrifying to him. The worldliness of his wife was the one thing he could not quite explain away, either to himself or to the Lord.

He was really a harmless man, quite stupid and good-looking. (There were moments in the night when Mrs. Simon found that a consolation, together with the fact that the tennis courts and her regimen of good food and holidays kept him young and vigorous despite the climate.) His smooth good looks were those of a man who somehow has remained forever a little boy, unaware of the currents of the lives about him, unaware of disaster or of suffering, whose motto was "Everything will turn out for the best." Even when he wrote home complaining of his colleague it was not himself who was responsible; it was Mrs. Simon who forced him into it. In the beginning he had written complaining letters and neglected deliberately to post them, but when no replies came from the home Mission Board his wife divined the reason and afterward she posted them with her own hand. What she hoped to accomplish was the recall of the Smileys so that she might have in the house across the drive a couple who were impressed by her, by her clothes, by her tea parties, by the provincial Englishmen she picked up in Poona, and most of all by the English subalterns in Ranchipur whom she corralled with difficulty by means of the tennis courts and the delicacies which they never tasted save at her house. She wanted too someone in the house opposite who would not be reminding her perpetually, day in and day out, that she was after all only the wife of a missionary.

She had designs. She did not mean to have her daughters Fern and Hazel waste their lives as mates to missionaries. In romantic moments she saw them both, or Fern at least, married into county families, living in England in an atmosphere and background of which she had read in novels but had never yet seen. There were times when she had designs on Ransome himself as the son of an earl and the grandson of old "Ten Percent" MacPherson, the millionaire. There were even moments when, behind locked doors, she experienced in her desperation a renaissance of faith, and kneeling, prayed, "Oh, God, help me to get Mr. Ransome to come to tea. Oh, Lord, make him come to tea just once."

In her heart she thought of him with irritation and at times with genuine hatred, but these feelings she never allowed to interfere with her campaign. She hated him because of his indifference to her fading prettiness and to her tea parties. He had a way of being perfectly polite but of making her feel at the same time with a disconcerting suddenness that she was wriggling her shoulders, tossing her head and rolling her eyes like a pie dog bitch. She hated him for the prestige which he achieved without effort because he was what he was, when she worked so hard without ever achieving it at all. She hated him because everyone in Ranchipur was always asking him to lunch or to dine or to come to tea, and because she knew that there were only two places he never refused to go—to the palace and to the Smileys. And she hated him because he would go to tea and dinner with Mr. Bannerjee, an Indian, and was a great friend of Raschid Ali Khan who was not only an Indian but a Mohammedan. Somewhere in the back of her baffled, muddled brain Mrs. Simon had two profound prejudices, one against people of darker complexion than herself, and the other a conviction that all Mohammedans were demons who had large harems guarded by eunuchs where the most lascivious orgies went on incessantly. In her ignorance of history, race, geography and all culture she lumped together Indians and negroes in one large sacrifice to her early "poor-white" prejudices.

She hated the Maharajah and the Maharani because in spite of their dark complexions they were supreme in Ranchipur, of greater importance, despite any arguments she could bring up in her frequent interior dialogues, than anyone, even Lily Hoggett-Egburry and the Resident himself. And she hated them because she and Mr. Simon were invited to the palace only once a year to dine in splendor with the Smileys and a few insignificant minor officials. She would complain to her husband, "I don't see why we should be treated the same as those 'hicks' across the drive. We aren't the same."

"My dear, we are the same to His Highness. We are foreigners and missionaries."

"You ought to explain the difference to the old man."

"He wouldn't understand. You must remember he is an Indian and an Oriental."

"It's humiliating."

"It'll come out all right."

"I'm sick of hearing that."

"What would you suggest that I do?"

"Make His Highness appreciate all you do for him. Demand an audience."

And then Mr. Simon would manage to put her off by saying, "We'll think about it. We'll find some way out." And she would say, "If you don't, I'll go to him myself. You ought to do it for the sake of Fern and Hazel. It's humiliating for us to be treated as if we were the same as the Smileys." And then Mr. Simon, rather desperate, would say, "We are the same in the eyes of the Lord," and Mrs. Simon would shout, "The eyes of the Lord, rubbish!"

But nothing was done although Mrs. Simon kept her husband in a perpetual state of terror lest she make good her threat and create a scandal at the palace. He knew that it was not beyond her, if she were exasperated sufficiently, to storm the palace gates and, knocking down the Sikhs, force her way into the royal presence.

He was at once weakened and strengthened by the knowledge that

[53] .

much of what she said was true, and being a muddled man who valued peace and the good will of others more than action or clear thinking, he remained in a perpetual state of compromise and unhappy confusion. He was meant by nature to have been a good citizen with a small shop in a Middle Western town where he could belong to innumerable lodges and be a moving spirit of the Rotary Club. Instead of that he found himself, bewildered and often hurt, in the depths of the Orient where the virtues of his simple nature were completely lost. Before the intrigues of the Maharajah's entourage, made simply out of love for intrigue and through no feeling against Mr. Simon himself, before the suburban snobbery of the tiny English colony and the rudeness of the subalterns who came to his wife's teas, he was simply lost. Both his wife and the Smileys were stronger than himself, his wife because, in her energy and singleness of purpose, she simply overrode all those things, and the Smileys because for them none of these things existed; they were simply unaware of them.

He knew how much the Mission had done for Ranchipur, not only by bringing the Maharajah's subjects into the Kingdom of Heaven, but in ways far less heavenly and far more real. In his heart he knew that the conversions meant nothing in a spiritual sense, because somehow in a fashion beyond his understanding, the Hindu religion, with a devastating indifference, managed mysteriously to swallow up Christianity and absorb its gods and prophets and saints. In Jaipur he had heard a holy man saying his rosary, calling out the names of Hindu gods, saying rapidly, "Krishna, Vishnu, Rama, Jeesu Kreest!" and in the court of the big temple in Ranchipur there was a cast-iron statue of the Virgin Mary. Although he always talked otherwise he knew that the whole problem of conversion was a hopeless one. The real benefits which the missionaries brought to Ranchipur were not heavenly but material. The intelligent among the Untouchables rushed into Christianity because, once converted, they ceased to be Untouchables in the true sense, exchanging this for the blasphemous and low state which all Europeans, even the Viceroy himself and the Emperor of India, held in the eyes of orthodox Hindus. Nevertheless the gates of conversion held rewards, and if the Untouchables were indifferent to heavenly ones they appreciated the rewards of a new economic and social status and the opportunity to go as converted

Christians where they chose and make their living as they saw fit. And conversion among the wild nomadic hill tribes meant that they embraced not only Christianity which they promptly turned back into a kind of witch-doctor religion, but they embraced agriculture and weaving and settled down in villages, ceasing to make the disturbance and trouble they had created constantly in their more primitive wandering days.

Ah, it was all very disturbing and discouraging and if Mr. Simon had not been an extremely easy-going healthy man, all of whose glands functioned perfectly, the whole thing would have thrown him either into an even deeper self-deception or a state of suicidal depression. As it was, he found his life pleasant enough despite his wife's ambitions and the problems created by the future of Fern and Hazel. One thing weakened all his half-realized decisions, and that was the knowledge that he himself and Mrs. Simon were really of very little value to the Maharajah or to India because their side of the mission was devoted entirely to spiritual conquest. It was the Smileys in the schools and workshops who did all the work and achieved the lasting good, and he was perfectly aware that the Maharajah knew it.

On the Saturday Ransome came to lunch with the Smileys Mrs. Simon had one of her moments of prayer. Kneeling beside the bed in her locked room, she implored God to send a call to Ransome to come to tea. Not trusting the question entirely to the Lord, she kept both eyes and ears well open in order to attack Ransome in person when he arrived at the Smileys. She knew that he was almost certain to come because on Saturdays he always lunched there at what, in moments of exasperation, she had referred to as Mrs. Smiley's "treasonable lunches" because the people who came there were interested only in India. Those "black traitors," Doctor Ansari and Mrs. Naidu, had both been there on the occasion of their visits to Ranchipur, and Raschid Ali Khan and Mr. Jobnekar who both lived in Ranchipur came there nearly every Saturday. Mrs. Simon wanted Ransome especially on this Saturday because it was a kind of farewell party before she left with Fern and Hazel for the hill station.

So when he drove up to the door in his battered Buick, before he had set foot to the still steaming earth, Mrs. Simon came out of the house and across her untidy lawn toward him, her blond hair freshly curled, her new silk dress crisp and as yet not dampened by perspiration. He knew what she was coming for, and after the first wave of weariness at sight of her (after all, he had come all the way to Ranchipur to escape people like her) he thought, "Hell, make it Thursday." He knew that they would be leaving soon and that there would be a respite of at least three months during which he would not be invited by Mrs. Simon to a tennis party. Besides, very faintly somewhere in the depths of him there had been stirring lately a desire to see people again, to see them indiscriminately, and be amused by them.

Mrs. Simon was holding out her hand, tossing her freshly made curls. Abstractly he recognized that she was a pretty woman of a certain age and he thought it a pity that she was unwilling to let it rest at that. She kept imposing her prettiness upon you, as if otherwise you might overlook it. And the eyes were perpetually giving her away. Far down in the depths of their blueness there was something as hard and cold as marble.

"I was thinking about you only this morning," she said. "We're having a farewell tea party and I said to my husband, 'we must ask Mr. Ransome.' He was going to stop by your house to ask you. Did he turn up?"

All this about stopping by the house was, Ransome knew, pure fabrication and he found himself suddenly in a position in which many people found themselves when dealing with Mrs. Simon. He was aware that he must help her with her lies. He began to play the game. He did not know why except that he felt a terrible necessity to save her from the shame of being caught.

"I suppose something has kept him in town. I just left the house. I couldn't well have missed him."

Mrs. Simon gurgled, "Well, anyway, I've caught you on the fly. You will come, I hope?" And she cast one of her most persuasive glances at him, a glance which, if she had been a more sophisticated woman, she would have understood could mean only one thing.

Ransome wanted to laugh, first at such a display of sex in the interests of so trivial a matter; and then at all the effort she was making when, if she only knew it, her game was already won. And suddenly in the midst of it he heard from the Smileys' house the angry voice of Raschid Ali Khan, booming and violent in a broken phrase.

". . . only got second raters now———men who don't come to India to
make a career of India, but just to pass the time."

And something about the juxtaposition of Mrs. Simon and Raschid
Ali Khan struck him not only as fantastic but as absurdly funny.

"Surely. I'd like to come," he said.

"Oh, I'm so glad! I'm so glad! It's always so hard to get you."

He smiled and put his topee back on his thick dark hair. The sun of
the monsoon was like a furnace.

"Please give my best to Mr. Simon."

"He'll be delighted. I can't see how he came to miss you."

She showed signs of lingering, and he began to feel that old uneasiness
which always crept over him after two minutes of her company. It was
an uneasiness mingled with exhaustion. What did you say to a woman
like this, who made gestures of invitation unaware of what she was
doing? What did you say to a woman who made conversation in which
there was no sincerity whatever? Always when he found himself trapped
by her his mind began to wander so that he made wrong answers. He
was aware that when she spoke to him her Southern accent grew doubly
rich, so that sometimes he had difficulty in understanding her. And with
him she referred a great deal to plantations and old "mammies," which
he felt was not only laying it on a bit thick, but insulting to his experience and power of discernment.

"You'd better not stand about in this sun. It's ferocious."

"Well, good-by," she said. "See you this afternoon. It isn't large. Just
some of the boys dropping in." She always referred to the subalterns as
"the boys."

As he walked up the path beneath Aunt Phoebe's orchids and petunias
he heard Raschid Ali Khan booming out again, from the kitchen this
time:

"The trouble is that they know they're only coming out here tem-
porarily and they do their job offhand, between times, just waiting for
the day they can go home on leave. If they've got any money they go by
the Italian line and get there quickly. If they haven't they go by P. & O.
They haven't any interest in India or Indians."

And then as Ransome entered the house he heard Raschid saying

[57]

"England has lost India because men like them won't sit down with an Indian to have a cup of tea." And he knew that Raschid was talking about civil servants.

There was no one in the drawing room so he went through the passageway into the big cool kitchen where he knew he would find them. In the center of the room the big Mohammedan was striding up and down, shouting in his excitement and pointing each gesture with the long radish he held in one hand. By the stove stood Mrs. Smiley in a clean apron, stirring something in a pot. In one corner sat Mr. Jobnekar, leader of the Depressed Classes, and in the other, seated in an authentic American rocking chair, was Aunt Phoebe, fanning herself with a large palm-leaf fan across which was printed in large black letters, "GO TO FREUNDLICH THE CLOTHIER, IF YOU WANT GOOD VALUE. 19 MAIN STREET, CEDAR FALLS, IOWA." She was a small thin old lady of eighty, with a body bent and worn by fifty years of life as a farmer's wife, but in the blue eyes behind the steel-rimmed spectacles glowed the light of youth. She was enjoying herself. She liked big, handsome virile men and Raschid Ali Khan was giving one of his best performances.

He was, like many Mohammedan Indians, well over six feet with a big muscular body through which flowed blood that was a mixture of Arab and Turk, Afghan and Persian, with perhaps a dash of Hungarian and a *soupçon* of Tartar. There was really nothing of the Hindu Indian about him. Beside a man like Major Safti, big and handsome as he was, one recognized at once the difference. In the Mohammedan there was a wildness and violence while in the Brahmin there was suavity and good nature. In Raschid there was a frankness and a positive quality which in the Hindu was supplanted by tact and a taste for intrigue. The Mohammedan was all for getting things done. He was a romantic and a visionary. The Hindu was passive and mystic. "Perhaps," Ransome thought, "that is why a few million Mohammedans can hold their own against three hundred million Hindus."

With fair hair Raschid would have been blond, for his skin was fair and his eyes a blue-gray, but the hair was blue black and curly. The sharp Arab profile gave him a proud fierce look. "The horsemen of Baber," thought Ransome, "must have looked like Raschid." There was no accounting in his appearance for the few drops of English blood that flowed in his veins. It was true, although Raschid never spoke of it, that his great-grandmother was an Englishwoman, the daughter of an East Indian merchant in Calcutta long before the mutiny.

Raschid did not remember her at all although she had lived to be nearly a hundred years old and stories of her at least must have come to him from his father and grandfather. He never spoke of her and did not, Ransome discovered, like to be questioned about her. It was as if he tried to forget that drop of blood come to him from the destroyers of the rotting Mogul Empire.

Ransome tried to imagine her, a young middle-class Englishwoman in the tiny world of Calcutta, eloping with the young prime minister of an obscure Muslim State. She must have been, he thought, one of those strange exotics which England in her middle-class respectability throws off now and then, exotics more fantastic than those produced by other nations—people like Byron and Lady Hester Stanhope and Doughty and Lawrence and Gertrude Bell and hundreds of others less well known who had found relief and spiritual peace in the midst of peoples as far removed from their own as night is from day. A portrait of her which Ransome had seen existed in Raschid's possession, but from it one could discover nothing. It was done in the deliberate decadent style of Persian miniatures at the end of the eighteenth century, stylized and artificial. She sat cross-legged, like a Muslim woman, on a cushion. Through the archway behind her there was a lovely blue sky diapered with mannered stars. From the portrait he gathered that she was dark, but the most important fact was that she, a Mohammedan woman, had been painted at all and that she was without a veil. When he spoke of this to Raschid, his friend, a little annoyed, said, "No, she was never in purdah, nor my grandmother, nor my mother, nor my wife. Mohammed said nothing about purdah. My great-grandmother always received her husband's friends and went about freely. She ruled not only him but his people. She knew all about his affairs and sometimes she gave him good advice. Pure Islam does not recognize purdah. It was a corruption which grew up out of war."

She must indeed have been a remarkable old lady. In her old age her husband had been knighted for his services in helping to bring peace to India after the mutiny, so in the end she died honored by her own people whom she had scarcely seen since she was a girl of twenty. Her own romantic blood, it seemed, had brought neither British balance nor a shopkeeper's calculation to the blood of her children. It was as if God had meant her all along to be a Muslim princess, and in the end she had found her place.

Raschid was a devout Mohammedan, less from tradition than from conviction, because the religion in its purity seemed to him the most honest and practical of all the religious systems devised for mankind. Islam included Christ among its prophets together with Moses and Isaiah, but Christ (thought Raschid) had been too impractical, too visionary, and all that he taught, which like the Islamic faith had been simplicity itself in its origin, had been corrupted ever since by priests and the church. He did not deny the corruption and the heretical sects of Islam, but he found them less mischievous and less productive of evil than the corresponding complex corruptions in Christianity. Priests had never had the same powers in Islam, nor the same worldliness nor the same hypocrisies.

He knew the history of Christendom far more profoundly and in detail than Ransome or any man Ransome had ever met knew the history of Islam.

"Neither one," Raschid would say, "is anything but a sorry spectacle. Perhaps the Russians are right to make a religion of the state and the brotherhood of man."

But somehow in Islam the idea of the brotherhood of man had been preserved. Raschid himself like any good Muslim, looked upon the blackest Moroccan or the yellowest Malayan as his brother in Islam. In this, he said, Christianity had failed since clots and clusters assorted themselves according to races and according to nations; that, he would say, has been the undoing of the West: "It is that which will destroy the West in the end. While Islam is still intact from the Pillars of Hercules to the China Sea, Christendom will be a howling wilderness once more preyed upon by marauding bands."

He would issue these statements in a thundering voice, his blue eyes flashing—these and others like, "Islam forbids any good Muslim to be a money changer or to loan money for interest. Did Christ ever speak of that?"

He spoke perfect English in a poetic and occasionally pompous manner, for he was Asiatic enough to enjoy long, pompous phrases and European enough to be excellent in the field of polemics. At moments, when he got thoroughly going, even his vitality could not save him from being a bore. He would have made, with his handsome physique and his huge booming voice, an excellent politician in the West, but his great fault as a politician and as a leader in India was his sincerity. Not only did the tactlessness which sometimes accompanies sincerity paralyze his own efforts but it confounded alike the intrigues of the West and the East, so that both elements refused to deal with him because he slashed through any intrigue straight to the heart of things. He would have been a leader in time of war or of revolution, but in times of bargaining and compromise he was of no value to any party. His tragedy was that he had risen in his prime too late and too soon, and that in his heart he was aware of this.

Now, at forty, he was head of the police in Ranchipur, a Muslim police official in a Hindu state. It was a less impossible situation than one might have imagined for there had been no religious riots, nor even any unpleasantness in the State of Ranchipur for twenty-five years. That peace which was almost unknown in the rest of India had come about through the work and the will and the absolute power of the old Maharajah. In Ranchipur religion was kept inside the temple and the mosque. There were no fanatics or agitators allowed—neither Mohammedan nor Hindu, nor those who sometimes appeared mysteriously from the world outside, armed with political rather than theological heresies. And Raschid himself was the soul of justice. No one, not even the most orthodox Hindu, had ever accused him of partiality toward his fellow believers in Islam. However profound his own belief, once he had stepped into the role of minister of police he became a fanatic for justice.

Across his forehead, cutting deep into his thick, blue-black hair, there was a scar which had been given him by bandits in the middle of the Arabian desert long ago, a year after the greatest war in Christendom. Alone, with one fellow Muslim, he had made the journey on camel back across the freezing desert from Haifa to Mecca to report on the damage done in the Christian war to the Holy City of Islam. It was a long romantic tale, that journey through the dust and burning heat and cold.

He had made it not because in his heart he believed there was any special holiness attached to the city or even to the shrine itself, but because he knew that the shrine was a symbol which held all Islam together from Morocco to Macassar, and when the great day came Islam would need such a symbol. It would need a consciousness of brotherhood. He had two loyalties, one to Islam and one to India, and sometimes they were difficult to reconcile.

On Saturdays Mrs. Smiley sent her cook into the city to enjoy himself, and herself took over the kitchen. It was the one half day of the week which she had to herself, and sometimes even that was snatched from her if there was illness or disaster among the families of the girls she taught all through the week. She liked cooking and she was a good cook, and there were times when she grew very weary of Indian cooking, excellent but always too highly seasoned when the cook undertook Indian dishes, and mysteriously pallid, pastelike and monotonous when he made the European dishes she had taught him. When she took over the kitchen she was able to cook the things which she and Mr. Smiley and Aunt Phoebe liked—things like candied yams (which grew in Ranchipur in abundance), lemon meringue pie and beaten biscuit. Saturday afternoon was a gala day and, as it was also the only time when the Smileys might see their friends, their kitchen on that day had long since become a kind of lunch club. The members included Raschid Ali Khan, Aunt Phoebe, Mr. and Mrs. Smiley, Ransome, Miss MacDaid when she could get away from the hospital, Mr. Jobnekar when he was not traveling, and sometimes Major Safti. After a few meetings Raschid, who liked good food and was an excellent cook, could no longer resist the temptation of the kitchen and himself took a hand, and from then on the Saturday lunches became a mixture of Mohammedan and Iowan cooking. Raschid made dishes of which pancakes were a principal ingredient, and *hodies* and croquettes of fish and meat. Mrs. Smiley undertook the desserts and the principal dishes. In all that odd assembly there was little trouble over the diet, for the Christians had no restrictions, nor had Mr. Jobnekar as an Untouchable, and Major Safti, the Brahmin had long ago forgotten that the cow was still sacred to millions of Indians. Only Raschid, the Mohammedan, drew a line, and that was at pork. He believed that the pig was a dirty animal and that in any case pork was impossible in so hot a place as Ranchipur.

Mrs. Smiley was a small woman with a thin body and a face, which although it had never been pretty was agreeable and had in it the light which is in the faces of good simple people. Both her body and her face, worn by the heat and the hard work of twenty-five years spent in Ranchipur, save for one year of leave in Cedar Falls, were those of a woman ten years older. But somehow this made very little difference, no more difference than her lack of interest in clothes. It was something else which you found in Mrs. Smiley, something which lay deeper than prettiness or fashionable frocks, something which you could not quite define but which made you notice her a moment or two after she had come into a room—notice her and think, "This is no ordinary woman." Mrs. Smiley had no consciousness of the effect she made; there was never any time for such things, any more than there was time for cosmetics and clothes. There were never enough hours in any day for all that she had to accomplish, for all that must be done until she was old like Aunt Phoebe and at last in her grave, never having had time in all her life to think for a moment of herself.

The friendship between Ransome and the Smileys was a subject of much muddled speculation, not only in the mind of Mrs. Simon but in the conversation of the whole European colony, who could not see what it was "a man like him" saw in "that dreary little woman" and her husband. What he saw in her was much simpler than anything they supposed. He liked her common sense, her simplicity, her contentment in life. He liked her toughness which, more through the spirit than through the body, had resisted the burning heat for twenty-five years as well as attacks of malaria and once a bout with typhus. He liked her lack of pretense and her integrity—that on Saturday afternoons she allowed all India to slither away from her and became for a few hours what she had always been at heart, a good Iowa housewife. He liked her because she was undefeatable, because deep in her soul there was a profound and solid philosophy which never permitted her, even in India, to turn cynical. Above the disillusionment, the disappointment, the betrayal, the pettiness, that was all about her in the vast country, in the state, in her own church, among the very Untouchable boys and girls to whom she

[63]

gave her life, she arose resilient and humorous, always saying, "Well, that's how things are"—a phrase which with her covered everything from a burned pancake to the paralyzing intrigues of Mr. and Mrs. Simon.

She was no professional cheer-giver like the Reverend Mr. Simon, yet from her presence you were somehow able to gather strength. That was why they all came to sit in her big kitchen on Saturday afternoons— Mr. Jobnekar, Ransome, Miss MacDaid, even the great dynamo of vitality Raschid Ali Khan—all those who sometimes grew low-spirited and fearful and discouraged. And he was certain that she had never once thought of why they came. She was only glad that they were there.

To Raschid Ali Khan Mrs. Smiley was always something of a mystery, but Mr. Jobnekar, the Untouchable, sitting on a stool in one corner, listening, understood her a little, because he had been to America. He was a small dark man, wiry and compact like a panther, with the tough smoldering vitality special to Untouchables.

"It is my theory," Mr. Jobnekar would say in his odd, thick accent, "that the Untouchables were a special race living in India since the beginning of time, who were enslaved when they were conquered by invaders. That's why they have greater powers of resistance. The others are newcomers. We have always been here. We are immune to most of the evils of India because we belong here."

Unlike Raschid who had been to school in Oxford and Berlin and Paris, Mr. Jobnekar spoke English awkwardly and with difficulty. He had learned it first in the mission schools from the predecessor of Mr. Smiley, and although four years in America had helped him it did not give him an easy command of the tongue. Now and then in the midst of an impassioned speech he would say, "You bet!" or "By Golly!"

It was the Maharajah himself who had paid for Mr. Jobnekar's education in America and now Mr. Jobnekar was the leader of the Depressed Classes and the only organizer they had in all the turmoil of people and races and faiths that was India. He traveled from one end of India to another, up and down and crosswise, into the great cities of British India, into obscure barbaric little states where a Hindu might kill an Untouchable and go unpunished on the plea that he had been defiled by

contact with his shadow. He knew them all, from his own people living
in comparative peace and freedom in Ranchipur, to those who lived like
vultures off the garbage and the donkeys and cows and goats which
died each night of starvation and old age in the streets and lanes and
byways of their towns.

It was not so long ago that this had been true in Ranchipur. Mr.
Jobnekar at forty could remember when he had played near a great
pile of animals, dead of starvation and disease, which always ornamented the dirty little square in the center of the Untouchable quarter.
In famine time the Untouchables suffered less than the other poor inhabitants, for there were always the beasts which fell each night to be
collected before the vultures got them. There were still places like that,
plenty of them, throughout India.

Mr. Jobnekar was patient and crafty. He was also intelligent and educated and an excellent speaker in spite of his odd accent. In a way Mr.
Jobnekar was a kind of symbol—the Untouchable Awakened! The
Maharajah was proud of him as a father might be proud of a gifted son.
Before Mr. Jobnekar there had been no leader and so his people had
been a football for the politicians and the sentimentalists. But that was
changing now, and it was Mr. Jobnekar, passionate, filled with the feel-
ing of a crusader, who wore himself out to bring about the change. Aunt
Phoebe liked little Mr. Jobnekar immensely. He always reminded her of
Job Simmons back in Wesaukee County as a young man.

At seventy Aunt Phoebe had discovered India, and at eighty-one she
was still discovering it, finding each day something new and fascinating
and unbelievable. She had come to Ranchipur when the Smileys returned
from the only leave they had ever taken, when twelve months of Iowa
seemed to them dull and unexciting after the first reception and the first
speeches of Cedar Falls were finished.

Mrs. Smiley explained to Ransome: "You see, we'd been away for
years and somehow we'd struck root in India just as if that was the place
to which we had always belonged. And in Cedar Falls we hadn't anything to do except visit friends and relatives, and they didn't like it
because we were so fond of India. After they got their curiosity satisfied
they got angry because, you see, they thought America and Cedar Falls
were the finest places on earth, and they wouldn't believe that there was

[65]

anything wonderful or exciting anywhere else. When we left India to go home we thought it would be wonderful to be back in Iowa again, seeing everybody and everything, but it wasn't. After a couple of weeks we both wished we were back here, and we kept worrying about the school and the people we'd left behind. It's funny, when we first came out here we both hated it—the dirt and the dust and the heat and even the people, and then slowly we got to like it. I don't think I'd ever want to live anywhere else. I missed it when we went home. Life back there seemed too easy and Cedar Falls seemed to have shrunk somehow. The houses, the streets, even the river were all so much smaller than we remembered them. And they seemed kind of dull and drab."

When the time came for them to return to India and they were packing their trunks, Aunt Phoebe drove in from the farm dressed in her best clothes. She sat about almost the whole of one afternoon and after much backing and filling she came at last to the point. She said, "You know, Bertha, I'd kind of like to go back to India with you."

"That kind of knocked me out," Mrs. Smiley told Ransome. "She was sixty-nine, but she was strong and full of life, and she was full of arguments."

"Being here is dull," said the old lady, "and I can leave my farm with the boys. I guess they'd kind of like to have me out of the way anyway and not meddling around and making suggestions. I'm going to die anyway some day and I might just as well die out in India. I'd like to have a little excitement before I die. I've never had any, like Pa had when he came out here and took up land and it was a wild country full of Indians. Iowa's always been kind of tame all my life. I've never been further away than Chicago. I'm good and strong and I've got a little money laid aside. I could help around the house. I'm sound as a nut and can work right alongside any middle-aged woman. It would be kind of a rest and recreation for me."

When her niece told her about the heat and dust and disease she was unimpressed. She said, "I guess I could stand the heat all right. I guess India's no hotter than Iowa in good corn weather. And old people don't catch diseases very easy, not nearly as easy as young people. As for dust, I'm not afraid of that. I'll pay all my expenses and I won't trouble you. Mebbe I'd be a help."

[66]

Nobody was able to stop her, not her sisters, nor her sons nor the Congregational minister. She had got the idea in her head and nothing was going to change her.

"It'll be," she said, "like beginning life all over again."

And so it was. She resisted everything—heat, dirt, disease. Instead of being aged or weakened by it, she seemed to take a new hold on life. She was ageless because she liked people and she was full of curiosity and so, as she said, she could begin life "all fresh in a new country with a lot of new people." She managed the household while the Smileys were at the Mission School. She even learned enough Hindustani to converse with Indians, and enough Gujerati to give orders to the servants. She managed them even better than her niece had done because they respected her on account of her great age and indestructibility.

Her humanity and her simplicity they distrusted at first, as they distrusted the humanity of the Smileys in the beginning. All the servants were Christians and they had been told about Christ's doctrine of the brotherhood of man, but none of them had ever experienced any manifestation of it, least of all from white people from the West. Presently their suspicions were quieted and they came to understand that the Smileys and Aunt Phoebe had no desire to exploit them.

What they never quite understood was Aunt Phoebe herself and all the background which had determined her character and her beliefs and her peculiar un-European behavior. Only Mr. Jobnekar, who was intelligent and had been to America and traveled there a great deal, had intimations of it, and even for him the intimations never passed beyond the state of rather vague emotional impressions which he could not reason out because he had always been a little confused by a life which was so different from anything he had ever known. He was aware that the simplicity and honesty and friendliness of Aunt Phoebe existed in the center of America, because for two summers, partly to earn money and partly in order to know America better, he had worked in the harvest fields of Iowa and Kansas and there he had discovered these qualities. He knew too that one never found them in the Eastern states. The Eastern states were, Mr. Jobnekar thought, rather like a false Europe. He did not know, as Aunt Phoebe knew, more by instinct than by reason, that what lay behind Aunt Phoebe was a vanishing thing. *She* knew it. That was one of the reasons for wanting to come to India. In her heart she couldn't bear to stay on there in Iowa watching the old life she had loved drooping and dying.

And so here she was at eighty-one sitting in the kitchen of a vast cool barrack of a house in Ranchipur surrounded by a whole new world, by a whole new set of friends made after she was seventy years old— Raschid Ali Khan, a descendant of Baber's conquerors, and Mr. Jobnekar, the Untouchable, and Ransome who was half English and half American, and Miss MacDaid, a Scotswoman born in Sourabaya. Here she was rocking and fanning herself and chuckling at the sight of Raschid pacing up and down, making a thundering political speech while he turned his pancakes.

Once she interrupted him in the middle of a great flood of orating to say, "Don't make the meat balls so hot, Mr. Raschid. Last week they burnt the lining right out of my stomach. You Muslims must have stomachs made of leather."

She was perfectly happy. There was only one fly in the ointment and that was the Simons. She thought the Reverend Mr. Simon was a humbug, which was not quite true, and she hated the snobbery and the airs of that "poor-white" woman, Mrs. Simon.

Presently they all sat down to lunch at one end of the big kitchen overlooking the enclosed part of the garden where the Smileys kept their little menagerie. They had no children and so they had all sorts of animals. In the enclosure there were two wild pigs, a gazelle, and a hyena which was tame as a lap dog and did not smell at all. The animals, all but two mongooses which keep running in and out in a dither of curiosity and excitement over the Saturday lunch, all lay now in the shade of the mangoes away from the scalding heat of the sun.

At the table there were two empty places. Mr. Smiley said, "I expect Miss MacDaid has been kept at the hospital. We won't take away her place. And I can't imagine what's happened to the Major."

And then they all fell to talking of the weather and whether more rain would come. Mr. Jobnekar reassured them. He *knew*. In him there was ten thousand years of India. Beside him Raschid and even Major Safti and their people were newcomers.

"You see the breeze," he said. "Look at the trees. The leaves are turning inside out. Look how the dust swirls. The breeze will rise. You'll see. We'll have rain, plenty of it before midnight."

The breeze was rising but it brought no relief. Instead it only carried the dust and the dreadful heat into the very heart of the cool thick-walled house.

Mrs. Smiley rose to take her lemon meringue pie out of the Indian oven. It was perfect, the beaten eggs lay bisque-colored across the top.

"These old-fashioned ovens are better than any new fangled ones," said Aunt Phoebe. "You can even get an even heat. I never made bread as good as when we used to bake it in an outdoor oven when I was a girl."

Outside a motor drove up under the trees and from it stepped Miss MacDaid and the Major. She looked crisp and cool even in the heat, but she had put too much rouge on her worn face. The Major was in high spirits.

"I can't stay," he said. "I've got to go and see Bannerjee's father. The old gentleman is having an attack of angina. I'll be back."

"It's a shame," said Miss MacDaid. "He never gets a moment to himself."

She watched him go out, climb into the motor and drive off. Ransome at the far end of the table looked at her and remembered suddenly what John the Baptist had told him.

"It's awful the way the Major has to work," said Miss MacDaid. "He should have an assistant or two who know about angina and things like that. I try to save him all I can, but that isn't very much. Oh, lemon pie! I forgot it was lemon-pie day. We're going to have rain tonight. The porter says so and he's never wrong. I hear Mrs. Simon is giving one of her routs this afternoon."

Ransome thought, "If she would only stop talking. She's trying to hide it and she can't. It's horrible."

"There were three cases of cholera in the lower town," she said. "We had to go down there this morning. Two of the patients died and the third was brought to the hospital."

"I hope that's not going to spread about," said Aunt Phoebe.

"It won't nowadays, at least not under normal conditions. We've got everything pretty well under control."

"I'll never forget nineteen twelve," said Mr. Smiley.

"It isn't the same now. It's lice that spread typhus and Ranchipur is eighty-five percent cleaner now than it was then."

"The monsoon's a bad time for it," said Raschid. "The plague dies out and typhus comes in."

"Well, there's not much use to worry about it. Ranchipur's a pretty modern state. Men like the Major manage to keep diseases pretty well under control. Mankind isn't the victim now that it once was."

She went on talking, leaping from one subject to another before any of them were exhausted, and all the time she was really thinking of the Major and seeing him, far more clearly than she saw any of those about her, probably at this moment bending over the heart of that old humbug, Mr. Bannerjee's father. And she was talking now, on and on endlessly, because in her heart she knew that her love for him was a little ridiculous and always she was haunted by the fear that anyone, himself most of all, would ever discover her secret. She never knew, as she should have known out of her long experience with the East, that it had been divined long ago, even by the little black Untouchable boy who ran errands for her.

And now one by one the Europeans would discover it. Ransome, watching her across the table, knew that what John the Baptist had said was true, and for a moment he was a little startled and frightened by the thought of how blind and cruel nature might be. For a moment, for the first time since the war, he felt a lump in his throat.

Across the drive Mrs. Simon took a short nap after lunch and arose feeling soggy and discouraged and worried. There were moments in her life, rare but terrifying, when suddenly she would ask herself, "Why do I make all this struggle? What's it all for? Why don't I simply quit and be lazy and enjoy myself?" But she couldn't be lazy no matter how hard she tried. Something drove her on and on until at times she worked as hard and got as little sleep as the Smileys.

Lying on the bed, dripping with perspiration, she worried about the cakes and the tea, about Fern's and Hazel's frocks, and about the weather. She too, like Mr. Jobnekar, knew that it was going to rain, although she knew for a different reason. Her bunion always told her. Half aloud, she was saying, "Oh, Lord, don't let it rain until after all the guests have gone home!" If it rained before then it meant that she would have to move the tea party indoors, and that in turn meant it would be a failure. On the lawn where there was plenty of room, with tennis and badminton in progress, things seemed to take care of themselves, but inside the house she became a nervous harried hostess aware that her guests were bored and desperately unable to do anything about it.

She hoped too that Aunt Phoebe wouldn't come and sit on the Smiley's front porch looking on. She had not asked the Smileys. She had given up asking them long ago, telling herself that it was because they always felt nervous and ill at ease among the distinguished people she entertained. To the Smileys their fall from the upper circle of society in Ranchipur had come as a relief, for they no longer had to put on their best clothes and stand about pretending they were enjoying themselves. In their simplicity they had always made a great effort to go to Mrs. Simon's teas, feeling that she would be hurt if they did not appear.

Mrs. Simon, lying on the bed, thanked God that a year or two earlier she had taken the bull by the horns and announced to Mr. Simon that she no longer intended to invite the Smileys.

"I won't have them standing around," she said, "stiff as pokers with their awful Middle Western accents. They hate it too. They'll be glad not to come. It's as if they just stood there reminding us that we're missionaries."

"Well, we are, aren't we?" suggested Mr. Simon.

"Yes, we are, but not their kind of missionary. We're modern missionaries."

So the Smileys had not bothered them any more. It was only Aunt Phoebe who annoyed her now. Aunt Phoebe did it after a fashion which was at once subtle and ostentatious. As soon as the subalterns and the small officials and Mrs. Hoggett-Egburry arrived she would drag her American rocking chair out on to the verandah and sit there, rocking and drinking lemonade and fanning herself with her palm-leaf fan. She rarely bowed to any of the Simon's guests because she knew very few of them, but she sat there, grim and grotesque, reminding them all that they were coming to a missionary's tea party. It was as if she made up for the role by wearing her dowdiest calico dress and dragging in all the most vulgar properties—the lemonade, the rocking chair and the palm-leaf fan from Cedar Falls, Iowa. Mrs. Simon could not order her off her own verandah and she suspected that Aunt Phoebe behaved thus out of malice.

Prostrate in the heat, Mrs. Simon fell to thinking of the rumored visit of Lord and Lady Esketh, wondering whether Ransome knew them and how long they meant to stay in Ranchipur and whether she would ever meet them. The last she admitted was unlikely unless she could induce Ransome to arrange a meeting. She knew Ranchipur, shrewdly and well, and she knew there was very little chance that anyone at her tea party except Ransome would ever see the Eskeths save as they rolled majestically along the streets in one of the Maharajah's Rolls-Royces. They would stay in the old summer palace and meet no one but the ministers and the General, Ransome and a few important Indians. Not even Mrs. Hoggett-Egburry or Mr. Burrage, the railroad manager, would be invited. All the really distinguished people, she told herself, would be ignored. In British India, she thought, it would have been different, and almost at once she began considering again how to induce Mr. Simon to ask for a change of post to a more civilized world. By civilization Mrs. Simon did not mean culture, sensibility, intellect, art, architecture or science. She had very definite ideas on the subject; she meant a world in which middle-class suburban society reigned supreme.

The hot breeze, rising, stirred the window shades, and with a groan she rose to pull them up and regard the sky. It was still cloudless, with the same scalding sun overhead. "So far," she thought, "so good," but she knew that the burning cloudless sky meant nothing. During the monsoon a violent storm might come up in two minutes.

Putting on a wrapper she crossed and opening the door called, "Fern! Hazel!" and a voice answered her from far down the huge hallway of the ancient barrack. It was Hazel's voice, of course. Fern, she knew, would not take the trouble to answer her.

"Put on your old tennis dresses and go down and see that everything is ready . . . not your new frocks or you'll be all sweaty before the boys arrive."

Her daughters were at once Mrs. Simon's pride and cross. Neither of them was perfect and neither of them was the instrument she would have chosen to help her carry out her ambitious plans. Fern, who was nearly twenty, was the prettier of the two. She looked rather like her mother, and she had a good deal of Mrs. Simon's wilfulness, and a great deal more petulance than her mother had ever had. In spite of her up-bringing, in spite of the fact that she had spent nearly the whole of her life in India, in spite of her mother's ambitious plans for her, she re-mained stubbornly what she was—an extremely pretty small-town Ameri-can girl. Designed by God and nature to lie in a hammock and strum a ukelele, circumstance had put her down in the middle of India, in an Indian state, where the only young men she ever saw were the young middle-class Englishmen with a fondness for "ragging," and to Fern "ragging" made all "the boys" in Ranchipur simply seem not quite bright.

Her happiest moments were spent in the fastnesses of her own room with the motion-picture magazines which her cousin sent her regularly from America in exchange for occasional exotic gifts from India—cheap shawls and bits of brocade for slippers; and when she was not reading the "Secrets of the Stars" she was turning over in her mind vast, misty plans for escape. It was not very clear in her mind where she meant to escape to but Hollywood seemed a likely place. Out of the movie maga-zines and the cheap novels she read she had evolved a philosophy of life which she revealed to no one, least of all to her mother. She knew that she was pretty and she knew that for her anything was better than Ranchipur. What she wanted was furs and jewels and lovers and mechan-ical civilization. In the solitude of her own room she came presently to develop a highly organized dream life in which she spent at least half of every day. To herself it came gradually to attain the proportions of reality, but by her mother it was referred to simply as "the sulks."

Her sister Hazel, with whom she had nothing whatever in common, was plump and rather moon-faced, and like her father she had that rather good-natured corn-fed look which many Americans from the Middle West possess. Unlike her sister, she was docile and never complained and never had "the sulks," but alas, so long as Fern was about, "the boys" were unable to see the more homely virtues of Hazel.

Mrs. Simon would think, "Oh, if only Fern had Hazel's disposition and Hazel had Fern's looks." She never gave either of the girls any peace. Fern she was always scolding for her ill humor and her attitude of superiority toward the eligible young men of Ranchipur. Hazel she was forever poking and prodding, ordering her to stand up straight and not to giggle so much, forbidding her to eat because her figure was already lumpy, forbidding her even to perspire. By this method she managed to destroy entirely whatever confidence poor Hazel had ever had. And before both of them she forever dangled the prospect of matrimony as the one goal of existence.

When she came downstairs at last, dressed in a flowered silk dress and with one eye still on the weather, it was after five o'clock and all the preparations for tea were complete. She found Fern alone in the living room and said, casually, "Mr. Ransome is coming for tea." To which Fern replied sulkily, "Is he?"

"I hope you'll be nice to him."

"He probably won't even look at me."

"What makes you say that?"

"I'm nothing to him. He never even notices me on the street."

"You've never known him very well. You should be nicer to him."

Fern was silent for a moment, engaged in putting powder on her face. In the heat the powder seemed to melt away. Her mother watching her wondered how best to get round her, and all the time Fern was aware of her plans.

She said, "If you're thinking that I might marry him, you're on the wrong track."

"Why not? He's rich and comes from one of the best families in England."

"That's just the reason why he wouldn't look at me."

"You've got a lot to offer him too."

"Anyway that's not the kind of husband I want."

"What is it then?"

"I want to be something on my own. I don't want to be anybody's wife."

"That's the best thing for a woman."

"Not any more. Not in America. Whoever marries me is going to be *my* husband."

Inwardly she was constantly giving interviews which one day would appear in the movie magazines: "Blythe Summerfield Adored by Her

Husband"——"Blythe Summerfield, the Languorous Child of the Orient"
——"Blythe Summerfield, the Screen's Best-Dressed Woman." For she
had already picked her name.

"Well, anyway, try to be polite to him. Try to be pleasant for once,
like Hazel."

"If I looked like Hazel I'd have to be pleasant."

"You ought to be ashamed of yourself."

"Well, I'm not and I don't see why you have to give these awful parties
anyway. I'd rather sit upstairs in my room. I hate everybody in Ranchipur."

"Now, Fern. Don't work yourself up."

Through the doorway Mrs. Simon caught sight of the first guests
arriving. They were Mrs. Hoggett-Egburry and one of "the boys." Mrs.
Hoggett-Egburry was, by virtue of many things, most of all by her own
assumption of importance, the acknowledged leader of the only society
in Ranchipur which Mrs. Simon recognized. The "boy" was Harry Loder
who, Mrs. Simon knew, had a liking for Fern despite her evil disposition. He was thirty-three, and scarcely a boy either in years or appearance,
but Mrs. Simon lumped him in with the others. He was good-looking
in a rather beefy fashion and had a maleness which approached brutality
and never failed to arouse in Mrs. Simon a little quiver of excitement.
Sometimes during those long hot hours in the early afternoons when she
was off guard against her own imagination, she found herself wondering
what it would be like with Harry Loder instead of the Reverend Mr.
Simon.

Now at sight of him she felt the old quiver of excitement, and said to
Fern, "Here come Mrs. Hoggett-Egburry and Harry. Do try and look
agreeable."

"Oh, to hell with Mrs. H.!" cried Fern. "To hell with everybody and
everything!" Suddenly she burst into tears and ran up the stairs, telling
herself that her parents had no right to bring her up in a place like
Ranchipur where there was nobody and nothing. "I didn't ask to be
born," she sobbed, "I didn't ask to be born!"

Flinging herself down on the bed she cried for a long time, and then
rising she bathed her face in water which was tepid from the heat, made
up her lips again and came downstairs. She moved slowly, with one
slender hand resting on the stair rail, then passed through the little group

of women in the living room and out across the lawn to the tennis courts and the pavilion covered with the brilliant flowers of the Indian bignonia. By the time she reached the bottom of the stairs she had recovered herself and slipped into the one state of mind which made her mother's parties bearable. It was not Fern Simon who greeted "the boys" but Blythe Summerfield, "Languorous Daughter of the Orient."

The people at Mrs. Simon's parties always seemed to Ransome extraordinarily like the flocks of silly sheep among which he had lived for a time in the high mountains of Nevada. Long ago, watching the flocks at sight of a coyote, he had suddenly thought, "Sheep are the middle-class animal. They should live in suburbs, always belong to the conservative party and be perpetually swindled by stockbrokers."

At the first sign of danger, of menace, even of change, the sheep would begin milling about, each one pushing and thrusting to reach the security of the very center of the herd. Like sheep, the people at Mrs. Simon's parties were without originality and without initiative. At sight of them he always began by feeling ashamed of the human race and ended by feeling ashamed of himself for feeling so damned superior. That was one of the reasons he refused the invitations nine times out of ten.

Like sheep they sought only security and enough grazing to keep them alive. The world of ideas, like the world of action, alarmed them. And he was sick to death of having heard all his life that this class, this whole society, evolved in little more than a century out of industry, mechanical inventions, shopkeeping and moneylending, was the ultimate in human aspiration and achievement. There were moments when it seemed to him that the middle class and the middle class alone was responsible, with its toadying and sentimentality and nationalism and muddleheadedness, for the sickness and decay that afflicted the West.

Here in Mrs. Simon's dusty shaggy garden, a little colony isolated in the imperturbable and terrifying vastness of the East, they seemed at their worst, like a culture of specimens set apart for examination under the microscope.

Filled with boredom simply at the prospect of the party, Ransome crossed the drive from the Smiley's house a little after six. The heat was still stifling and the sun was like hot brass in the sky, but the breeze had begun to assume the proportions of a real monsoon wind born far off somewhere in the Arabian Gulf or the Indian Ocean. It was as cool now beneath the Simon's trees as anywhere in Ranchipur, save perhaps the icehouse or the inner courtyards of the great palace.

On the Simon's lawn he found exactly what he had expected to find. There were no Indians, and grouped about the tables and in the arbor covered with trumpet vines he found exactly the same world he would have found at the same sort of party in England or America, save that here, against this hot Eastern background, all the qualities both of class and individual seemed to have become exaggerated to the point of fantasy. Voices were pitched a little higher, snobberies were pushed a little further, and the accents, a queer mixture of Cockney and Middle-Western and something earnestly believed to be Oxford, together with Mrs. Simon's "mammy talk," made speech at times very nearly unintelligible, and all communication, especially for Ransome who had not frequented the set sufficiently to have discovered the key of tongues, almost impossible. Here in this remote isolated world there were no dukes and duchesses, no millionaire bankers, no prime ministers, no chamber of commerce presidents, and so each individual, unawed by the constant presence of these phenomena, expanded and sought to fill the places of the missing giants and giantesses.

Mrs. Hoggett-Egburry, a large florid woman who had created an accent entirely special to herself, stepped into the role of duchess and referred constantly to her relatives as county people in Shropshire (here in Ranchipur it was easy to refer to them thus for no one could possibly discover that they were simply honest dairy farmers). Mr. Burrage, who had something to do with the state railway, became the local Lord Esketh and Mr. Burgess, who was a kind of head accountant in the Ranchipur Bank became something which was a blend of chancellor of the exchequer and head of the Bank of England. And "the boys," with their polo and pigsticking, became Lord Lonsdales and Lord Derbys. Lost and hidden away in a powerful Indian state, far from the pomp and gold braid and rococco splendors of Delhi, they abandoned manners on the assumption that rudeness showed breeding, ignored civilization and allowed their souls to expand into a middle-class idea of what was aristocratic.

Only Mrs. Simon, as wife of a missionary, was left with no great role to play. The only missionary she could think of who had ever been renowned was Livingstone, and there was nothing very smart or worldly in pretending that she was Mrs. Livingstone.

Moving among them, watching them, it always astounded Ransome that this tight little world existed, day after day, in utter ignorance of the splendorous world which engulfed it, unaware of its beauties, its magnificence, its tragedy, its squalor. Yet, like sheep, they were aware of the terror. It was always with them, the fear of being swallowed up and forgotten; and so to give themselves courage they became arrogant and comic. Among themselves they referred to this process as "keeping a stiff upper lip." Like sheep in their fright they huddled together, all save Miss MacDaid and the Smileys and Aunt Phoebe and those two strange spinsters, Miss Dirks and Miss Hodge, who ran the Maharani's High School for Girls and were never seen by anyone. And so all these were outcasts among the sheep, mavericks who wandered alone. The spectacle of the tea party, Ransome knew in his heart, was more pitiful than annoying. The bleating, the arrogance, the odd affected accents were like the whistling in the dark of a small and frightened boy. Yet there were compensations. Here in Ranchipur all these people experienced a certain prestige and importance; when they returned home they would be lost in a vast swamp of suburban mediocrity.

Ransome was aware that he was not popular with any of them but he was aware too that every one of them, save perhaps one or two of the more cocky subalterns, was impressed by him. The sight of him crossing the lawn created a sudden stir in the little party. The men turned to look and the women became more animated, and Mrs. Simon swept forward to greet him, clinging with one hand to the picture hat which kept rising from her head at each gust of the rising monsoon wind. He thought, "If I were simply myself, a man, unknown to them, poor and without relatives who have titles, they would not look twice in my direction."

There was a tennis match in progress with the Reverend Mr. Simon, his big amiable face dripping and red, and Mrs. Burrage on one side, playing Hazel, obliging, clumsy and perspiring freely despite her mother's orders, and a dapper little subaltern called Hallett. At one end of the courts in the arbor sat most of the others grouped about Mrs. Hoggett-

Egburry who, seated in a large wicker chair, was playing graciously the role of the local duchess who had just opened the bazaar. She was a large woman, not fat but with a large blond milkmaid body which seemed not to have faded but simply to have spread. Thirty years ago she had been a beauty and she still dressed in the Edwardian tradition, in flowing chiffon and an enormous bazaar-opening hat with which the monsoon wind kept playing tricks.

For nearly thirty years she had lived in India as the wife of an official of the Imperial Bank, and in those thirty years she had come to use a language which was an odd jargon of English and Hindustani and East of Suez slang. With her a whisky and soda was always a *chota pieg*; a letter was always a *chit*; rupees were *chips*. Her husband she always referred to as the *burran sahib* and people were classified in her simple mind simply as *pukka* or not *pukka*. Her capacity for brandy was the highest in Ranchipur, higher even than that of Ransome himself. Her husband saw her infrequently: a good part of the time he was occupied with business in Calcutta or Madras or Bombay, and when he was in Ranchipur his own engagements nearly always failed to coincide with hers. She had no children and nothing whatever to do with her time save to drink quietly and go calling or coquette with "the boys." Ransome and Miss MacDaid and the Major always called her "Pukka Lil."

After a certain point at Mrs. Simon's parties a spirit of unrest began to manifest itself among the men because nothing stronger than lemonade and ginger beer ever made its appearance, and after an hour or two of the same games and the same gossip their spirits began to flag. In her heart Mrs. Simon felt that serving only lemonade and ginger beer implied loss of caste, but the shadow of the Board of Foreign Missions was always there forcing her, like Aunt Phoebe, to remember that she was only the wife of a missionary.

She was a nervous hostess, unwilling to let well enough alone and forever stirring up her parties and separating people the very moment they began to get on, in order to make new and unsympathetic combinations. She suffered profoundly and the only pleasure she got from these occasions was the illusion, after everyone had gone home, that she had come a long way from Unity Point, Mississippi. Now she kept circling round Ransome like a sheep dog, conducting him from group to group as if, now that she had got him to come, she must distribute his favors without partiality. Meanwhile she kept one eye on the storm and the other on the verandah of the Smileys' house, praying that Aunt Phoebe, for once, would not appear with her lemonade, her fan and her rocking chair to sit there watching like an angel of judgment.

When Ransome was thrust at last into the group surrounding Mrs. Hoggett-Egburry, they were all talking of the Eskeths, and Mrs. Hoggett-Egburry, the Edwardian, was explaining about Lady Esketh.

"She was Edwina Doncaster," she said, "Ronald Doncaster's daughter, you remember. He was a great friend of the King. King Edward of course. The family comes from my part of the world—from Shropshire, that is. Mr. Ransome must know her."

And graciously she reached out one large soft unsteady white hand as if to draw him physically within the circle. A little startled, he said, "No, I'm afraid not."

He had lied, partly out of a desire for security, partly because he was startled by the announcement of Lady Esketh's identity, for he did know perfectly. The moment Mrs. Hoggett-Egburry, out of her "Court and Society" knowledge, used the name "Edwina," he knew at once. He had known somewhere in the back of his consciousness all the time, but in all that had happened to him in fifteen years he had forgotten. When he had turned his back long ago on people like Edwina he had managed to forget what had become of a good many of them. Now suddenly he saw her again not at Mrs. Simon's tennis party but against the background of after-war London, surrounded by crowds of people all smartly dressed, with a jazz band playing somewhere in the background—— young, pretty, smart in handsome clothes which were probably not paid for, with a reputation already tarnished.

Once he had fancied himself in love with her and now the memory of her brought him a sudden wave of warmth and sympathy, because once he had belonged in her world and in a way her sickness had been his own—an illness which journalists had a way of fastening upon one generation and one small group. But it was an illness more widespread and profound, of which Edwina and himself were only the exaggerated symptoms. The old, living in the illusion of a security which was gone forever, could neither understand nor divine it and the young, being born to it, accepted it as the normal state of affairs.

With a fixed polite smile on his face he slipped away from the conversation of Mrs. Hoggett-Egburry and her friends to thinking about Edwina, wondering what she would be like now. He was quite certain that he knew; she would have followed the pattern of the women of her class and time.

Then Mrs. Simon left him to occupy herself with the refreshments, and suddenly out of nowhere he saw her daughter Fern standing in front of him. She was saying, "Mr. Ransome, could I speak to you for a moment?"

He had never really noticed her before and now he saw that she was very pretty and that her prettiness had been augmented by her blushing and confusion. His thoughts still entangled with memories of Edwina, he found himself comparing the two; Edwina was never fresh and young like this girl. There was never anything feverish and excited about her, and he found himself wondering whether in all her life she had ever blushed.

He managed to say, "Of course. Whenever you like."

Hesitating, blushing, she said, "Do you mind coming on to the verandah? It's rather private . . . what I want to ask you."

As they crossed the burnt seedy lawn the wind suddenly increased, stirring up little swirls of dust which had already formed since the downpour of the night before. He noticed as they passed the Smileys' that Aunt Phoebe had taken up her position on the verandah and was staring at the party, and that Mr. Jobnekar was waving to him as he sailed down the drive on his bicycle through the very midst of the party. From the direction of the tennis courts he received no greetings nor even an acknowledgment of his existence either as an Untouchable or as the leader of millions of people.

At the far end of the verandah there was a corner hidden by moonflower vines and a swinging seat, and it was here that Fern led him.

He saw that she was making a great effort. She said, "Of course, I know I'm nothing to you. You don't even know I exist."

He interrupted her to assure her that he was aware of her existence and had been ever since he came to Ranchipur. He could not say that

[81]

to him she had always been a child; indeed until this very moment he had not thought of her as a woman at all.

"Maybe you'll think I'm crazy," she said, "but there isn't anyone else I can talk to. If I even mentioned it to any of those people, everybody in Ranchipur would know in half an hour." And then she plunged: "You see, I've got to get away from Ranchipur. I'm going crazy." She wasn't Blythe Summerfield, Pearl of the Orient, now. She was just Fern Simon, a bored unhappy restless girl who in her spirit had never left her own country. "I'd rather be any place than here. I can't stand these awful people. There isn't anything to do or any place to go. I've got to get away."

Ransome's eyes opened a little wider and he thought, "Maybe she's better than I believed." And not knowing what to say he waited, aware that she made him, with her enthusiasm and unhappiness, feel immeasurably old. "I'm only thirty-eight," he thought, "about twenty years older than she is." But he knew the difference was much greater than twenty years.

She said, "I want to find out about boats and things. I've got some money saved up and I want to take a boat from Bombay, and by the time they find out it'll be too late to stop me."

"Where will you go?"

For a moment she hesitated and then she said, "Hollywood."

He laughed because he could not help himself and then, a little ashamed, said seriously, "That's not so easy."

"If you want a thing badly enough you'll always get a break. I'm still young and I'm prettier than most of them."

Silently he appraised her. It was true that she was prettier than most of them. Perhaps if she had her chance—who could tell? He was aware that he felt vaguely miserable, for as he grew older and more solitary he resented the confidences of people. He hated the responsibility of decision which they always thrust upon him, why he did not know, unless there was something special about him which he did not understand that encouraged them. Now he found himself trying to discourage her, again without knowing why, for he did not believe in meddling in the lives of other people, and even while he was talking he kept thinking, "I must be growing old and respectable. Once I'd have encouraged her to run away and find as much adventure as she could squeeze into a life which is far too short."

Instead of being persuaded by him, she began suddenly to cry, not quietly but with great hysterical sobs, pouring out all her troubles and the persecution she suffered from her mother.

"She's determined to make me marry one of those pipsqueaks. She doesn't even see that the lousy little snobs will never ask me. I can't stand them any longer. I can't! You've got to help me. There's no one else in Ranchipur."

"Be quiet first and then tell me what you want to do. It'll make a fine piece of gossip for Mrs. Hoggett-Egburry if she should come up here and find us like this."

Gulping, she said, "I want you to lend me some money. I only need about fifty pounds more."

He laughed, "Well, that's something. But it isn't the money I mind."

"I'd pay you back. I promise I would."

"It isn't that, my dear child. Don't you see? It's the position it puts me in."

She gave him a sharp hard glance. "I didn't think you were going to be respectable like all of them out there," and she began to cry again, more noisily than ever. "I won't go to Poona with her! I won't . . . and have to see all those awful people again!"

Despite anything he could do he began to laugh, until he was shaking in his efforts to suppress his mirth. He was aware that something must be done quickly. The wind was rising and the sky was suddenly black with clouds and at any moment the entire tea party might be forced inside.

He said, "If you'll be quiet and go upstairs and wash your face, I'll promise to help. I'll do what I can."

At once her sobbing ceased and again she gave him a sharp, appraising look from her clear blue eyes.

"You promise?"

"I promise. If you'll only be good now and go upstairs."

"I won't forget." And he thought, "No, she won't," and again he began to laugh at the spectacle of himself, a man who certainly knew his way about the world, being quietly blackmailed by Fern Simon in whom he had not the least interest.

And then he was aware that beyond her, by the tennis courts, some disaster had overtaken the tea party. Most of the women, clinging to their hats, were running toward the house. Two or three had climbed on to the tables at the side of the tennis court and somehow Mrs. Hoggett-Egburry had managed to scramble unsteadily up one side of the arbor. "The boys," armed with chairs and tennis racquets, had formed themselves into a circle to cover the retreat of the women against a menace which was not yet visible to Ransome. Leaving Fern he ran to the end of the verandah and discovered the cause of the panic. There in the middle of the lawn, ambling genially toward the tea party in quest of a biscuit, was the Smileys' tame hyena.

Shaking inwardly and making strange suppressed noises he leapt off the verandah to the rescue. The big brute recognized him and ran at once in his direction, making small, affectionate noises. Siezing him by the scruff of the neck he led the hyena away from the tennis party, across the drive to the Smiley's. Between gulps and chuckles he managed to call back over his shoulder, "He's harmless. He wouldn't hurt a baby," and then almost at once he realized that with "the boys" still in formation, armed with chairs and tennis rackets, and Mrs. Hoggett-Egburry still clinging in all her Edwardian finery to the lower end of the arbor, he had been tactless. "Like sheep," he thought, chuckling. "Exactly like sheep."

As he passed the Smileys' verandah Aunt Phoebe leaned forward in her rocking chair and said tartly, "I might have gone and fetched him home myself only I wasn't invited to the party."

Looking up at her Ransome caught the shadow of a twinkle in her bright blue eyes, and then he *knew*. Aunt Phoebe had left the gate of the enclosure open deliberately, so that the amiable hyena might escape and go to the party, and all at once he knew why she had always seemed familiar to him, even on their first meeting. She was very like his grandmother MacPherson who had forced "Ten percent" MacPherson to marry her at the point of a six-shooter.

As he turned the hyena into the enclosure and fastened the gate, the rain began again in big splattering drops. It seemed to him that each drop must contain half a teacup of water. The Simons' tennis court was empty now and the Untouchable servants were scurrying to rescue the refreshments while Mrs. Simon, who had given up the struggle with the monsoon wind for the possession of her picture hat, shouted directions against the howling of the rising storm.

The rain caught Mr. Jobnekar on his way home from the Smileys' and Ransome found him standing under a mango tree outside the alcohol distillery. When he had taken him and his bicycle into his car he told him the story of the hyena and his suspicion of Aunt Phoebe's guilt.

"That's what I mean about Aunt Phoebe," Mr. Jobnekar said. "That's how she's different. She makes big fat vigorous jokes. She loves people but she can't bear to see them making fools of themselves. I used to know old men and women like that in the West in America. I could always be sure they'd be kind and friendly to me. Most of them had never seen an Indian before—any kind but a redskin—but it didn't make any difference."

They drove across the bridge by the zoological gardens, past the statue of Queen Victoria with an inscription written by Disraeli, down to the part of the town where most of the Untouchables still lived. The quarter was an irregular network of streets and alleys grown up without plan over a period of a thousand years and all centered about a square which contained the tank and the wells of the Untouchables. Once not so many years before it had been a filthy place with a great heap of dead animals— the bounty and communal property of the quarter—at one end; but all that was changed now and the quarter was clean and well ordered, cleaner indeed than the quarters occupied by most of the caste Hindus. For part of the change, Mr. Jobnekar explained, the Maharajah himself was responsible, but a great part of it came from the energies and the teaching of Mr. and Mrs. Smiley. As they crossed the square toward Mr. Jobnekar's house the steaming rain cascaded in a waterfall down the steps of the tank.

Mr. Jobnekar said sentimentally, "Look at it. What is more beautiful than water? The nourishment of the earth."

Mr. Jobnekar's house was very like the other houses which surrounded the square save that it had a second floor and had been painted a bright pink that was already discolored by spots of damp. At the windows there were cheap curtains of lace which together with the pink plaster gave it a curious bedizened likeness to the villa of some small shopkeeper in Nice or Toulon. At the house next door an old woman, drenched by the rain, was hastily removing pats of cow dung from the house wall before they became wet and unfit for use as fuel.

Mr. Jobnekar refused to let Ransome go without a cup of tea and so they got down and walked through a narrow passage and up the stairs to the main room of the house. There they found that Mrs. Jobnekar was entertaining Miss Dirks and Miss Hodge, the mistresses of the High School for girls.

Mrs. Jobnekar came out of the shadows at the far end of the room to welcome them, a tiny woman with enormous black eyes and skin the color of copper, clad in a sari of pale blue cotton stuff. Although she had never been out of India her English was very nearly perfect, and for that she had to thank the conscience and devotion of the two spinsters who now sat on stiff chairs at the far end of the room. Behind Mrs. Jobnekar trailed three small children aged four, three and two. It would have been difficult to judge their ages exactly for there was something miniature and ageless about them, like Persian dolls or midgets of extraordinary beauty and perfection.

Tea was already under way and Miss Dirks and Miss Hodge, sitting like two strange birds beside the sewing machine, were having theirs. In this house, where by habit everyone sat on the floor and there were no tables, there was something grotesque not only in the sight of the two spinsters but in the very cheap chairs upon which they sat.

Jobnekar said to Ransome, "I'll fetch a chair for you directly. They're kept downstairs except when we entertain visitors," and Ransome went forward to speak to the two schoolmistresses.

He scarcely knew them, for in all the years he had lived in Ranchipur he had seen them only twice and then only on occasions when he went to visit the school. They led a life apart, without contact of any sort either with Indians or Europeans; they never entertained and they only went out on occasions like this when their duty toward the school seemed to demand it. One never saw them at the palace nor in Mrs. Simon's set, nor at Mr. Bannerjee's nor even at the Smileys'. They lived

[86]

in a neat bungalow opposite the great gate of the palace on the Engineering School Road.

At sight of them Ransome thought, "They belong in some village in the north of England living in a house made of granite where the sun only shines ten times a year." And here they were living in India beneath a sun which blazed day in and day out from morning until night from October to June.

Miss Dirks was tall and thin with iron-gray hair, and she wore a topee with a scarf which fell down the back and a suit of white linen as practical and as uncompromising as one of Major Safti's operating costumes. Her face, the texture of leather, was seamed and lined and utterly plain save for the fineness of the eyes in which there was a dark expression of suffering. Miss Hodge was less hard-bitten in appearance. She had rejected the topee and veil and the grim practical costume of Miss Dirks and wore a hat of white felt ornamented by a single artificial rose and a frock of pink gingham ornamented with little frills at the throat and wrists. But her face was as plain as that of her companion. It differed only in the fact that instead of being rough hewn from granite it was lumpily molded from clay. The pair of them filled Ransome, who was not a shy man, with shyness. When he shook hands with Miss Dirks he felt rather like a friendly dog being greeted politely by a woman who has the conviction that all dogs are unpleasant and smelly animals.

They affected Mr. Jobnekar in the same fashion but instead of throwing him into an awkward silence they forced him, as an Eastern host, into an exaggerated display of friendliness and hospitality which rang all the more false for the effort he put into it. As Mr. Jobnekar returned with the chairs a sudden silence fell upon the room and poor Mr. Jobnekar redoubled his efforts at conversation. Mrs. Jobnekar went to fetch more tea and for a few moments they all talked of the weather, of the school, of the typhus and cholera cases which had broken out alarmingly in the poorer quarters—stiff stilted conversation during which Ransome discovered that Miss Dirks seemed to have lost all capacity for contact with her fellow creatures. Miss Hodge, although rusty and shy, had moments when conversation would gush forth like a spring freshet and then suddenly dry at the source, and immediately beneath the pallid skin there would appear something which might have passed for the ghost of a blush.

The conversation could not have lasted more than ten or fifteen minutes, and during all that time Ransome was aware that the grim Miss Dirks was eager to be up and away. It was as if both Mr. Jobnekar and himself were infected with plague. He thought, "We've spoiled their call." And wanting to make some kindly gesture, he said, "I'll drive you both home. You can't possibly walk through this flood."

Miss Dirks said primly, "Thank you very much but we like walking. We came prepared. We have galoshes and umbrellas and mackintoshes downstairs."

Ransome laughed, "Well, even all those things aren't any good against the monsoon," and then he was sorry because she looked at him sharply and he divined that she thought he was poking fun at her.

Miss Hodge started to speak and then suddenly, with her mouth already open, thought better of it and was silent. Mrs. Jobnekar came forward bearing garlands of jasmine and marigold which she sprinkled with rose water and put over the heads of the two spinsters when they stood up to go. Then she gave them each a fragment of coconut and a bit of brocade sari cloth, and Miss Dirks and Miss Hodge in turn shook their hands together Indian fashion, and bowing to the two gentlemen Miss Dirks led the way out of the room. But in the doorway Miss Hodge turned and addressed Ransome with sudden boldness across the whole length of the room.

"Thank you for your offer, Mr. Ransome," she said. "Perhaps some other time. You see, we came prepared to walk. We get so little exercise." She lingered a moment longer, shy, awkward and uncertain, until the voice of Miss Dirks came up the well of the stairway:

"Elizabeth, what are you doing?"

"Coming . . . coming," cried Miss Hodge and hurried down the stairs. Ransome, watching her, had the feeling that she would have liked to have stayed behind.

From the window overlooking the flooded square he watched them picking their way between pools of water around the tank and into the mouth of the street which led toward the old abandoned palace facing the cinema. Miss Dirks walked a little ahead as if she were a trapper guide, erect and rigid, the end of her scarf hanging from the topee like the tail of a racoon cap, with Miss Hodge scurrying along at her heels. They wore the garlands over their mackintoshes and each carried the bit of coconut and brocade in her free hand.

There was something sad in the sight of the two lonely women which filled Ransome with a sudden impulse to do something to brighten up their lives, but what it was he could do and how he could do it he had not the faintest idea. Long ago when he had spoken of them to Miss MacDaid she had shaken her head rather solemnly and said, "There isn't anything to be done. You see they're like that. They might just as well be in Birmingham as in Ranchipur. They're doing their duty. They'd have the same life anywhere. I tried to be friendly but it wasn't any good. It just made them suspicious of me. They disapprove of me I think, because I feel quite as much at home with Indians as with anybody else. You see, they do their duty, but they never feel at home."

Standing at the window Ransome saw beyond their two drab figures into the background from which they had come. He *knew* what it was because there was nothing rare and unusual in it. The West was filled with just such tiny worlds—narrow, nonconformist, respectable, with just enough money to carry them through from one year to another, worlds in which there was never any color nor any fire, worlds in which the father went to an office at eight in the morning and returned at eight at night, hardworking, innocent, loyal to the employer who kept him and his family forever on the edge of starvation. Suddenly he *knew* all about the tragedy of the two lonely women. They had never lived. They had scarcely even breathed. Even India meant nothing to them. By the time they were old enough to have loved a man all love and all men had been made ugly and forbidding by the little world out of which they came.

Behind him, the three children clinging to her sari, Mrs. Jobnekar was pouring him another cup of tea. He turned to her thinking how pretty she looked and how well the pale blue sari suited her copper skin. Beyond her through the high window stretched the open country—the mango orchard and the burning ghats and then the fields of maize and millet, all the way to the fabulous mountain, Abana, rising out of the dead flat plain, its summit crowned by a cloud of white Jain temples.

"They're very odd," he said, meaning Miss Dirks and Miss Hodge.

"But they're very kind," said Mrs. Jobnekar. "If you were in trouble Miss Dirks would do anything for you and hate it if you spoke of her kindness. They're like lots of Englishwomen. They can't show what they feel. Believe me," she added as she passed him his tea, "I know how good they are."

Mrs. Jobnekar was smiling and he wondered how she, who had never been out of India, could understand the souls of two women who in their hearts had never left their own country. The very idea of Miss Dirks and Miss Hodge having tea in the house of an Untouchable seemed too preposterous to be believed. For a long time afterward he kept seeing them, plodding flat-footed through the monsoon flood in mackintoshes garlanded with jasmine and marigold that had been sprinkled with rose water.

Still in silence, Miss Dirks always walking a pace or two in front, the two schoolmistresses crossed the square before the old palace where so much evil had taken place, continuing past the tank and the music school, beginning now to be clamorous as the day's work ended and one by one the students began to arrive, past the great gate of the palace where the Maharajah's military band was giving its evening concert, until at last they came to the gate of their little bungalow. Here Miss Dirks took out a key, opened the gate and held it open for Miss Hodge to enter.

The bungalow was no longer new and its nondescript architecture was entirely lost beneath the creepers and passion vine which made it damp in monsoon time and bad for Miss Dirk's rheumatism. It had been built especially for the two schoolmistresses when they had come to Ranchipur twenty-five years before, by an Indian contractor who admired Liverpool suburban architecture. It was not well adapted to so hot a place as Ranchipur and, if the vines which covered it had been ampelopsis and Virginia creeper instead of trumpet vines and passion flower, it could have been transported intact to any English suburb and worn the name "The Nook" without startling anyone. Inside it had grown with time to become a perfect shell for the two women. Like caddis worms they had surrounded themselves gradually through the years with bits and pieces, until at last the inside of the little house had the air of a charity bazaar. There were innumerable cushions, and every available spot was covered with doilies and covers of the lace which Miss Hodge worked in moments of leisure during the hot still evenings. And there were bits of Indian embroidery and cheap brasses from Benares and a great many nostalgic framed photographs of places like the Grampians and Cheddar Gorge and Windemere.

Once inside the house the two ladies put down their umbrellas and shook the water from their mackintoshes, hanging them carefully on the golden oak hall rack where they or their predecessors had hung for twenty-five years. Despite umbrellas and mackintoshes they were both thoroughly soaked, partly from the rain itself and partly from the effect of the mackintoshes which, designed for the chilly climate of Scotland, simply became walking steam baths during an Indian monsoon.

Miss Dirks, shaking out her mackintosh, said, "Go at once and have a bath, Elizabeth. I'll see to the supper."

But Miss Hodge protested, "No, I'll do it. You take the first bath."

"Please, Elizabeth, do as I say."

And then began one of those interminable pointless arguments which occurred between them, day after day, arguments which were subtly selfish because each of them sought the fruits of martyrdom for herself. Once long ago the arguments, less frequent then, had been sincere and filled on both sides with genuine solicitude, but as the years passed they had become perverted somehow and twisted into mockeries of sincerity. It was as if each of them sought to martyrize herself in order to hurt the other by exhibiting the scars, with the implication, "Look how I have suffered for your sake. Look how many times I've given in."

They wrangled over the subject of the bath for nearly ten minutes and in the end it was Miss Dirks, the more grim and powerful of the two, who won.

From the great Persian gateway across the road the music of the Indian band drifted in through the open windows—wild, barbaric, strident and monotonous to the Western ears of the two schoolmistresses, now rising in volume, now fading away, a cacophonic clamor to which Miss Dirks had never grown accustomed. When she was exhausted by the heat and the damp the magnificent sounds became almost unbearable, especially when in her heart she was homesick for a good band concert on Bournemouth pier.

Now she burst out, saying, "I can't stand that music any longer! It's driving me crazy! I'm going to demand another bungalow."

Miss Hodge said, "We could escape it for the summer. It's not too late to take a P. and O. boat and have two months in England. We've plenty of money saved up."

"I'm not going back! I'm never going back! I've told you that, a thousand times."

For a moment the outburst silenced Miss Hodge and then wistfully she said, "I think you're wrong, Sarah. The change would do you good. We've both been away for such a long time."

Then Miss Dirks went alarmingly white and looked fiercely at Miss Hodge: "Do you want to go back there, ever again? After what happened? You must be crazy! I never want to see England again." The angry tears came into her eyes and Miss Hodge was suddenly frightened, not only by the sudden burst of feeling on the part of her companion but by old memories of injustice, of shame, of lies, of deceit which still, after twenty-five years, had the power to frighten and confuse her. In a low conciliatory voice she said, "That was twenty-five years ago."

"I don't care whether it was a hundred years ago. I'm never going back." And turning, she ran from the room, slamming the door to lock herself in with her loneliness and nostalgia and shut out from her mind the picture of a soft green country with lovely gardens where there were never any snakes or monsoons or earthquakes and no wild horrible barbaric music.

Miss Hodge made no effort to follow her and presently she went quietly to her bath.

For a long time now she had been dimly aware of a strange restlessness which had invaded her worn middle-aged body, raising a curious intangible barrier between herself and Sarah. It was a sensation which made her feel strong and miserable at the same time, and the odd thing was that in her heart there were times when she cherished it. In its weakest manifestations it was a desire to cross Sarah, to irritate her by disagreeing upon every subject, to turn even the smallest incident into a "situation." At its worst it showed itself as a wild craving for some excitement or adventure to break the narrow monotony of her existence, a fierce desire for freedom from the intricate web of habit and duty and devotion which had grown about her, more binding and more bitter with the passing of each year. At such times it was as if she became another person, forgetting the loyalty between herself and Sarah, forgetting that all either of them had in the world was each other. The feeling came over her at times in great waves against which she found herself powerless, and as each wave passed she would be overcome with remorse for having hurt Sarah and be filled with a desire to make amends. She would try to apologize to Sarah without apologizing, to explain without speaking, by the tone of her voice when they discussed simple things like the weather or the evening meal, by little gestures of solicitude and attention; but each time she was swept by a wave of feeling she was aware that like a wave breaking up on a beach, when it had passed, it left her a little further removed from Sarah. Never was she quite able to recover exactly the old feeling of devotion and understanding. Each time a little ground was lost and each of them became a little more solitary. Lately it had made her feel more and more miserable and muddled and confused until there were moments of terror when she thought she was going crazy.

Now lying in her bath, listening to the wild music from the gateway, one of the greater waves swept over her. With Sarah locked in her room weeping, it was as if she had won a great victory which left her feeling independent and strong. It was as if in some way she was enjoying vengeance, how or for what she could not say, because during these waves she did not trouble—indeed it was impossible for her—to be reasonable. In all their years together she had never seen Sarah weep, but she knew that there were times when Sarah wept because she had heard the sobbing through locked doors.

More and more as the music, played each evening at sunset, had affected Sarah's nerves, she herself had come to like it. Now it made her feel almost savage so that she really found pleasure in the knowledge that Sarah was growing old and ill while she herself was still strong. It brought her a strange excitement in which she imagined all sorts of

[93]

things which might have happened to her if her life had been different. There were moments at that hour when the daylight, fading, lingered and then quickly vanished, when, listening to the wild music, she seemed to escape from her plain rather plump body and soar to great romantic heights, when she became a woman like the heroines of Flora Annie Steel.

When she got out of the bath and dried herself she regarded her face for a long time in the mirror, studying its lines and bumps, trying her thin hair in new ways, now this way, now that, attempting to imagine how she would have looked as a girl if she had done herself with a little more dash and had not had a nose that was too snub and too fleshy at the bridge, and if her chin had been firm instead of weak and her skin lovely and white instead of blotched and oily. And then as she dressed she allowed her mind to wander about the subject of Mr. Ransome, thinking that he was very good-looking and that she would have liked to have stayed behind at Mr. Jobnekar's to talk to him. She liked his Scottish darkness and blue eyes, the leanness of his face and his nice manners. And the fact that he had a reputation for loose living and dissipation only made him the more exciting and opened up exciting vistas of mysterious things which she was unable even to imagine.

And then she tried to think what it would have been like if she had never met Sarah and had perhaps married a nice dull little clerk (she could not have hoped for more) and had a family and a semi-detached villa with a back garden in Birmingham. Sarah had taken her away from all chance of that; she had enveloped her in a web of devotion and protection, and then given her nothing in return, nothing that the hypothetical clerk could have given her.

And then all at once the music across the road stopped and outside it became swiftly dark, and the wave of independence and romance and bitterness left her as if she were a child's toy balloon pricked by a pin. It was too late, too late! There was nothing to do but go on and on with Sarah until the end of things. She would die and be buried here in this dreadful country where the earth was never cool and damp as at home but always hot and dusty. Remorse took possession of her and suddenly she began to hurry with her dressing so that she could have supper ready and on the table before Sarah could recover herself and see to it.

When she had dressed she went into the kitchen to look in upon the two Untouchable girls who worked for them after school hours, and when, fussily, she had seen to it that each dish was made to look as attractive as possible, she put on her mackintosh and went into the garden to gather a few sprigs of bougainvillea. Then she returned and going to the cupboard took out the best lace tablecloth she had worked, the one they only used once a year when the Maharani and her women came to tea. When she had reset the table she went to Miss Dirks' door and knocked to let her know that supper was ready.

When at last Miss Dirks came out her eyes were swollen and she looked tired and old, and for a moment terror struck at the vacillating heart of Miss Hodge. Only a moment earlier in the bathroom her mind, beyond her control, had been hovering about the idea of Sarah's death and the freedom it would bring her, and now frightened she could only think, "What would I do if anything happened to Sarah? What would become of me?"

The spectacle of Miss Dirks and Miss Hodge and the contemplation of all that had gone into the making of their tragedy threw Ransome into one of the periods of melancholic reflection which attacked him from time to time like an illness; and then on top of that he had been upset by the talk of Mr. Jobnekar about the work he was doing among his people. The little man, seated uncomfortably on a stiff chair out of politeness for his European guest, had talked long and eloquently after the departure of the schoolmistresses, his black eyes glittering all the while with excitement and hope. He had found a new man in Bombay, like most of the Untouchable leaders, a Christian. Each time he found a new worker it was, he said, like waking on a bright cool morning with the sun shining brilliantly. The new man was called Mr. Bikaru and he came from the United Provinces.

"It's spreading," Mr. Jobnekar said with excitement. "It's spreading all over India, much more quickly than anyone could hope. By Jesus! we're beginning to get somewhere. You see, we're organized now. That's one of the things we've learned from the West—organization, banking, even

[95]

things like engineering. By golly! We'll have all our own engineers before very long, to make steel and cotton mills and build dams. The British have taught us a great deal and lately we've been learning from the Americans. We're waking up. It has a huge body—India—and it takes a long time for it to waken."

"Don't learn too much," Ransome wanted to say, "or you'll only destroy yourselves the way the Japanese are doing," but he held his tongue in the face of Mr. Jobnekar's faith and enthusiasm. It was the faith of men like Mr. Jobnekar and Raschid which he envied. They believed in something, in a marvelous, almost mystical future for which they might give their souls and their bodies. What was there to work for in England or France or America? Where was there to go? You could make money and pick up worldly honors but that wasn't living. You couldn't live without faith. You merely existed in a dull squalid fashion.

Suddenly he took his pipe from his mouth and interrupted Mr. Jobnekar: "That's what the enemies of Russia won't see. Faith! They don't see, or perhaps it's beyond their understanding, that faith is more exciting than silk stockings and the mass production of pins . . . that it's the most exciting thing on earth, the only thing which makes life worth living."

What man or what people had faith in Europe? Who was there that desired anything beyond middle-class security and a chance to make money? No, the West was tired. There was no one, no man, no people, strong enough and young enough to make the effort.

Feeling the old depression stealing over him, he rose and said, "I must go now." For when he felt thus he was not only impossible company but he found anything save solitude unendurable.

Mrs. Jobnekar came in with a garland of marigold and jasmine and put it over his head. The gesture touched him because he knew that he had been an unexpected guest and there had been no garland prepared. It pleased him too that Mrs. Jobnekar and her sisters made no attempt to become imitation Europeans. They had the integrity which must accompany faith.

Ransome knew exactly the moment when he had been aware of the illness for the first time. It had come over him one evening in Flanders a little after his twentieth birthday and two days before he was wounded for the second time. It was evening, a still blue evening in summer with a long fading twilight so different from the quick nightfall in Ranchipur, and he had been sitting on the ground with his back to the wall of a house which had been hit the night before, listening, with half his mind, as one always did, to the distant roar and crackle of the German shells that were reducing to dust, with systematic thoroughness, the villages among the low hills beyond Boschaepe. He was full of thin Flemish beer and cheese and his whole body was relaxed and peaceful in the knowledge that he would have one more night of respite from the lines, for it had long since ceased to be exciting. Even to a boy of twenty it was only a dull horror.

He had been thinking about the quiet green village of Nolham and what his father and mother were doing, and wondering whether when the war was finished, if it ever was, he would go back there and take over one of the farms, or go up to Oxford for a while, or simply clear out for Canada or South Africa and find a new world where he could build up a life of his own, free of all the things he hated at home. And slowly through his daydreaming he became aware of the shrill sound of a fife, a perky, gallant sound, and turning his head, he saw coming down the street from the direction of Ypres a dozen companies of soldiers from the Midland regiment which had been hustled in to take over the Belgian lines. They had been there for ten days or more and there was nothing strange about them; he had seen them again and again. Only this time he seemed to see them with a kind of second sight, not as men, but as monkeys, a whole regiment of monkeys, but tragic without the grotesquerie and humor of monkeys.

They marched toward him and then past him, half a regiment of men, none of them much over five feet tall, gnarled, hard, brave little fellows, but all rickety and twisted and deformed. Past him they went swinging along to the sound of the fife, rank after rank, and presently he was aware of a profound feeling of pity and affection for them. It seemed to him that he saw beneath the drab ill-fitting uniforms, beneath even the tough skins of the twisted undernourished little bodies, bleached by years of mines and factories, into the hearts and beyond even that, into the womb of time and what it was that had made this whole regiment of gnomes. He saw them born out of the smoke and filth of factories, out of the damp and blackness of mines, out of starvation and misery and strikes, the greed of mankind and the black sanctimonious hypocrisy of the nineteenth century. None of them had ever had a chance at life, nor their fathers and mothers for generation after generation before them, until at last they had emerged from the womb of time, whole regiments of men, small and wretched and deformed. In his half-dreaming state their numbers seemed multiplied vaguely into thousands and millions coming not only out of the Black Midlands but out of France and Germany and America and Italy, from all the Western world, marching and marching, a cloud of men. For a moment in a kind of vision the whole dreary Flemish landscape, the low hills in the distance, the very sky itself seemed filled with marching men.

And then as the sound of the fife died away he wakened, feeling sick and depressed, thinking, "I must be going balmy," but oddly enough he knew in his heart that what he had dreamed was truth. All that night— that one precious night of peace—he had not slept at all, and the next morning he went back again to the lines filled with a sense of numbness and despair which made the discomfort and danger and misery seem no longer anything at all. And then two days later he had thrown himself forward at the head of his men to attempt a desperate thing and received a bullet in the thigh. And for that, months later, they gave him a decoration, never knowing that he had charged forward not because he was valiant and brave and full of faith in his action, but because he had hoped to be killed in order that he would no longer have to suffer that sense of shame for being a man, one billionth part of what was called "the Civilized West."

During convalescence the sense of depression clung to him, and when his father came to him proposing that he be transferred to a "cushy" job to which he had a right as a man who had been twice wounded and given the V. C., he surprised everyone by accepting. He was finished with the indiscriminate killing of men. He knew then that if ever he killed again he would know the man he killed and it would be for a reason.

And then when the War had finished the neurasthenia did not go away. It remained, growing a little stronger each time it returned, so that there was no way for him to return to normal life and to find for himself a place in the civilization that was England. He tried a dozen things but each time he abandoned them in the end—business, a chance to go into the Foreign Office, a farm in Sussex. Each time it was the same story; there would come a moment when he was overcome by apathy and disgust, a moment when it was no longer possible to apply himself or even to have any interest any longer in what he had undertaken. Always he was aware of the world outside himself, of the sickness which was not his alone but the sickness of a whole nation and a whole civilization; and then he would plunge himself into dissipation and debauchery as if by doing so he could emerge once more, clean and fresh. For a little time it was effective, but he came presently to have the name of being vicious and undependable, a rake and waster, and then one day when he had wakened from a long bout with drink and women he sailed for America, from which his mother had come; and since that time he had not seen England again.

What he sought in America was a vague thing, which became clear to him only after he had married and spent years there. It was, he thought, something which came down to him in his blood, a heritage from his grandparents. He had run away from England partly because Europe had become insufferable and partly because he had hoped to find in America a country and a people that were less tired. Dimly he was aware of an impulse to return to the source of something he had once known very well, which went back to his youth; and always in his mind, what he sought was associated with the small energetic figure of his grandmother, not the Countess of Nolham but Mrs. "Ten percent" MacPherson; and so he came at last to Grand River which was the only town that he really knew in America.

She had left Grand River as a girl of seventeen to accompany her father to California to find gold and she had come back to Grand River after she had married MacPherson and was fabulously rich, to build herself a huge turreted house overlooking the Ohio River. There Ransome's mother had been born and her brother, and there his grandmother had always returned, no matter what glamorous adventures or what brilliant people she had encountered in New York and London, and Paris. There she returned after her husband had served as Ambassador to the Court of St. James', for Grand River and the huge turreted house she loved better than any place in the world.

Long after she was dead Ransome thought of her a great deal, seeing her with a clarity he had never known during her lifetime, for she had died on the day he was wounded the second time in Flanders when he was still only a boy of twenty. And the older he grew, the more he suffered, the more he came to understand her. He understood that she had had a simplicity and an integrity such as he had never encountered in any other person. It was her integrity that forced her always to return to Grand River where she knew everyone. That was her country. The people of Grand River were the people she knew and understood and loved. That was the world in which she felt at home, where she could barter with the tradesmen and call half the population by their Christian names, where she could, when the spirit moved her, take off her famous pearls, go down into her own vast kitchen and bake a cake or make pancakes which were better than the most expensive chef could create.

Of all her grandchildren he had been her favorite, and because he was the youngest son his parents made no objection to his spending summer after summer with her in the turreted house in Grand River, summers which were a mingling of delight and misery because he had there a freedom which he had never known in England and because he earned in the beginning the mockery of the other boys for his neat and elegant Eton accent. Long afterward he came to understand that his childhood had been extraordinary, divided as it was between an English public school and a thriving town in the Middle West. There were moments when it seemed to him (during those bitter, clinical examinations which he made of himself) that this experience lay at the root of all his later misery and defeatism and neurasthenia. It was in a way simply one shock and change after another, a kind of perpetual readjustment which was too much for the stability of any child. It was like a childhood divided between a Manchu family and a Scottish Presbyterian household.

Because she had loved him she had spoiled him, and when old MacPherson died she took him over as her own, talking to him sometimes as if he were a grown man, confiding in him, telling him in the evenings when they dined alone in the huge ugly paneled dining room stories out of her extraordinary life. Sometimes they were stories of the Nevada mining town where she had run a boarding house for miners at the age of twenty, sleeping always with a revolver beneath her pillow; and sometimes they were stories of the King or of ambassadors and prime ministers. She was eighty-two when she died and during the last summer he spent with her, the very year the war began, she told him things she had not told him before, things which perhaps she had never told anyone. It was as if she was aware that she was dying and felt the necessity of confiding to him many things which otherwise might have been lost forever. Among them was the story of her marriage.

When she was nineteen she had found herself alone in a small Nevada mining camp, her father dead in an accident, with no money at all and so, because she was a good cook, she had opened a boarding house for the miners and made it pay. And among the miners there was a young fellow of Scottish descent from Pennsylvania, a big brawny good-looking young man who fell in love with her, and presently she fell in love with him too, so much in love that there was never any other man in her life.

"It was a little place," she said, "just fifty or sixty shacks on the side of a rocky canyon and there were only seven other women in the camp and none of them better than they should have been. If you're lucky, my boy, you'll fall in love in the same way with a girl who will be just as lucky if it happens to her, but it doesn't happen very often . . . not to one person in ten thousand, so don't hope for too much. There wasn't any church in the place and there wasn't any preacher nearer than Sacramento and that was a good three hundred miles away, so we didn't wait for the preacher. It would have been foolish. You never saw your grandfather as a young man, but no woman in her right senses would have sat about waiting. She'd have been a fool if she had. . . ."

And then she discovered that she was going to have a baby and suggested that after all they had better leave the mine for a month and go to Sacramento to be married.

"He didn't want to go very much," she said. "He had a strange feeling that if he kept on digging he was going to strike it rich. I guess he felt in his bones all the time that the gold was there. He kept putting me off and saying he'd go next week or the week after but I was determined I was going to be married before the baby was born. He was always like that. When he had something big on his mind, he let everything else slide until he got it done. That's how he was successful in whatever he undertook. He wouldn't give in till he got the thing done. That was the way he courted me. Well, a month passed and then another month and then a third and then I decided that the time had come to take affairs into my own hands, and so one morning I packed up everything and took my pistol and went to the mine. He was working there, finding traces of gold and excited because he knew there was more where it had come from. So I pointed the pistol at him and said, 'Jamie MacPherson, we're going to go to Sacramento to be married!' At first he just looked at me as if he couldn't believe what he saw was true, and then he sat down and began to laugh. I never saw a man laugh harder. He shook and shook and went on laughing until I said, 'Hurry up and get through with it and come down the hill and pack.' So he came, still laughing, and packed up his things and we set out for Sacramento on two mules. It took us about two weeks to get there because the going was awful, with hardly any trail at all. And all the time I kept possession of the gun and most of the time he kept laughing. Afterward he told me that he'd never loved me so much as when I stood there pointing the pistol at him. He'd never had any intention of not marrying me, and I knew that too, but I knew how he put things off.

"Well, we got married and went back to the mine and pretty soon I had a son who was your Uncle Edward. He's always been pretty tough and tenacious. He had to be, I guess, to stand all the jolting on that trip to Sacramento and back. And two days after he was born your grandfather struck the lode, and with a son and a million-dollar gold mine he was something to watch. I thought for a couple of days he was going to burst.

"I guess your grandfather never regretted the marriage. It brought him luck and sometimes when he was in a tight hole I was able to help him out. Anyway I was in love with him all my life, just as much as I was in the beginning and I still am now. Sometimes in the night I wake up and think about him and me and the days back there, and it's almost as good as living them all over again."

As Ransome grew older, she became to him the most vivid figure in all his memory, far more vivid than his own mother, her daughter, for with the daughter's generation the softening process had already begun. Ransome's mother liked Europe better than Grand River. She married an Englishman, against the will of her mother, and slowly she lost what character she had and became merely the appendage of a tradition. She was dead now and there were moments when Ransome found it difficult to remember her very clearly—a pale woman who grew a little more sad each year, lost and rootless. In the end, just before her death, she drank secretly.

In a way he went back to America and to Grand River after the War to find his grandmother or to find what she had been and what she had stood for, but he never found her nor did he find any of the things she had been. He discovered that in a powerful fashion she had given her own color to the town; his impression of the place had really always been an impression of the old lady herself. When he returned he found neither her simplicity, nor her sense of equality, nor her integrity and her downrightness. He found instead a town that was an imitation of Europe, a place in which there was no longer any simplicity and people were valued not for their character and their eccentricities, as they had been in her time, but for their money. And he found the same sickness that he found in Europe, the same weariness and recklessness, the same despair stifled by drink, the same misery among the working people. In a city a little over a hundred years old he discovered the maladies of cities which had been in existence for a thousand years. In some ways it seemed to him worse than the old cities, for it was senility imposed upon adolescence and so it became grotesque and exaggerated and some-times terrifying. He found no faith here either save in the automobile factory and the stock market.

And insanely he married.

Now in Ranchipur, years afterward, there were moments when it seemed to him that his marriage had never happened at all, so dim and so unimportant had it become. But he knew that he had married partly because Mary Carstairs had caught his fancy for a little time and partly because he had wanted to settle himself into Grand River to rediscover that lost world which had been his grandmother's. He took his wife to live in the old turreted house, closed and empty since the death of old Mrs. MacPherson. He did his best but it did not work. He knew afterward that it could never have succeeded and that the fault was his, because he remained forever a stray and an outcast in the community to which his wife belonged. And once he had had enough of her physically, he saw her clearly in all her superficiality, her cultural shallowness, her snobbery, her trivial ambitions, her reckless barbarity. He had deceived himself for a little time but the deception could not have lasted; and she in the end found him a tedious prig who would not take her to England, to the world that was his by right and which she found, from a great distance, so glamorous. And so one day he had quietly gone away and she divorced him. It was all as if it had never happened. And almost at once she married the son of the president of the automobile factory, and now she lived, not in the old turreted house which was pulled down, but in an imitation French chateau furnished by decorators from New York.

From Grand River he had gone into the Far West to the country where his grandparents had been married. He had expected to find a new country but he found that it was already old and not very different from the thing he had run away from. People talked big of frontiers and democracy but these things, he discovered, no longer existed in reality. In two or three generations the things they boasted of were gone forever, as if they had never existed; and a little way from the town where his grandmother had kept a boarding house he found coal mines where starving miners and their wives and children were shot down by gangsters imported from the East and paid by a pious Baptist who had so many millions that he gave them away wholesale, not to the starving miners who did an honest day's work, but to charities and good works which might gloss over the greed and hypocrisy and dishonesty upon which the vast fortune was built.

Now and then, here and there, Ransome had found a single old man or old woman who had known that vanished world which had existed for so short a time, never in Europe but only in the West of America.

But their point of view, their very manners were regarded as obsolete and eccentric and even comic. It seemed to him that out of the simplicity he found in them might have grown something splendid and wonderful. That was why he had loved Aunt Phoebe Smiley the moment he saw her in Ranchipur, that and because she made him think of his grandmother.

In his heart he knew that he was more American than English and that in spite of everything he had always been a stranger in England, rebelling against rigid formulas of living, economic inequalities and the system of caste which at moments seemed to him as uncompromising as the system he found in India. He was not European at all but neither was he a good American, accepting the American faith in panaceas, or deceiving himself as Americans did. Nor did he accept its worship and awe of success and wealth.

He was neither one thing nor the other but only, as he knew bitterly in his heart, a dated and useless liberal in a sick world which demanded violence and ruthlessness and revolution to set it right—a disappointed idealist, solitary and bitter toward his fellow men because they were greedy and hypocritical and predatory. Bitterest of all he had come at last, slowly and grudgingly, to the knowledge that he himself was useless, paralyzed by his own dark pessimism, as useless even as the holy *sadus* sitting naked on the steps at Benares.

In Ranchipur he had found peace for a little time. In Ranchipur he had come dangerouly near to accepting that death in life which the Hindus offered, but in time that temptation had passed and now the danger was gone. He had been saved, he knew, because out of his own bitterness and despair he had discovered what it was to hate; and out of that, he was aware, strength might come, for in his time hate and violence were the only means by which the great sickness might be cured.

It was Raschid's capacity for hate which attracted Ransome to him in the beginning, for the big Muslim came of a race and a faith which had never placed faith in gentleness and nonresistance. Its hate, its zeal for reform had never degenerated like that of Christianity into a preoccupation with theology and private morals. Raschid in his Islamic faith looked upon greed and hypocrisy and knavery as infinitely greater crimes than adultery or polygamy or perversion. The Christian church, thought Ransome, having profited again and again by crimes against humanity, now overlooked them in its morbid concern over sex. Raschid had faith, he had power. He was the new Islam, yet he was as old as Mohammed. He himself had no faith, for there was none in the Christian world. But he was beginning to know hate, and through hate he might be saved.

On his way home he went around by the music school. Once he was rid of Mr. Das he would listen to the music alone, for the singers never addressed him. It was Jemnaz Singh and his two apprentices who again played and sang for him, and this time there was no lightning and no thunder. Outside the rain fell with a faint steady roar, destroying at last even the violence of the wind, and against the accompaniment of the rain Jemnaz Singh, exquisite, cross-legged and beautiful in his brilliant Rajput turban and *atchcan*, sang a song of thanksgiving to Krishna for the deliverance from drought and famine. It was an ancient song, thousands of years old, of which Ransome understood scarcely a word since Jemnaz Singh sang in the tongue of the Rajput warriors, but while he listened peace began to come once more into his spirit, for there was something eternal in the song which said, "Nations come and go. Kings rise and fall. Millionaires come into being and are destroyed overnight, but we, the Earth and the people, go on forever."

It was dark when he left the music school still wearing the garland of marigold and jasmine. The spectacle of a European man garlanded with flowers driving a five-year-old Buick through the monsoon rains did not strike him as ridiculous. Once the newness wore off, once you had ceased to be merely a tourist, there was nothing ridiculous in all of India. It was so ancient, so vast, it sheltered grudgingly so many peoples, so many faiths, so many customs that all of them were mixed together and swallowed up in an indiscriminate fashion, as the Hindu faith quietly swallowed up Jesus and Mohammed and Buddha.

At the smaller bridge near the zoo he was forced to stop and wait while one of the Maharajah's great Rolls-Royces, spattered with red mud, rolled heavily across it. Inside, sitting rather like wax works beneath the top light, sat two people, a pretty blonde woman of no age at all and a heavy blond man with a purple face. The woman stared at the old

Buick as they passed without even changing her expression. The man took no notice but kept on making notes on a folded bit of paper.

Ransome thought, "It's the Esketh's. They've been taken to visit the waterworks."

He would not have recognized her if he had not known that it could have been no one else. It was not that she had changed greatly but that the face he saw was a dead face, like a mask made with great realistic skill. The perfectly done hair was like a wig, and the costume of white silk was too perfect and too unspoiled to be worn by any woman in the midst of an Indian monsoon. Not knowing that he was in Ranchipur, she could scarcely have recognized him in the man driving the sunburnt old Buick with a garland of marigolds round his neck. Perhaps she would not even remember him. A good deal had happened to them both since they last saw each other.

"She is," he thought, "exactly as I knew she would be."

Thinking of her, he stalled the old car when he attempted to start it, and once it was stopped he made no effort to restart the motor but stayed there for a long time near the cast-iron statue of Queen Victoria carrying an umbrella and a reticule. The river was no longer a still green canal, reflecting a mosaic of stars; it was moving now, yellow and turbulent, lapping higher and higher against the low flat steps which led from the water up to the jewel-box shrine of Krishna, and its wild coming-to-life fascinated him as it always did. Presently, step by step, it would rise to the level of the road and of Krishna's temple, until you could hear its roaring all through the damp hot nights. There was a story that once, long ago, during the rule of the wicked Maharajahs, the river had not stopped at the level of the road but had risen and risen until the temple of Krishna was drowned, and the roaring water, bearing trees and dead beasts and men, had swept over the whole city of Ranchipur. It must have been, he thought, a splendid and savage spectacle—that of an angry Nature destroying what the puny hands of man had raised. And afterward there had been famine and pestilence and death. He regarded the dumpy statue of the Queen and thought, "If that happened again the good Queen, the housekeeper of a whole empire, would be drowned like the temple of Krishna."

But it couldn't happen again, for the Maharajah, fearing such a disaster, had taken the most violent and writhing curves from the river and left it moving quietly through the center of the town, like a cobra crossing the garden path.

Dreamily he fell to thinking of Edwina and of himself as they had been long ago, just after the War, and the thought of them as they were then made him feel suddenly sad and immensely old. He had always liked her and for a time he had been in love with her, and looking back now from a great distance it seemed to him that perhaps if their lives and their ancestry and the time in which they lived had been different, they might have loved each other profoundly and been married and found the stability which neither of them had ever found. But he knew that with his strange spells of melancholia and debauchery he would have made a wretched husband, and that she with her upbringing and giddiness and lack of any moral sense would have made any man a dreadful wife. How could they have been faithful to each other when there was nothing in life in which they believed? They had snatched at pleasure on two week-ends, without scruple or remorse, and then suddenly they had become bored and the whole thing had come to an end, leaving them the best of friends, with so little interest in the adventure that, so far as he could remember, they had never spoken of it again. And now, thinking of it, it seemed to him that they had scarcely ever been alone. Always they had gone about in crowds as if solitude held some terror for them. It was Edwina and her sort—his own sort for that matter—who had driven him in the end from England and from Europe. The sick ones . . . but no sicker than all the rest, the millionaires, the politicians, the bankers. . . .

"We were the bright young people," he thought. "We were the first of Modern Youth. And now look at the God-damned thing."

Gradually the sound and the sight of the yellow rushing water in the wet twilight seemed to hypnotize him, and he thought that it would be quite easy to slip from the bridge into the wild stream and never be seen again. No one would ever find your body; the crocodiles would see to that. This was the time to do it; in a day or two, if the rains held, it would be full of snakes and floating debris and even the bodies of those animals who had escaped the vultures and the jackals only to be devoured by the crocodiles. It was the first time for months that the idea of suicide, once continually with him, had returned. It would be easy and rather magnificent to slip over the edge and disappear. Certainly no one at home would miss him—neither Mary safe in the security of her Grand River French chateau, his brothers nor his father. Very few would miss him here in Ranchipur. Perhaps Raschid and the Smileys and Mr. Jobnekar, perhaps even the Maharajah. But after a week or two his death would make very little difference even to them, for he was in no way a part of their lives, in no way necessary to them as Raschid and Mr. Jobnekar were necessary to the future of India and the Smileys, whose death would leave half the poor and wretched of Ranchipur bereft and lost. No, logically, there was no reason why he should not destroy himself, save that he no longer wanted to do it.

Through the mist of his thoughts and the roar of the river he was aware of the sound of little silver bells and the clop-clop of horses' hoofs, and then a tonga passed him and a hearty voice shouted a greeting. Still at a trot, the tonga rattled across the bridge into the gathering darkness and rain, but by its lights he could see that it was a gay little tonga painted bright red and decorated with bits of looking glass. And the voice and the great figure huddled beneath the too low roof he recognized as that of Raschid—Raschid the Saracen, the Warrior, born too late and too soon, driving home from his office to his wife and his seven handsome children. He pressed his foot to the starter and drove off past Queen Victoria, feeling suddenly cheerful again.

At home he found that John the Baptist and his friends had replaced the tiles the monkeys had thrown from the roof of the shed and were huddled inside, gossiping and playing the flute.

In the house he found two notes. One was from Mr. Bannerjee asking him to dinner on Thursday to meet Lord and Lady Esketh. The other bore the Maharajah's turban, star and scimitar and was a summons to the palace to dine there with the same distinguished visitors. As he finished reading them darkness came down outside in the garden, suddenly, like a curtain. Switching on the lights he noticed that mildew had already formed on the wall of the dining room. For a moment he fancied that the river had already begun to roar and that he could hear it. Against the faint sound came the thread of music from John the Baptist's flute. For a long time he stood quite still listening, as if to catch still another sound, fainter than the others, so faint that it scarcely existed outside his imagination. It was the sound of things growing, of roots thrusting, of buds bursting, of vines writhing with vitality—the sound of a whole vast continent come to life with the rains.

It was the last dinner of ceremony at the palace until the monsoon was over and important people began once more to circulate back and forth in dusty trains across the burnt red plains of India, not humble people like the Smileys and Aunt Phoebe and "Dirks and Hodge," or even people like Mr. Jobnekar and Raschid Ali Khan—for they never went to hill stations where it was cool, high above the clouds which flooded the plains —but viceroys and millionaires, and generals and maharajahs, and people like Lord and Lady Esketh. No dinner of ceremony would have been held so late in the year save for the untimely visit of the Esketh and the request of His Highness' friend, the Viceroy, that they be entertained splendidly.

No one expected to find much enjoyment in it, neither the Maharajah, nor Ransome, nor Esketh himself, nor even Raschid whose own vitality made almost everything seem enjoyable, but least of all the old Maharani and Lady Esketh. For Her Highness it meant that she would have to be magnificent and a little pompous and polite all evening, and long ago she had ceased to find pleasure in any of these things. For Lady Esketh it meant nothing at all, for even that first faint curiosity about the bizarre magnificence of India was satiated now. The person to whom it brought the greatest enjoyment was one who was not invited at all.

This was Miss Hodge. At seven-thirty she was already seated on the verandah of the bungalow opposite the great palace gateway, her face a little flushed with excitement, embroidering and waiting for the first vehicle to arrive. A little earlier in the evening she had been upset again by the sound of the wild military music and there had been another stifled incoherent scene with Miss Dirks over leaving the gate of the front garden open so that she might see the guests as they arrived. It was quite true, as Miss Dirks had pointed out, that it would be too dark to recognize any of the guests, but this argument had no weight with Miss Hodge; she knew every vehicle from the tonga which Mr. Jobnekar hired by the month to the purple Rolls-Royce which was used by important guests like the Eskeths, and she could imagine the people inside. This time the strange unsatisfactory quarrel had ended without a climax, without tears or reconciliations, leaving behind it a sense of incompleteness and misery.

Seated on the verandah, Miss Hodge was taking a superior attitude and trying to forget it all, but somehow she could not and in her heart there was a sense of shamed triumph. Again she had won a victory; the garden gate was open so that she had a clear view of the palace driveway. She kept talking to herself about Miss Dirks, not audibly, for Miss Dirks sat just inside the window, but with such fervor that her lips moved to form the words without her knowing it. She kept telling herself that it was absurd of Sarah to want the gate closed so that no passerby could look into the garden.

It was an exaggerated neurotic feeling. You'd think, instead of asking simply to have the gate open, you'd asked her to walk naked across the great square by the cinema. It was perfectly ridiculous, Miss Hodge told herself, and morbid and showed no sense of proportion. If there had been any reasonable objection she would have yielded without a word. Sarah certainly knew that she scarcely ever disagreed with her. But this time surely she was in the right. That was why, after they had quarreled, she simply walked out of the house down the path and opened the gate. Sarah could have gone out and closed it again, but she would only have opened it once more. She could not allow herself to be forever browbeaten by Sarah. Now and then she had to assert herself.

But Sarah hadn't closed it. She had simply looked at Elizabeth as she re-entered the house and taken up her book without a word. And now she was taking her revenge by being tired and dignified, perfectly polite but cold, so that if Elizabeth attempted to begin a conversation it would die almost at once, chilled and frostbitten by the tone of Sarah's voice. Nevertheless Miss Hodge was glad she had asserted herself. It brought her a sense of excitement and palpitation. Ever since she had walked down the path and opened the gate her heart had been beating too rapidly and her cheeks had been hot.

Opposite her beyond the gateway the huge mass of the palace, glittering now with lights, rose black against the stormy sky. For a moment the rain had ceased and the wind fallen and here and there you could see little patches spangled with stars between the broken flying clouds. In the covered gateway two of the Maharajah's horse guards, turbaned and dressed in scarlet and gold, sat their black horses silent, immobile, their lances, carrying the purple and gold pennons of His Highness, pointing straight upward, as motionless as the men themselves. They were Sikhs, professional fighters, who never shaved, and now on duty they wore their long black beards neatly folded into little nets beneath their chins.

For twenty-five years Miss Hodge had seen them there, day in and day out, and she never quite come to take for granted their lean straight bodies, the proud narrow-nosed faces, the handsome tunics of scarlet and gold. They were men, beautiful men, fierce and bearded, who lived on horses, and all that was too much for Miss Hodge's romantic nature. She had no idea why they fascinated her, and because she was a little ashamed of the stormy feelings they roused in her she never attempted to discover what or why it was. It was a muddled emotion, partly literary by way of Flora Annie Steel and partly mere glandular reaction. Sometimes, when Miss Dirks was out of the room, she would stand at an upper window, push back the curtains and look at the Sikhs. Each time she peeped she felt faintly excited, her heart beat a little faster and she felt gay. It was exactly like taking a drug, and like taking drugs the peeping had become a habit and a necessity. Slowly she had come to know the Sikhs apart, although they were all of a type—lean, hawk-faced and tall. She had never even heard their names, but as time went on she invented names for them herself, good English names because she had never heard any Sikh names. She had her favorites. They were called John, Geoffrey, William, Herbert and Cecil. Some of them she had seen grow from boys into middle-aged men. Now and then one would fail to appear and never be seen again. Occasionally there were new ones, whom she would study carefully each time they came on duty, giving them each a fair chance until she had rejected them or listed them among her favorites. Cecil had been the favorite of favorites, and when he left the regiment to go back again to the North she experienced for weeks afterward a sense of depression each time she looked at the gate.

She kept hoping that he was ill or on a holiday and would return, but he never did. She had not even any way of discovering what had become of him.

While she watched the two horsemen standing beneath the great lanterns of pierced copper, the guests began to arrive. She recognized the great form of Raschid Ali Khan huddled in the gay little tonga ornamented with bits of looking-glass, and Mrs. Raschid all in white, sitting beside him; and she knew the Dewan's old-fashioned French motor, and Ransome's five-year-old Buick which had belonged to Monsieur Descans, the Swiss engineer, and Major Safti's mud-spattered Ford, and the Packard which she thought must contain the General, and the baby Austin driven by Mr. Bannerjee with his handsome wife at his side, and presently, with a sudden excitement, the lumbering purple Rolls-Royce with Lord and Lady Esketh inside. The light inside the car was turned on and so she had a glimpse of them, the famous millionaire peer and his fashionable wife. She knew all about them. She knew that Lady Esketh had been Edwina Doncaster, one of the "bright young people," and at one time a great friend of the Prince of Wales, for she kept up on her news of Court and Society. She knew every birth and death in the "Morning Post" which arrived in Ranchipur a month or two after it had been printed, in a world which she had never seen and among people she would never know.

Last of all came Mr. and Mrs. Jobnekar clopping along in their hired tonga. Then after waiting a long time she turned and said, "That seems to be all the party, Sarah—the Esketh, Mr. Ransome, the Raschids, the Bannerjees and the Jobnekars."

There was no answer from Miss Dirks and Miss Hodge thought, "Oh, so she's not going to speak to me? That's carrying things a bit far."

When she turned to look she saw that Miss Dirks was sitting with her eyes closed. Her book on new methods of teaching algebra had fallen into her lap and one thin hand was pressed against her stomach.

Frightened, Miss Hodge jumped up and called out, "Sarah! Sarah!" Miss Dirks opened her eyes and seemed to come back from a great distance.

"Yes, Elizabeth, I'm sorry. I was thinking."

"You're not feeling well?"

"Yes, I'm all right. Just tired, that's all." She sat up straight and picked up her book.

"I'll make you a cup of tea," said Miss Hodge.

"Don't bother."

"Yes, I will. You can't stop me." And she went off to the kitchen to heat the water, trembling and filled with remorse, ashamed of her petty victory over the open gate, wanting to make amends, to apologize, to regain the ground which had been lost between them.

Miss Dirks had not been sleeping. She had been thinking, with her eyes closed, fighting pain.

It had grown worse of late and now for a long time she knew that there was no use any longer in combating it by power of will or in pretending that it did not exist. It was there all the time, now withdrawing a little way, now returning to attack her with savagery. She no longer believed, even in moments when it withdrew a little, that it would pass away presently and leave her well again and strong. She had known perfectly well for weeks now that she should have gone to a doctor long ago, but in all Ranchipur there was not a doctor who would understand such things save Major Safti, and she could not face the ordeal of undressing and being pawed over by a doctor who was not only a man but an Indian and young and good-looking. She might have gone to Bombay but in Bombay there were only men doctors, and after all, in the whole of India and the East, there was no surgeon as fine as the Major. But she could not face it. The very thought of it made her feel ill. She would rather die first.

The pain was bad enough but she could have borne that alone, as she had borne many things in her life which were worse, but she was tired too and troubled and frightened and there was no one that she could go to, no one she could tell about it, least of all Elizabeth, who would grow silly and hysterical and make it all the worse by fussing and showering her with unwanted little attentions that would never allow her to forget the pain, even when it went away for a little time.

In a little while Miss Hodge returned with the tea. It did nothing to ease the awful gnawing pain but it made Miss Dirks a little happier because the gesture wiped out a little her shame for the childishness of her friend.

The palace was an immense structure set down in the midst of a vast park laid out long ago in an attempt to imitate the lushness and the well-ordered disarray of a great English estate. Turrets and domes and spires rose without restraint or balance from a great mass of galleries, arches and balconies in a style which included something of North Africa, something of Persia and something of India. If you saw it first by daylight it struck you, if you were a European, as a kind of architectural nightmare; if you saw it by night with the stars overhead in the blue Indian sky and all the lights glittering in the hundreds of windows, it was a fabulous and enchanted structure out of the *Arabian Nights*. With all the hardness of brick and stone melted away into shadows, its huge bulk rose above the trees on moonlit nights like the magical city in the "Tale of the Fisherman."

The park itself, with banyans and mangoes and eucalyptus trees and palms taking the place of the elms and oaks and cedars of an English park, was no less fantastic than the palace. In the beginning the Scotch gardener employed by the Maharani had tried, stubbornly and with heroism, to make English plants and shrubs and trees grow in the reddish heavy soil, but in the end India would have none of them and one by one they shriveled and died beneath the burning sun.

Even the little lake had a bottom of cement so that the precious water would not seep away during the dry season, and it raised toward the brazen sky, not the cool pellucid surface of an English pond bordered by sedges and flags, but a face that was pallid and dead and green and faintly streaked by the oil spread on it to keep down the malaria-carrying mosquitoes. In a year like this one, when the monsoon came late and water became more precious than wine, the little pond was allowed to evaporate altogether, leaving a shallow shell of cement, the ugliest travesty of a lake, with the gawdy little pleasure boats stranded here and there beneath the blazing sun.

Ransome had never become reconciled to the park, where the sense of travesty was heightened by the presence of galloping troupes of sacred monkeys, but slowly, as he ceased to be a tourist and began a little to *know* India, he came to understand that the fantastic palace was not only exactly right but that it was a triumph of architecture. It had none of that distressing, lonely, barren look which his own Belgrave Square house had had until he managed to conceal its classic Georgian façade beneath a tangle of flowering shrubs and vines; nor did it give the effect of the government buildings in Delhi, constructed in the hope of impressing India and succeeding only in looking like Regent Street set down amid the magnificent ruins of the Mogul Empire. The palace belonged there, in India, with all its fantasy and extravagance and disorder, as if it had been born of India herself out of an excess of vitality. It was as right as if, like the mango and banyan trees that replaced the dead oaks and elms, it had grown out of the very soil of the country. If you had planted a bit of the seed from which Indian palaces grow in the reddish heavy soil, surely this fantastic structure would have sprung up, a giant among palaces. Presently Ransome discovered that not only was it right; it was beautiful.

It had been built against the heat and so the doors and windows were enormous and the ceilings high, and distributed through the center of it there were seven great courtyards in which plants and trees grew and water trickled in fountains all day and all night. Arica palms pushed their way upward through orchids and hanging vines toward the light that fell from above the open marble galleries, and in the center of each there was a marble basin where goldfish swam above flowers made of jade and chrysoprase and other semi-precious stones in designs taken from the old Mogul palaces at Agra and Fatepur-Sikri. High up, in gilt cages, hanging from the arica palms there were myriads of birds, the extravagantly colored birds of India, and above them suspended from the marble eaves there were great nests of Indian bees, living perpetually in one gigantic swarm, crawling over and over one another, until presently one by one they died and were replaced by those which had hatched in the center of the swarm. In all Ranchipur there was no refuge so cool as these damp shaded gardens, open at night to the sky, where the brazen sun never entered.

All about the open courts clustered the rooms of the palace—on the second and third floors the apartments of the royal family and their *entourage*, below stairs big rooms which were useless and empty save for a strange conglomeration of furniture and *objets d'art*. They were like vast warehouses in which furniture had been thrust away without plan or discrimination, and so cabinets and embroideries and vases of marvelous and lovely workmanship, brought long ago out of the old deserted palace of the wicked Maharajah, found themselves standing side by side with atrocious bits of *art moderne*. Paintings of the Munich school hung above priceless bowls and vases of jade and agate and pink quartz collected by the Maharani; Persian tapestries from the time of Abkar ornamented walls opposite windows adorned with Nottingham lace.

Some of the horrors the Maharani had bought herself long ago when she first went to Europe to the great expositions which were held to exploit the horrors turned out by machines; the complicated slickness of the objects had impressed her, but later when she grew used to Europe and her own taste came to assert itself she knew that nearly everything she had bought was a horror, and so she had stuffed them away helter-skelter, together with the overflow of palace treasures, in these big deserted rooms where no one ever came.

Some of them had come to her as gifts from Edwardian visitors and from Indian societies whose causes either she or the Maharajah had helped at one time or another. In the far end of the great hallway, which ran the whole length of the palace, there was a room where the gentlemen who came to dinner left their hats and in the corner of it was a group of objects which never failed to arouse Ransome's mirth. It contained a Landseer of two bloodhounds and a terrier, a magnificent Chinese god in bronze, an elaborate modern statue of Psyche in alabaster probably purchased from a peddler in the street in Naples, and a Mogul prayer rug of the most exquisite design and color.

One by one the guests arrived, coming up the great staircase of white marble into a room that was all blue, the color of Indian night, with the Maharani's famous collection of Mogul paintings set into the walls among the silver stars. It was a high room with windows which overlooked the park with a view of Mount Abana in the distance, and across the great windows were hung nettings of white cord to keep out the giant bats and defeat the curiosity of the sacred monkeys. From the center of the room hung a huge chandelier of crystal, blazing with light and filled with thousands of bees. Just beneath it the rulers of Ranchipur stood to receive their guests.

The Maharani wore a sari of white bordered with silver, Mahratta fashion, with a giant fish-tail train which passed between her tiny feet and swept behind her as she walked. And she wore no jewels but emeralds—emeralds in her ears and about her throat, on her wrists and fingers and even on her toes, emeralds collected here and there throughout the world to satisfy her passion for jewels, from Fifth Avenue and Bond Street and the Place Vendôme, from Moscow and Jaipur and Peking. Tonight she was not the spirited old lady who played poker like a professional gambler in a mining camp—shrewd, witty, malicious and sometimes Rabelaisian—but a woman intelligent and, in the depths of her nature, still half-savage, who was a great queen. She was a small person, made with the delicacy and perfection of a Tanagra, yet now she gave the illusion of stature and majesty. She carried herself erect with the sureness and poise of a woman who has never known the tottering heels of fashionable Parisian bootmakers.

Ransome, regarding her from the doorway as she stood in the blaze of light from the bee-filled chandelier, thought again, "The last queen." In the West it was the fashion of queens to be as nearly as possible like middle-class housewives. In that lay their last security.

The ancient Dewan was already there and Raschid and his dark modest little wife and Mr. Bannerjee and the cold and beautiful Mrs. Bannerjee, and the Maharajah himself, looking old and tired and full of dignity, all in white with a single great diamond, set round with emeralds, blazing in his scarlet Ranchipur turban. And there were staff officers and aides-de-camp and the two old Princesses of Bewanagar, intimates of the Maharani. Out of all the group it was Mrs. Bannerjee who caught his attention. She was standing against the wall beside one of the great windows netted against the giant bats, very still and aloof and beautiful like a woman out of one of the miniatures which adorned the wall. She was tall for an Indian woman and very fair-skinned and there was an air of insolence and contempt about her which was at once provocative and irritating, and an air of stillness and indifference which permitted her to dominate any room.

[118]

For a long time she had fascinated Ransome far more than any woman he had encountered in India, and it had happened without the faintest effort on her part. To his weariness it was not only her beauty which held an appeal; her aloofness, her air of detachment, as if she endured life without enjoying it, stirred his curiosity. It was as if she were always just beyond his reach, mocking him, a new adventure, something he had never before experienced. Falling in love with her was out of the question, for they were too strange to one another and would, he knew, always remain so no matter how profound a physical intimacy they might know. One might as well have hoped to fall in love with a beautiful statue made of ice, yet the sight of her always excited him, raising a kind of perverse passion to conquer her, to humiliate her, to violate her and bring her pride to earth. He knew well enough that this would be an exciting thing but how it could be accomplished he had not the slightest idea. Again and again he had tried to discover some approach to that glacial summit upon which she appeared to have her existence. He had talked of the *Swadeshi* movement in which she displayed an interest; he had tried talking of philosophy and love and of the animals—the Pekinese dogs, the parrots, the ibises, the cranes and the honey bear—which she kept in her garden, searching for something which might interest this childless beautiful woman; but it never led to anything more than polite rather absent-minded answers which left him with the conviction that in everything—in thought, in feeling, in background and in emotion— there was no way of reaching her. Sometimes he thought, "She is India. One day when India is reborn she will come alive"; but that awakening was, he knew, something which neither of them would ever see because they would both be dead before it happened. And sometimes when he was alone and had been drinking he would think, "She is really nothing at all. She is simply beautiful and lazy and stupid."

She never spoke save to answer a question and she was never made uneasy by long silences as Western women were. She would sit watching and listening or drifting off into some realm of meditation beyond the comprehension of the others, indifferent, outwardly bored and yet some- how more complete than anyone else in the room. There were moments when the steady level gaze of the black eyes grew disconcerting, as if, by her mere presence, she had the power to paralyze the conversation, even the human contacts all about her, and render them trivial and idiotic.

Tonight when she found Ransome staring at her she looked at him for a moment beneath her long lashes, inclined her head in an arrogant gesture of recognition, and seating herself on a divan took out a neatly rolled *pan* of lime and betel leaf from a box of jade and began to chew. In most Indian women there was for Ransome something cowlike in their taste for *pan*, but with Mrs. Bannerjee it was quite different. Watching her he was aware again of the old excitement which always made him feel hot and a little suffocated. He thought, "She hates me because I am not an Indian."

And then across the room, among all the brilliant clothes, he saw the Eskeths come in. His Lordship, stifling in a swallow-tailed coat, looked bleary and purple and rather like a peevish bull. Beside him his wife appeared incredibly fragile and pale. Then for the first time in nearly fifteen years Ransome really saw her. She was dressed like the Maharani, all in white, but instead of emeralds she wore against the white of her gown a mixture of diamonds and emeralds and rubies, very nearly as magnificent as the jewels of the Indian queen.

Against the deep blue of the wall, beneath the blaze of brilliant uncompromising light from the crystal chandelier, she was all white and pale gold, as beautiful as Mrs. Bannerjee but in a fashion as different as it was possible to be. With the Indian woman one had intimations of fire, sullen and smoldering somewhere beneath the ice, but with Edwina Esketh one divined almost at once that if there had ever been any fire it was extinguished now forever. It was her boredom which struck you almost immediately—a certain deadness of reaction to everything and everyone about her, as if she had experienced too much so that nothing, save perhaps jewels and clothes, had any longer any power to stir her. When she smiled at the Maharani it was a tired smile full of sadness, but without self-pity. It was a smile as old as time.

She said, "Your Highness has been so kind to us. I don't know what we should have done otherwise"; and the voice was curiously tired and flat.

The Maharani laughed, a full throaty laugh: "It's nothing. We're pleased to do anything we can for a friend of the Viceroy." There was fire in her dark eyes and vitality in her voice, and Ransome thought, "She's twice Edwina's age but she's the younger of the two."

Even when Edwina spoke it was as if she spoke automatically, with a perfect grace and politeness and even a charm that was a little threadbare and worn because it had been used so many times, for so many centuries. There were moments when the weariness became almost an insult.

Then she turned and saw Ransome, regarding him for a moment blankly and then with growing interest as slowly she understood that this was a face out of her past which she had once known very well. For a moment she came almost alive.

"So, it's you, Tom? Somebody told me about a person called Ransome who was living in Ranchipur but I never dreamed it was you."

"I wondered if you were going to remember me."

"It's been a long time—seven or eight years."

"A good many more than ten."

She laughed, "And now we're all middle-aged."

"Not quite, but very nearly."

For a moment she seemed to brighten, as if suddenly the sight of someone out of her old world had set her heart to beating more rapidly. It had been a small and intimate world, gay and wild and sometimes despairing, but small at least and friendly, without these hordes of strange and boring and important people whom she had seen since she married Esketh, day after day, for a moment or two and then never again.

"What are you doing here?"

For a moment he hesitated. No one had ever asked him that question before and now in a moment he found it difficult to answer. He said, "Nothing in particular; a little painting, a little drinking, a little messing about."

"It doesn't sound very exciting."

"It isn't."

"You must meet Albert."

"I met him once or twice long ago when I thought I was going to become a great business man. He probably doesn't remember me."

Lord Esketh did not remember him, but then it was his habit to remember only the people whom he might use or from whom he might gain something, a little group which each year grew smaller until now it contained only a handful of bankers, the royal family, a quite large group of unscrupulous politicians and two or three men more powerful than himself, whom he respected because they had made greater fortunes than his own. To anyone save those few, he no longer troubled even to be civil. If you were not among them you felt that he gave even the time to say "How d'you do?" grudgingly and with annoyance.

Then the General arrived, followed too closely for his dignity and comfort by Mr. and Mrs. Jobnekar, the Untouchables, looking rather like a pair of bright-eyed mice. He had met Lord Esketh before and they did not care for each other, since neither yielded anything to the vanity and egotism of the other.

"They're both preposterous," thought Ransome. "But the one is evil and dangerous. The General is a little like the Great Auk. The Empire is built. They don't need him any more, and now they're leaving it to Esketh to destroy it.

The "small" white dining room to which the guests were led was an immense room with great arched windows on two sides like the window of the blue room, covered with nettings in which a great bat entangled itself now and then to struggle and squeak until it was freed by one of the servants. On one side the windows opened into one of the courtyards from which the sound of falling water rose among the betel palms. Through the other windows there was a view of the park and distantly of the great tank and the square with the cinema on one side and the sinister old palace on the other. The rain had stopped now for a time and the lights of the square were swimming in the tank.

The dinner was Indian because Esketh had requested it, a dinner typical of Ranchipur, with its famous curry of crayfish, sugared guavas and hearts of palm; in the distance on the roof of another wing of the palace there was an orchestra, organized by the Maharani herself in defiance of the tradition which allowed musicians to play only in groups of two or three. There were thirty musicians in it playing lutes and drums, Indian violins and flutes, even bowls of soapstone tuned by lowering and raising the level of the water in them, and the lowly melodeon which had come to India long ago with the missionaries to accompany the singing of hymns and had long since become the traditional Indian instrument for dancing girls and for playing hymns to Shiva and Krishna. The sound of the music drifted across the endless turreted roofs of the palace, distantly, into the white marble dining room.

Ransome found himself between Mrs. Bannerjee and Mrs. Jobnekar so that he sat diagonally across from Edwina Esketh and the old Maharajah. The nearness of Mrs. Bannerjee stirred him faintly but he had no more success with her than he had ever had. She was silent, eating elegantly and rather greedily, taking no notice of the party, her lovely hands dipped now into the rice, now into the sauce of the curried crayfish, now into a sweetish dish made of coconut. Mrs. Jobnekar was pleasant and chatty but with Mrs. Bannerjee beside him and Edwina across the table he found his mind wandering away from her, so that sometimes when she asked him a question he had to rouse himself violently to give an intelligent answer. About the middle of the dinner he became aware that Edwina was watching him now and then, stealthily, speculatively, and that when he glanced in her direction she turned back at once to the Maharajah.

Remembering back a long way, he kept seeing her as she had been when she came down to the farm in Sussex. Then she had had the same porcelain white and gold beauty, but she had been alive, with a wild, hysterical kind of life, as if she felt that there was not enough time to encompass all the excitement, the adventure, the love there was to be had. And he thought again, "She is just what I imagined she would be." That was her tragedy and his own—that they had both burned the candle at both ends for too long. Now on the verge of middle age, there was nothing left to burn.

They had been greedy for experience and cold-blooded, and at the same time (an odd combination) they had been both disillusioned and foolish. There had never been any romance in anything they did, and he was aware now, when it was much too late, that neither of them had ever known what love was like because without romance, without sentiment, there could be no such thing as love, but only curiosity and sensual desire too quickly satisfied. To love, to make love endure, one had to be a little drugged by something which perhaps had no existence in reality. Either by nature you took willingly to the drug or you used it deliberately, hypnotizing yourself, the way you might work yourself up on a

[123]

night like this with the wild barbaric music in the distance and the sound of the water falling among the arica palms and the squeaking of the bats which entangled themselves in the nettings. He thought, bitterly, "We've had no luck, Edwina and I. We had all the romance, all the sentimentality knocked the hell out of us before we ever began."

He had never thought of it before but now he saw himself from a great distance as he had come back from the War, bitter and unhappy, greedy for women and pleasure and experience, as if somehow he had had to make up for what he had lost during the three best and most romantic years of his life. Nobody could give that back to you; nobody could blame you for trying to get back what belonged to you, snatching pleasure and experience wherever you found it, in whatever form, with that old hysteria always inside of you, that feeling that life was too short and that you might have only another hour or two to live. The old ones had never known what it was and the young ones would never know. But he knew and Edwina knew. The wounds in his thigh and in his back were nothing; the flesh grew again somehow making itself whole. But the spirit was different; somewhere in some book he had read long ago something which came back to him now:

Dans la damnation le feu est la moindre chose; le supplice propre au damné est le progrès infini dans le vice et dans le crime, l'ami s'endurcissant, se dépravant toujours, s'enfonçant nécessairement dans le mal de minute en progression géométrique vers l'éternité.

That was it—that was Edwina's case and his own.

Suddenly he heard the voice of Esketh above the murmur of talk and the sound of the distant music, even above the amiable chatter of little Mrs. Jobnekar to which he listened with only half an ear. Esketh was shouting at the Maharani and it occurred to Ransome that perhaps she had been baiting him, as she baited the General.

"It's a damned outrage!" Esketh bellowed, and Ransome, seeing the twinkle in the black eyes of the old lady, thought, "It's no use his trying to bully her." The methods he used in the West would come to nothing here, save that they would amuse Her Highness.

Esketh's face looked swollen, and Ransome thought, "He's ill. There is something the matter with him. No man who wasn't ill would shout like that." In the protruding blue eyes there was a dull look as if they were covered by a film. And he wondered if Esketh made scenes like this with Edwina.

Then the dinner was suddenly at an end and the Maharani in her white and emeralds was leading the way from the room, the long train of her Mahratta sari trailing far behind her between the tiny feet covered with emeralds from the four parts of the earth.

In the room with the blue walls the entertainment had already begun, and seated on a small dais with her back to one of the huge arched windows sat Lakshmi Bai, one of the great singers of India. She sat cross-legged and wore a sari of blue and silver. She was neither a beautiful woman nor a plain one and she was no longer young, but neither her age nor her appearance were of importance in her performance. It was not a woman that one saw and listened to but a work of art, in which every tiny detail contributed a little part toward the whole—the scarlet lips, the lacquered nails, the glimpse of jeweled foot from beneath the blue and silver sari, the exquisite style with which the beautiful hands, more delicate and more sensitive than the hands of any European, picked the strings of the lute. It was the hands which fascinated Ransome, and even Edwina, sitting beside him now, was interested, it seemed to him, for the first time, in something, a creation, which was very like herself, possessing the same half-decadent perfection.

They alone in the room were silent, watching, and listening, for the Indians looked upon the music merely as a background for conversation and talked among themselves, and the General and Esketh had no interest in such goings-on; and sitting beside her, Ransome was acutely aware of her perfection, of her breeding and poise, of her clothes, her jewels, her hair, her grace of manner and the way she sat, leaning back a little, listening and watching. It seemed to him suddenly that he had discovered the very essence of her existence. He thought, "She is the last example of something which will soon be gone from the world because there is no longer any time or place for it." She was not, like Esketh, a kind of crude fungus growth, sprung up overnight out of the confused *ordure* of his time; she was the product of hundreds of years of leisure, of privilege and responsibility won and carried on by generation after generation. And now even the civilization, the epoch to which she belonged, was nearly at an end and there was no longer any place for her, or for himself for that matter, and both of them were touched by the decay of something which was too old, from which even his grandmother in the vast turreted house back in Grand River had not been able to save him. They were, he knew, both rotten at the core, and suddenly it occurred to him that it was Esketh and his crude gods that were destroying them.

Presently Lakshmi Bai finished singing, and as she left the room a little band came in and seated itself in front of the dais, and then the two dancing girls appeared. Like the singer they were not young, and one of them was definitely old. They were mother and daughter who had come long ago from the temples of Tanjore into the service of the old Maharajah, but neither their age nor their plumpness had anything to do with the beauty of their dancing. If they had been young and beautiful, thought Ransome, their beauty would have distracted you; you would have been aware of bodies rather than of the archaic patterns, thousands of years old, refined now to the point of decadence, which their bodies made as they danced. Again none save Ransome and Edwina paid any attention to the performance, and in a little while first one and then the other of the two dancers discovered their interest and put a certain fire into their dancing. They danced the legends of Krishna and the Gopis and the story of Rama and Sita, but there was no longer any realism in their dancing, for each incident, each action, had become thousands of years ago merely a pattern, a filigree, exquisite in itself and related to nothing. It was a pure art beyond which there was nothing save decadence, destruction, and a new beginning.

When they had finished and gone away again with the little band Edwina sat for a moment leaning back, with her eyes closed, and presently Ransome asked, "When are you leaving?"

"The end of the week. We're taking the *Victoria* from Bombay."

"It's a pity to meet again and then separate almost at once."

She gave a little laugh that was at the same time a sigh: "Well, that's the way the world is nowadays."

She told him about the visit to India, about coming to Ranchipur because of the Kathiawar horses, about the heat, the dust, the misery, and the boredom of the long official dinners.

"I don't see how you emerge from it all, looking as if you'd come out of your own house in London in the middle of the season."

Again she laughed: "It's simple enough. It's nothing but a question of money. I have two maids with me and one of them is an excellent hairdresser. It's different from the old days when I did my own hair and could only afford the hairdresser once in three weeks."

"You looked just as well then."

"I was younger then. It didn't matter so much."

"It doesn't matter now."

She looked at him slyly and then laughed: "Just the same I like it better this way. I'm luxurious by nature. I like all the things money brings."

He wanted to ask, "*All* the things?" but had not the courage. They had not recovered enough lost ground to risk a question so intimate. All the same he knew that she was talking to him as she would have talked to no other person in the room. There was a kind of bond between them after all, an odd feeling that they belonged to a small and dying world which together they would defend to the very end, even though there was no end save defeat and decay. The others in the room could not know what it was. Slowly he became excited at seeing her again, at having someone beside him to whom it was unnecessary to explain, to analyze, to justify, someone who understood exactly how desperate you were, how useless, how rotten.

"You must come round to me and have tea some afternoon," he said. "I live in a damp mildewy old Georgian house and mess around with paints. It's very untidy but it might amuse you."

"Why do you stay here through the monsoon?"

He grinned: "I don't know. I might as well be here as anywhere else."

"I'll try to come. I'll have to squeeze it in somehow. There's so much arranged for us"; and she looked at him almost as if she were appraising him and thinking, "Could it be worth while for us to begin all over again? Could we ever recapture what is lost?"

He did not say, "Bring your husband," because he did not want Esketh there, impatient and bored, destroying this feeling between them.

"Make it Thursday," he said.

"Thursday." She lighted a cigarette. "Are you by any chance going to Mr. Bannerjee's to dinner?"

"Day after tomorrow?"

"Yes," and with a sensation of satisfaction he saw that she was pleased.

"What's he like—Mr. Bannerjee?" she asked; "I mean inside. I can see from the outside—a rather fussy little man who looks Chinese."

"It would need a whole book to describe him—a kind of symbolic book. He's the Indian who is lost between the East and the West."

She was silent for a moment and then she said, "Who is that man over there. The one who looks like a pale copper Apollo?"

He knew without looking whom she meant, for the description was inspired. It was the Major. He was talking to the Maharani, by command, Ransome knew, so that she would not be bored.

He told her about the surgeon and she listened, distracted, almost as if she were Mrs. Bannerjee, without taking her glance off the Major. He praised the Major's qualities, but after a moment he was aware that what he was saying did not hold her interest. He saw that it was not the Major's virtues which interested her. Her blue eyes had a fixed expression in them as if she were speculating, appraising the clean good-looking young Brahmin doctor. And Ransome felt suddenly angry and jealous because somehow she had slipped away from him, and he thought, "I didn't know she was as bad as that."

"He looks very romantic," she said.

"Well, he isn't. He's a surgeon and a scientist. No one could be more cold-blooded." And then growing brutal he added, "Love to him is just copulation—something to be studied with scientific detachment." And almost at once he knew that he had said exactly the wrong thing to kill her interest in the Major, and he thought, "Slut!"

He did not hear her reply for her words suddenly were drowned in the roar of falling water. It was as if a gigantic waterfall had struck the palace. The rains had begun again.

She laughed and raised her voice against the downpour: "It's not much like the good old English drizzle. Isn't there another room we might go to? I hate sitting here, shouting, with everybody listening."

"We might take a look at some of the other rooms. It might amuse you. Her Highness wouldn't mind. I'll ask her permission."

The Maharani was talking now to the Dewan about the new wing that was to be built at the Girls' High School, and when Ransome asked her permission to take Lady Esketh through the lower rooms she gave a little laugh: "Of course. Go where you like"; and as he turned away she said, "Good luck," and then returned to her conversation with the Dewan.

He found himself suddenly confused by the remark. It was as if she said, "I know your Englishwomen of that sort—sensual, decadent, cold-blooded, promiscuous." It annoyed him as insulting to Edwina, and then it occurred to him that the old lady was right and that it might be agreeable to have happen what the old Maharani had hinted at, not only agreeable but a necessity. It *had* to happen.

So he told the aide-de-camp that he knew his own way and that they needed no one to accompany them.

They went from one to another of the deserted empty rooms below-stairs, to the great Durbar Hall, all done in gold leaf and sandalwood, to the courtyards drenched now in the downpour, and presently into the smaller rooms where treasures and monstrosities stood side by side. At first he felt nervous and excited, as if instead of being experienced and jaded he were a boy again, aware of desire for the first time, timid and ignorant. Presently they talked less and less of the things about them as if the conversation were too artificial and in the heat talking against the roar of the rain, too great an effort; and after a while they walked in silence save when he spoke absent-mindedly and without interest or conviction, to point out some special treasure or some incredible horror. At last they came to a small room at the far end of one wing of the palace just beneath the room where a little while before the Maharani's band had been playing.

Edwina said, "Let's sit here for a moment and have a cigarette. I'm exhausted by the heat."

So they both sat on the divan and after the cigarettes were lighted they both fell silent until at last the silence became unendurable, when Ransome said, "Are you thinking what I'm thinking?"

She laughed, "Of course I am, you ninny."

For the first time in many years he was aware of a romantic feeling. He said, "You're looking very beautiful—more beautiful than you were then."

"It's a long way from Tipton Farm. We've both come a long way since then."

"It's as if it were meant to be, you know, the two of us meeting again like this in a Maharajah's palace. Something about the whole evening —the music, the dancers, the rain. It's set me going."

She laughed. "It's all very Elinor Glyn."

"Don't do that."

"Even to the tiger skin," she said, kicking the skin on the floor with her toe.

"You're a perverse bitch. Anyway it's a panther skin." But inside him the excitement kept on mounting.

She laughed again: "In the middle of the monsoon—with the heat and the rain. It's all very provocative and savage."

He rose then and closed the door and pushed a chest against it and put out the light. Then he made his way toward her in the darkness.

"Wait," she said. "Don't be in such a hurry. Mind my cigarette."

Upstairs, in one of the smaller rooms, Esketh was trying to bargain with the old Maharajah for a Kathiawar stallion and three mares, and the bargaining was not going too well.

His passion for horses had begun long ago when as a boy he had never missed a running of the Grand National. As a boy he had stood in the crowd watching the arrival of the rich, the powerful, the fashionable. As a boy, when he had a holiday, he would cycle for miles across country simply to catch a distant glimpse of pink coats flying over a hedge. And later on as a young man, selling cutlery and cotton goods in the Far East, he was driven always by the knowledge that one day he must have horses, because horses were a kind of label, a label which no Simpson had worn since the race of Simpsons had existed. One day he meant to have a racing stable and a half-dozen hunters and the prettiest and most fashionable woman in England for a wife. And to have these things one had to have a great fortune.

He had them now, his horses, and a wife who was the peer of any woman in the British Empire for position, for sporting qualities, for smartness. He had come a long way, Albert Simpson of Liverpool. He had bought his hunters and his racing stable and his wife and his title, and now he meant to buy the four most beautiful Kathiawar horses in existence.

But it seemed that the old Maharajah did not understand bargaining, at least not the methods Lord Esketh had learned long ago selling cutlery to Chinese merchants in the Malay States. He was willing to sell Esketh three mares and a stallion of the Kathiawar breed but not the ones the great Lord had picked out after three or four visits to the stables. He was a shrewd judge of horses and he had chosen the finest stallion and three of the best mares that existed in the world. He was angry now because he could not have his way and baffled and furious because for once he had set his mind on something which he could not buy simply by offering more money, and while he talked to the Maharajah his irritation increased, stimulated by one discovery after another.

It was always humiliating for him to encounter someone richer than himself, and doubly humiliating when he was forced to bargain with the person. He knew well enough that the gentle old man sitting opposite him could have bought him up—his jute and rubber and munitions and newspapers and steamship lines—for cash and still have a great fortune left. It was annoying too that the wealth of the old gentleman existed in concrete form, in reality, and not as credits and papers in a complex tangled system which even Esketh himself did not at times understand. His own wealth might be increased a million pounds one day and decreased a million pounds the next, without much rhyme or reason. But the old gentleman sitting opposite was not troubled by depressions, disasters and financial blunders for he was quite independent of that gigantic clumsy fallible structure which the West called big business. It was like dealing with a tough old peasant who *owned* his land and had a sock full of money under the mattress. The Maharajah, like the peasant, was down to brass tacks and the realization of the fact made Esketh feel shaky and insecure. He was a man who could not gracefully accept a sense of inferiority, and he was ill.

And His Highness did not pound the table and shout. He did not grow angry nor did he talk of his horses being worth four times their real value. He did not lose his composure. He was suave and smiling and dignified. He did not even talk of the value of his horses at all, because to him they were above price.

"I cannot sell you the stallion and the mares," he said, "because I am very attached to them. I bred them myself. If I sold them to you I would be throwing away the product of fifty years of work and selection. They are the most beautiful Kathiawar horses in the world, perhaps the most beautiful horses in the world. To me they are, and so they are to my friend Mohammed Begg who has managed my stables for thirty years. If I let them go it would break his heart. You see, quite aside from anything else, I am unwilling to do that."

Esketh crushed out his cigar with a vicious gesture which said, "To hell with your friend Mohammed Begg! To hell with all of you!" Aloud he said, "I will pay you anything you like. I will build you a school or a whole railroad system. I will feed your starving poor."

"We have no starving poor, you see."

"I'll pay you what you like." It was as if his passion for horses had slowly centered itself in the beautiful stallion, Asoka, and the mares, as if he could not live if he did not have them.

"It is not a question of money. You, Lord Esketh, who have a stable should understand what I mean."

"I don't want to take back to England a string of second-rate stock."

The Maharajah did not lose his temper: "There is no second-rate stock in my stables. You need have no fear of that. If you take back to England the horses I am willing to sell you, they will be as good as the best horses in England."

Esketh started to answer him angrily and then thought better of it for with this old man he felt strangely unsure of his ground. In his shrewdness he knew the Maharajah was sure of his, and slowly he was beginning to feel that the old gentleman knew all about him, everything there was to know, more perhaps than Edwina knew or even himself, things which he would have preferred to keep hidden.

He said, "Then I must take the mares and stallion Your Highness will sell me and be satisfied."

"I'm quite sure that you'll be satisfied with them. You'll find them wonderful and beautiful creatures—intelligent, capable of any endurance It would be interesting to cross their breed with some of your best racing stock. Let me know when and how you want them shipped and Mohammed will see to it. I only ask you not to ship them now, during the heat. It would be very hard on them."

"Then, there isn't anything more to be said?"

"No, I should like to please you. I'm sorry about Asoka but I could not break Mohammed's heart." And then very quietly he said, "Please let me make you a gift of the other stallion and the mares. It would give me great pleasure."

The blood rushed into Esketh's face and he felt a wild insane desire to shout, "Keep your horses and be damned! I'm not accepting gifts from any bloody Indian!" But he was uncertain whether the Maharajah had spoken from sincere generosity or whether he had meant the speech as an insult, the condescending gesture of a king to a tradesman. His anger, confused and impotent, was roused not only by the suavity of the old Maharajah but also by the memory of a man dead now for many years. Edwina's father, a bankrupt, had always treated him thus, courteously and condescendingly; and sometimes Edwina herself treated him in the same fashion—Edwina, who owed him everything, whose bills he had paid when he married her.

"Thank you," he said, "I couldn't accept that. You have been too kind already."

"As you like," said the Maharajah gently. "But I meant the offer sincerely."

And suddenly Esketh felt, from the manner of the Maharajah and the tone of his voice, that he had been made to seem boorish by his refusal. The little scene had put him somehow, mysteriously, into the position of a small shopkeeper or a moneylender who valued everything in life in terms of shillings and pence. And it made him seem an awkward, bumptious boy.

In his other mission Esketh had no greater success.

The Dewan was an immensely old man, with a long and beautiful white beard, who dressed always in white and looked rather like one of the more fabulous patriarchs of the Old Testament. No one knew exactly how old he was but he had been important and powerful in Indian politics for fifty years, and he was still shrewd and vigorous. For twenty-four of the fifty years, ever since the Maharani had driven out the Brahmin Dewan and caused a scandal he had been prime minister to the Maharajah of Ranchipur, helping him to build and reform and bring peace and order and prosperity to his people. The old Maharajah accomplished things by simplicity and directness, but the Dewan was Machiavellian. Believing that the end justified any means, he succeeded by craft and intrigue where the Maharajah in his simplicity often failed. In his pride as an Indian he desired to accomplish the same good ends as his master, but he lacked his master's faith in the goodness of men and he had a mischievous delight in intrigue for intrigue's sake, and so for fifty years, while he had accomplished great things, he had had fun.

In his faith he was a devout Hindu, not what might have been called an orthodox one, but a Hindu purist, for he went far back for his faith to the very beginnings of the religion when it had been simple and strong and good, uncluttered by superstitions and defeatism and innumerable gods, ranging from Vishnu to the phallic symbol set in a mud shrine at the crossroads. He ate no meat and lived a simple life, apportioning his day like the Greeks, into periods of action and repose, of intellectual and physical exercise. He had been known to rise and leave political conferences because everyone had talked too long and the hour had come for him to be alone and reflect. And so, whatever immense age he may have reached, he was still wiry and spry and brilliant.

To him Esketh was simply another game. As soon as the Englishman mentioned Bombay mills he knew what it was he wanted. But he pretended that he did not understand, forcing Esketh to put aside all delicacy and crudely show his hand. The old Dewan knew all about the mills, more even than Esketh had discovered in all his investigations, but he pretended that he knew nothing at all and was astonished to hear that the Japanese competition was cutting into their markets. He forced Esketh to come into the open and say that he would like him to use his influence with the Khojas and Parsees in Bombay to make them reasonable in their demands.

The old patriarch listened to him quietly with a gentle smile while he

[134]

explained that if he took over the mills and put in the latest methods of action and organization they would pay.

"It would mean work for thousands of starving Indian mill workers," said Esketh. "But I cannot undertake it unless I can buy into the mills at a reasonable price."

He agreed with all Esketh's arguments, even with his threats, but he committed himself to nothing and gave him no encouragement until at last Esketh, after much roundabout talk, said, "Perhaps you'd be interested in working together with me. I should see that you would not go unrewarded."

"How?" asked the Dewan.

"Perhaps a share in the profits of the mills or some such thing."

Now the old gentleman had gotten what he wanted. He had forced this powerful millionaire from the West to propose bribery like any shabby merchant in the bazaar. With a twinkle in his black eyes, he said, "No, you see, in my position it is impossible to meddle in business." And his smile seemed to say, "I should not mind meddling in business but what you propose is unsound. I know a thousand better investments."

"Then you are unwilling to help me?"

"If the opportunity comes to put in a word for you, I shall not overlook it."

But Esketh was aware that he had accomplished nothing whatever, no more than he had accomplished with the old Maharajah. For the second time he had been unable to buy what he wanted. He had come to Ranchipur to swelter, traveling five hundred miles through heat and dust, and nothing had come of it.

He was in a furious humor when he returned to the blue room and found the Maharani dismissing her guests. Edwina and Ransome came into the room at almost the same moment and, noticing them, he thought, "Ah, she's found one of her own kind. Now there'll be hell to pay! She'll be grand again for days!"

He walked over to her and without a word to Ransome, he said, "We're going home now."

"I'm quite ready whenever you are."

[135]

Before they left Ransome managed to say to her, "You'll be coming to tea with me on Thursday."

She smiled, "If I can manage it. It'll be difficult."

She was smooth and serene, all white and gold porcelain again, as if nothing whatever had happened.

As he said good night to the Maharani she looked at him for a second, her eyes dancing with amusement, just long enough to say without saying it, "I know what you were up to below stairs.' And quite suddenly he was ashamed of himself, for something in her look made him feel cheap and clownish. To her, what had happened below stairs was funny, like a cheap dirty story.

When the guests had gone Her Highness dismissed all the aides-de-camp, the ladies-in-waiting and her friends, the two old Princesses of Bewanagar, and stayed for a moment alone with her husband. It was one of those moments, so rare when, alone, they needed no longer to be King and Queen but simply husband and wife, humble people who might have lived in the quarter of the Untouchables. The proud old lady seemed to shed all the majesty, all the pride she had shown a little while before. Instead of speaking English or French or Hindustani they spoke together in Mahratta, the language they had both spoken as children long ago in the dusty sunburnt villages of the Deccan.

"How is your gout?" she asked.

"A little better tonight." But he sat down all the same, to ease the pain in his knees and feet.

"We must go to Carlsbad at the end of next week. You shouldn't stay any longer in this heat."

"If the rains keep on we can go."

"You didn't give in to him about the horses?"

"No. I didn't give in."

"The Viceroy sends us some odd packages now and then."

"He's obliged to. He can't help himself."

"This Esketh is the worst in a long time."

The old man was silent for a moment, reflecting: "He's not a very happy man."

The Maharani chuckled: "And while he was bargaining with you like a Bunya, his wife was downstairs behaving like a bitch in heat."

The Maharajah looked amused: "With whom?" he asked.

"With Ransome."

"Ransome! He's not a very happy man either. If it made him happy . . ."

The Maharani chuckled again: "It didn't."

Then they went away, each to his own apartment, and the blue room was left empty and silent save for the wild sound of the rain and the buzzing of the wild bees in the great crystal chandelier, until an Untouchable boy, coming in to free a giant bat entangled in the netting, put out the lights.

In the hallway outside the old gentleman's nurse, Mr. Bauer, was waiting with his wheeled chair. Mr. Bauer was a big blonde fellow about thirty-four or five who had been with the Maharajah since the day, five years before, when His Highness found him teaching people to swim on the beach at Ouchy. His Highness had the Indian liking for beauty and he preferred to have near him a nurse who was pleasant and handsome to one who was dull and scrawny. Bauer was placid and conscientious and amiable and he possessed the same beauty as Asoka, the stallion. It had worked well since the beginning, but the Maharajah was troubled sometimes lest his nurse become bored in Ranchipur, for he could not see how Mr. Bauer fitted in any possible way into the small, special life of the place.

Together, Mr. Bauer pushing the chair, they went along corridor after corridor until they came at last to the wing of the palace which overlooked the town. Here in the antechamber were waiting Major Safti and Raschid Ali Khan, the Muslim and the Brahmin sitting side by side, smoking cigars and exchanging stories. His Highness greeted them, saying, "Gentlemen, if you will wait for a moment, I will have Mr. Bauer put me to bed and then I'll talk. You see I am a little tired."

The silver bed was placed near one of the windows where the Maharajah might look out over the park and the town. When the Swiss had put him into it and arranged the nettings at the windows and over the bed, he said, "Is that all, Your Highness?"

"Yes, Bauer. If you'll tell the doctor he may come in now."

"Good night, Your Highness."

"Good night."

In a moment Doctor Safti came in: "Well, Your Highness, the gout seems better tonight."

"Yes, my knees are better."

"You shouldn't have stood up all the evening."

"I only stood when it was necessary. There are certain politenesses one has to observe."

"Quite right. Still Your Highness can do as he pleases."

The old gentleman laughed: "It's not as easy as that. You'd soon find out, Doctor, if ever you'd like to change places. . . ." He made a little gesture: "But that wouldn't work. You could do my job but I could never do yours."

"What Your Highness needs is a change. You should get off to Carlsbad."

"I shall as soon as I'm able."

When the Major had finished examining him and saw that his medicines were arrayed properly on the lacquer table beside him, he bowed and turned to go.

"Wait, Doctor!"

"Yes, sir."

"Sit down. I want to talk to you for a moment."

"Yes, Your Highness."

"It's about something serious."

"Yes, Your Highness."

"Why haven't you ever married, doctor?"

Major Safti grinned: "I don't know." He seemed to reflect for a moment, as if he had never thought about it before: "When I was in England there was nobody suitable and then when I came here I was so busy at first it never occurred to me, and now I've got used to not being married."

"But what do you do about it? Light your cigar, you'll feel more comfortable."

Major Safti grinned again: "Thank you, sir." He lighted the cigar and then said, "Well, at first it was difficult, but I've had it fixed up now for a long time. At first it got in the way of my work and then I found a girl. That was three years ago. Everything's been fine since then."

His Highness waited and Major Safti divined that he was full of curiosity. "It's Natara Devi," he said, "one of the dancers from the school. You know, Your Highness, the little one from the North with blue eyes and very black hair."

The Maharajah smiled: "Very pretty too, but dancers are expensive. They have to lay aside money for their old age."

Major Safti grinned again, a little sheepishly; "She doesn't ask much —a trinket now and then. I think, sir, she's in love with me."

"Are you in love with her?"

The Major thought for a moment: "I've never considered it before. No . . . I don't suppose so. She's a nice little thing."

"Then it wouldn't make much difference if you gave her up?"

"No, she isn't necessary . . . not Natara Devi herself. Any pretty, good-natured woman would do."

"Then if I found the proper wife for you, you wouldn't object to being married?"

"No . . . not if I liked her. But you see it's difficult. I'm a Brahmin and not orthodox. I'm not religious at all. My mother has talked to me about getting married but she's never been able to find anyone. There was always something wrong. You see, I couldn't properly get on with an orthodox woman and I wouldn't ask her to try to get on with me. I've got a lot of ideas that most Indian women and their families wouldn't put up with."

"Yes, that's true," said the Maharajah. "But I know a girl who might suit. Her father is a friend of mine. He's a great scholar, in Bombay, and her mother is an American woman from San Francisco. They met when he was working in the museum there. It's difficult for the girl too to find a proper husband because she's not one thing or the other."

"Is she pretty?" asked the Major.

"Very pretty. She'd make exactly the right wife."

"All right, sir. I see no objection unless she takes a dislike to me. I'm very easy to please."

"I'll write to her father then. In the autumn when I come back I'll invite them all to visit me."

"Very good, sir." Major Safti rose from his chair: "You may count on me."

"You understand why I am interested?"

"I think so, Your Highness."

"It's because we need more Indians like yourself. I hope that you will have plenty of children."

The Major grinned: "I hope so too, sir. I see no reason why I shouldn't have."

"Will you ask Raschid to come in? Good night, Doctor, and thank you for all you've done for me."

The Major's face grew serious for the first time. "It's my duty, sir. It's the thing which is the most important of all . . . to keep you well for all our sakes, for the sake of Ranchipur . . . for the sake of India."

"Good night. I know you aren't rich and neither is the girl I've spoken of, but I'll see to that."

Then Major Safti left, and as he walked along the endless corridors it was not of Natara Devi, oddly enough, that he kept thinking, but of plain middle-aged Miss MacDaid. His getting married would hurt her and he was fond of her. She knew about Natara Devi and didn't seem to mind, perhaps because she knew the East so well and understood it; but getting married was another thing. The poor old girl would be jealous and annoyed and she would try not to show it, but it would make their work together more and more difficult; and their work was more important than anything, good or bad, which might happen to either of them. Presently an odd thought occurred to him, almost without his thinking—that he had been putting aside the thought of marriage for a long time on account of Miss MacDaid. Perhaps if she would understand that he was only marrying in order to have children, lots of them, in order to help along their plan, she would not mind; and as he drove off through the rain he decided that he would explain it all to her when the proper moment arrived.

At his bungalow he found Natara Devi already there, waiting for him,

[140]

small and slim, the color of pale *café au lait*, with a body that was like a lovely poem; and for an hour or two the Major forgot India and Miss MacDaid, the Maharajah and the Untouchables. That hour or two belonged to him, not Major Safti, the surgeon or the political leader, but to a man who was young and strong and loved life and all the sensual pleasures he might wring from it in the few short years there were, who knew that for the pain a man suffered from his body it owed him in return a great debt of pleasure. In Natara Devi he lost himself as he was not able to lose himself otherwise even in sleep.

And at daylight she went away again back through the rain in a little red tonga ornamented with bedraggled plumes and tiny bits of looking-glass, to her house near the old wooden palace.

For a long time the Maharajah and his police minister talked in Hindustani of affairs of state, of changes to be made at the jail farm, of plans for settling the wild hill people on state land, because the old gentleman had come long ago to trust the honesty of Raschid Ali Khan and to seek his advice, sometimes so violent and headstrong, but always intelligent. He knew that Raschid would never understand——because he was Arab and Afghan and Turk——that in India one had to go slowly, sometimes with heartbreaking slowness. But where his Hindu advisers, however enlightened, sometimes retarded progress by the very intricacy of their plans, Raschid always saw a way of accomplishing a reform efficiently and energetically. It was this balance between Muslim impetuosity and Hindu intricacy which the Maharajah had sought all through the fifty years of his reign. It was not a new formula. Akbar, who had ruled India wisely and well, had discovered it three hundred years earlier.

And presently while Raschid sat, big and powerful and heavy on a frail gilt chair, setting forth his plans for the hill people, the Maharajah came to the point.

"You see," he said, "I am very ill, more ill than anyone knows but the Major and unless things get better I must make plans for when I die."

"No, Your Highness. There's no danger."

"All the same, Raschid. One has to think of these things and there is

[141]

no one to succeed me but a boy of fifteen. That's what I wanted to talk to you about. Her Highness will be regent. I suppose she'll live for a long time yet. She's luckier than I am. She has always known how to amuse herself. In some ways she is just as young as when I married her. I mean to leave the state to her. She has worked with me for fifty years. She knows better than anyone what I've tried to do and she wants the same thing. But the job is too much for her alone, vigorous as she is. She'll need someone to help her, and so I've arranged for two persons. One is the Dewan. . . ."

His Highness saw the shadow of an expression of distaste cross the honest countenance of the big Muslim. He and the Dewan did not like each other. That much the old gentleman knew and out of that dislike he saw the hope of a fine balance of judgment and energy and method. Her Highness could manage the two of them. He meant to give her sufficient power to cope with them and their dislikes and their quarrels, with the Dewan's intrigues and Raschid's fiery tactless honesty.

". . . the other is you," he continued. "With the three of you, Ranchipur ought to be safe and well governed. Do you think you can manage it?"

Raschid Ali Khan frowned. "I don't care for the methods of the Dewan," he said.

The Maharajah smiled: "Neither does Her Highness. In that you'll have her on your side."

"And Her Highness is very quick-tempered."

"And so are you, Raschid. The Dewan can pour the oil."

"I accept, of course, Your Highness, but I have to think of the difficulties."

The old gentleman laughed: "There will be plenty of difficulties. My grandson won't be difficult. I think already that he wants for Ranchipur what Her Highness and I have always wanted. I suppose he'll come into his powers at twenty-one, and before that I want him sent round the world to see what it is like. I want him to have a sense of proportion, to know how unimportant Ranchipur is and how important. And I want him to know all kinds and colors and races of people. Perhaps you would go with him?"

"If Your Highness asks it."

The Maharajah was silent for a moment, fighting the pain in his legs. Then he said, "Very good. We'll talk of all this later in detail, perhaps tomorrow . . . say at three o'clock, if you're free."

"I shall be free, Your Highness."

Painfully the old gentleman pulled himself up in bed. Then he said, "Come here and take my hand"; and when Raschid Ali Khan came to the bed and lifted the mosquito netting, the Maharajah took his hand and said, "Thank you, Raschid, for what you've done for Ranchipur." It was not a Hindu gesture. In his simple heart the old man had no thought of caste, or creed or race. He and Raschid were working for the same thing and so Raschid was his brother. To him it did not matter whether Raschid was Muslim or Christian, Hindu or Jew, Buddhist or savage.

In the vast hallway below stairs Raschid Ali Khan found his wife sitting upright in a huge imitation renaissance chair, waiting for him. She was a quiet little woman, shy and always a little startled at being the wife of so important and so fiery a person as her husband. To her he was God, mankind, everything in the world, save her seven children. As they drove home through the pouring rain in the little red tonga he told her that His Highness meant to make him coregent with the Maharani and the Dewan, and when he had finished talking she said, "You will be a great man yet, Raschid." And then they fell to discussing the party and the Eskeths, whom both of them found puzzling, and presently as they turned in at the gate of their own house Mrs. Raschid said, "While I was waiting I saw that Russian maid of Her Highness going through all the rooms downstairs. She didn't know I was there. She was going from room to room as if she were looking for something. What do you suppose it could mean?"

Raschid laughed: "I don't know. With the old lady, it might mean anything."

The Maharajah, left alone, did not sleep. Sitting propped up in bed, he struggled against the pain until presently the morphine left his mind free but weary and a little confused.

Alone now in the vast bedroom overlooking the town, he was not alarmed at the prospect of death. In his weariness he rather welcomed it, as a tired man welcomes sleep. And examining his heart and his conscience he found there little with which to reproach himself. He was a good man and a simple one and in his simplicity he saw himself exactly as he was, without brilliance, without extraordinary gifts, a man who had tried as long as he could remember to do what was best for his people. Lying there, he knew well enough that all his vast wealth, all his absolute power, all his prestige had come to him long ago simply by circumstance and not through any achievement of his own. Without them he might now have been a simple and beneficent old villager, somewhere in the vast dusty stretches of the Deccan.

But given all the wealth and the power and the prestige, he had abused none of them. He had used his wealth to bring schools and libraries and hospitals to Ranchipur, to put an end forever to floods and famines, to erect factories and workshops which would bring his people wealth, and his power he had used to battle the ancient prejudices which were like festering sores on the huge body of India, to drive into exile scoundrelly priests and parasite Brahmins, to release the Untouchables from the filthy square where superstition had imprisoned them. He had never been bigoted or tyrannical or depraved although fate had given him opportunity for all the tricks of tyranny and bigotry and depravity. And all this he had done not as the friend but the enemy of religions, taught long ago by an Englishman to abandon the pettiness, the corruption, the superstitions which were a part of every sect, for a higher faith, to be found not in idols or invisible incredible gods but, like that of the great Akbar, in mankind itself.

And he had had staunch friends and known many fine and noble people. There was Raschid and Miss MacDaid and young Doctor Safti and the Smileys and Mr. Jobnekar, who had all rewarded his faith and trust many times over. And there were those two strange Englishwomen, Miss Dirks and Miss Hodge, always beyond his understanding, so cold, so devoted to duty, so lonely and lost and unwomanly, who had given their whole lives in a strange singleness of purpose to help him and the women of Ranchipur. Although he had never said more than a few words to them in all the twenty-five years they had been in Ranchipur, they somehow understood his plan and shared it with him.

[144]

And there was always Her Highness who, he had known from the beginning, was more brilliant and more gifted than himself, but he had known too that she was more passionate and more erratic, and that beneath all her suavity, all her dignity, all her beauty, a part of her had always remained savage and untamed. They had quarreled, again and again, for she was wild and headstrong, but never had they been able to do without each other. For nearly fifty years they had been together, through disappointment and humiliation, through satisfaction and triumph, through the deaths of their sons, one by one, tragically unsettled and corrupted by their education in the West. Always they had worked for the same thing, with a strange united singleness of purpose, himself because long ago John Lawrence had taught him to be a good ruler, she because in her arrogance and pride of race she meant that India should waken and live again as it had lived in the times of Asoka and Akbar. For that she had fought to free the women of Ranchipur from ignorance and superstition. For that, although she was a religious woman, she had put aside her faith to free the Untouchables. He knew that now, as an old woman, she had found a faith greater than the faith in gods and rituals and superstitions.

Now, looking back over fifty years, her whole life and character seemed incredible to him. He saw her again as she had been at thirteen when she came down from the hills to marry him, still a child who could speak only Mahratta and could not even read or write, haughty and fierce and shy and savage like a sleek panther cub. There were times still when she was haughty and savage but there was no longer any shyness about her. He loved her now, not for her beauty nor for her greatness, but for her humanity—that she was so filled with curiosity and mischief and malice, that she made him chuckle at times when otherwise it would have been impossible for him to smile, that she had remained forever young. He was glad that he would die before her because without her there would no longer be any savor in life.

Lying in the dark, listening to the rain which brought fertility and salvation to Ranchipur, face after face returned to him out of the past, without relation or discrimination, more clearly now than they had come to him since his boyhood—faces of men who had served him, good and evil, stupid or clever, trustworthy and treacherous; the face of the Maharani who was the widow of the evil Maharajah he had succeeded, a strange, clever woman, robbed of a power and a wealth she might have used better than himself; the faces of ministers he had had from time to time over fifty years; of his dead sons, so wild and brilliant, slain by the civilization of the West. But clearest of all he saw the face of his old tutor, of John Lawrence who had been sent to him long ago by the British when he was a boy of twelve who could neither read nor write and knew only the tongue of the warlike Mahrattas.

It was a long gentle face with very clear blue eyes and large shaggy blond mustaches, a face which had given him confidence when he saw it for the first time as a child, fresh from the mountains where he had been herding cows. Now in his old age he remembered exactly how it felt, how shy and terrified and defiant he had been, his ragged cow-herd's clothing replaced by the most magnificent silks and brocades, his mud-walled room exchanged for the splendor of the old wooden palace that now stood deserted on the square opposite the cinema. Beneath his shyness and defiance he had thought, "I am a warrior of warrior people. I must bear myself well before these pale-skinned men from beyond the sea." For then he had never heard of Europe and he only knew vaguely that beyond the borders of India there was a vast sea, so vast as to be beyond the imagination. And he had been sullen too and suspicious, watching the pale men, how they ate, how they spoke, even how they walked, thinking, "I am a King and a Warrior. I must not be shamed by them." And then there were too moments of dull misery when he had wished to be back again in the barren dusty hills watching the cows and goats. It was John Lawrence who had saved him from bitterness and defiance and evil, for he knew now that without Lawrence he might have become one of those evil princes, depraved, extravagant, tyrannical and mad, of whom there were all too many in India. When the face of John Lawrence had appeared among all the other strange faces which surrounded him, the boy of twelve had known at once that he might trust him forever.

It was John Lawrence who had taught him to read and write, not only English and Hindustani but French as well. It was John Lawrence who had opened up for him the whole world, not only of the East but the West. The Englishman, he knew now, had seen the world with detachment and without passion, not as an Englishman or as anything else, but as a man, pointing out to the Indian boy, whose whole world had begun and ended with the borders of the half-savage Deccan, the virtues and vices alike of governments and vast empires and peoples, so that it became clear and simple for him to recognize what was just and good. It was John Lawrence who taught him that he was simply a man like all other men, to whom fate had brought a vast responsibility. Out of his own intelligence and goodness John Lawrence had planted goodness and humanity in the boy who one day would become the absolute ruler of twelve million people. It was John Lawrence who had made him see that religions were compounded largely of superstition, born of a common human impulse out of the fear of mankind and out of its helplessness, and it was John Lawrence who had chosen the great Akbar, a Muslim, as the model for the boy to follow, a ruler who was wise and just and who dreamed, for his people, things that were forever beyond their reach because they were not worthy of them.

He could see his tutor very plainly now, sitting across the big table from him in a room in the old wooden palace or in the garden of the house where Ransome lived now and where John Lawrence had lived then with his plump wife and their eight children. It seemed to him that there were no longer any men like John Lawrence come out of the West. Now they were all like Esketh, greedy and ruthless and evil or like Ransome, warped and barren and tired. Ransome, he knew, was an ill man and his illness was the illness of Europe. Esketh was evil and had another kind of illness, but it too came from the West.

Lawrence, he saw now, had had a dream that was the same as the dream of Miss MacDaid and Mr. Jobnekar and Major Safti and the Smileys—a dream which the tutor had passed on to himself. For John Lawrence had loved India. He had gone back to England but, like Miss MacDaid, his heart had stayed in the East and in the end he had returned to die in the house where Ransome now lived. The old gentleman saw it all clearly now. John Lawrence had seen that half-savage boy of twelve as an instrument, and he had molded and sharpened him out of his love for India into a man and a ruler who would cherish the dream and carry it a little way further along the way to fulfillment. For a moment he was tempted to chuckle. The British who were, like Esketh, interested in India only for the profits to be got from it, had made a mistake in sending him a tutor like John Lawrence.

Sighing, he reflected that the English no longer sent men like John Lawrence out to India, but perhaps, he thought, there were no longer any men like him. If only there had been more of them, so much bitterness, so many conflicts, so much evil might have been avoided. India, on the day she awakened, might have been England's greatest friend. But that part of the dream was lost now, forever, through the pettiness of mankind.

The morphine stole over him, filling him with sleep. He had only one reason for wanting to live, and that was to see India, united and proud, freed from poverty and superstition and ignorance, a great nation. But for that one would have to live the lifetimes of many men, and he was old and tired and sometimes discouraged.

Half asleep, he put his hand out to ring the bell for Mr. Bauer and then remembered that very likely the Swiss nurse had been asleep for hours and he had not the heart to waken him.

But Mr. Bauer was not asleep. He was not even in his room. A little while later, still dressed at three in the morning, he opened the door softly to see that all was well with the old gentleman and then went away.

"That Russian woman" whom Mrs. Raschid had seen going through the lower rooms of the palace was the daughter of a Moscow professor, and near to the Maharani she occupied an unofficial position as confidante, companion, gossip, guardian of the fabulous jewels and the vast wardrobe, interpreter and bargainer. Penniless and adrift and discouraged, she had been found by the Maharani a little while after the Revolution in the Kurhaus Park in Carlsbad. It was the curiosity and humanity of the old lady which brought them together. Her Highness wanted to have an intimate personal account of what the Revolution had been like and how it was to live under Soviet rule. So for a magnificent dinner and a bottle of champagne Maria Lishinskaia had given her an account, somewhat superficial because that was Maria's nature, and very bitter because she had lost everything in the debacle——father, fiancé, home and money. But the bitterness did not last. Long before the end of the dinner Maria was aware of her opportunity, and the bitterness became transmuted into charm and gayety which, Maria being a Russian, was, strangely enough, genuine.

It was her gayety that made the Maharani take a liking to her—her gayety and her philosophy of indifference (if she hadn't a meal today, one would turn up tomorrow and it always did), her independence and her cynical humor. Also she had understanding. When it was necessary, for show, she would address Her Highness in the most groveling fashion, creating the illusion of abjectness; but the moment they were alone she became simply a friend, full of humor and a sense of the spectacle of life, with a liking for intrigue and a mocking cynicism. Here, Her Highness, discovered at last, was a European whom she could understand.

Maria Lishinskaia wasn't just one or two things like most Europeans, clean cut and blunt. She was not simply Ambition, or Lust, or Sentimentality, or Fidelity, or even just a combination of two or three of these things. She was a mixture of all of them, and a great deal more thrown in, and so she was changeable and contradictory and amused Her Highness. She could be savage one moment and overcivilized the next, straightforward at times and incredibly devious at others, now trustworthy, now completely false, now cynically humorous, now sentimentally and romantically melancholy, for she was an Asiatic at heart and not a European at all; and so Her Highness understood her and found the companion she had been seeking for thirty years, to accompany her to theaters and casinos and night clubs when she was in the West and share her magnificent isolation when she lived in the huge palace in Ranchipur. When she was in the East she had someone with whom she might gossip in the royal bedroom, someone who understood alike the idiosyncrasies of Indians and Europeans. In the West she had someone who would explain to her why Europeans sometimes behaved as they did, and someone to bargain for her with hotels and jewelers and dressmakers. Maria Lishinskaia understood the Oriental pleasure that was to be had in bargaining and she went into the game with zest. Although she knew that the Maharani could have bought the best palace hotels in which she spent a few weeks now and then and not have missed the money, she knew too that it gave Her Highness far more pleasure to bargain for rooms or discover an error in the bill. In a jeweler's shop in the Place Vendôme the Maharani would plan the campaign and Maria Lishinskaia would carry it out, occasionally contributing brilliant touches of her own, so that the jeweler confronted by the two of them—Maria Lishinskaia prompted by Her Highness—would find himself, before he quite understood what had happened, selling his finest jewels to one of the richest women in the world at bargain prices. And Maria had too that incredible smoldering vitality of the East. Like the Maharani she could stay up gambling in the casino until daylight and be out shopping at noon without the slightest sign of dullness or fatigue.

And sometimes it was convenient for the old lady to have Maria Lishinskaia at hand when her nerves were on edge and she felt the need of torturing someone.

When the Maharani returned to her own rooms Maria Lishinskaia was lying on the *chaise longue* reading a novel by Mauriac. She was a woman of perhaps thirty-five or six, neither plain nor handsome but with a fine voluptuous figure and greenish eyes that slanted a little in Tartar fashion. There were moments when the Maharani thought she looked very like Raschid Ali Khan and that the likeness was not only one of physique but of indefatigable vitality. The Maharani said, "Your ancestors must have gone down one side of the Himalayas into Russia when Raschid's came down the other side into India." But there the likeness ended, for Maria Lishinskaia had none of Raschid's faith or purpose in life. She believed in nothing. She was an opportunist without faith, without any longer even a country.

As the Maharani came in the Russian woman put down her book, stood up, yawned and said, "Well?"

"It was terrible . . . terrible," said Her Highness in French.

"And the Eskeths?"

"Terrible . . . terrible."

The Untouchable maids began undressing the Maharani, massaging her face, rubbing oil into her fine black hair. The old lady opened a small gold box and began chewing betel nuts.

Maria Lishinskaia helped her to take off the heavy emeralds, and one by one laid them into their boxes.

"Comment, terrible?" she asked.

"He is a big money king and a bully and a brute and she is . . . one of those fashionable English sluts. She disappeared with Ransome. She was gone most of the evening. They said they were going to look at the rooms downstairs."

"Yes?" said Maria encouragingly. "What happened?"

"What do you suppose?" asked the Maharani. "But I never heard it called looking at rooms before."

"I had an idea Mr. Ransome didn't care about women," said Maria.

"What do you mean by that?" And the Maharani looked at her sharply. She was fond of Ransome and Maria Lishinskaia was jealous of him as she was jealous of everyone to whom Her Highness showed favor.

"Oh, nothing . . . anything." And then aware that the feeler she had put out was received with displeasure, she became noncommittal. It was a kind of game that went on between them when they gossiped.

"He is tired," said the Maharani.

"That's what I meant," said Maria brightly. "He's tried everything."

"Perhaps."

The old lady was aware shrewdly that the bit of gossip had excited Maria and that the mind of the Russian woman, stimulated, was now rushing this way and that, speculating, imagining things, gloating.

"Do you like Ransome?" she asked.

"I don't know," said Maria. "I scarcely know him. He's good-looking . . . in a special kind of way. Does Your Highness know it happened?"

"How can I *know*? You can only *know* about those things when you are under the bed."

"But couldn't you tell when they came back?"

"Not with the English. You can't even tell the moment afterward any more than you can tell if a man has had a glass of water. Why don't you go down and see for yourself? If it happened, it was in one of the rooms downstairs."

"Oh, no, I couldn't do that!"

But Her Highness knew that very likely after she herself was in bed Maria Lishinskaia would go from room to room downstairs trying to find out. Suddenly the old lady saw that Maria was like the other two, like Lady Esketh and Ransome. Weary, faithless, bored, sceptical, she had come, like them, to the last resort—the body. When everything else failed there was always lust and sensuality. She thought, "What will she do if Mr. Bauer should go away?"

Maria was asking, "Does Your Highness know when we shall be leaving for Carlsbad?"

The old lady knew that very likely they would be leaving at the end of the week, but she had no desire to give Maria Lishinskaia the pleasure of knowing it. The shadow of the Eskeths still hung over her, creating a curious sense of irritation, so she said, "It depends on the rains. If they keep on like this we shall be able to leave soon. His Highness won't leave until he knows the rains have settled in for good."

Maria was thinking, "Once I can get Harry to Europe I can get him to marry me. Then he won't be able to get away, and our future will be safe with Their Highnesses. They'll fix us for life." For there were moments when she grew weary of her own rootlessness and the uncertainty of her future. Aloud she said, "I suppose Your Highness will want to sleep early tonight?"

"I'm not tired," said the Maharani; and at the same time she was thinking, "This must be one of Bauer's nights." And the temptation came to her to keep Maria Lishinskaia by her side for a time, restless and full of desire, to read to her.

"You might read to me for a little while." And she saw the disappointment in Maria's face and her heart softened a little. She thought, "I'll ask her to read and then after a little while pretend I'm sleepy and let her off." So she said, "You might read out of that French book—that classic one."

"*Les Liaisons Dangereuses?*"

"Yes, that's it. I'm always interested in knowing how the French go about such things. They're very like the Chinese, the French. I've been thinking about it. They've got a form and an attitude for everything."

So when the Maharani was in bed with all her creams and oils well applied, Maria Lishinskaia sat down beside her and began to read out of *"Les Liaisons Dangereuses,"* against the faint dull roar of the rain. She read on and on, passage after passage analyzing love and desire, describing intrigues and jealousies and reconciliations, all written with a minute and passionate skill, each word an aphrodisiac, each comma stimulant to desire. And beneath her long eyelashes the Maharani watched with satisfaction and entertainment. She observed that Maria Lishinskaia began presently to breathe with difficulty. She blundered over passages as if the words danced before her eyes. Little beads of sweat came out on the wide olive-skinned forehead. And she knew that Maria scarcely knew the sense of what she was reading. It was all confused with her passion for the white athlete's body of Mr. Bauer. He was good-looking, thought the Maharani, and had a beautiful body, but he was stupid. Scarcely listening to the words which were torturing Maria, she wondered how it was possible to have so stupid and servile a man for a lover, no matter how beautiful he was. And she speculated for a time upon the horrors of being a slave to one's body, so that you suffered as Maria Lishinskaia was now suffering from her desire for the Swiss swimming instructor.

Scarcely listening to the words which were torturing Maria Lishinskaia, she watched her with a curious detachment and satisfaction. There were moments when out of the bitterness of her life, out of the exasperations and the humiliations and the bafflement, there came a need of cruelty to quiet her stormy soul. Once long ago such a queen as herself could have sent for a slave or a criminal and inflicted pain upon him until her exasperated nerves were appeased, but that no longer was possible, and so she had to think of intricate and devious ways. She knew that if she had not thus tortured Maria she herself could not have slept. Presently, after Maria had been reading for an hour or more, she felt sleep stealing over her, and turning on her pillow, she said, "That will be enough, Maria. There's just one thing more."

"Yes, Your Highness." Her voice was weak now and exhausted and as she spoke she passed a handkerchief over her face.

"Go downstairs and see if you can find the room, and discover if it really happened."

"Yes, Your Highness."

"And come back and tell me. If I'm asleep, don't trouble to waken me."

"Yes, Your Highness."

The Russian woman looked pale and limp like a cloth which has been dampened and then wrung dry.

With her eyes half-closed, the Maharani watched her leave the room. On the poor lost Maria Lishinskaia she had taken a little, a tiny fragment of the vengeance which her pride and spirit demanded of Europe for the humiliations she had suffered for nearly half a century.

Dizzy and nearly fainting, Maria Lishinskaia stumbled down the stairs and along the corridor, visiting room after room without finding anything in disarray. She kept saying to herself, "It will be the next room and then I can go to Harry. Oh, God, make it the next so that I may go to him!"

And presently, when she had visited room after room in vain, she grew cold with terror at the thought that if she did not return soon he might grow tired of waiting and go back again to his own room next to the Maharajah, where she dared not follow him. "Oh God, keep him there!" she kept saying aloud, "God-damn all these empty useless rooms. Oh God, keep him there till I can go to him." And at last she came to the room. She did not remain long, for no more than a glance was necessary—the divan, rumpled and in disorder, the panther skin kicked aside, the burnt cigarette ends crushed out in haste on the floor. She saw them all in one swift glance. She thought, "The bitch! the bastard! To make me all this trouble! They didn't even trouble to put the room in order."

Running, she went back through all the rooms and along the interminable corridor past Mrs. Raschid, without even seeing her, until she reached the apartments of the Maharani. When she safely pushed open the door of the bedroom she heard the old lady breathing easily and closed it again in the belief that she was asleep. From behind her dark lashes the Maharani watched her, and when the door closed she fell asleep, her spirit at peace.

Mr. Bauer was still waiting, angry and impatient and ill-tempered, but, thank God, still waiting. Nevertheless she was unaware of his anger, and when peace came to her again she forgot herself so far as to begin to nag him again about marriage. Lying by his side, she told him that she would kill herself if he did not make her his wife, but Mr. Bauer,

[154]

also at peace now and no longer angry but only filled with a desire for sleep, yawned and was unmoved by her threats.

He had no intention of ever marrying her because the last thing he wanted as a wife was an hysterical Russian woman who was always threatening suicide and complaining because she hadn't enough of him. He had other plans. When he returned to Europe this year he meant to marry Lina Storrel. She was the proper kind, solid and reliable and economical. And while he was in Europe he'd start their first child and then come back to India with His Highness. One more year and he'd have enough money to buy the vineyard above Montreux. Now that he was at peace again he felt full of contempt for Maria Lishinskaia. Why couldn't she understand that this was good now and then for the health of both of them, especially in a hot country like this? Why did she keep trying to make it into something else—romance, marriage, etc.?

Mr. Bauer knew what he wanted. He was a peasant and primitive. There was nothing ill about him, very little indeed that was civilized.

While he dressed, Maria Lishinskaia kept sobbing and saying she would throw herself out of the window, but he took no notice of her and only went on stolidly putting on his clothes, for he knew well enough that she would do nothing at all that would cause a scandal and make her lose the soft place into which luck had landed her. And he knew too that she would always be there, waiting for him whenever he sent word.

Driving away from the palace, slowly, along the winding avenue, Ransome kept losing his way continually in the blinding rain. The lights of the old Buick were of no use save when now and then they revealed directly in front of him the trunk of a tree or a withered bed of flowers beaten flat by the downpour. By the bridge he narrowly escaped driving into the little lake with the bottom of concrete. It was filling now slowly with water, and the tiny pleasure boats, canopied and gilded, and ornamented with fretwork, no longer tilted on their sides but were beginning to stir and float and come to life. The rain was like a thick wall against which he could feel the car pressing its way.

It was slow going and until he got the feel of the thing he had no time to think of anything save whether in the next moment he would

[155]

hit something, or slip into the lake. It was like driving a motor again at the front without lights. Then, slowly, as his lean hands got the "feel" of the thing, he became aware of a profound feeling of depression, the feeling that came when he had dissipated all his strength and gone without sleep for days at a time. It was a curious lost feeling, heavy with a sense of futility and despair; not only was his body weary but his spirit as well.

He had no feeling of shame save at his own foolishness in believing that by embracing Edwina for a few short moments he, and she with him for that matter, might recapture something of the feelings they had known long ago. He knew now that such raptures were forever beyond recapture because both of them were too old and too experienced and neither of them had anything left of fire or recklessness. It was not recklessness when you risked nothing, when what you did made no difference to anyone, not even to yourself. The only excitement they had won from the experience lay in those few precious moments of almost animal excitement, filled with anticipation. The rest was flat and dull and routine. He could not even find satisfaction in the knowledge that he had fed a little his hatred for Esketh by taking Esketh's wife. There was no satisfaction in it unless Esketh discovered it, and he was certain that Edwina would see to it that he never did. Pushing the idea still further he felt doubtful suddenly whether Esketh would care, because the quick cold viciousness of her embrace and ease and shame-lessness of her whole behavior argued a hundred such casual affairs, "love" snatched here and there in haste—in corners, on yachts and beaches, in motors. He had known from the moment she came into the room, into the glare of the bee-haunted chandelier that she was "dead" but he had never believed her to be as dead as that. Esketh must have found her out long before now.

Alone, driving through the rain, he felt a sense of disgust and re-pulsion, as if Edwina had been more guilty than himself of what had been a trivial and callous folly, but he thought, "That's an illusion. That's the old double standard coming up again." But he was unable to argue himself out of the feeling, for his instinct was more true and more profound than any argument he might bring against it. What *had* hap-pened *was* worse in her than in himself. It should not have been so and

[156]

yet it was, because he knew that somehow sooner or later, if it were not already true, *she* was certain to be the victim of her own viciousness. There was something terrifying in the glance he had had for a moment of that abyss. He saw now that in what they had done there was nothing of sentiment, nothing perhaps more than curiosity, perhaps nothing but an animal gesture, like the *accouplement* of two *pie* dogs, but without its realistic necessity.

Out of the adventure the figure of the Maharani appeared to him now more clearly than that of Edwina. Thinking of her it seemed to him that she always knew everything about everyone, not merely the gossip and the intrigue which came to her naturally in a million different underground ways, but hidden things in the very characters and thoughts of people. There was the Maharani he knew across the poker table and the Maharani who was a great queen, doing her duty magnificently; these two he understood, but beyond them there was someone whom he never saw at all, at once complex and secret, savage and overcivilized, full of astounding intuition. There were times when he had seen her change before his eyes, while he was talking to her, from a woman who was everything that was European and understandable, into a savage hill princess, unfathomable and capable of the utmost cruelty and lack of scruple. At such times she both fascinated and alarmed him, and he was afraid of her now, for what reason he did not quite know. She alone knew what had happened belowstairs. At this very moment she was probably discussing it with that tiresome, arrogant Russian woman. It did not matter to him who discovered it, and he knew that very likely it mattered even less to Edwina, and yet the thought of the Maharani's knowledge made him uneasy, with a dull sense of dread and shame. It was a puerile, silly feeling, like that of a child fearful and shamed at having been caught in a nasty act.

Again he thought, "Perhaps I am ill. Perhaps I ask too much of every experience, too much of every person . . . more than anyone is able to give."

From the sound of the river he knew that he was near the bridge, and in a moment the lights of the old Buick suddenly revealed the stubby figure of Queen Victoria, still standing staunchly on her pedestal, her umbrella and reticule grasped firmly in her chubby iron hands, solid, imperturbable in the midst of the wild storm. Then he passed Mr. Bannerjee's house and caught a glimpse of a light in Raschid's house and at last came to the gateway of his own garden, thinking how dreary it was to come home alone to this damp empty Georgian mausoleum. If his marriage had been a success he wouldn't be coming home now to an empty house in Ranchipur; indeed he would not be coming back to a house in Ranchipur at all, but to that great turreted castle of his grandmother in Grand River.

He drove the old car under the *porte cochère*, and then for the first time he noticed that, although he had given stern orders to John the Baptist about keeping the house dark on account of mosquitoes, there was a light in his bedroom, and instead of going in by the door that led from the carriage drive he walked in the dark along the verandah until he reached the window of his own room.

There in his own easy chair he saw the figure of a woman, wearing a cheap raincoat and soaked and shapeless hat. She was sitting with her back to the window, for having heard the sound of the motor she had put down the "Tatler" which she had been reading and was watching the door.

At the old summer palace Lord and Lady Esketh got down from the purple Rolls-Royce and in silence climbed the red carpet which covered the marble stairs. At the top they separated to go to their own rooms, and casually Lady Esketh turned and said, "Good night," adding, "Are you all right? You're not feeling ill?"

He answered, "It's all right. There's nothing the matter with me but this damned heat and these damned Indians. I want to get out of here tomorrow. Bombay won't be any worse than this. At least it'll be a little more like Europe. This is like living in a madhouse."

"Whenever you like," she said. "I've had enough of India. I never want to see it again."

It was true that she had had enough of India. While she was undressing she thought about it indolently, allowing her mind to wander where it would, and presently she came to the conclusion that she might just as well never have come out at all. The only memories she would take back with her were unpleasant ones—of heat and dust and smells, of tiresome official dinners, of boring civil servants and their more boring wives and plain daughters. There must be, she thought, an India which could arouse even her languid interests, but where it was she did not know. There must be something in India to have held an intelligent restless man like Tom Ransome for nearly five years. Now and then, for a moment, she had been dimly aware of such an India, but whenever she attempted to approach it, it seemed to withdraw from her. When she talked with Indians—something which she had avoided whenever possible because of the effort—it was always with Indians who had been at Oxford, who seemed to hide from her everything that was Indian; they became simply European and talked about cricket and night clubs and horses, as European as any men she might have met at dinner in London. And then it occurred to her for the first time in her life that not only India but almost everything in life had always been hidden from her. It was as if she had always been protected, sheltered and hedged round by luxury, by convention, by manners, by the very privilege which went with being Edwina Esketh, and before that Edwina Doncaster. In spite of having been for half her life without a penny she had been robbed by her very position of a knowledge of what poverty was like, because there were always people to give her credit and do things for her, even to providing her with money which they never expected to be paid back.

For a moment she had an envy of the dullness of the lives of all those little people who carried on the work of governing India, envy even of the lives of the families of little clerks in suburbs everywhere in the world. Their lives could scarcely be duller than her own, but it was in any case a different dullness. And she suddenly experienced an extraordinary feeling of loneliness, as if she were a sort of spirit living in the world but without any contact with it, a shadow without substance or reality. The only real thing, she suddenly saw, was her body and the pleasure she found in adorning it, in keeping it young, in using it to make love.

Thinking of making love, she began to think about Tom Ransome again, admiring him because long ago in the very midst of it he had turned his back on the life to which he had been born and made an effort to find something else. What he had found or whether he had

[159]

found anything at all she did not know, but at least he had tried and that was something. It was too late now for her to make an attempt to escape, even if the desire persisted until morning. She had no illusions about herself; she would rather go on putting up with Esketh than make the effort it required to escape. And then she remembered something Tom had said to her in the room belowstairs, something in American slang which she had not at first understood, so that it had been necessary for him to explain it to her.

"My God!" he observed, "but you're cold turkey."

When she had gotten into her *peignoir* she gave all the bracelets to her maid and said, "Good night, Parker. That's all."

"Me lady looks tired."

"I am a bit. It's the heat and the dampness. I'll be glad to go to Cannes."

Then when Parker had gone, suddenly and for no reason at all, she was overcome by a sense of loneliness and terror. She was frightened of India, of its vastness, its violence, of the heat and the dust and the millions of people and animals, of the jackals and the vultures and the hostility which she felt about her, a hostility shared by the animals, the people, the climate, by nature itself. She was terrified by the sound of the incredible rain beating upon the roof of the old palace and pouring in torrents from the flooded eaves. What if anything happened to prevent her escape? What if she had to stay on here forever in this vicious abominable country? For a moment it seemed to her that her nerves could not stand it any longer. She wanted to scream, to cry out, to throw herself on the floor. She wanted to run out of the palace and go to Bombay now, tonight, to a city which would be a little more like Europe, a weary and boring Europe, but at least unlike this malevolent India which terrified her.

Then she set her jaw and pulled herself together, thinking, "I must be breaking up. I've never been like that. It must be the heat." And going over to her traveling case, she opened it and took out stuff to make her sleep. When she had taken twice the ordinary dose and was in bed with the mosquito netting drawn about her, she felt more calm, and presently the medicine made her feel drowsy and voluptuous and she no longer wanted to go away the next day. She wanted to stay at least until the end of the week as they had planned so that she might go to have tea on Thursday with Tom. Lying back in the bed she gave herself up voluptuously to thinking of him.

She liked his lean hardness and his vigorous dark hair and the lean ridges at the back of his neck. She liked his straight nose and his full lips and she thought, "He's practically unique. He has intelligence and a fine physique as well. Why is it that most athletes are so stupid and most intelligent men have pot-bellies?" But when she tried to think of what Tom was like inside, she did not know; she had not the faintest idea. The Tom Ransome she had seen tonight was simply the Tom she had known long ago in London. When they talked at all, they had talked of the old days and what had become of the people they knew then. If he was as pleasant, as gentle, as lovable as he seemed, then it might be worth while going on with the affair, for presently she might discover in him the thing which in spite of everything, she thought, must exist, although she had never found it nor even come upon its tracks. "Perhaps it's my fault," she thought. "Maybe I've never found it because I've never been able to get beneath the surface."

She did not think, "Perhaps I could be happy with Tom," because the question of happiness or unhappiness had not occurred to her for a great many years in any sense save a physical one. She did not deceive herself. If happiness ever existed for her, it was at such moments as she had experienced tonight when she had gone to the palace expecting one more dreadful official dinner and then found Tom Ransome and the quick hurried adventure in the little room belowstairs. In a way the only excitement which any longer existed for her lay in such adventures, in the unexpectedness of finding an attractive man, in the perverse pleasure she found again and again in betraying Esketh. Coldly, she thought, "I am a promiscuous, abandoned bitch! So what! There isn't anything I can do about it."

Rarely after such an adventure did she want to see the man again and when she saw him again she managed to freeze at once the slightest attempt at continuing the intimacy. It was luck if the man were attractive enough to give her any desire to continue. Now she wanted to see Tom again, not merely for the pleasure it gave her or because he was a good lover, but because she had been left with a sense of incompleteness. She did not know how he felt about her. Perhaps at this very moment he was thinking of her with disgust, as a slut; because he was, she knew, complex and given to attacks of virtue and remorse, and that, she found, was attractive. She even experienced a faint sense of shame, which astounded her, and a desire to see him again in order to justify herself in some way, or at least to charm him out of the idea.

And then she was aware that the door leading to Esketh's apartment had been opened and the light was shining in, and Esketh himself came in wearing the dressing gown she hated. She had given it to him at Christmas four years before, thinking that it would please him, and she had succeeded only too well. It had been cleaned countless times and was worn and shabby, but he would not be separated from it. Whenever she suggested chucking it away he always told her that it brought him luck. It was covered with a design of horses—horses racing, horses clearing hedges and ditches, horses rearing, horses in full stride at the finishing post.

Without speaking he came over to the bed and, lifting the mosquito netting, sat on the end of it. She meant to say, "Go away, please go away just tonight," but in the next moment she saw that he did not mean to stay. He looked ill and sullen. At the corners of his heavy jaw there were little knots of hard muscle which always came there when he meant to make a scene.

He said, "Edwina, who is this fellow Ransome?"

"You know him perfectly well. He's Nolham's brother. You've even met him yourself, years ago."

It never occurred to her that he might suspect the whole truth for he was always making scenes like this, nearly always about men like Ransome who gave him a sense of inferiority; he did not mind her friendship with sporting men. It was that eternal, inverted snobbery of his, that hatred of anyone born with the things he had never achieved and would never be able to achieve. "That," she thought, "is how the caste system works at home."

"You seem very friendly with him."

"I used to know him very well. We were friends in London just after the War. I hadn't seen him for nearly fifteen years."

He set his jaw a little harder: "Where has he been since then?"

"I don't know. Wandering about the world. He's living here now."

"By choice?"

"By desire."

"He must be a damned fool."

"I don't think so. He's been trying to straighten himself out."

"What's the matter with him? What has he got to straighten out?"

"It's not a very interesting story. You'd find it boring."

He took out a cigar and lighted it. She wanted to say, "Please don't smoke in here"; but again she thought. "If I let him do as he pleases he'll go away that much sooner." She was suddenly feeling very sleepy.

"One of those damned radicals, I suppose."

"You might call it that."

"Well, he ought to be at home working to help out his government. Why do you always pick out asses like that?"

She laughed and the laugh was a secret one, against his stupidity. She hadn't any particular taste for radicals and intellectuals or anything else. She wasn't attracted to men by their ideas and their brains. It was so much simpler than that. "It's comic," she thought, "how a husband is always the last to understand the truth."

She was tired, not physically, but in the spirit, because she had been through these scenes so many times. She knew all the questions and answers, and at this sort of thing she was much the quicker-witted of the two.

He went on bitterly and abusively and having heard it all so many times before she did not trouble to listen but continued with her own thoughts: "What if I took up with an Indian? That would fix him"; and while he talked she began thinking about the Indians she had met, and the one she remembered most clearly was that Major Somebody-or-other who Ransome told her was the chief surgeon in Ranchipur. She began to see him, quite clearly, with his big shoulders and fair skin and blue eyes. Yes, that might be fun. She began to wonder what making love with an Indian would be like, and presently she noticed Esketh again and saw that his big face had become lobster-colored and that his eyes seemed to be covered by a film. For a moment she thought that perhaps he had been drinking more than usual but almost at once she realized that he never looked like this when he was drunk. At moments he seemed to be making a great effort to speak. Then she was aware of

[163]

the loathed dressing-gown again, and in her boredom it seemed to her that the horses had come to life. They were all in dizzy motion, jumping, striding, rearing, so that the sight of them put her teeth on edge.

Because it did no good she never lost her temper and never answered back during the scenes of jealousy and now it was not Esketh who made her angry but the dressing-gown and the awful rearing and prancing horses. She heard herself saying, "Why do you always pick on men like Tom Ransome? Is it because you hate all gentlemen? Because you know they're better than you?"

For a moment he stared at her, his heavy mouth half-open, so astounded that he seemed unable to find words with which to speak. Then he asked, "What do you mean by that?"

"Nothing in particular."

"Well, don't get any silly ideas. I'm proud of being Albert Simpson. I'm proud of having made my way. I'm proud of everything I've built up. It's more than any of your sickly down-at-the-heel gentlemen could do."

And again she astonished him by saying, "Yes, that's quite true—if that's what you value most." And before he could speak she said, "What is it you want of me, Albert? If you don't like men to speak to your wife then you should have married a plain respectable middle-class woman and not me. Sometimes I think you didn't marry me for any reason save that I was Edwina Doncaster and what I am. You wanted to show people that you could take what you wanted from the world, away from anyone. I was a kind of prize who had had a lot of cheap publicity in the illustrated weeklies and you wanted to show me off. You didn't really want *me*. We've never had the least understanding or sympathy. You just wanted the idea of me. A gentleman by the time you married me wouldn't have wanted me at any price."

For a time he regarded the end of his cigar without speaking. She knew what he was doing. He was pulling himself together, counting ten before he spoke, so that he would say nothing which he need ever take back. He was being a shrewd business man. She had caught him at it now and then when he was talking to other business men. But in truth it was that and much more too, for suddenly in his tired muddled brain he saw that for the first time since he had married her he had a chance to learn the truth, and he was afraid. For a moment he hesitated, wondering whether it was not better to continue in ignorance and doubt, and then like a man hesitating to dive into icy water he set his teeth and plunged. "Why did you marry me?" he asked.

"Because my father and I were stony and had a lot of debts. Because you offered me a big settlement, because I thought it would be nice to be colossally rich, and because I really didn't much care who I married." For a moment she was silent, thinking, and then she added, "I think it was the settlement that did it. That meant that whatever happened I'd always be independent."

He looked at her for a moment, understanding for the first time the fathomless hardness of the woman he had married. Then silently he rose and crushed out the end of his half-smoked cigar on the marble top of the old-fashioned Victorian dressing table. It was a concentrated brutal gesture and she thought, "That is what he would like to do to me but he's afraid. He's not the great bullying Lord Esketh now. He's poor, bumptious, awkward Albert Simpson scared of the gentry."

He started to speak and then merely said, "Good night," and went out of the room, closing the door behind him, leaving her aware that she had hurt him who she thought could not be hurt. She had found the vulnerable spot in the great Lord Esketh, born plain Albert Simpson, and she was not sorry. It avenged her for many things, for his brutality and arrogance, for his vulgarity and lack of all sensibility, for his brutal cold-blooded love-making, taking her as if she were a glass of brandy to be downed quickly without finesse or technique or understanding. Perhaps now he would leave her in peace forever. Anyway with the settlement she would always have enough money.

The effect of the sleeping medicine had worn off now and she switched on the light and tried for a time to read a book called, *India Distraught,* which the jacket said explained everything about India, but which seemed to her to explain nothing at all and bored her so profoundly that she found herself reading whole pages without having the slightest idea of what she was reading, and through the printed words she kept seeing the big figure of the Indian surgeon with his blue eyes and perfect white teeth, a wholly beautiful and attractive man. That would fix Albert!

At last, giving it up, she rose and took some more sleeping medicine and a final cigarette, and as she regained the bed there was a knock on the door and she called out, "Who is it?"

A voice answered, "It's Bates, me lady."

"Come in."

In the heat the damp skin of the valet looked whiter than ever. He came in, respectful and rather cadaverous. The climate was getting him too. "What is it?" she asked.

"Sorry to disturb Your Ladyship, but I think there's something wrong with His Lordship. He's not well."

"What is it, Bates?"

"I've no idea, me lady, but he most certainly has a fever. I wanted to take his temperature but he wouldn't hear of it. You know how he is? He'll never admit it when he's feeling seedy."

"What about a doctor?"

"He wouldn't hear of that, either. He said there wouldn't be any good doctors among these Indians." The ghost of a smile appeared on Bates' face and he added, "He used much stronger language than that, but that was what he meant."

That was what she disliked about Bates. It was as if the grin said, "You and I understand the old bastard," and that wasn't playing the game. They both might hate Esketh, but so long as they were with him neither of them should give any sign of it to the other.

For a moment she was silent, thinking of many things. Then she said, "Thank you, Bates. If he's not better in the morning I'll find a doctor. I can persuade him, I think."

"Thank you, me lady. Good night."

"Good night, Bates."

When he was gone, thinking about Bates, she decided that he was a bad servant, not because he was inefficient or stupid but because he was less interested in the welfare of those he served than his own. "Secretly," she thought, "he is probably a communist. He is the kind of servant who is involved in detective mysteries and lodging-house murders." He gave a professional impression of utter discretion but her instinct told her that she could not trust him for a moment. The interview left her with a curious sense of distaste as if somehow Bates had managed to make her his accomplice. He had betrayed himself in no way whatever, neither by glance nor word, nor even by the intonation of his voice, but she *knew* that he was thinking of Esketh's death and finding pleasure in the thought and that he knew she too had been thinking of it.

She did not want him to die; she did not *wish* it, yet she could not keep herself from thinking how much simpler life would be with him dead and how pleasant the freedom would be with all the money which he would certainly leave to her in addition to the settlement, no matter what she said to him or how she treated him.

Presently she put out the light again but even then she did not sleep for a long time. The sound of the flooding rain and the buzzing of the insects which blackened the surface of the white nettings annoyed her and for a moment, while she lay between sleep and wakefulness, the hysterical terror of India seized her a second time. And then again just as she was falling asleep she had a strange dream in which she was searching desperately for something, but what it was she did not know. She was aware of a terrible anxiety and of wandering through great dusty fields and ill-smelling streets and at last through a jungle in which she seemed to *hear* the plants, the trees, the ferns, the vines, growing all about her, closing her in. And then, just as she knew that she would find what she was searching for beyond the next hill, she wakened screaming.

For a moment while Ransome stood on the verandah looking in through the window a whole procession of women went through his mind, women of every sort and description out of a despairing and reckless past when indiscriminately he had made love here and there, as the occasion arose, throughout half the Orient. Which one, he asked himself, had come all the way to Ranchipur now in the midst of the monsoon to run him to earth? Which one had cared enough? Which one had thought him worth it? Uneasily he remembered the planter's wife in Malaya who had grown hysterical when he left, the Russian tart in Shanghai who had said she would never abandon him, the English girl in Colombo who might have heard that he had stopped wandering at last and settled in Ranchipur. It might be any of them or any of a half-dozen others, perhaps even one of those whom he could no longer remember without effort, and he could not think what he would do with any one of them in a tight little world like that of Ranchipur, save to marry her, a thing which he had no intention of doing. It all happened in the space of a second——the speculation, the rush of memories, even the certainty that out of the lot he would have liked seeing the Russian woman again but not here, not in Ranchipur.

Then he stepped through the doorway and at the sound of his footsteps the woman turned and he saw with sudden relief that it was only Fern Simon.

She was dripping wet. The old tennis dress she wore clung to her tightly, and for the first time he was aware that Fern not only had a pretty face but the loveliest of bodies. She looked at him with a shamed smile and said, "Hello," very casually, like a woman of the world, as if she had come to meet him at a rendezvous, but her voice was a little unsteady like that of an actress uncertain of her role who is in terror of forgetting her lines.

"Hello," he said. "What are you doing here?"

"I've run away from home. I'm never going back."

He grinned, thinking, "Well, this is a nice mess," and then said, "You can't do that."

"Why not?"

"Because I can't take the responsibility." And then he saw that the unsteadiness of her voice and the uncertainty of her manner came from the fact that in spite of the damp heat she was shivering and trying to keep her teeth from chattering. The old terror of fever came over him, not for himself but for her.

"You're going straight home," he said. "I'll take you back right off."

But she was unmoved. She even planted her feet more firmly, a little apart, as if she meant to resist him physically in case the necessity arose. Her defiance and determination amused him and for a second it occurred to him that perhaps she was not such a silly fool as he thought. Looking at her, he knew that if he attempted to force her to leave in her present mood she might fling herself on the floor and scream and cry like a child, and that would never do.

"You'd better put on some dry clothes first," he said. "You can't stay any longer like that. You're shivering."

"What will I put on?"

[168]

"It'll have to be something of mine. I haven't any women's clothes here."

She offered no objection, for now her shyness was melting away a little and she felt herself well into the role of Blythe Summerfield, the Pearl of the Orient. Changing her clothes would give her a little more time to gain control of herself; and it was really a brilliant idea for a scenario——that she should put on the clothes of the man she loved and appear in the next sequence dressed as a boy. She waited while Ransome brought a towel and a pair of shorts and a shirt.

"Now," he said, as if he were talking to a child, "go into the bathroom and dry yourself thoroughly—rub hard—and put these on and then I'll take you home." He looked at her closely: "You've never had malaria, have you? You haven't a fever now?"

"No . . . I don't know why I'm shivering. I'm not really cold." And he thought, "Good Lord, a child like that can't be trembling for any other reason."

While she was gone he went and fetched a bottle of brandy and two glasses and hung up the old raincoat and the battered hat she had left behind. And all the time he was chuckling deep inside himself at the spectacle of the Roué and the Virgin and feeling a sudden perverse desire to have Edwina know what was happening. It would amuse her; and she would see how funny it was. And then he remembered John the Baptist and the sense of mirth went out of him. If John the Baptist knew she was here he would certainly not keep the news to himself, and his gossipy flute-playing friends would tell it in turn to their friends and sooner or later everyone in Ranchipur would come to hear of it.

Putting down the bottle and glasses he went out on to the verandah and looked toward the garden house where John the Baptist slept. In the darkness there was no sign of life, and he thought, "He sleeps like an animal. He doesn't know anything about it." For a moment he considered crossing the garden in the rain to make certain, but he knew that he could not run those few feet and back without becoming soaked and so he abandoned the idea and went back into the house, thinking, "To hell with it!"

When she came out of the bathroom she was no longer shivering. The tennis shirt was too large for her but the shorts, because he was slim about the waist, fitted her perfectly, and she had gained from the costume a kind of smartness, a perkiness which she had not had in her own dowdy clothes. She was no longer the rather frumpy daughter of a missionary in a little middle-class community. She had, he saw, possibilities; and for a moment, in his enthusiasm, he thought, "Almost limitless ones." Then drawing back, he said to himself, "Steady now . . . steady."

Aloud he said, "Here take these pills and drink this, and when you get home take two more, and two in the morning. Put the box in the pocket of your shirt."

She took the glass of brandy and water and said again, "There's nothing the matter with me. And I hate the taste of quinine."

"Nevertheless, do as I say." She looked at him for a second with an expression of astonishment in her clear blue eyes. Then, like an obedient child, she swallowed the two pills, washing them down with brandy and water and making a little face.

"I'm not a child," she said.

"Nobody said you were, but you can't meddle with fever."

"I haven't got any fever. I was just shaking from excitement."

He picked up the mackintosh and hat and said, "And now you're going home." But she sat down suddenly and repeated, "I'm not going home. I can't . . . I'm never going home again."

"Why not?"

"Because I left a note saying I was going away forever. I can't go home now. I couldn't face my mother after that."

He grinned and said, "You ought never to leave notes in case you change your mind."

"Don't make fun of me."

"I'm not. Anyway the note doesn't make any difference. Nobody will find it until morning. You can tear it up before anybody sees it."

Suddenly she began to cry, the way she had done on the afternoon of the tennis party. "I can't," she sobbed, "I can't go back. I'm through with all that lousy life."

The sound of her sobbing alarmed him until he realized that it could not possibly reach the house where John the Baptist slept through all the downpour. Weeping women always made him helpless and filled him with a desire to run away. He had run away before, again and again, when women became emotional and refused to accept the limits of the thing he was willing to give. But this time he was innocent; he wasn't giving anything at all but advice, and anyway it would do no good. He didn't want to run away from Ranchipur. He didn't mean to be driven away by a girl who meant absolutely nothing to him.

"My mother says I have to marry Harry Loder," she sobbed, "and I won't!"

Vaguely Ransome sounded his mind to remember which of "the boys" was Harry Loder, and then the picture came to him. Harry Loder was the big beefy one whom, in the rare moments when he thought of "the boys" at all, he disliked the most. He was a bully and drank too much. So Harry Loder wanted to marry her? The news astonished him——that Harry Loder with his slick army snobbery should be willing to marry the daughter of a missionary; and then he saw, he thought, why it was. She was the prettiest European woman anywhere in Ranchipur, one of the prettiest in India, and Harry Loder wanted her and must have discovered that that was the only way he could have her. When he'd had enough he'd neglect her and carry on with any woman he found at hand, and all the time he would never forget nor allow her to forget that he had done her a great favor by marrying her, the daughter of a missionary. That was a story he had seen played out in India before. No, she couldn't marry Harry Loder. That was out of the question.

Then for the first time in a long while his youthful sense of chivalry came alive. Once it had been exaggerated and fantastic and got him into all sorts of trouble, but for a long time now he had been on his guard against it because it always paralyzed his common sense and made an ass of him. There wasn't any longer any place for chivalry in the world. It only made you look a fool.

"No," he said, "obviously you can't marry Harry Loder. Did he ask you? . . . properly, I mean."

"Yes, he asked me and he told my mother too. That's how she knows. Everything will be worse than ever now."

Then growing cautious again, he said, "There isn't anything I can do about it. It's none of my business."

She stopped crying and looked at him with that expression of determination which had impressed him before. "Yes, there is," she said, and

[171]

then looking away from him, "If you were only big enough. I thought you were when I came here."

He wanted to laugh but he only asked, "What do you mean by that?"

"If you'd let me stay here tonight . . . if they found me here in the morning so that everybody knew it, then Harry Loder wouldn't want to marry me, and my mother would have to send me away from Ranchipur with everybody talking and gossiping. Don't you see? Then I'd be able to get away and have a life of my own. I'd never come back." Then after a moment she said, "I don't care what people here say about me."

It was clear that she knew what she wanted. The desire to laugh turned into a sudden admiration for her strength of will. "What about me?" he asked.

She answered him so quickly that he knew at once she had already thought of all the questions and answers. "It wouldn't matter to you," she said. "You've lived. You've been through so much. It wouldn't hurt your reputation. I don't see why you should care."

What she said and the patness with which it came out made him suddenly see with a sense of swift intuition how that small world which he held in contempt regarded him. In their hearts, beneath their snobbery and toadying, they saw him as a roué, a waster, a cad, a remittance man, capable of any low act; they must have talked of him thus, sometimes before Fern. Yet they were willing to accept him, even to run after him if he so much as smiled in their direction.

Suddenly he was violently angry, not at the girl, but at the world out of which she had come. "Those God-damned bootlickers!" he thought. "They have a nerve to judge me!"

"What makes you think that?" he asked. "Where did you get such an idea?"

Her answer was disconcerting and took the force out of his anger: "Well, I mean you don't care anything about nasty things like respectability. You don't care what people think or say about you. You're not like them. Don't you see, you'd be doing a noble act?"

"Did you read all that some place?"

"No, I thought it all out." Suddenly she forgot her tears in her eagerness: "Don't you see, I *understand*. I know what you're like, really like. You hate the kind of life they lead, and so do I. I want to be myself.

[172]

I want to get everything there is to be had out of life. I don't care about being respectable or any of those things."

So she thought of him like that. Well, once he was like that, a long time ago, and suddenly he felt ashamed that he was weary and bored.

"That's all very well," he said, "but it isn't easy. You have to be strong . . . stronger than I am to get away with it. Maybe nobody is strong enough."

"I'm not looking for things to be easy."

"Why did you come to me? If that's what you wanted you could have gone to almost anyone . . . one of 'the boys,' say?"

She leaned forward and took a cigarette off the table and lighted it. The match was damp and she blundered and missed, and her face grew red with confusion. But she persisted and the second time she succeeded and began to puff in an inexpert fashion, like a spinster smoking for the first time. While he waited for her to answer he watched her, rather touched and charmed because she was so young.

"You're the only one I could go to because you're the only one who would understand and not take advantage of me." Then after a silence she said, "And because I like you. Sometimes I think you're the only person in the whole place I don't hate." Then he knew she had picked up the cigarette in order to make herself feel worldly and give herself courage.

"But you don't know me."

"Yes, I do."

He grinned: "The big strong silent man . . . mysterious and cold and different."

"Don't tease me. Don't act as if I'm a child. I'm not a child, I don't want to be. I want to be a woman."

For a moment he felt himself wavering. He said, "You never let me know that you liked me. You hardly ever spoke to me." And then he checked himself, aware that in that direction lay danger.

Her hair had begun to dry now and stood up in blond ringlets all over her small head. In spite of anything he could do it was impossible for him not to be aware of her body, of her virgin slimness and the long slender legs and small ankles. The clothes certainly suited her. But the situation began to seem grotesque——that he, of all men, should be re-

[173]

sisting so much loveliness, so much freshness thrown at his head, his for the taking. He poured himself another drink and felt suddenly dizzy. "Perhaps, after all," he thought, "what happened with Edwina was a good thing. Perhaps it has kept me from making a fool of myself with this girl. Funny how things work out." He told himself that he should force her to leave at once, but he was not strong enough; the temptation, even though he meant not to yield to it, was enjoyable and exciting. It made him feel as he had not felt in a long while, young and interested in something beyond the sensual satisfaction of the moment.

Then he saw that she had finished the whole glass of brandy and water he had given her and he thought, "I shouldn't have given her so much. Probably that's the first drink she's ever had in her life."

She was saying, "I've liked you for a long time. I've watched you on the street. I've waited at the window every Saturday when you went to the Smiley's, to see you. I've always liked you, only you always treated me as if I were a child. You never even bothered to speak to me."

No, he thought, she's not three years old. She knows what she wants and nothing will stop her. The second drink made him think, "Why not? What difference would it make? Life is so short and so lousy."

But aloud he said, "Now, you're going home before it's too late." He had been leaning against the table and he stood up suddenly and put down his glass to give his words force.

"Don't make me go. Please let me stay."

He leaned against the table once more. "If you stayed, what would you do afterward? I won't ever marry you."

"I wouldn't want that. I don't want to be tied down myself."

"Then how do you think it could possibly work out?"

Again she had her answer ready with amazing quickness: "I'd have to leave Ranchipur whether my mother liked it or not. I'd get away to America where I'd have a chance. I could go to Hollywood. I know I would make good."

"That's not easy. It's tough to get a good break."

"I'd do anything."

He looked at her sharply without speaking, and avoiding his eyes she went on: "Yes, anything. I mean anything. What is anything if it can give you your freedom . . . to do what you want to do? A thing like

[174]

that doesn't matter. It's all over in a minute. Anyway the body doesn't matter. It isn't you, really."

Again he felt suddenly dizzy and thought, "It's impossible. I'm not really hearing all this. It's funny that once I too thought that."

"It can be awful," he said. "You haven't the least idea how awful men can be."

"That's why I came here." She hesitated as if gathering her courage, and then plunged: "That's why I wanted it to be you, for the first time. I knew you wouldn't be like that and I wanted the first time to be with somebody I liked. Don't you see? Don't you understand? Afterward what happened wouldn't matter so much. I'm not asking so very much of you."

Trembling a little, he thought, "Good God, there are things Saint Anthony never dreamed of!" Aloud he said, "Yes, I understand . . . all too well. That's why you're going home now. If you don't I shall have to go and fetch your mother." He went over to her and held out the damp mackintosh. "Come," he said.

But she did not stir. She only began to cry again. "No, please keep me here. Don't make me go home."

Then suddenly he felt tired. He felt himself slipping back into his old weakness. He knew that he would begin soon to compromise, to procrastinate, to make promises that he never meant to keep. That was what he had done on the verandah the day of the tennis party and it had only gotten him in more deeply. "You'll have to give me time to think over a thing like this." And hearing himself say this, he began to laugh.

"I can't go back now. My mother would wake up and ask me where I'd been. She'd hear the motor."

But he was prepared for that: "No, we won't go near enough to the house for that. I'll stop the motor down the road and take you to the Smileys'. You can spend the night there and slip across the drive to your own house early in the morning. You can tear up the note before anybody finds it."

"I won't go to the Smileys'. Mrs. Smiley hates me."

"You don't know Mrs. Smiley. She doesn't hate anyone. She hasn't time for that."

She had risen from the chair, still crying and saying, "Don't make me

[175]

go! I don't want to go! I won't go unless you'll promise to see me again and be kind to me."

"I promise."

"And you've got to help me."

"I'll help you."

"Because it isn't true what I said. I don't like you. It's more than that." She began to put on the mackintosh: "I guess I love you. If I didn't I wouldn't be going home now."

"Oh, my God!"

Along the road the water streamed in the ditches and in one place it lay spread across the road in a small lake into which the old Buick, its lights veiled by the wall of rain, bucked head on, splattering them both with water. They rode side by side in silence, for since the moment of her confession an odd barrier had come up between them, partly of shyness and partly a kind of paralysis which made it impossible to speak. It wasn't fun any longer; it ceased to be a farce in which he was playing the role of wise guy, and he was aware that Fern wasn't play-acting any more but in dead earnest. He didn't know what role she had been playing because he knew nothing about Blythe Summerfield, Pearl of the Orient, but he knew well enough that she had slipped out of the part which obviously she had written for herself before she ever came to the house.

For a time he tried earnestly to find something to say, in the belief that by casual conversation he could pull their relationship back into the realm of common sense, but he could think of nothing whatever to say that would not sound banal and ridiculous and betray his intentions, for he understood now that the girl was not stupid. There was something in her directness which made small talk quite impossible at the moment. She sat a little away from him huddled sullenly in her seat, and although he did not look at her he was aware of her nearness and knew exactly how she looked in his old tennis shirt and shorts——trim and appealing and a little wild. It was odd how clearly he saw her now, when a couple of hours earlier he could not have told what she looked like if anyone had asked him.

A little beyond the alcohol distillery he stopped the car and said, "We'd

[176]

better walk from here and then the sound of the car won't waken anyone."

"I can go alone," she said. "You'll get soaked."

"It doesn't matter. I'll be going straight home. How is the chill?"

"It wasn't a chill. There wasn't anything the matter with me."

"So she *is* like that," he thought. "Maybe I am a fool." And as he splashed along beside her through the rain he had a moment of clear vision as if suddenly a light had been turned upon himself, and he was a little shocked because he found that all the while, all through the hour or two they had been together, a part of him had been appraising her bit by bit, in cold blood—her throat, her breasts, her thighs, her blond hair— speculating upon what the experience would be like. "I'm senile," he thought, "a broken-down old lecher," because while he had been appraising her he hadn't thought at all what she was like inside. "I shouldn't be like that. I'm only thirty-eight. Maybe that's all there is left. Maybe that's the only thing remaining which can rouse me."

The Smileys' house was in darkness but they had no trouble in finding the door and entering, save that he received a glancing blow on the side of the head from one of Aunt Phoebe's swinging pots of petunias. The door was never locked, the windows never closed. Day or night one could walk directly into the heart of the house. In the beginning it had been entered two or three times, but after a while the story got about that the Smileys' possessed nothing which was worth stealing and after that there had been no trouble.

Ransome knew his way in the darkness. He left Fern standing in a corner of the hallway and made his way along the passage with the aid of his cigarette lighter until he came to the door of the Smileys' bedroom. There he knocked. He had no fear of startling the Smileys because they were accustomed to being wakened at any hour of the night when there was sudden illness or death among the Untouchables and low-caste people. Twice he knocked, and then the sleepy voice of Mr. Smiley said, "Hello! What is it?"

"It's Ransome," he said. "Could I see you for a moment?"

Then the voice came back, awake and alert, "Sure. Just a minute."

When the door opened Mr. Smiley came out, clad in a cotton dressing

[177]

gown, with Mrs. Smiley following him in a kimono, her hair done in a screw on the top of her head.

Mrs. Smiley switched on the light and Ransome, grinning, said, "I'm sorry to disturb you, but the circumstances are a bit extraordinary."

Then he explained to them about Fern running away from home and why she would not return but was willing to spend the night in the Smileys' house. He told only enough of the story to make it believable, giving them to understand that he had not found her in his bedroom but walking along the road in the rain. The Smileys did not appear to be astonished. Even when they turned and saw Fern standing sheepishly at the end of the hallway, dressed in Ransome's clothing, they gave no sign of surprise.

Mrs. Smiley said, "Oh, hello, Fern!" as if they were the best of friends, and went forward to welcome her. It wasn't easy for Fern, who had always held the Smileys in scorn as pious, hard-working fools, but some, how Mrs. Smiley, who perhaps had never noticed Fern's high-and-mightiness, made it all seem easy and natural, as if Fern had just run across the drive to borrow a teaspoonful of baking powder.

"I'll put you in the room next to us," she said. "Then you won't need to be afraid."

"I'm not afraid," said Fern, and Ransome saw suddenly that she was still a child.

The Smileys begged him to stay and have something to eat. It was, he thought, exactly as if he had been a stranger caught in a wild storm and the Smiley's house was a cabin on the frontier. They displayed no astonishment and asked no questions and were full of hospitality. And then a door opened a little way down the hallway and the head of Aunt Phoebe appeared.

"What's the matter?" she asked. "Anything I can do?"

"No," said Mrs. Smiley, "it's nothing."

But Aunt Phoebe had caught a glimpse of Ransome and of the daughter of "that poor-white" Mrs. Simon, clad in man's clothing, and she came out dressed as she was, in a nightgown with a high collar and long sleeves and her thin white hair all in curl papers, to find out what was going on. And Ransome, knowing that she would not hesitate to ask pointed questions, fled. But before he went he said good night to

Fern. She looked at him directly, so directly that for a moment he felt uneasy, and said, "Thanks." But he divined that she was making an effort to convey to him the knowledge that it was not finished between them and that putting her off with promises was no good.

When, drenched and miserable, he left the car under the *porte cochère* it occurred to him for the first time quite clearly how near he had come to doing something which would have made Ranchipur forever impossible for him. When he had rubbed himself down and finished what was left in the brandy bottle, he saw it all even more clearly, knowing the very moments when he had felt himself growing reckless and dizzy, thinking, "The hell with it! It's the only thing that matters in life. If I don't do it, some day when I'm an old man I'll regret."

He knew already that very nearly the only regrets he had in life were for the things, both good and evil, which he had not done; they were there in the fabric of his existence like holes left by a careless weaver, spoiling the rich effect of the stuff. And one could never go back and repair the holes. When a thing was done it was done. And the awful part of it was that the elements which seemed so important now—honor, the fear of gossip, the responsibility—would one day be of no weight whatever. "Perhaps," he thought, "the strong people are those who know all that, who are aware and still act ruthlessly," for he did not feel that he was strong, or that he had been strong a little while before, with Fern sitting opposite him provocative and eager. All those things would one day have faded away, leaving him with only a dull sense of regret that he had turned away from an experience which might have been glowing and wonderful. And that thought brought him sharply to the philosophy of Major Safti—that the body which caused so much pain owed in return a great debt of sensual pleasure.

"Damn it!" he thought, drunkenly. "It's always the moralist and the gentleman in me which paralyzes me and makes a mess of everything." Not even all the wilful cold-blooded debauchery, into which he had thrown himself again and again to kill that thing in him, had succeeded in killing it. It was still there, lying asleep for long periods to waken suddenly when he least desired it, throwing him, despite everything, into a role which long ago, in disgust, he had consciously, by a deliberate effort of will, chosen to reject.

And as he put out the light and climbed into bed beneath the mosquito netting, he thought, "I've never once made love, enjoying it directly, brutally, like most men. I've never lost consciousness. I've always been a little outside, watching myself, aware that I am futile, shameful and ridiculous." Perhaps the day would come when at last he had beaten down all these things and found the direct way, but that day, he knew, even in his drunkenness, would mean not only the liberation of his body but the death of everything which was himself.

Lying sleepless and restless in the heat, annoyed by the buzzing of the thousands of insects attracted by the light, he had not even the solace of feeling noble to dull the edge of his regret, because in honesty he knew that it was not himself but Edwina who was responsible for the departure of Fern still in the role of *virgo intacta*. If it had not been for what happened with Edwina he might have been driven by boredom and demands of his own body to have done what that strange girl asked. Yes, strange she was, and even fascinating. There was something there, deep within her, under all the naïveté and nonsense and revolt against her parents and their world, that was worth discovering.

"Funny," he thought again, "that it should have been Edwina—cold-blooded, poisonous Edwina—who saved Fern without ever knowing it." Saved her from what? echoed in his brain—from something which was certain one day, before very long, to happen to her, something which might after all release her. "I, at least," he thought, "could have made it pleasant for her."

And then he was aware that someone was crossing the verandah outside his window. In reality he neither saw the dark figure nor heard the step of the naked feet. In the heat and restlessness he *felt* a presence. Springing out of bed, he took up the electric torch and stumbled on to the verandah. The light fell against the wall of rain, blunted and dissipated by the falling water, but even so it was strong enough for him to distinguish a dim brown figure like a ghost, quite naked, running across the garden into the garden house.

Aloud he said, "God-damn it!" And returning to his bed he laughed, thinking, "I might just as well have done it. Now I'll have the credit for it sooner or later."

There was no use in trying to threaten John the Baptist or in offering to bribe him, for neither reward nor punishment, he knew, would make any difference when so juicy a morsel as this could be dropped into the circle of John's gossiping musician friends. The story would grow and grow in repetition like the ripples made by a stone thrown into a quiet pond, until presently, having passed from servant to servant, it would reach the ears of someone like Mrs. Hoggett-Egburry and then the jig would be up. He knew Ranchipur. By the time it reached the ears of "Pukka Lil" he would have first gotten Fern thoroughly drunk and then raped her.

"I might just as well have done it, God-damn it! It just goes to show. . . ." But what it went to show he could not make out, because he was beginning to feel profoundly muddled and weary and drunk. It seemed to him that the night which had begun with Edwina entering the room at the palace, white and cool, all pale and gold, had gone on forever.

Just before he fell asleep he raised his head and listened for a moment. This time it was not his imagination; it was unmistakable. He could hear it even above the sound of the torrential rain. The river had begun to roar.

Then he remembered Edwina again and thought, "Yes, I suppose that's what whores are for."

At the Smileys' Fern stood waiting sheepishly while Mrs. Smiley and Aunt Phoebe fetched bedclothes and a cotton nightgown and made her comfortable. They talked about the rains and about the difficulty of keeping the bedclothes dry in such weather, but never about Ransome or the way Fern was dressed or how she came to be walking along the road in the rain after midnight. Aunt Phoebe looked at her once or twice with sharp penetrating looks which, oddly enough, were neither hostile nor condemnatory, but only curious and rather appraising. There was in them something of admiration, a little astonishment, and a great deal of curiosity. It was as if the old lady said, "Well, I never thought you had that much spunk in you."

Awkwardly, paralyzed by embarrassment and shyness, the girl watched the two older women working to make her feel at home. Aunt Phoebe fetched a bottle of water and placed it on the table beside her bed. Mrs. Smiley draped the mosquito netting over the frame, chattering all the time about the way the netting rotted almost before you had it sewed together properly and sending Aunt Phoebe for a bit of thread and a needle to darn the holes which had appeared since she had last used it.

Now and then Fern said, "Oh, thank you, Mrs. Smiley!" or "I'll be all right, don't take too much trouble," or "I can do that. Let me!" And all the while she was beginning to understand for the first time what Mrs. Smiley was.

For the first time Mrs. Smiley ceased to exist for her as a drab sort of shadow which was simply a symbol of all dreary missionaries living perpetually like a menace in the house across the drive, the ever-present proof that after all, whatever dreams she had, she was only the child of missionaries condemned forever to live in a "missionary" atmosphere. She saw Mrs. Smiley quite suddenly as a person who was alive and had reality and perhaps knew the same passions and weaknesses and despair as herself. And dimly, without quite understanding it, because she was so young and so innocent of experience, she divined that in Mrs. Smiley the passions and disappointments had long ago been subdued and put into order. Vaguely too she was aware that Mrs. Smiley had in some way disentangled the messiness of living and clarified its muddledness. "It must be nice," the girl thought, "to be so easy and sure," for you did not have to *know* Mrs. Smiley to discover the calm and sureness that was in her; it was apparent in the way she moved and smiled at you, in the brisk efficient way she whisked the sheets on to the bed, the ease and skill with which she mended the holes in the mosquito netting.

Something in the presence of Mrs. Smiley, at just this moment when the senses of the girl were excited and acute, made her know exactly what it was that had driven her out of her own home into Ransome's bedroom. It was not that she had gone because she was bad or vicious, nor because she was driven by curiosity, nor because she was really in love with Ransome outside the realms of her romantic imagination, but because she had had to escape from that muddling false world which her mother and her father had created and kept in existence all about her shutting her in and making her miserable. She had wanted to straighten things out and there had seemed only one way to do it—by running away and leaving Ransome to do for her what must be done for every woman before she is able to understand the full depths and the full richness of living.

When Mrs. Smiley and Aunt Phoebe had gone away and she lay in the darkness, clad in one of Mrs. Smiley's cotton nightgowns, she did not fall asleep. The brandy and the excitement had sent her mind to working, swiftly and clearly, as it had never worked before, and presently, thinking about it all, she came to understand that, although she had gone to Ransome driven by all sorts of reasons save that she was in love with him, what had been merely a romantic idea was now all at once a reality. Sitting up in bed, she thought, "I am in love. So that's what it feels like." It wasn't a bit like the things she read about in the picture magazines nor the way they showed it in the cinema.

She knew she was in love because she felt "different." Not only toward him but toward herself. She saw that he was not, as she had believed him, a romantic hero, silent and melancholy and mysterious, who made speeches such as men made in novels and in the films. He had talked to her simply, with perfect honesty, and had shown himself so much easier and so much "nicer" than she had pictured him during the scenes she had invented while walking through the rain to his house. She saw now that nobody had ever talked to her in quite that way before, as if she were grown up and a real person. She could not think of anybody in the world about her who had ever talked like that, because all the others were always pretending this or that so that everything they said or did was false and complicated and maddening. It seemed to her now that the others were afraid of everything—of poverty, of gossip, of respectability, of snobbery, of a million things, so that everything they did or thought became cramped and distorted and unhealthy. And she saw that she herself in the role of Blythe Summerfield had invented a world which wasn't true any more than her mother's world was true, or her father's or Mrs. Hoggett-Egburry's or that of "the boys." She had even written a part for Ransome in which she made him hard and mysterious and cynical and a little violent, and that wasn't true either. And now, alone in the dark, she felt herself blushing at the things she had done and said while she was with him because so many of them were false and ridiculous; and she knew suddenly how kind he had been to her.

She knew too that even if the thing had happened which she had wanted to happen she would now be suffering no remorse or sense of sin, because it would have been *right* in a way which she could not quite explain to herself. "I'm in love," she kept thinking; "so this is what it's like." It was so much nicer, so much warmer, so much more exciting than any of the silly things she had imagined.

He did not exist for her now as a shadowy mystery, because he came out of a world and out of a life of which she knew nothing at all, but as a reality. She wasn't afraid of him. She *knew* him. Without knowing it until this moment she had discovered all sorts of things about him—the way the thick dark hair grew on his sunburnt forehead, the little rueful almost sad grin that came over his face sometimes in the very middle of a speech, the exact sound of his voice, a nice pleasant caressing sort of voice which she could hear now perfectly clearly while she was alone in the solitary darkness of a strange house, and the shape of his hands which were beautiful, and the way they shook slightly when he raised his glass.

For a moment Blythe Summerfield returned and she found herself saying half aloud, "His hands, his dear hands," and then again in the darkness she blushed and was ashamed of herself because she had betrayed her new-found reality.

But most of all——the thing which made her love him most of all—— was the knowledge, of which she had not dreamed before, that he was as unhappy as herself.

Oh, she began to see now how it was that he was so friendly with the Smileys, and came so often to their house, and why it was that he came so rarely to her mother's; and she knew that even when he did come to her mother's house he was not really there at all. He simply sent someone else in his place who was kind and polite and pretended to believe in that crazy world which existed there. She thought, "He and Mrs. Smiley know something that we don't know on the other side of the drive," and suddenly she had intimations of another kind of world which was the one, she was vaguely aware, where she belonged—a world in which there was a richness, in which suffering had depth, ambition, grandeur, and pleasure substance.

She was no longer a little girl. When at last she fell asleep it seemed to her that the night which had begun with her stealing out of the house into the rain had gone on and on forever. For the first time something had happened to her. For the first time she discovered that life was not simply a thing ticked off by the clock in seconds, minutes and hours. Sometimes it did not move at all for days, perhaps for years, and then all at once one could live years in an hour or two. It was a funny idea. . . .

When Mrs. Smiley went back to her own room the light was still burning but Mr. Smiley, on his side of the double bed where they slept winter and summer, was already dozing, and she did not waken him because she knew that he needed every minute of his sleep. Carefully she climbed under the netting so that the worn springs would not creak and disturb him. She had no great desire to waken him and talk about Fern because she already knew all about Fern and what she had been up to and she was quite sure that Mr. Smiley also knew. There was neither need nor time to hash over the whole story, picking it to bits, speculating and inventing things. She knew well enough that Fern was unhappy and she knew why; she had known for a long time. And she understood why Fern had run away to Ransome of all people in Ranchipur, and she knew too that nothing had happened, because Ransome, whatever his low opinion of himself, was like that.

She knew all these things because, although very little that was exciting had ever happened to herself, she could divine what it was like, and because in an odd way she had been born understanding human folly and suffering.

This was perhaps because Mrs. Smiley had no ego whatever; she had no idea of her own of what she was like; she scarcely knew her own appearance because there had never been any time to study it. She used a mirror just long enough to arrange her hair in the morning so that it would not fall down, and even while she was using a mirror she did not see her own face but only her hands and her hair as if her hair was something detached from her like a pie or a loaf of bread. She had never had any ego even as a child, for she was born, it seemed, with a kind of innate humility which had been preserved rather than corrupted by being one of nine children. It had never occurred to her that she had been neglected, or abused, or insulted by anyone. As a young girl back in Cedar Falls she had been perfectly content to be thrust into the background by others more handsome, more clever or more assertive than herself. Indeed she had found a kind of pleasure and satisfaction in watching and listening, and she always felt happier herself when others were enjoying themselves. So it was inevitable that she should be the confidante of everyone who came near her, and that while she was still young she had ceased to be shocked or astonished by anything at all, and presently that she came to have more wisdom about living than most of those who lived passionately and violently, committing over and over again the same sins, the same blunders, the same errors. And although she rarely attracted admirers she never pitied herself because she was always so busy and so interested in the spectacle of others; indeed there were moments when she felt an honest simple pity for people more brilliant and attractive than herself, because it seemed to her that all their beauty and all their gifts only drew upon them unhappiness and suffering. Quiet, mouselike, in her own corner, she had never known jealousy or envy, bitterness or disappointment, and so she felt that she was luckier than the others.

And then Mr. Smiley happened along, unworthy, humble and frowned upon by her family because he was only a Baptist, and dared in Cedar Falls to court the daughter of a Congregationalist family—Mr. Smiley with his innocence and correctness and his shy warmth, the only person who saw people and things the way she saw them. But she married him in spite of everything and became a Baptist and a missionary and went to India with him, not through faith or hysteria, or exaltation, but because it was the most natural thing for both of them to have done and because it was a career which was a perfect expression of her own nature. They lived always in other people and never in themselves, without possessions which might be stolen, or pride which might be hurt, or pretensions that might be vanquished, or ambitions that might fail. That was the secret of which Ransome had become slowly aware.

After Mr. Smiley came along she was never lonely, nor was he. She never pretended to herself that they had married out of a passionate love for one another, and she knew that neither of them had any aptitude for such raptures. They had married because both of them possessed humility and understood each other and saw people in the same way and because both of them found the profoundest happiness in serving others. She knew nothing of the raptures of the flesh and made no attempt to imagine them, but she found Mr. Smiley gently and warmly comfortable.

For a little while she lay awake wondering how she might be able to help Fern Simon. She had known for a long time that the girl was lonely and unhappy but she had known too that it was no use in going to her. Now that Fern had come to her, or rather been delivered to her by Ransome, it might be easier.

She fell asleep at last, but she was awakened a little after dawn by a knock and found outside the door one of the boys from Mr. Smiley's classes. He was from the potter's caste and he came to tell her that his mother and his brother were both ill with typhus. There were four other new cases in the quarter where the potters lived.

She dressed herself and went with him, thinking a little wearily, "They are slipping back again. Where there is typhus there must be lice." She and Mr. Smiley would have to begin one of their campaigns, and they had done it already so many times that for a moment she was tempted to think that it was all hopeless, all their work and their efforts. And she was worried too. Four new cases in one quarter in a single night was too many.

Before she went out, she wakened Fern and sent her across the drive to her own house.

Quickly, miraculously, the rains had changed the whole landscape and the whole life of Ranchipur. In a few hours the vines in Ransome's garden sent forth long tender shoots of a lettuce-green color which crept everywhere with a strength and a persistence out of all proportion to their fragile appearance. Into crevices in the walls of stone and mud, into drainpipes and even through open windows they pushed their way. Round pillars and garden chairs and the ancient banyan trees and even the pump that served the vast deep well, they writhed and thrust, attaching themselves in a kind of vegetable ecstasy and voluptuousness to whatever they round at hand. In the borders and in the midst of the barren paths tender seedlings sprang up, nourished only by the downpour of warm rain. Even the tired and dusty marigolds and hollyhocks became young again with leaves and buds no longer cooked by the sun before they were well open. And now the old banyan and the huge mango trees appeared in the full dignity and splendor of their deep green, for the dust was washed away and the leaves no longer turned yellow and wilting beneath the scalding sun.

And in the palace garden the dusty little lake filled with water and on its surface the frivolous little pleasure boats, no longer stranded on a sea of cement, came to life and rocked gently in all the gayety of their scarlet and gold. The vast borders of flowers, only a week earlier dusty and dying, grew suddenly more extravagant and vigorous than flowers in any garden in damp England. Beyond the windows of Mr. Jobnekar's house the wide bare fields of maize and millet changed from golden brown to emerald green as if a vast cloak had been flung over the countryside from the edge of the Untouchable quarter as far as the magical mountain of Abana and the dead city of El-Kautara. And in the garden of the American Mission Aunt Phoebe's petunias and geraniums and orchids, hanging beneath the dripping trees in their old tin cans and boxes of bamboo, began to grow and to blossom with such exaggerated strength that the old lady, in a mackintosh, went out into the monsoon with a tape measure to mark the growth between one morning and the next, so that she might include the statistics in her annual description of the monsoon when she wrote to Cedar Falls, adding as she did each year, "I am not exaggerating. I measured the growth myself. Four inches in twenty-four hours," which was always two or three inches more than the truth. At the cottage where Miss Dirks and Miss Hodge lived, opposite the palace gates, the vines, gorged by rain, grew across the very windows, turning the light that came through to a pale green color so that the two spinsters seemed to eat and sleep and embroider and correct school papers under water like a pair of virginal middle-aged mermaids.

And the snakes came out—the pythons and the cobras, the kraits and the Russell's vipers, languidly at first and then with quickening appetites, swarming in fields and gardens and along the edge of the river, and at the hospital the burdens of Miss MacDaid were increased by the cases of snakebite which they treated by cutting away the flesh and giving injections of serum. They could save the people bitten by cobras and vipers if they had good hearts, but for those bitten by the ugly little krait there was nothing to be done.

In the houses and in the vast palace mildew came in great spots on the walls, and fires were kept burning all day to dry the bedclothes which grew heavy with moisture during the night. The insects increased by billions until there were times when, wakening in the night to put on the light, you would find the netting so black with their bodies that it was as if a stifling cloak of black stuff had been thrown over the bed, shutting you in. In the daytime they lurked in clouds behind pictures and under cushions and beneath furniture, providing a feast for the squeaking little lizards which dwelt in the reed-filled roofs.

In the bazaar and in the square before the old wooden palace the vendors of sweets and eskimo pies vanished along with the crowd. Business was no longer done in the open under a blazing sun but in dark small rooms like caverns, heavy with damp. The steps of the great tank were empty save when, for an hour or two, the rains ceased, and then the square would be filled suddenly by whole processions of *dhobies* coming to the tank to beat their clothes.

The rains had come, with a force and extravagance which swelled the river and filled the tanks to overflowing in four or five days. Within the memory of the oldest living man in Ranchipur there had never been rains like these. So violent were they that, once the hysterical rejoicing at their arrival was over, people began to feel a vague sense of alarm and to talk of the legendary great flood which had happened in the days of the evil Maharajah.

But the straightening of the river channel was effective and the stream held its course, torrential and unhampered, through the very midst of the city and across the green plains to the hills beyond Mount Abana. The steps below the temple of Krishna disappeared beneath the yellow flood and the base of the temple itself was littered with the broken branches of trees, the bodies of animals and all manner of rubbish, so that Raschid Ali Khan, noticing the wreckage on his way home from work, ordered a sweeper posted there day and night with a long pole to push away the debris. It was odd that the Hindus themselves did not

[189]

mind, but to Raschid's Muslim soul it seemed indecent that the steps of a temple should be littered with garbage and rubbish and dead animals.

One by one whole families of importance left for the hill stations where there was no mildew nor any snakes and insects——the General, the Commanding Officer and his family, Mr. Burgess from the bank with Mrs. Burgess, her aunt and her sister, the Dewan with his whole patriarchal household including his sister and his two nephews, his two sons and four grandsons and their wives and seven great-grand-children. At the palace Maria Lishinskaia and the Maharani planned what jewels and what saris Her Highness would need in Carlsbad and in London and Paris, and the Maharajah himself at last gave orders for departure by the *Victoria* from Bombay on Saturday. But he had no interest in the voyage for he felt no desire to leave. He was tired and ill and he wanted to die in Ranchipur among his own people. It was the Maharani and the Major who persuaded him. They were persistent and laughed when he told them that in his horoscope it was written that he would not last out the year. They laughed—but he *knew*.

In the dampish old house Ransome stayed behind, willingly, filled with the excitement which the spectacle of the monsoon always brought him. On the day after the dinner at the palace he wakened feeling ill and depressed, and it needed a long time for him to reconstruct all that had happened the night before. He knew that he wanted to see no one— neither Edwina nor Fern nor even John the Baptist. When the boy brought his tea he showed no sign of knowing what happened the night before. He was silent as usual and Ransome asked him no questions, thinking it better to make nothing of the incident in the hope that John the Baptist would not find it extraordinary and believe that all European women behaved like Fern Simon.

When he had finished tea and shaved and dressed he decided what he meant to do for the day. He would drive alone far out into the country to the dead city of El-Kautara. That was, he knew, the only way to avoid society, for in spite of his solitary habits there was no such thing as privacy in Ranchipur. People were always coming and going. In the streets it was impossible to avoid friends and acquaintances. Door and windows were always open. There was no way during the monsoon of locking oneself in to be alone.

Lord Esketh failed to carry out his threat of leaving Ranchipur in the morning, for when morning came he was far too ill.

At eight o'clock his wife was wakened, with difficulty, by Bates, who told her that now there was no mistake and that his Lordship was so ill that he could no longer pretend that the illness was nothing. Wearily, her brain still dulled by all the medicines she had taken the night before in order to sleep, she listened to him, trying to remember that she was in Ranchipur and not in the house in Hill Street.

His Lordship, so Bates said, had not wakened properly. He appeared to be in what Bates called "a comber," and now that he was no longer able to resist Bates had managed to take his temperature, and found that it was seven degrees above normal.

"I'm afraid, me lady," said Bates, "that he has one of these Eastern fevers."

She wanted to say, "You're not afraid at all. You hope he has." But pulling herself together with a great effort she said, "I suppose we should send for a doctor, but I don't know whom to send for or where to send for him."

"Perhaps if me lady wrote a note to Her Highness, I could send it round by one of the boys."

"I'll go in and see him first and then write a note. Go along, Bates. I'll be in in a moment."

When she had made up her face and set her hair in order and put on a *peignoir* she felt a little better, although her brain still seemed as if it were encased in cotton wool, and when she raised her hand it was leaden and strange as if it did not belong to her.

It was the first time she had gone into his room, and for a moment the sight of Esketh in the vast red-carpeted Victorian bedroom tempted her to laugh. He lay, grotesquely, in a vast bed of teakwood ornamented with bits of mother-of-pearl, and the sight of him filled her with a sudden sense of shock and distaste. It was as if she had never seen him properly before—how gross, how heavy he was—for now, lying there half-conscious, the spark, the vitality, the energy which had always ani-

[191]

mated all his great bulk and turned mere weight into strength was gone, and he appeared dull, inert and heavy, the hard line vanished from his jaw, the muscles of his big face all flaccid. He had suddenly become simply a repulsive mass of flesh.

And then she remembered a little vaguely what had happened the night before in the palace and the quarrel that had taken place in her bedroom, and she was filled suddenly with shame and a loathing for herself, not because of Ransome or even because she was promiscuous—she felt no shame for any of the adventures she had had outside marriage—but because she had lived for nearly ten years with this gross mass of flesh which lay in the bed of teakwood and mother-of-pearl, that she had yielded herself again and again to him with indifference. All the other men—all of them—had at least been beautiful in one way or another, and she thought at once of Ransome and how different his body was, how slim and hard in spite of all his drinking and dissipation. Looking down at Esketh she thought, "Whether he lives or dies I'll never sleep with him again." But she wished shamelessly that he would die, for she knew that as long as she lived she would always see him thus, betrayed by his illness, heavy, gross, purple-faced, with his mouth hanging open a little; and each time that she saw him she would remember that she had prostituted her fine slim body to him again and again. Only with him, her husband, had she ever been a prostitute. With all the others there had been pleasure and even sometimes love. Esketh alone had ever paid her.

Leaning over the bed, she knew that Bates was watching her, dankly curious to see how she would behave, and she knew that she must put on some sort of show which, although it would probably not deceive Bates, would make him believe in her good intentions. She was aware that in his servant's way he already knew too much about her.

She said, as if she were a devoted wife, "Albert! Albert! It's Edwina." The dull pale blue eyes opened a little way but they only looked into space, far beyond her, without focusing. He made a faint grunting sound and the eyes closed again. A second time she tried with no more result, and then she said, "I'll write a note, Bates. We'd better send it off at once. I'll bring it to you. You'd better stay here to watch."

In her own room she took out her writing case and a bottle of smelling salts and began to write, but she got no further than "Your Highness" when she understood that it was not to the Maharani but to Ransome that she must send the note, for she knew suddenly that she was afraid of the old lady—why it was she could not say—but there was something about her, something in her presence, her manner, her dignity, yes, and her shrewdness which made her feel uneasy and a little ashamed. She saw her again as she had seen her the night before, standing beneath the blazing chandelier filled with bees, a look of mockery in her eyes. "She knew what we were up to," thought Edwina. And she felt too the scorn of the old lady as if she said, without saying it, "You were born to position and to responsibility. You have a place in life to hold up, even a little corner of the civilization which your ancestors helped to create; and you let it down every time. You let down yourself and the others about you. You had a job and you funked it."

She understood now, suddenly, how the Maharani felt about her, an Englishwoman, of the race of conquerors and merchants. No, she could not write to the Maharani and ask her to send the attractive Major Something-or-other. Her Highness would see through it. Smiling, she would read the note and think of Lady Esketh as if she were the dirt beneath her feet. To Ransome she could write asking him anything she liked. He would see through her too, but with him it did not matter because he, like herself, had let everyone down and so he would understand. And he was not an Indian.

She had no conscious prejudice about Indians because she was at once intelligent and abandoned, but all of them seemed quite strange and incomprehensible to her. When she thought of it at all it seemed to her that this feeling must be the vestigial remains of that legend of British superiority which Esketh was always trying to pound into her. It was all that was left, like the joints and bones in the fins of a whale. "Perhaps," she thought, "some day all English will be like me, with only fins instead of arms and legs, fingers and wrists"; and seeking to justify herself, she thought, "Maybe through Major Something-or-other I could begin to discover India. Maybe he would be able to kill that last vestige of prejudice."

To Ransome she wrote:

Dear Tom,

Albert is really ill this morning and needs a good doctor. I don't know what's the matter with him. There was an attractive fellow at the Palace last night, a Major Something-or-other who, I hear (all this had to be very casual) is an excellent physician. Could you send him a note and ask him to come round?

It's all a bloody bore when we were planning to get off today to Bombay. I forgot you didn't know that. I wasn't lying to you last night. We only decided it after we came home. It may make us miss the *Victoria* and then God knows when we'll be able to get away.

If you have a moment to spare, drop in and see me. I need cheering up. You'll probably find me in bed. In weather like this there doesn't seem to be anything else to do and I've seen the waterworks, the jail, the asylum, etc. Better still, come and have lunch with me. The cook isn't bad. Anyway I'll see you tomorrow night, at Mr. Bannerjee's dinner. I mean to go if Albert isn't *too* ill. It's better than sitting here reading books *about* India. And anyway now I can come to you on Thursday.

Edwina.

When she had finished the letter she put it without rereading it into an envelope and sealed it with special care, not only against the prying eyes of Bates but, remembering sinister stories she had heard in Simla, against the curious eyes of any Indian into whose possession it might come.

A boy from the palace came with the note at the very moment Ransome was stepping into the car to go to El-Kautara, and when he had read it through he tipped the boy and sent him away telling him to say that he would come over at once. But he had no intention of changing his plan; he would not pay a call on Edwina and he would certainly not lunch with her. Last night he had welcomed her presence and slipped willingly back into the feeling of his youth, but now this was the last thing he desired. All the brandy he had drunk the night before made him feel physically ill and there still lingered with him a confused feeling, made up of equal parts of remorse and satisfaction, over the way he had behaved with Fern; and this, he felt, must be resolved into terms of common sense before he would have any peace. And something in the adventure with Fern made Edwina seem much less desirable to him, as if she were an old story, told too many times.

As Edwina suspected he saw through the letter at once, through the elaborately casual reference to Major Safti and the hint about *knowing* India instead of reading about it; and the note made him suddenly angry, not at her shamelessness which left him as indifferent as if she had been a machine instead of a woman, but because he did not want her muddling up the life of the Major. He trusted his friend but he could not forget that all too often an Indian lost his head completely when a European woman showed him attention, especially a pretty woman like Edwina who would clear out when she had had enough. And he thought too of poor Miss MacDaid; if the Major took up Edwina's challenge it would not only upset his work but make poor Miss MacDaid frantic.

And then he remembered the monkeys in the garden and grinned and thought, "No! Hands off! I mustn't take to playing Jehovah with a catapult."

In any case there was nothing that he could do. In all Ranchipur, in all India, there was no doctor as clever as the Major and it would, he knew, be quite impossible to keep him from so important a fellow as Esketh. You couldn't leave the health of a great industrial king like Esketh to a poor little fellow like the Major's assistant, Doctor Pindar. While he tore up the letter he thought, "She should never have come out to India. She doesn't fit into the picture. She's nothing but a disturbance. It's bound to end in some sort of a mess. It's like bringing the wrong chemicals into contact."

Neither the Major nor Miss MacDaid was at the hospital. They had gone to the old barracks near the jail to see about putting it into order to receive the cholera and typhus cases. There he found the two of them on the second floor walking along the echoing hall, giving instructions to a whole procession of servants who followed them about cleaning and disinfecting and installing beds. He saw at once that they were both in high spirits and he divined the reason. They were both excited at the prospect of a task which would keep them working day and night; nothing like this had happened in years. And Miss MacDaid knew that

[195]

as long as the epidemic continued the Major would belong to her alone, sleeping at the hospital, forgetting even Natara Devi. The Major had a big cigar in his mouth and was laughing and talking loudly. The sight of them aroused a sudden pang of envy in Ransome.

When he told them his mission the Major said, "I'll come right along. Miss MacDaid can finish up here. We can't let a big bug like Esketh get ill and die in Ranchipur. His Highness and the Viceroy would never forgive us, not to mention all the shareholders."

"I didn't know the epidemic was so bad," said Ransome.

"It isn't bad really," said Miss MacDaid, "but there were eleven new cases this morning and the only way to stop it is to step right up and take it by the throat." She turned to the Major: "I suppose he'll want a nurse."

"He'll probably want two or three."

Miss MacDaid frowned: "Under the circumstances he'll have to get on with one. I suppose you'd better send Miss de Souza. She speaks the best English."

"I'll tell her to pack up and go over."

"Anyway," said Miss MacDaid, "it's a nuisance. We've enough work without that. He might have gone to Bombay to be ill."

At the old summer palace the Major announced himself to Bates, and Ransome waited in the hallway, seating himself on a horsehair sofa opposite a dreadful mildewed portrait of the Maharajah done by a student of the Bombay Art School. He had no desire to see Edwina for he knew perfectly well that she had no need for comfort or consolation, save perhaps for the fact that she would undoubtedly miss her boat back to Europe. Twenty minutes passed and then a half-hour, and he thought, "Well, she must have met her young doctor!" And then the portrait opposite him began to get on his nerves. It was an absurd production in which the Indian instinct for style had been mingled in an extraordinary way with what the artist believed to be modern painting in the West. Beneath the mildew the picture had not one virtue save that of quaintness, for the marriage of the two styles had succeeded only in creating an effect that was grotesque and childish. The picture, he thought, was like Mr. Bannerjee, not quite certain what it believed or whither it was bound.

He was still studying it when the door opened and Edwina came out, looking cool and lovely in a *peignoir* of lettuce green. She said, "Why didn't you come in? I only just found out that you were here."

"I thought it was none of my business. Is he very ill?"

"Yes. Major Safti doesn't know what it is."

(So she had found out his name? Progress! He wasn't Major Something-or-other any longer. The bitch!)

After a moment he said, "Well, that is a mess. I suppose now you won't be able to leave."

"Not for two or three weeks at the best."

He grinned: "Well, you'll find out in earnest what a monsoon can be."

"Are you going to have lunch with me?"

"No."

"Why not?"

"I don't feel in the mood." (Why wasn't the Major enough to occupy her for the moment?)

"It would be a help. I need cheering up."

"No. I can't."

"Is there any special reason? I promise to behave myself."

(Why in God's name couldn't she leave him in peace? Why did she keep stirring him up, prodding the past into life again? Why in hell had she ever come to Ranchipur?)

"No, there's no special reason except that I'm a bloody neurotic and I've got to be alone. I've got the jitters."

"I can give you a drink."

He looked at her with sudden fury: "Did you understand what I said? I'm ill. I'm a damned bloody useless fool and I've got to be alone. I don't see why you ever came here."

"I'm sure I don't know. I never wanted to. I won't bother you any more. When you're in a better humor and think you can stand me, let me know. I'm going to be awfully bored."

He almost said, "Oh, you're not going to be so bored with that fine specimen of manhood, Major Safti, coming in and out every day. I know what you're up to." But he held his tongue, lighted a cigarette and said, "I'll let you know. I'll probably be all right tomorrow."

"Have you any books I can borrow?"

"Send around and take anything you like."

"Thanks."

And then she was gone, leaving him to consider the extraordinary quality of the brief conversation, how it consisted mostly of one hiatus after another. What they had said was of no importance. It was what they had not said: "We understand each other too damned well. We understand each other because we're both bastards."

A moment after she had disappeared the Major came out, and like a *voyeur* Ransome regarded him sharply to discover, if it were possible, whether she had made any progress. But the Major gave no sign. Ransome said, "Well?"

"I don't know what it is. It's too early to tell. It might be any one of three or four things."

"Serious?"

"Well, bad——malaria or typhoid or typhus or even plague."

"How could he have got any of those things?"

The Major grinned: "Even great English Lords have been known to have been bitten by fleas." He took out a fresh cigar and said, "Do you know anything about him?"

"No, nothing."

"I should say he was an alcoholic. That isn't going to make it any better."

The rain had stopped for a moment and as he drove across the square by the cinema the whole place came suddenly to life, with people rushing out of shops and houses to take advantage of the respite—servants on errands, women bound for the bazaar, merchants bartering, washerwomen hurrying to the great tank. From the square he turned past the music school into the Engineering School Road. It was actually called Beaconsfield Avenue but nobody ever used that name. It was always spoken of as Engineering School Road. And then as if God had pulled the chain of a gigantic shower bath the rain began again in a flood, and a little ahead of him on the right he spied the figure of Miss Dirks trudging along in a mackintosh and a man's felt hat. He thought, "I'll stop and ask the poor old thing if she wants a lift. If she refuses then I'll never have to ask her again."

She must have been thinking of something very far away as she trudged along through the rain, for when he drew up beside her and called out she looked at him in a startled way, almost without recognition, as if she had come back from a great distance.

"Can I give you a lift?" he asked.

She did not smile. She said, "Good morning. No thank you. I like walking. I get so little exercise."

(All right then, walk! I'll be damned if I ever ask you again!)

As she spoke her face grew suddenly flushed in the most extraordinary way so that Ransome wondered if speech with a man always affected her thus. He had put his foot on the clutch to start on his way to El-Kautara when she spoke again.

"It's funny," she said, "I was just thinking of you." Then she coughed and said, "Could I come and see you this afternoon?"

His first impulse was to make an excuse, but pity for her and curiosity checked him. Something about her made him feel suddenly very English. He was aware of the closeness of his blood to that of the grim spinster and he felt suddenly their loneliness in this rain-drenched town where nothing was what it seemed to be. He saw that both of them were in a way exiles from everything that touched them closely.

He said, "Of course. But I could save you the trouble. I could come to you."

But she objected quickly: "No. It had better be at your house. At home we wouldn't be alone. . . ." Again she coughed: "You see, it's rather personal."

"All right . . . as you like. What time? Will you come for tea?"

"Yes. That will be fine. I couldn't get away from school before then."

"I'll expect you about five."

The flush went suddenly out of her face, leaving it the color of death. She said, "It's very kind of you. Good day," and awkwardly, abruptly she turned and went on her way.

The road toward Mount Abana was thick with mud, and beneath the new bridges built by the Swiss engineer the yellow water slid past with only an inch or two of clearance. He thought, "They should have been built with higher arches. If there was a flood they would only act as dams to the water."

Slowly as he drove along the road the great mountain appeared out of the rain, taking form above the flat plain like a gigantic pyramid. There were few pilgrims now that the rains had come, and the great stairway which led from the plain to the summit crowned with temples was no longer crowded with worshiping Jains from every part of India, going up and coming down in an endless pageant of color. At the top of the mountain in this season the priests were living a damp solitary existence —a good life, thought Ransome, if it were not for all the other priests.

He was forced to drive slowly because of the thick mud and the danger of slipping off the road, but after two hours he arrived at the huge ruined gateway of El-Kautara. It was made of red sandstone and the elaborate Mogul carvings were half-hidden by the tangle of vines and small thrusting plants. It stood at the very base of the mountain, this dead and silent city, its thick walls surrounded by a wide ruined moat which had filled with water, so that for a moment he had an illusion of what the city must have been like in the days when its squares and mosques were filled with merchants and soldiers, courtesans and dancing girls, horses and elephants. But the illusion passed quickly. It was a dead and ruined place which the earth had begun to claim again as its own.

Among the ruins in the streets and squares a path had been cleared just wide enough for a motor to pass and along this Ransome drove slowly, avoiding the deep pools of water that stood here and there. In the courtyards and sometimes within the walls of palaces and houses wild fig trees and banyans had sprung up, cracking and thrusting aside the tiles that had been brought long ago from the north, from Delhi and Agra and Lahore.

As history went in India it was not an ancient city; it could not have been more than a hundred and fifty years since the last Mogul subject looked back for the last time at its deserted walls. But already it was lost, its history swallowed up. No one knew why it had been abandoned and allowed to die. India was like that, thought Ransome. It swallowed up everything, human ambition and faith, cities and conquerors, fame and glory. Only Akbar survived and his successors who, as time went in the

East, had lived only yesterday. Asoka and the great Alexander and the rest were already legendary, half-man, half-god, like Rama and Krishna. In the empty courtyards the trees were hung with flying foxes waiting for nightfall to sweep in clouds across the plains toward Ranchipur. Again and again, where the fragment of a roof still remained, he caught a swift and sinister glimpse of a wild face framed with long greasy black hair peering at him from behind a ruined arch, and presently he came to have the feeling that as he drove along the empty streets he was being watched. They were the Bhils, the wild aboriginal people from the hills beyond Abana, who when the rains came sought the shelter of the ruined mosques and temples for their children and their goats.

At last in the great square before a huge ruined mosque he stopped the car and sat there for a long time, filled at last with a sense of peace, the sickness gone from him. In the solitude there was bitterness and a kind of sinister pleasure, for the spectacle said to him, "See! Here was once a rich and powerful city. It is gone now as all the others which followed it must go." It seemed to say to all the world—the dictators, the politicians, the bankers, the "great men" of the world—"See! This is what you must come to through greed and folly and evil! See! One day what you have built will fall and its ruins will be the haunt of bats and panthers and savages."

When she was dressed and everyone had gone away, even Bates, Edwina went into Esketh's room and sat for a long time, watching and thinking. She did not sit beside the bed but in a chair across the room, from which he appeared to her objectively, free from any bond of any kind. He did not stir when she came in and gave no sign of knowing that she was there. He simply lay bloated and heavy, his face swollen and more purple than it had been three hours earlier. Major Safti had told her that she should not enter the room until Esketh's illness had been properly diagnosed. If it were plague, he said, it would be dangerous for her. But she had no feeling about the danger because deep within her there was a consciousness, like the belief which some soldiers have in battle, that nothing would touch her. And she was by nature a gambler. If she was to have the plague, she would have it anyway.

She had been driven to return to the room by a kind of horrid fascination which Esketh, ill and unconscious, seemed to have for her. And because it gave her a perverse pleasure to look at him, helpless, downed, beaten for the first time. And while she sat there she thought: "There you are—not the great swaggering Lord Esketh, boasting and bullying and buying what you want, but just plain, vulgar Albert Simpson, the son of a small building contractor in Liverpool, who got beyond himself. You've never done a good deed for anyone unless it brought you profit and glory. And you've ruined men and women who trusted you for the sake of power and money. Oh, you've given money to charities in large lumps well advertised in your newspapers, but it never cost you anything. You never missed it and it made people who didn't know you say you were generous, and it served to whitewash your character and cover up a lot of sculduggery and stifle the criticism of your enemies. You'd betray your own country if it would bring in another shilling or another ounce of power. Long ago you sold rifles and shells to Turks to kill at Gallipoli boys who came from your own country, men better than yourself who went off to their death while you stayed at home and made money out of the tragic needs of your own people and wrote wild leaders in your own papers to keep the war going. And now, only a fortnight ago in Delhi, you wrote a leader to be printed in all the Esketh papers that was certain to make ill feeling and bitterness and lead to more wars. It cost you a nice lot to cable it all the way from Delhi but that didn't matter because if there was a war you'd get back the money a billion times over. You didn't know that I read it first, but I did. There are so many things you don't know about me and what I know of you. Bates and I together could write a biography of you that would put you in jail or in an asylum for mad men. Oh, you're very shrewd . . . using your newspapers, your mines, your factories, your steamships, round and round in an endless chain, turning out profit for yourself at the expense of workman, of shareholders, of humanity itself. You've never had a friend that you didn't buy. You even bought your own wife and a bad bargain she was—probably the worst bargain you ever made. What was it that happened long ago, perhaps when you were a small child, that made you want all those things for which you sacrificed everything decent? Were you thinking about all this long ago when you were selling cheap knives and watches in Malaya? Who

[202]

hurt you? Who put into your head the idea that all this power and all this money were the only things worth having in life? What made you think that you could buy things in life—things like love and fidelity and respect and breeding? What are you like inside? What must it be like to be *you*? What does it feel like to be so ruthless, so bitter, so alone, hating everybody who does not lick your boots? You'll never tell anyone because you don't know yourself how it feels. You've never known. You can't know, because you're like a man born with a horrible physical deformity who can never know what it is like to be fine and straight and young and beautiful. Your brain, your soul must have some horrible deformity which is all the worse because it cannot be seen. You must have been a horrible child—grasping and calculating how to make money even out of your mother. But it's all destroyed you too. Because you're a finished man, Albert Simpson. The world is finished with you and you are sick of yourself and tired and worn down by the thing you built up with so much trickery and ambition. You're going to die in the India which you hate, of a loathsome disease; and no one will ever care, not one person in the world, not even your wife or your servant or the secretary you sent ahead to Bombay. That wonderful private railway carriage which you thought made you seem greater than other men will go back without you. Maybe your ashes will go home on that swift beautiful boat and maybe they won't. But you're finished. God-damn you! You'll never get out of that horrible bed alive, to sleep with me again like an animal. You'll never again shout at servants as if they were dogs. You'll never again make me ashamed in public that I ever knew you. You did something horrible to me, to my very soul. Oh, I let you do it because I was tired and didn't care, but you could have helped me a little. You might have seen what I needed—oh, so little—to have saved me, but you didn't see. You never had time. All you did was shove money at me. Well, you're finished. You're going to die and rot and in a few years nobody will remember who you were. You haven't even an heir to leave behind you. I'm glad that vile blood of yours won't go on living because I bore you a child. I'm glad I saw to that. You're finished and nobody cares. Go on, slobber and snore, like the gross animal you are. There were times when you thought you could break my pride and make me as coarse as yourself, but you never did. In the end I've won. Even last night I won

[203]

when I sent you skulking out of my room. You hadn't any kindness or any morals or any ethics, so nobody could touch you but me. I knew you well enough to know where it would hurt, and you made me use my knowledge. You forced me to do it. I'm not sorry. I wish it had been more cruel. Oh, if you only knew how many times I'd betrayed you, and never once with a man who wasn't better than yourself—kinder, warmer, more decent, more beautiful. Yes, and every one of them was a better lover than you. People grow to look like what they are, Albert. You were a hog and you've grown to look like a hog, lying there, snoring and slobbering in your own spittle. Well, you're going to die. This is the end of you; and the whole world—even little brats in the streets of India and China—will be happier and have a better life because you are dead."

And presently she felt a wild desire to cross the room and spit on him, but she did not do it because it occurred to her almost immediately that such a spectacle would only be extremely funny. "What's happened to me?" she thought. "Perhaps I'm going to be ill too. I shouldn't be here in this room. But even if I caught something, what difference would it make? I shouldn't care. Why should I suddenly care so profoundly about Albert's nastiness? Why should I be hysterical?"

Leaving him, she went back to her own room and threw herself down on the bed, and in a moment she found that she was crying without making a sound. The tears streamed down her face and made a nasty little puddle on the pillow of pink *crêpe de Chine*. She could not think why she was weeping; certainly it was neither for Esketh nor from fear of death. She had never been afraid of that, not half so afraid as she had been of growing old and losing the white smoothness of her skin and the shine of her blond hair. She could not remember having wept since she was a schoolgirl and now this was the same sort of weeping, from nerves, over nothing at all, a relaxing, satisfactory performance, touched by the same voluptuousness and melancholy.

"But I've never had nerves," she thought. "It must be this damned country and this damned climate—the bloody rain and heat and boredom."

After a time she felt better and, sitting up, she took her mirror and looked at herself, a little shocked that her hair was in such disarray and her eyes so red and swollen. Looking at her reflection she thought,

"Is that really me? It can't be," for what she saw was a woman who was no longer elegant and smooth and beautiful, but a rather plain disheveled creature on the verge of middle age. And then in fright she put down the mirror.

"What if I should never escape? What if I should have to stay in this awful country forever? If my looks go what will I have to offer a man?" "No," she thought, "I must be quick. I must snatch everything while I can." And she wondered whether she looked to Major Safti as she had looked just now in the mirror. She had wanted to look her best because he was more attractive than she had remembered. But for him she would pack up and leave now. To hell with Albert! To hell even with the Major! She leaned across the little table to push the bell for the maid, to tell her to begin packing at once, but in the middle of the gesture she stopped herself. You couldn't do that, even to Albert.

Miss Dirks was late for tea, not because she had failed to leave the high[1] school in plenty of time but because she had stopped a great deal on the way—in shops, at the library and even at the museum where she pretended to be looking for some new Persian designs which the younger girls might use in their embroidery and water-color work. When she had first come to Ranchipur, people—even Indians who are rarely astonished by anything—had turned and looked after her in the street, not only because of her strange sexless appearance but because there was something about her which set her apart from other people, something direct and determined; duty was a master little known and scarcely recognized among Indians. But now they no longer noticed her because she had become a kind of fixture, like the statue of Queen Victoria on the middle buttress of the Zoological Gardens bridge.

It was not an easy thing for her to do—this going to have tea with Ransome. A half-dozen times she very nearly lost her courage and would have turned back save that her sense of obligation amounted to an obsession. She had engaged herself for tea and Mr. Ransome was waiting for her to arrive and in order not to fail him she would have passed through fire and water, battle and plague.

For the first time in twenty-five years she was calling on a European and for the first time in her life she was calling on a man. A year or two earlier, when she felt strong as a horse, it would have been easier for her, but now when she was weak and tired there were moments as she walked through the rain when she felt a strange animal desire to crawl into a thicket of bamboo and quietly die, alone, leaving the world to deal with all the troubles which tormented her, to lie down and quit like a faithful old horse who could not go one step further. As she trudged along in her heavy boots the temptation became an obsession, the kind of luxury which one would encounter only in heaven. And her weariness seemed too to drag her back and back across all the years of isolation into her childhood as if she were already a very old woman, so ancient that she forgot what happened yesterday and remembered only those things which had occurred when she was very young. She wasn't any longer Miss Sarah Dirks, distinguished and able head-mistress of the Maharani's High School for Girls who had done an extraordinary job under the most discouraging circumstances, but plain awkward Sally Dirks, daughter of the Nolham draper, going to the castle to help at the annual bazaar for the benefit of the orphanage.

At the prospect of having tea with Ransome the same vague awe and confusion filled the heart of this tired woman of fifty which had filled the same heart at the age of seventeen. It all returned to her with remarkable clearness, the whole picture of the castle, the great lawn with the little booths all about it and the showers which always interrupted the gayeties, and in the midst of the scene Ransome's mother, Lady Nolham, all in lace with a big picture hat, moving about fussily and aimlessly, always in spite of everything a stranger, greeting the townspeople. She could remember too the figure of the child of three or four who clung to her hand, a good-looking child with dark curly hair, the youngest of the family, who had grown up into Tom Ransome.

It was absurd, she told herself, that she should be upset at the prospect of calling upon a man who was young enough to be her son. She tried to argue herself out of the feeling but in spite of every argument she still felt herself to be what she had been at seventeen, pale, unattractive and shy, the daughter of the village draper permitted inside the grounds of the Castle on the occasion of the annual bazaar and horticultural show. For three hundred years the people of the Castle had looked after the people of the village conscientiously and well.

At five-thirty she arrived at last, her heart beating wildly to find Ransome waiting for her on the verandah, drinking brandy. "He looks like his father," she thought. "But his drinking is beginning to tell." She thought he looked tired and middle-aged. The drinking probably came from his mother. In the last letter she ever had from Nolham her sister had written that Lady Nolham (so she had heard) was unhappy and drank secretly.

For a moment it seemed to her that she had not the strength to climb the five steps to the verandah, not only because she felt tired and ill but because she was bearing the weight of a whole flood of new memories, which had come rushing back to her at sight of him.

He was very kind to her and put an extra cushion into the deep chair when he had taken her mackintosh. He did it gracefully and with sincerity of feeling. "They were always great gentlemen," she thought. He did it just as his father would have done. She could remember old Lord Nolham well, coming into her father's shop to pass the time of day. He too had had that same quiet look of desperation. He was, she remembered, a very handsome man who wore side-whiskers like Lord Lonsdale.

She said, "I hope I haven't been a nuisance, coming in like this?" and at the sound of her own voice she felt her confidence returning a little.

He laughed pleasantly, showing very white teeth, and it struck her that it was a pity so handsome a young man should apparently be set upon destroying himself by dissipation.

"I've nothing to do," he said; "I never have. After all, life in Ranchipur is very simple, especially when you have nothing to do like me."

John the Baptist appeared with the tea, silent, but observing everything out of his large dark ox-eyes, and Miss Dirks said, "Shall I pour it?"

"Please. No, I won't have any."

She poured her own tea, her big bony hands shaking with weakness and excitement. "I heard that you painted," she said; and again he laughed: "No, not really. I haven't any talent. I do it to kill time."

It was not easy at first. There were little halts and pauses, and he discovered that in her shyness Miss Dirks had developed a stammer which made it difficult sometimes to understand what she was saying. It was awkward because they were both waiting for something—Miss Dirks to tell the reason for her visit, and Ransome to discover what it was. They talked of the rains and the cholera, of the school and the Maharajah's impending departure, and after a time Ransome began to feel that weariness which came over him when he talked with people who were not frank but held back a part of themselves. It always gave him a sense of fencing with a shadowy opponent, of trying to find something which he knew was there but could not find. All the while Miss Dirks sat bolt upright, with an air of authority, as if she were conducting a class. He noticed that now and then the muscles of her face would contract with sudden harshness and she would grow deathly pale.

John the Baptist returned presently to take away the tea things and then Miss Dirks plunged.

She said, "How long has it been since you last saw Nolham?"

At the mention of the name he put down his brandy glass suddenly: "Nolham? Oh, ten years at least. What do you know about Nolham?"

"Do you remember Mr. Dirks, the draper?"

"Old 'Dacy' Dirks? Of course I do. Oh, I see. You're some relation?"

"I'm his daughter. He only had two children. My sister still lives in Nolham and keeps the shop."

The thing was done now, the barrier broken down and she felt suddenly free. All at once it was as if they were old friends, and Miss Dirks felt a wild desire to cry.

"Why didn't you ever tell me before?"

"Well, you see, I scarcely knew you. I couldn't think that it mattered very much, really. I thought it would be . . . " She hesitated miserably and then said, "I thought it would seem presumptuous."

"You should have told me. I never connected the names—yours and Nolham, I mean. I never thought of it. You see, your father died when I was still a boy and I haven't been back to Nolham since my brother succeeded."

"My father has been dead twenty-one years this autumn."

"That's right. I must have been about eighteen. I remember the funeral. I went to it with my father. I was home on leave."

"Yes, he died after I came out here."

"What do you hear from Nolham?"

A shadow crossed the grim face of Miss Dirks. "I don't hear much," she said. "You see, I've rather gotten out of the habit of writing home. I haven't had a letter for a good many years." After twenty-five years, she still thought of Nolham, with its green common and the little river full of reeds alongside, as home. India was still "out here."

"I know," he said. "One does lose contact. It's been three or four years since I've had any news from there. The last was from Banks, the estate agent, about some things my father left me."

"Not old Morgan Banks? He's not still alive?"

"No, his nephew . . . you remember, the red-headed one."

They were getting on now. Miraculously, suddenly, they had slipped back into the ancient relationship from which they had both broken away so long ago. Nothing had really changed that feeling between Castle and Village. It was exactly the same as if neither of them had ever left Nolham and they had met now by chance in the Peacock Tea Room instead of on the verandah of a house in Ranchipur.

They talked about characters in the town, about the changes which had taken place since they both had left. There was something in her eagerness which made him feel inexpressibly sad. She flushed and grew excited and at last she confessed, "You don't know how I sometimes longed to talk with you about Nolham, but I couldn't get up my courage. You see Elizabeth—that's Miss Hodge—had never seen Nolham. She comes from Birmingham. She's city bred. She'd never understand what Nolham was like."

He had quite forgotten that she had come to see him about a matter which was "personal" until she grew suddenly rather stern again and said, "But that wasn't really what I came for. It was to talk about something else—to talk about Major Safti, to be exact."

"He's a great friend of mine."

"Well. That's just it. You see I've been ill for several months." She flushed and added, "I may have to have an operation. I wanted to know about him."

"There's no better surgeon in India."

Again a wave of color came over her face: "I didn't mean that. I know that. I meant what kind of a man is he?"

Then slowly the preposterousness of what she was seeking struck him.

He felt a ribald desire to laugh and managed to translate it into a reassuring smile.

"Oh, he's a fine gentleman," he said, "one of the finest I've ever known. Charming and human too." And in order to make it clear he added, "He's immensely understanding and his attitude toward things like that is absolutely scientific and professional."

"Then you'd advise me to go to him?"

"I should think he was the one man in all India to go to. You needn't feel shy with him. He won't make you feel shy."

(My God! Now I'm becoming adviser to old maids with female complaints.)

"Well," said Miss Dirks, "I must say I've never heard anything against him. It was only that he was Indian. I've never gotten over feeling that Indians are a little strange."

"He's the same race as you and I. Even his eyes are blue."

"I know . . . I know," said Miss Dirks, "but they always *seem* different."

He had thought that she meant to leave but she remained, slipping off again, temporizing, talking about his garden and John the Baptist. At last she said, "That wasn't all I wanted to ask you. There was another thing . . . about Miss Hodge."

"If I can help in any way, I'll be delighted."

The color rushed back again into Miss Dirks' face: "You see, we've been friends for a great many years and she has come to be dependent upon me—rather too dependent. She doesn't even think for herself any more except"—she hesitated for a moment and then plunged—"except in moments of rebellion; and at such times she hasn't any judgment or balance. She's like someone who tries to get up and walk for the first time after having been in bed for years." She fumbled with the worn handbag in her lap and looked away from him: "Lately she's been getting worse. You see at times it seems almost as if she were a little . . . well, unbalanced." She hurried on as if she were forcing herself: "You see, I've lost touch with all my friends and relations at home and the same thing has happened to her. What I'm worried about is if I should have to have an operation and anything should happen to me."

Tears rose suddenly to her eyes, but they did not fall. It was the gnawing pain and the weakness which made her cry. With a terrible effort she stopped the tears almost before they had begun to flow. Ransome, listening, thought, "If only she could say all that is in her heart. If only once she could let herself go." But it was too late now. She, like Miss Hodge, was paralyzed, but in a different way.

"You see," she went on, "if anything did happen to me, Elizabeth would be left all alone in the world. Whatever money I have, I'm leaving to her. It isn't much but it's enough to make her comfortable—a little I've saved and what my sister paid me for my share of the shop in Nolham. You see, there were only two of us and my father left it to us jointly. My sister . . . she married Tom Atwood, son of the chemist. Maybe you remember."

"Of course. Perfectly."

"Well, she wanted to buy my share, so I sold it to her. But to get back to the point . . . I can't think of Elizabeth being left out here all alone. She's so nervous and flighty. You see, what I wanted to ask you about was finding someone who might act as a kind of trustee for her to look after the money and see that she didn't get into some scrape or other. I came to you because you were the only possible person. It isn't only that we really don't know anyone out here, but you were the only one I could think of who might understand. If anything happened to me, I'd prefer to have Elizabeth go back to England. I hope it's not too presumptuous . . . I hope . . ."

Ransome said, "I couldn't do it myself. I'm not what you'd call a responsible person. And I might clear out and leave Ranchipur for good at any time, but I could ask the family solicitor to take the responsibility. He'd do it for me and then you could be sure that her income would always be safe."

Again the tears rose for an instant in the clear blue eyes: "That's so good of you. You don't know what a relief it is. You see, I feel responsible for Elizabeth. I feel as if it were my fault, as if I'd brought her out here where she's lost touch with everyone at home. I was always the strongest and I've always had wonderful health. I never thought that something would happen to me first. I never thought that anything like this would happen. It's very kind of you. It makes everything much easier."

"You can trust him. He'll know exactly what to do."

"Some of the money is at Lloyd's in Bombay and the rest is at home in England. There's enough here to get her safely back." Again she hesitated for a moment: "Of course it's not all as simple as that. If anything did happen to me, it's quite possible that it would throw Elizabeth completely off her balance, for a time anyway. I was wondering if you could look out for her and see that she was treated kindly and got back to England all right. I know I'm asking a great deal, but I didn't know who to turn to. I worried about it for a long time and then I thought of Nolham. . . ."

He said, "I'm sure that there's no need to think about anything happening to you. I'm sure everything will be all right, especially with the Major. You can trust him."

He divined what it was she thought although she never quite said it, perhaps because she did not understand it quite clearly and had not the words to express it. In her extremity she had gone back to her roots, to a system, a civilization which had almost vanished, from which both of them had cut loose long ago; she had come up from the Village to find help at the Castle, and ironically she had come to him, the one member of the family who had revolted and refused to accept the responsibility. He was pleased that she had come to him and at the same time he was ashamed of the half-feudal pleasure he found in it. It was at once warming and deceptive to be thrust suddenly into the patriarchal position of the Lord of the Manor. And he thought suddenly of his grandmother at home in her great turreted house in Grand River, seeing her in the same circumstances, accepting the responsibility of Miss Hodge and of helping poor Miss Dirks, not as something medieval but as something simple and human. If she were only here now there was so much that she could do to help these two poor lonely old maids which he could never do because he was a man and because, in spite of everything, neither he nor they could ever quite forget the relationship of the Castle to the Village.

"I think now," she was saying, "that perhaps we were wrong in living so much apart. Sometimes Elizabeth did want to call on people and ask people to tea, but in the end, somehow, we never did it and so now we really don't know anyone."

While she was speaking his mind slipped quickly and naturally from his grandmother to Aunt Phoebe and from Aunt Phoebe to the Smileys, and then he saw exactly the course to take. The Smileys were precisely the ones to care for Miss Hodge if anything happened to Miss Dirks. One more burden he knew, would scarcely be noticed by them. And they would do it simply and kindly, as if Miss Hodge were a neighbor just across the street who had fallen ill. He found himself saying, "Maybe it's not too late. Maybe it would be a good idea to have Miss Hodge come to know some of the nice people." He saw that she winced a little as he said "nice people," but he went on: "I'm sure nothing is going to happen to you, but if it did, then she wouldn't find herself quite alone. Maybe it would be a good idea if I gave a tea party. Would you come and bring Miss Hodge?"

She did not answer him at once, for she was struggling again with the terror and paralysis which attacked her whenever the question of human contacts arose. At last she said, "That would be very nice of you." And then the seamed harsh face went white: "But I'm afraid it's impossible. You see there are so many people who wouldn't come if they knew we were going to be there."

"Oh, I'm sure that you imagine that."

She looked at him directly, searchingly, as if judging whether he would understand what she had to say and then, like Fern Simon, she found in his face something which gave her courage and she plunged: "You see, some of the people here have spread nasty stories about Miss Hodge and me."

He smiled, "Oh, I hadn't meant to ask those people. I never see them myself. I had meant to ask friends of mine—the Smileys and Mrs. Smiley's aunt and Miss MacDaid and Major Safti and maybe Raschid Ali Khan and his wife. Raschid might be very useful to Miss Hodge."

The whiteness left her face and she hesitated for a moment on account, he knew, of the Indians. Then she said, "Yes, that would be very nice. And then perhaps we could give a party too at home. I think that would make Elizabeth quite happy. For years she's wanted people to see the house and how very attractive she's made it."

"Very well, then. I'll do it. I'll let you know what day I can get them all together."

She rose now and took up the mackintosh, and when he helped her with it he saw that she was trembling from head to foot with the effort the visit had cost her:

"And I'll speak to my friend the Major about an examination. I know he'll see you whenever you like. You needn't be afraid of him. He's a kind man and very understanding."

"That would be very good of you. You've helped me so much today."

"It wasn't much I've done. We must have another talk soon about Nolham. It's made me homesick." And he knew at once that he had said the wrong thing because he had raised up for her a picture of the little town which her spirit had never left and her body would never see again. She choked and said, "Yes, sometimes I get very homesick for the common and the river and my father's shop."

She would not let him drive her home but went alone down the drive into the rain, leaving him with his brandy and soda; and when she had gone out of sight he himself returned to Nolham which had come back to him with extraordinary vividness. Talking about old "Dacy" Dirks and Morgan Bates and Tom Atwood, the chemist, had suddenly peopled the common, the square, the "pub," with figures, alive and moving about within that frame which none of them had ever left. It was far enough away now for him to forget the things he had hated— the awful patronizing Victorian qualities of his father, the arrogance and snobbery of his older brother, the bewildered unhappiness of his ineffectual mother whose money it was that kept Nolham intact, the quality of lifeless, paralyzing artificiality which he always felt on his return from the easy freedom of Grand River—all that rigid feeling of caste which he found even in the scullery. All these things seemed unimportant now and, sentimentally, he saw only the virtues of a system into which he had never fitted—the stability, the peace, the sense of obligation accepted alike by Castle and Village. But even that was already going. They were represented by a Socialist M. P. and bit by bit the land had been sold until there remained only one or two farms and the vast useless park which surrounded the castle. Even his mother's American fortune, dug long ago by his grandfather out of the hills of Nevada, was not enough to preserve it.

Out of all the figures from his boyhood old "Dacy" Dirks the draper emerged the clearest of all, perhaps because there had always been about him a sinister quality almost of menace, standing in the doorway of his shop, clad in the unchanging long-skirted coat and white tie, looking angrily across the little square toward the "Hare and the Jug" where so many fine young men were being ruined. "It was extraordinary," Ransome thought, "how well I divined, on that day at Mr. Jobnekar's, the background out of which Miss Dirks had come—divined it without even so much as a hint."

Old "Dacy" belonged to the Plymouth Brethren and in his household there was never any fun. The rooms back of the shop where "Dacy" and his family lived must have been as dreary and sunless as the shop itself. On the Sabbath there was never anything but the Bible. His daughters never saw any boys their own age and they were taught that all men save "Dacy" were predatory creatures and that love was an unfortunate necessity like going to the privy in the back garden. Out of that Miss Dirks had stumbled only a little way, crippled and hampered, to die at last in India on the other side of the world from green quiet Nolham, having never known any pleasure save the grim tyrannical satisfaction of having done her duty.

For she was going to die. He knew while she sat there talking to him that he had entertained at tea a woman who was already dead. He was wrong only in the supposition that she herself did not know it.

As Miss Hodge hurried through the rain across the square by the cinema it struck her as extraordinary that Sarah had made no comment on the fact that she had worn her new foulard to teach in all the afternoon. It was quite possible that she had not noticed, for there were so many things that escaped her lately; still, the new foulard which she had bought two years ago at the Army and Navy store in Bombay and worn only three times, once to the Maharani's Durbar and twice on school prize-days . . . No, it was extraordinary and very lucky.

When Miss Dirks left her on the square before the cinema, saying she had some errands to do and would not be home before six, Miss Hodge had continued craftily on her way past the tank in the direction of the Engineering School until her friend was out of sight. Then abruptly, like a redskin, she had doubled back on her tracks and turned into the street which led through the bazaar.

She was having one of her "waves" when she was filled with defiance of Sarah, a "wave" so violent that she had even dared to put on the new foulard which might have betrayed her. But really, she told herself, she did not care. If it had come to a show-down she would have faced Sarah down and gone anyway. She was not a child and she was certainly not Sarah's slave. And she was sick of never seeing anyone but Sarah when Ranchipur was so full of interesting people.

From the bazaar she turned through the street by the mosque and presently she came to the gate of the old Summer Palace which she entered, passing between two beautiful Sikhs in red and gold whom she had never seen before, and walked up the streaming drive to the palace Halfway to the portico she forgot her excitement in a wave of shyness and confusion, confronted by a problem which she had never faced before. How did you call on someone who was living in a palace? At the Durbar it was simple enough. You just found your place in line and walked in. But an informal visit like this, just a dropping-in . . . dropping in on a palace was not easy. Did you knock or ring? Or were you announced? For a moment she was tempted to turn and run but, knowing that if she stood much longer making up her mind she would be soaked through, she went as far as the shelter of the *porte cochère*, and there a decision was thrust upon her when a servant, wearing the purple and gold livery of the Maharajah, spied her and salaaming deeply asked what he could do for the *memsahib*.

Flushing and trembling she advanced up the steps, and opening her bag to find her cards her hands shook so violently that she dropped the bag and its contents spilled over the floor. When the servant returned the bag to her she found the cards, and gathering her courage gave them to him and said, "Lady Esketh, please!"

She had not used a card in twenty-five years, and when the idea of "branching out" came to her she thought of the cards she had had printed long ago at Stebbins' in Birmingham, and remembered exactly where she had put them—in the teakwood chest along with her diaries and some essays about the Dominions for which she had won a prize at the age of seventeen. But when she opened the chest she discovered to her dismay that the cards were yellowed and mildewed by the damp of twenty-five Indian monsoons. Luckily they had been placed neatly in layers in a cardboard box so that the ones near the center were fresher than those on the outside and from among those, when she had gon/ through the lot, she found two that were quite presentable, free from mildew and only a little yellowed around the edges. They looked almost as if they had been made that way—"Ivory white," she thought, "shading into white." They read, "Miss Elizabeth Hodge, Heathedge School," but neatly crossing off Heathedge School she wrote instead, "Assistant Principal, The Maharani's High School for Girls, Ranchipur."

She hadn't seen Heathedge School since that awful time when she and Sarah were asked mysteriously to resign, and the sight of the name brought back to her the shadow of that faint, sickish feeling she had known after Miss Hillyer, the principal, dismissed them both from her study. Even now she was not quite sure why they had been asked to go and Sarah had never really explained it to her, telling her not to ask silly questions but to keep her dignity and not try to stay where she was not wanted. The sickish feeling passed off quickly because all that had happened long ago and was finished and the exciting thing was that she meant to call upon Lady Esketh.

Even as she sat in the big reception room near the door of the palace it did not occur to her that Lady Esketh might be out or that she might not receive her, because Miss Hodge, from long years of solitary existence imposed by circumstance upon a naturally sociable nature, had come to live a large part of the time in an imaginary world in which she had the most extraordinary adventures. There were, for example, occasions when she hobnobbed with duchesses and bishops, when she constructed scenes and conversations in which she was charming and made a vivid impression upon the most distinguished and fashionable personages. After she left, the bishop would turn to the duchess and say, "Who was that intelligent and well-informed woman who knew so much about India?" and there were long dialogues full of "I said" and "then the Duchess said to me." So that now, sitting there while the servant took up her cards, she had no misgivings. She had lived through the whole call from beginning to end and knew exactly how it would be. And the room itself gave her confidence, with its turkey red carpet and its plush upholstered furniture, the mildewed invisible landscapes in huge gilded frames, the palms on stands of teakwood. It was all, she thought, exactly like St. Mary's Assembly Rooms in Birmingham.

Lady Esketh had had lunch in bed—curried lamb and rather soggy potatoes and wooden carrots in cream sauce, a very pallid and pasty pudding, *papaia* that tasted like a rather poor cantaloup, and weak coffee. Since she left her husband's room nothing whatever had happened save the arrival of the nurse, a plain dark Goanese woman with Portuguese blood who spoke a kind of curious phonetic English with a lisping accent—a woman, she felt sure, who was a suffocating bore, and was called Miss de Souza which sounded like the name of an American show-girl at the Palladium. The boy whom she sent to Ransome's house to fetch books had simply vanished into the rain, and in desperation she had tried reading in turn *India Revealed*, *The Problem of the Empire* and *The Indian Muddle* which Bates brought her from Esketh's room, but in the end she abandoned each of them because none of them seemed to tell what she wanted to know. They did not tell her what Indians were really like but only what some Anglo-Saxon professor thought they should be; and there was an incredible amount of statistics which to her detached and uncomplicated mind seemed to prove nothing at all except that India wasn't such a good investment any longer. And each writer, so far as she could see, seemed to contradict all the others. Each had his own theory of what was the trouble with India.

When in turn she had thrown the books on the floor in disgust, she tried for a time to sleep simply in order to kill the dragging hours; but that was no good either and after an hour she rose and began to walk up and down the room, thinking, "Now I understand why animals in the zoo pace back and forth." From the window one had a monotonous view of the small park which surrounded the palace, simply a vista of trees, vines and shrubs beaten down by the rain, nothing save greedy vegetation without even a glimpse of a coolie or a *dhobi* to provide animation and distraction. And suddenly she was aware that the mere effort of walking up and down the room had filled her with a feeling of suffocation. She, who never perspired and always appeared cool and elegant, was dripping with sweat.

At about five o'clock she called her maid and dressed, filled with a desire to do something, no matter what, if only to go out and walk up and down the streets of Ranchipur in the rain. And she could spend money, which was always what she did when bored, only she could remember having seen nothing in the bazaars of Ranchipur which she wanted to buy. When she tried to remember what was there she could only think of things made of imitation silk and bolts of cotton cloth and cheap silver ornaments, and jade of no value. And anyway she had no proper clothes. What she needed in such a downpour was oilskins and men's boots and all she had was a fragile raincoat of oiled silk and sports shoes from Greco. The maid fetched them, protesting, but Lady Esketh remained firm in her decision. Even if she had to go naked into the streets, something which she would not much have minded doing, she had to escape the throbbing monotony of these dull Victorian rooms. She was so bored that it seemed to her she could feel every nerve in the complicated network which ran through her body.

And then just as she was ready to go out a servant brought in two cards, both of which read, "Miss Elizabeth Hodge, Assistant Principal, The Maharani's High School for Girls." For a moment she stared at the cards in indecision and then she thought, "Why not? It might be funny. Anyway it's better than nothing." And she asked the servant to bring Miss Hodge up to her sitting room, and when he had gone she felt a faint sense of excitement. "If Tom is going to behave like a bore," she thought, "then I'll launch out for myself."

She told her maid to ask for tea.

When she entered the room Miss Hodge was sitting on the edge of a plush sofa, plump and dowdy in her Army and Navy Stores foulard, examining with her near-sighted eyes the furniture, the pictures, the fantastic collection of bric-a-brac which had found its way somehow from the four quarters of the earth into the old summer palace. At the sound of the opening door she got up quickly and came forward, blushing and trembling.

"I'm Miss Hodge," she said, "from the Girl's High School."

Edwina answered, "How d'you do? I'm Lady Esketh. Do sit down."

"Yes," said Miss Hodge, sitting down, well forward on the sofa, "I've seen you once or twice in your motor. I'd have recognized you anywhere from your pictures." She coughed, and then: "I hope I haven't been a nuisance, dropping in this way, informally. But it occurred to me as I was walking home from the school this afternoon that you might want to meet some English people. I know the guests of His Highness don't often see any of the English colony and I said to myself, 'Perhaps Lady Esketh would like to see the other side of Ranchipur.'" It was a speech which she had rehearsed again and again walking through the rain and now it came out with astonishing glibness, all in one breath, like a poem recited by a small child.

"That's very kind of you," said Edwina. "As a matter of fact I was just dressed to go out. . . ." Miss Hodge started up as if to leave at once. "Oh, don't think you kept me in. I was only going out because I was dreadfully bored and there wasn't anything else to do."

"Perhaps I should have written you a note."

"I think it's very kind of you to have thought of me at all."

Miss Hodge fumbled with her bag, uncertain of what to say next, and then the weather occurred to her. "I suppose," she said, "that this is the first time you've ever seen a monsoon."

"Yes, you see it's the first time I've ever been to India."

"I suppose you find it very interesting?"

Edwina was about to say, "No, I think it's deadly," when she understood that she must not say this to Miss Hodge. You might say it to people at dinner in London or to Indian generals or even to the Viceroy himself, but not to Miss Hodge, to whom India must be everything in life—everything. So she said, "Yes, but I've seen too little of it. It might be interesting if I knew it better. But that seems to be very difficult."

"I suppose," interrupted Miss Hodge, "you've seen the waterworks. They're the finest in India. They . . ."

"Yes, and the asylum and the jail and the distillery . . . but that isn't quite what I mean. I'd really like to see Indians and know how they live and what they think and what they're like inside." And as she spoke she was thinking of Major Safti. In the boredom of the long afternoon she had thought a great deal about him. And in the middle of the speech she felt a desire to laugh at the spectacle of Miss Hodge and herself,

[220]

thinking, "It's a good thing she can't see into *my* inside and discover that she's calling upon Messalina."

The first impulse of Miss Hodge was to say, "Well, I must say I've never been able to fathom Indians myself. I don't know any more about them than on the first day I came here twenty-five years ago"; but from somewhere out of the shadows appeared an unsuspected Miss Hodge who was an opportunist, one of those unsuspected Miss Hodges which were always stealing up on her to take possession of her body and make her say things which astonished her. The unsuspected Miss Hodge said, "Well, perhaps I could be able to help you. You see, we see a good deal of the families of the girls at the school—Miss Dirks and I, she's the principal and a great friend of mine. We've been here for twenty-five years, so naturally we've come to know a good deal about Indians—how they live and what they think and what they're like inside."

"Twenty-five years? How interesting! I suppose you do go home now and then."

"No, we've never been home." And Miss Hodge slipped from reality into one of those conversations which she was perpetually having with the duchesses and bishops in the bathtub and in bed at night. "We've meant to go home several times, but at the last moment we never seem able to manage it. It seems impossible to tear yourself away, once the Orient gets into your blood. It's very fascinating . . . so strange and different and colorful."

(And then the bishop would turn to the duchess and say, "Who is that interesting woman who seems to know so much about India?")

"I think you're very lucky," said Lady Esketh, "to know it the way you do. All I've seen is official dinners and waterworks. I've met a few Indians . . . your Mr. Raschid and a doctor . . . Major Safti."

"Oh, yes, of course," said Miss Hodge, "a charming man and a wonderful surgeon. We're very lucky to have him here in Ranchipur."

"He came to see my husband this morning. He's ill, you know."

"Since last night?" asked Miss Hodge, for all Ranchipur knew already that the Eskeths had dined at the palace and what had been said and what hour they left. "Since you dined at the palace?"

"Yes, it's some sort of fever."

[221]

"Dear me, I hope it's nothing serious. There are so many awful diseases out here . . . horrible diseases we never dream of at home."

Edwina thought, "I hope it's as serious and horrible as possible. I hope he has the most loathsome of the lot." And again she felt an almost hysterical desire to laugh.

Aloud she said, "Major Safti doesn't know just yet quite what it is. We'd planned to go to Bombay tonight but now no one seems to know when we'll be able to leave."

In her plump breast Miss Hodge's heart leapt. Perhaps Lady Esketh wouldn't be able to leave for weeks. Perhaps they would come to know each other very well. She was so charming and made you feel so at home. Perhaps . . . anything might happen. . . .

"Yes," she said, "sometimes they last for months."

"In that case I should certainly leave and go back to England," thought Edwina. Aloud she said, "It would be very kind of you to show me about. I'd love to see your house and go to the school and meet some of the Indians you know."

"Of course a good many of them don't speak English at all."

"Then you speak their language?"

"Yes," said Miss Hodge modestly, "I speak Hindustani, of course, and a little Gujerati. You see, Hindustani is a sort of universal language in India and Gujerati is the language of the people of Ranchipur."

"How very clever of you."

Then a sudden silence fell between them and Miss Hodge felt all at once like a whale stranded on a beach, struggling and wallowing helplessly, and even Edwina felt that the possibilities of conversation were somewhat limited. She had not been on her good behavior like this for years and the effort was a little exhausting. It was like opening a bazaar at Barbury House. She was aware that her caller had a way of running into conversational blind alleys and bumping her head against a wall. Yet she was interested, far more interested than she could have believed possible. Sitting opposite the dowdy little figure in foulard, it seemed to her suddenly that Miss Hodge was quite as strange to her as an Indian. She had not the faintest idea how Miss Hodge lived or what she thought or what she was like inside under the badly made-up face. And, watching her, the envy of small serene orderly lives, which she had felt for a moment on the night before, returned to her now more strongly than ever. Miss Hodge probably lived in a house like a bird's nest and every day for her had a wonderful monotony of peace. Out of the vast and spectacular disorder of her own existence it occurred to her that it might be very pleasant to be Miss Hodge for a little while.

A boy brought tea which fell like rain upon the conversational desert.

"Won't you have a cigarette?" asked Lady Esketh, holding out a case of ribbed platinum and gold, and Miss Hodge who had never smoked in her life took a cigarette because she could not do otherwise. It was as if she were under a compulsion. The sober Miss Hodge of the class room was dead and vanished. But when she took the cigarette she felt suddenly confused and helpless and laid it on the table, saying, "I'll have it when I've finished."

"I like to smoke with my tea," said Lady Esketh. "I love the taste of smoke with bread and butter," and she apologized for the tea, saying, "I suppose one really only has good tea in an English household."

"I'd love to make you a good cup of tea," said Miss Hodge, "with very thin bread and butter. We have lovely bread. It's baked for us by one of the girls. She learned how from Mrs. Smiley . . . that's the wife of one of the American missionaries."

"Perhaps you'd let me come to tea with you some day," said Lady Esketh; "I haven't had a bit of decent bread since I've been in India."

Miss Hodge heard herself saying, "Oh, would you come? I'd be delighted."

It all happened without her knowing how it had come about and before the words were well out of her mouth she remembered Miss Dirks and was terrified. But beneath the spell of Lady Esketh the terror slipped away quickly. It was like something out of a fairy tale. After all those years of wanting people to see how nice and cozy she had made the bungalow, of wanting them to see what a lovely tea she could serve, it happened at last, and with Lady Esketh! Suddenly nothing mattered, not even facing Sarah.

"And I hope you'll let me come one day very soon," Lady Esketh was saying; and Miss Hodge, still enchanted, found herself saying, "Any day you like, Lady Esketh."

"I could come tomorrow or Friday."

[223]

Cornered now and in desperation Miss Hodge said, "Perhaps Friday would be best. You see Thursday is prize day at the school and we shouldn't be home until quite late." Anyway Friday would be one day further off. It would give her one more day to appease Sarah.

"Yes. Friday would be fine."

The tea was finished now and it was clear to Miss Hodge that it was time for her to leave, but in her excitement and her fear of Miss Dirks she could not seem to pull herself together and think how to bring the conversation to an end and make a graceful exit. Edwina, aware that her caller was uncertain of how to make a getaway, made more effort and asked questions about the school, about the English colony, about the Maharani, so that the conversation became a kind of cross-examination of Miss Hodge. Presently as Lady Esketh began to feel completely exhausted, there was a knock at the door and her maid appeared to say, "The doctor is here again, me lady"; and Miss Hodge, seizing the interruption with a sudden relief, rose and said, "Well, I think I had better leave now. I must be getting home."

Edwina, a gracious mechanical Edwina, said, "It was very kind of you to think of me."

"Then we'll expect you on Friday, about five."

"That's right," said Edwina. "And we must arrange to meet some Indians . . . real Indians I mean, not the kind who have been to Oxford."

"Yes . . . yes," said Miss Hodge; "I'll arrange that." But how she would arrange it, she had no idea.

"Good-by."

"Good-by." And Miss Hodge, trembling and blushing, backed out of the door. There wasn't any way out now. She would have to face Sarah. Anyway she had escaped having to smoke the cigarette. It still lay on the table. Lady Esketh, it seemed, had not even noticed it.

Despite the rain Miss Hodge took the long way home, going all the way round by the Untouchable quarter instead of through the bazaars. It did not matter to her now whether her foulard was ruined. She had seen Lady Esketh and talked to her in the flesh and she was coming to tea at the bungalow—Lady Esketh of whom she had read week after week in "Court and Society" since Lady Esketh was a little girl going

Windsor to stay with her godmother, the good old queen. She had been kind and friendly and talked to her just the same as if she had been one of the neighbors back in Agatha Terrace in Birmingham. "No," Miss Hodge kept assuring herself, "there's nothing in the world quite so splendid as an English gentlewoman."

She was no longer sick of Ranchipur. She no longer minded the heat and the rain and the monotony. At last something had happened to her, something that was like the wild dreams she had at the sight of the Sikhs and the sound of their music. Now that she had "branched out" everything would be changed. The lives of Miss Dirks and herself would become interesting and the bungalow would always be filled with distinguished and fascinating people. In the end Sarah would thank her for having shown so much initiative. Anyway what Sarah really needed was a change. That was all that was the matter with her—she'd been queer and solitary for too long. Think of it, having Lady Esketh come to tea just like anyone.

And as she walked she began to live out the whole tea party, seeing herself pouring tea while Sarah sat by, charmed with the graciousness of Lady Esketh. And Sarah would be able to talk in a much more interesting fashion than herself. She would simply sit by as the hostess. And cigarettes . . . she must not forget to buy cigarettes tomorrow in the bazaar. She would put on the best lace tablecloth and have the thinnest bread with fresh buffalo butter, and serve the whole thing on the East India Company china. Sarah would say it was too precious but she would get round Sarah. She'd wash it herself afterward instead of leaving it to the girls.

Then as she turned into Engineering School Road something of the first excitement deserted her suddenly, leaving her cold and a little alarmed. Perhaps it was the sight of the familiar rows of pepper trees, the walls, the bungalows, the Indian Club, all saying to her as she passed them, "You're going home. You are going to have to face Sarah. Every step is bringing you a little nearer. How are you going to tell her?"

As she stepped on to the verandah she saw that Sarah was already home. Through the doorway she saw her seated at her worktable, reading and marking the prize-day essays on "What I like about Ranchipur." When she had hung up her mackintosh and her hat in the entry she walked into the room, trying to behave as if nothing had happened. Sarah, looking up from her work, said, "Where on earth have you been?"

She had meant to say, "I've been calling on Lady Esketh," and take the wind out of Sarah's sails at once, but she found herself saying, "Just for a walk"; and then a little defiantly, "I get so tired being shut up here all the time."

"But you're soaked through."

"Oh, that's nothing."

"Just the same, go at once and have a bath and put on some dry things."

"I mean to presently."

She tried to be easy and full of assurance the way Lady Esketh had been, but in her heart she had a sick feeling that Sarah saw through her. She could tell by the way Sarah looked at her. And, wet as she was, she seated herself and took up the "Morning Post" and began looking through it. It was already a month old, but time in India was merely relative. Sheltered behind it she knew that Sarah was pretending to go on marking the essays written by the senior-class girls, and that her mind was not on her work. She knew that Sarah was looking up now and then, trying to see her face, trying to discover what she had been up to. It made her feel brilliant and triumphant. And she began to imagine what it would be like to read her own name in "Court and Society," something like . . . "Miss Elizabeth Hodge of Ranchipur City, India, is the guest of Lord and Lady Esketh at Barbury House."

But in the midst of her dreaming the voice of Sarah interrupted her: "Elizabeth, do as I say. Go and put on some dry clothes and stop in the kitchen and see if the girls are getting on with supper. I must finish these papers."

The color rose in Miss Hodge's face, and flinging down the "Morning Post" she rose and flounced out of the door into the kitchen. Really, Sarah might have left her in peace for a moment instead of ordering her about as if she were a child or only a school teacher who had to keep an eye on the cooking. Very well, she'd keep on her wet clothes and catch malaria and then Sarah would be sorry.

In the kitchen she found everything going well, and as she unlocked the cupboard where the supplies were kept and took out the sugar and tea and the mustard and chutney bottle she decided that she would break the news to Sarah at supper when she was in a mood of relaxation; and as she locked the cupboard she saw through the window a boy coming up the path, a boy whom she recognized at once as Mr. Ransome's servant, and her heart began to beat a little faster. What could he want? What if it was an invitation from Mr. Ransome? So many things had happened today. If it was an invitation she meant to defy Sarah and go without her.

Hurrying, trembling with excitement, she left the kitchen in time to encounter the servant on the verandah. Salaaming, he gave her a note addressed to Miss Sarah Dirks, saying that he would wait for the answer. It was maddening not to be able to open the note, but Sarah was so funny about things like that. When she gave it to Sarah, Sarah spitefully held it in such a way that she could not read it over her shoulder. Then she rose and taking the note with her went to the door and said to the servant, "Yes, tell Mr. Ransome that everything will be all right."

She returned from the door looking rather white, and she said to Miss Hodge, "Mr. Ransome has asked us to tea"; and Miss Hodge, like a child, said, "Oh, Sarah, I want to go."

"Of course," said Miss Dirks, "we'll both go," and for a moment Miss Hodge was left speechless, unable to believe her ears. Sarah had spoken exactly as if there was nothing strange about the invitation, as if they had been in the habit of going out to tea two or three times a week every week for twenty-five years. She seated herself and went back to work on her papers, saying without looking up, "He's asked the Smileys and Miss MacDaid, Mr. and Mrs. Raschid and the Jobnekars."

"What day is it?"

"Friday," said Sarah without looking up.

"Friday . . . *this* Friday?"

"Yes, day after tomorrow."

For a moment Miss Hodge felt dizzy and confused. She did not speak and presently Miss Dirks looked up from her work and said, "What's the matter? Why are you standing there gaping at me?"

"I can't go on Friday," said Miss Hodge.

"Why on earth can't you?" Then Miss Dirks' long patience suddenly gave way and, sitting up, she said, "What on earth have you got to do?

[227]

And what on earth is the matter with you? Why are you running about in soaked clothes looking as if you'd swallowed a canary?" Miss Hodge simply looked at her, paralyzed, with her mouth open. "Why can't you? Have you become a deaf mute?"

"Because I've asked Lady Esketh to come to tea."

"How is she coming to tea? You must be out of your mind, Elizabeth. You don't even know her."

"I do know her. I called on her this afternoon. She's so nice." And suddenly Miss Hodge began to cry, partly from vexation and disappointment and partly from shame because in Sarah's uncompromising blue eyes she received an intimation that she had been ridiculous. She had made a fool of herself.

"What on earth ever possessed you to do such a thing?"

"I wanted to see her. You don't know how nice she was and how kind."

"Well, you'll have to put her off."

"I can't put off Lady Esketh."

"And why not?"

"Because I can't. It's impossible."

"Well, you'll have to."

"Tell Mr. Ransome you'll come another day."

"I can't do that."

"Why can't you? He's always been so polite and kind. He wouldn't mind."

"I can't because I really asked him to have the party."

"You asked him . . . ?" In her astonishment Miss Hodge stopped crying for a moment.

"Yes, I thought we should see more people."

The shock of this second announcement again made Miss Hodge mute. Miss Dirks said, "Just sit down and write Lady Esketh a note explaining. She'll understand. Tell her to come another day . . . any day. She won't mind. Two old maids can't be very exciting to *her*."

"You needn't cast slurs at her. Anyway I can't do that."

"Why not, pray?"

Miss Hodge saw that her friend was losing her temper, and she grew terrified. Sarah very rarely lost her temper; it had happened only two or three times in all their life together, but when it happened she could be terrible and cruel because she was so much the cleverer of the two.

"Because she's so lonely and bored."

Sarah laughed, wickedly, cruelly: "Lady Esketh lonely and bored? You must be losing your mind, Elizabeth. I suppose you think it's going to be exciting for her to come here to tea . . . with two dreary old maids? Really, I don't know what's come over you lately."

"I won't put off Lady Esketh for a lot of Indians and missionaries."

In perfect silence Sarah regarded her for a moment, with a look so cold and so terrible that for a moment Miss Hodge felt like fainting. It was the terrible look of a sensible intelligent woman who had put up for years with triviality and silliness, with stupidity and shallowness, out of an affection born in a weak moment of loneliness twenty-five years before, a look rich with contempt revealed for the first time in a cold fury. For twenty-five years, ever since the scandal, she had been kind to Elizabeth Hodge and protected her and covered all her blunders and silliness, and now suddenly she could bear it no longer.

In a terrible voice she said, "Go to the writing desk this minute and write a note to Lady Esketh. I knew you were stupid and silly and a fool but . never thought you were a snob and a bootlicker."

Miss Hodge went suddenly mad. For a moment she stared at Miss Dirks as if hynotized, her blue eyes wide with horror, her mouth hanging open. Then she cried, "A snob! A bootlicker!" I'm not a snob! I'm not a bootlicker! I won't put her off! Now I know! You hate me! You hate me! You've always hated me!" and she ran from the room screaming to lock her door. She did not sob quietly, from nerves, as Miss Dirks did. She screamed. She wanted everyone to know how she was treated, how she suffered, how cruel Miss Dirks could be. She wanted the Untouchable girls in the kitchen to know and the Sikhs in the great gateway on the other side of the road and the passers-by outside the garden.

When she had gone Miss Dirks rose and closed the door and the windows lest passers-by should hear her screaming. Then she sat down again and covered her face with her hands. Her whole body was trembling and she wanted to die, now, at once, for it seemed to her that she no longer had strength to go on. And tomorrow she would have to go to the hospital and undress and have Major Safti see her and touch her.

From the moment her maid announced the doctor Edwina forgot all about Miss Hodge and her envy of small lives and the invitation to tea. Even the last few words of farewell were spoken mechanically with a graciousness which did not come from the heart but from long-established habit. It was the kind of absent-minded graciousness bestowed upon servants and inferiors. She was thinking only of Major Safti and seeing him in her imagination, clean and good-looking, gentle and intelligent, good-humored and vigorous; and Miss Hodge, like a dream, simply faded out of the picture. All afternoon, tossing in the heat on her bed, she had thought of him with a kind of vicious abandon born of her boredom, until in her fancy he had become more tempting, more mysterious, more exciting than any man could possibly be in reality. While the rain beat monotonously on the roof and the bamboo screens before the windows, she had endowed him with all the qualities which could arouse a *grande passion*, for that, she knew now, was the thing she had dreamed of searching for and had never found without ever knowing what it was. She made of him a lover so great of spirit as well as of body that in her daydreams she was no longer Edwina Esketh, possessing a body which was simply an instrument and a spirit which was detached and sensual and calculating and quickly bored with every new adventure, but a woman in whom body and spirit had been welded together in a blaze of radiance and ecstasy.

And so when the door opened and the Major came in she felt a sudden twinge of disappointment, that he lacked somehow the magnificence with which she had endowed him, that he looked at her not as the lover who had been with her all the afternoon, but simply as the family doctor calling upon the wife of a man who was ill, that he was unaware of all that had happened between them during the long hours when she lay on her bed on the misty borders of sleep. She, like Ransome, spoiled, felt suddenly greedy, thinking, "If I do not have him I shall spend the rest of my life regretting it."

He did not sit down. "I can only stay a moment," he said; "I still don't know what your husband is suffering from, but whatever it is, it is erious. You must not go near him. It is so serious that even the nurse ᴍust keep her face covered until we know. I've sent a specimen of blood to the Institute in Bombay. It will go by the Bombay Mail and we should know the result by tomorrow evening. I have asked them to telegraph me."

"What do you think it might be, Major?" she asked him, making an effort, as she did in front of Bates, to give the illusion of concern where there was none, because she knew that this man was an idealist. She knew it from his face, from his voice, his humanity and kindliness and from the look in his eyes. She knew that if she was to seduce him he must not think badly of her. While she talked to him a strange wild hysterical thought came to her out of nowhere: "Perhaps he is the one. Perhaps he could save me."

He did not say what it might be: "There is no use in alarming you needlessly. In any case it's certain that your husband won't be able to leave for weeks."

"How many weeks?" She, who had been bored and eager to leave only a little while before, now wished that he had said months instead of weeks. The heat, the rain, the monotony no longer existed. She felt herself trembling and put her hands behind her.

"Four or five at the least." He looked at her directly, saying, "I'm very sorry on your account. For you Ranchipur must be deadly." And suddenly she felt very young and very happy, "No, it really isn't."

"I must go now, Miss MacDaid is waiting for me at the barracks."

Quickly she said, "Won't you have a drink or at least a cup of tea?" He could not go now, as quickly as this, still in the cold professional role of doctor. Somehow she must change that. Somehow she must lead the thing onto a different plane.

Then he smiled for the first time, and the charm and simplicity in his smile made her feel suddenly ill. "If it's all ready you might give me a cup."

"It's cold now. I'll send for some fresh."

"It doesn't matter. I'll take it as it is. I haven't time to wait." And out of her instinct and a long experience she knew by the way he smiled and looked at her that he had forgotten for a moment that he was the doctor. For a moment he had seen her as a woman. And she said to herself, "You must not go too fast. You are not in Europe and this is a kind of man you have never met before. You must not give your hand away. He must think you are something which you are not . . . he must think you are a decent woman."

So she kept her voice and eyes in control and poured him a cup of tepid tea and even drank a cup herself, although there was nothing she loathed so much. And for five brief minutes they talked, pleasantly and easily, for the great vitality of the Major made him easy company; and as they talked she watched him greedily, seeing his big sensitive hands, his great muscular shoulders, his fine head and the perfectly sculptured nose and full lips, studying them so that she might see him clearly after he had gone away, finding in him through her intelligence and her experience infallible signs of all the things she had hoped to find.

And then he finished his tea and took up the cigarette left behind by Miss Hodge and said, "Now I must be off. I'll drop in again in the morning. I've done what I could to keep down your husband's temperature. There's nothing to do but wait until the symptoms become clearer."

And he went away without telling her what he had discovered that morning, that at the royal stables the rats were dying like flies and that one of the stableboys would be dead by tomorrow morning, all his glands horribly swollen, his tongue dry and burnt by the terrible fever.

When Fern crossed the drive from the Smileys a little after daylight she found her room undisturbed and the note exactly where she had left it, pinned to the pillow the way people pinned notes in the cinema; but now the note, like so many other things, seemed to have changed. The sight of it filled her with shame as if she were another Fern from the one who had left it there a few hours before. It seemed to her that a silly child had pinned it there and run out into the rain, a child whom she saw quite clearly now as if she were another person. But the Fern who stole into the house through a window in the wet light of the early dawn she could not see at all. She did not know her, what she was like or whither she was bound. It was not that she had changed so much as that she was changing, and that an odd thing had happened to her. Before she "ran away forever" she had always been inside herself. Herself had been the beginning and end of existence. Nothing happened save inside herself; all else was vague and unreal unless it happened to touch her momentarily. And now, for a moment or two, she had somehow got outside and saw herself from a distance. It gave her a strange feeling of excitement and made her feel grown-up and strong. It seemed to her that she was aware of other people for the first time and that until now she had been quite blind, not seeing them at all in reality, but only as shadows which did not touch her. She had "seen" Ransome and Mrs. Smiley for the first time, and now she might go on "seeing" other people.

Almost at once she fell asleep again and when she wakened it was to the sound of her mother's voice calling her to breakfast. She answered and then, throwing one arm over her head, buried her face in the pillow and slept again.

Belowstairs where Mr. and Mrs. Simon and Hazel, still rather bleareyed because she always wakened slowly, sat at breakfast, Mrs. Simon announced that Fern again had "the sulks" and that she supposed it was "over this Harry Loder business." But when Fern did appear at last, a little before lunch, she was neither ill-tempered nor sulky, and when her mother announced that Mr. Simon had found it possible to get away to Poona on Saturday Fern said perfectly quietly, "Then I suppose we should get started with the packing."

All through the afternoon and the evening until she went to bed she appeared astonishingly sweet-tempered, so gentle and so agreeable that Mrs. Simon, while they all sat together like a united happy family in the sitting room after dinner, began to consider plans for the wedding; but she did not yet dare to speak of it lest it set Fern off again. It was only after Mrs. Simon had gone to bed and Mr. Simon was asleep at last that she began to grow suspicious. A Fern who was too sweet-tempered might be up to something. And then the following morning, while Fern was helping her put away the woolens and linens, she discovered that her suspicions were correct, when Fern suddenly stopped in the midst of the work and said, "Mama, I don't want to go to Poona."

"You don't want to go to Poona? What on earth do you mean?"

"I mean that I want to stay here. I hate Poona."

"Stay here all through this awful weather? Why, *nobody* stays in Ranchipur during the monsoon."

Fern wanted to say that some twelve million people stayed behind in Ranchipur, among them quite a few Europeans like Ransome and Miss MacDaid and the Smileys, but she held her tongue because she was determined to have her way and give her mother no opportunity for starting a quarrel about something which had nothing to do with the main issue. That was what always happened; somehow in every argument which concerned Mrs. Simon the subject of the original discussion always managed to be lost.

"Why, pray, don't you want to go to Poona? Don't you meet lovely people there? Isn't everyone nice to you? Why, Hazel loves it."

"I'd like to stay here. Everybody in Poona is 'phoney.' Everything is 'phoney.' Everything they do is 'phoney.'"

Mrs. Simon, perplexed, regarded her with astonishment. Then she said, still having no idea what Fern meant, "I wish you wouldn't use words like that. People here don't know what you mean, and it makes you sound common. I don't know where you pick up all this American slang."

For a moment Fern came very near to losing her temper. There was something maddening in her mother talking of "commonness," as if she knew what it was. That was one of the things which mysteriously Fern had learned over night—what commonness was. In a way she had always known, but now she saw quite clearly. She knew what was common and what was not, and the knowledge made her feel sick and ashamed for some of the things she had done before she knew. Her mother, she knew, thought Harry Loder and Mrs. Hoggett-Egburry the very apotheosis of everything that was refined and distinguished, and nothing would change her conviction.

She only said, "I don't care whether people think I'm common or not."

"Well, I do and so does your father. We've both tried to give you a refined bringing-up. Anyway the whole idea is preposterous. Why can't you be pleasant and agreeable like Hazel?"

"Because I'm not like Hazel." What she meant was, "I'm not a born slattern. I'm not sloppy and good-natured."

"Hazel," continued her mother, "never tried to destroy the happiness of our family life."

The happiness—where was it? Fern knew now that it had never existed. Certainly she was not happy, nor her foolish bewildered father, bullied and tormented by his wife, nor even Hazel, unless one could say that cows were happy. And her mother with her envy and hatreds and baffled ambitions was the least happy of any of them.

"I won't even think of your staying behind," her mother went on. "A girl of your age alone in Ranchipur. What would Harry think?"

"I know what Harry would think," said Fern.

"What?"

"He'd try right off to get me to do what he wants me to do if he married me."

"Harry Loder is a gentleman."

"Well, don't drag him into it. I told you I wouldn't marry him if he was the last man on earth." And she kept seeing him and Ransome side by side in her mind as if they were put up on exhibition—the one smug, contented, bullying, the other gentle, defeated, despairing. She thought, "He needs me. I could do so much for him."

"Besides," she said, "I wouldn't be alone."

"Why wouldn't you be? Everyone we know is going away."

"Because there would be the Smileys. I could stay with them."

"The Smileys!" Her mother dropped the blanket she had been folding and sank back on her knees as if she had been struck. "The Smileys! You must be crazy! I thought there must be something the matter with you to go a whole day without the sulks."

"I'm not crazy. The Smileys wouldn't mind looking after me."

"They hate us . . . the Smileys."

And into Fern's mouth came the words of Ransome, "The Smileys don't hate anyone. They haven't time to hate."

A dull flush came over Mrs. Simon's face. It was an evil sign and Fern knew them all; once she had been confused and even frightened by these displays of her mother, but now she didn't care. Deep inside her she felt strong in the certainty that Ransome would understand her if no one else did. Moisture began to appear in Mrs. Simon's marble blue eyes. Presently she would begin to cry, and at last she would fling herself on the nearest sofa screaming that no one loved her, that her husband was a fool and her children ungrateful. She would cease to be a plump mature woman of forty-one and become a nasty spoiled child.

[235]

"You taking the side of the Smileys . . . against your own mother," she cried, "siding with that woman against the mother who bore you!"

"I'm not siding with anyone. Anyway there aren't any sides. The Smileys haven't got any feud."

Her mother stopped moaning and looked at her with suspicion: "How do you know so much about the Smileys?"

"I've been thinking about them. It's easy to see."

"Yes. You're very clever. Smarter than your mother or your father or anyone. Let me tell you, my girl, I could tell you things about the Smileys."

"What?" asked Fern.

"Don't be impudent. But plenty of things . . . about letters they've written home behind our backs. They're jealous of us because we know nice people." She began to cry again: "Siding with them after all the humiliation they've heaped upon us!"

"They've never heaped any humiliations on us. They've never paid any attention to us."

"Don't talk like your fool of a father. What would Mrs. Hoggett-Egburry think of your staying with the Smileys? After all I've tried to do for you. . . ."

This time Fern was silent. She went on folding linen and woolens, placing them in the teakwood chest, knowing that there was nothing she could do, nothing she could say now that would stop this outburst because her mother meant to go through with it to the end. It was never any use. You could never get the smallest thing settled. Somehow you always became mired in emotions and tears, and the muddled victory went to Mrs. Simon. For a moment she thought that she had been a fool not to have stayed at Ransome's, not to have gotten into his bed and screamed if he threatened to put her out. She knew now, more than ever, that there was no other way out; and anything was better than this. It would almost be better being married to Harry Loder, and she was frightened at the thought that if she had not run off to Ransome and come to know the Smileys she might one day have weakened out of weariness and said "yes" to Harry Loder. Now, that was impossible!

She did not look at her mother because she knew that if she looked at the faded swollen face and the eyes red with weeping she would be sick, but she could not help hearing the sobs and the sniffles and the blowing of the nose. She knew now that she hated her mother and that she had always hated her, even as a child, without knowing it. When she had said to herself as a little girl, "I don't want to be like mama," it was because she knew all the time in her childish mind that her mother was a fool and unscrupulous and selfish and common. It was awful to hate your own mother but more horrible still to be ashamed of her. Even if she did escape one day, even if she did marry somebody like Ransome, her mother would always be there, forcing her way in, shameless and common.

When Fern remained silent Mrs. Simon took to the sofa as if she were overcome, but Fern went on working as if she were alone in the room because she knew that that gave her power; and presently her mother rose and left the room, slamming the door so violently that bits of mildewed plaster fell from the ceiling just above it.

Fern knew where she would go. It was a simple matter of routine. She would go to her bedroom and lock the door and pull down the shades and have what Mrs. Hoggett-Egburry called a "migraine," which was refined for headache. She would not come down to lunch and no one would see her all day until late that night she would unlock the door and admit the consolation of her husband.

Bending over the chest Fern thought, "Anyway, we shan't have to see her for the rest of the day;" and she began to cry, quietly without a sound, not out of self-pity like her mother, but simply because her mother made the world so ugly a place, and because she was tired, not physically for she was young and strong, but weary of her mother and Mrs. Hoggett-Egburry and Harry Loder and all the rest. Big tears rolled down her face and fell on the linen as she packed it away.

Lunch was a dreadful meal, with the rain falling outside and the heat steaming under the windows. Fern did not speak at all and Hazel was tearful as she always was when her mother had one of her spells, and Mr. Simon—pretending that nothing had happened because his wife's spells always filled him with shame—read the "Missionary News." The meal was no less friendly than it was day after day, year in and year out, but the absence of Mrs. Simon made a difference. She had a way of holding the family together, of keeping up the illusion of friendliness

[237]

and sympathy where in reality there was none. She "made" conversation which was sometimes more tiresome than silence. She pressed food upon her husband and daughters. Sometime, somehow, in her Mississippi past she had been taught that one should be "elegant" at meals because they were ceremonies not distantly related to weddings and funerals, at which there were certain formulas of speech and set conventions to be employed. Being indifferent toward food herself, she had no special interest in the quality of the food set on the table, but she believed that it was refined to behave as if all of it were delicious and that conversation was necessary whether one had anything to say or not. Chatter at meals was to Mrs. Simon as necessary as salt and pepper. And so they missed her clatter and felt lost because none of them was able to create the same effect.

When the meal was finished Fern went to her own room and after a while she fell asleep from the exhaustion and excitement of the last twenty-four hours, to be wakened about six o'clock by the sound of a motor outside the window. Because you could count the motors of Ranchipur on the fingers of one hand she rose and went to the window, thinking that it might be Ransome calling on the Smileys and that she might at least have a distant glimpse of him, but she found only the motor of Mrs. Hoggett-Egburry and Mrs. Hoggett-Egburry herself descending from it. It was a tiny motor, so tiny that a stranger seeing Mrs. Hoggett-Egburry standing beside it might have thought that she was meant to contain the motor rather than the motor Mrs. Hoggett-Egburry, but because motors were rare in Ranchipur it contributed to her prestige, and she always descended from it (while it rocked and swayed under her weight) as if she were a duchess descending from a Rolls-Royce to lunch at Claridge's.

Fern, watching her from the upper window, thought, "Someone has told her."

Belowstairs Mrs. Hoggett-Egburry, after a moment's wait, was summoned to the bedroom of Mrs. Simon. In all Ranchipur she was the only person ever admitted to the presence of Mrs. Simon during one of her spells.

For a little time Fern sat on the edge of the bed trying to plan what she would do if Mrs. Hoggett-Egburry *had* been "told." She was not fright-

ued now but cold and felt rather calm and superior, and presently she
-orgot Mrs. Hoggett-Egburry altogether and decided to write a letter to
her cousin back in Biloxi, feeling that for once she had something to
write, something as exciting as the things her cousin wrote to her . . .
about picnics and swimming parties and young men, the kind of young
men Fern longed to know, not like "the boys," but young men of her
own kind who had never heard of "rags" and "ragging."

She began the letter "Dear Esther," but before she had written two
pages she understood that something had gone wrong and that what
she had put on paper failed somehow to convey the quality of her adventure with Ransome. When she reread it she saw that it sounded
trivial and schoolgirlish and rather silly and it had not been at all like
that. Even her description of Ransome and of her feelings for him became something different. Ransome emerged simply as a kind of romantic cinema adventurer and her feeling for him seemed no different
from the palpitating descriptions which Esther wrote to her each time
she met an attractive young man. It was a feeling for which she could
find in her small vocabulary no words—a feeling, a secret feeling, which
seemed to make over the whole world, to bring to her a sense of freedom
and independence. Now she could see her mother exactly as she was,
and that gave her a secret power of which she was aware each time she
came into the room where her mother was. Nothing of this could she
write to her cousin because on paper it seemed idiotic and complicated.
She suddenly felt older and wiser than Esther and superior to her. Esther
who only knew boys her own age who were "swell" or "attractive" or
"marvelous." It was extraordinary how many young men she seemed
to know who fitted these three, her only, adjectives. None of these words
suited Ransome, and Fern, considering the problem for the first time,
doubted that Esther would understand any others. She saw now that in
a good many ways she was really older than Esther. For that she could
thank this strange isolated unnatural life which she led in Ranchipur.
And Ransome was a man, not a boy like the young men Esther wrote
about.

After a fourth attempt she gave up the idea of writing to Esther about
falling in love. Three days ago it would have been exciting to write

to Esther that she had had a proposal, even though it was only from Harry Loder, but now it scarcely seemed worth while. The drafts of the letter she carefully tore into tiny bits so that it would be impossible for her mother to piece them together. Then there was a knock at the door and one of the servants said that the *memsahib* would like to see her in her bedroom.

The moment she entered the darkened room Fern knew that her mother had been "told." Mrs. Simon lay propped up in bed with a wet cloth on her forehead, moaning faintly. Fern did not speak. Trembling a little she sat down and waited.

Her mother said, "I want you to tell me the truth, Fern."

"Yes."

"Is it true what Mrs. Hoggett-Egburry has just told me?"

"I don't know what she told you."

"That you've been going to Mr. Ransome's house at night . . . after dark!"

For a moment Fern hesitated. She saw at once that the story had grown rampantly, luxuriantly, the way stories grew in Ranchipur, and she saw that it was quite useless to deny it. It was no good even to say that she had been there only once and that nothing had happened, because in her mother's present mood that would not be bad enough to satisfy her. So she said, quietly, "Yes, it's true."

Mrs. Simon said, "Oh, my God!" and began to moan again. "How could you do such a thing? With a man of his reputation! Everybody in Ranchipur will know it."

Fern thought, "She's not thinking of me at all. She's only thinking of how she'll suffer." Aloud she said, "Yes, Mrs. Hoggett-Egburry will see to that."

"Don't you dare to say anything against Lily Hoggett-Egburry. She was right to come and tell me."

"How did she find out?"

"She found out from the servants, but it doesn't matter how she found out."

It was the first time Mrs. Simon had ever called Mrs. Hoggett-Egburry "Lily" and the sound of it infuriated Fern. The word "Lily" seemed to throw into relief all her mother's groveling snobbery. And it made

Fern suddenly see the two women, bound together in a common cause in a way she had never thought of them before—two fading belles, aware of their waning power, jealous of her because she was pretty and years younger than either of them. For a moment she had a quick picture of her mother talking to Ransome, shaking her "touched-up" curls, ogling him, talking very "Southern," and she saw now that all along her mother had wanted his admiration for herself. She had a horrible vision of what her mother would have been if she had not been the wife of a missionary forced into the mold of respectability, frustrated and bitter, hedged round by conventions and hypocrisies. She could see Mrs. Hoggett-Egburry and her mother, their heads together, excited, morbid, angry, talking about her and Ransome. It was all horrible and made her feel sick; and then she knew that she was going to strike back. She would hurt them both, for suddenly she knew how it could be done.

She heard herself saying, "Yes, it's true! It's all true! I've lived with Tom Ransome and I'm in love with him and he loves me!"

That did it! When she saw the effect upon her mother she wished suddenly that Mrs. Hoggett-Egburry was there too.

Her mother screamed and then threw off the damp cloth and sat on the edge of the bed looking, in her pale pink nightgown trimmed with lace, her hair bedraggled and still damp from the cloth, strangely like the fading "kept" women Fern had seen in the cinema.

"Now we'll have to leave Ranchipur . . . all of us. You've ruined and disgraced your father and Hazel and the mother who bore you, who's given up her whole life to you, who wanted to see you married respectably to a good husband!"

Fern did not speak. She simply sat, shaking and terrified, thinking, "Now I've done it. How am I going to get out of it?"

Her mother sobbed for a time and then stopping suddenly she asked, "How did you get in and out of the house?"

"I went out after you were in bed and . . ." Recklessness swept over her. "I stayed with the Smileys and came across the drive early in the morning before anyone was awake."

As she spoke she saw the faded pretty face of her mother grow hard, the jaws set, the lips part a little over the too small teeth.

"The Smileys," she said. "So that's it? Mrs. Smiley is a procuress, is she? I've always known it. God knows what orgies go on over there with all those dirty Indians coming and going. Oh, I've heard about Indians and what they do. . . . You're mother's not the simpleton you may think!"

The long-suffering Mrs. Simon became suddenly the Mrs. Simon of action. She began to walk up and down the room in her nightgown and then, stopping abruptly, she pulled it off over her head and for a moment stood naked and unashamed, while she snatched up her stockings and underwear.

"I know what I'll do. I'll go and see Ransome myself. There's only one way of putting everything right. He'll have to marry you."

Fern sprang up: "No! No! I won't marry him. He doesn't want to marry me. He said so. You mustn't go and see him. You mustn't!"

Mrs. Simon, clad now in a chemise and one stocking, stopped dressing and looked at her: "You won't marry him, won't you? Well, we'll see about that. What kind of a daughter have I anyway . . . a . . . ?"

"Yes," said Fern, "a whore!" She pronounced the letter "W" because she had never heard the word spoken and it was a word that was not common in the cinema. Mrs. Simon resumed her dressing. "I'm going straight to Ransome," she cried; "and as for the Smileys, I'll fix them!" Her mouth grew hard and the blue eyes more than ever like marble at the thought of the Smileys delivered thus into her hands.

Fern began to cry: "Please don't! Please! It isn't true any of it. I was lying."

"Oh, don't try to get out of it now, young lady. He's going to marry you, all right. Just leave it to me."

The girl fell on her knees and tried to hold her mother's legs to stop her but Mrs. Simon kicked herself free.

"Don't!" cried Fern. "I'll do anything. I'll promise anything."

"Don't even speak to me. I ought to put you out of the house. But I won't. Oh, no! That's what you'd like . . . to go on the streets."

Fern was lying on her face now, moaning, and Mrs. Simon, pulling her dress over her head with fury, thrust one arm through the lining instead of into the sleeve and was trapped, so that her words came out through the cloth, muted and confused.

Then Fern sat up quietly on the floor watching her as she sat before the dressing-table mirror prettifying herself with cold deliberate fury. There was something horrible in the scene which brought to Fern a sudden calmness and even dignity, as if this woman putting powder on her nose before the mirror existed at a great distance, a stranger having nothing to do with her. A kind of cold relief came to her. It was all over now, they need never again pretend even to like each other.

She rose and said quietly, "All right. Do what you want. You'll be sorry. I'm through. I hate you!" But in her terrified heart she knew that nothing, no threat, would stop her mother, and all at once she saw that without knowing it she had played into her mother's hands. Her mother thought, "Now Ransome will have to marry her. Beside him Harry Loder is nothing at all. His brother might die and he might be an earl and then I'd have a fine place to spend my old age. . . . The mother of a countess! I never dreamed of anything as good as that." Fern understood suddenly why in all her mother's fury there had been a note of triumph.

Without another word she left the room, thinking only that she must go at once to Ransome to warn him. She had learned one more bitterness —that maternal love could be a delusion, that it could serve as a cloak to hide selfishness and egotism and evil. She knew that she had been deceived by a fraud for twenty years, since the day she was born.

Mrs. Simon scarcely noticed her going. Before she put on her hat she sat down and wrote a letter to the Mission Board about the Smileys, a letter which surely now would mean their ruin and recall. When it was finished she took the motor and, swollen with triumph and evil, she drove to the station where she posted the letter so that it would catch the Bombay Express and the Saturday boat to Genoa, not knowing that it would be the last time for weeks that any mail would leave Ranchipur.

While he dressed for dinner Ransome had two more drinks. It was difficult for others, especially strangers, to know when he was drunk; one had to know him very well in order to recognize the point at which he became a trifle too polite, a bit too ironic, a *soupçon* too considerate and too interested in what you were saying; but Ransome knew. It was the point at which that eternal feeling of melancholy and depression left him, the moment when he no longer felt paralyzed and incapable of action or decision because in the back of his mind there was always a consciousness that no decision and no action was of any importance. It was not that drinking brought him either strength of will or faith, but that drinking made the lack of these things seem unimportant and trivial. Drinking made the world become a bright and careless place in which nothing mattered and one was no longer troubled and tortured because it did not matter. The change came slowly. The faint surliness, the irony, the sarcasm, the bitterness which afflicted him sober, vanished to be replaced by a good-natured recklessness which was infectious because of his charm and so extremely dangerous to others. Drunk he was happy and that was the only reason for his drinking.

Now as he fastened his tie he knew that he was drunk and was glad, because whatever happened at Mr. Bannerjee's dinner he would neither be bored nor restless nor disagreeable. One was offered cocktails at Mr. Bannerjee's because it was smart and European, but Mr. Bannerjee himself did not drink because of religious scruples, and so he never knew that his cocktails tasted rather like mouthwash and there were never enough of them. He had never before been bored at the thought of going to Mr. Bannerjee's because the whole household was preposterous and because in the midst of it there was always Mrs. Bannerjee and her frigid beauty to lend interest to the evening. He dreaded it now only because Edwina was going. "Edwina," he thought, "with her bored weary European point of view." Edwina was certain to afflict the whole party with a kind of social paralysis in which the very air itself would seem charged with weariness and boredom.

For two days, avoiding her, he had not seen her at all save for that moment or two in the hallway of the palace before he drove to El-Kautara. Now, drunk, he knew perfectly well why he had avoided her; she upset him. He detested her because her very nearness filled him with weariness, but if he had only detested her she would not have troubled him. At the same time he found her attractive, with her cold-blooded abandon, her lovely viciousness and her perfection as a woman of elegance. All these things attracted him because once a long time ago, with her humor, her beauty and her wildness, she had been able to save him for a time from his own morbid nature. That she could no longer do; for that she had less power than the brandy he drank; but her

[244]

presence, her voice, her tired smile did serve to excite him. He knew now that he hated her because she made him feel sordid, because she was in a way a mirror of himself. And she made him feel frightened too. He had been a little frightened ever since the snatched mechanical delight of that weary adventure at the palace, because in the depression which followed it he had looked for a moment into such an abyss of emptiness and negation and despair that drunkenness, drugs, death itself seemed far better than the desolation he divined; anything was better that would blunt the edge of the consciousness so that it was no longer possible to regard the ruin of oneself.

Now, even drunk, he regretted that he had not made some excuse to stay away from the dinner. John the Baptist hovered about naked in the heat, handing him his clothes, brushing off bits of invisible dust, watching him stealthily, vaguely fascinated, he knew, at the spectacle of his master slowly making himself drunk.

John the Baptist was very good at watching. Never once did Ransome, even when he turned quickly, ever catch him staring directly, but all the time he knew that the servant was studying everything he did, every change of expression in his face. He could feel the boy's eyes on his back, and he became fascinated by the speculation of what it was that John the Baptist saw and what it was that went on inside his round black head. And at last as he turned from the mirror he said suddenly, "What is it you see? What are you looking at?"

But John the Baptist was not to be caught. His face went cold and opaque. In his soft Pondicherry French, he said, *"Je ne comprends pas. Je ne vois que vous, Sahib."*

"But what do you see? Am I different? Why are you staring?"

"Rien de différent," said John the Baptist. And then he understood that it was impossible ever to discover what was going on inside the head of his servant. Perhaps John the Baptist was only interested in the process of a man's getting drunk. Perhaps he was glad or maybe he was sorry. Or it might be that John the Baptist saw him as he did not see himself even in moments of self-reproach, as a broken, useless, dissipated man to whom it was worth while to be devoted because the place was good and easy and there was money in it. Perhaps he was thinking, "One more European going the way of the others. One more European

who soon will be finished." For five years they had been together but he had not the faintest idea of what his servant thought of him . . . and suddenly he was filled with shame.

At last he was dressed and as he turned to put on his jacket he saw Fern standing in the doorway. She wore the same old raincoat and felt hat, and she had been running, yet she did not look flushed but pale and frightened. He knew at once that he was glad to see her and the thought went swiftly through his muddled brain that it would be much more agreeable to stay here all the evening with Fern, but he knew too that such a thing was impossible in Ranchipur.

"Hello!" he said. "Come in." And to John the Baptist he said, "That's all"; and the servant passed Fern on the verandah and ran across the garden to his quarters.

"Something awful has happened," she said. She did not cry as she had always done before.

"What?"

"My mother has found out."

He laughed. In his present mood, it did not matter. It was merely funny. "I thought she would," he said, "but not so soon."

"It was Mrs. Hoggett-Egburry who told her. She got it out of her servants."

"The black bastard!" thought Ransome. "He didn't waste much time." Even through the pleasant haze of drunkenness he was aware that Fern had changed. She seemed older. Even the faint pudginess which made her pretty instead of beautiful seemed to have gone from her face, and she was not hysterical now.

"That's not the worst. We had an awful quarrel and I lost my temper and told my mother that it was true and that I'd been coming here all the time and living with you."

Again he wanted to laugh, because at once he understood the quarrel and knew why it was that Fern had confessed to something which had never happened. His mind leapt quickly.

"Has your father a shotgun?" he asked.

She looked at him, puzzled, and then said, "He's not like that. He'd never do anything."

[246]

"Oh, it's your mother who keeps the shotgun." And this time he laughed aloud.

"It isn't funny," Fern said. "It's awful."

"I was only laughing at the picture of your mother arriving with a shotgun. Anyway we know it isn't true."

"That doesn't make any difference. Don't you see, she wants it to be true?"

"Why?"

"So you'll *have* to marry me. Don't you see?"

He did see. She did not have to humiliate herself by explaining what her mother was—that she would like nothing better than having her daughter ruined as long as it was accomplished by the brother of an earl.

"She's forgotten already all about Harry Loder."

"Yes," he said soberly, "I see the difference in the candidates and I think she's quite right."

"You'd better get out right away. She's on her way here."

Then he sat down and began to laugh and he was tipsy enough so that it was difficult to control himself. Fern watched him for a moment and the tears came into her eyes.

"Don't laugh . . . please don't . . . please!" A kind of pleading came into her voice, so evident that it sobered him. "It isn't funny," she said in a very quiet voice. "Don't you see it isn't funny? You're making it so awful."

"No," he said, "it isn't funny. I'm sorry. I've been . . ."

"I know," she said. "But please go. Please go tonight to Bombay."

"What about you?"

"It doesn't matter. I don't care any more. I can take care of myself."

He was aware of a faint note of reproach in what she said.

"What will you do?"

"I'll face the music. I don't mind."

For a moment he was silent, wishing that he was sober; and then he said, "What if we *did* get married?"

"I wouldn't marry you for a million dollars."

"Well, that's that!" But he was, she suddenly saw, too drunk to understand what she meant. There was a look of hurt in his face and she

[247]

knew that he thought she would not marry him because he was a drunkard and no good. She wanted to explain that it was her pride that made her say it, but the same pride held her back. She could not do it.

"Look here," he said, "you mustn't go home. You can't do that. You can't put up with another row."

"If only I had a little money I could do as I please."

"That's right. It's a pity. No, you can't go home. Go to the Smileys."

"I can't do that either. I've already made enough trouble for them. I told her about them too."

He grinned again, "That wasn't very wise."

"I didn't know what I was doing."

"I can't ask you to stay here. That would only make it worse." And an idea came to him: "You could go and stay with Raschid."

"I couldn't do that. I don't know him."

"I do. He is minister of police and he has a wife and seven children. Nothing could be more respectable."

"But he's an Indian."

"What difference does that make? He's a fine fellow."

She remembered what her mother had said about "the dirty Indians" who went to the Smileys. "It doesn't make any difference to me, but it might give her an excuse to make trouble . . . you don't know what she's like. She might take it to Delhi—even to the Viceroy. She might do anything."

Yes, he saw what she meant, and again he wanted to laugh. It was preposterous the way the perfectly harmless escapade of a romantic schoolgirl had become an extraordinary affair, and now it was threatening to become an "incident" which might unsettle the peace of India, a scandal of international proportions which might become historic. And for the first time he saw inside the thing that was the Indian question, all the infinite complications which could be made by small people, the hopeless tangle of meanness and jealousy and fear and pettiness and prejudice. He was aware, even through his drunkenness, for the first time of how Indians must feel. He understood the subtle and sinister quality of the humiliations and the insults compounded by second-rate people like Mrs. Hoggett-Egburry and Mrs. Simon. A girl of European

[248]

origin could not seek refuge from a sluttish mother in the house of the most honorable and upright of men, because he was an Indian.

"Yes," he said gloomily, "it's a sick world . . . a lousy world."

But Fern was direct, without interest in politics or philosophy or mankind. She said, "No, there's only one thing to do. I'll go back home now. I'm not afraid of her any longer. I think maybe she's afraid of me now. I know she is. But you've got to go away. You've got to! See?"

He saw that she was no longer trusting him. She had come to him thinking that he might be able to help her and he had been able to do nothing because he was drunk and muddled and useless, because in his heart at this moment he did not care what happened, because he was unwilling as always to accept responsibility, because it all seemed no longer serious at all but only funny, inexpressibly funny.

"I don't know," he said feebly. "You go back. Tomorrow . . . when things are different . . ."

"It's all right. Don't worry about it too much. It's all my fault anyway. I don't know how any of it happened, except that I must have been crazy. I'm sorry I was such a fool!"

He looked at her for a long time, seeing even through the haze of drunkenness how young she was and how charming and earnest, and he saw too that now she was no longer looking to him to help her. It was the other way round. Then he said, "No, you weren't crazy. You aren't crazy at all." He thought, "I wish I had you with me always, forever"; but it was too late now.

Abruptly she said "good by" and went out of the house into the rain. He sat for a long time in the chair opposite the door and at last he remembered Mr. Bannerjee's dinner and rose and took another drink to drown the somber thoughts which had taken possession of him and to give him the strength to go to the garden house and send John the Baptist away because he had gossiped and betrayed his master. It was a disagreeable task and although he had no idea what John the Baptist was like inside, he knew that he was used to him and even fond of him. But when he reached the garden house it was already empty. The servant had not gone away for good because his few belongings and the little wooden chest which contained them was still there. Ransome thought, "He does know me better than I thought. He has disappeared

[249]

because he knows that tomorrow I will not send him away because by then it will have become too much trouble to find a new servant and because tomorrow I will see that his gossiping was, after all, unimportant and only human. He knows that tomorrow I will understand that it was not he who caused the evil but Mrs. Simon and Pukka Lil and all those like them."

Mrs. Simon arrived five minutes after he had left and found the house quite empty. In the anticlimax all the righteous indignation which she had carefully preserved all the way to the station and back oozed out of her and curiosity took its place. For three years she had wanted to see the inside of this house and now she satisfied her desire, going from room to room, even into his bedroom where the sight of his brushes and pipe and bed gave her a certain voluptuous excitement for which Mr. Simon would have to pay later on. It was a disappointment, the house, because it seemed so simple and so bare and not at all like her idea of what the house of an English gentleman should be, not at all the way the houses of such men were in the cinema, not at all like Lily Hoggett-Egburry's house.

When she had examined everything she drove directly to the Smileys' and there made a terrible scene in order to relieve her baffled spirit. The Smileys, bewildered, attempted at first to explain in terms of simple humanity, but after a moment it became evident that simple humanity was something beyond the understanding of Mrs. Simon and they both fell silent. It was Aunt Phoebe who answered her at last in her own language. When she could bear the tirade no longer she called Mrs. Simon "a poor-white slut" and told her to go across the drive and never enter the house again.

Part II

Part II

Mr. Bannerjee's house was that rare thing in Ranchipur, a house constructed of lath and stucco. It was in every way a very odd house, designed and built cheaply seventy-five years earlier beneath the eye of Lady Streetingham, the eccentric wife of the Resident during the reign of the Wicked Maharajah, to house her guests. Being a woman of great sociability and considerable wealth, married to a bore and exiled by her husband's duties to a barbarous state, it was her habit to invite everyone she met to come and stay with her as long as he liked; and so she had constructed a house which was rather like a tavern with a great many ramshackle outbuildings to house the servants.

The house itself, perhaps because of its odd shape, had a bizarre charm. It was octagonal, with a piazza on the ground floor, and a balcony on the second which ran the entire way around the house, and the roof was flat, with a stairway leading up to it, so that the guests might use it in the fashion of the East and on hot nights lie there in the open air beneath a brilliant blue sky spangled with glittering stars. At the back, like a clumsy tail, there was a barrack-like wing added as an afterthought when the main house became too small to house all the adventurers and remittance men who accepted the invitations of the Resident's rich and eccentric wife; for the building quickly became a kind of boarding-house for people who were down and out, until at last it achieved a spectacular notoriety and brought about the recall of the Resident himself. In its day, it had done more to lower the prestige of Europeans in Ranchipur than any other element in the history of the place. The sight of the piazza dubiously ornamented by the figures of Lady Streetingham's strange guests, the rumors of the debauchery and drunkenness which took place inside its walls, the murder of a servant and finally the murder of one guest and the suicide of another—all these things and many more had given the house such a name and such a legend that for years after the retirement, it remained tenantless, and even the lowest coolie never passed it without a faint scornful curl of the lip. This, the people of Ranchipur told themselves, was a spectacle of what European civilization was like.

In those days it took a long time for news to find its way across the whole of India from Ranchipur to Government House in Calcutta, and an even longer time for those in power to believe that things in the guesthouse of the Resident's rich and eccentric wife were as bad as they were reported to be. The murder and suicide put an end to the Resident and his wife and to the guest-house itself, but by that time the damage was done and for thirty years afterward the legend of its bawdiness lingered, corrupting the opinion of the twelve million inhabitants of the great rich state of Ranchipur, making it a difficult state filled with troubles and complications and smothered rebellion. But in an odd way the legend of the guesthouse had been a great help to the old Maharajah in his efforts to enlighten his people and fill them again with the pride which had once been theirs, because it had weakened and corrupted that mysterious weapon which the European called "prestige," and brought to the natives of Ranchipur a sense of equality. It weakened, too, the authority of the central government, which before long discovered that the guests of Lady Streetingham had rendered it extremely difficult to manage the people of Ranchipur, and so the people and their Maharajah were given a free hand. The central government turned away its face for the sake of peace, and permitted Ranchipur to go its own way.

The house was already falling into ruin when the Maharajah reclaimed it as a residence for his librarian, Mr. Bannerjee. The librarian was by nature rather like old Lady Streetingham, extremely hospitable and indiscriminate in his hospitality; luckily his taste was more conventional. The Resident's lady had not much cared whom she had for guests so long as they were outwardly human, could talk, and remained sober enough to play whist with her; Mr. Bannerjee, on the other hand, behaved rather like a professional Mayfair hostess. He was the leader of a society which was neither Indian nor European, but a mixture of the two. Mr. Bannerjee was a snob. He had been educated at Oxford, and there, largely by observation and instinct rather than by contact, he had acquired a snobbery which in its essence was not British, but something purer than that; it was English. His snobbery lay imposed like a veneer on the darker Indian side of his character. He was very like his own parties, a strange mixture of elements which he was never quite able to bring together into a harmonious whole. As the leader of the cosmopolitan set in Ranchipur, important guests of the Maharajah were sent to him for at least one dinner or tennis party. The British suburban set, ruled over by Lily Hoggett-Egburry, professed to hold him in scorn, although in their hearts they were eaten up with rage and envy that the real plums like Lord and Lady Esketh were always entertained by Mr. Bannerjee and seldom seen by themselves. On the other hand, the real Indians distrusted Mr. Bannerjee and his Oxford ways and held him in scorn because he seemed forever unable to decide upon which side of the fence he meant to descend. But Mr. Bannerjee had created a world and a position of his own, a world which at times seemed a little like the world which had used his house as a club in the time of Lady Streetingham. It was known as "Mr. Bannerjee's set" and his awareness of this filled him with pride and made him bear himself in Ranchipur with a strange manner in which arrogance and timidity were in perpetual conflict. And he was rich, as a leader of society needs to be, for when the older Mr. Bannerjee, his father, had retired from an extraordinarily prosperous counting-house and insurance office in Calcutta to withdraw into a life of meditation, he had given everything he possessed to his son. Mr. Bannerjee also had a beautiful wife and a position of eminence and authority and even power, but he was not a happy man, for there was a great deal which Mr. Bannerjee had to conceal from the world.

There was his own indecision and the weakness of a character and a personality that was cleft exactly in twain. Only someone with an all-seeing eye could have known this, for only someone with an all-seeing eye could have believed that the Mr. Bannerjee, debonair and a little arrogant, passing out cocktails at a tennis party and talking about the theater in London and the races in Paris, was the same man who in the early morning crept out from the octagonal house into the maze of ramshackle outbuildings at the far end of the compound to cut the throat of a goat before a small and monstrous statue of Kali already smeared with the blood of a hundred sacrifices. And no one but himself could know those awful moments in the very midst of a worldly and cosmopolitan dinner party when suddenly he became cold with fear and terror, when in a second of horror it was as if he saw Kali the Destroyer appear above the head of one of the guests to accuse him of having betrayed his blood, his race, and his faith. Only Kali herself could know that he had no children, not because his beautiful wife was barren, but because her silent scorn of him was so great that from the very beginning he had never been able to exercise his rights as a husband. She had never said anything. She talked to him scarcely more than she talked to the European guests beside whom she found herself seated now and then entirely by circumstance. The scorn was the same terrifying silent scorn of which Ransome himself had been aware again and again; it had tantalized Ransome with a perverse desire to humiliate her; Mr. Bannerjee it merely frightened into impotence.

Ransome went frequently to the Bannerjees' because, next to the palace itself, it was the only place where one sometimes met people who appeared to have brains. Now and then, there appeared in Ranchipur, a scientist or a writer or an architect or someone interested in Indian music or painting or sculpture or history. Ever since Mr. Bannerjee had come to Ranchipur, thirteen years before, the old Maharajah had cherished the illusion that at Mr. Bannerjee's the state guests could obtain a glimpse of real Indian life, although what one found there was neither Indian nor European but simply Mr. Bannerjee's somewhat fantastic idea of what a fast party was like in Park Lane in the time of Edward the Seventh.

But Ransome was fond of Mr. Bannerjee in a way, and sorry for him, because at times he came very close to understanding that Mr. Bannerjee's indecision and misery were not so different from his own. And of course, there was always Mrs. Bannerjee, cold and beautiful, chewing her *pan* and gossiping and giggling in a corner with some woman friend, exciting him only to leave him baffled and unsatisfied. But he was not happy at Mr. Bannerjee's house and he could never remember ever having enjoyed himself at one of the parties. What it was that depressed him he could not define exactly, save that it had the quality of something sinister. From the moment he entered the house until he left it he always felt faintly ill at ease and even awkward, as if somehow, instead of being

Ransome, the man who had seen everything in the world and had known every sort of person and was able to hold his own anywhere, he was simply a small boy at his first party. In the beginning he had merely been uneasy and bored, but when it happened again and again, he began to wonder at it and made an effort to analyze the feeling. At first he had told himself that in some half-mystical fashion it was the aura of the house itself, with its memories of two murders and a suicide, of drunkenness and debauchery, indulged in long ago by people now dead and in their graves. There were, too, the personality of Mrs. Bannerjee and the atmosphere of bitter marital unhappiness and the knowledge that always in the house only a little way from you, behind a wall or even perhaps behind a screen, there lurked the presence of Mr. Bannerjee's father, whom no one in Ranchipur save the Bannerjees and Major Safti and one or two servants had ever seen.

Once or twice in the enclosed garden at the back of the house where Mrs. Bannerjee kept her pets, Ransome had caught a glimpse of a white robe disappearing among the dustry shrubs. But the face and the figure of old Mr. Bannerjee he had never seen. Now and then his son spoke of him, quite casually, as if there was nothing mysterious about him, but into the face of the son there always came a look of reverence and awe at the mention of the old man's name. He told Ransome that the elder Mr. Bannerjee in his old age had given up all worldly pleasures to find wisdom, to contemplate, to prepare himself for another life; and the reverence and awe in the voice of the son impressed Ransome, not because he had any special respect for the Hindu faith, but because it seemed extremely odd that a worldly man like the son could be so profoundly moved by the old man's accession of holiness. And once, but only once, he asked somewhat irreverently, "What is this contemplation? What is it that he contemplates which is beyond the understanding of the rest of us? What is it he contemplates that he might not contemplate while living in the midst of his fellow men?"

Politely but with a certain coldness Mr. Bannerjee answered, "It is difficult to explain. It is something which you would not understand if you do not already see it." And then quickly he had changed the subject; but Ransome was aware he had been quietly snubbed and that suddenly Mr. Bannerjee had become frightened. In the way in which his face twitched a little and his eyes avoided those of Ransome, he was like a frightened hare.

He did not suppose that the air of sinister mystery about the house had anything to do with secret nameless sacrifices or hidden orgies of the kind cheap journalists had a way of ascribing to Hindu rites. It had its origin, he was certain, in nothing so obvious and sensational as that; yet it was, he came to feel more and more, a perfectly real and almost a tangible thing. It was *there*. If you had sharp eyes and ears and any sensibilities whatever, you felt it each time you went to the house. It hung like a subtle rather corrupt fragrance about the personalities of Mr. Bannerjee and his wife. It was in all the rooms. At moments it came sharply to light in an intonation, in a frightened glance, in the way the personality of even Mrs. Bannerjee herself could change suddenly while you were talking to her and become, instead of something which, however cold and aloof, was real and even familiar, something shadowy and half-savage and frightened. It was not an experience which Ransome found confined to the Bannerjees alone; he had encountered it a hundred times, a thousand times before in Indians; even the old Maharani, fierce and proud and independent, he had seen change suddenly in the same mysterious fashion while he was talking to her. In the Bannerjees' house it was simply more acute because Mr. Bannerjee was a Bengali and because all Mr. Bannerjee's pretenses at being an enlightened Indian and a model of European behavior, made the contrast more painful and the mystery doubly noticeable.

It was, Ransome slowly became convinced, the thing which set most Indians and Europeans apart, dividing them in the very midst of intimacy, desiccating the closest friendships and leaving them withered and empty. It was that thing which writers referred to vulgarly as "the mystery of India," yet Ransome, in his intelligence, could not accept this any more than he could accept the cheap tricks of the *fakirs*. He did not suffer mysteries easily, because he had found that in the end mysteries, even the most esoteric Hinduish ones, always had explanations which were perfectly simple.

After a time he began to ask questions of Indians whom he looked upon as friends, but he made very little progress until he went to Major Safti. It was no good, he soon discovered, in asking Raschid Ali Khan.

No Muslim understood it; indeed the bluff and hearty Raschid held the opinion that it was this mystery which made the Hindu cowardly and treacherous and unreliable and lay profoundly at the root of the troubles between all Muslims and Hindus. It appeared to irritate and puzzle the Muslims far more than it irritated and puzzled Ransome himself.

But Major Safti was a Hindu, a Brahmin who was "free," freed perhaps by ancestors who, instead of cowering before the mystery and the terror, had fought it, freed too perhaps by his own faith in science and the power of man's intelligence against the evil of Nature enshrined in the bodies of mysterious gods.

"It is," he said, "the great Indian sickness. You might call it the Hindu evil. It stifles and suffocates and paralyzes. It is like the stench which hangs over the poor quarter when there is an outbreak of plague or smallpox."

They discussed it again and again, sometimes on the verandah of Ransome's house, sometimes in the Major's office at the hospital, when Miss MacDaid would come in for a moment to listen, and then snort in scorn that they should be wasting their time talking about things which made no sense. All that was needed to save India, she would say, was education and cleanliness and enough to eat.

The Major liked talking about it, as if each time he talked of it, the thing became somehow a little clearer to himself. And each time he made it seem a little clearer to the reason and understanding of Ransome himself.

"It is mystical in its origin," he said, "and still, I suppose, mystical in its manifestations. To understand it you must know and understand the whole history of the Hindu religion—its origins, its rise, its decay. I don't know anything quite like it in history save perhaps the strange hysterical faiths of the Dark Ages in Europe when hermits took to caves to 'contemplate' like that mysterious old fraud, Mr. Bannerjee's father. Men of intelligence went into monasteries because that was the only place left where they might keep alive the flame of culture and civilization. It is like the cloud which hung over all Europe in those times . . . a cloud of what might—yes, what must, I suppose—be called faith and religion despite all its baseness and superstitions, when Christianity became for a time an evil compound of the teachings of Christ strangely mixed with

Druid paganism and superstitions born long before in the swamps of Germany, sprinkled with a seasoning of Roman and Greek ideas and superstitions. It entered every house and the life of every man save those shut away in monasteries or living like animals in caves. It filled the minds and lives of even intelligent people with hosts of witches and demons and incubi and made them live by terror and faith in evil rather than faith in good. It occurred during the break up of a great empire, of a whole civilization.

"You see, a retired insurance agent like old Mr. Bannerjee is afraid and so he retires to become holy because all his life he has not been holy at all. All the money he has piled up did not come from too holy a beginning and he is afraid, of what he doesn't quite know, but he is afraid. And Bannerjee himself is afraid. For all his fine manners and his high talk he is a coward and now and then he becomes terrified by the vast imponderable mass of things beyond his understanding."

He chuckled suddenly and said, "Even the old Maharani is afraid sometimes. I've seen her when she forgets that she is enlightened, that she has founded a high school for girls and put through a law which makes it honorable for Hindu women to divorce their husbands. It doesn't make any difference. Sometimes the *thing* takes possession of her and makes her again the half-wild, superstitious creature she was when they brought her here from the hills long ago. It hangs over all India like a cloud . . . a religion which has never known a reformation, a religion which, like all faiths, was born out of nature itself and rose once to great heights and now has descended again, corrupted and wasted to the level of a savage religion of images and taboos, which worships the principle of evil and destruction as much as the principle of good and creation. Perhaps in its manifestations it is more savage and terrifying than the pagan Christianity of the Dark Ages ever was, but that is not because the people are different. It is because of India itself . . . not the people, but the earth, the sun, the sky, the very life of India which is cruel and ruthless. It is a country of burning sun and dry plains and wild cloudbursts where nothing is ever wholly peaceful and green and pleasant, a country crawling with life and where the very principle of life itself seems at times to become menacing and evil and destructive . . . a country filled with snakes and wild beasts and floods and droughts and earthquakes, where even nature itself is more hostile than elsewhere. And yet a continent swarming with life . . . as overcrowded, as overfertile, as Africa is empty and sterile."

And then the Major would suddenly grow still and grave and even sigh and say, "You see, that's what it is . . . this India. That's why it has always been tortured and tormented . . . why its rulers have always been incredibly splendid and barbaric, why its misery and sickness are beyond the misery and sickness of other nations. It is a country of savage exaggerations where cruelty is more cruel than elsewhere and beauty more beautiful, and out of that came an all-embracing faith which rose to great heights and then decayed again into a worship of the savage principle of destruction. Anywhere in the world nature is always an enemy until subdued by the hand and the intelligence of man, but in India nature is a monster whom we have never tamed even a little. One has, I suppose, to worship her in the figure of Kali because nothing else seems logical. Miss MacDaid is partly right. We can educate Indians. We can feed the children properly. We can try at least to stamp out disease, but in the end nature will always win. We have gone a long way in Ranchipur, but in the end we may be defeated by India herself, India the continent, the unconquerable.

"What Mr. Bannerjee is afraid of is not simply these vague symbols which have been set up as gods, but of something far more savage and profound. He is terrified of India itself. The gods are only shadows. It is the drought and the monsoons and the earthquakes, the leprosy, the plague, the typhus, the burning sun and the barren sky, which lie at the root of his terrors. But Mr. Bannerjee is not very intelligent, so he thinks it is Kali whom he fears. He is aware, and rightly, that in spite of all his Oxford education and his talk of London and Paris he is Indian and that he can never escape India." Again he sighed and added, "Perhaps we shall be defeated. I don't think it is as simple as Miss MacDaid believes. Anyway, we can try. But it's not easy when all your people live by fear instead of by faith. You in Europe are dying because you no longer have faith, but sometimes I think no faith at all is better than ours. Because it is fear that we have to overcome, fear and denial and negation. That's where our friends the Muslims have the upper hand. They aren't afraid of anything on heaven or earth . . . not even of India. They came hearer to subduing her than any men have ever done, but they too were defeated. She has never been conquered even by the British. They are here by sufferance until one day India with all that is evil and good stirs in her sleep and gives one mighty roll, and then they will tumble off like Asoka and Alexander and the Moghuls and the Tartars and the Chinese."

In the voice and eyes of the Major there were sadness and defeat, the sadness and defeat which Ransome had seen so many times in so many Indian eyes, but there was, too, a kind of smouldering triumph and pride, perhaps in the knowledge that he was a part of the vast, unconquerable, tragic continent. The Major had neither the tough optimism of Raschid Ali Khan, forever proudly aware of his conquering blood, nor the bird-like cheerfulness of Mr. Jobnekar, freshly released from the servitude and oppression of centuries. The Major was more intelligent than either of them and he had, as well, the instinct and the sensibility of a race and a caste whose age could scarcely be measured by time.

There were moments when even the Major was frightened. For Ransome that was a part of his fascination—that he was at once a boy and yet as old as time, that he found life too painful to be borne save by plunging full into the midst of it, by losing himself in its very horror and confusion. For the Major it would be forever impossible to withdraw into the deep negation of the contemplative life.

Ransome left the house on foot to go to Mr. Bannerjee's because he was drunk and filled with a sudden fierce conviction that contact with the monsoon storm might free him from the depressing sense of petti-ness and evil with which Fern's story had infected him. Tipsily he felt that despite the old mackintosh and felt hat he wore, the rain would wash him clean. "Cleanness," he said, half aloud. "That is what I want, cleanness."

He thought, "If it is raining hard when I come home, the Major can drop me off."

He did not want to be brought home by Edwina. He did not even want to make the short journey of two minutes in the same car with her. And he knew well enough that if she came to the door she would come in and talk and have a drink, for she was a child of the night who hated sleeping save by day, and was never properly awake until after sundown. By daylight there was at times something faded and tired about her, but at night she always appeared fresh and cool and lovely. It was as if the darkness brought her vitality and fascination. She would want to come in and talk, and he knew how that would end. They would drink and talk until presently even talk would grow wearisome and then they would repeat what had happened at the palace on the night of the dinner, for no reason at all save that the same weary, perverse attraction would drive them to it, as if they were under a compulsion born of satiety and exhaustion. And in the morning he would feel sick again and soiled and degraded. No, drunk now, walking through the rain, he saw the whole thing that drew them together quite clearly for the first time. It was if they were tired and frightened and embraced as a weary gesture of defiance at the rest of the world. They were like naughty, insufferable children thumbing their noses. He knew now. It was as if that night at the palace they had said to all the others, "—— you!" in a gesture of defiant exhibitionism, aware that no matter what they did or how they did it, the world would go on accepting them because they were both attractive and most of the world was so dreary and so mean, so like Mrs. Hoggett-Egburry and Fern's awful mother. There was even in Edwina's weariness and depravity something bright and dazzling . . . yes . . . something even that was clean. That was what made her power of corruption so devastating. God had given her too much, long ago in the beginning.

And then halfway to Mr. Bannerjee's the rain almost stopped and for a moment a sultry sun appeared just above the horizon, bathing everything in an evil sulphurous light. The houses, the walls, even the freshly washed green of the trees seemed to absorb and then give back the unearthly yellow glow. It was the kind of light, he thought tipsily, which must be provided by God to illumine the end of the world—a sick, leprous yellow light with the quality of decay and horror in it. It fell now full on Mr. Bannerjee's octagonal house, even touching the figures of the guests whom he could see through the opened windows; and the old feeling that the place was invested by some evil power returned to him more sharply than ever. Mr. Bannerjee's house, it seemed to him, should always be illumined thus.

Then, before he was halfway down the muddy drive, the sun vanished quickly below the horizon and left the still air damp and heavy and green once more, filled with that strange ominous sense of fertility which infected it during the rains when the air itself seemed so thick and so rich and damp that the plants and trees might live by air alone, drawing nourishment from it without the need of roots or soil. By the time he reached the verandah the yellow light had faded so that the sinister old house itself lay in darkness, its windows lozenges of light in which he saw the figures of the Bannerjees and Edwina, Miss MacDaid and Major Safti and Miss Murgatroyd talking and drinking cocktails.

As he climbed the steps he noticed that the barren aspidistras and rubber plants which ornamented the verandah had burst miraculously into bloom. From their dull green leaves, as if by some piece of magic, the blossoms of the marigold, the zinnia, the hollyhock, the begonia, the carnation had burst forth in a riot of color. It was a spectacle of madness and decadence in the world of plants which offended the gardener's sense in Ransome; and then he understood. The strange flowering was the work of old Mr. Bannerjee, who evidently considered the dinner one of the greater occasions in the social life of his son. On gala evenings he ornamented the sterile rubber plants and aspidistras with the blossoms of more showy and fortunate plants, tying each flower carefully on with a bit of thread. This time, Ransome thought, the ornamentation must be in honor of Edwina. Even old Mr. Bannerjee in his retirement and meditation was a snob.

There was never any need of being announced at Mr. Bannerjee's. The sound of a footstep on the verandah was enough to raise a chorus of shrieks and growls, screams and yappings, from Mrs. Bannerjee's Pekinese and from the dozens of parrots and macaws and parakeets who lived in cages and on perches the whole length of the verandah—a chorus which, like the plague, spread to all the birds and animals and children which lived in that huddle of outbuildings at the far end of the compound. Mr. Bannerjee's house and garden were a kind of India *in petto*, overcrowded, confused, swarming with noisy life.

Inside the house Mr. Bannerjee, very neat and smart in white clothes made in Savile Row, was pouring cocktails for Edwina, Miss MacDaid, and the Major. In a corner on a divan sat Mrs. Bannerjee and her confidante, Miss Murgatroyd, a little apart from the group, removed not alone by space but by an atmosphere of psychical detachment, as if their corner, hidden behind an invisible barrier, remained inviolate and Indian.

Miss Murgatroyd was a thin little spinster in her late thirties who acted as assistant to Mr. Bannerjee in the management of the libraries. She belonged neither to the Indian nor to the European world of Ranchipur and she had never married, partly because she was neither rich nor very attractive and partly because there was no one for her to marry save an Anglo-Indian like herself, and Miss Murgatroyd regarded all Anglo-Indians, sometimes even herself, with contempt. Although everyone in Ranchipur knew her secret, although anyone with the feeblest perception could guess it at once, although the odd color of her hair, the muddy texture of her skin, the blue eyes surrounded by yellowish whites, and the thin collapsible Indian hands all betrayed her, Miss Murgatroyd went through life cherishing the illusion that no one *knew*. She always said that her parents had died while she was a child and that her father had been a magistrate in the Madras Presidency, and she always dressed in European clothes which did not suit her and made her seem even plainer than she was. In a *sari* she might have passed for an Indian and kept a certain authenticity and even a certain dignity, but European clothes gave her a kind of fancy-dress appearance, full of falsity. The effect was the same as that of a middle-aged thoroughly Anglo-Saxon spinster dressed in a *sari* and bangles for a fancy-dress party. It was not only that she dressed as a European woman, but that she chose her frocks as badly as possible, selecting costumes which would have suited only the palest and fluffiest of blondes. Now, sitting primly beside the handsome and exotic Mrs. Bannerjee, she wore a gown of pale-blue taffeta ornamented with little garlands and rosettes of tiny flowers.

Ransome never saw her save at the library or at the Bannerjees' and apparently she had no other life. There was something timid and frightened and groveling about her which always made him feel a little sick, not only at the spectacle of Miss Murgatroyd herself, but at the human cruelty and prejudices which had deformed her whole character and personality, as disease may slowly deform a whole body which should have been sane and healthy. For the handsome Mrs. Bannerjee she was a kind of slave, fetching and carrying for her, flattering her, giggling with her in corners as she was now doing, applauding with gratified bitterness the mockery with which Mrs. Bannerjee treated nearly everyone who came her way. It was, Ransome thought, as if she were revenged through Mrs. Bannerjee upon all those, both Indians and Europeans, who snubbed her, as if it were only through Mrs. Bannerjee that she could discover enough self-respect to go on living.

The relationship existed, Ransome was certain, not because of any fondness Mrs. Bannerjee felt for her, but because on the one side Mrs. Bannerjee found her useful, and on the other Miss Murgatroyd would have found life unendurable without the little fillip of confidence which the relationship provided. After a long time, after having watched them together at dinner after dinner and tennis party after tennis party, the suspicion came to him that Mrs. Bannerjee, the proud Bengali, tortured Miss Murgatroyd, the timid Eurasian; Miss Murgatroyd, he suspected, was a kind of whipping-boy upon whom Mrs. Bannerjee might vent her hatred of everything European. But Miss Murgatroyd, it seemed, bore the cruelty and even welcomed it because it was the only thing in her life which made her seem important. Her worship of Mrs. Bannerjee was like that of the dullest, plainest girl in the school for the one who was most gifted and beautiful.

When he came over to the divan, Mrs. Bannerjee only stirred languidly but Miss Murgatroyd sprang up and began to gush.

"Oh, good evening, Mr. Ransome," she said. "It's been such a long time since we've met. I was hoping you'd be here. I was afraid you might have gone off to the hills."

"No," said Ransome, "I never go away any more."

Even through his drunkenness he felt the old nausea returning; the spectacle of Miss Murgatroyd, squinting and gushing, always made him despise the whole of the human race. She was so like an ill-used mongrel puppy, wagging his stumpy tail, crawling toward you on his stomach, full of friendliness but secretly terrified of receiving a beating. The gushing of Miss Murgatroyd he had, he knew, brought upon himself because in his impulse to make up to her for the snubs and ostracism she suffered, he had always paid her a kind of exaggerated attention, as if he really had an interest in her. He spoke to her when others ignored her; he always made it a point of saying good-night to her when others walked out of the room without so much as looking in her direction. He did not in the least mind Miss Murgatroyd being an Anglo-Indian; he did mind her being an appalling bore.

Mrs. Bannerjee said good-evening and went on chewing her betel leaf as if impatient for him to leave her in peace. Miss Murgatroyd went on gushing, until Ransome, in desperation, murmured something about a cocktail and left them to join Edwina, who seemed to have withdrawn a little from the others and to be waiting for him.

Edwina said, "Do you think you ought to have another cocktail?"

He grinned. "Why not? One more or less can't make much difference."

"Some night you'll take just one more and fall flat on your face, and then, I suppose, people will suspect that you drink. Anyway, I'd like to have you make sense when you're talking to me."

"Am I as bad as that?"

And while they were talking he became suddenly aware that behind Edwina on the divan there was a fresh outburst of whispering and giggling and all at once he was certain that Mrs. Bannerjee and Miss Murgatroyd were talking of Edwina and himself. He was certain that they knew what had happened in that lower room at the palace. He was a fool to have supposed that everyone in Ranchipur had not heard the story within twenty-four hours. By tomorrow, the other story would be about too, enlarged and garnished until it had become a melodrama in which he had raped Fern Simon. And while he went on talking to Edwina, he thought: "Perhaps Fern was right. Perhaps I should clear out of Ranchipur," and suddenly, for the first time, Ranchipur with all its intrigues and gossip seemed unendurable to him—worse even than Grand River had been when his marriage with Mary had begun to go on the rocks.

Aloud he said to Edwina, "How is your husband?"

"The same . . . delirious. I suppose I should have stayed at home by his bedside, only the Major forbade me that. Anyway, I can't begin doing that now if we're going to be kept here for weeks."

Now, suddenly, he felt drunk enough to risk asking what he had wanted to ask from the beginning. He said, "Do you care very much?"

Deftly she avoided the answer. "About having to stay on here? No,

[267]

I've made up my mind to it. It'll be a good story to tell back in London. I can dine out on it when everything else fails."

He was aware that she was evading him and he was determined that she should not slip out as she always slipped out of everything. "No, I didn't mean that," he said. "I mean do you mind very much about your husband."

"No, I don't."

"I didn't think you did."

"I never pretended, did I?"

He laughed. "No, it might have made you seem more human if you had."

"What's wrong with you? Why the evil temper? Being drunk used to make you more agreeable."

Through their talk he could hear the voices of Mr. Bannerjee and Miss MacDaid and the Major talking about the cholera, about the terrifying speed with which the river had risen, and beyond that the giggles of Mrs. Bannerjee and Miss Murgatroyd, apart, aloof, as if they had nothing to do with the dinner party, and above everything the dull roar of the rain and the sound of the river itself and the persistent coughing roar of one of the lions in the zoo on the other side of the bridge.

"And the doctor . . ." he said.

"He seems to know his business."

Neither her eyes nor her voice betrayed her, so he said, "Are you finding out about India instead of reading about it?"

She did not answer him at once, and when she did, she spoke looking him directly in the eye. She said, "Why are you doing this?"

"What?"

"It's because you're drunk. Everything that's nasty and feminine in you is coming out."

"I apologize."

"And don't be grand and ironic. It isn't because you're jealous."

"No . . . yes . . . perhaps it is."

"No . . . not directly jealous. It's very complicated."

"Yes, I suppose so."

"If I know anything, it's about things like this."

His only answer was a grin. She put her hand on his arm and said,

"Listen, Tom. We've double-crossed nearly everybody in the world. We mustn't turn on each other." And even through the haze of drunkenness he was aware that she was appealing to him, that all the trivial hardness had slipped away from her for a moment. He thought, "Edwina the glittering, Edwina the fortunate, Edwina the heartless . . . the self-sufficient Edwina, is frightened."

Aloud he said, "No, we'd better stick to each other. Neither of us has anyone else."

"Let me have my fun. Don't be nasty about it."

"All right. Do as you please. It's all the same to me. I wasn't worrying about you. You can pick up and sail and that'll be an end to it. I was thinking about the evil you might leave behind you."

"You can be an awful bastard sometimes."

"Perhaps that's my proper rôle."

She started to speak, quickly, and then checked herself. He waited, and when she remained silent he asked, "What were you going to say?"

"No, I couldn't say it. You wouldn't understand me. You'd only make a crack and think I was sentimental. I don't understand it myself."

And now the Major joined them and he saw at once that either she could not hide the effect he had upon her or she was shameless, or it was possible that no one but himself could read the signs. No one else could notice that the blood seemed suddenly to course a little faster beneath the lovely pale skin, that a new richness came into her voice. No one but himself could see the light which came into the lovely blue eyes—eyes, he thought bitterly, which in spite of everything, were innocent, as if they were always expecting something which could never be, which perhaps had never existed. And suddenly, intimations of something he had never thought of before came to him, filling him with a sense of melancholy. Never once before had he ever thought of her like that, and almost at once he said to himself: "No, it's no good in being sentimental. That doesn't help anything."

There was no escaping it. In the end they were closer to each other than he would ever be to anyone in Ranchipur, or to anyone in all the world, for that matter. They were bound together beyond escape. He was afraid for the Major, whom he loved and respected, and jealous of him because until now it seemed to him that the Major was the only

[269]

man he had ever known who had not disappointed him. Nevertheless, he must always, in spite of everything, be on Edwina's side. He thought, "If I were not drunk, I would never have understood suddenly that look in her eyes."

And then he noticed Miss MacDaid. She was talking to Mr. Bannerjee, but clearly she was not hearing anything he was saying. She was looking straight past his dapper little figure at Edwina and the Major, and as he watched her plain worn face with its ridiculous coating of rouge, he knew that she had divined what was happening and was in agony.

The dinner, it seemed to Ransome, went on interminably. Something, he could not discover what, although he attempted dully to discover, had altered the effect which drink usually had upon him. It still made him believe that nothing mattered, that nothing was important, but the knowledge did not make him gay now, but only filled him with a kind of aching despair. It was a mood very near to suicide. It was worse even than the pain and despair which attacked him when he was sober. Seated between Edwina and Miss Murgatroyd, he heard neither the sharp comments of the one nor the gushings of the other, but he was aware persistently of the sound of the rain and the roaring of the river; it was like an awful ringing in the ears. He thought, "Maybe this once I have taken too much. Maybe Edwina was right. Maybe this is what the beginning of delirium tremens is like." And then above the sound of the river there rose again the sound of lions roaring in the zoo, not one now, but three or four or five—the lions which had been sent to the Maharajah by the Emperor of Abyssinia. There was something ominous in their roaring, something which filled him with distress and anxiety. He had wakened in the night many times to hear them roaring, but always it was a solitary lion or at most two of them, never this chorus of coughing roars that was at once so beautiful and so terrifying.

Presently Edwina paid no more attention to him, but talked to the Major across the table or to Mr. Bannerjee, whose small Nepalese face was alight with the knowledge that he was entertaining here in his own house one of the most fashionable peeresses of England. And then suddenly the dinner was ended, and Mrs. Bannerjee was rising and the ladies were leaving the room. He saw them hazily, full of disgust that he was betrayed by his own drunkenness, aware that never before had he felt like this.

And as Ransome turned politely in his chair and looked up at Mr. Bannerjee he discovered a look of terror in the face of his host. It was not anything obvious; if Ransome had not seen it there many times before, he would never have divined its significance. Mr. Bannerjee was frightened, by what Ransome did not know, unless it was the sound of the rain and the river, or the unearthly roaring of the lions. Mr. Bannerjee wasn't any longer a dapper, worldly little man in white clothes from Bond Street; he was a frightened villager from the remote jungles of North Bengal.

He glanced at the Major, and the Major grinned. "He has a rendezvous with Kali," he said in a low voice. "To appease her for having caused the death of the skinny chickens we've just eaten."

Ransome made a desperate effort to pull himself together, thinking, "This is the first time in my life I have ever been ashamed of myself quite thoroughly. This is the first time I have ever seen myself through the eyes of someone else. I am looking at myself through the eyes of Safti, and a pretty spectacle I am."

The Major was leaning across the table toward him now, smiling. He said, "You look ill. I wouldn't take any of that brandy."

"I feel ill," he said. "Perhaps you're right."

There was a little silence and the Major said, "There's something I'd like to say, but I'm not sure how to do it." Ransome did not answer him and he continued. "I don't want you to think me impertinent or priggish." His hand came across the table and touched Ransome's. Then slowly, gently, it took Ransome's hand, and then the Major said: "Look here, old fellow, if there's anything I can do to help, you must call on me. I know that sounds bloody sentimental. It took a lot of nerve to get it out, but it's done now. I only wanted you to know."

Ransome looked away from him at the glass of brandy and murmured, "That's good of you. I understand. But there isn't anything you can do. There isn't anything anyone can do." And at the same time he thought, bitterly, "What a pretty spectacle this would be for the General,

[271]

for all those boys who talk about prestige! I've let them all down . . . all of them. Prestige, s——!"

Then the Major withdrew his hand and lighted his cigar and said, "I've a couple of pieces of bad news. Could you take them now or would you rather I kept them until tomorrow?"

"I can take them," Ransome said, sullenly. "What are they?"

"One is about our poor friend Miss Dirks."

"Yes, I think I know what that is."

"Well, the worst that you can think is true. If she'd come to me months ago I might have been able to do something. There isn't anything to do now. It isn't any use thinking of operating unless we wanted to kill her. That might be better. . . ."

Suddenly Ransome began to laugh, drunkenly, hysterically, but the sounds he made were not laughter. They were worse than the sound of wailing. While he laughed he saw poor Miss Dirks as she had been that day on the verandah, sitting with her hands in her lap, hidden beneath her jacket, white-faced, clutching her stomach when the pain became overwhelming. His own voice inside his brain kept crying out to him: "Poor Miss Dirks! Old Dacy Dirks' daughter who never had any fun! Poor Miss Dirks! She knew she was already dead!" He went on laughing, aware that the Major was watching him, not alarmed but somehow understanding his awful drunken mirth. "Oh, my God! Poor Miss Dirks!"

Then presently the paroxysm came suddenly to an end and, choking, he drank a glass of water and said, "I'm sorry. I couldn't help it. But do you know why she didn't come to you long ago?"

"I think I know."

"You're right. It was because she couldn't undress in front of a man. The poor old thing is dying because Dacy Dirks and all the ugly people behind him for generation upon generation taught her to think that men were lascivious and evil and the body something to be ashamed of. The poor old thing is dying of slow torture because of a thousand evil Nonconformist clergymen . . . a thousand perverted Christians." Then suddenly he felt quite sober and said, "Did you give her stuff to help the pain?"

"She won't have any more pain. I gave her all she needs . . . and more . . . to use as she sees fit."

"She'll never use it that way. Maybe she won't use any of it at all. She's like that."

"I know," said the Major. "She's very English. She must have been going through agony day and night for weeks."

"What's the other thing?" asked Ransome. "It couldn't be as awful as that." He was aware again of the roaring of the lions. The great coughing roars seemed very close now, just outside the windows.

"No, it's pretty bad, but not so awful as that. It's only that Esketh has plague."

After a moment Ransome asked, "Are you sure?"

"There isn't the faintest doubt. I sent a blood sample to Bombay. The telegram came just before dinner."

"Where could he get such a thing?"

The Major gave him the same answer he had given him that morning in the corridor of the old Summer Palace, only this time he did not grin. "Even great English lords have been known to have been bitten by fleas." And then he added, "It must have happened at the stables when he went to look at His Highness' horses. The rats are dying there. Two stable boys are already dead."

For a moment Ransome felt something that must have been a little like the terror of Mr. Bannerjee, a terror of the monstrous evil of Nature. Then he asked, "Have you told her?"

"No. I thought it might be better coming from you as an old friend." Then he looked sharply at Ransome. "Will she take it very hard?"

He was still sober enough to think before answering. Through a haze he knew that he could answer in such a way that it would put an end forever to her chances with the Major. He had only to tell the Major the truth; and then he heard her voice again saying, "Let me have my fun. . . . We mustn't go back on each other;" and saw again that unsuspected look of innocence in her eyes, and again he thought, "I mustn't play Jehovah." Soberly he said, "I don't know. It isn't a pretty situation. He's always been rather a brute. She's stuck to him through a lot more than most women would put up with. In a way, I suppose she's been very gallant. She's had . . ."

He never finished the sentence, for suddenly the table shook so that all the glasses jarred together with a singing sound. The curtains at the window opposite him seemed to stand out into the room as if blown by a wind, but there was no wind. The floor rocked and two of the Persian miniatures fell from the wall, followed by bits of plaster from the ceiling. He thought, "I must be passing out," and at the same time he saw a look of extraordinary astonishment on the face of the Major and then the lights went out. Above the clamor of parrots and macaws and Pekinese he heard the hysterical screams of Miss Murgatroyd from the other room.

It was the Major who acted. Calling across the table to Ransome, he said, "Come along. We must get the women out of the house."

Stumbling in the darkness, knocking over chairs and glasses, Ransome followed him toward the drawing-room. On the way he stepped in the darkness full on the face of a Moghul painting which had fallen from the walls. At the feel of his heel grinding the glass into its fragile beauty he sprang away as if he had stepped upon a snake.

In the other room Miss Murgatroyd was on her knees in the darkness, still screaming, not hysterically now, but efficiently at perfectly regular intervals as if she found a kind of enjoyment in the noise she was making. Miss MacDaid was trying to pull her to her feet and drag her to the comparative safety of the verandah, but Miss Murgatroyd, behaving as if Miss MacDaid were attempting to drag her off to torture, simply kept on screaming and resisting. From across the room Ransome could see their figures outlined against the faint light in the doorway. Then suddenly Miss MacDaid slapped the Eurasian woman with all her force, saying, "Come on, you bloody fool! One more like that and the house will be down on all of us!"

The slap did the work and Miss MacDaid dragged her through the doorway on to the verandah. Then there was a moment of extraordinary stillness, with only the sound of the river and the falling rain, and then the lions began again to roar, and from the huddle of buildings at the end of the garden there rose a sound of screaming and wailing that was like a single voice of terror and despair.

With a great effort Ransome resisted the hazy temptation to let everything slide, to hope that a second shock would come quickly and destroy them all. It was as if physically he took hold of his own body and slapped it, as Miss MacDaid had slapped Miss Murgatroyd, back into sobriety and action.

In the darkness he called Edwina's name, and out of the darkness her voice came back to him, not frightened, but queer and strained.

"Are you all right?" he asked.

"Yes," her voice came back. "Extraordinary, wasn't it?"

"Maybe it isn't finished yet."

"What are we going to do now?"

"I don't know. Better leave it to the Major."

The Major had been collecting them, urging them off the verandah into the shelter of the *porte cochère*, the one spot which was at the same time safe and sheltered from the awful flood of rain. Suddenly he asked, "Where are the Bannerjees?"

No one seemed to know. If Miss Murgatroyd knew she was unable to answer. She did not scream now, but whimpered with terror.

"For God's sake stop that noise!" Miss MacDaid said. "It's bad enough with all that yelling from the compound."

The Major shook her and said, "Where is Mrs. Bannerjee?" but all she did was to go on sobbing and saying, "I don't know. I don't know." And almost at the same moment Mrs. Bannerjee appeared, coming down the stairs, carrying an old-fashioned paraffine lantern and surrounded by a feathery ripple of yapping Pekinese. She moved slowly, as if there were no danger and no reason for haste, walking very erect with a kind of dignity which Ransome had never seen in her before. The light shining upward threw the planes of the beautiful face into relief, bringing a new modeling to the high cheek bones, the faintly slanting eyes, the finely chiseled nose, and even in the midst of the confusion Ransome, watching her, thought of what Miss MacDaid had once said . . . that beside the beauty of an Indian even the most lovely European face seemed an anemic pudding.

And then as she moved across the room a new sound came from the verandah overhead . . . a single isolated sound of wailing and terror, the voice of Mr. Bannerjee raised in prayer; but almost at once it was drowned by still another sound, faint at first, like the distant hissing of a million snakes, then growing louder and more distinct, increasing in

[275]

volume, and as the group beneath the *porte cochère* turned, it grew into the unmistakable sound of rushing water, and across the darkness there appeared a narrow white line of foam about the height of a man which seemed to gather out of the thick darkness every faint ray of light that came from a moon completely hidden by clouds, light which otherwise was not apparent and now seemed phosphorescent. It came toward them swiftly, smashing the distant mud wall of the garden, as the hiss changed into a roar which drowned the distant wails, the roars of the lions, the barking of the Pekinese, and the terrified moans of Mr. Bannerjee.

Ransome pushed Edwina before him into the house, Miss MacDaid took care of herself, and the Major picked up Miss Murgatroyd like a sack of meal and shouted, "Make for the stairs! It's the waterworks. The dam has broken!"

Ransome was the last to gain the stairs. He reached the bottom step at the very moment the wall of water struck the old house. For an instant the walls trembled as if shaken by a second quake, and Ransome thought, "This is the end. It can't hold against this." But it did hold. The flood poured in at the windows and doors, rushing halfway up the stairs at the very heels of the refugees.

Outside, the wall of water swept across the garden and engulfed the buildings at the end, stifling the sound of wailing and despair in the fresh sound of broken beams and brickwork. Then the roaring began slowly to die away again into a distant hissing, and from the city there rose a new veil of sound made by the voices of those who had seen death coming toward them across the great square before the old wooden Palace.

In the hallway at the top of the stairs there was no sound; even the dogs of Mrs. Bannerjee, huddled about her feet, were terrified into silence. Still holding the lantern, she stood leaning against the wall. At her feet Miss Murgatroyd had collapsed unconscious from terror into a huddle of blue taffeta and garlands and rosettes. The Major and Miss MacDaid stood looking at each other, listening, an expression of horror on both their faces, and Ransome knew that it was not of themselves they were thinking, but of their hospital and the helpless patients inside it, of the destruction which had come in an instant to everything for which they had given their lives. Opposite Mrs. Bannerjee, Edwina leaned against the wall. She was not looking at any of them, but beyond them, it seemed, through the very walls. There was a curious light in the blue eyes and her lips curled a little at the corners as if she were smiling in spite of herself.

Ransome was quite sober now, the fogginess gone completely from his brain, and in the midst of the disaster he was aware of a melodramatic beauty in this scene in the Bannerjees' upper hallway—Mrs. Bannerjee and Edwina, opposite each other, the one so dark, the other so blonde and fragile, the dogs huddled about Mrs. Bannerjee's feet, the pathetic crumpled pale blue of Miss Murgatroyd's silly taffeta gown, the Major and Miss MacDaid regarding each other with fixed looks of horror, the whole scene lightened by the yellow glow of the lantern.

Then outside the house the night was still again save for the sound of one or two distant isolated screams rising from the heart of the town on the opposite side of the bridge, which died almost at once, leaving only the sound of the river and the flooding rain. The lions were still now, for good, and Ransome thought, "Poor brutes! Drowned in their cages." There was in the sudden stillness something more awful than all the noise and confusion of the earthquake and the flood.

Miss MacDaid said, in a strange dead voice, "My God! We've got to get to the hospital somehow." And from the upper verandah the voice of Mr. Bannerjee was heard again, praying in Bengali to all the Hindu gods.

Long afterward, whenever Ransome thought of that night, the memory of it came to him without reality, a little because the catastrophe had happened at the very moment when in his drunkenness the world was becoming unreal and fantastic, and a little because in its suddenness there had been no time for either the body or the mind to adjust itself. In one sense his having been drunk gave him an advantage over all the others because each sound, each impression of the catastrophe, did not strike him directly but came to him, muffled and veiled, with a lag between the moment of the impact and the moment of realization. That was why he had not been terrified—that and because he alone, out of all the little group, had had no fear of death, but, on the contrary had been indifferent to the prospect. And so he had taken it all—the shock of the earthquake, the flood, the despairing cries from the huddle of the houses at the end of the garden, the distant wail from the square, and the death of the lions calmly, with detachment, as if all these things were simply part of a play which he was watching from a great distance. That was why, in the very midst of the confusion, he had experienced a sharp sense of pain, almost of anguish, at the feel of his heel grinding the broken glass into the lovely painting of Jehangir and his courtiers practicing the art of falconry, and why for a second he had been aware of the theatrical beauty of the scene at the top of the stairs. That was why the Major, instead of himself, had acted, taking command of the situation while he, functioning more slowly, simply obeyed.

It was only at the moment, when the first violence had passed and Miss MacDaid spoke, that he turned away from the others lest they should see by the light of Mrs. Bannerjee's lantern that he was laughing. It was laughter that was quite beyond his control, like the savage laughter which took possession of him when the Major told him that poor old Miss Dirks was dying; but this laughter was different in quality, laughter born of the ridiculous and the sudden memory of Miss Murgatroyd screeching methodically until Miss MacDaid slapped her into silence; of Mrs. Bannerjee coming quietly down the stairs surrounded by Pekinese in the midst of an earthquake; of the sound of poor little Mr. Bannerjee's voice raised in terror; of the vision of all of them—the able Miss MacDaid, the capable Major, Mrs. Bannerjee and her dogs, Edwina, one of "England's most fashionable peeresses," and Miss Murgatroyd, the Eurasian librarian, carried like a bag of meal, all bolting before the flood. Whatever their secrets, their despair, their trouble, they had all wanted to live, desperately. And so it was funny, but it was more than that. Deep inside him he was aware that the scene brought him a sense of satisfaction. If only the flood and the quake between them could have encompassed the whole world . . . if only he could have witnessed bankers and statesmen, millionairesses and labor leaders, journalists and dictators and politicians, scuttling for safety in Washington and Whitehall, the Quai d'Orsay, the Quirinal, and Unter den Linden . . . if only he could have watched that. . . . What if in the end the prophets of the Old Testament *were* right? That would be a good joke with a bitter laugh in it.

He felt the Major shaking him and saying, "Miss MacDaid and I are going to make a try at the hospital. You'll have to look after the others. Bannerjee is no good."

"Okay," said Ransome. "But you're crazy. It can't be done." And he thought, "They mustn't be lost. Of all the people in Ranchipur, in all India, they are the most precious just now." And aloud he said, "You've no right to take any risk."

"We won't take any risk. Here, give me a hand with Miss Murgatroyd." Between them they lifted her and carried her into a room where there was no furniture save cushions and an Indian bed. Edwina followed them and Mrs. Bannerjee with the lantern.

Then, surprisingly, Edwina said, "I'll stay with her," and to Ransome, "Get some water and some brandy if you can find any."

Mrs. Bannerjee, still carrying the lantern, led the way down the stairs just as a servant, shaking and moaning and almost naked, appeared in the hallway. In Gujerati Mrs. Bannerjee told him to stop whining and fetch some candles.

Water still covered the floor of the drawing-room to the depth of a foot or more, and even while they stood at the bottom of the stairs, looking about at the wreckage, a fresh wave, but a tiny one this time, no more than a foot in height, poured through the doorway.

"You can't make it," said Ransome.

"Well, anyway, we can have a try at it," said Miss MacDaid.

"If it doesn't rise any more, I think we can make the bridge."

Miss MacDaid hitched her evening dress above her knees and, following the Major, with Ransome holding the lantern, they reached the verandah. One corner of the *porte cochère* had been swept away so that the roof hung, sagging, above their heads. The Major's Ford lay on its side in a tangle of grass and wreckage on the verandah itself. The aspidistras and rubber plants were gone, and a large part of the railing.

The Major looked at his motor, grinned, and said, "Well, that's that!"

"I'll come with you," said Ransome.

"No, you'd only be a liability. No special use and maybe a hell of a lot of trouble."

Miss MacDaid said, sharply, "Don't be a fool," and Ransome knew that she did not want him to come because it was to be their expedition —hers and the Major's. The presence of anyone else would spoil it.

"There's no special reason for you to come along," the Major said to her.

"Nothing could make me stay here. A lot of good you'd be without me," and a look of excitement came into her lined and painted face, and a note of exultation into her deep voice.

Ransome thought, "The Major will belong to her alone." There was no one else who could be of the least use. She was indispensable.

Then he watched them set out, the Major walking ahead, carrying the lantern, Miss MacDaid following, her skirt tied about her waist in a knot at the back like a bustle. From the verandah above them the monotonous voice of Mr. Bannerjee went on and on in a kind of high-pitched drone, like the sound of the bees in the great chandeliers at the palace.

The muddy water came to their waists and they had to struggle against it, although there was almost no current now, but only a little wave now and then crested with a line of white foam, which each time forced them back a step or two. Watching, he waited until the lantern disappeared at the end of the drive behind what remained of the compound wall.

When he turned, Mrs. Bannerjee was still standing on the steps with the whining servant, who had found candles and another lantern. As he approached she said, "You'd better look for the brandy in the dining-room. If it hasn't been swept away, it's in the cabinet." He found the brandy, and when he returned, she said, "You'd better fetch the bridge cards out of the secretary. They're in the top drawer," as if there had been no earthquake and no flood and the evening was going on just as she had planned it.

The secretary had been whirled completely about by the force of the water but it still stood upright and in the top drawer he found the cards, not too damp, and he thought, "Maybe I'm crazy. Maybe we all are."

He gave the cards to Mrs. Bannerjee and took a lantern from the servant, saying, "I'm going to the end of the garden. There may be some one there who needs help."

Then as he splashed through the water on the verandah, his world began to expand, no longer confined to the people in the house and what had happened to them, but including all of Ranchipur. And first of all he though of Fern, feeling thankful that she had gone home instead of

[280]

to Raschids. The Mission was nearly three miles away and stood on higher ground, and the flood, he knew, must have followed the course of the river. She would be safe if the quake hadn't brought down the old stone barracks of a house on the top of all of them. He saw now that Mr. Bannerjee's house had stood up against the quake because it was light and made of wood and therefore flexible. A stone house might have collapsed. And all at once he was aware that he was frightened for the first time, not for himself, but for Fern. Nothing must happen to her. The thought that he might never see her again was unbearable to him, and suddenly he could not picture life in Ranchipur without her.

Struggling, he came at last to the spot at the end of the compound where the huddle of houses had been. Holding the lantern above his head, he tried to find some mark by which to guide himself, because he found nothing at all and believed that he must have taken a false direction. The huge banyan tree which grew in the very center of what had been the compound was still there but there was no trace of a single house, not so much as a post or a beam emerging from the muddy water. And then he knew what he could not believe was true. The houses with everyone in them, men and women, children, babies, grandparents, a whole tiny village, had been swept away completely into the mad current of the roaring river by that first wall of water.

He was there alone, horribly, terrifyingly alone; standing in water up to his waist, holding the lantern above his head in the presence of death, only there was no sign of death, but only a sea of muddy water beaten by the rain and covered with floating bits of rubbish and the branches of trees. And then he noticed that above the town the clouds were turning a yellowish pink with the reflected glow of fire, and in a moment the flames were visible through the mango trees, from the direction of the square.

Quickly he thought of the Smileys and Raschid, and the Jobnekars and their fragile, silly pink house in the low part of the town near the wells of the Untouchables, and of Miss Dirks and Esketh, one dying of cancer in the tiny bungalow and the other of plague in the old Summer Palace, and the Maharajah and Maharani in the vast new palace with its dozens of fragile towers and pinnacles and minarets.

He thought: "I've got to get out of here. I've got to find out what's happened to them," and pushing with all his strength, he found his way, against the water, back to the house, but as he climbed on to the verandah it seemed to him, by the reflected light from the burning town, that the water was rising again. Inside the drawing-room he was certain of it. On the stairway it was a whole step higher than when he had left. Going to the front of the house, he waved the lantern and shouted the names of the Major and Miss MacDaid, but there was no answer. Against the wall of rain his voice could not carry more than a few feet.

In the little house perched on the rim of the dam close by the safety gates there had never been more than two guardians, and on the night of the disaster there had been only one, for the head *jobedar* had gone down into the town to spend the night with his wife, an excursion which did not save his life, for he was drowned with all his family when the great wave crushed their house. The guardian who remained behind was a timid black little man, and at the first shock of the quake he rushed out of the little house into the rains along the wall of the dam. There he found no safety for almost at once he heard before him, above the sound of the rain, the roar of rushing water through the broken barrier and when he turned and ran in the opposite direction the same sound came toward him out of the darkness. Trapped and in terror, he threw himself on his face in the rain and called upon Shiva and Krishna and Rama and even Kali the Destroyer, to protect him, but even while he was praying the stone beneath him crumpled and gave way and he plunged, lost in a mass of rocks and pouring water, to the top of the electric plant a hundred feet below. Then the safety gates tottered, groaned, and fell, and suddenly the whole lake, seven miles long and three miles wide, poured out with a wild roar into the valley below.

The electric plant, with the thirty-one men who worked there, was simply overwhelmed and swept away and afterward nothing of it was found at all but only a great hole where it had been.

Down the wide flat valley the wall of water rushed, sweeping away two villages and a hundred farms, carrying with it men, women, and children, cattle and donkeys, goats and sacred monkeys, following the course of the already swollen river, sweeping over the low ground and curling round the higher parts. At the edge of the town it struck the barracks of the beautiful Sikhs whom Miss Hodge admired, drowning half those who had not already been killed or injured in the quake. It lapped hungrily at the distillery and the chemical plant, destroying all the expensive apparatus the Maharajah had had brought from Germany. It rushed, shallow now, because it was on high ground, across the tennis courts at the Simons' house and into the Smileys' garden, carrying with it the hyena, the barking-deer and the wild pigs from the little inclosure at the back. It rushed across Engineering School Road, avoiding the high ground about the great palace, licking the sides of the bungalow where Miss Dirks and Miss Hodge lived; across the tank into the great square before the old wooden palace filled now with terrified men, women, and children who had sought refuge beside the tank from the quaking houses and cinema; through the bazaar where one by one the little wooden buildings collapsed like paper houses; through the first floor of the old Summer Palace where the first Lord Esketh lay abovestairs, tortured and swollen with plague; through the low-lying Untouchable quarter where the mud houses melted away as if made of sand; through the zoölogical gardens where the beasts were drowned in their cages; across the burning-ghats and once more into the open country—a tempest of water and houses, corpses and uprooted trees.

Across the plain it followed the course of the river toward Mount Abana, checked for a second or two by the two bridges with the low-lying arches, until at last it reached the narrow gorge where the river passed through the ring of hills, and here it became dammed by a barrage of its own making, by a horrible accumulation of rubbish and trees, of the bodies of men, women and children and animals which it had carried on its breast for twenty miles. Driven higher and higher by the wreckage, the torrent of water presently became almost still and began quietly to spread back and back toward the ruined city, fed always by the terrible rains and the roaring torrent of the river, until at last over all the drowned valley and the stricken city there was only silence.

At the moment of the disaster, the Maharani, bored and restless in the heat, sat playing six-pack bezique with Maria Lishinskaia. The game went badly and the Maharani found that she beat her companion too easily to find any pleasure in the contest. She was bored with the cards, bored with Ranchipur, bored with Maria Lishinskaia. Maria, like herself, had had too much of the monsoon. She looked pallid and ill, and seemed to have little spirit.

"Perhaps," thought the old lady, "things are not going too well with Mr. Bauer, or perhaps she is just tired." After all, Maria wasn't young any more. The Maharani wondered how old she was, and presently she asked not, "How old are you, Maria?" because she knew Maria would lie in answer to any question so direct, but "How old were you when the war ended?" and Maria, caught, answered quickly and truthfully, "Twenty-one."

Yes, the Maharani calculated quickly, that made her thirty-nine, and at thirty-nine one wasn't young and fresh any more, especially if you'd led a life like Maria's. There were times when Maria looked younger than her age, and times when she looked much older. She was, the old lady had observed, very changeable. In those moments when she was more Asiatic than European she became as old as time itself, old and frightened and despairing.

"Would you like me to read to you?" asked Maria.

"No, I think I'll go to bed."

Maria lighted a cigarette and fell to playing patience, and while she was laying out the cards, an extraordinary change came over the palace. The air seemed to grow insupportably heavy and suffocating and there was a sudden silence as if the world itself had been checked in its turning. More and more slowly Maria laid down the cards until suddenly, as if she were aware of some danger, she stopped, listening and waiting, a look of terror in her eyes. Her sallow face grew white as wax, and opposite her the Maharani braced herself unconsciously in her chair.

The old lady knew what was about to happen and suddenly she was transported back again across more than fifty years into the dusty little village in the Deccan from which she had come to be Maharani of Ranchipur. She knew that feeling in the air. It made her see again the whole village collapsing into the streets in a cloud of rubbish and dust. She heard again the cries of those buried in the wreckage of the fallen house. . . .

And then the floor seemed to heave beneath their feet as if there were an enormous monster just beneath them. Bits of plaster fell from the ceiling and the nets which kept out the giant bats swayed at the windows. And then one by one the towers and pinnacles of the vast palace began to fall and the lights went out. Sitting in the darkness, they heard the towers crash through the roof, one by one, with a horrible slow interval between each collapse, and presently Maria Lishinskaia began to scream wildly and horribly, the screams rising above the sound of wailing and terror which had risen from all over the palace.

Savagely the old lady shouted at her, "Stop that bloody row! Stop screaming! It helps nothing!" And in the voice of the old woman there was the timbre of a terrifying authority and scorn, as if she felt only contempt for a woman who grew frightened and hysterical in the face of death, abandoning the dignity without which man became something a little lower than a dog.

Then the faint rocking and sound of the falling towers ceased and after a moment she said, "It's over now. The palace is going to stand. Go and fetch my electric torch. Don't be a fool!"

There was no answer, but in the darkness the Maharani knew that Maria Lishinskaia had obeyed her. In a moment the companion returned, preceded by a little circle of light. The wailing in the palace seemed to have taken on a rhythm now, rising and falling, loud enough to drown the roar of the water descending on the city from the broken dam.

The old lady took the torch from her and said, "Come. We must go to His Highness," and Maria, no longer frightened now for herself, prayed, "O God, don't let anything happen to him! Keep Harry safe for me!"

The fierce timbre of the Maharani's voice, the absolute ring of authority and command in her speech, were like a violent slap on the cheek: it had shocked the terror out of her. Suddenly she felt calm and resigned and Asiatic; and as they made their way along the hall over shattered glass and fallen plaster, past the wide arched windows, she saw herself suddenly with complete objectivity, perhaps for the first time in all her muddled existence. She thought, "How did I come here . . . I, Maria Lishinskaia, born in Kieff? What am I doing trailing along the hall of an Indian palace after a Maharani in the midst of an earthquake?" And she knew that she was no longer afraid, not because she was courageous, but because she was tired, so tired that she no longer had any desire to go on living, tired from all that had happened to her, tired from the ravages of her passion for Harry Bauer, so tired that she saw everything quite clearly now, as if she were already dead. There was nothing left to her but her body, and now her body, too, like her spirit, was tired and worn.

And this Harry Bauer, who was he, that she should ever give herself to him . . . she, Maria Lishinskaia, with a wit and a brain and childhood filled with exciting and important people, none of whom would have accepted Harry Bauer save in the rôle of a servant? Who was he? Nothing but a fine animal with a lovely body, without wit or sensibility or brains or cultivation. And against the sound of the wailing she saw herself almost as if she were watching a picture in the cinema, sitting in her father's flat in Moscow long ago, beside a round table covered by a bit of plum-colored plush which fell to the floor; and on the table was a green-shaded lamp of the sort students use, and beyond it sat her father, his round Tartar head bent over a book—Nicholas Michailovitch Lishinsky who knew more of organic chemistry than any man in Russia, a leader of the Liberals who had been too weak, too intelligent, believing too much in the goodness of mankind, believing that only liberty and education were needed to turn all men into angels. And then in a little while the door would open and her mother would come in from the theatre, perhaps with the make-up still on her face, to ask if Leonid had gotten off safely from the Central Station . . . Leonid who was going away to be killed in the Carpathians because his battalion had been sent cartridges which did not fit their rifles and because bayonets, backed by all the courage in the world were no good against Skoda shells and German machine-guns . . . Leonid who should have been the father of her children, sitting now on the other side of a table with a green lamp on it, as her own father had sat long ago. And where was he now, her father? In some ditch outside of Kieff, his bones all mixed with the bones of other intellectuals, of other Liberals like himself, who had been fools enough to believe that man was essentially intelligent and good. . . . And her mother dead of pneumonia because she had not had enough to eat and there was not enough coal to keep her warm . . . her mother who had been so gay and pretty and clever and carefree.

No, she had had too much. Before now when she threatened to kill herself she had always known in her heart that she would never do it, because she had neither the courage nor the indifference; she had not had the courage even that time in Prague when she was beaten with a whip by a fat, elderly commercial traveler, nor on that night of horror in a bedroom filled with red plush and crystal and mirrors in a hotel in Leipzig. No, she could do it now. It was easy when you were tired, too tired to reach the end of the corridor. It would be wonderful never to wake again, never to have to begin another day . . . just sleep, eternal sleep, just oblivion, nothing more.

The sound of the Maharani's voice shouting in Gujerati shocked her out of the hazy state into which she had fallen. Before them in the circle of light from the old lady's torch lay two Untouchable serving-women, flat on their faces, wailing. Savagely, with contempt, the Maharani kicked them with her bare jewelled foot and again shouted in Gujerati. Then one of the women raised her head and, finding herself in the royal presence, forgot her terror, prodded the other, and rose to her knees to salaam again and again.

Beyond the two women the way seemed barred by a great pile of mortar and stone where one of the towers had fallen through the roof, but after a moment the Maharani found a way through, and climbing over the rubbish, they found themselves in the passage which led to the Maharajah's apartments. There the Maharani pushed open the door of the antechamber and hurried past the guards, who still stood in their scarlet and gold on either side of the bedroom door as if nothing had happened. Inside, the old Maharajah was leaning on a chair by the window overlooking the town. Harry Bauer stood beside him, supporting him with one arm about the old man's body and when the ex-swimming-teacher turned toward them and Maria Lishinskaia saw the stupid beauty of his face and the set of his shoulders, she forgot death, saying to herself, "Thank you, God! That he is still alive! Thank you, God!"

In all the room she saw nothing but him. She did not see the face of the old Maharajah as he turned toward them, nor the look of horror and tragedy in his eyes. Distantly she heard the faint wailing that rose from the square as the people there saw death coming toward them. What was wailing now, and what death? She did not hear the cry of the

Maharajah, nor that of his wife, as she saw the old man, despite the strength of Harry Bauer, slip to the floor. Half-aloud she said, perversely: "Thank you, God! Send him to me tonight in the midst of horror and disaster, for that is all you have left me."

And then she knew what it was she found in him, not sensuality, nor even physical satisfaction; it was at once more complicated and more simple than that. There was something about him that was vigorous, uncorrupted and uncorruptible, as old as time, yet eternally new. He had in him the strength of the earth itself, with all its simplicity and beauty. He had come from the earth and he would return to it, untroubled by doubts or theories or ideals, unchanged and unchangeable. He was the antithesis of fear and weariness, for he belonged to the eternal earth. Without him she was lost, already as good as dead.

When the first rush of water had passed, Miss Dirks dragged Miss Hodge to the sofa, and in the darkness found her way to the cupboard where the brandy was kept. After five minutes, when Miss Hodge had been slapped and given brandy, she opened her eyes and said, "Where am I?" and began almost at once to cry, and Miss Dirks patting her, said, "You're all right. There's been a flood and an earthquake. Something must have happened at the waterworks. Do stop crying and try to pull yourself together."

"I'm doing my best," sobbed Miss Hodge. "I really am. It was so silly of me to faint."

"Not so silly. It was enough to make anyone faint. There's still six inches of water on the floor."

"Did it hurt anything? Did it break the East India Company china?"

"I don't know," said Miss Dirks. "Do be quiet now for a moment."

She kept stroking Miss Hodge's head and Miss Hodge, closing her eyes, felt for a time very dizzy and then presently she felt very happy because this was the the first time in years that Sarah had stroked her head thus, and it made her feel again like a small child who was being petted and spoiled and for that she had been hungry now for so long. They stayed thus by the faint blue light of the alcohol lamp which Miss Dirks used in ordinary times for her chemistry experiments, having come so close to death that when it had passed they emerged cleansed

[288]

and purified, both of them aware in the precious moment of stillness that they were close to each other once more. All the bickering was gone, all those waves of emotion that were forever stranding Miss Hodge higher and higher on the beach of discontent, all the pettiness and neurasthenia which was forever corrupting their friendship.

Presently Miss Hodge said, "What's that funny noise?"

"It's the natives wailing," said Miss Dirks. "You know how they grow hysterical at the least excuse." And after a time she said, as if she had been considering the question, "They have no self-control. They can't stand anything. That's what is the matter. They're soft. Are you feeling a little better?"

"Yes . . . much better. I'm such a fool. I'm never any good in a crisis. I'm always a burden. I've always been a burden all my life to somebody." And she began to cry again.

Miss Dirks started to answer her, and then, caught by a paroxysm of pain, was made speechless, and before she had recovered Miss Hodge said, "I wanted to tell you something, Sarah. I've been wanting to tell you all day. I'm ashamed of myself for behaving as I did about the tea party. I'll write a note to Lady Esketh this very night and leave it at the Summer Palace on the way to school."

"I don't think it matters now. I don't suppose, after this, that people will be thinking of tea parties. And I don't think there will be any school tomorrow. Maybe there never will be again."

"Why? Is it as bad as that?"

"We're on high ground here and we're half under water . . . and there was the earthquake, too."

"Was there an earthquake?"

"That's when you fainted."

"I wonder how bad it really is."

"I'm going out presently to discover."

Miss Hodge seized her hand hysterically, "No. No. Don't do that. Don't leave me."

Miss Dirks did not answer her. She only said, "Elizabeth!"

"Yes?"

"You've never regretted it, have you? I mean coming out here with me."

[289]

"No, Sarah, no. I suppose I've had a more interesting life than I had any reason to expect. I suppose it's been a lot more interesting than Birmingham would have been."

"I didn't mean any of those horrid things I said to you."

"I know you didn't, dear."

"It was nerves. My nerves have been so bad lately. I wanted you to know, that's all."

"I did know," said Miss Hodge.

And then Miss Dirks fell silent and embarrassed and after a long time she said, quite simply, "I'm going out now."

"No . . . no. Don't leave me."

"Don't be foolish, Elizabeth. You'll stay here. I couldn't rest without knowing what's happened to the school and all those lovely new books from home. It would be awful if they were all ruined now because no one moved them upstairs."

"I'm afraid. I'm afraid."

"There's nothing to be frightened of. You'll stay here. I'll be back in half an hour."

"It'll be all dark at the school."

"I have my keys. I know my way about."

"I'm afraid," murmured Miss Hodge.

"If you want to help you'll behave yourself and stay right here till I come back. There's no danger now. The water has passed." Then she rose with something of the decision she had always shown, and said, very practically, "If you feel afraid, take a little more brandy. Take as much as you like. I don't even suppose it would matter if you made yourself drunk tonight."

Then Miss Hodge started up from the sofa. "I'll go with you. I couldn't think of you going there alone."

Miss Dirks was already putting on her worn mackintosh. "No, my dear," she said, firmly, "you'd only be a nuisance. You might faint again and then what would I do with you?"

Then Miss Hodge felt suddenly dizzy and lay back on the sofa because she could not sit up. "Don't go. Don't go," she kept on repeating. Miss Dirks poured a whole glass of brandy slowly between her lips and again began stroking her forehead, and Miss Hodge, crying, said, "Forgive me, Sarah, for having been so mean and horrid."

"There wasn't anything to forgive you for, my dear. I understood all that. Now lie back and be comfortable. I'll be back before you know I've gone. Try and sleep."

And then she was gone before Miss Hodge, in her dizziness, was aware of it. Presently she tried to rise again, but fell back weakly, calling out, "Sarah! Sarah! Wait for me! Wait for me!"

A second time she tried to rise and this time she succeeded. Staggering a little, she made her way to the little entrance hall and, taking down her mackintosh, put it on and went down the steps of the bungalow. As she descended, the water crept slowly up to her knees. She was terrified of snakes at night but now in her haste she forgot them.

"Sarah!" she cried into the darkness. "Sarah! Wait for me! Wait for me, Sarah!"

In the gateway she halted, standing in water up to her waist, listening, but no sound answered her save the distant ghostlike noise of wailing from the palace. Again she cried out, wildly this time, "Sarah! Where are you? Wait for me! It's Elizabeth! Sarah! Wait for me!"

Still no answer came out of the darkness. She listened again, cursing herself because she was weak and silly and incompetent, but there was only the gurgling sound of the dark water which, dammed to the east of Mount Abana, had begun again to rise. The clouds above were bright with the light of a fire burning somewhere near the center of the town.

In the night school beyond the bazaar the Smileys herded together the twenty-seven boys of the class and led them onto the roof of the one-story extension. The building was new and built of reinforced concrete with a steel frame, and although it rocked and cracks appeared in the walls, it stood fast, and there on the roof there was little danger even if a second shock followed the first. From the roof they heard the roar of the approaching water and the cries of terror from the square before the old wooden palace. They heard it rushing toward them up the street of the bazaar, knocking about the ancient wooden houses as it approached, and Mrs. Smiley falling on her knees, closed her eyes and prayed. She had not prayed in months because she had never been able to find time and because she knew that somehow God would understand and forgive her, and she prayed now not for herself or Mr. Smiley, but for the twenty-seven boys, huddled in terror at her side who still had all their lives before them, lives which would be unbelievably better than the lives of their fathers because she and Mr. Smiley had worked for them. She prayed, too, because she knew that only God by some miracle could save them, and she really believed in God, or at least in the vague principle that in the end good did win over evil.

As the water struck the night school, the heavy building shuddered and new cracks appeared in the roof beneath the feet of the refugees and from all about them out of the darkness came the sound of crashing walls and falling timbers as the little houses in the bazaar crumpled and were swept along by the flood; but the school itself stood fast, like a rock in the midst of ruin, a refuge for twenty-seven low-caste Indian boys and Mr. and Mrs. Homer Smiley of Cedar Falls, Iowa.

As the roar of the flood died away Mr. Smiley peered over the side of the house with caution, straining to discover what remained of the familiar street after the passing of the flood, and Mrs. Smiley, aware now that the miracle *had* occurred, opened her eyes, rose from her knees, and said, "What shall we do now, Homer?" And in Mr. Smiley some impulse, some instinct, some power dormant since he was born, stirred and came to life. It was almost a physical sensation like waking from sleep, not drowsily and unwillingly, but with pleasure and confidence and a sensation of vigor and strength. In the blood of the humble, quiet Mr. Smiley there came to life a whole procession of ancestors of whose presence there he had been quite unaware until this moment. . . . Jed Smiley, the Indian fighter, and Grandpa Smiley, who had carved a rich farm out of a wilderness, and Morgan Downs who had been the companion of Daniel Boone during his Kentucky adventures, all of these with their heroic female companions and their tough and vigorous offspring, all capable of inhuman endurance, endowed with a genius for surviving in the midst of disaster, resourceful and courageous to the point of recklessness. They were all there in his blood and now suddenly they came to life. Within the slight, colorless middle-aged body of Homer Smiley heroism and the excitement of adventure unexpectedly asserted themselves.

Heroism there had always been—the dull, dogged, unspectacular heroism which was needed for fighting filth and ignorance and disease, but for this new peril a new kind of heroism was needed, and now, without searching for it, Mr. Smiley, with a sudden pleasant sensation of excitement, knew it was there—the spectacular heroism which called for a cool head, for resourcefulness which demanded the triumph of vanquishing impossible obstacles.

The blood ran more quickly through his small wiry body and he felt young and strong—younger and stronger than he had ever been at eighteen. And when, out of rain and darkness, he heard Mrs. Smiley's voice addressing him, he knew that he was not alone. He knew from the very sound of her voice that in her thin tired body the same capacity for heroism had come alive. Together they would be equal to anything, to floods and earthquakes, to all the assaults of a malignant Nature. He knew then that it did not even matter if, losing, they were destroyed, because they would go down together, fighting, full of trust in each other. And for the first time in all his gentle existence, Mr. Smiley experienced intimations of what passion might be, of its full glory, its excitement, of the *catharsis* it brought with it . . . not the comfortable affection he had always had for Bertha Smiley, but something magnificent and glowing, not lyrical but savage. In darkness and disaster Mr. Smiley became aware that he was a male, as much a male as the noisy, violent Raschid or the handsome Major. And without knowing it, he had been waiting all his life for that moment.

He answered his wife in a voice which Bertha Smiley knew was different, a voice which told her that she could count on him through everything as a guide and a protector.

He said, "We'd better get out of here on to high ground. I'll go downstairs and have a look around. You stay here with the boys and keep them from doing anything silly."

He left them and, re-entering the school building, went down the stairs. There was a metre or more of water still in the rooms on the ground floor, but for the moment there was no danger. When he returned to the roof he said, "I'll go out and do a little reconnoitering" (exactly as if he were preparing a sortie from a blockhouse in a wilderness infested by redskins).

But Mrs. Smiley objected (exactly like a pioneer wife). "No," she said. "You might get lost or cut off from us. We'll be just as safe going with you as staying here, and at least we'll be together. It's much better that way." She had to shout to make herself heard above the sound of the rain and the terrified whimpering of her charges.

It was difficult even to get the twenty-seven boys under way because six or seven of them had become paralyzed with fear and would not stir until Mrs. Smiley told them in Gujerati that they would be left behind, and even went so far as to make a feint at leaving them. The feint forced them into action, for all of them were terrified now of being left by these two middle-aged Europeans who did not seem to be afraid. With Mr. Smiley leading the way, and Mrs. Smiley bringing up the rear like a faithful sheep dog, the party straggled down the stairs and, in water above their knees, made their way into what remained of the street. In the darkness it was impossible to see more than three or four feet on any side, but the going was less evil than Mr. Smiley had expected because most of the houses and the wreckage had been swept clean away. There was no use in attempting to follow what had been the street. There were no landmarks, and even if they had existed, one could not have seen them. So Mr. Smiley had to rely upon his sense of direction, something which until this moment he had never been called upon to use. He knew perfectly well what he meant to do. Avoiding the site of the bazaar, he meant to execute a circle based roughly upon the Summer Palace and the Girls' High School, swinging round in the end across Engineering School Road into the high ground where the great palace stood.

The little procession advanced with abominable slowness, not only because of falling constantly over wreckage and into holes filled with water, but because the boys were terrified and unmanageable. Once Mrs. Smiley, putting out her hand to save herself, seized at something white floating near her, only to find that she had seized the thigh of a floating corpse, and again Mr. Smiley very nearly took hold of a small python which had wrapped itself firmly about a floating beam. Every few minutes as they advanced, Mrs. Smiley kept calling the roll of the class, shouting out their names in order to make certain none of them had gone astray. She had no faith in them, for she knew the weaknesses of the

Hindu spirit which in terror and despair might, like the male camel, suddenly lie down and die simply because the desire to go on living was no longer there. Now, in their terror, most of them were like small, irresponsible children and not like boys who would be men in another year or two. Not one of them, she knew by now, felt any responsibility toward the others or even toward himself and she knew that to God she and Mr. Smiley were responsible for all twenty-seven lives; so, stumbling and falling, drenched and out of breath, her hands bleeding, she kept prodding them on, barking at their heels, calling out their names, threatening them when they weakened before the horrors of floating snakes and corpses.

And presently from the head of the line, she heard the voice of Mr. Smiley shouting back, "It's all right. I missed the Summer Palace, but here's the High School. It's still standing." And the building, partly wrecked, loomed out of the darkness, twenty feet to the left of them.

As they passed it, Miss Dirks, standing on the steps, heard the voice of Mrs. Smiley shouting threats and encouragement in Gujerati and calling the roll for the tenth time, and for a moment, standing there with her hand on the door of her precious school, she felt, like an old sheep dog which has been left behind, a sudden desire to join them and help in the shepherding. Vaguely above the biting pain, she felt a sudden envy of Mrs. Smiley, wishing that all her girls, half of them probably drowned by now, might have been herded together like the Smiley low-caste boys and driven to safety, with herself barking at their heels. For a moment she felt an impulse to call out to them as they passed, to join their little procession on its way to safety, to return once more into the current of life, to build as she had done before all that had been destroyed in a moment; but almost at once she knew that she was old and tired and no longer had the strength, the terrible strength and the terrible patience that were needed and she thought, "What am I thinking of? I, who am already dead."

So she kept silent, still pressed against the door, as if to hide herself from the little procession she could hear but no longer see, thinking, "No, this is much the best way. It will be so much easier for Elizabeth. It is much the quickest and the easiest way." Still listening, still wishing in her spirit to follow the little procession, she waited in the darkness as the voice of Mrs. Smiley, encouraging and threatening her little flock grew fainter and fainter until at last there was only the sound of the rain and the rising water lapping about her feet.

Beyond the High School, Mr. Smiley, still swinging in a great circle, stumbled into the Engineering School Road and made the discovery that the water had begun to rise again and that they had made their escape with scarcely a second to spare. Staggering in the darkness, he came suddenly upon the wall of the park exactly where he had expected to find it and felt a quick thrill of satisfaction at his cleverness. He was uncertain of the exact spot where he had come upon the wall, but after a moment he decided that if he turned to the right he would come presently to the Great Gate where the Maharajah's band played each evening at sunset. Again the instinct of the pioneer was right, for after hurrying along the wall, he came presently to the Great Gate itself rising, it seemed to him, up and up into dark infinity. Calling out in Hindustani to the guards, he got no answer and found that the niches where the Sikh horsemen usually stood were empty. Then, halting the procession for a moment, he read once more the names of the class to make certain that none had been lost, and he was about to give the order to go ahead when Mrs. Smiley called out, "Listen, some one is calling!" and out of the darkness and the rain and above the distant sound of wailing, he heard a woman's voice from somewhere on the opposite side of the road calling out, "Sarah! Wait for me! Sarah! Sarah!" and he knew that it was Miss Hodge.

Mrs. Smiley called out, "Shall we go back for her?" and in an instant Mr. Smiley was forced to make a terrible decision. The water, even in Engineering School Road which was comparatively high ground, had risen almost to his waist. Five minutes more and it might be over the heads of the smaller boys. Thinking quickly, he called back, "No. We'll get the boys to the palace first and I'll come back for her." It was the life of one middle-aged old maid against the lives of twenty-seven low-caste boys who had scarcely begun to live.

"Hurry!" he called out, and in Gujerati, he urged the boys through the great silent gateway and along the curving drive, for there was still a good five hundred yards to cover before they might consider themselves safe.

As they staggered along the drive, one of the smaller boys whimpered and lay down in the water to die. Mrs. Smiley would not have known it save for the cries of the boy nearest to him, whose hand he had been holding. Groping her way, she found him and yanked him to his feet. Then she slapped him, and herself took his hand, dragging him, whimpering and crying, through the water.

Presently the ground began to rise beneath their feet and the water to grow more and more shallow until at last they were walking on earth that was soaked but free of flood water. It was easy enough to follow the contours of the metaled drive and in another moment or two the enormous mass of the half-ruined palace, bare now of pinnacles and towers and turrets, rose in front of them, visible only because it was more opaque than the darkness. Then they were safe within the dubious shelter of the broken *porte cochère* and Mr. Smiley climbing the steps, led them toward the Hall of Honor. But he had gone only a few feet when he found the way blocked by masses of stone and plaster which was all that was left of the great tower. He knew then what had happened— that the great tower had fallen, blocking the Hall of Honor and crushing all the gold leaf and mosaic and sandalwood in the Durbar Hall. The faint perfume of splintered sandalwood hung in the damp air, and from a distant part of the palace came the sound of wailing and lamentation. Then close by him there rose a sound of scuffling and chattering and a troop of sacred monkeys scuttled away into one of the anterooms.

Then for the last time he made certain that none of the boys were missing, and said to Mrs. Smiley, "I'll go back now and see what I can do for the old maids."

And Mrs. Smiley found herself crying out, "No! Don't go! Don't go! There's nothing to be done now." And then abruptly she was silent and ashamed of herself, for she knew that Mr. Smiley *had* to go, that nothing could stop him, and that she herself had no right to attempt it. In her spirit she knew that she had no desire to stop him, that if he had stayed behind now he would have lost some of the new glory with which the rescue and escape had endowed him in her eyes. It was her body which cried out, the body which until now had always been docile and indifferent, a mere machine which had served the spirit. Her spirit had always loved Mr. Smiley, but now her body was in love with him, with his resourcefulness, his bravery, his determination. He was a new Mr. Smiley, and suddenly, in some strange way, she was a new Mrs. Smiley. The sensation glorified and puzzled her. In the darkness and confusion she felt a great singing inside her, a kind of exaltation because together they had defeated the earthquake and the flood and all the horrors of the darkness and the rain. She heard him saying, "But I must go, dear" in his familiar gentle way, and at once she answered, "Of course you must, but do be careful!" feeling at the same time that the words she spoke and her voice itself were pitifully inadequate and banal beside what she was feeling inside her.

She was aware that in the darkness he was trying to find her, and putting out her hand she found his and drew him to her. Quickly they embraced and then he was gone into the wall of rain, but she knew from the way he kissed her that he was feeling what she felt, and again the sense of exaltation, more wonderful than anything she had ever experienced, swept over her. And presently she began to cry, feeling wonder that she was a woman and no longer simply an instrument of God, and after a time her tears ceased and she fell on her knees again to pray, and this time she prayed alone for the safety of Mr. Smiley.

For two hours she waited, now praying, now keeping watch over the low-caste boys who lay huddled together near her, some of them asleep, some of them still shivering and whimpering. And every few minutes she went as far as the ruined *porte cochère* to call, "Homer! Homer!" again and again into the darkness, terrified by the lonely sound of the voice that was stifled so quickly by the rain.

After a time the sounds of lamentation from the distant parts of the palace died away and the night grew still save for the gurgling sound of the water. It was still rising, for each time she went to the *porte cochère* it was a little higher on the steps. The perfume of shattered sandalwood still hung in the air, and after a time, in spite of hope, of desire, of faith, she began to doubt that he would ever return, and vaguely her brain began to consider how she would carry on without him, especially now after what had happened to her. And then out of the darkness she heard his voice, calling, "Bertha! Bertha!" a voice that was weak and hoarse from exhaustion, and she felt suddenly faint and sick with joy.

Almost at once he sank down on the marble floor and said, "I couldn't get anywhere near them. I had to swim for it myself. It's nasty. The water is full of snakes now." And then he slipped into unconsciousness, his head lying in her lap. And at the same time out of the darkness, into the ruined hallway, staggered the figure of a white man, a European whom Bertha Smiley had never seen before. By a flash of lightning she saw a narrow white face with a long nose and narrow eyes and saw that he was dressed oddly in a morning coat such as the British officials wore at the durbars of the Maharajah. The man stumbled over one of the Untouchable boys and fell without making an effort to rise. It was Bates.

From Ransome's house, Mrs. Simon, agitated by an odd mixture of emotions which included rage, exultation, triumph, suppressed lechery, and confusion, drove in her ancient Ford to the bungalow of Mrs. Hoggett-Egburry. It stood at some distance from the town on the edge of the parade-ground. When Mrs. Simon arrived she found her friend alone, seated morosely in a vast chair, corsetless and clad in a flowing *peignoir* of pale pink and lace, brooding over the absence and neglect of Mr. Hoggett-Egburry, who had gone off, as usual, alone, to Delhi, leaving her behind to swelter in Ranchipur. She was not drinking, because she had reached the saturation point a little after she had returned from her trip to Mrs. Simon's to relate the "news," and once the saturation point had been reached more brandy only made her feel sullen and sick. Most of Ranchipur knew when Mrs. Hoggett-Egburry had reached the saturation point; she became petulant and quarrelsome and the curious accent which she had invented for herself slipped away beyond control, replaced by her native Putney cockney. Also she ceased to talk *pukka* and had even on occasion been known, while saturated, to use such expressions as "God blimey" and "bloody."

In spite of her saturation she brightened a little at the sight of Mary Lou Simon stepping out of the old Ford. Immediately she said, pouting a little as if she were still nineteen and possessed of a flossy prettiness: "You must stay to tiffin and keep me company. I have a terrible migraine."

Mrs. Simon accepted at once and sent a servant to say that the Reverend Mr. Simon was not to expect her. It always flattered her that Lily Hoggett-Egburry should desire her company, and now she was full of exciting news—the revelation about the depravity of the Smileys, the outrageous behavior of Fern, the description of the interior of Ransome's house which had "intrigued" Mrs. Hoggett-Egburry for so long, but above all the prospect, which she knew would dazzle her friend, of Fern's marriage to Ransome. In fact, she was fairly bursting with items certain to titillate the bank manager's wife, saturation or no saturation.

All this Mrs. Hoggett-Egburry had been waiting impatiently, too impatiently, perhaps, with a brandy bottle in the house, to hear since five in the afternoon. At once Mrs. Simon proposed that they go into the sitting room where what she had to tell was less likely to be overheard by some barefooted servant.

This room was as overcrowded as Ransome's rooms had been empty. In it were crowded masses of bric-à-brac, Benares brass, photographs, cushions, dubious objets d'art, including an enlarged, colored, and life-sized photograph of Mrs. Hoggett-Egburry in her prime, at the moment she had made her first appearance on the stage in "Puss in Boots." All these things were arranged without plan of any sort; in fact, the room very closely resembled the inside of Mrs. Hoggett-Egburry's head at the moment her friend had discovered her on the verandah.

Amid the magpie collection of souvenirs they put their heads together while Mrs. Simon, breathless, recounted all the terrible things she had discovered since they had last met two hours earlier, and here Harry Loder found them a little later, just at that point in the story where Mrs. Simon related how she had written a letter to the Missionary Board in Iowa and "fixed" the Smileys once and for all.

He was a big man of thirty-one, beefy rather than muscular, with black hair and brown eyes and a fine complexion which, despite a good deal of drinking, had remained fine and high-colored instead of going white and pasty like the skins of most Europeans in India. He had survived the heat, the climate, the drinking through a heavy animal vitality. He was healthy, rather stupid, male, full of blood, and coarse. There was an animal beauty about him which struck both women whenever they saw him, and now as he charged into the room, a certain perkiness entered their manner. Now in their forties they were able to appreciate a man like Harry Loder, and tonight he seemed more impressive than ever, more agitated and more red-faced, more charged with rich masculine promise.

When he had checked the first bull-like rush of his entrance, he said, "Excuse me for crashing in like this, but I wanted to see Mrs. Simon." To Mrs. Hoggett-Egburry he said, "I'm sorry, but it's very important," and then they both knew that he too had "heard."

Mrs. Simon said, "It's all right. Mrs. Hoggett-Egburry knows everything."

Now, at sight of Harry Loder she began to weaken a little in her determination to have Ransome for Fern's husband. After all, if he wasn't as rich as Ransome and his family wasn't as good, there were things about him. . . . And he was much easier to snare. She would have liked him herself (she even half-admitted it) but failing that . . . then Fern. . . .

"I meant about Fern," he said, and his nostrils dilated and he breathed heavily.

"Yes, about Fern," and in a lowered voice, appropriate to the circumstances, she added, "It was Mrs. Hoggett-Egburry who told me." She took out her handkerchief, and although there was no moisture in her eyes, she wept in pantomime . . . and her heart beat with an odd excitement when Harry Loder shouted, almost like an old Southern gentleman: "I'll shoot the blackguard! Such things aren't done!"

"No," said Mrs. Hoggett-Egburry, with tipsy wisdom, "you certainly can't do that."

"Why can't I?" Loder roared back at her.

"Considering who he is," continued Mrs. Hoggett-Egburry, her idea becoming a little clearer to her, "It's not as if he was a common soldier or even an inferior officer."

"I suppose you mean because his brother is a bloody earl?"

"Captain Loder!"

"I beg your pardon, but my feelings got the better of me."

Mrs. Simon, at the fine spectacle of a professional male in jealous rage, grew a little more excited, and forgetting even Fern, said, "In mah part of the South, they call that kind of man a nigger-lover."

And then like the vengeance of God the earthquake happened, noisily, with a clatter and bang because there was so much brass and bric-à-brac to fall all about them. Both women began to scream, and still screaming they were dragged to the verandah where Mrs. Hoggett-Egburry promptly fainted. Then while her friend and Harry Loder were reviving her, the flood swept down the valley, just below them, roaring and whining above the distant sound of wailing, and as Mrs. Hoggett-Egburry raised her head for the first time and moaned faintly, it occurred to Harry Loder that he should be back at the barracks where all sorts of terrible things might have happened, and not here on the verandah with two hysterical middle-aged women.

He said to Mrs. Simon, "Now she's all right, I'll leave you and get to the barracks," but Mrs. Simon cried out, "No, no. You can't leave us now."

"That's where I belong," he answered. "Stay here and I'll come back for you as soon as I'm able."

Then Mrs. Hoggett-Egburry cried out that she could not be left, and Mrs. Simon, intoxicated a little by the spectacle of Harry Loder in male action, said, "No Lily, let him go." And to Loder she said, "Go! Go! Do your duty!"

Then suddenly he was gone and Mrs. Hoggett-Egburry heard the strange horrible sounds from the town below them and said, "What is that?"

"It's people yelling," said Mrs. Simon, and again she turned to where Harry Loder had been, and said, "Go! Your place is at the barracks." But he was already gone.

Skirting the edge of the flood, he drove the wheezy old Morris through the rain, sometimes on the road, sometimes across the sodden fields, for he knew every inch of the way only too well, so well that he was damned sick of it, even now in all the excitement; and as he drove he was frightened, not by the fear of death which he had never experienced, but by a kind of vague, indescribable animal fear, like the panic fear of a startled buck in thick jungle, a dread of something which he did not understand. It was terror of that damned interminable rain, of the fiercely burgeoning vegetation, of fevers, of snakes, of the hatred he sometimes felt about him everywhere, a fear of the dank stillness that preceded the quake and a fear even now in his excitement of his own Indian troops, so sleek and obedient beneath his iron hand, and yet somehow so evasive and insolent and in their spirits disloyal. It was a dread of the very land-scape which he could no longer see in the driving rain, and of the very trees whose branches seemed to reach down into the yellow circle of light to seize him from the car.

He had been like that—nervy—for a long time, he knew now; he could remember the definite feeling coming over him for the first time about three years ago, but it had, he knew, been going on much longer than that beneath the surface of his healthy skin, from the very moment he had arrived in India, hating its smells, even the pleasant smell of jas-mine and spices which other men, men whose health had been broken long ago, found nostalgic and agreeable. He had hated the whole bloody thing and most of all had hated the Indians themselves. He couldn't, when he tried, think of one you could trust. He couldn't understand them. Hindus or Moslems, it was the same kettle of fish. If you were friendly, they turned arrogant and insufferable; if you treated them as a soldier should, the sly bastards had a way of making you feel inferior, as if you were some kind of half-savage animal. For ten years he had stuck it out, hating the country and the landscape and the people, home-sick for Devonshire and wishing all the time he were in Burma, which was at least lush and green, or Shanghai or any bloody place but India. It hadn't even hurt his health, the vulnerable spot with most men. It had struck him from behind, subtly, undermining the nerves of a man who had no nerves. Not even the pig-sticking and panther-shooting, not even the pleasure of killing that was always in his blood, the pleasure of an expert thrust of a spear or a perfect shot from a high-powered rifle, could make up for the other thing, that horrible nameless dread that had been eating into him for so long. Once in the hills beyond Mount Abana when he had been panther-shooting, he had had a mild attack of fever and experienced a horrible dream in which he kept on killing panthers, one after another until there was a great pile of corpses before him and his aching arms could no longer hold up the rifle. They had kept on coming, leaping at him from the top of the heap of carcasses until at last when he no longer had strength to fire, one leapt at him and dragged him to the ground. And in the dream each panther was India.

Driving faster and faster along the road, the dread overcame even the rage he felt that Ransome should have gotten Fern Simon before him, the rage which he had managed somehow to turn from jealousy and injured vanity into outraged virtue and honor with the peculiar dull hyprocrisy of men who live by what is called a "code." He forgot even that he had planned to do the same thing and had not done it simply because the girl would not have him. And in his vanity there was a kind of physical pain that such a girl, the daughter of ordinary common missionaries, should prefer a bloody drunk like Ransome to himself, to whom most women fell victims at once. But through the fury and dread he saw that Mrs. Hoggett-Egburry was right. He couldn't shoot Ransome. He wasn't worth it, or that little tart, either! After all, he had his future to think of, and what happened to Fern wasn't important. Now he didn't want her any longer, but his vanity wanted balm. No, he wouldn't shoot Ransome, but he'd beat the hell out of him the first chance he got.

Then in the lights of the car he saw the white corner post of the race-course road and knew that he was only a little way from the barracks, and at the same time he heard wild shouts and cries and the sickening un-nameable fear took entire possession of him again and he thought, "Maybe they've turned! Maybe they're murdering the boys!" and in the next moment the lights of the car turning in at the drive, struck the place where the barracks should have been, only there were no barracks now but only a great heap of rubble with jagged and broken beams emerging here and there. He heard the wild cries of the Indian soldiers scurrying like ants in the drenching rain to clear away the shattered stone and mortar, and at the same time he thought, "That's where the mess was. They must have been at mess. They're all beneath it . . . Cruikshank and Culbertson and Bailey and Sampson." Then the soldiers came run-ning toward him, staring into the lights, shouting things which he did not understand, and he thought, "This bloody country! This God-damned bloody country!" and began to sob.

Without stopping the motor he jumped out and cried in Hindustani, "Where is Lieutenant Bailey? Where are the officers?" and the three men who had run toward him no longer shouted, but stood half in the circle of light from the motor, paralyzed and tongue-tied, and then one called Pashat Singh, a sergeant, choked and blurted in Hindustani: "He's in there. All the sahibs are in there. The house fell on them." Then the men began to make incomprehensible noises and to salaam again and again in the most unmilitary fashion as if they were in some way responsible for the disaster.

Loder cried out, "Get to work, you bloody bastards! Get to work! Dig them out of there!" He shouted and swore to cover the sound of his own sobs, for his men must not know that he, a British soldier, was sobbing; but he could not stop the sobs now, even by stiffening every muscle. The sobs were a physical paroxysm which shook him from head to foot like spasms, and between the paroxysms he shivered in his drenched clothing. He thought, "God help me to pull myself together! God help me!" He had not felt like this since he was a child of four, frightened by the great dog which had jumped into his crib in the middle of the night once long ago at his uncle's house in Surrey.

And as he ran toward the mass of stone, he saw that there was no use in hurrying to get them out . . . Cruikshank and Bailey and Culbertson and Sampson . . . nobody could be alive beneath all that mass of stone and beams and mortar. He would never again see them alive.

With Pashat Singh beside him he began to tear at the heap of stones, cut long ago from the depths of that eternal Mountain Abana, wildly and without plan, cursing and sobbing, and almost at once he came upon the piano, that poor, awful, tinny piano, ruined by heat and dampness, which Cruikshank used to play after tiffin in the evenings. He thought, "Perhaps he was playing the piano. Perhaps we'll find him here." And then suddenly they found the body of poor Cruikshank beneath the battered piano, crumpled, broken, bloody and quite dead, and clenching both fists, Loder raised them toward the pouring sky, shaking them and crying out, "This bloody country! This bloody awful country!"

For a long time after Loder left them, the two middle-aged women remained huddled together on the floor of the verandah, Mrs. Hoggett-Egburry sobbing hysterically, Mrs. Simon trying to comfort her, and then presently they both were silent from emotional exhaustion and sat listening, straining to hear the distant sounds from the stricken town which came to them, muffled and hideous through the rain, as if in some way they could read them and discover what had happened.

Then Mrs. Simon said, in a low voice, "I wonder what has happened to the boys . . . and to Hazel and Mr. Simon."

Mrs. Hoggett-Egburry said: "Thank Gawd 'erbert wasn't 'ere. 'Is nerves could never 'ave stood it."

"I've got to get home. I think I can drive the car."

Then Mrs. Hoggett-Egburry began again to cry drunkenly: "Don't leave me. You cawn't leave me."

"Get me your driver."

"I can't move. I cawn't get up. Call him. Call the 'ouse boy."

Mrs. Simon clapped her hands, but there was no answer and then she tried shouting the name of the head boy, weakly at first and then louder and louder as the terror grew again.

"Dalji!" she shouted, "Dalji!" again and again, and when no one answered she fell silent, filled with terror worse than her terror of the quake. Beside her the "Duchess," the wife of the manager of the Ranchipur Bank who came of county people in Shropshire, with an accent she had invented for herself, began to scream again, this time in cockney. She wasn't any longer the "Duchess," but simply the vulgar beauty she had been long ago when Herbert Hoggett-Egburry married her out of passion and weakness and innocence, to the ruin of his whole career, a woman who had been left behind in Ranchipur because in Delhi he was ashamed of her, now that her beauty and his passion were spent. The two middle-aged women, one from Unity Point, Mississippi, and the other from Shropshire, clung to each other, deserted, terrified, forgotten.

In the Summer Palace the solid ancient walls cracked at the first shock of the quake and for a little time, held together by their own vast weight, tottered before falling, the east side inward, the west side outward upon the ornate *porte cochère* over the beds of cannas and geraniums. The east wall buried Miss de Souza, the nurse, Lady Esketh's two frightened maids and four Indian servants, and the west wall put an end to the two Sikhs and the porter on guard at the entrance. The servants who escaped ran from the house into the park in the direction of the bazaar, and here the flood caught them, sweeping them to death in a wall of water and corpses and broken houses. In what remained of the palace Lord Esketh, in the teakwood bed ornamented with mother-of-pearl, alone remained alive. The wall and part of the roof slipped away and the driving monsoon rain swept in, striking his face, soaking the bedclothes, rousing him for a moment to consciousness out of the delirium which for fourteen hours had kept him writhing on the bed, crying out at the phantoms which tormented him, now cringing, now trying to throw himself on the floor, for the fever and pain were violent and drove him to behave like a madman. Two hours before the quake the glands in the groin had begun to swell and the dread buboes to appear beneath the arms and in the throat, and with them came the lancinating pains which burst even through the wall of morphine which the Major had built between him and torment, dragging him by its awful violence back to a kind of consciousness in which he was aware clearly of his own misery and agony.

Now, wakening slowly in little gusts of consciousness beneath the flood of the monsoon rain, he thought at first that he was back again in the luxury of the house in Hill Street and that a pipe had burst in a room above his head. He would try to shout for Bates, and then the delirium would seize him again, thrusting him back into a horrible world of dreadful shapes; but with each returning wave of consciousness his mind became a little more clear, and each time the wave lasted a little longer, until presently he was able to understand by the glare from the burning town that he was in a strange place, in an unfamiliar shattered room, and that the water which fell on his face came not from a broken pipe, but from the sky itself, a sky thick with clouds which reflected the light of the flames on the earth below him. The glowing clouds seemed to press down onto his bed, and in his groin and beneath the arms there was a terrible grinding pain, and in the distance the sound of wailing as of souls in torment.

Again he tried to cry out the name of Bates, but this time he found that no sound came from his mouth. It was filled, choked with some substance which, when he attempted to speak, seemed to suffocate him. Then slowly he understood that he could not speak because the curious substance was his own tongue, so swollen now that it filled his whole mouth, and wildly, half in delirium, he thought: "I am dead. I am already in hell" and horror took full possession of him.

Then mercifully the delirium intervened for a time with horrors more kind than the horror of the conscious pain and the monstrous swollen tongue, and he tossed and struggled until the morphine, receding again in waves, freed his consciousness once more and again he tried to cry out the name of Bates; but his mouth made no sound. And at last a little before midnight the morphine wore away altogether, leaving his mind quite clear but still a prey to pain which made him clutch his own body as if by tearing it apart with his own hands he could find peace from the agony. Throbbing with each beat of the powerful heart, the pain came and went in spasms, and in the intervals it became slowly clear to him where he was and how he had come there and he wanted to cry out: "Where are you? Why have you all left me here in this hell?" And then he remembered the bargaining with the Maharajah over the horses and the bargaining with the Dewan over the mills, and clearest of all the quarrel with Edwina, and again he tried to shout, not the name of Bates this time, but of Edwina, thinking, "She can't leave me here like this. She doesn't hate me so much as that. It is not the sort of thing she would do." But again his throat contracted and the muscles of his jaws worked desperately but no sound came from the swollen tongue.

Then, half-delirious, half-conscious, he began to live over again in snatches the whole of his life—the days when as a boy he had gone out of Liverpool on his bicycle on holidays to watch the gentry riding over hedges and ditches in their pink coats, the day of his final quarrel with his father and mother when he had run away to London never to see either of them again, the days in Macassar and Borneo, and then the Malay States when, as a young man, planning and scheming the future, watching people, studying them shrewdly, he had sold cutlery and cheap watches. Between stabs of tormenting pain and moments of delirium he lived again that feeling of triumph touched with bitterness and contempt for his fellowmen, a feeling which he knew each time he swindled one of them and made a great coup. And at last he came to this final voyage, to this India which he hated, this India which was being ruined as a great market because there were stupid men in the India office who refused to treat the Indian people harshly, as one must always treat those from whom profit is to be drawn—this hateful India where there were men like the Maharajah and that wily Dewan. It all passed through his brain, muddled and confused and shot through with the pain and the new misery of the chills brought on by the soaking rain. And in a sudden moment of clearer vision, he thought: "I must not die. Not till I've done all I mean to do . . . not till I've got all this bloody world owes me. . . ." Not till he had more wealth and more power and had written all those leaders with which his newspapers were to smash the bloody Bolsheviks and those weak bastards who were all crying out for peace. Who wanted peace? Whoever made profit out of peace? Look at the bloody League of Nations. . . . Wildly he thought, "I must get out of here . . . I must get away."

Raising himself with a frantic effort, he tried again to make the hideous swollen tongue articulate the name of Bates. Then desperately he managed to slip to the side of the bed, where the jagged knife was thrust again into his groin and turned this way and that while he slid to the floor, every muscle cramped by the awful pain. Then it passed and only the throbbing which came from the bull-like heart which would not let him die, remained, and the obsession returned: "I must get out of here . . . out of this bloody place and this bloody country." And crawling on his hands and knees, he struggled toward the door.

Inch by inch he made his way under the beating rain across the Turkey-red carpet. Twice he fell, stabbed again in the groin and the armpits and the throat by that dreadful knife, by those worms, those horrible microscopic animals which were devouring him; and at last he reached the door, and with a surging of that monstrous vitality, raised himself slowly until at last he was standing, tearing at the gilt door handle. But the door did not move because behind it there lay tons of fallen stones and beams and the crushed bodies of Miss de Souza and Edwina's two maids. Wildly he tried to force it open, gurgling and choking in an effort to make the swollen tongue cry out: "Help me! Save me! I am Lord Esketh . . . the great and powerful Lord Esketh. I'll pay you what you want. I'll give you everything I have, only get me out of here. Help me! Save me!"

But the tongue was silent, so swollen now that it had begun to choke him. Then in the wild delirium he had a sudden vision of the face of Bates, cold, white, damp, hating him, full of contempt. The door handle came away suddenly, and in a final paroxysm of pain he fell with all his huge weight, and his aching, burning head struck the marble top of the Victorian washstand. Then mercifully he was beyond pain, beyond delirium, and in the reflected glow from the burning city he lay still at last on the soaked Turkey-red carpet beneath the flood of the monsoon.

It was the Untouchable quarter which suffered worst of all because it lay in the lowest part of the city just across the river from the burning-ghats and on it fell not only the weight of the water itself, but the whole burden of shattered trees and wrecked houses and corpses which the flood bore upon its angry breast.

At the first shock of the quake Mr. Jobnekar, taking his wife and three doll-like children with him, had gone down into the little square to join the crowd which had gathered there, but before he was able to speak and reassure even his nearest neighbors, the distant roaring began, and above it the curious muffled sound of terror which rose from the city above them, not the sound of a thousand separate voices raised in terror, but the sound of a single voice as if the whole city had seen destruction coming toward it and had cried out in agony.

Mr. Jobnekar, quicker, more intelligent, more educated than the others, understood the meaning of the sound and cried out, "Flood! Flood! Take to the roofs!" and all about him the cry was picked up and carried along until the voices in the Square of the Untouchables joined the sound of terror that rose from the upper city. Seizing two of the children, with Mrs. Jobnekar carrying the smallest, they ran back again into the little pink house with the Nottingham lace curtains, up one flight of steps and then another until they came to the roof. Neighbors pushed up the stairs at their heels, all screaming and shouting with terror. Behind them the panic-stricken mob poured out on to the flat roof until there was no more room and children disappeared, trampled in the agony of fear. Mr. Jobnekar had only time to pull his wife close to him and shelter the three whimpering children between them when the flood with a wild roar struck the square, sweeping aside one house after another, crushing with its weight of wreckage and corpses the few miserable men, women, and children who still remained in the square itself. And at the same moment Mr. Jobnekar knew that there was no hope and tried wildly to gather his wife and the crying children all within the compass of his

The awful woman opposite her, that vulgar, strange, ravaged woman, went on and on talking, telling her things she did not want to hear, things which had nothing to do with her, which in an odd way made her feel ashamed of herself.

She was saying now, "I wasn't good to him as often as I should have been . . . he never asked me outright, but I knew and sometimes I shut him out."

Lady Esketh wanted to cry out, "What is that to me? Why should you be telling me all this?" But she could not bring herself to speak. She wanted to say, "I don't give a damn about a husband I never saw," but she kept silent, still watching the raddled face that was no longer coquettish and hard, but raddled and old and flabby.

"I've had so much misery. You've no idea what it is like to have to live here in Ranchipur . . . always . . . always. It makes you mean and queer and horrible inside."

Then perhaps through her tears Mrs. Simon saw the shadow on the face of Lady Esketh, the hard, rather set look of distaste, and she said, "Please let me talk to you. There isn't anyone else I might talk to." And Lady Esketh thought, "I suppose that at home I would have said that she didn't show a decent restraint . . . but I'm not at home." No, she was sitting here in the midst of India in a world that was suddenly shattered and terrifying.

"You see," Mrs. Simon said, "I've just begun to feel what has happened. I couldn't feel it before. It wasn't real. I didn't believe it in my heart. It's only now that I *know* he's dead under all those stones. It's the first time I've *known* I'll never see him again."

The jackals began their ghostly wailing again, and above the chorus rose the wild laughter of a hyena. "Dead," thought Lady Esketh. "The whole place is full of dead and the jackals and hyenas are dragging the dead about." And she remembered suddenly the clouds of vultures and kites she had seen distantly from Mr. Bannerjee's balcony, swirling round and round, circling lower and lower, not darting cleanly like eagles and falcons, but swooping lazily down because their victims were dead and there was no reason for haste. She thought, "I will waken and it will be over and I will discover that I have never been in India at all." But she knew that the sound of the jackals' crying was real, as real as the cheap, bitter grief in the face of the awful woman who kept watch with her.

It was true—what Mrs. Simon had said. Neither the catastrophe nor the death of her husband and daughter had had any reality for her until suddenly in the stillness of the half-ruined kitchen it had become suddenly as real to her as if they had both died slowly in their beds under her very eye. Before that, the shock, her own sense of the dramatic, the confusion, the terror and the excitement, had somehow numbed her consciousness and distorted the whole world about her so that her own persistence and heroism in the rescue of Lily Hoggett-Egburry had obscured all else. And then something in the eyes of the Englishwoman opposite her had changed everything. What it was that suddenly made the difference she could not explain to herself, but there was in the eyes a kind of coldness and honesty which had eaten away layer after layer of pretense and hysteria until at last she had begun quietly to cry the first real tears which she had shed in twenty years. For the first time in nearly twenty years she felt as she had felt long ago as a girl, soft and warm and at peace. The tears she shed were not for the middle-aged, plumpish man who lay crushed and dead under all the stones across the drive, but for a boy of twenty-one and for herself as she had been long ago. They were tears, too, for what had never been between them and might have been, something which now, weary and terrified, with the world about her demolished and standing still at last, she divined dimly for the first time. They were tears, too, of self-pity for her own muddled life, and because suddenly she knew that in spite of everything she was old, older even than she should have been at forty-three, worn out by anxieties and envy and petty jealousies, older by a hundred years than this cold beautiful woman who sat opposite her and could not be many years younger than herself. And beneath her tears and regrets she kept thinking, "It isn't fair. It isn't fair that she should have had everything and me nothing."

She found herself saying, "I can't help talking like this to you. There isn't anyone I can talk to in all Ranchipur." There wasn't even Lily any longer, for she had found out about Lily, found her out so thoroughly that she could never again envy or even respect her. And for that too she wept. Burying her face in her hands, she leaned forward on the table and for a moment she felt that she was about to faint or to die, and then quietly she fell asleep in the candle-light.

Opposite her, Lady Esketh thought, "Thank God!" but at the same time she felt ashamed of her own hardness.

The night dragged on and on. For a long time Edwina sat upright on the stiff wooden chair, Harry Loder's pistol on the table before her. Opposite her, Mrs. Simon slept, leaning forward on the kitchen table, her head buried in her plump arms. It was a sleep like death, born of all the terror and hysteria and exhaustion of the past forty-eight hours. Edwina herself felt no desire to sleep; it was as if she would never sleep again. And presently she rose and walked about Aunt Phoebe's kitchen, clean now and spotless as Aunt Phoebe always kept it. She opened cupboard doors and examined kettles and the odd Indian stove with its series of tiny fireplaces, and slowly the place took on a kind of wonder for her. It was all so small, so neat, with a kind of charm about it like the charm of a doll's house for a child. This was a tiny realm belonging to the odd, rather matter-of-fact, direct old lady. Within its walls there was a scrupulous order and an obviously efficient organization. And presently Edwina thought, "What fun it would be to have a kitchen like this—a kitchen which belonged to you, in which you were a queen, out of which you produced with order and efficiency the meals three times a day for a whole family." And again there occurred to her intimations of that peace which was a part of all small lives, a peace which was desirable and even wonderful for all its monotony. She saw suddenly that never in all her life, not even during those pinched days long ago in the Florentine pension, had she ever known a life that was orderly and secure and pleasant; for even then in the three small rooms overlooking the Arno, she and her father had had in a sense "camped out" like gypsies, awaiting always a turn in the wheel of fortune which would throw them back into a world of impersonal luxury and debt, where there was a certain splendor and even glamour but neither security nor order nor peace. "That was it," she thought as she inspected Aunt Phoebe's orderly kitchen, "I have always lived a disorderly life as far back as I can remember."

She had been trained somehow, without ever having had any training, to believe, even to feel in the marrow of her bones, that for her there was some special privilege which set her aside, some obligation imposed upon the world to see that things were done for her; and so she had never known the sureness and satisfaction of that bird-like old lady to whom all this unearthly mixture of refugees—Hindus and Europeans and Americans alike—had turned in the moment of catastrophe. And suddenly she understood for a second the profoundness of the satisfaction which Aunt Phoebe must know, a sense of fulfillment, of having done one's duty, so great that it annihilated fear and boredom and disorder and even the terror of death. No, that she had never known. And she thought, "I am intelligent. I am strong as an ox. I have never been of the least use to anyone. I might still make a try. I might find something more wonderful than I have ever known. I might some day come to have in my eye that look of peace which is in the eyes of that old lady and in the eyes of that funny, disagreeable Scotswoman who runs the hospital for the Major."

Like a schoolgirl she began, in the silence of Aunt Phoebe's kitchen, to have dreams and ideas about another existence. The catastrophe had broken the line of her life. Now, alone, she knew that circumstance had freed her and given her another chance, perhaps the last she would ever have. Albert was probably dead by now, dead as she had predicted on that morning, years ago it seemed now, when she had sat across the room from him, realizing for the first time all her hatred and contempt. Yes, he was probably dead (the fact left her cold and without feeling) and she was free, free not only of him, but of all that life of which she had been a part. She need never even go back to the house in Hill Street or to England. She could become another person. She would go to the Maharani, to Aunt Phoebe herself, to old Miss MacDaid, or to the Major and say, "Here I am, strong and healthy. In all this death and misery there must be something I can do to help. Tell me and I will do it."

And suddenly she was seized with excitement, of a kind she had never known before. That was it! She would work in the hospitals. She would work with the Major. Somehow she would cling to the edges of that feeling, that emotion, which Tom said those others had about India, the India that was to stir and, shaking herself, rise and return to her old dignity and grandeur. She, who had always been spoiled and lecherous and useless, could still save herself. The room seemed to her suddenly small and stifling, and going to the door she pulled away the chair and table and opened it and went out into the Indian night.

For a moment the sky had cleared here and there, and among the scattered clouds there were patches of deep sapphire sky filled with shining stars. It was still now save for the occasional cry of a jackal and a distant sound of roaring which troubled her as if it were the prelude to some new catastrophe. Before her, beyond the barrier of prickly pear and the shattered mud wall, stretched the Indian plain, that vast plateau which extended on and on as far as the Gulf of Bengal, a plain which could swallow up England and France and Germany, more than half of Europe, and still be empty. Far off, miles away, near the barrier of corpses and wreckage which Harry Loder and Raschid had gone to destroy, rose the dark mass of Mount Abana, its white Jain temples dimly glistening in the light of the Indian sky. While she stood there she experienced, for the first time in all her crowded and confused existence, a sense of solitude and insignificance, which to her feverish spirit was like a bath of cold clear water; and with the solitude came a kind of peace. And then all at once she was terrified—of what she did not know, unless it was the revelation of her own smallness.

Then out of the stillness from behind her came a noise like the cry of a jackal, the voice of Mrs. Simon filled with terror.

"Lady Esketh! Lady Esketh! Where are you? Where are you?" and the dreams, the peace, the solitude were gone and she was filled with anger and exasperation. In a fierce whisper she called toward the plump figure outlined against the dim candle-light which showed through the open doorway, "Here I am! Be quiet! You'll wake all the others!"

"Oh, you frightened me so! I thought you might have been carried off by those awful Bhils."

Then as the rain began again the clouds swept over the sky. The faint phosphorescent whiteness of the distant temples faded away into the darkness and she went back into the shuttered house to listen once more to the shaming confidences of Mrs. Simon.

In Mrs. Bannerjee's bedroom Fern waked as the first light of dawn appeared over the shattered city. She had slept long and wearily and as she opened her eyes and threw back one arm she did not know where she was and for a long time, half between sleep and consciousness, she experienced a slow feeling of horror, of what she did not know. It was like the horror of a nightmare from which she could not waken. And then in the dim gray light she became aware of the netting that enclosed her and of the hardness of the strange, rope-woven bed on which she lay. Sitting up, she pushed aside the netting and at the same time she remembered all that had happened—the horror of the quake itself, the trip in the little red-and-gold boat, the dreadful scene with her mother, and the scene with Ransome, drunk, mocking her and himself.

In the gray light she saw the figure wrapped in a *dhoti* lying on the floor at her feet, and in sudden terror she thought it must be a strange corpse. Fascinated, she stared at it for a time, and seeing that the body inside the *dhoti* breathed and moved, she bent over it and saw that one hand emerged, a hand which she knew very well, one of the two hands she had found so beautiful, and for a moment she felt that she was going to faint. But she thought, "No, I mustn't do that. Not now. I must not faint." And pulling herself together she knelt and gently lifted the cloth so that she might see the face beneath it. The face she could not see, as it was hidden in the crook of the arm, but she knew the head with its strong lean neck and curly, crisp, dark hair, the head which she somehow knew so well without ever having consciously noticed it. The sight of it made her want to cry. Quietly she slipped down beside him, and lay there pressing her cheek against the curly head.

When he stirred he turned his head and looked at her with a dazed expression of wonder in the dark eyes. Then slowly the crooked grin which always made her feel weak spread over the tired face, and he put his arm about her and held her close to him. As her cheek touched his, she knew that he was crying.

Outside, in the rising dawn, the choked river had begun to roar again for Harry Loder had done his job well and the barrier of wreckage and bodies was gone.

When they left the room and came out on to the frail wooden balcony, the daylight had come and with it the flood water had disappeared. From the balustrade the little gilded pleasure boat dangled, like a drunken man after a night of revelry, from the cord of Mr. Bannerjee's Bond Street dressing-gown. Then for the first time they were able to see the devastation wrought by the flood. Of the village at the end of the compound nothing remained of the clustered huts and shrines. Against the shattered wall lay three bodies, those of a man, an old woman, and a child. In the lower branches of the great banyan tree there was another body caught and held there by the cheap cotton *dhoti* which the man had worn in life. In another tree there hung suspended grotesquely the carcass of a dead donkey. In the landscape close at hand only two structures remained standing, the phallic temple of Shiva and the stout cast-iron statue of Queen Victoria. Half the bridge had collapsed, but the buttress which supported the Good Queen remained, and on it she still stood, clutching firmly her umbrella and her reticule. Weeds and branches formed a kind of boa scarf about the short plump neck, trailing backward as they had been drawn by the current of the flood.

"We can walk now," said Ransome. "I suppose we had better go to the Smileys'. We can't get across the river."

So they descended the stairs of the wrecked half-empty house and set out along the drive past the Major's overturned motor toward the Racecourse Road. Everywhere there was wreckage and red mud, mud so thick that it sucked at their feet as if trying to draw them back into the earth with all the other dead. They passed Raschid's house, where they saw Mrs. Raschid and her seven children already engaged in dragging soaked bits of furniture on to the verandah. And then Ransome's own house still standing but with half the roof shattered and a gigantic crack disfiguring the Belgravian façade. Then they reached the open country and the walking was easier, for the flood had swept past here and left the metalled road bare and shining.

They walked in silence, both still dazed and incredulous at what had happened to them. Ransome scarcely saw the shattered landscape about them. It was as if he moved without effort, as if he had no consciousness of reality of the moment—that Fern, dressed in his own shorts and tennis shirt and himself in Mr. Bannerjee's Bengali *dhoti* made a grotesque picture. Now, grotesqueness which even in ordinary circumstances counted for so little in India, had ceased utterly to exist. He knew now what poets meant when they wrote of "the singing of the heart." Something had happened to him, something which he had sought, sometimes without knowing it, the whole of his life. He had for a time lost himself, that awful, introspective self-pitying, boring self which always destroyed all satisfaction. And it had happened easily, without planning, without self-consciousness, with a kind of simple beauty and naturalness, like the thrusting of green shoots after the first downpour of the monsoon rains. For a second the old self returned as he knew it would return again and again once this first intoxication was passed, and he thought, "I am a man at last, a human man like those who are blessed by God with simplicity." Not all the debauchery, not all the weary promiscuous experimenting, had made of him a man. It had been that simple, fine and lovely thing, merging into the borders of sleep and dreams, which had happened in this shattered, evil-haunted house of Mr. Bannerjee. It was a new feeling, filled with a kind of glory which seemed to blind him and fill him with an extraordinary sense of confidence and of strength that was physical.

She was there beside him, walking with her fingers entwined in his. And he dared not to look at her for fear that the whole thing, all the sense of exaltation, all the simple beauty of what had happened, even Fern herself, might simply vanish in illusion, as all else had always vanished. As he walked he felt prayerful and kept repeating, not with his lips, but in his brain, "Thank you, God! Thank you!" for he knew that whatever else happened to him in the rest of his life, he had, for one moment, known what few men ever know. It was a sense of fullness, of fulfillment. At last he was a man. Most men died without ever knowing what that meant. And it had happened in the midst of desolation and death.

Beside him Fern walked, thinking over and over again, "I am happy! I am happy! I love him!" and she too knew, without all the weary experience of Ransome, that she was among the blessed of God. Now she did not even think that with her father and sister dead, and death all about her, she should be sad. In all that ruined world only two people existed any longer—herself and Tom Ransome.

As they came in sight of the Smileys' house, they saw among the trees the rusty gray figures of the elephants, and Ransome said, "Raschid must be there, and Harry Loder." But when they arrived at the house Harry Loder was not there, but only Raschid Ali Khan still dressed in the ill-fitting uniform, surrounded by the others, by Edwina and Aunt Phoebe, Mrs. Simon and Mrs. Hoggett-Egburry and the Bannerjees and a half-dozen low-caste Hindus who had turned up from somewhere. He looked gaunt and weary and he was telling them about the death of Harry Loder.

Harry had succeeded in blowing up the barrier with dynamite, but somehow, Raschid did not know how, something had gone wrong and in the darkness, in the very midst of the operations, his escape from the barrier had been cut off, and as the explosion occurred and the mass of wreckage and bodies heaved and broke, Harry Loder was swept away with it, down the narrow canyon.

The big Muslim told the story simply, and when he had finished, he said, "He gave his life to save many others. He wasn't even an engineer. He knew nothing about such things. He acted as a soldier and a hero."

For a moment there was silence and then Raschid, the warrior, the Muslim, the enemy of the British Empire said, quite simply, "It was an Englishman doing his duty."

Watching him, listening, Fern understood suddenly the look on the face of Harry Loder when he had stood here in the same room the day before without seeing her at all, as if she had ceased to exist. It was like the look in the face of Miss Dirks as she sat on the verandah of Ransome's house, drinking tea and talking nostalgically of Nolham, the look of one who was already dead. What Fern could not have known was the story of the nightmare he had had long ago in the mountains when he had killed one panther after another as they sprang at him; until at last in weariness his arm had fallen and that last one which he saw was India, had sprung upon him, dragging him to the ground.

Then Mrs. Hoggett-Egburry, dressed once more in her dried but still mud-stained *peignoir*, began to cry and Mrs. Simon led her from the room. They had both known Harry Loder well; the sight of his full-blooded, beefy body entering a room had stirred them both. And now in death he was a hero. Now their itching, troubling desire was still; together they might weep for what they had never known.

[383]

When they had gone, Raschid said, "I must get back now to the other side of the river." And to Ransome he said, "You'd better come with me. I imagine Her Highness will want to see you."

But Aunt Phoebe would not let him go until he had had coffee and toast and the last two eggs in the house. "It's no good," she said, "asking a man to do work on an empty stomach."

So while they waited he wrote a note in French to John the Baptist and sent one of the Untouchables on Aunt Phoebe's bicycle back to his house for proper clothes. Now suddenly, with Mr. Bannerjee in the same room, he saw that in spite of everything he must look ridiculous in a Bengali *dhoti*, and he found it unmanageable; it kept tripping him up and slipping off his shoulders. Then for the first time he became aware of Edwina, sitting in a corner, dressed in Mrs. Smiley's calico dress. She looked at him and gave him a tired smile, and he thought, "She knows what has happened, but of course she would."

She knew and Aunt Phoebe knew. They had known, he understood now, from the moment he and Fern had entered the room. He tried to catch Aunt Phoebe's eye, but when he met her gaze it was blank, too blank to be convincing.

Raschid's account of Harry Loder's death had saved Fern and himself the ordeal and embarrassment of coming into the room to meet at the same time the combined gaze of Aunt Phoebe's strange house party. The others had all been listening to Raschid, and scarcely noticed them. They would perhaps have thought the worst, but they could not, like Edwina and Aunt Phoebe, have divined it. On the way from Mr. Bannerjee's house, in his mood of exaltation and release, he had thought of that old world of gossip and smallness as shattered and finished, but now he knew that it still existed. It was still there all about him so long as people like Fern's mother and Mrs. Hoggett-Egburry and Miss Murgatroyd remained. They had a power, a strong and maddening power, of altering the whole quality of what happened about them. Once their distraction over Harry Loder's death was gone, they would talk, and in talking of what they could not understand, would tarnish and complicate and bespatter the thing with their hypocrisy and respectability. There returned to him the memory of Fern's visit just before Mr. Bannerjee's dinner, of her misery and his own drunkenness, and the hopelessness of going for aid to Raschid Ali Khan and his wife. But it seemed now all very far away, as if he had been another man who was now dead.

Exhaustion, the exhaustion which follows shock and the long strain of work and responsibility, seemed to have seized them all. Mr. and Mrs. Bannerjee drifted away silently, with Miss Murgatroyd, subdued and weary, following them, and there were left in the kitchen only big Raschid and Edwina, Fern, and Aunt Phoebe bending over the stove. Even her spare, tireless figure seemed to droop a little. They sat in silence until Edwina said, "But what happened to you? You haven't told us that."

For a second Ransome did not answer her; he did not want to answer her until he was sure how she meant the question, whether she had asked simply out of curiosity, whether there was still in the question something of the old maliciousness, or whether she had asked only to embarrass himself and Fern. A sharp glance and he saw that the blue eyes were innocent. She *knew*, but she had not asked in order to embarrass them.

"Nothing much. On the way back, it got dark and I got myself lost. ⁓ spent most of the night in the boat tied up to a banyan tree."

He watched Aunt Phoebe's back. She did not even turn from the stove, and then, with a little shock of astonishment, he knew that she had approved of what had happened, and he thought again of his grandmother and the story of how she had not waited for a clergyman and had ridden pregnant, three hundred miles across the Nevada mountains on muleback to make her child legitimate. In both old women there was something, some force and grandeur, it seemed to him, which one no longer found in the world, something which was of the world, real, not "modern" and transient like the morality of such people as himself and Edwina, but something eternal. The sight of Aunt Phoebe bending over the stove, so ancient and wise and dependable, made him feel suddenly young, like a boy who has gotten himself into a scrape.

He and Raschid and Fern began to eat, and to his astonishment he saw Edwina rise from the stiff wooden chair and help Aunt Phoebe to serve the eggs and coffee—Edwina who for years had never raised a finger even to dress herself. He looked at her, and in the blue eyes he

[385]

saw the shadow of a smile. She was too tired and the burden of misery was too great for her to smile, but the look of understanding was there —that she knew he thought the spectacle funny. But there was, too, in the sudden glance something appealing, as if she said, "You see, I can be useful. I'm not a useless fool," and he remembered the sight of her on the day before, with her white evening gown hiked up and fastened about the waist, making her way across the muddy red plain. A sudden flash of delight went through him because people, in a crisis, were better than you expected them to be—even people like Edwina and himself.

Opposite him, Raschid said, "Look! Here come Homer and Bertha!" and through the open door they saw a little procession coming across the plain toward the house from the direction of the shattered Sikh barracks. At the head walked Homer Smiley; after him trailed the twenty-seven Untouchable boys from the night school and at the rear like a sheep dog, came Bertha Smiley.

They brought news, good news, that there still remained a bridge— the steel bridge two miles above the city which carried the narrow-gauge railway across the Ranchipur River. The force of the flood and wreckage had jarred it loose from its foundations, but it was still solid enough to provide a way from one side of the town to the other.

In the joy of finding the Smileys still alive, the little group forgot for an instant the catastrophe. The Bannerjees and Miss Murgatroyd, Mrs. Simon and Mrs. Hoggett-Egburry returned, drawn by the sounds of welcome, and Ransome was treated to the extraordinary spectacle of Mrs. Simon kissing Mr. Smiley while tears ran down her plump face. Even Mrs. Simon was more human than he had believed possible.

When they had all heard the Smileys' story, Raschid said, "What is the news from the other side?"

"The Maharajah is dead," said Homer Smiley. "The hospital is still standing. The Summer Palace is wrecked. The Engineering School and the Law Courts have burned. Her Highness is living in a tent in the park. She sent word that she wanted to see Raschid and Ransome if they were still alive."

"And the Major?" asked Ransome without looking at Edwina.

"The Major and Miss MacDaid are alive. He was nearly drowned, but God saved him by some miracle. It must have been God who saved the man who is most needed."

Still Ransome did not look at Edwina.

The Untouchable boy who had been sent for Ransome's clothes appeared with the message that John the Baptist would remain to guard the house. The wild Bhils, said the boy, had come down from the hills and begun looting deserted houses.

"He needn't have stayed," said Ransome. "There isn't anything to guard. They could take what they like so far as I am concerned."

Then he changed and with Raschid set out on the elephants for the other side of the river. A little crowd sped them on their way, and as they left an idea came to Ransome. Calling Homer over to him, he said, "What about setting the boys to work to find the bodies of Mr. Simon and his daughter. In this heat, the sooner they're found the less horrible it will be."

For nearly three miles Ransome and Raschid rode the elephants through the rain across the devastated plains. They sat upright, each behind a *mahout* on the shoulders of the elephants. It was a slow and ponderous progress, with the red mud sucking at the feet of the great beasts. The *mahouts*, all Muslims, seemed unmoved by the whole affair. They sat very straight, crying out now and then a command to their elephants.

As they passed the house of Mrs. Hoggett-Egburry, four wild Bhils emerged, carrying with them pieces of bric-à-brac and Benares brass. At sight of them, Raschid had the procession of elephants turned in their direction, but the greasy aborigines only ran away toward the river. One of them carried a statuette of Psyche in Naples marble, another two embroidered sofa cushions, a third the enlarged and tinted photograph of Mrs. Hoggett-Egburry in her prime.

At last the bridge appeared. It had the air of floating on the river itself, for the surface of the water was just touching the rails. The elephants, it was clear, would have to swim, since walking the naked railway ties was impossible for them. So Raschid and Ransome slithered down the sides of their great beasts and set out on foot. On the other side of the river they came upon what remained of a tiny village; there

[387]

was nothing save a broken wall or two and a shattered village temple to mark the place where a hundred souls had once lived.

Along the road which had led from the city to the shattered reservoir they walked, picking their way among bits of rubbish and wreckage deposited by the receding waters. Here and there among the torn prickly pear that bordered the road there was a body, distorted and grotesque, beginning to swell in the damp heat. They walked hurriedly and in silence, and as they neared the city itself there came toward them even through the wall of rain, a faint sickly sweetish odor which stirred in Ransome old memories of mud, of shattered bodies, of decaying flesh in another part of the world. He knew now why Raschid had been in such haste, why he was striding along now like a madman. The whole city would be a pesthouse, filled with people wailing and paralyzed by the calamity. Half those with authority, with experience or talent for organization, would be dead. Harry Loder and The Boys were all dead. The Dewan was in Poona. The Maharajah dead. And somehow, quickly, all this desolation, all those multitudes of corpses which had not been swept away by the flood would have to be destroyed or there would be epidemics of cholera, of typhus, even of plague which in horror would be worse than the earthquake and the flood. And somewhere among the wreckage of the Summer Palace would be the corpse of the great and powerful Lord Esketh, bloated and rotting now in the damp heat. That corpse, he knew, must be rescued and shown at least a decent respect before the vultures found it.

They were flying overhead now, sailing slowly down on the plain and on the outskirts of the wrecked city, and here and there a little distance on either side of the road there were black struggling clusters of them, pulling and tearing and gorging themselves. There were more vultures than he had ever seen before; they must have come from the outlying villages, from the hills, from the dead city of El-Kautara. The spectacle was not revolting now; he wished there were more vultures, millions of them to swoop down and destroy the corpses all about them.

On the edge of the town they came upon the first people they had seen, a half-dozen women, three men and a child collecting bits of shattered wood from the wrecked houses to make a funeral pyre. The child had been given a stick to frighten off the vultures which soared above three bodies laid neatly in a row against the broken wall of a house. The little group stopped gathering wood and stared at them until one of the men recognized the Minister of Police dressed grotesquely in the uniform of the Conquerors. Then they all fell on their faces and, salaaming, pressed their foreheads into the mud.

A little further on as they passed a shattered house, a woman, wailing, ran into the street and threw her arms about the knees of Raschid, crying out in Gujerati. The big Muslim tried to thrust her aside, but she clung to him, still wailing.

"Her husband and child are ill," he said. "She wants us to save them."

In Gujerati he spoke to the woman and, still salaaming, she led them to the door of the broken house. There on the floor, in the filth, lay a man and a child. For a second he looked at them and then bent over the child, and after a moment turned and spoke again to the woman, in Gujerati. Throwing herself on the floor, she began to wail more loudly than ever.

Quickly Raschid turned away from her and into his blue eyes came a look that Ransome had never seen before in the handsome fierce warrior's countenance, an expression of terror and horror and compassion.

"It's cholera," he said. "Cholera already. The child is dead. It's too late to do anything for the man."

Then as they hurried on toward the Great Palace, Ransome was afraid, with a fear he had not known since the first days at the front. He was afraid now of death. He knew a sudden physical horror of being trapped here in this ruined city, surrounded by the dead and dying. The chill indifference to life and death was gone. For a moment, as the first terror passed, he was filled with wonder, and the old self cried out, "Why? Why now suddenly are you afraid of death?" Then he knew, and feeling again oddly young as if he had been reborn, he thought: "Fern! I must send her away if there is any way of sending her—at once, today, tomorrow!"

A mangy *pie* dog sitting on its haunches howling, suddenly stopped its outcry as they passed, and sniffing at their heels, followed them. It was followed then by another and another hungry animal until behind them was a whole procession. The sickly sweet smell of death grew stronger, and then, passing the shattered Music School, they saw in the distance the hospital which seemed scarcely damaged at all and beyond the Great Gate the Great Palace, its towers and pinnacles shorn away, a gaping hole where the Durbar Hall had been.

In the Park, the flowers, the shrubs, the vines, the trees, grew wildly in the rebirth of the monsoon. Already vines had thrust tentacles across the wrecked drive as if to close it and take possession once more of the land wrested thousands of years ago from the jungle. The little lake was filled to overflowing but the pleasure-boats were gone, swept away by the first onrush of the flood. By its side stood the pavilion where the Maharani had set up her court. It was a huge striped tent of many rooms which the old Maharajah had used when the court went to shoot lions, tiger, and panthers in the Kathiawar hills. It stood upon the permanent stone emplacements built for the tents which housed the overflow of guests during jubilees and durbars and other great state occasions.

At the door stood two Sikhs in their scarlet and gold, their handsome faces as blank as if nothing had happened, as if half their number had not perished in the disaster. At sight of the Police Minister they presented arms and permitted Raschid and Ransome to enter an outer room of the great tent. There an aide-de-camp rose and came toward them. His face was gray and his eyes dull.

"Her Highness has been awaiting you," he said, "since daylight. Major Safti is with her and Mr. Gupta, the town engineer."

They passed through another room and then came to the largest of the compartments. Along one side the fabric of the pavilion had been lifted a few feet, high enough to admit light but to keep out the rain. Then for the first time Ransome had a clue to what had happened to the Maharani. It was as if at the moment he and Raschid stepped through the curtained doorway they had gone back across the centuries to the time of Akbar or Asoka.

Whatever had been European in the background of the old lady was gone now. At the very end on a dais sat the Maharani herself, cross-legged on a great cushion of Benares brocade, and all about her on the earth and on the walls there were Moghul and Persian prayer rugs. She herself was dressed all in gray, the mourning color of Ranchipur, and she wore no jewels, but to Ransome, in the half-light that came in beneath the borders of the tent it seemed that she had never been more beautiful. There was at once an air of authority, of dignity, of tragedy about her that was new, and a beauty about the whole scene that was archaic like the delicate, vigorous beauty of a Moghul miniature. He thought, "This is a Mahratta queen, living in her tent, waging war, regal, untamed."

And as they moved toward her, he found himself not bowing as he had always done, European fashion, but placing his hands together and making a low obeisance as Raschid was doing. Then he saw that the Major was there and Mr. Gupta and Nil Kant Rao, the palace steward, a compact Mahratta with fierce mustaches. At sight of him Ransome thought, "Thank God he is still alive! He is a capable man." Behind her in the shadows sat one of the old Princesses of Bewanagar and, uncomfortably, cross-legged on her haunches, the Russian woman.

The Maharani said, "It is good you are here. We have much work to do. This is all there are. The others are all away or dead—the others who might be of use. All save Colonel Ranjit Singh. He is now driving off the Bhils."

As they came in, the men who had been sitting stood up, and now as she finished speaking he was aware that the Major had moved nearer to him and suddenly he felt the Major's hand clasping his own in a sudden fierce grip. It was as if he had said, "We are all here together— to help each other and to save our people. We are depending on you. We have faith in you." For a second Ransome was overcome with astonishment, and then he returned the pressure, and at the same time something like a lump came into his throat. It was not only that the sudden clasp of the great delicate hand had said, "I am a friend." It also meant: "You are one of us. We trust you. That is why Her Highness sent specially for you." It was the first time in all those lonely years in Ranchipur they had told him that. And now he knew what before he had sometimes suspected—that he loved these people, the old Maharani, the Major, and the burly Raschid, as much as he had ever loved any people in this world.

Then the old lady told one of the servants to bring a chair for him, but when the chair arrived he refused it, saying, "No, I have sat on the floor many times. I can do it as well as the others."

Then the Maharani set forth her plan. It was that the little group assembled about her was to constitute a kind of council of war. These, she said, were the ones she had chosen after long reflection. These, together with Colonel Ranjit Singh, were the ones who could meet the catastrophe—these and the Smileys and Miss MacDaid, but Miss MacDaid could not leave the hospital. She would have her hands full organizing and carrying out the care of the sick and wounded. When she had finished the first short speech, Raschid said, "Your Highness, I think that first of all we should know what the situation is—how bad it is. There is so little time. There is already cholera in the town and there will be typhoid and typhus."

And so, one by one, each of the little group told what he knew, what he had seen, what he had heard. And then for the first time the full picture of the catastrophe emerged, a picture far more terrible in its reality than any one of them had imagined.

There was no more telephone or telegraph, no more electricity. What motors remained would be useless in a day or two because the only petrol was what remained in the tanks at the palace stables. Between the city and the outer world, the railroad which followed the shallow valley had been swept away. Roads there were none beyond the dead city of El-Kautara but only the tracks over the distant hills to the desert and salt marshes beyond, tracks over which only bullock carts and elephants might pass, slowly, painfully. The granaries in the middle of the city were half-destroyed and the rice, the millet, the grain stored there would be fermented and useless in a day or two. The wells where the flood had passed were now only sources of corruption and sickness, and the people must be prevented from using them. There were corpses everywhere beginning now to rot which must be gathered and burned in heaps regardless of religious prejudices. Force had to be used if necessary.

For two hours the little council sat there—Mohammedan and Mahratta, Hindu and European, striving to bring some order out of the terrible chaos. Only a few things were settled, only a beginning was made. Mr. Gupta, the engineer, was to concern himself with the repairing of bridges, the opening of roads, the demolition of wreckage, the gathering of wood for the great pyres to burn the bodies. Colonel Ranjit Singh was to use what was left of his Sikhs and of Raschid's disorganized police to stop the looting and seal the wells, posting a guard at each one to prevent the people from using the water which would poison them. The Smileys and Aunt Phoebe were to be given the task of sheltering and feeding the orphans and the low-caste children. The Major and Miss MacDaid would have the hospital and the horror of the epidemics which each one in his heart knew had already begun. To Raschid fell the task of commander-in-chief, the duty of being everywhere at once, of seeing that commands were carried out, the gathering of food from the villages and districts, and of attempting what at the moment seemed an impossible thing, the establishment of communication with the outside world. And Ransome, it was agreed, was to help him, to have somewhere a headquarters where information might be gathered, where orders might be given, where the helpless and ignorant, the hundreds and hundreds of them, might apply for food and for shelter. He would have the nephew of Nil Kant Rao, the palace steward, for interpreter, and a half-dozen Untouchable boys for runners. To Nil Kant Rao of the fierce Mahratta mustaches fell the task of apportioning the scanty supplies of grain and rice to the hungry. And above them all stood the old Maharani herself, the dictator, the absolute monarch, with the power of life and death in her hands.

Before the council had ended, the curtains at the end of the pavilion parted and Colonel Ranjit Singh came in. What he had to say was brief. He had driven away the Bhils from the east side of the river. Twenty-three of them he had put against the wall of the ruined Engineering School and shot as a lesson to the others. "Twenty-three poor, half-naked aborigines from the hills," thought Ransome. He heard Ranjit Singh saying in Hindustani, "I regret the matter, Your Highness, but it was necessary. They were caught in the Girl's High School with two Parsee girls they had carried there. The girls are at the hospital now. They are the children of the Parsee called Ginwallah who keeps a restaurant in the Engineering School Road."

Suddenly Ransome understood what it was had happened. The state was isolated. All the vaunted modernity had vanished overnight as if it had never existed. The old Maharani living in her pavilion furnished with the loot of the long vanished Moghul Empire, was a despot once more, ruler of a state which had become half-savage again. And the heir, her grandson, was at Eton, learning to be a gentleman.

Then as the others left, the old Maharani signaled to him, and when he came up to her she said, "There is the question of your friends, the Eskeths."

"She is safe. I don't know what has happened to him."

"He is dead," said the Maharani. "She must be told. There is the question of what to do with what is left of him. He is an important man. Even a thing like that may make trouble later on."

"Yes."

The old lady looked at him sharply. "She must be got out of here."

"Yes, Your Highness, I think she'll be willing to go if we can find a way."

"I don't like her being here."

"I understand."

She was thoughtful for a moment and he saw that there was a sudden, quick sadness in her face. It was as if the body were old and tired; but the spirit in the black eyes was unflagging, indefatigable. He thought, "She has been waiting all her life for this. Now she is queen. Now she is absolute." For a little while not even the power of the British Empire could touch her. He was pleased that she should have placed this trust in him, that she should think him worthy of being summoned with the others—Raschid, and Nil Kant Rao and the Major. Why should she trust him? Why should she believe that he was anything but a waster, a remittance man? She liked good-looking men. She had always surrounded herself by them. He was, he knew, tolerably handsome, better than Homer Smiley or the Reverend Simon or most of the Europeans in Ranchipur, but that was no reason for believing he might be worthy of the trust she was placing in him.

"And the other Europeans—they ought to leave, too. I don't mean the ones like Miss MacDaid and Miss Dirks and the Smileys . . . but the others, the ones who don't belong here."

"It is a question of how to get them out." It was extraordinary how much she knew of the state, he thought, even of the Europeans there whom she rarely saw.

"We shall have to find a way," she said. "They will only be a nuisance and make trouble."

He was aware suddenly of the sallow face of the Russian woman just behind her. He did not like Maria Lishinskaia, although he barely knew her, and he did not like her here now, listening, prying, with her pale green eyes and despairing lascivious mouth. There was something hungry, something almost greedy, about her which always made him feel uncomfortable.

As if she divined what he was thinking, the old Queen said, over her shoulder to Maria Lishinskaia, "Go and fetch my gold box—the one with the rubies."

When the Russian woman had gone, the black eyes of the Maharani narrowed a little and she said, suddenly, "You are better than you think."

He could not think what to answer to the extraordinary remark, but he managed to say, "Perhaps!"

"You can help us now."

"I want to help, Your Highness."

"That is all. I wanted you to know why I asked you to help."

Still he did not know why she had chosen him, but he dared not to ask her. She was, he knew, his friend, but now he dared not to be presumptuous, to talk to her intimately, as he had done sometimes during those poker games long ago in the now ruined palace. Something had changed and the change was subtle, indefinable. It had to do with this luxurious tent and the new authority he discovered in her. It was as if he had been transported suddenly back across hundreds of years to the time of the Moghul Emperors. He was aware all at once of the absurdity of himself, in shorts and tennis shirt, standing there before the magnificent old Mahratta Queen.

She said, "I suppose you think the shooting of the Bhils was barbaric?"

"No," but his answer was polite and doubtful rather than sincere and she divined the reticence immediately.

"This is India," she said. "We can be thankful that the people here

[395]

are only Gujerati—a mild people. Especially the Europeans can be thankful."

Then Maria Lishinskaia returned with the gold box. The Maharani opened it and took out a handful of cardamon seeds and began chewing them.

"You might try to find Miss Dirks," she said. "She has disappeared."

"And the other one?"

"Miss Hodge. The Sikhs rescued her. She was on the roof of the bungalow. But she's a fool and no use to us. It's Miss Dirks who has the head."

They gave him for an office the quarters of the *jobedar* in the great gateway opposite the bungalow of Miss Hodge and Miss Dirks. In the great niches no Sikhs in scarlet and gold now sat on their black horses; they were needed elsewhere to guard polluted wells and shoot marauding Bhils and see that the orders of the Major as to the burning of the corpses were carried out. He was tempted for a moment to cross the road and try to discover what had become of Miss Dirks and Miss Hodge, but a second glance told him that the place was deserted. There was a thick coating of mud on the tiny verandah and from the windows the rain-soaked curtains flapped in and out dismally.

In a little while the nephew of Nil Kant Rao appeared, a sturdy, small, muscular Mahratta about twenty years old, rather like the terrier police-men of Bombay. He wore his small Mahratta turban at a rakish angle with the same air of dash and recklessness. He was a bright boy who had been educated in Bombay and spoke English and Gujerati as well as Hindustani and Mahratta. One needed a lot of languages to get on properly in India.

His name, he said, with a white-toothed grin, was Gopal Rao and he was willing to do anything. The disaster, it seemed, did not appall him; rather he seemed to find it exciting, and his attitude made Ransome feel far more cheerful. He thought, studying the boy, "The Mahrattas are the toughest people in the world, bred in a burning desert upon hardship and catastrophe and disaster." And he was young so that horror seemed less horrible to him.

They had not to wait for long. The news of the office in the Great

Gateway had spread in the mysterious way of news in India, and presently there was a little line of those who had survived the flood and earthquake extending along Engineering School Road. Some wanted to find lost relatives and friends; some wanted food and shelter; one silversmith complained that his shop had been looted by one of the state police. It was an interminable story which concerned a prostitute and her passion for silver trinkets, and while he told it, others in the line grew impatient and complained. One rich Parsee came to offer the store of grain he always kept in his own compound. It was dry and in good condition and would help feed the population until grain could be brought in from the districts, only he wanted to be assured that it would go only to the part of the population which was Parsee. Just as he finished his story there came through the grilled window the sound of quarreling, and when Ransome and Gopal Rao went outside to discover the cause, they found that two Bunyas, reverting to the times before the Good Maharajah, had thrust a mason and a potter roughly out of their place in line. Now the whole group began quarreling over the ancient rights of caste. Blows were struck and one of the Bunyas began whining that he would have to go through purification rites because he had been struck by a brickmaker.

It was the Mahratta, Gopal Rao, with his contempt for other races and his unorthodox feeling about caste, who bullied the line into respectful silence. He hit those who remained quarrelsome and cursed them in three languages, and when there was silence at last he told them that the death of the Maharajah had made no difference and that the Maharani was still alive to carry out his orders; that in Ranchipur all subjects were equal and had the same right to a place in the line. Then he and Ransome went inside once more, but the Bunya who had to be purified kept on whining and complaining about the expense of the rite.

Toward the middle of the day Ransome looked up from his table and saw in the doorway an extraordinary figure dressed in the impeccable costume of a London butler. The man had a long sallow face and a long nose and washed-out blue eyes, with straw-colored hair. He wore a morning coat and trousers that were wrinkled and spattered with mud, and in his hand he carried a small metal box.

When Ransome spoke to him he saw that the man was trembling. "Come in," he said. "What can I do for you?"

"I'm Lord Esketh's man," he said, "Bates is my name. They sent me to see you, sir. I've been everywhere, but I've only seen Indians, and none of them seemed to know anything. I've got 'Is Lordship's papers and the jewels 'Er Ladyship left behind. Can you take them in charge, sir?"

He saw that the man was frightened, that probably he had had nothing to eat and no shelter for two days. The spectacle he made was at once pitiful and comic. Ransome told Gopal Rao to go on with the work and he took Bates into a corner of the room.

Immediately he began to pour out his story. On the night of the quake he had gone out for a little air and had walked as far as the Engineering School when the world seemed to come to an end all about him. The shock, he said, had thrown him to the ground, and when he picked himself up he ran, where he did not know, but luckily in a direction away from the path of the flood. There was a good deal he did not remember at all.

"The shock," he kept repeating, "was 'orrible," and the terrified people he met could not understand what he was saying and he could not understand their language. For hours he had wandered about, and at last he stumbled into an archway which he discovered afterward was the great portico of the palace. There he had found a lot of Indian boys and two American missionaries. He could talk to them, at least, but they hadn't seemed very talkative.

The next morning he set out to find His Lordship but because of the flood he couldn't get anywhere near the Summer Palace and he took up a refuge in the wrecked Engineering School, where at least he could keep out of the endless, horrible rain. And on the third day when the flood water went away, he made his way back to the Summer Palace and there, climbing over the wreckage, he managed to make his way to the second floor, where he found His Lordship.

" 'E was dead," he said, dully, "lying alone on the floor of the bedroom. 'E must have died of the fever 'e 'ad. There wasn't any mark on him but a gash on the side of his 'ead. I don't know what 'as become of the nurse and 'Er Ladyship's maids. Maybe they're alive and maybe they're under all that wreckage. 'Is Lordship is an awful sight, sir. 'E ought to be buried, but I thought I'd better see about 'Er Ladyship first if 'Er Ladyship is still alive." He held up the black tin box. "I didn't know what to do with these things. Could I leave them with you, sir?"

"No. I think you'd better take them to Lady Esketh. She's alive." He reflected for a moment and then said, "I suppose you'll want something to eat."

"I 'aven't 'ad anything for two days, sir."

"You'd better go to Lady Esketh." He told Bates that she was at the American Mission and gave him directions and even made him a map showing him how to reach the only bridge that remained standing. Then Bates thanked him and said, looking down at himself ruefully, "I'm afraid I don't look very presentable, sir."

"I wouldn't worry about that. Lady Esketh will understand."

He was about to leave when Ransome said, "Wait. I'd like to send a message by you to Lady Esketh." Quickly he wrote a dozen lines, folded the bit of paper and gave it to Bates. Then almost at once he said, "Wait," and wrote another note, and addressing it to Fern said, "And give this to the young woman you'll find there at the Mission. That's all."

Then he took Bates to the arch of the Great Gateway and showed him the way. For a little time he stood looking after the stoop-shouldered dreary figure in the bespattered morning coat. He thought, "What can all this mean to him?" And for a second he was tempted to laugh.

When he returned he found his young assistant hard at work, brusquely dispatching one by one this line which kept growing longer and longer in spite of all their efforts. He did it with energy and decision, abruptly, and Ransome thought, "He's better at the job than I am. They only thought of me because I'm European and they think all Europeans are efficient." So he sat down by the Mahratta and said, "You go on with it; I'll keep the records."

It was not until after the railway bridge that Bates lost himself. Through all the nightmare of *pie* dogs and vultures, dead and dying and desolation, he made his way along the smooth metaled road. A half-dozen times, people seeing him dressed in the costume European officials wore to the Durban, ran out of wrecked houses or sprang up from the ditches beside the road to throw themselves on their faces in the mud and ask for food and protection, but Bates, understanding none of their gibberish, only went on his way doggedly, freeing himself with a kick when some woman grasped his knees in hysterical supplication.

He was weak now from hunger and exposure and the morning coat soaked by the rain seemed an intolerable weight, but he could not bring himself to throw it away. Lord Esketh's man did not appear walking through the streets, even of a ruined city in the midst of disaster, clad only in shirt, trousers, and braces. And so he bore the weight, stumbling along, frightening flocks of vultures who only rose and flapped a little distance, to return to their feast as soon as he had passed.

He moved in a daze, uncertainly, from side to side of the road, beyond horror, in a realm which bordered upon delirium. There were moments when he felt a wild desire to fall beside the road and remain there, but he kept being driven on by habits and instincts stronger than his own body. He had to find Lady Esketh and deliver into her hands the tin box. Then and only then would he lie down and rest, sleeping on and on and on. And then when he woke perhaps all this would only be a nightmare and Lord Esketh would not be simply a bloated corpse, but alive and red-faced and irritable. Then Lord Esketh would take him back to England, and he would give notice and go to Manchester and live for the rest of his life in a semi-detached villa with his sister. And never again would he leave Manchester, even to go as far as London. As he stumbled along he saw the villa, exactly as it would be, and to him in that moment it was as magnificent as the Paradise of the Revelations.

He should have gone away from His Lordship without even coming out to this horrible country. It had all been a mistake, he saw now; he had been led into it by the descriptions in the newspapers of the magnificence and romance and color of India, the Pearl in the Crown of the Realm. It hadn't been like that at all; it had only been hot and dusty and miserable, and had made His Lordship more irritable than usual and Her Ladyship more bored and restless. In Government Houses and hotels it had been no better, with no proper quarters for a self-respecting servant, and shower baths and water closets which never worked properly.

For a moment on the railway bridge, with the flooded river rushing along beneath his feet, he had come near to falling, and slipping to his knees he remained for a long time, dizzy, his head going round and round, clinging with one hand to the tin box and with the other to the rails. After a time he regained control of himself, but he had to make what remained of the journey to the other side on his hands and knees. He had to deliver the box and he had to reach the semi-detached villa in Manchester.

But between the Distillery and the Sikh barracks, he could go no further. Slipping in the mud, he fell on his side and fainted. There Mr. Smiley found him, the tin box still clutched in his hand. On a window shutter Mr. Smiley and two of the Untouchable boys carried him back to the Mission. There was no brandy to revive him, but Mr. Smiley stripped the soaked clothes from the skinny body and Aunt Phoebe wrapped him in hot sheets, and in a little while he opened his eyes and drank a little hot goat's milk. When he was able to speak he asked for his clothes, and taking from a pocket of the trousers some keys and the two damp notes, he asked Mr. Smiley to deliver the one to Fern, and then asked to speak to Lady Esketh alone. Before Mr. Smiley left he asked to have the tin box set on the bed beside him.

When Lady Esketh came into the room, still dressed in Mrs. Smiley's calico dress, she saw at once that he was shocked by her appearance. Strong, he might have concealed the expression which came over his face, but in his weakness the disapproval was as clear as if he had spoken it. She thought, "He would rather see me wearing the evening dress and all my jewels in the middle of the afternoon." But in her turn she was shocked by his woebegone appearance. As she entered he sat up on the army bed and clutched the cotton sheets high about his throat, leaving exposed one skinny arm, knotty with muscles, the heritage of generations of underfed ancestors. She was shocked, too, by his pallid ugliness, but most of all by the tired ugliness of the skinny arm.

She said, trying to smile, "Well, Bates?"

"It's been awful, Your Ladyship . . . 'orrible."

"I know, Bates. I suppose, though, we ought to be thankful we escaped."

" 'Is Lordship is dead, me lady."

"Yes, I know that."

"I found Your Ladyship's jewels. I think they're all here. I would be thankful if you checked them up."

He had placed the key in the tin box. She had only to turn it and lift the lid.

They were all there in small boxes—all the diamonds, the emeralds, the rubies she had brought with her, all save the ones Aunt Phoebe guarded pinned into her petticoats. As she opened the box and looked at them she had a sudden feeling of their glittering uselessness and unreality. What could she do with them now, in this wrecked world? They were meant for balls in London and Casinos in Cannes and Le Touquet, those remote places which seemed scarcely to exist any longer.

"Yes," she said, "they're all here."

"The nurse is dead, too," he said, "and the two girls. I suppose they never knew what hit them."

For a second a vision of Bates, correct and slightly pompous, on the night of the quarrel with Albert, returned to her now—the sly, insinuating Bates, who had implied by a look that they would both be glad when Albert was dead.

"There's a note, too, from Mr. Ransome," he said, and gave it to her. Then out of weakness he was forced suddenly to lie down again, drawing the sheet carefully up to his chin, concealing this time the knotted, skinny arm.

"I'll go away now and let you sleep," she said. "You'll be all right here. Old Mrs. Smiley will look after you."

"Thank you," he murmured in a weak voice. "I'm sorry, me lady, that I'm useless."

"Don't worry about that, Bates. As soon as you're strong again we'll send you home."

"Home?" asked Bates.

"Yes . . . England."

"And Your Ladyship?"

"I don't know, Bates. Don't think about that now."

He made one more effort. "His Lordship's papers are in the box, too. All I could find. I 'ope they're all there." For a second he looked at her with the old slyness. "I brought everything," he said, "just as I found them in his drawer. I didn't know which ones might be important."

"Thank you, Bates."

She left him then and took the note and box into the next room, where the Smileys slept at nights in the tired old double bed. The note from Ransome was brief. It told her of the job they had given him, and asked what was to be done with Albert's body. It had to be disposed of before nightfall. Did she want it buried or burned? He advised against burial. There was no proper ground. If the body was burned she could take back to England with her what ashes might be gathered up.

Then she opened the tin box again and took out the jewel-boxes and underneath them she found the papers, neatly tied in a bundle. As she untied the string her glance caught a name that was familiar, written in Albert's handwriting. She read "Henri de Rochefort," and thought, "How could Albert have known anything about him?"

Taking up the papers, she saw that the name was part of a list. It read:

Henri de Rochefort
Perry Molton
French Boxer (?)
Austrian at Monte Carlo
Tom Blashford
Nolham's brother (?)

She saw clearly enough the significance of the list. All of them but one had been her lovers, but how could he have known? For a long time she sat staring at the list in a kind of voluptuous revery.

Rochefort from the Embassy had been satisfactory. It had been a silky, decadent affair, very Latin in quality, and it had lasted longer than most, until he had grown tiresome and jealous and complicated. He had threatened to kill himself when she broke it off, but deliberately she had put an end to that by telling him brutally that as a lover he was satisfactory, but that she had never been in love with him. That was not altogether true, but it had served to make him seem ridiculous, for it had insulted his Latin belief that to sleep with some one you had to feel romantic about them. He had called her a cold-blooded, depraved English bitch, but she had not resented the accusation because in that sense at least she was a realist and had no pretensions. And it had served to end the affair without a scandal.

And Perry Molton didn't count. He had come to her room twice simply because he happened to be in the room across the hall at Barbury House. He was handsome in his good English way and had the body of an athlete, but there had been nothing very exciting about those two occasions. The next morning she had to think hard to believe that it had ever happened at all. No, that was just a house-party affair, of scarcely more significance than shaking hands. And Perry was so clumsy and stupid.

And Albert need not have placed a question mark beside the French boxer. It had happened all right, again and again in that ugly little villa at Èze. And it had been satisfactory. Even now, years afterward, the memory made her heart beat more rapidly and the fever to rise in her cheeks. His name, she could have told Albert, was André Simon. He had a body like a beautiful machine, and he was tireless and brutal. There had been something primitive and earthy and vigorous about him which she had never found in any other man, something which made of her a woman like the peasant women who dragged harrows in the fields. What she had experienced with André she saw now, sitting in the Smileys' bedroom, was not depravity; it was life; it was generation; it was what love and creation and sleeping together should be, at once brutal and tender, satisfying and sometimes cruel. Unconsciously she smiled now at the memory of the other women who, one way or another, had tried to gain him for a lover; because he was so good-looking and his manners were so good that he went everywhere on the Côte d'Azur and met all sorts of women. Out of the lot he was the only one that she regretted, but the regrets were old now, and she shuddered a little to think that then, for the only time in her life, she had nearly lost her head and considered for a time chucking everything and running away with him. But she thought, too, "Maybe if I had done that, life would have been more satisfactory. Maybe it would have had a biting earthy flavor and a reality I've never known." But she knew, too, that he would have been unfaithful to her as he had been even during those six weeks she met him secretly in the ugly little villa. And some day he would have grown tired of her and left her, and then. . . . No, she had always had to be master of the situation. In the end she had left him because she was afraid, of blackmail, of violence, of what she did not know, but the fear had made the breaking away easy at the time. She had made him a gift of two hundred pounds in bank notes, told him to buy himself a motor which they could use together when she came back from London, and then she had never returned and never seen him again. Now the memory of him was more painful than the parting had been, because she had not known then that she was losing a satisfaction which she would never again discover in all her reckless searching. She did not even know what had become of him; perhaps he kept a *bistro* now in Marseilles or Toulon and was no longer beautiful with a body of marble, but middle-aged and fat with a plump black-eyed wife and a half dozen black-eyed children. That was the destiny made for him . . . to breed and breed and breed fine animals like himself who would grow up and bring a fierce and salty satisfaction to people like herself who were born too old, too lecherous.

And the Austrian at Monte Carlo. On the list Albert had placed no question mark against his name. He had been sure about him and he had been wrong. She remembered his face and his body, although she could not remember his name. She had done her best to seduce him, for he was beautiful in a curious, decadent fashion, but even when she tricked him into a rendezvous nothing had happened. He neither loved nor desired her, and then one day she heard that he did not desire any woman, and she had been humiliated, resentful, and furious because she had made a fool of herself.

And Tom Blashford. He was nothing. Just another week-end party like Perry Molton.

And Nolham's brother . . . Tom Ransome. Albert need not have put a question mark beside his name. She had lived with Tom before she had even heard of Albert. And Tom, she knew now, was the only man who had brought her near to knowing what love might be. He was not brutal and satisfactory like André. He was too much like herself, a little rotten at the heart, but lovable and sympathetic and wise in a despairing fashion as none of the others had ever been.

The list was incomplete. There had been many others, some half-forgotten, some like André, still vivid, but none so vivid as he. And what an odd thing life was, that after so many years she had found Tom Ransome again in Ranchipur, of all places. And now perhaps all that was finished and there was nothing before her but dreariness and monotony.

She sighed, and then was struck again by wonder that Albert should have known so much and never once betrayed his knowledge. That he was simply complacent she could not, knowing him, believe; it must have been then that his snobbery was more profound even than she had believed on that morning when she sat hating the swollen, helpless body in the bed of teakwood and mother-of-pearl, or perhaps he had known her far better than she suspected, better even than she knew herself, and divined that she was hopeless and the less said the sooner mended. Perhaps he had gone his own way; perhaps he had had mistresses, too. But she doubted this, knowing that he could never bring himself to take the time which mistresses demanded. And he had been too exigent of herself. Perhaps he visited brothels or picked up women in Jermyn Street, or perhaps she herself had been enough for him; perhaps he had used her all along simply as a convenience, a necessity like the necessity for food and drink. He was, she knew, very English and middle-class and so he had been materialistic; women were for him a necessity but never a glory. She knew that, God knows, from his own love-making. There had been times while he made love to her when she had suspected that his mind was occupied with other things, with columns of figures or plans for some great coup.

"Perhaps," she thought, bitterly, sitting there on the Smileys' battered old double bed, "the joke was on me, after all. He could show me off outside working-hours, and then take me home and use me to quiet his desire and his nerves and leave his mind free."

And all at once she was wild with rage, that he should have tricked her, that at the very end, on that last night when they had quarreled, he had had the laugh on her, knowing that it was he who had the victory.

And he was dead now, and she could never discover the truth and perhaps salve the wounds of her humiliation.

"And yet," she thought, "I got what I deserved. He had either to divorce me or treat me as he treated me." And divorce he would not face or any scandal which might have endangered his precious position, that position to which he had fought his way up from the suburbs of Liverpool. There was, too, his vanity, which would never permit him to announce to the world in a divorce court that the woman he had purchased had not found him satisfactory or sufficient. It must have been that his suspicion of Ransome was the last straw, that on that last night after they had quarreled and he had left her, he had considered divorcing her for the first time and written down this list of men whom he knew about; and it must have been when he had finished the list that he decided the humiliation of a divorce court was no worse than the knowledge that half the world must have known one way or another of her infidelities, and that these six men must have laughed at him as a cuckold. And he must have known that there were others whom he had never discovered.

Bates, she thought, must have told him, for Bates knew her better and knew more about her than Albert had ever known. Perhaps he had cornered Bates on that last night and bullied or bribed him into telling what he knew. Perhaps that was why Bates was so sly and insinuating when he came in to tell her that Albert was ill. If Albert were alive she would have gone to Bates and accused him and discovered the truth, but now it did not matter; it was not even worth a disagreeable scene. Bates would be gone soon on his way back to England, out of her life forever. And then she saw that Bates, whether he was the one who had betrayed her or not, knew the list of lovers. He had himself placed it there on top of the other papers when he made up the bundle. It was stupid of Albert and caddish to have left such a thing lying about.

Then suddenly she felt very tired and bored with the whole thing, and tearing the paper into tiny bits she thrust them into the pocket of Mrs. Smiley's calico dress and began looking at the other papers. Most of them meant nothing to her; there were notes on a new special leader for the Esketh papers. She did not even bother to read them, but went through the rest of the lot until she came to the will.

It struck her as odd that he should be carrying it about with him; perhaps, in spite of his swaggering, he knew that he was an ill man and might never reach England alive. Perhaps he had meant to alter it, cutting her off with nothing. He had been shrewd about the marriage settlement, making it cover her rights of dowry so that if he chose he could always die without leaving her a cent. That was it; on that last night he had decided to divorce her and cut her out of his will. He could have added a line or two with Bates and one of her own maids to witness the signature. Witnesses were not supposed to know the contents of a will or to be included in it. And then, as she held the paper in her hand, she thought, "Perhaps that is what he did do"; but when she glanced hastily at the end there was no sign of a codicil. Quickly she began to read it through.

It was long and contained a number of showy bequests to charities and schools and hospitals. In life he had been mean about gifts to such organizations unless he felt he must make them to buy respect for himself. But now, because he could not take the money with him, he was generous. And there was a provision about his newspapers which she did not trouble to read, and then she came to the list of personal bequests—five thousand pounds to that lower middle-class brother of whom he had been ashamed, never allowing her to see him, and a thousand pounds to two maiden ladies she had never heard of, perhaps his aunts or cousins, and five hundred pounds to Bates—Bates who had betrayed him and mocked at him and hated him.

And the rest, the residue of the estate, was left to her.

She had never believed that it would happen. She had thought that he would leave her something, but not everything, not the hundreds of thousands of pounds, perhaps a couple of million pounds, perhaps even more. The will lay there in her lap and for a moment she felt for it a curious, indescribable horror. That bit of paper made her one of the richest women in the world, and the thought gave her no pleasure, nor even much excitement.

"I had enough with the settlement," she thought. "What can I do with all this?"

By a chance it was hers. She found herself thinking again of the Florentine pension, of the days when she could not afford a hairdresser more than once a month, when she had worn the dresses of her fashionable friends which were misfits or failures. Then a windfall like this would have been in the realm of the wildest fantasy; it would have changed all her life and her father's life. She would never have married Albert. She might even have been more honest and less of a slut.

She tried to feel as she would have felt then, but the effort ended only in a sensation of dullness; now there was nothing she desired in the world which could be bought with money. Now, it was too late.

She thought, "I suppose I had to earn it. Now I must think what I shall do with it."

He had meant to divorce her and cut her off, but the decision had come too late. This horrible country, this monster with its plagues and terrors, its splendor and shabbiness, its hospitality and its cruelty, had killed him too soon. Then she saw the bitterness of the will—that in all the world there was no one to whom he might leave this huge fortune he had built up out of ambition and trickery and ruthlessness, none but herself, who had always been contemptuous of him, who had betrayed him again and again from the very beginning. For a moment she tried hard to think of some one to whom he might legally have left his wealth, but there was no one. She saw suddenly that she had been right; he had never had any friends.

Half aloud, she found herself speaking as if Albert were still alive in the room with her instead of having to be buried before sundown for sanitary reasons. "But I don't want it. What am I to do with it?" and thought, "I may never even go back to England." For now she knew that there was only one thing she wanted and that was something that money could not buy, as she had bought André Simon, the boxer, long ago.

Thrusting the paper and jewels back into the box, she closed the lid and locked it, thrust the keys into the pocket with the torn bits of paper, and crossed the room to the battered mirror where each morning Bertha Smiley did her hair.

It was not like the glass on her dressing-table in Hill Street, made with a pinkish tinge to flatter her. The quicksilver which backed it was blotched and had peeled off in spots from the heat and dampness, and the whole thing had a bilious yellow tinge. When she saw herself

[409]

it was with a sense of shock, for she saw a tired, pale woman who looked more than her age, with hair that hung limply against her face.

"In a day or two," she thought, "the parting will begin to lose its color. I suppose I must have reached the bottom of something this morning." But what it was she did not know.

Then through the sense of defeat which had overcome her she heard the sound of music, incredible music, for it was hymn-singing. Somewhere near at hand in the garden people were singing, "Now the day is over" as they used to sing it at the little church next to the house in England where she had lived as a child. There were only four or five voices and they were accompanied by a tiny organ. For a moment she thought, "Maybe I've gone mad. Maybe I'm seeing and hearing things." Nevertheless, she walked to the window to make certain that she had not lost her senses.

There, beneath the trees, standing in the rain about a little mound of fresh earth, were Mr. and Mrs. Smiley and Aunt Phoebe and that girl Fern. They were singing in quavering voices to the accompaniment of a melodeon played by one of the Christian Untouchables. And then she understood; they were burying what remained of the missionary and his daughter.

Across the drive from the Smileys', on the tennis-court where The Boys had once come to play tennis, Mr. Smiley and the Untouchable boys had built a great pyre of beams and shattered furniture salvaged from the ruins of the Simons' home. They found the bodies of Hazel and the Reverend Mr. Simon in what had been the dining-room, for they had been having supper while Mrs. Simon was with Mrs. Hoggett-Egburry and Fern was pushing her bicycle through the rain from Ransome's house. When they brought the news to Mrs. Simon she became hysterical and only the firmest persuasion on the part of Mrs. Smiley and harsh words from Aunt Phoebe prevented her from rushing across the drive to throw herself upon the bodies of her husband and daughter. When she was a little more calm Mr. Smiley said that they meant to burn the bodies and that he would read the service. This threw her into a fresh attack of hysteria in which she cried out against the burning as "heathenish." But when Mr. Smiley explained that there were no coffins in Ranchipur and no wood and no coffin-maker, and that the bodies had to be disposed of as quickly as possible, she yielded again and fell into a low moaning which continued for the rest of the day.

So at last, wrapped in sheets, all that remained of Mr. Simon and poor Hazel was placed on top the pyre; and Mr. Smiley, exhausted and troubled, read the service, and when he had finished set fire to the oil-soaked mass of wood, and the bodies of the Baptist missionary and his daughter were burned as if they had been no more than Hindus. The rain came and went away, in gusts and showers and torrents, but the wood was old and dry and oil kept it burning fiercely, and at last there remained only a heap of rain-soaked ashes. With these Mr. Smiley reverently filled two of the glass jars which Aunt Phoebe used for her chutney preserves, and these, with a second short service, were buried in the Smileys' garden beneath the trees hung with orchids and petunias and ivy geraniums.

Mrs. Simon, moaning on her cot in the storeroom, took part in none of the service, but Fern was present to the very end, even raising a shaky voice to join in "Now the day is over."

Mr. Smiley had not allowed her to witness the burning of the bodies and she was thankful to him for that. She had meant to be present, why she did not clearly know save that she had a confused feeling that poor Hazel and her father would be less lonely if she were there. Mr. Smiley in his kind way must have divined her thoughts, for he had said to her, "There is no reason for you to be present, Fern. There is nothing left that was Hazel or your father. What is left is only clay. The Hindus know that, too, even better than ourselves."

And so, with a handful of Untouchable boys to help him, he had gone about the grisly task, leaving her alone to comfort her mother. She had no great desire to be with Mrs. Simon and she could not think what to say to her. It was odd, she thought, that Mrs. Hoggett-Egburry, her mother's bosom friend and companion, had not remained to comfort her. She had always been the only person Mrs. Simon would see on the occasion of her migraines, and now Mrs. Hoggett-Egburry had gone off in the dirty peignoir, waddling a little in her high-heeled shoes and accompanied by two of Mrs. Smiley's pupils, to revisit her house and discover what had happened to it.

So there was nothing for it but to go into the big storeroom where her mother lay on a cot, moaning, with a damp cloth on her head.

She opened the door quietly, still thinking that she might by some lucky chance find her mother asleep and so escape, but the door creaked and Mrs. Simon, removing the cloth, stopped moaning for a moment and looked up to see who was entering the room. When she saw it was Fern she said, "Come here, my child, and sit by me," and awkwardly, reluctantly, Fern obeyed her.

She sat on the very edge of the bed, as far away as possible from her mother. In a way she suddenly felt sorry for her, because in the last two days she had aged so much. The fresh look which always made people say, "But you can't be the mother of a daughter of twenty," was gone now. She was collapsed, crumpled, frightened, and tired. Fern thought, "She is the one who is alone now. With Poppa dead she isn't anything any more—not even a missionary. What will become of her?" and for a moment she was almost frightened by the picture of her mother alone, gone to pieces, with no one to bully but herself who would no longer be bullied, with no husband to lie beside her. That, Fern divined in her new wisdom, had always been important to her mother, although such things were never mentioned among people like themselves. What now would she do? She was in a way still young—only forty-two, and sitting there on the edge of the bed, fragments of a conversation she had overheard between her mother and Mrs. Hoggett-Egburry, long ago, returned to her. She had been in the hall upstairs and the door of her mother's room was open, and she had heard the two voices, and being only fourteen or fifteen years old, she had listened and heard Mrs. Hoggett-Egburry saying, "No, Herbert has his own room. He hasn't come near me for nearly three years. I think he must be incapable because I can't see that there could be any other woman in Ranchipur. If there was another woman the servants would hear of it."

And then there had been a silence and she had heard her mother's voice saying, "Of course, our husbands are very different, but I can't imagine Elmer wanting a room of his own. I don't know what I'd do. I'd be so lonely."

At the time, because she had never been told anything, she did not understand the significance of what the two women were saying, but she had felt, without knowing why, that it was shameful and even vulgar. Now, long afterward, she understood the conversation and pityingly she wondered if her mother had ever felt about her father as she felt about Ransome. It would be terrible if anything happened to him. She did not think of him as "Tom," but always as "Ransome" and sometimes even as "Mr. Ransome." In the two or three times they had been together she had never addressed him by name, she had never called him anything at all. All this morning when she had lain there beside him on the floor in Mr. Bannerjee's house, she had called him "my dear" and "my darling."

Then her mother turned toward her, and opening her eyes once more looked at Fern and said, "We shall have to stay together now, no matter what happens. You're all I have in the world."

A sensation of horror swept over Fern. She had thought herself free; she had never imagined the personal consequences of the earthquake. She found herself saying: "There's always Mrs. Hoggett-Egburry. I thought she would be with you now."

"No," said Mrs. Simon. "That's finished."

"What's happened?"

"The night of the flood I found her dead drunk in her own house."

So that was what was the matter with Mrs. Hoggett-Egburry. That was why she was so strange and muddled at times. Mrs. Hoggett-Egburry drank secretly. At the moment it struck her as incredible how innocent she herself had been up to that night she went to Ransome's house to wait for him. She had been an idiot. No wonder he had always thought of her as a child. Mrs. Hoggett-Egburry's drunkenness was only one detail in a world which, she saw now, had been fantastic in its unreality. Her mother must have known all along and pretended not to know, because she was a snob.

Her mother was saying, "You'll never know what I went through on the night of the flood. I did everything for her. I saved her life and she wasn't even grateful."

Then there was a knock on the door, and when Fern went to open it Aunt Phoebe was there with the note from Ransome. She closed the door again, opened it and read it on the far side of the room away from her mother, but the ruse did no good, for one of the marble-blue eyes, she knew, was watching her from beneath the damp cloth.

[413]

It was short. It simply told her what he was doing and that he could not return to the Smileys' all day and perhaps for several days. She must, he wrote, remain there at the Mission. The town was already full of cholera and typhoid and the stench was horrible. *"You must not think of coming here,"* he wrote. *"Not now, my dear. Nothing must happen to you."* And when she read that, happiness engulfed her again, shutting out all else, all anxiety and sorrow and misery.

From across the room Mrs. Simon said, "What is it, Fern? Don't stand there saying nothing."

"It's a note for me," she said.

"What's it about? Who's it from?"

And then suddenly Fern thought, "I'll tell her. I'll tell her everything. I *am* free now. My life is my own." So aloud she said, "It's from Mr. Ransome."

"Oh!" said Mrs. Simon. "What does he want?"

"He wants me to stay here at the Mission and not go into the town."

"Of course, and quite right he is."

Fern thought, "She beats anything. She's already accepted him as a son-in-law." Crossing to the bed, she said, "I'm not going to stay here. I'm going into the town."

"You must be crazy. You can't leave me here alone with the Smileys. You can't let anything happen to you now. You're all I've got. Where on earth did you get such an idea?"

Quite calmly Fern said, "I'm going because I can be of use at the hospital or some place. And I'm going so that I can be near him."

Mrs. Simon for the first time sat up on the cot. "Am I nothing to you? Haven't you a thought for your own mother?"

With a sudden feeling of triumph Fern thought, "She can't touch me any longer. I'm not afraid of her or her scenes. She can't touch me." It was true. She was free. She said, "Of course I'm thinking of you, but I'm going just the same. That's where I belong. No matter what happens, I have to be near him. He doesn't know how to take care of himself."

"Fern, do you realize what you are doing? Do you want everybody to think you no better than a street-walker?"

"It doesn't matter what people think—the few of them that are left.

[414]

What happened has changed all that. It doesn't matter about marriage licenses or anything just now. Maybe it will again some day, but it doesn't now."

Her mother started to speak, but in the onrush of new confidence she stopped her and said, "I was lying that day when I told you I had lived with him. I was lying because I was unhappy and frightened. But it isn't a lie now. It has happened. It happened this morning. I love him more than anybody or anything in the world. I'd do anything for him—anything at all!"

Her mother covered her face with her hands. She was too tired now, too old, to make one of her melodramatic scenes. She only covered her face with her hands and said, "Fern, my child! My little girl!"

What she meant by the action and the speech was not clear to Fern. She did not know whether it was a gesture of tragedy and reproach or one of satisfaction. But knowing her mother, she understood that she saw what had happened as only a prelude to marriage, and such a marriage would, of course, solve her mother's problems. She would be provided for; she would have a future, more brilliant than anything she had ever known.

Now she said, "Come here. Sit by me." And when grudgingly Fern sat on the edge of the cot, Mrs. Simon took her hand again, and said, "It isn't the way I would have wanted it to happen, but I hope you are going to be happy."

And then Fern knew that never again would her mother trouble her. She was, Fern saw as from a great height, childish and futile. From now on she would have to be cared for, told what to do. The capitulation, the whole collapse, was too sudden; it left Fern undecided and a little frightened. And suddenly Mrs. Simon was crying, whether out of relief or sadness or satisfaction Fern could not divine.

At that moment Mrs. Simon was not thinking of Fern or Ransome or anything that had to do with them. She was seeing suddenly a dead oak tree hung with Spanish moss, and in the moonlight beyond, the silvery sheen of the Mississippi. The revival meeting was over and on their way home she and Elmer had climbed a fence of rails and lain down beneath the tree. It had happened there in silence without a word spoken. They had even turned aside and climbed the fence as if they were a single person. It had happened quickly in a burst of adolescent passion stirred by the singing and the hysteria of the meeting. They had been drawn by something stronger than either of them, stronger even than the Baptist church and the teachings of the little freshwater college. And afterward she had not been stricken down by the wrath of God; she had gone on living, terrified of having a baby, and so they were married quietly, much sooner than they had planned. No one save Elmer and herself had ever known of it, and never again had it been like that.

Suddenly she took her hands from her face and looked at Fern. "What if you should have a baby?"

"I hadn't thought about that. I might have."

"You had better be married right away."

She did not make any answer, seeing that it was useless to expect her mother to see the thing as she saw it. Whatever happened, even if she had a baby, she would never ask Ransome to marry her. She did not want it to be like that. She would not have it spoiled. So to her mother she said, "You'd better lie down again and rest. Sleep if you can."

"I couldn't sleep. I couldn't close an eye." But her mother lay down again and began to moan, and presently the moaning ceased and Fern saw that she had fallen asleep. Oddly, mysteriously, she had become older and wiser than her mother. In a little while she rose quietly from the edge of the cot and sat in a rocking-chair, and presently she too, out of sheer exhaustion, closed her eyes and slept.

A long time afterward she was wakened by a gentle touch on the shoulder, and waking saw Mr. Smiley standing in front of her.

"I'm sorry to wake you, my child," he said, "but we'll have to read the burial service now. I must go to the school and I may not be able to come back tonight or tomorrow or the day after. Will your mother want to be present?"

"No," said Fern. "Let her sleep."

So with Bertha Smiley and Aunt Phoebe carrying the glass jars with the ashes, they had gone out and buried them beneath the banyan tree. It was over very quickly. It was, Fern thought, no more than a symbol, and Mr. Smiley had done it so nicely, so gently, that there was something beautiful in it. And she thought now, "Only three days ago they were both alive. Only three days ago I talked to them both."

It was Homer Smiley who guided them across the plain past the Sikh barracks and across the half-ruined bridge into the town; for they went together, Fern Simon and Lady Esketh, stubbornly, against the protests of all the little party at the Mission, against the protests even of the gentle Mr. Smiley, who could not see how either Fern or Lady Esketh could be anything more than a nuisance in the desolation of the city. He knew the will of Aunt Phoebe and the firmness of his own wife, but with these he was seldom forced to deal; he had never encountered anything like the stubborn wilfulness of these two women, and he yielded at once.

Mrs. Simon, sleeping the sleep of exhaustion and grief, was told nothing. Aunt Phoebe volunteered to deal with her hysterics when she wakened and found that her Fern had gone away into the pest hole of a city.

Mr. Smiley led the way through the red mud, with the two women following silently at his heels, and on their way to the bridge they had their first of two encounters. It was with Mrs. Hoggett-Egburry, who appeared suddenly from behind the ruined Sikh barracks. She was walking unsteadily, attended by her bodyguard of Untouchable schoolboys. She had changed her costume and was wearing a short dress of flowered cretonne and carrying a purple silk umbrella and a workbag, and had the air of just having opened a county horticultural show in the pouring rain. The umbrella did little good, for it leaned now this way, now that, permitting the monsoon rain to soak the flowered dress. From the workbag protruded the neck of a brandy-bottle.

At sight of her Mr. Smiley frowned, but with the firmness of a martyr continued straight on his course. She did not see them at first, but when she recognized them she began to cry, and as they came near she cried out, "They've stolen everything, even the sewing-machine and my hats and my enlarged portraits."

They stood there in the rain, polite and falsely sympathetic, while she recounted all the Benares brass, the bric-à-brac, the embroidered sofa cushions which had been looted by the Bhils.

"I shall make a claim against the state," she cried, tipsily. "All the things I've collected for years. No protection. It's an outrage! An outrage! My enlarged portrait! Wait until Herbert hears of it."

The little group of Untouchable boys stood about, watching her with fascination. One of them giggled now and then. In the midst of her recital Mr. Smiley managed to whisper fiercely in Gujerati to the oldest. "If she falls down, you're to carry her. You must get her safely to the Mission."

Mr. Smiley tried to reassure her, but Lady Esketh grew impatient and said in a low, fierce voice, "We have things to do. We can't stand here all day talking to that bloody fool," and so they left her, looking after them, a little bewildered and startled when she recognized the fashionable Lady Esketh of whom she had taken no notice. To make up for the error, she made a great effort and waved her hand at the retreating backs of the little party.

The second encounter occurred just as they had made the dizzy, perilous crossing of the railway bridge. On the way over they had held hands, making a chain to steady each other in case the roaring, rushing water made any one of them giddy, and when they had reached solid land and looked up once more, there right in front of them was standing Miss Hodge surrounded by a group of villagers, all chattering at her.

In her confusion and bewilderment she heard and understood nothing that they said, that they were asking her for food, for news of their children, for security. They were low-caste people with whom she had little contact, and they spoke in a variety of jargons, but even if they had spoken Gujerati or Hindustani, she would not have understood them because she was paralyzed by fear and horror, by all the sights she had witnessed after her escape from the hospital and now by the spectacle of the narrow, tottering bridge over the rushing water which she must cross if she was to reach her adored Lady Esketh.

She did not understand that the dirty low-caste people clustered about her had confused her character and personality with that of Miss Dirks. They knew that if they asked Miss Dirks for help she would not refuse them, and Miss Dirks and Miss Hodge had been together for so long that the little group had come to think of them as a single manifestation, a single phenomenon. So they went on appealing to her, throwing themselves on their faces, grasping her knees again and again, as often as she managed to shake herself free. To them Miss Hodge was the only visible remaining vestige of the great British Empire. But Miss Hodge alone, without Miss Dirks, was as confused and useless as a fluttering sparrow trapped in a room.

For forty-eight hours she had scarcely slept at all, and for twenty of the forty-eight hours she had sat perched on the roof of the one-story bungalow in the rain, watching the rising waters carry past her debris, dead cattle, snakes, and corpses. Now and then in the darkness she had cried out in a voice which steadily grew more hoarse and feeble, the name of Sarah, but there had been no answer out of the rain. And at last in the early morning light she had seen one of the pleasure-boats from the palace lake coming toward her, and in it one of the lovely Sikhs; which one she could not make certain for they all looked so much alike. Despite the fact that he rowed straight toward her, she tried to call out to him, but when she opened her mouth no sound came out of it. Even in her weakness and terror she felt a wave of excitement sweep over her, one of those waves which turned her into another creature and deranged all the monotonous peace of her life with Sarah.

He spoke to her in Hindustani and when she tried to rise she only sat down again suddenly on the low sloping roof. So the tall Sikh had bent down and gathered her up easily in his arms and placed her in the gaudy little boat. For a moment she had nearly fainted from the combination of weakness and excitement, for when her soft middle-aged body became aware of the great chest of the Sikh and the powerful biceps of the two arms which grasped her, she was like a woman ravished. Her heart stopped beating. She closed her eyes and the world, the flood, the ruined town spun round her. When she opened her eyes she was lying in the bottom of the little boat, and the Sikh, his black eyes looking straight before him over her head, was rowing toward the ruin of the Great Palace.

Then an extraordinary thing happened to her. She was seized suddenly by all the craft of a prostitute. She pretended, with consciousness of what she was doing, that she was still fainting and watched him between half-closed lids. She saw him as she had never seen a man before; she looked greedily at the shiny black beard, the fiery black eyes, the red sensual lips, the great shoulders, the breast and the powerful arms, outlined now, as if he had been naked, by the rain-soaked tunic of cotton. Her eyes in a kind of wild insanity, swept his body from the jaunty turban to the naked powerful foot, and what she did not see she imagined with a terrifying lewdness. Shame touched her for a moment faintly, but was swept away by a powerful wave of voluptuous abandon. It was as if she felt her whole plump, pudgy body changing, as if it had become a stranger to her, glorified and frightening. And in the midst of the sickening emotion a sudden wild and vicious thought came into her head, "It's Sarah's fault," she thought, bitterly. "It's her fault I have never known anything. She would never let me know."

She wanted the rescue to go on and on forever in this orgy of wild emotion. The Sikh never looked at her at all, but straight before him, except when he turned his head to make certain that he was steering in the proper direction, and then she saw the muscles of the powerful throat and felt again that she was going to faint. But so far as he was concerned, she might have been no more than a bag of meal. Waves swept over her, shutting out the world in a hot glow of ecstasy. And suddenly the little boat bumped slightly and ceased to move and the Sikh in Hindustani told her that they had arrived at the Great Palace. She tried to rise and could not, and once again the Sikh gathered her up in his powerful arms against the powerful chest, and once again the ruined world whirled about her in a chaos which was like the beginning of creation.

When the world about her grew real once more, she had opened her eyes at the sound of Mr. Smiley's mild voice and saw him standing over her, surrounded by a cloud of dark faces, and she felt a faint shock of disappointment that it was not the Sikh or at least Lady Esketh, but only meager Mr. Smiley. He gave her a drink of toddy and water (which he had found in the ruins of the palace kitchen) and then he said, "The water is going down. In a little while you can get to the hospital."

But the shock of the toddy cleared her head a little, and she said, "I don't want to go to the hospital. Where is Sarah Dirks? I want to go back to the bungalow."

Mr. Smiley said he did not know where Miss Dirks was, and then slowly, haltingly, with an effort she related how Miss Dirks had run off into the rain and flood like a mad woman to save a few school books newly arrived from England. In her poor muddled brain it seemed to her that the flight of Sarah had happened years ago, as long ago as their flight from England, but Mr. Smiley kept assuring her that the earthquake had happened only day before yesterday.

Mr. Smiley, on his side, listened, trying patiently to make clear to her all that had happened, but thinking ruefully all the time, and shamefully, too, that it was a pity it was not Miss Dirks who had been saved instead of this poor, pudding-faced, addle-pated creature. For he did not doubt now that Miss Dirks had perished; as nearly as he could make out she had gone from the bungalow to the Girl's High School at about the moment he and Bertha and the boys reached the wall which surrounded the Park of the Great Palace. They themselves had escaped the rising waters by some miracle in the very nick of time. Miss Dirks, going back into the very center of the town, could not possibly have escaped.

But he said nothing of this to Miss Hodge. He only reflected that it was always the weak, the incompetent, who escaped because somehow they were always taken care of; it was people like Miss Dirks who were dutiful and took risks who were lost.

When the water had receded he told his wife that he would take Miss Hodge to the hospital, discover what news he could and return as quickly as possible.

Then Miss Hodge, sitting up, asked, "Where is Lady Esketh?"

"I don't know. She went to dinner with Mr. Bannerjee."

And Miss Hodge began to cry, saying, "She was coming to tea with us. Now I suppose she won't be able to come." And that made her remember the quarrel with Sarah over the conflicting tea parties, and she grew all muddled again, and was seized suddenly with an obsession that she must return to the bungalow because Lady Esketh was already there waiting for her.

It was that which gave Mr. Smiley his cue as to how he might deal with her. Patiently he explained all over again the circumstances of the flood and how it was impossible for Lady Esketh to have reached the bungalow. Very likely they would find her at the hospital, along with Miss Dirks.

It was not that Mr. Smiley meant to escape the responsibility of poor Miss Hodge, but only that he knew well enough how much work there would be for him to do, and that he could not possibly drag Miss Hodge with him wherever he went. At the hospital they would at least have means of caring for her.

He gave her another drink of toddy, and when she was able to stand up she consented to go with him as far as the hospital and they set out down the drive among the shrubs and flowers which overnight had become a jungle.

At the hospital they found Miss MacDaid, somehow fresh and neat in her nurse's costume, and the Major, his head bandaged, a rueful grin on his face. Although the water had scarcely left the first floor of the main building, they were already at work, putting things in order with the aid of the hospital servants who had not perished. In the center of the town the hospital alone remained, shaken, but at least a shelter and a refuge. Everywhere about it there was only desolation, the ancient earth swept clear of any vestige of the swarming life which had once been.

But at the hospital it was no better with Miss Hodge. When she heard that there was no news either of Lady Esketh or Miss Dirks, she wanted to go away again and search for them. She began to cry, repeating over and over again, "But Lady Esketh was coming to tea"; and then suddenly she changed the refrain and said, "No, we were going to Mr. Ransome's. That was it. We were going to Mr. Ransome's. It's such a pity, too, just when I'd gotten Sarah to the point of going out and seeing people."

It was Miss MacDaid who lost patience, and taking Miss Hodge by her plump shoulders, shook her violently in an effort to bring her back to her senses. Miss MacDaid had no cosmetics on now. Her face was gray and formidable. She looked old, but fierce and vigorous.

"You fool!" she cried, "We've got other things to think of besides tea parties," and to the Major she said, "Give her something to quiet her and I'll take her up to my room."

So the Major gave her something, and they managed, after a time, to get her up the stairs where they made her a bed on the floor of the room which Miss MacDaid occupied on the nights when her presence

[422]

was needed at the hospital. In Miss MacDaid's own bed lay a low-caste woman they had managed to snatch from the maternity ward just in time to save her from the rising waters. She lay now, with the baby born in the midst of the disaster lying in the crook of her arm, watching the scene with dark untroubled eyes. The baby was a boy, strong and well, and that was enough for her.

Miss Hodge slept for a little while, but about noon she wakened, her head more muddled than ever from the effects of the drug. She did not know where she was or how she had come there or what had happened, and when she tried to speak to the woman in the bed in Hindustani and Gujerati, the woman only looked at her with frightened eyes, for she spoke only the dialect of her own people and understood nothing Miss Hodge said.

Then slowly things grew a little clearer to her and she knew that there were two things she must do: escape from this place and find Lady Esketh. Lady Esketh would need her help; she would not know where to go in Ranchipur and she could speak nothing but English. So after a time she rose from the bed on the floor, and opening the door, made her way along the corridor. It was empty; the stairway was empty; and presently she was in the compound, and then among the ruined houses and shops of the bazaar, and presently she reached the bridge on Race-course Road with its statue of Queen Victoria and the Shiva temple. The bridge was broken and the turgid river rushed through the break, but the statue of the Queen and the jewel-box temple still remained standing.

She went to the bridge that led from the Great Palace to the Sikh barracks, but that too was shattered, and so she continued on her way, not knowing very clearly what she meant to do, along the course of the river. In the town, no one noticed her. People were beginning to come in from the villages and the districts, but she knew none of them and they only stared at her. It was only when she reached the outskirts of the town, on higher ground, that people recognized her and wailed and cried out to her and seized her about the knees. Again and again she managed to shake herself free and continue on her way. She scarcely saw the prostrate bodies or heard their cries of misery and despair. She had to find Lady Esketh, and if only she kept on, she would find a place where the terrible roaring river might be crossed. Her clothes were soaked and she was spotted with red mud and filth to the waist, but she kept on, and after an hour of struggling she arrived at the railway bridge which she had not the courage to cross. There she was surrounded at once by a score of people all crying out to her for help; and then suddenly she was aware that Lady Esketh was there beside her, speaking to her, only it was not the Lady Esketh she had called upon at the Summer Palace, smart and worldly, the way she looked in the pictures in the weekly pictorials, but a strange woman in a calico dress, looking much older, weary, and untidy. Miss Hodge stared for a moment into her face, and in her mixed brain occurred the thought, "It is the same woman, but it isn't. Something has happened to her." Then suddenly she felt shy with the agony of shyness which had swept over her that afternoon at the Summer Palace when she had taken a cigarette and had not known what to do with it.

She was aware that Mr. Smiley was saying something to Lady Esketh, and the shyness vanished in a wave of anger and she cried out, "Don't you believe anything he's saying. I know what he's saying. He's saying we couldn't have you to tea because we had to go to Mr. Ransome's. It's not true. He's lying. He's only a missionary. And, anyway, Sarah is dead; she can't bully me any more."

Then Lady Esketh put a hand round her shoulder and said, "I know he's lying. You come along with me. I'm going to the hospital. I'll take care of you. Don't you worry."

The crowding, dark faces all about them, grown silent for a moment at the spectacle of Miss Hodge's outburst, began again to wail, even drowning out Mr. Smiley's assurance that they would be helped, and the little procession started off again along the road through the mud and filth, between the shattered houses, the *pie* dogs and the vultures.

In the gatehouse, Ransome and young Gopal Rao labored on and on, pausing only to eat the rice and curry sent them from the Maharani's pavilion. Even this they had to eat, one at a time, apart, because there seemed to be no end to the growing line of the homeless and hungry beyond the Great Gate. And the repast of Gopal Rao was interrupted again and again when Ransome, who knew only Hindustani and a little

Gujerati, had to summon him to interpret. They ate in a small, dark room of the *jobedar's* lodge because Ransome was unwilling to torment the long line of hungry by the sight of food; yet he and Gopal Rao *must* eat, as Miss MacDaid and the Major, the Maharani and Raschid and Colonel Ranjit Singh and the Smileys *must* eat, because this ruined world depended upon them.

The line of refugees filed past the little table, on and on, eternally it seemed to Ransome. There were Kathis and Kolas, Nagas and Modhs, Mochis and Pomlas, Dhodhias and Vasawas and Naikas and even three or four Bhils who slyly came in the hope of free rice. Each one was required by Gopal Rao to give his name and his caste; these Ransome wrote down in a little book, why he did not know, save that it seemed to bring order from chaos and would, he knew, give satisfaction to Doctor Mukda, the recorder, with his passion for statistics. But he was learning things he never knew before, small details out of the lives of these people who bred like swarming maggots—differences in caste and the incredible variety of castes and sub-castes, of odd religious beliefs, from degenerate Hinduism to the witchcraft of the Bhils. And slowly, as the day wore on, he saw how incredibly complicated, how hopelessly tangled, were the problems of people like the old Maharajah and the Major and Miss MacDaid who were fighting to bring light to these people.

They were, most of them, diseased and rickety, with a kind of dumb, animal despair and resignation about them, and slowly, as he listened to Gopal Rao talking with them, he discovered that they had not come here to the Great Gate driven by any definite hope or plan, but because the Great Saracen Gate represented to them everything that was the Maharajah. The news had got about that their Father had sent men to the Great Gate to care for them, and so they had come swarming from all parts of the ruined city, even from the nearer villages, like frightened children. They did not know what it was they wanted except that they clamored for food. Few of them yet knew that the good old Maharajah was dead.

As the day passed in damp heat like a steam bath into the afternoon, Ransome grew more and more fascinated, forgetting for long periods of time Edwina and the Major and Miss MacDaid and even Fern. For five years he had lived in Ranchipur and for five years these people had not existed for him, or if they had existed, it was only as strange figures which stepped aside when his motor passed, looking up at him through the cloud of red dust with black eyes burning with hunger and privation. His Ranchipur, he began to understand, had been incredibly small and limited—the palace and Mr. Bannerjee's set, and the tiny group which had dedicated their lives to the rebirth of India. Now, slowly, he began to see beneath the surface, and to divine the misery which lay beneath layer after layer of ignorance and hunger and superstition. The miserable people passing the little table, one by one, quarreling and reviling each other in their haste and terror, became human to him.

Beside him Gopal Rao, the young Mahratta, went on with his work efficiently and with a kind of contempt hovering in his black eyes and about the red, full lips. Gopal Rao was a warrior. A hundred years earlier he would have led a band of Mahratta horsemen charging down from their barren plain to raid the riches of the rest of India.

Ransome thought, "I must learn to speak better Gujerati and learn Mahratta and one or two other tongues." But what were one or two other tongues or four or five or a dozen in the swarming, bewildering complexity of India. Even the clever Gopal Rao with a half-dozen languages at his command was stumped again and again by some obscure dialect. Light was what they needed, all these miserable creatures, light and one or two common languages, and he thought of the boys and girls educated by the Smileys and the transformation which learning achieved in them—how the eyes brightened, how the bodies grew straight and strong, how the whole world became changed for them. But what was that—all the work of the Smileys and the Major and Miss MacDaid, Raschid and the dead, tired old Maharajah? No more in the vastness of swarming India than a pebble dropped into the sea.

Suddenly he understood what he had not thought of until now, that in the back of his mind, in his soul, there had always been the quiet knowledge that he would live on and on in India, that he was caught now by the East as Miss MacDaid had been caught long ago in childhood. Europe seemed a remote thing, half-dead, dying at least, slowly. Europe he might never see or feel again. And in his heart there was no regret.

Mechanically he kept writing on and on in the little book, the long list of low-caste names, phonetically because he had not the slightest idea how they were written in European script. Now and then Gopal Rao turned a sharp black eye toward him to ask in English some bit of information. Tomorrow he could leave this work to the young Mahratta and find something at which he would be more useful. By tomorrow, the clever Gopal Rao would know all the answers. By tomorrow it could only be worse instead of better, more starving people and less food unless they could clear a road over the mountains by which lorries could pass. A hundred ox carts had gone already and a few of the elephants were on their way, but ox carts and elephants were slow. Hundreds might starve and die of cholera before they returned.

Then slowly he became aware that even his wiry body, which had withstood so much dissipation, was beginning to feel the misery and hardship of the past three days, the lack of food and sleep, the horror and the strain. His head ached and the inside of his mouth was dry and he felt an overwhelming desire to lie down there on the floor of the *jobedar's* lodge, to sleep on and on forever. He had never known weariness like this which seemed to enter the very marrow of his bones.

Dully he thought, "Perhaps it is cholera or typhus or plague. Perhaps I shall die." And he knew that he did not want to die and the thought of death made him think again of Fern. Now, weary, all the exhilaration gone from him, he was ashamed of what had happened. What was he to do with her? What right had he to change all her life? Supposing she had a baby. Neither of them had given a thought to that.

"Pomla," Gopal Rao was saying. "They make brooms and baskets."

Through the doorway Ransome saw a strange group beneath the Great Arch with its huge pierced copper lantern—Smiley and Fern, Edwina and Miss Hodge. They looked as dirty, as bedraggled as any of the low-caste people in the line. Their fine clothes, their jewels, their background, their superiority—where was it now? Prestige! Prestige was of the heart and not something which could be imposed. Mr. Smiley had it by good works and perhaps Miss Hodge; but Fern and Edwina—Edwina looked haggard and weary.

Then he noticed the strangest of things—that Edwina was holding Miss Hodge's hand as if she were a child. Edwina and Miss Hodge! Of all people in the world.

He rose and went to the door, saying to Gopal Rao, "Go on. I'll talk care of these." The young Mahratta glanced at him. It was a question of a second, but in the black eyes he divined a queer look of hostility as if he were saying, "Yes, they're your people, Europeans. They do not have to wait in line like the others." The look astonished Ransome. He had looked on Gopal Rao as a friend as he looked on all Indians like him as friends. He wanted to say, "It isn't like that! Believe me, it isn't like that!" but there was no time. In the line a quarrel had broken out again, but now there was a Mahratta policeman to keep them in order. Up and down the line he went, barking his orders like an aggressive terrier. This was the sort of thing he liked.

They were, they told him, on the way to the hospital and had passed by the gate to ask him for news and to tell him theirs. To Fern and Edwina he said, "You shouldn't have come. You should have stayed at the Mission."

"We've come to work," said Fern. "There's nothing for us to do out there."

It surprised him that she had said "we," for there had never been anything but hostility between her and Edwina. He allowed it to pass without comment, only saying, "It's not safe here. You would have been safer at the Mission." He was troubled suddenly about the Major and Miss MacDaid. The Major might not mind having them at the hospital, but Miss MacDaid would not want Edwina; that knowledge he had read in the eyes of the head nurse on the night of Mr. Bannerjee's party.

He looked at Edwina. She was still holding Miss Hodge's hand, and the gaze she returned had in it something almost of defiance. It was a look he had never seen in her eyes before and it startled him. Like Miss Hodge, he thought, "Something has happened to her," but the look didn't alter his suspicion that she was going to the hospital because of the Major. He said to Miss Hodge, "Is there any news of Miss Dirks?" but Miss Hodge only stared at him and then turned again to Edwina with a look of adoration.

Mr. Smiley said, "She must have been lost. She went to the school just as the water began to rise a second time."

Edwina, indicating Miss Hodge by a nod, said in a whisper, "She's potty."

So that was it. Miss Dirks had gone off into the flood, meaning perhaps to die, knowing that Miss Hodge would go potty. And now he had Miss Hodge on his hands.

"Will you look after her," he asked Edwina, "until I have time to do something about it?"

"I suppose I'll have to," said Edwina. "She won't leave me."

Then they went away again, but before she left, Edwina said they had better burn Esketh's body rather than bury it. As they left, Fern suddenly seized his hand and pressed it. She had not spoken again. It was a curious, barren visit which left nothing accomplished. It might just as well never have been made. For a moment he stood in the doorway, looking after the bedraggled little procession. As he turned to enter the gatehouse once more he saw an elephant picking its way among the wreckage that littered Engineering School Road. It was the dead Maharajah's great beast. He carried a mourning howdah and in it sat the old Maharani, swaying as the elephant moved. She was returning from a visit to the ruined city.

Suddenly he wanted a drink more than anything in the world. A good stiff brandy would set everything right and kill the weariness and the aching head. But there was no brandy. Very likely there was no brandy in all Ranchipur except in his own house, and perhaps even those bottles had been destroyed.

When the Major and Miss MacDaid left Mr. Bannerjee's house, they struggled through the flood toward the Racecourse bridge, the Major holding high the hurricane lantern with one hand, while with the other he held firmly to that of Miss MacDaid. As they neared the bridge the current grew so strong that he was forced to let go of her hand in order that both of them might cling to the rail of the bridge itself. Above the roaring of the water and the wailing that rose from the stricken city they had to shout to each other in order to be heard. Step by step they worked their way across, past the statue of Queen Victoria toward the Shiva temple, and then just as they had reached the other side the tall Major stepped into a hole in the road, lost his balance, and, springing forward, found only water beneath him. The hurricane lantern went out and Miss MacDaid was left standing alone up to her waist in the rushing current.

"Major!" she cried out. "Major! Where are you?" but the only answer was the roaring of the water and the distant wailing. Again she called out and again there was no answer. It was as if with darkness and beating rain the Major had stepped off the edge of the earth itself into infinity.

For a second she was terrified, so terrified that she was sick, and then all at once she was cold again and clear-headed. Clinging to the balustrade of the bridge she thought, coldly, "He is gone! He is dead!" and for a second she thought, "Why should I not join him?" What was not possible in life would be possible in death. She was old and she was very tired, weary not from the exertions of the perilous journey as far as the bridge but weary from all the long years of work, from bouts of malaria, from the despair which had seized her at the moment of the earthquake when she knew that all they had worked for had been destroyed in a single spasm of nature. Standing there, with her eyes closed, the water swirling about her, she thought, "Why should I not join him? Why should I not have rest and peace?" In the face of death she knew in an instant many things which she had never had time to consider—that she was tired, that she was too old to begin again all the struggle of the past twenty-five years. But most of all she knew that for the last few years she had worked day and night, never sparing herself, not any longer driven by that dream which was born on the day the old Maharajah came to her in Bombay, but because of the Major, in order to be with him, to see his face with the grin that began at the eyes and then seemed to spread from them until his whole body, his great shoulders, his fine hands, his straight legs, were all laughing. It was for him she had gone on and on beyond her strength, wearing her body thin, bringing new lines of weariness into her face. And now all she had accomplished was swept away and the Major was dead.

"Why should I not die? Why should I not have peace?"

It all happened quickly, in the space of a second. If she had been a sentimentalist she would have let go the balustrade and allowed the rushing water to sweep her away. But she was not like that. She had always known that she was plain and powerful; she had always known that while her love for the Major was in itself fine and true, the spectacle of it was ridiculous. And now, once the moment of temptation had passed, she knew well enough that easy death (for death by drowning was easy) was not her destiny. It was work, eternal, endless work. And there came into her mind the vision of what the city would be when the flood subsided, of the misery and sickness and death. With the Major gone there would be no one but herself to stand between the people of Ranchipur and the cruelty that was India. For that she was stronger even than the Major himself. She knew all the tricks, for she had played the game all her life.

And so after a little time she let go the balustrade and struggled on into the street which led toward the hospital. Away from the bridge itself, the current grew weaker, but even so she was swept again and again across the road against the stone wall of the Zoölogical Gardens. Inch by inch she fought her way along, aware presently that the water was rising again and that she must hurry. There was no time now to think of the Major. And presently she felt the earth rising beneath her feet and the water growing more shallow. She knew every inch of the way, every tree, every stone. In the darkness and the rain, she made her way from landmark to landmark until presently out of the darkness rose the opaque mass of the hospital itself—most of it still standing.

Aloud she said, "Thank God!" and made her way up the shallow stairs into the familiar hallway. There she found a chair and sat down, the rising water still about her ankles, and when she had recovered a little she called out the name of Mrs. Gupta, and presently from the stairs she saw the faint glow of a candle and heard her voice.

Quickly her assistant came down the stairs, and when she reached the hallway she told Miss MacDaid that the hospital had escaped destruction by some miracle. Most of it still stood, but there were no lights. The patients had been taken to the upper floor. One of them was having a baby at this moment.

"Where's the Major?" asked Mrs. Gupta.

Miss MacDaid wanted to say, "He was swept away. He was delayed," but her honesty made her say, "He disappeared on the Racecourse bridge. He is dead." Then quickly she said, "Where have you put the woman?" There was no time now, no time even to think of the Major. For the harness was about her once more and in some way she knew that work would make it easier. Wearily but quickly she rose and followed Mrs. Gupta up the wide shallow stairs.

It was a difficult delivery and this time there was no Major to be called upon for advice and skill. With Mrs. Gupta at her side, they labored until the first gray light began to appear over the city, and at last the child was brought into the world. But almost at once the mother began having hemorrhages, so that the work, instead of being finished, became more desperate. And there were the other patients, more than fifty of them, clamoring for food and water, for bandages, and most of all for the presence of Miss MacDaid or one of the nurses to reassure them and ease their terror. It was always Miss MacDaid they wanted, no more than the sight of her, to calm them; for they seemed to have no confidence or faith in their own people. The sight of the girls who were being trained or even Mrs. Gupta did not silence their terror and wailing. So twice Miss MacDaid had to leave her bleeding patient to walk through the rooms to show herself to the terror-stricken patients.

As she walked through the wards a pool of silence created itself about her as she moved. It extended as far as the beam of the candle she carried in one hand. As she passed the hot, disheveled beds the patients grew still and followed her with their great dark eyes, only sobbing or whispering a little; but when she had gone and the light of her candle had disappeared into the corridor, the terror and the wailing began again.

Now as she moved among them, touched by their simple faith in her presence, she was ashamed, ashamed to the point of sickness, that she had ever, in that moment of weakness on the bridge, thought of abandoning them for a rest which would have gone on forever and ever in unbroken peace. She was ashamed now before the memory of the Major, and she was afraid, too, that he or his spirit or whatever remained of him might know the weakness which had seized her and would find her unworthy. Such weakness would have been beyond his understanding. No, whatever happened now, she must go on and on until at last she dropped into the grave.

When she returned the hemorrhages had stopped at last, but the woman, already anæmic from malnutrition, had turned a ghastly yellow color. She saw at once that there remained but little life in the patient. She sent Mrs. Gupta for brandy and for an injection, and seated herself by the side of the bed, and taking the damp, cold hand in her own, she began to chafe it. The woman shook so violently that the whole bed trembled and creaked.

While she held the poor thin hand she began to talk to the woman in a low voice, speaking Gujerati slowly and carefully, so that the woman who spoke only her own caste dialect would be able to understand her. Always she had fought like this even for patients doomed by cholera and plague, but now she was driven by some special inner compulsion. This woman must live. Somehow by force of her own will and vitality she had to overcome the woman's apathy, her utter willingness to die. She had to live in order to wipe out that moment of weakness on the bridge by the statue of the old Queen. If she brought this woman, who was already dead, back to life, then she would never again need to feel ashamed.

Leaning down to the woman, she said in Gujerati, "You have a fine son, as beautiful as the moon, as strong as the panthers which roam the hills beyond the mountain called Abana, as quick as the leopards and as clever as the Maharajah's great elephant. Forget not the joy of your husband in so fine a son, that he will make much of you, and when the period of purification is finished he will lay garlands upon your shoulders and thrust the scarlet flowers of the silk-cotton tree in the black of your hair. And among all Gandhies you will be the most honored and honorable of wives. Come, open your black eyes and look upon your son who will bring you honor and glories and riches."

It did not matter that the child was a skinny thing, uglier than any sacred monkey, or that the husband might mistrust and abuse her a month or two afterward. It did not matter that the feast would be no more than the rice and saffron and a few fly-specked, sweetened rice cakes. It did not matter that the garlands would be of withered marigold and withered jasmine, and the flowers of the silk-cotton tree limp in the damp heat. It did not matter that this skinny child, grown to manhood, would force her, like all the others, to shave her widow's head and cover it with ashes and work as slave to his own wife. The woman had to live. It was for this that Miss MacDaid had given up all the joys and pleasures and horrors that other women knew; it was for this she had come back again into the huge swarming East. The woman had to live!

"Know you," she said, "what it means to have a fine son? To have your people bow down as you pass along the street, to go honored by the father of your husband. The drums will be beaten and the zither played and there will be dancing and rejoicing in the village."

Nearer and nearer she leaned over the dying woman, willing her back to life, willing into the drained, undernourished body something of that terrible vitality which had driven her on and on through heat and intrigue, disaster and strife and disease.

Presently the woman slowly opened the immense sunken eyes and looked at Miss MacDaid as from a great distance, and for a moment the lips twitched and Miss MacDaid knew that she was trying to smile, to smile perhaps for the first time in a life which had known only misery and starvation. Then the tired lips of the woman moved, and although no sound came from them, Miss MacDaid knew that she was saying in her ugly dialect, "My son," and gently she released the hand of the woman and lifted the baby against her sallow drooping breast. The eyes closed again wearily, but about the blue lips there still hovered that wan ghost of a smile, and Miss MacDaid thought in triumph, "I have won. Now she will fight to live."

And turning to take from Mrs. Gupta the syringe and the brandy, she found that it was not Mrs. Gupta who was standing beside her, but the Major, naked save only for a breech-clout and a clumsy bandage on his head. He had been standing there for a long time, listening while she bent over the low-caste woman, willing her back to life, talking to her in the poetry which she would understand. In his blue eyes there was an odd look of wonder, as if for the first time he had really divined the greatness of poor Miss MacDaid.

She had never before seen him like this, naked, and the sight at first shocked her and then brought a lump into her throat. The smooth body, the fine chest, the beautiful muscles of the shoulders, the abdomen, the arms, gleamed now, golden in the dim candle-light. She saw now how beautiful a thing a body might be, the body which until now had only been something that one poked or cut open or dosed. It was of a beauty beyond anything she had ever seen. There could be nothing evil, nothing

[434]

ridiculous, in loving anything so beautiful. But it was too late now for love, for what she saw, she knew, was not the flesh, but a ghost, for the Major was dead, swept away in the flood from off the Racecourse bridge.

Even when he touched her, gently laying one hand on her shoulder, she could not believe in what she saw, but went dizzy and for a moment thought that she, Miss MacDaid the war horse, was going to faint.

He began to talk, telling her what had happened, and as she listened she came, slowly, to believe that he was living, and as she listened she felt for the first time in her busy life a mystic sense of belief, for surely what had happened was a miracle.

He was saying, "I must have been swept against the wall of the zoo. I don't remember anything more until I waked in the limb of a tree."

He had bandaged the wound in his head with his shirt, and when he had regained a little of his strength, he had started for the hospital, naked, now swimming, now fighting his way breast deep in water among the snakes and corpses and debris, until he had come against the ruins of the Music School beside the great tank and knew where he was.

"I met Mrs. Gupta in the hall and I came straight here. I was afraid that something had happened to you. I knew if you were alive I should find you here." Then he said, quietly, "You'd better go and visit the wards. It will quiet them to see you. I'll take care of this woman."

"You'd better let me bandage your head properly."

"When I've finished here."

So she went again into the wards, this time stopping at each bed where there was a whimper or a moan, calming the terror and easing the pain, but all the time she scarcely knew what she was doing. It seemed to her that she was moving in a pool of glory. That was it—a pool of glory. There were those two miracles—the miracle which saved his life and the miracle of the young and golden body. She knew now what that beauty could mean. Somehow it changed everything. It was a mad, crazy feeling full of worship without desire. It made up for all she had missed in life, for all her self-consciousness and humiliation. That she was old now did not matter, because she was no longer ridiculous. Now she had something definite to worship; the love, vague, yearning and absurd, had been transmitted into something as hard and definite as if the lovely body had been made of gold instead of flesh. As she bent over the beds in turn, stilling the terror of the ill, she saw him as she had seen him when she turned expecting to find plain, pimply, faithful Mrs. Gupta at her shoulder. She saw him all naked and shining in the light of the candle looking down at her with an odd, soft expression in the blue Brahmin's eyes. It was a look which told her what she had wanted to hear for so long, that he trusted and honored her, that although the years and her plainness made love between them a ridiculous thing, he worshiped and loved her none the less. And surrounded by the pool of glory there was in her soul the deep peace of a woman who turns away at last from her lover, satisfied and at peace, with a body reborn.

In the late afternoon the Major saw the little procession from the upper window, arriving by the main driveway between the rows of mud-soaked hibiscus—first Fern and Smiley, and then Miss Hodge clinging like a child to the hand of a woman whom he did not at first recognize. All his interest concentrated upon the figure in the calico dress, and as it came nearer he saw that it was Lady Esketh, whom he had never seen before save immaculate, smooth as porcelain, and covered with jewels. For a moment he was annoyed that they were coming here to the hospital to add their burdens to the complications which kept piling up as patient after patient was brought in and fresh reports of typhus and cholera cases outside in the town appeared on the records. There were sick lying everywhere now, even in the hallways and in the X-ray rooms, people with shattered heads and broken limbs and torn bodies. Most of them would die because they had been neglected too long, but until they died they would have to be cared for. And none of these people would be of any use, neither that silly missionary girl nor poor addle-pated Miss Hodge nor Lady Esketh, spoiled and accustomed only to luxury. Only Smiley could possibly be of any help, and he would have problems, end-less problems, of his own.

But he thought it was better that he should receive them than Miss MacDaid, so he turned and walked down the stairs as they came through the doorway.

It was an odd meeting. Little Smiley quite unexpectedly put his arms about the big Major and embraced him as if he had been a little boy found after having been thought dead. The Major hugged him suddenly, lifting him quite off the floor. Smiley had no weight at all. It was like lifting a cloud, so poor and meager was the flesh on his bones.

Then he said, "Lady Esketh has come to see about the burial of her husband. And Fern thought she might be of use."

"I can work, too," said Lady Esketh. "I'm perfectly strong."

"I too," echoed Miss Hodge, still holding Lady Esketh's hand. "I'm strong as an ox."

For a second the Major looked sharply at Lady Esketh. His eyes met hers and he saw that she was looking at him defiantly, boldly, as if she were saying, "You think I'm a fool. You think I'm a spoiled, luxurious ass. Well, I'm not. I've got as fine and strong a body as your own. And when I choose to be I'm as clever as you are."

The look, its meaning so clear, astonished him so that he didn't speak for a moment. He had not expected to find this bold confidence in her, of all people. It was all right for her to believe that she was beautiful, luxurious, and lecherous, because that was true, but for her to assert that she was also clever and strong and capable— The color appeared in his tired face and he said, "I'll go and find Miss MacDaid. She's the one to talk to. I can't offer you chairs because there aren't any. They've all been taken away to make room."

He left them standing among the sick, and at last found Miss MacDaid at the far end of the maternity ward, where she had gone for a second to direct two Untouchable women in the task of sweeping out the mud and making it once more habitable. With her eyes on the two women she listened to him, and when he had told his news, she turned to him, as he had suspected she would, and said, abruptly, "They'll be more trouble than they're worth. What do any of them know about anything? Better send them back to the Mission."

He too had thought that on sight of them, but now he was not quite certain.

"They don't know anything—any of them," Miss MacDaid continued. "None of them can speak Hindustani but Miss Hodge, and now that Miss Dirks is gone she'll be nothing but a nuisance."

He didn't yield entirely. "We might give them a try. If they can do anything, even scrub the floor or carry water to the wards. . . . We need them desperately."

[437]

She softened a little. "Maybe you're right. I'll come along in a minute.' She spoke in Gujerati to the two women and then turned and went with him out of the room. "But that Englishwoman is no good to me. That sort of woman is the most useless thing on earth." And slyly she glanced sidewise at him. His face betrayed nothing at all.

At sundown Ransome and Smiley, who, in the meanwhile, had been to the horrible desolation of the Untouchable quarter, appeared at the hospital to fetch Lady Esketh for the funeral of the great Lord Esketh. They found her bathing a Bunya child of ten whom the Major had operated upon for a tumor two days before the flood. When she saw them she looked up and said, "I'm nearly finished. Two minutes more."

At the sight and the sound of her voice, Ransome felt a wild, illogical desire to laugh. Without turning, she said, "Is it absolutely necessary for me to go?"

"It's only an affair of a minute," said Mr. Smiley. "Just the reading of the service."

"Very well."

She pushed the black hair back out of the eyes of the child and passed a damp cloth over his face. Then she rose, and taking up the basin and towels, she said, "Shall we go?"

Together they walked past the great tank through the ruined streets of the bazaar, until they came to the Park of the shattered old Summer Palace. The city appeared empty now. Here and there, men who had somehow escaped from the disaster poked and prodded among the ruins of their shops, searching for trinkets and silver bells and cloth that had not been pilfered by the looting Bhils. But there were no longer sick and dying to wail at them from the shattered doorways. Here and there among the ruins flames and smoke leaped up from great funeral pyres where a dozen, twenty, fifty bodies were being burned at once. About each pyre there was a little guard of Colonel Ranjit Singh's Sikhs stationed to keep the wailing relatives from throwing themselves into the flames. There was, thought Ransome, something hellish about the scene with the corpses, the flames, the writhing, wailing bodies. It was like a picture out of Doré's Inferno. The odor which filled the air now was not of decaying bodies, but of burning flesh.

arms, turning his back against the flood in a last gesture of protection. As the flood struck the house, it swayed, creaked and groaned, and almost at once the far end collapsed with all its weight of terrified humanity. Then the rest gave way, slowly, like a stricken animal sinking to its knees, and Mr. and Mrs. Jobnekar and the frightened, crying children, slowly sank with it beneath the torrent. As the water closed over his head he pressed the children closer to him as if to comfort and reassure them, and thought, "I must not die yet, when there is so much to be done. . . ."

When the flood had swept on across the flat plains toward Mount Abana, not one house remained in all the Untouchable quarter.

For twenty-three years since the day the dam was finished as one of the wonders of India the fault had remained hidden. For twenty-three years the Maharajah in his pride, the Dewan in his wiliness, Raschid the Police Minister, Mr. Jobnekar, the councilors of state and the humble of Ranchipur had believed in the great dam with a faith that was like their faith in the ring of hills and the unchanging desert beyond, like the faith they had in the sacred mountain of Abana rising eternal, crowned with white temples against the brazen sky; for in the hearts of all of them save perhaps the old Dewan, who was as old as time, there was a kind of mystical child-like faith in the miracles which could be worked by the great engineers from the West . . . things which no Indian could conceive or execute. Had they not built the huge barrages of the north and the great bridges over the Ganges and the Brahmaputra? And who among them could be trusted more than the smooth and plausible Aristide de Groot, who had, he said, built dams and bridges and factories in Switzerland and Austria, in Italy and Sweden, in Brazil and China?

After nine thousand people had lost their lives in the great flood there were those in Ranchipur who remembered Aristide de Groot and even recalled suspicions, partly imaginary, which they had had long ago that he was not as he had said, a Swiss, nor anything else very definite but simply a man without a country, an adventurer, and a swindler. They remembered him as a swarthy squat little man who already spoke a half dozen languages when he came to Ranchipur and who learned Hindustani and Gujerati with astonishing swiftness. He had been plausible and even engaging company, with no prejudices as to race or creed or color,

[311]

with a tongue which had a lightning quickness like the tongue of a Russell's viper. One or two clever people like the Dewan and the old Maharani remembered Aristide de Groot, twenty-three years afterward, only as a pair of eyes, cold eyes like those of the deadly *krait*, which must have regarded all men as exactly alike simply because they were potential victims of Aristide de Groot. But his viper's tongue had been smooth enough to persuade not only the lowly and the good and the simple like the Maharajah, but even men like the worldly Viceroy himself, that he was a great engineer.

After the disaster when the first news of its horrors reached the Dewan, surrounded by his innumerable family in Poona, the old man, running his lean fingers through the long white beard, thought, sadly, "There was some fault in the dam. I can scarcely remember that man de Groot save for his eyes. In his eyes was hidden the whole tragedy of European greed."

He knew, sitting there in his cool garden, that long ago he should have trusted the instinct which had never failed him; but that knowledge did little good now. After a morning of contemplation the memory of the *krait's* eyes made him think, "Men like that should be stamped out like serpents. If they are not stamped out, the West is finished. It will destroy itself." And sitting there, immensely wise and immensely old, the thought did not displease him. But the memories of old suspicions did nothing to restore to life the nine thousand men, women, and children who were dead, nor save from destruction all that it had taken the old Maharajah more than fifty years of struggle and heartbreak to create.

And the fault in the dam was nothing which anyone could prove, least of all in a court of justice where Aristide de Groot would sit surrounded by rich and corrupt lawyers; and there was always the shock of the earthquake which accompanied the flood as an excuse for the collapse. Nevertheless it was plain to be seen after the flood when the great reservoir lay empty, that the construction of the shattered dam had been shoddy, that the reinforcements and the steel work had been insufficient, and that sand from the sea, impure and filled with salt, had been used because it was near at hand and cheap. It was quite impossible to prove that any of these things had been responsible for the disaster; the worst verdict to be expected was that Aristide de Groot had been a bad builder, and such a verdict would have made little difference to de Groot, for he had other irons in the fire and had forgotten long ago that he had ever been a contracting engineer.

It was the British Government which uncovered in detail the rise of the famous Aristide de Groot since the comparatively lean and shoddy days when he had constructed the great barrage of Ranchipur. Those who had the investigation in charge discovered that he was no longer, as indeed he had never been, a proper engineer, and that long ago he had abandoned any pretentions in that direction; now he had interests in oil and foreign exchange and munitions and even more shady under-takings. Out of the misery of bankrupt nations and the death of men he had built a fabulous fortune which was vague and untraceable. Some of it was in New York, some in London, a little in Paris, some in Amster-dam, and some in Sweden. And the British Government discovered that behind a dozen petty wars and revolutions and disorders there always lurked the sinister presence of the man with eyes like a *krait* and the tongue of a Russell's viper, a man with a genius for creating markets for rifles and shells and cannon and machine guns. It discovered too that he had swindled a *de facto* Chinese Government out of two million pounds on a munitions contract, that he had smuggled arms into Afghanistan, that he had had a strange association with the early Hitler and had an interest in a huge underground syndicate which dealt in drugs.

And almost at once Aristide de Groot became the beloved "mystery man" whom the journalists are forever seeking, and vanished from his château near Compiègne wearing dark glasses and bound for a holiday in Peru. He need not have taken the trouble to run away, for the British Government discovered that there was not much to be done about Aris-tide de Groot since he numbered among his intimate friends too many "statesmen" and senators and bankers in continental countries. He was as well protected as possible. The British Government even discovered with a certain shock that four or five important men in London, including Lord Esketh and his journalist rival, Lord Pakington, had spent week-ends with Aristide de Groot on his yacht or at his château near Compiègne or his house in Biarritz. The Government discovered that the tragedy of Ranchipur could even be listed as one of de Groot's minor crimes; but even about that there was nothing to be done unless as Lord Pakington (who outlived Lord Esketh) wrote in one of his famous leaders "we are willing to unleash the whole spirit of Bolshevism to work its deviltry upon the unprotected women and the countryside of England." Suddenly everyone felt that the less said about Aristide de Groot the better, and after a little while he returned from Peru to rejoin the wife he had found long ago in a Trieste brothel, in their handsome Louis Treize château not far from the gate where Joan of Arc was captured.

And, anyway, it did not matter very greatly to a Christendom tormented by its own festering wounds that nine thousand heathens had been crushed and drowned in a few minutes, or that Ranchipur, the best-governed state in the East had been crippled by the disaster for a whole generation. All that was very far away, although it was alarmingly nearer than it had been half a century earlier. Still, it was far enough away so that the disaster did not add its anguish to the burden of threats and conferences, civil war, secret alliances, intrigues, greed bigotry and bitterness and hatred which already festered in the repository of Western civilization.

The dam had been in a way a kind of symbol—the symbol of Oriental faith in Occidental practical achievement and honesty, organization and superiority, a faith which like the dam itself had long since cracked and fallen.

Part III

Part III

O<small>N THE</small> frail wooden balcony which ran round the second floor of
Mr. Bannerjee's house Edwina and Ransome awaited the swift Indian sunrise. From there, through openings in the masses of peepul and
banyan trees, they had a view of that part of the flooded burning town
which lay in the low ground between them and the Great Palace. Most
of the fires had been drowned quickly by the torrents of rain or by the
flood itself, but three or four of the more important buildings—what
Ransome judged to be Great Market, the Courts of Justice and the Central Administration offices—still burned stubbornly, throwing up sudden
jets of fire which cast on the thick clouds overhead the sullen menacing
reflection of flames. The strange sound of a whole city wailing with a
single voice was gone presently, and there was only silence save for an
occasional distant solitary cry of anguish and chill terror, like the howls
of the jackals when they came out of the jungle in the evening to hunt.

Once he said, "I'll fetch you a shawl. It's silly standing there dressed
as you are. You'll be soaked. You don't know what this monsoon rain
is like. Roofs mean nothing. The dampness penetrates everywhere." He
spoke quite simply as if, instead of watching the death of a great city,
they were watching a cinema, but the sound of his own voice startled
him a little, as if there was something of bad taste in his speaking at all.

He found a Kashmiri shawl that was used as a covering for one of
the Indian beds, and when he had wrapped it round her shoulders,
over the white dress and all the jewels, they were silent again, watching. At moments when the flames of one building or another leapt high
in the air, the reflected light from the clouds illumined the water, re-
vealing there all sorts of nasty things floating just beneath the surface.

Tom thought, "Tomorrow it will begin to stink. Tomorrow will be
horrible, and the day after, and the day after . . . with all this heat and
rain." But the jackals would feed well and the vultures and the croco-

diles, risen now in the flood out of the thick smelly mud of the river. They could swim anywhere now, into the very heart of the town.

Then the wind, rising, tore apart the clouds for a little while, and in the velvety blackness of the open sky the stars appeared again, the Indian stars that were different from stars elsewhere, more brilliant than ever now in the clean-washed air. But in a little while the stars disappeared again and there was only the low roof of blood-red clouds. Inside the house the wailing of Mr. Bannerjee began once more, a wailing in which there was the terror of a hurt animal.

Edwina said, "I wish that nasty little man would stop making such a noise. That's worse than everything else."

She had come to India wanting something to happen to her, and now as she stood on the balcony the realization came to her that it was happening to her and happening with a vengeance, something which surpassed anything within the scope of her imagination. She was not dead, but she might be dead before many days passed, or hours or even minutes, for that matter. She had never thought much about houses before, but now the house of Mr. Bannerjee, even though it withstood the double shock of flood and quake, seemed to her a fragile, puny thing, ridiculous in the face of the catastrophe which had surrounded them; and when she thought of the house, it made her think suddenly of herself and her own utter fragility and uselessness. There was something ridiculous in facing a spasm of Nature, clad in a single garment of white crêpe, wearing half of one's jewels. A little amused, her mind began to wander, thinking how one should dress properly for such an occasion. "Shorts, I suppose," she thought, "and a silk shirt. That would be smart as well as sensible."

A great many times in Hill Street, in Cannes, in country houses at moments when she had lain in bed, bored with reading, half-asleep, she had speculated lazily and voluptuously on what it would be like to find oneself suddenly faced by death with the knowledge that one had a few hours to live. Pushing the idea further, she had wondered what she would do, bored and cold-blooded as she was, if she found herself facing death alone with an attractive man. She had thought then,

"There would be only one thing to do to kill the time. Anything else would be a bore."

She had thought, too, that making love under such circumstances would have a kind of fierce added zest, springing from some primitive atavistic necessity deep in one's nature. Now, slyly, she looked at Tom, who was leaning on his elbows on the fragile wooden rail, his profile silhouetted against the red clouds, and she thought, as she had thought many times before, "He is an attractive man . . . in that way surely one of the most attractive of men." But now, strangely, the sight of him left her without emotion. There was nothing on earth to prevent them making love. Three nights ago, on sight, in the palace they had not hesitated, but now the idea did not even interest her. It was not at all as she had imagined it.

Quite logically she thought, "What if he had been any one of the others?" But she could think of no man out of her past who could have aroused her interest in the same circumstances. In any case, none of them any longer interested her. She was fonder of Tom than she had ever been of any of them, and the affection for Tom persisted somehow, surviving boredom and surfeit, luxury, idleness, everything. And again she thought, "Perhaps I ought to get rid of Albert and marry him. Perhaps it would bring stability into both our lives." But almost at once she knew that she was not ready to marry yet, not, at any rate, in the sense which meant a settled, tranquil life. There were still adventures to be had. She did not love Tom. She was only fond of him.

And suddenly she found herself wishing that it was Tom who had gone off into the flood and darkness with Miss MacDaid, leaving behind the Major, and almost at once, a little startled, she thought, "So that's the way the land lies. That's what has happened to me." And in a kind of decadent voluptuousness she gave herself over to thinking of the young doctor, seeing him again, greedily, as she had seen him during the hours of restless boredom before the fantastic Miss Hodge had come to call. He was the one! And she thought, "If I do come out of this alive, I will be free for a little time; there will only be confusion so terrible that no one will notice me or what I do. I will no longer be Lord Esketh's wife, but nobody at all. I'll be, for a little while, no more than the wife of one of those little clerks."

[319]

She saw the Major very clearly now carrying the hysterical, scream-ing Miss Murgatroyd up the stairs like a bag of meal. She saw him with his great shoulders and fine dark face and blue eyes and the funny half-grin that was born, she divined suddenly, out of an odd mixture of animal vitality and high spirits, with the sadness of melan-choly and tragedy just beneath. It was Tom, in his drunkenness, who had been useless.

The Major couldn't be dead now, swept away by the flood like all the screaming, terrified people in the compound, because the thing wasn't finished yet. It was for that, she told herself with a half-hysterical mys-ticism, that she had come to India against her will, against the advice of everyone; it was for that she had come here in the wrong season, drawn here by this thing which had to happen. Two days ago, even an hour ago, she would not have cared whether she lived or died, but now she had desperately to live, because this thing had to come to an end in fulfillment, this thing for which she had been searching always, which she had dreamt of in a wild nightmare only a few nights ago. No, he couldn't be dead, because it was he who would save her. In him she was going to find the thing she had been searching for; and suddenly she was aware that it was not simply his good looks which attracted her, but something else—his coolness, his defiance, his fear-lessness in setting out into the flood with that rather grim old maid, Miss MacDaid, and by something that was in his face, shining there like a light, something which was goodness and pity and understanding and strength which she had never encountered in any man she had known before.

But then she thought, "I have never known any decent men except perhaps Tom, and he's eaten up by defeat and bitterness. All the men I've known have been cheap and common or bounders or weaklings or men like Albert." And again she was aware of a whole world which existed, which had always existed, outside the realm of her experience and understanding. The realization was like a brilliant light which made her blind suddenly to Tom, to the flood, to the disaster, to all the hor-rors. And then the sudden revelation faded quickly, so quickly that she had not time to seize and hold it, and again she was simply Edwina

Esketh, bored, intelligent, cold, cynical, and sensual—Edwina Esketh, a rich and fashionable slut.

When she could bear the unnatural stillness no longer, she said to Tom in a whisper, "Do you think they got through?"

For a moment he did not answer, and she thought, "He is contemptuous of me and shocked. He thinks I'm shameless, but it isn't like that. It's different, only I could never make him believe that it isn't simply the other thing all over again."

Tom was saying, "If they managed to reach the hospital and it's still standing, they're all right." And then, after a moment, he added, "But I should think the chances were one in a thousand."

A little before dawn, after the rain had begun again, Mrs. Bannerjee, calm and beautiful and still steel-bright with excitement, came quietly up behind them and said, "My father-in-law has had an attack. I think he is dying."

When Ransome offered his aid, she refused it, saying: "No, there is nothing you can do. The excitement was too much for him. He's an old man. It's just as well. If Major Safti had been here he could have done something, but it was meant to be like this. In his horoscope it is written that he should die in a disaster." For a moment she was silent, and in the darkness Ransome felt that she was smiling. "My husband's wailing," she said, "you must not take too seriously. It relieves him."

Then she was gone, and after she had gone it seemed to Ransome that there had been in her voice something of pride and triumph, as if she had said: "You have not conquered India. Nothing has ever conquered her . . . you pale, puny Europeans least of all." And he thought again of the Major's long speeches about the cruelty of India.

As the rim of sky beneath the clouds began to turn pink and gray in the east he turned and said to Edwina, "Perhaps it would be better if you had a little sleep. I don't suppose there'll be much rest or comfort for a long time to come."

"No, I couldn't sleep now . . . I want to see what it looks like when the light comes up. I want to see if the Summer Palace is still standing." She did not look at him, for fear that he would divine her deceit and make her ashamed, for in her heart she did not care a fig whether the Summer Palace was gone; it was the hospital she must know about.

Again the sense of freedom returned to her, the same extraordinary sense of having come to the end of something, neatly and cleanly, and she thought, "If only this place would remain isolated forever. If only I would never have to go back to Europe again."

Once more she glanced at Ransome, and now in the rising light she could see the unhappy face quite clearly and it seemed to her that she found in it a kind of bitterness and tragedy she had not seen there before, not the trivial bitterness which made him speak so often with mockery and scorn, but something deeper, as if a fine spirit and a great intelligence had been wasted and that he was aware of the waste and the folly. Perhaps he was suffering even now, not for himself, but for the people in the drowned city whom he did not know and perhaps had never seen. And it occurred to her that perhaps that new look was not new, but only strange to her because until now she had never before been able to see it. She thought, "It is the Major, whom I scarcely know, who has made me see." And with shame she remembered that Tom had never talked with her save in a trivial way, as if he thought her unworthy of anything better. She had never known him at all. She did not know anything about him. And suddenly she felt a quick wave of affection for him, an emotion that was clear and clean and uncomplicated and different from any feeling she had ever had for him before, and at the same time she was swept by an emotion of terrifying loneliness, as if both Tom and the Major existed on a plane far above her, which she could not reach, which neither of them would permit her to reach, and that between the two men there was a kind of understanding which forever shut her out. For the first time in all her life, there was no arrogance in her, but only humbleness and fear, a greater fear, a far greater fear, than any terror she had experienced during the earthquake and the flood because it was a fear of something unknown, of some vague thing which lay before her.

Tom turned to her and said, "Look, the towers of the Great Palace are gone."

It was light enough now to see the silhouette of the great structure on the heights on the other side of the river. The light was gray and murky, for the low heavy clouds had come back again and stifled the beams of the rising sun, and as it increased it became clear that nothing remained of the town save here and there the half-wrecked mass of some important building. From the balcony of Mr. Bannerjee's house they could make out distantly the ruins of the Music School, the shattered mass of the Maharani's Girls' High School, the Engineering School. As it grew lighter, Edwina pointed into the gray rain and asked, "Is that the Summer Palace?"

"Yes."

"It has fallen in."

"Not all of it. He might still be alive there." And at the same time he remembered what he had forgotten until this moment—that the Major had said that Esketh had the plague, and he thought, "Better that the whole palace fell on him." And then he thought about poor Miss Dirks, old Dacy Dirk's daughter, and for a moment he doubted whether all this had not been a kind of nightmare. The memory came back to him hazily and he thought, "That is because I was so drunk." It was not possible that a man like Esketh could catch the plague. It was not possible that there could be such cruelty as the lonely suffering of poor dutiful Miss Dirks.

Then he heard Edwina saying, "The hospital . . . where is the hospital?" and he answered, "You can't see it from here. It's behind the trees." And when he looked at her he saw that she had turned away her face so that he could not see it.

Then for a long time they watched the desolation in silence, fascinated by the spectacle of bodies and trees and snakes, and in the shock and unreality of what had happened to them, calloused to the full horror of what they saw, Tom thought, "It was that way in the war. In the normal person something must happen to deaden the sensibilities when a catastrophe occurs." The war had never upset him in that way; he had simply grown sick, horribly sick, at the endless idiotic killing.

Behind him some one was saying, "Goodness! there's nothing left at all," and turning he saw Miss Murgatroyd, her sallow face swollen with sleep, her gown of blue taffeta with its garlands of pale-pink rosebuds, all bedraggled and soiled to the knees with muddy water. It struck him as odd that her terror was all gone. The dull, muddy face betrayed no emotion of any kind.

"You're not frightened now?" he asked.

"Oh dear, no! I'm sure we'll be rescued," and she smiled at him that silly bright smile of admiration which always made the pit of his stomach contract with boredom. She was play-acting now, in front of himself and Edwina; she was being British, the daughter of that mythical magistrate in Madras, and as he watched her he understood the full depths of her loneliness and her morbid egotism. She was not frightened now; she was even insensible to the whole tragedy because she was safe and Mrs. Bannerjee, who was so cruel to her, was safe, and perhaps himself who had been kind to her. That was all she had in the world, the only friends she had known for years, and here they were, the three of them, isolated together by the flood in Mr. Bannerjee's house.

"Old Mr. Bannerjee is dying," she said, brightly, as if the news made her, in some way, more interesting.

"I know," said Ransome. "Perhaps there's something that we could do to help Mrs. Bannerjee."

"Oh no," said Miss Murgatroyd. "She sent me away. She said I'd only be in the way."

Very likely Mrs. Bannerjee had not put it as kindly as that. He thought, "O Lord! that means she's going to stay with us."

Edwina said, suddenly, "Do you think there's any way of making a cup of tea? It would help our spirits."

Ransome looked at Miss Murgatroyd as the intimate of the household.

"I expect so," she said, "Mrs. Bannerjee keeps a primus stove in her room just for making tea at night. I'll go and see." And suddenly important and useful, she turned and re-entered the upper hallway.

"I hope the old gentleman doesn't die," said Ransome.

"Yes, I suppose it would add to the complications."

"It's worse than that. Bannerjee will want to burn the body before sundown so that he can throw the ashes into the river. The old man meant to die in Benares. He was going there next month to sit on the bank and wait for death. It was a piece of bad luck, the flood. . . ."

Edwina smiled.

"What are you smiling about?"

"I know it's not in the best of taste, but I can't help seeing you and myself here on this balcony, worrying over such things as what is to become of old Mr. Bannerjee's body."

The wailing of Mr. Bannerjee, the son, was less violent now, as if the exertions of the night had worn him out. It had sunk away into a kind of low, monotonous keening, rising and falling now into a moan, now becoming distant like the buzzing of the bees at night in the great chandeliers of the palace.

"I'd like to have a picture of Bannerjee just now to frame and send to the Oxford Union." As he spoke he knew that Edwina's smile and her remark had been born of the weariness and hysteria which had followed the excitement of the night before, an excitement to which neither of them had yielded at the moment. Now he felt it in himself, the sudden desire to laugh and make flippant remarks in the very face of death and tragedy. Now that all the brandy and cocktails had worn off, his head ached and he began to think longingly of the brandy bottle he had salvaged from the flooded dining room. At the same moment Miss Murgatroyd returned.

"The stove is all right and there's tea, but there isn't any water."

Flippantly he said, "What, no water?" and Miss Murgatroyd answered, "You know what I mean, no drinking-water." She pointed to the flood and said, "If we used that water we might get cholera or typhus or something."

"Fetch me the kettle," he said, and when she returned, he went to the pipe which carried the water from the roof to the ground and kicked loose a section of it. The clean rain water poured out from the broken pipe and the kettle was filled in a moment.

"There," he said, "there's plenty of water. Do you suppose there's anything to eat?"

"The cookhouse is under water. There's part of a tin of biscuits in Mrs. Bannerjee's room."

"Well, fetch them when the tea's ready, and tell Mrs. Bannerjee. Perhaps the old man would like a cup of tea."

"He's beyond that," said Miss Murgatroyd.

She went away happy, bustling now with importance and content to be serving these two members of a conquering race, whose blood, diluted, mixed in her veins with that of a low-caste Indian woman.

Edwina said, suddenly, "Has the house got a tin roof?"

"No, it's slabs of stone."

"Then it's all right. He could burn the body up there."

"That wouldn't stop him. He's so scared by now, he'd set the house on fire and burn us all out if there wasn't any other way."

Then from inside the house the wailing of Mr. Bannerjee suddenly took on a new energy, hysterical, louder even than it had been at the onset of the flood. For a moment Ransome listened, and then said, "The old man must be gone."

In the doorway Miss Murgatroyd appeared, looking like a dreary A.B.C. waitress in fancy dress. She carried a tray with the teapot and two cups, and a plate of biscuits. She said, "Will you hold this a moment while I fetch a table?" Obediently Ransome took the tray, thinking, "Perhaps, after all, the poor thing is good for something."

In a moment she returned with a cheap bamboo table, and after placing the tray on it she asked, as if there was nothing whatever unusual in the scene about them, "How does your ladyship like it?"

"As it comes," said Edwina.

"Old Mr. Bannerjee is dead," said Miss Murgatroyd, brightly.

All that day they did not see Mr. or Mrs. Bannerjee, but Miss Murgatroyd, bright with the delight of finding some one to worship, came and went, reporting the progress of the ceremonies of mourning. Toward noon Lady Esketh retired to one of the bedrooms to sleep for a time, and Ransome, after he had finished what remained of the brandy, went to another room to sleep. There was no use in thinking of lunch, because there was nothing to eat. When he wakened he went out again to the balcony, but nothing in the scene of desolation had changed save that two or three of the fires had burned themselves out. The water still moved sluggishly, its surface clotted with wreckage. Still in all the wide landscape not one human figure was visible, not one sign of life save for the passing of an occasional python wrapped round a floating beam or the branch of a tree, and the distant chatter of the sacred monkeys in the trees somewhere in the direction of Ransome's own house.

A little while later Edwina joined him, and presently she said, "Aren't there any boats in Ranchipur?"

"Not many, and those were along the river. They must have been swept away."

"It doesn't seem to trouble you."

"There isn't anything we can do about it. You're not in Europe now, you know."

"Won't anybody do anything about it?"

"I think it unlikely. It depends on who has been left alive. I should think everyone is pretty badly disorganized. Raschid we could count on, and the officers of the Indian regiment, and some of the Mahrattas. I wouldn't trust the Gujerati at a time like this. Very likely they're all behaving like Bannerjee or trying to save their own property."

"I was only thinking that it's beginning to be a bore."

Then Ransome, who was himself beginning to feel restless, remembered the playing-cards Mrs. Bannerjee had rescued before everything was covered with water. "We might play patience," he said, grinning.

"I consider that a bad joke."

"No, I really mean it." So he fetched the cards, and for a time they tried playing patience on the top of the bamboo table which Miss Murgatroyd had furnished with the tea. It was too small to allow them a double game, too small even to play a single game in comfort, and they both had to stand because there were no chairs. After a time in which Edwina kept repeating, "Red jack on black queen" and "Black eight on red nine" she said, suddenly, pushing the cards from the table, "I'm sick of being British."

"What do you mean?"

"Taking it like this, coldly, as if nothing had happened. I'd like to know what's happened to the maids and Albert and even Bates and the Major and that nurse."

"Of course I could swim to the Summer Palace and stop by at the hospital on the way back."

"Don't be a bloody fool!"

"Patience, my dear girl, is a great game in more senses than one."

"I must say I wish Indian houses had a little more furniture. I'm sick of standing up or lying down. Don't they ever do anything else?"

"They sit on the floor. There are plenty of chairs downstairs for entertaining people like us."

The afternoon wore on and Edwina's temper grew a little worse. Presently she said, "Are you inhuman? Don't you care what has happened to your friends?"

And quickly his face grew white and he said, "Don't talk like a Goddamned fool!" And she was ashamed again.

Then Miss Murgatroyd reappeared, carrying fresh tea, and they knew that it must be four o'clock. There were only four soggy biscuits on the tray.

"That's all there are," said Miss Murgatroyd.

"Perhaps we'd better go on rations," said Ransome.

"Oh, the water will go down or some one will turn up," said Miss Murgatroyd, and suddenly Ransome understood another reason why she was neither frightened nor bored. Something was happening to her. For the first time in her dreary librarian's life something was happening.

"Won't you join us?" he asked, politely.

"No. I've had tea with Mrs. Bannerjee." She handed him his cup and then said, "They're going to burn old Mr. Bannerjee on the roof." There was a hint of a giggle in her voice and she added, "These Hindus certainly do the most extraordinary things." And Ransome felt his stomach contract again with dislike. At the same time, from the inside of the house came a sound of wood being smashed, and Ransome turned toward the door, listening.

"It's Mr. Bannerjee and the house servant tearing up the floors to get wood."

"The servant?" said Ransome, "Did he have a family?"

"Yes, a wife and four children."

"What happened to them?"

"They were in the houses in the compound."

After Miss Murgatroyd had gone, the sound of hammering and smashing continued for a long time. Then as the darkness began to close in, it died away, and in its place came the dim, ghostly sound of bare feet ascending and descending the stairway to the roof. The sound continued until it was quite dark outside, and then presently from the roof above their heads the sound of Mr. Bannerjee's wailing began again, louder now, for his voice was rested, and then after a moment from the roof above them appeared a glow which illumined the leaves of the trees all about, a glow which grew and grew, accompanied by a crackling sound. Ransome thought, "I suppose I should stand by with water in case the house takes fire," but he did nothing. He was aware now of a kind of apathy which had transformed everything, changed all values, made nothing seem worth while. Edwina disappeared again to try to sleep, and, alone, he waited on the balcony.

While he watched there he saw that the body of old Mr. Bannerjee was not the only one being burned. Here and there all about the rim of the flood little fires leapt up against the stormy sky, puny, feeble flames of superstition, perhaps of faith, wherever the bodies of friends, of mothers, of children, of wives and husbands, had been found. The Major and Mrs. Bannerjee were right. No one would ever conquer India.

While he listened to the sounds from overhead he became aware presently that a flame had sprung up on the roof of the shattered palace, tiny at first, no more than a pinpoint of light, growing and growing until Ransome understood that there, too, a body was being burned. The wind blowing toward Mr. Bannerjee's house carried the smoke across the water and presently Ransome fancied that he divined the ghost of sandalwood scent in the deep air. He thought, "Perhaps it is the old gentleman. Perhaps he was killed by one of the falling towers. That would be the worst calamity of all." Now, more than ever Ranchipur would have need of the old Maharajah's simplicity and courage.

About ten o'clock—Ransome did not know exactly the time, for in the excitement his watch had stopped—the glow from the roof overhead began to die away. The house had not caught fire, perhaps because there was some magical quality in the slabs of stone which had been brought long ago from the sacred mountain of Abana to roof the house built by the dissolute Lady Streetingham to house her wastrel guests. The wailing, too, had ceased, perhaps because the voice of Mr. Bannerjee had failed at last. When it was quite dark he went into the house and called as softly as possible the name of Edwina. She was awake and answered him from one of the rooms along the hallway.

"Come in," she said. "I'm not asleep. I couldn't stand on my feet any longer. But I think a light would help, and some tea."

From the doorway of the roof he called to Miss Murgatroyd as softly as possible, and in a moment Miss Murgatroyd appeared out of the thick blackness, feeling her way along the wall.

"Do you think we could have some tea?"

"There isn't any more alcohol."

"What about a light?"

"The parafine is all gone, too. Mr. Bannerjee used them both to start the fire."

"Blast and damn!" said Ransome, and out of the darkness from the bed behind them he heard the sound of Edwina's stifled laugh.

All through the night they spent their time sleeping, talking, and watching. Outside, the last of the great fires burned itself out, so that there was no longer a tragic but magnificent spectacle beneath their eyes, but only velvety darkness and the sound of the horrible, monotonous rain. When dawn came there was nothing to see save the unchanged panorama of water and rubbish and bodies and shattered and burned buildings. And then about eight o'clock Edwina cried out, "Look! Look! What is that?" And Ransome, turning, saw one of the Maharani's tiny pleasure boats, all gold and gilt, coming through the lower branches of a great banyan tree. It was driven by some one whose figure was not yet visible, for the canopy of the little boat had become jammed in the branches of the tree and the oarsman was struggling, half-concealed by the leaves, to free it.

Then suddenly it shot free of the branches and the figure they saw was that of a white boy clad in shorts and a shirt. For a moment it nearly lost its balance and fell into the muddy water, but as it regained its feet and took up the oars once more they saw that it was not a boy at all.

Ransome said, "My God! It's Fern!"

"Who is Fern?"

The question puzzled Ransome for a second because, without thinking of it, it seemed to him that Edwina had been in Ranchipur for weeks, even for months, and that she must know quite well who Fern was. Then, with a shock, he remembered that only five days had passed since her arrival, and he said, "She's the daughter of the American missionaries."

The boat was quite near now, near enough for them to see that one of the oars was painted scarlet and gold and clearly belonged to the boat, but that the other was an improvised affair, made of a pole and a bit of wood. And Ransome now recognized the clothes he had loaned her to wear home on the night she had run away. She did not shout to them. She did not even stop rowing to raise her 'arm and wave. Instead she kept rowing steadily, awkwardly, her progress crippled by the makeshift oar, driving the fragile silly little boat against the sluggish current nearer and nearer to them.

"She's very pretty," said Edwina, "and very young."

Ransome did not answer her.

Fern had left Ransome's house, meaning to go straight home. Angry, she went away, out of the house to the *porte cochère*, where she had left her bicycle, and then when she mounted it she discovered that even the bicycle had let her down. One of the tires was flat and the discovery made her burst into tears. It meant that she had two miles ahead of her on foot through the rain, unless she went back and asked Ransome's boy to repair the damage, and she could not go back now for fear she might see Ransome again, and as she left the house she told herself that she would never see him again, no matter what happened.

Walking beside the bicycle, wheeling it, she got as far as the end of the drive, and there she discovered that she was no longer angry, but only defeated and tired, more tired than she had ever been in all her life, not only of Ranchipur, of her mother and father and Hazel, everyone she knew, but tired even of Ransome. Because she was very young she thought, "If only I could die now. It would be so easy. There isn't anything to live for. If only I could lie down here on the racecourse road and die of exposure." But she knew that in the warm, sticky air of Ranchipur in monsoon time, she might lie there for days without any ill effects, and then at night at this season there was always the question of snakes, and snakes terrified her. They were everywhere now. At night one might encounter them anywhere crossing the road . . . pythons or Russell's vipers or kraits or cobras.

The failure of the tire changed her mood suddenly, so that she was no longer angry at Ransome, but only sorry for herself. It seemed now to her, as she trudged along through the sticky mud, that he had never done anything but let her down. He had never treated her seriously, and tonight, worst of all, when she had come to warn him, he had been drunk and behaved as if she were a child or an idiot. She had never seen a man really drunk before (once or twice she had seen one of The Boys when they had had too much, but it seemed to make them only gay and rather silly) and the sight of Ransome frightened her and made her feel ill. It seemed to her that he might have been less drunk than mad, laughing as he did at the things which frightened her and made her so miserable, laughing even at the prospect of scandal and scenes and trouble in which he himself was certain to be involved.

Why had she ever told that horrible lie? Why had she ever said that she had lived with him? It wasn't only that she had played directly into her mother's hand; it made her seem, when she tried to deny it, nothing better than a silly fool.

As she passed the garden of Raschid Ali Khan she thought, wildly, "I *will* go in and stay there. That will fix them all. Then they'll all be sorry." But almost at once she saw that such a course was impossible because the one it hurt most was certain to be Raschid Ali Khan, who had never done her any harm. She scarcely knew him by sight and she did not know whether she would like him or not. She did not even know whether or not she liked Indians, because she had never really known any except the converted half-savage Bhils who worked about the Mission. And they were aborigines and not really Indians at all. But she told herself that they must be all right if Ransome liked them so much, for even in her anger and disappointment she did not accuse him of being a fool. To her he still seemed, in spite of drunkenness, in spite of everything, the wisest person she knew. Then the thought that she would never see him again made her weep once more, so that she was blinded now not only by the driving rain but by her own tears; but at the same time that curious warm feeling which she had experienced in the darkness after she had gone to bed at the Smileys' returned to her, and even in her youth and inexperience she knew in her heart that she loved him and that she would always remember him and think of him with a catch at the heart even when she was an old woman.

Then, plodding along in the mud, she reached the corner by the Distillery and as she turned toward the Mission she noticed the lights of a motor coming along the road over which she had just passed. At once she thought, "That is momma coming home from town," and without hesitation she switched off the light of the bike and plunged into the *nullah* alongside the road. She knew now that she dreaded the snakes less than she dreaded seeing her mother. Very likely her mother was returning from Ransome's. Very likely she had seen Ransome and told him that he had to marry her. Terrified, she waited in the *nullah* until the car had passed above her, showering her with mud. She recognized the old Ford, and then, out of terror, anguish, and sheer misery, she was suddenly sick.

Once on her way again she saw that every step was bringing her nearer home, nearer to her mother, who by now had perhaps told her father and Hazel the whole story. She still walked, automatically, almost without conscious effort, in the same direction, because there seemed to be no other direction in which to go. Sobbing, she stumbled along until ahead of her the lights of the Mission appeared through the wall of rain, and at sight of them a new idea came to her. She would not go home at all. She would go to the Smileys' after all and ask them to hide her. The harm she had done them was already accomplished. The awful letter filled with disgusting accusations had already been sent. Nothing worse could happen. And the decision brought her a sense of peace. The Smileys would understand. At least they would shelter her for a little time until she got over the shock of the call on Ransome.

But the Smileys weren't at home. As she reached the door she saw only Aunt Phoebe alone in the sitting-room, and remembered that of course the Smileys at this hour would be at the night school. For a moment she hesitated again, for Aunt Phoebe frightened her a little, not because she would be hard and unsympathetic, but because in the wisdom of her great age she seemed to know everything. Her eye was too sharp, and her common sense frightened and shamed what little there remained of Blythe Summerfield, the Pearl of the Orient.

But again, as in the *nullah*, the thought came to her that she would rather face anyone or anything now, than her mother, and she understood that it was quite impossible to go all night walking round and round Ranchipur in the rain. So resting her bike against the rail of the verandah she knocked, and Aunt Phoebe, looking up from her tatting, said, "Come in."

At sight of Fern a dim expression of surprise came into the bright eyes of the old lady, but she suppressed it quickly, perhaps moved by the swollen eyes and the look of despair on Fern's face.

Then Fern was embarrassed, so embarrassed that without any prelude she said, abruptly, "I can't go home. Will you let me stay here for a while?" and overcome with self-pity and the image of herself as a homeless orphan, she burst into tears.

"Heavens on earth!" said Aunt Phoebe, springing up from her rocking-chair. "What's the matter?" She put her arm around Fern's shoulders and said, "But you're soaking wet. I'll get you some dry things and then you can tell me all about it." Left alone for a moment, Fern flung herself down on the settee and sobbed loudly and without restraint.

When Aunt Phoebe returned she was carrying a complete costume belonging to Mrs. Smiley, as well as a large towel. Gently she touched Fern's shoulder and said, "Come now. Rub yourself dry and put on these things of Bertha's, and then you can tell me what's the matter."

Fern had no desire to dry herself and change her clothes. She wanted only to weep, to keep the soaked clothing on her until she caught pneumonia and died, but there was something in the dry manner of the old lady which made her feel a fool and compelled her to obey.

Then by the time she had changed, the hysterical sobbing had stopped and once more she felt on the defensive. But again it was no good against the determination of Aunt Phoebe, who said, "Now, listen to me, child. You've got something on your mind and you're going to tell me about it. I can kind of guess what some of it is, but you can tell me the rest. I don't say I'll be of any use, but it'll take the load off your mind."

Then Fern heard herself saying, "Could I tell you? Will you let me?" And she realized all at once that in all Ranchipur it was only the Smileys who could possibly understand why she had been such a fool. It was only the Smileys, too, who would not judge her or give her advice or laugh at her. She did not like the plain gingham dress belonging to Bertha Smiley because it was ugly and too long, but it gave her a kind of confidence as if it were invested with the quality of

Bertha Smiley herself, and suddenly she found herself telling Aunt Phoebe everything, just as it had happened to her, why she had done this and that, why she hated her mother (she admitted even that), why she had gone to Ransome's a second time, and throughout the recital Aunt Phoebe was silent, save that now and then she made a clucking sound to indicate her concern and her disapproval of certain foolish incidents.

When Fern had finished with the account of her second visit to Ransome, Aunt Phoebe said, "I must say he didn't behave much like a gentleman. It doesn't sound like him. Maybe it was because he was drunk."

"That's it," said Fern, herself suddenly seeking excuses for him. "I'm sure that's it. I shouldn't have come to you at all . . . not after all the trouble I caused you the last time, not after my mother wrote that letter to the Mission Board."

"Never mind about that," said Aunt Phoebe. "It ain't the first letter like that she's written. And, anyway, evil never triumphs over good. I'm an old woman, and in the end I know that's true. The trouble is your mother wasn't raised right. Southern women never are. All they're taught is to get a husband for themselves. They can't even think of anything else."

"I don't know what to do now," said Fern. "I don't know where to go."

Aunt Phoebe stood up. "I guess," she said, "the best thing for us to do is get a bite to eat. We've all had supper and I guess maybe the cook-boy has gone out, but I can rake up something. I'd kind of like a bite myself. I'm used to scratching up odds and ends when I get hungry. We'll make up a good cup of coffee and some eggs and maybe some fried yams."

She took Fern's hand and led her toward the kitchen. Aunt Phoebe's hand was old and thin and gnarled and worn by the hard work of nearly seventy years, but Fern found it soft and comforting. It was an experience she had never had before in all her nineteen years, and it made her want to begin crying all over again.

The old lady kept on chattering, perhaps to spare the frightened girl the effort of saying anything. "The trouble is," she said, "that you don't belong in a place like Ranchipur. It's bad enough for grown-up people with all the heat and filth and mud and dust. I like it, but sometimes it gets on my nerves and makes me cantankerous so that I get sharp even with Bertha and Homer. It ain't natural, this climate, but it's awful interesting."

While Aunt Phoebe bustled about, she set Fern to helping her as if she knew that the best thing for the girl was to have something for her hands to do. As Fern worked, the sense of hysterical tension began to leave her and presently she knew that there was still something she wanted to tell the old woman, the one thing she hadn't told her, the most important thing of all, that she was in love for the first time in her life. Again when she tried to think of some one to whom she might tell her secret, there was, after all, no one in Ranchipur except Aunt Phoebe and perhaps Bertha Smiley, and she was not sure even that Bertha Smiley would have understood. Of Aunt Phoebe, who was so old, she felt more confident. It was as if Aunt Phoebe had lived so long that she had completed a cycle and become young again.

She wanted desperately to talk about Ransome with someone. Even her attempt to confide in her cousin by letter in far-off Biloxi had been a failure because with every word she put on paper she knew more surely that her cousin would not understand, or that if she had even a hint of understanding, she would somehow make the whole thing cheap and trivial. She remembered Aunt Phoebe's sudden contemptuous speech about her mother—that Southern women were never taught anything but to get a husband for themselves, and she thought, "Now when we sit down to eat I will begin to talk about him." Again the warm feeling came over her, and she felt her own heart expand again with goodness and a desire to help to save him from drunkenness and despair.

When at last they sat down to a snack of eggs and yams, toast and tea and gingerbread, Aunt Phoebe, as if she understood everything, said, "It's such a pity about Mr. Ransome. He's such a nice man. It's awful when drink gets a hold on a man like that. Most drunks don't matter, because they were never any good, anyway. I had a brother like that . . . like Ransome I mean—he died of drink when he was fifty."

Fern's heart warmed again, and she was about to tell the old woman everything, when suddenly her tongue was checked, with the very words

[336]

at her lips, by something physical outside of her, a kind of menacing stillness in the hot damp air. It was as if she had started to speak and then suddenly became aware that she was interrupting some more important speech, some communication being made to herself and old Aunt Phoebe by all of Nature. She saw that Aunt Phoebe was aware of the same intrusion; it was as if a ghost had entered the room and commanded the attention of both of them. The old lady looked at her and started to speak, and then the world about them seemed to come to an end. The tiles beneath their feet crinkled and broke apart. The table rocked and the tea was spilled on the fresh cloth. There was the sound of stone and mortar crackling and crumbling, and the lights went out as the distant power-house was buried by the wall of water from the broken dam.

Then in the darkness Fern heard Aunt Phoebe saying in a funny flat voice, "I guess that must have been an earthquake."

Fern, paralyzed, did not move or speak, and the old lady said, "Stay where you are. I think there's a flashlight in the cupboard," and Fern heard her, rustling like a mouse, across the broken tiles somewhere in the darkness and then the sound of a cupboard door being opened and then there was a light again in the room, the dim light of an electric torch with a battery which was almost exhausted. Then she found candles of which there were an abundance because Aunt Phoebe had never in her heart trusted lights which might go on and off without warning at the touch of the hand of some Indian filled with curiosity in a power-house ten miles away.

"I suppose we ought to go outside at once," said Aunt Phoebe. "That's what my sister Doris said she always did at Long Beach when they had earthquakes. But I don't hanker after going out in that rain. I suppose it would make more sense if we went to see what had happened to the house. From all the dust and smell you'd think the whole place had come down."

The calmness of the old lady, which wasn't perhaps so much calmness as indifference, brought Fern back to her senses, and she thought, "What has happened to our house? And to Ransome? Where was he?" And then she remembered that he had gone out to dine with the Bannerjees, and thought quickly: "Anyway, that's not a stone house. Maybe a wooden house is better in an earthquake."

Half of the Smileys' house—the front half looking on to the Distillery Road had collapsed, but there remained intact three bedrooms and a vast empty storeroom which had not been made over when the rest of the house was converted from barracks into mission. In some freakish fashion the earthquake had demolished the one end and left the other shaken but still standing. The old lady, followed by Fern, regarded the wreckage, making a clucking sound at the sight of the ruins of a house which she had always kept in such fine order.

To Fern she said, "I guess it was lucky we were in the kitchen instead of the sitting-room." And at the same moment they were both aware of a strange sound coming toward them distantly from the direction of the town, a sound vague and distant, compounded of the rushing of water and the wailing of people which filled the emptiness of the silence that succeeded the quake. Each with a candle in her hand, they stood, the old woman and the girl, listening, frightened now by the new sounds which were less sudden and, being mysterious and less immediate, were more terrifying.

Aunt Phoebe, pulling herself together, was the first to speak. "What on earth do you suppose that could be?" and then: "I guess Bertha and Homer will be all right. The night school is a new building and good and strong."

"It sounds like yelling," said Fern. "I want to go and see what's happened to our house."

She was afraid now, deeply, sickeningly afraid, because from the house in the other garden there had come no sound. If her mother was there, or Hazel, they would have screamed because that was their nature. One of them would have come across the drive, no matter how much they hated the Smileys. From the window she could make out nothing in the thick darkness . . . nothing but rain and the great branches of the banyan trees reaching up and up toward the black sky.

The house of the Simons had gone down, like the regimental barracks, into a mass of beams and mortar and broken stone. By the time

[338]

Fern and Aunt Phoebe reached it the cloud of dust raised by the collapse had been stifled by the downpour, and feebly, in silence, by the aid of the worn-out electric torch, the girl and the old woman circled the wrecked house, calling out in faint, shaken voices, searching for some sign of life. Now Fern felt a sudden terrible calmness come over her—the calmness that follows a horrible shock. It left her mind unnaturally cold and clear. There was no reality in the scene. Her consciousness rejected it as something nightmarish and impossible—that she and Aunt Phoebe should be here in the rain, searching the ruins of the shattered house for some sign of her father, her mother, and her sister. The weird sound of wailing which came toward them from the distant town had nothing to do with life; it too belonged in a nightmare.

Then suddenly it seemed to her that if she called their names loudly enough they might appear, safe and alive, out of the rain-drenched darkness, perhaps from the tennis-courts or along the road, and she began to call in a wavering hysterical voice, "Poppa! Momma! Hazel!" but her voice was muted by the flood of rain and no sound came back to her save the ghostly wailing from the stricken town.

She heard Aunt Phoebe saying, "Maybe they weren't at home. Maybe they're safe somewhere else."

A wild and dreadful thought crossed her brain, "Perhaps they're all dead! Perhaps I'm free!" and she felt suddenly sick with shame. Again, for the last time, she called into the blackness, "Hazel! Hazel!" For plain, stupid Hazel couldn't be dead. The earth seemed suddenly to rise beneath her feet and the blackness closed in on her, swallowing her up as the sound of the wailing grew fainter and fainter, until it died away.

When she became conscious again she was lying wrapped in a sheet on the broken floor of the kitchen. There was a taste of brandy in her mouth which made her think at once of Ransome and that first visit to his house, and over her was standing Aunt Phoebe who said, "It's all right, my child. You fainted and I dragged you in here. That was all. Here, take a little more of this. I always have it around for a time like this."

She drank the strong, cheap brandy, choking a little, and then slowly the memory of what had happened came back to her. Now it had a kind of dull, sickening reality. The nightmarish quality was gone and she knew that the earthquake had happened and that very likely her mother and father and Hazel were dead. Tears came to her eyes and began to trickle down her cheeks, and in spite of herself she began to whimper. The old lady took her hand. "You mustn't do that," she said. "It doesn't do any good. You'd better put on some dry clothes. I couldn't get you dressed. It was about all I could do to get you in here and get the wet clothes off you."

"I won't do it again. I promise. I don't know what was the matter with me."

And then from out of the darkness they heard faintly a voice calling. For a moment the wall of rain made the sound blurred and weak. Sitting up, Fern listened. A second time the voice came to them, shrill, wavering, hysterical, but clearer this time, so clear that Fern recognized it as her mother's, and holding the sheet about her scrambled to her feet. The third time the voice became clear. In the darkness and rain her mother was calling, "Elmer! Elmer! Hazel! Fern!"

"I'll go and fetch her," said Aunt Phoebe.

"I'll go with you. I'll go! I'll go!" And with the sheet wrapped about her, she followed the old lady out into the rain.

By the weak light of the torch they found their way toward the sound of Mrs. Simon's voice. They discovered her on the drive, a little distance from the house, and when they came near they saw that she was not alone. Leaning on her, being dragged along, was the overblown figure of Mrs. Hoggett-Egburry.

At sight of the light, Mrs. Simon called out, hysterically, "Who is it? Is it you, Elmer?" and Fern answered, "It's me, Momma."

"Where are they? Where's your father? Where's Hazel? O my God! what has happened?"

Then Mrs. Simon flung her arms about Fern and, sobbing, cried out: "Oh, my darling! I know they're dead! I know they're dead!" and Mrs. Hoggett-Egburry, unsupported now, slipped to the muddy driveway and remained sitting there, upright, murmurous and complaining, in the drenched peignoir of lace and baby-blue satin.

Left alone with Mrs. Hoggett-Egburry on the verandah of the deserted bungalow, Mrs. Simon had waited for a long time, listening to the moans of her stricken friend and the sounds from the town. She did not at first know what she was waiting for, but presently it was borne in upon her intelligence that they might stay there until doomsday without anyone coming to help them. Slowly, too, it dawned upon her that her friend was drunk and therefore useless. It was rare that she ever saw Mrs. Hoggett-Egburry so late in the evening, and never before had she seen her helpless. That part of Mrs. Hoggett-Egburry which had always remained sober enough to permit an illusion of dignity had now, it seemed, succumbed to the added intoxication of terror; and for a moment Mrs. Simon hated her profoundly because in such a crisis she was silly and useless, because she was only a burden, because she was stupid and soft and idiotic. Her instinct told her to go off, leaving her friend there alone on the floor of the verandah, but experience told her that this was impossible. Twice she slapped her, with no effect save to increase the volume of the moans. Then taking one arm and placing it over her shoulder as if she were saving a drowning woman, she got her to her feet.

She cried, "Pull yourself together, Lily. We've got to get out of here." But Mrs. Hoggett-Egburry only moaned and remained sagging and heavy and inert. Now, in the midst of catastrophe, Mrs. Simon was no longer impressed. In some mysterious way the importance of Mrs. Hoggett-Egburry had melted away. She was no longer afraid to call her Lily to her face, as she called her behind her back; she called her even worse things. Now she made no effort to conceal her hardness. She cried, "Come on, you damned drunken fool. I've got to get home!"

Just as Mrs. Hoggett-Egburry seemed to collapse, so the small female figure of Mrs. Simon seemed to gain strength. The coquetry, the exaggerated femininity were nowhere in evidence now. She became suddenly a woman of iron. Half carrying, half dragging her friend, she negotiated the steps and thrust her, still moaning, into the back of the old Ford. Mrs. Hoggett-Egburry fell on the floor and lay there with one plump leg hanging out of the car, but Mrs. Simon savagely thrust the leg inside and banged the door shut. Then, without a backward glance, she climbed into the front and drove off.

By now the fires had begun in the town and the reflected glow lighted up the road all the way to the Distillery. At the Distillery corner, which was on lower ground, the Ford plunged in a jet of spray into a foot or more of water. The road itself was invisible but she was able to discover where it lay by the lines of Java fig trees on each side. Steering by these, she made another half-mile, sometimes on the bare road, sometimes driving through water which nearly covered the wheels. She kept thinking, "If only I can get to the racecourse milepost we'll be on higher ground," and then just as she had almost reached it, the water entered the carburetor and the old Ford died.

Again and again she tried to start the engine, swearing now, using words which she had heard long ago as a girl on hot nights, used by drummers on the verandah of her father's hotel in Unity Point, Mississippi, words which she did not even know that she knew. And at the same time she began to cry, more out of exasperation than from fear. She thought, "We can't stay here all night. The water might rise. I've got to get back to the Mission and I've got to drag that drunken fool with me. After this she can never again put on airs with me."

When at last she gave up all hope of starting the Ford, she climbed down, filled with terror of snakes, into the tepid water. It rose above her knees, muddy, smelly, and uncomfortable. Pulling open the door, she cried, "Get up out of there, you fool!"

By the glow of the reflected fire, she saw that Mrs. Hoggett-Egburry lay exactly as she had fallen, and at once she divined that there was no way of getting her out of the car save by pulling her out feet first. Bracing herself, she managed this by a series of tugs and jerks, so that presently the bank manager's wife was able to sit up on the floor with her feet outside. This position was better, Mrs. Simon realized, and with one more effort, she said in a wheedling voice, as if she were addressing a child, "Now, Lily, help yourself a little. Put your feet down and stand up." Mrs. Hoggett-Egburry, moaning, obeyed her hazily, but the heel of one ostrich-feathered mule caught on the fender and she plunged face forward into the water.

The shock of the water and perhaps the terror of death by drowning sobered her a little and gave back something of the will which she had cast away a little time before in a kind of drunken feminine voluptuousness. After a struggle she managed to scramble to her feet, and cried out, vaguely, "Where am I? Where am I? How did I get here?"

"You're on the Distillery Road, you fool! And we've got to walk. The Ford won't run."

With a little help from Mrs. Simon she managed to walk, whimpering and unsteady, until they were on higher ground and were free of the flood. Then, almost at once, she began to moan again and to collapse every thirty or forty feet. At last they passed the racecourse milestone and presently came to the foot of the Mission drive. Here, exhausted and in despair, Mrs. Simon had begun the screams which presently Fern and old Aunt Phoebe heard in the kitchen of the Smileys' half-wrecked house.

All the way from the banyan tree as far as the Bannerjee house, Fern continued rowing across the submerged gardens without once looking up. From the moment she had nearly capsized in trying to free the boat from the limbs of the tree, she had seen him there on the balcony, standing beside a strange woman, and now she was shy, not only on account of Ransome, but of the stranger. She thought, "It must seem to him that I am always running after him," and he might not want to be rescued. He might want to stay on there. The single glance at the stranger told her that the woman was very pretty. In her directness, she did not think or care about rescuing the stranger or the whole of the Bannerjee family. It was only of Ransome she had thought when she found the little boat drifting on the flood near the Distillery. It was only of him she had been thinking when she waded out to it up to her waist in water to drag it ashore; only of him when she patched together the crazy oar out of two pieces of wood Aunt Phobe had found for her. Her mother had become violent at the idea of the rescue, screaming and crying and wringing her hands and saying, "I forbid you to go out in that crazy boat. Haven't I suffered enough? Haven't I lost enough without losing you, too?" And Fern had paid no attention, but had gone on hammering away, and when she had made the contrived oar she stalked out of the house dressed in the clothes of Ransome which had been left behind on the night she spent with the Smileys.

She wasn't free, after all. Her mother was still alive and in her heart she knew that she would rather have lost her mother than her father and Hazel. But something had happened to her during the night of terror and tragedy. She knew now that, even if her mother was alive, she was none the less free of her forever. Slowly, another discovery about life dawned on her . . . that distance, that escape, had nothing to do with freedom. Freedom was something which existed inside of you, no matter where you were. She had not escaped and run away, she was still in Ranchipur, yet she was free, freer, perhaps, than if she had succeeded in escaping to Hollywood without having lived through the tragedy of the last few hours. She had proven stronger than her mother, for although she was sick and miserable and terrified, she had kept her head. She had found dignity, and her mother, in the crisis, had lost whatever dignity she had ever had behind the silly pink-and-white façade of the perpetual ingenue.

Even when she appeared dressed in Ransome's shorts and tennis shirt and her mother, at sight of them, gave a low cry as if she had been mortally hurt, she was not impressed. Setting out on such an expedition, it would, Fern knew, have been silly to wear any other clothes. Even in the midst of tragedy her mother had managed to cry out, "What will people say if they see you dressed like that? What will the natives say? They won't have any respect for us."

She did not, Fern noticed, say, "What will Mrs. Hoggett-Egburry say?"

Mrs. Hoggett-Egburry was still lying on her back, plump and inert, naked, beneath the sheets in the Smileys' double bed. The peignoir of pale-blue silk and lace, covered with mud, hung over the back of a chair in the kitchen to dry before the fire, and Mrs. Hoggett-Egburry, collapsed and ridiculous, was snoring. No, Mrs. Hoggett-Egburry and the threat of what she would say was finished forever.

And then, just as she was about to set off on the expedition, Raschid Ali Khan and Harry Loder appeared out of nowhere. The big Muslim was dressed in bits of officers' kit which they had found while searching the ruins for the bodies of The Boys. The jodhpurs he wore were too tight for him and the great muscular wrists protruded from the sleeves of a tunic which was meant for a man of half his size. And Harry Loder no longer looked the spick-and-span polo-playing dandy of the Indian army. The ruddy color was gone from his face and he was shaking a little as if he had a chill.

At sight of him Mrs. Simon, frightened, began to cry again, but Aunt Phoebe said, "You'd better have some brandy."

"A nip wouldn't be bad," he answered, in a voice that seemed like the voice of another person, and while Aunt Phoebe went for the brandy, he told them that all the Boys except himself were dead and already buried by the soldiers of the regiment. Then Mrs. Simon, hysterically began to scream and say that they must help her to find the bodies of her husband and Hazel, and Raschid Ali Khan, in a brusque voice (a voice, she thought afterward, he should never have dared to use to her as a European) told her that there was no time for the dead while there were living to be saved.

Then Aunt Phoebe returned, having found the brandy bottle empty among the sheets of Mrs. Hoggett-Egburry's bed, to say that she had made a mistake and there wasn't any brandy, after all. Almost eagerly but with a curious coldness, they exchanged grim bits of news. Not even the hysterics of Mrs. Simon checked them. Raschid's wife and seven children were safe because the house was built on an American plan and had stood up against the quake, but they were isolated by the flood, with only a little food. As soon as it was light, Raschid, naked, had plunged into the water and swum through the flood to dry land. He could, he said, rescue the family later. He had arrived at the Barracks as naked as any sweeper, but clothed still in the boundless dignity of a true believer.

They had, he said, to find boats or build rafts; they had also to discover what it was that blocked the canyon far off near Mount Abana and held back the waters.

To Fern, Harry Loder seemed a person she had never seen before—not the boisterous, beefy fellow who had tried to get her alone in corners where he might try to kiss and maul her, but a man who was ill and frightened. She listened to them, never speaking, and she said nothing of the frail little boat hidden in the half-drowned guava orchard near the Distillery, for fear that they would take it from her; and she had to have it to find out if Tom Ransome was still alive. After that they could have the boat. After that they could take anything they wanted from her. Now she was not afraid of Harry; she did not even dislike him and he did not seem to be aware of her at all. She was afraid that one of the others might betray her secret, but Aunt Phoebe was busy with the Untouchable cook-boy, who had come back at daylight, cooking eggs and toast for the two men. Mrs. Simon only moaned hysterically, hypnotized by her own loss.

Raschid, he said, was going to the Philkana to bring out the elephants. Harry's motor had run out of petrol halfway from the Barracks. They had tried Mrs. Simon's old Ford, stalled near the Distillery, but there wasn't enough petrol in it to be worth salvaging. The tanks at the Barracks had collapsed and the great petrol tanks in the town, if they still stood, were under water. Mechanical civilization had failed them. There remained only the elephants, rocking back and forth in the dubious shelter of the Philkana. The elephants could go anywhere, even swimming the flood, if necessary. Only some one—it was Raschid who meant to do it— would have to swim the mile or more of flood to give the *jobedar* orders to fetch them out. With the elephants they could go down the valley to Mount Abana to discover what it was that dammed the waters. Harry thought it was a barrier of debris and bodies. While the police minister swam to the Philkana, Harry meant to go to the army warehouses for dynamite.

Then the eggs were ready and Raschid and Harry Loder sat down to them, scarcely talking at all, save to answer a question now and then from Aunt Phoebe about the hospital or the Maharani's Girls' High School. But about the part of the town which lay on the other side of the river they knew very little more than she herself.

Fern, still terrified lest her mother come to her senses and betray the existence of the pleasure-boat, watched and listened, and as she watched, she grew fascinated by the spectacle of Harry Loder, tired and white, his tunic all stained by mud and plaster. He had not looked at her directly, and as she watched him it seemed to her that although there was something dead in him, something which she had never seen before had come to life. What it was she could not define because she had been taught nothing and had so little experience and knew so little, but it seemed to her that the new look in his face was a little like the look of grimness she had seen now and then in the face of that strange woman,

[346]

Miss Dirks, when she had encountered her by accident in the bazaar or in the great square . . . the Miss Dirks who seemed always intent upon some urgent errand, who in passing her might have been passing no more than a tree or a rock.

Suddenly they had finished their eggs and coffee and Raschid stood up, absurd but rather magnificent in his ill-fitting tunic and jodhpurs, Raschid, of all people (thought Aunt Phoebe) wearing the uniform of the conquerors. Harry said, "I'll be back with news as soon as I have any," and to Aunt Phoebe, "How are you for food?"

"We can get along for two or three days. I was never one to have a house empty of food. I'll get up a regular meal for you next time."

Then Harry Loder looked at Fern for the first time, with an odd unseeing look. "You'd better not run about," he said. "There aren't any police. You don't know what might happen. The Bhils may even come down from the mountains to do a bit of plundering." To Aunt Phoebe, as the one in authority, he said, "Have you got a gun?"

"No," said Aunt Phoebe. "Who needs a gun?"

"There's nothing to eat in Ranchipur. You can't tell what may happen." He unstrapped the revolver he wore beneath his tunic and said, "Here, keep this. I'll send around a guard." He was silent for a second, looking down at the big muscular hands scarred and still bloody from the struggle with the stones and broken beams. Then he said, "But I can't even be sure of my own troops . . . what's left of them."

At that Mrs. Simon began to weep noisily, crying out, "What do you mean? Don't go away and leave us. Don't leave us alone. We may be killed or anything. . . ."

It wasn't Harry, but Raschid, who answered her brusquely, with scorn. "You'll be all right, madame. You can be thankful we've got nothing worse than Gujerati to deal with."

Then they went away, and when they had gone Aunt Phoebe strapped the revolver to her waist over her apron and set about clearing up the dishes and taking stock of the supply of food. She'd lived through this sort of thing before, twice through prairie fires as a girl, and she'd heard stories of red-Indian raids and massacres in her father's day, and she didn't expect to be left in peace with only Fern and Mrs. Simon and poor drunken Mrs. Hoggett-Egburry in the house. In her tired tough old heart she was troubled about Bertha and Homer Smiley, but there wasn't any use in speaking of that, what with Mrs. Simon, hysterical and useless, Mrs. Hoggett-Egburry drunk in Bertha's bed, and poor Fern eating her heart out about a man whom nothing could save from drink. The best thing she knew was to keep as busy as possible.

But now as the silly boat sidled to a position just beneath the balcony on which Ransome stood, Fern wasn't thinking of Harry Loder, but only that perhaps for a second time she had made a fool of herself. She could not bring herself to look up at him as he called out directions, leaning over to hold out the cord of one of Mr. Bannerjee's Jermyn Street dressing-gowns. Now that she was here, now that she had achieved the rescue, she did not know what to do. She only wanted to leave the boat and go away again. And as she caught the cord and fastened it to one of the fluted gilt columns of the boat's canopy, she knew that she was miserable, not so much because of Ransome as because of the woman with him . . . that lovely woman dressed all in white and wearing a great many diamonds and emeralds, a woman out of another world of which Fern knew nothing save the specious shadow of the reality as Hollywood saw it.

This woman belonged to his world. When they talked to each other each would understand almost without words what the other meant. There wouldn't be the awkward pauses and misunderstandings that made him grin suddenly in a way which caused herself to blush and made her love him at the same time because he was so kind and tried so hard to be elderly and wise in order to help her. It was the woman who troubled her . . . that woman whose very clothes and jewels were insolent and assured, that woman who to Fern seemed not bored and on the verge of middle-age, but incomparably perfect and lovely. She did not see or even suspect that she herself, in Ransome's old shorts and tennis shirt, had a freshness and charm for which the woman would have exchanged all her fine clothes, all her jewels, everything she possessed.

Then for the first time she was forced to look up because Ransome was calling out to her, now that the pleasure boat had been made fast, to take his hand so that he might draw her up to the second-floor balcony. She saw his face and her heart leaped because she saw by the look in it that, after all, he was glad she had come; she saw that he was pleased to see her, even proud of her, and that at the same time he was amused by the preposterousness of the whole scene. For the first time it occurred to her, who had never analyzed any emotion or thought, what it was that made her love him so much. It was the kindness and the grin, that grin which came and went so easily and quickly, like a light turned or and off, a light illuminating depths which she might divine but not yet understand.

The hand and arm were strong, with more strength than she had believed possible in the body of a man so slim. He drew her up to the edge of the balcony and there she let go of his hand quickly and climbed over the railing, feeling helpless and awkward.

Ransome said, "You're a very clever girl," and she was suddenly angry because he was treating her again as if she were a child, and humiliated because the other woman was there to watch them. The tears were just beneath her eyelids, waiting to rush forth, but with a great effort, an effort worthy of the iron control of poor Miss Dirks, she checked them. In a sudden wave of self-pity the death of her father and Hazel became for the first time a reality. Until now it had been like something seen in the cinema, but now it was true. She knew now that whatever happened she would never see either of them again. And Ransome dared to grin and call her a "very clever girl."

Then he said, "This is Lady Esketh" and Lady Esketh said, in the most charming way possible, "We owe you a lot. It was very courageous of you. We might have died here of starvation and boredom."

"Where on earth did you get the boat?" asked Ransome.

"I found it near the Distillery. Aunt Phoebe helped me make the oar. It only had one." And suddenly she felt proud again and almost happy. Then poor Miss Murgatroyd appeared in the doorway in her bedraggled *robe de style* of blue taffeta, and at the sight of her Fern felt assured and confident, for the appearance of Miss Murgatroyd at that moment would have brought confidence to any woman.

Miss Murgatroyd cried out, eagerly, "For Heaven's sake, how did you get here?" And when Fern answered, "I've got a boat," Miss Murgatroyd turned and ran into the house, crying, "Mrs. Bannerjee! Mrs. Bannerjee! We've been rescued!"

While Miss Murgatroyd was bearing the tidings to the Bannerjees,

Ransome and Lady Esketh asked for news. Fern told them of the death of her father and Hazel and the wiping out of The Boys when the barracks collapsed on them, and the grin died out of Ransome's face. He took her hand and said, "I'm sorry, my dear" and again her heart warmed and again she felt a little stab of shame that she should be so happy when her father and sister were lying dead beneath the ruins of the Mission.

Lady Esketh asked, "The Summer Palace? What has happened to it?"

"I don't know."

"And the hospital?"

"The hospital is standing. Raschid Ali Khan said so."

Then Ransome said, "Where is Raschid?"

"He swam out from his house. He's gone to get the elephants."

"And his family?"

"They're all right. They're still at his house."

"And the Smileys?"

"I don't know. Aunt Phoebe is safe."

Suddenly Lady Esketh asked, "Are the people in the hospital alive?"

"I don't know."

And Ransome, divining what lay beneath Edwina's question, asked, "The Doctor and Miss MacDaid?"

"I don't know."

"They tried to get from here to the hospital when the flood happened."

Then an odd silence occurred again, and the sense of excitement died away. Fern, awkward and shy, was again aware for a moment of the horrible reality of the tragedy. She thought, "Tomorrow it will be real and the day after that and the day after that, but it isn't real now. It never happened."

Ransome said, "I suppose we ought to get away from here on to dry land, at any rate. If there was another quake, the whole place might come down." He turned to Fern. "My house? You must have passed it."

"The verandah and the cookhouse have fallen in. It's half under water like this, but it's still standing. Your boy was sitting on the roof." (So John the Baptist hadn't run away. He'd been hiding there in the house all the time.) "You'd better go to the Smileys'. Aunt Phoebe said to tell you. She's awfully good at looking after people. Momma is there with Mrs. Hoggett-Egburry."

"I'll take the boat," said Ransome. "We'll only be able to go off one at a time. There isn't room for more. Have you had any sleep?"

"Not much."

"You ought to lie down for a bit and I'll come for you after I've taken off the other women."

"I couldn't sleep."

"No, but just lying down for a bit would be a help." He took her arm and said, "Come along. Do as I say. It isn't over yet—it's only begun."

She did not want to lie down. She didn't feel tired now. She only felt bewildered, and so excited that it seemed to her that very likely she would never be able to sleep again; but it was nice having him care whether she was tired or not. It was nice to have the chance of being alone with him, if only for a moment. It was nice to have him away from that Lady Esketh and her superiority, for even in the crudeness of her instinct she had divined that the speech and manner of Lady Esketh were not sincere, but the casual products of long habit and breeding. Lady Esketh had seemed unconcerned about the whole thing, except the hospital. Fern couldn't help being interested in the way she cared so much about what had happened at the hospital.

In one of the rooms she lay down on the hard Indian bed, and Ransome said, "Your clothes are wet. You ought to take them off."

"Not much. The canopy kept off the rain."

"I'll fetch a couple of shawls."

He went away, leaving her happy and full of peace, and when he returned he was carrying two Kashmiri shawls which he wrapped about her, carefully and gently. Then casually he laid a hand on her forehead and said, "You've had a tough time, my dear. Try and sleep a little." Without knowing what she was doing, without willing it, her hand reached up and touched his, but he drew it away quickly as if the touch hurt him and said, "Now go to sleep like a good girl" as if she were a child.

On the balcony Edwina was still waiting. First she said, "I wish we could get more news."

The speech angered him because it seemed to him to illuminate shamelessly the profundity of her selfishness and egotism. So he said sourly,

"We'll get more news as soon as we get out of here, but I don't imagine we'll find out what's happened to the Major."

"I didn't mean that. It's bitchy of you to think it."

"You did mean it and you ought to be ashamed of yourself, if not for the fact, at least for betraying it. Do you want to go ashore first?"

"It doesn't make a damned bit of difference when I go unless you want to be left behind with your little bit."

"What do you mean by that?"

She laughed, "You're not going to tell me that there isn't something up between you?"

"I'm not going to tell you anything. Because you behave like a Piccadilly whore, don't believe all other women do the same."

"All right. Have it your own way. But if ever I saw a girl suffering from calf-love, it's that one. When you speak her face lights up like fireworks. But I suppose you like being treated as if you were God." Then she put her hand on his arm, gently and disarmingly, so that he had again the feeling that with him, and perhaps before all the world, she always made herself appear far worse than she was. She said, "If you remember, that's what broke it up between us a long time ago . . . because I never treated you as if you were God, but just as bad as myself."

"My God! the things you can think up."

But he was ashamed now and his shame went back to the thought he had had two days ago—of how amusing Edwina would find the story of Fern's determination to seduce him, how amused she would be by the idea that she had saved Fern's virtue, because a little while before they had experienced a bored and passionless embrace in that forgotten room of the palace. It did not seem funny now. The idea of repeating the story to Edwina was disgusting and made him feel a little sick. He thought, "I must be worse even than I believed." He told himself that it was not because he was in love with Fern. Such an idea was preposterous, and if she were in love with him, something must be done to put an end to that. Whatever else was true, Fern deserved someone better than himself, at any rate someone fresher and younger and cleaner. But he was troubled now for the first time because he no longer knew what he felt.

[352]

Then it occurred to him that it was he whom Fern had come to rescue. It was for his sake she and Aunt Phoebe had contrived the clumsy necessary oar. It couldn't have been the others, whom she scarcely knew. And he thought, "It must have been that! I'm a bloody fool! I've been a bloody fool all along."

The rest of the day was spent in journeys back and forth between Mr. Bannerjee's house and the Distillery corner. It was not an easy task in the frail boat with the sluggish currents moving now this way, now that, and he had to go in a roundabout way to avoid the clumps of trees in the Maharajah's Park and the long row of Java figs that lined the Distillery Road. From the landing-place the wrecked Mission was distantly visible in its dark clump of banyan trees, and one by one as the refugees landed from the little boat they made their way along the road and across the muddy fields to the haven presided over by Aunt Phoebe. First went Miss Murgatroyd, then Mrs. Bannerjee carrying with her three Pekinese, some jewels, and the inevitable gold box in which she kept her *pan*, then Lady Esketh still in the white gown from Paris, a Kashmiri shawl wrapped round her shoulders.

The rain came and died away, sluicing down suddenly from the low overburdened clouds, and there were moments when the silly boat was threatened by the violence of the wind as well as by the water. It had been built long ago to drift at fêtes over the surface of a shallow pond littered with flower petals and illuminated by Bengal lights, and now each shift of the current, each clutch of the passing branches at the silly gilt canopy threatened it with disaster.

Miss Murgatroyd, during her voyage, squealed a great deal and giggled when Ransome, with that old feeling of illness at the pit of his stomach, grimly told her to sit very still unless she wished to join the corpses that floated past them. Mrs. Bannerjee was still and dignified and silent, chewing her wilted betel leaves with the calm and indifference of a sacred cow; chewing with assurance and confidence as if this India, torn, shattering, and dying, was the true India to which she belonged, as if only now, with the famed modernity of Ranchipur destroyed, she had come into her own. Only the Pekinese made a nuisance of themselves, squealing and barking at the corpses and wreckage and snakes that drifted slowly past.

Ransome, sitting opposite her, no longer felt any desire to conquer or humiliate her. As he watched her, chewing indifferently, it seemed to him strange that he should ever have found her exciting. Now he admired her in a kind of abstract fashion for her calmness, her indifference, even for the humor she had shown over the wailing of her husband, but he no longer thought of her as a desirable woman; she had become, somehow, a kind of inhuman and sexless curiosity. Her peculiar fine-drawn beauty, the great glowing eyes, the exquisiteness of the pale hands with their lacquered nails—none of these had changed, save perhaps that their quality had been augmented by excitement. Only yesterday he had desired her out of boredom and perversity. Today she was strange, even a little repulsive, because she seemed inhuman.

At the landing-place near the Distillery they found the faithful Miss Murgatroyd, her pale-blue taffeta drenched now, the hem of the skirt stained with the red mud of the fields. She wore a shawl over her head. She had pretended, when Ransome put her ashore, to set out toward the Mission, but the moment he was gone she had turned back to wait for her beloved and precious Mrs. Bannerjee.

Edwina, throughout her rescue, was ill-tempered. Now that the excitement was over, she was bored, dismally and profoundly, the victim of a kind of gnawing impatience. As the little boat made its way through the dripping trees, she talked now and then, irritably. She was aware only of the mud, and that she was soaked through, and that there was no way of discovering what had happened at the hospital, and that this was something that she could no longer discuss with Ransome because somehow he had slipped away from her overnight; the Tom she had met on that first night was gone. It seemed to her, as she watched him slyly (because she did not want to meet his eye) that even his face had changed, that it had grown mysteriously thinner and that the angle of the stubborn jaw had grown a little sharper. The change made her angry and she thought, sullenly, "Now, if the Major is still alive, I will have him in spite of every one. Nobody can really care. I shall have him, and after that we shall see. After that I'll have to go back to that bloody awful life at home." She had to have him now after all those hours of thinking of him, of trying to imagine what it would be like. Even though he proved to be a poor thing, simply another changeable, intriguing Indian, only another lover like all the long procession before him—she had to have him, because that was the only cure for the malady which she herself had perversely created. She had to be crushed by him, to be humiliated and subdued. It would be, she thought cynically, like a purge, and afterward she would be free. But all at once she was ashamed, thinking, "I never dreamed this could happen to me."

Ransome was saying, "You should have accepted one of Mrs. Bannerjee's *saris*."

"No. Even this dress is better than a *sari*. What would I do with all that stuff hanging about me? What I want is a bath and some practical clothes . . . a shirt and some shorts like that girl was wearing."

Quietly Ransome said, "Oh, you mean Fern Simon?"

"Yes, if that's her name."

"You know it is."

"Let's not begin all over again."

He grinned and said, "You can't be jealous of her. You haven't any right to be. I never pretended anything . . . not even that night at the palace."

"Neither did I."

"All this seems pretty trivial and silly considering the circumstances." He allowed one oar to drift and pointed to a naked corpse wedged head downward in the low branches of a neam tree. "It wouldn't matter very much to him."

And then he saw that he had been silly himself and melodramatic and priggish. With all Edwina's upbringing, with all that had happened to her, the body of a low-caste Hindu could mean no more to her than the corpse of a goat or a cow. With all the feeling of caste behind her in England, she would be no more impressed by the spectacle than an orthodox Brahmin. Once the sight would have left him unmoved because it was beyond his comprehension; in certain aspects it still was. Even now in his heart he could not believe that this man, whoever he had been, was not better off dead than alive. His death could not have made much difference to anyone, least of all to the man himself.

She said, "The trouble with you is that you're a bloody sentimentalist. . . ." Then after a moment's vague thought, "The kind that gets sentimental over cities and armies and history. If you were a little more personal you wouldn't always be in a mess."

She had spoken, he knew, out of instinct, because although she was intelligent, intellect was a quality unknown to her, and yet what she had said was true, so true that it threw a great light suddenly upon him and all his life. She was right. He had always been a Universalist. He had fallen from the beginning into the error of Descartes. He had separated humanity from the individual and that made you at once sentimental and a little less than human.

They passed the blank wall of the Distillery and the little boat thrust its nose into the red mud of the shore. He stepped out, took her hand and then began to laugh.

"What's so funny?" she asked.

"Just the picture of the two of us. The world is a more wonderful place than I thought."

"Yes, it's pretty funny. I'm not sure it's our proper rôle."

"Why?"

"I'm not sure we can live up to it."

He turned and pointed toward the Mission. "That's it, over there," he said. "Tell Aunt Phoebe that I recommend you to her care. I'll be along when I fetch the others ashore."

Then he put off in the boat again, and when he had gone a little way he let the oars rest and turned to look after her. She had thrown away her slippers and was walking barefoot through the mud. The trailing skirt of soiled white crêpe-de-chine she had hitched up and fastened about her waist with the girdle of rhinestones. Her legs were bare to the thighs. The Kashmiri shawl she had thrown over her head.

Grinning, he thought, "Maybe it wasn't necessary to recommend her to Aunt Phoebe. Maybe the old lady will understand her quality of indefatigability." And again he thought, "She's personal. . . . God knows, she's personal."

When he came once more in sight of the house he discovered the figure of Mr. Bannerjee already waiting for him on the balcony. It was clear at once that he had reverted with a vengeance. Gone now was every vestige of Bond Street. He was wearing a white *dhoti* Bengali fashion, draped over his shoulder, and the black hair which usually shone with brilliantine was covered with a paste of ashes. In the crook of one plump arm he carried a big lacquered box which Ransome divined at once must contain all that remained on earth of the elder Mr. Bannerjee.

"The old gentleman," he thought, "is going to the Ganges, after all." The flooded Ranchipur wasn't holy enough to receive the ashes of the retired insurance broker.

As the boat drew nearer, Mr. Bannerjee suddenly caught sight of it and immediately he began to moan once more and beat his breast with the free hand. The costume did not become him and he had lost, somewhere between Calcutta and Oxford, the knack of wearing it properly, for the *dhoti* kept slipping from his fat shoulder, so that now and then in the midst of his breast-beating, he was forced to give it a hasty tug in order to keep it in place. Bond Street had managed better than the Howrah bazaar to conceal the soft rotundity of Mr. Bannerjee's figure and now Ransome discovered that he had the great kimono arms of a prima donna past her prime.

But the moment the canopy of the little boat touched the balcony the wailing and the breast-beating ceased and Mr. Bannerjee, as if still pursued by the vengeance of Kali, plumped over the side, lacquered box and all.

"Easy!" cried Ransome. "You'll sink the boat."

He was angry suddenly, so angry that if it would not have capsized the boat he would have given Mr. Bannerjee a good kick in the behind. His anger illuminated the distaste he had long felt for him; he disliked Mr. Bannerjee because he was a fool and had no dignity, because he was at the same time a coward and a humbug. And he was angry, too, at the obvious arrogant conviction of Mr. Bannerjee that he himself at that moment had no importance to the world save as ferryman for Mr. Bannerjee and the ashes of Mr. Bannerjee's father. Dressed in Bond Street clothes, Mr. Bannerjee had been obsequious and, at times, groveling. Now he had taken a leaf from the book of his wife. He was still frightened, so frightened that the yellow white of his eyes showed in the ash-colored face. A person so terrified could not at the same time afford to be arrogant.

"Sit tight," said Ransome. "If you capsize the boat I shan't try to save you. There's too much work to be done."

Mr. Bannerjee did not answer him. It seemed to Ransome that in his terror he must have lost the power of speech. With one hand he clung to the edge of the pleasure-boat; with the other he clutched the lacquered box containing the ashes. Once clear of the balcony, he closed his eyes and seemed to go into a trance, and Ransome, watching him, remembered what the Major had once said—that the Bengalis were the Irish of India. It was odd that the same race could produce two people as unlike as Mr. and Mrs. Bannerjee.

As he passed the house of Raschid Ali Khan, the figure of Mrs. Raschid surrounded by children of all ages appeared in a broad upper window. In Urdu she called out to him that she and the children were all safe and could hold out for another day, and in Hindustani he called back that he would come to fetch them either tonight or early the next morning. Then as they passed the drowned world of his own compound, he caught sight of John the Baptist, naked, perched on the cracked roof in the rain. Through the downpour, John the Baptist shouted to him in his soft French. "All the plate is safe. It's on the first floor with all Sahib's clothes."

"Better go inside. I'll come for you later."

"Très bien, Sahib," and the boy slithered down the drain-pipe like one of the monkeys and swung into an upper window.

At the Distillery, Mr. Bannerjee, still meditating, opened his eyes long enough to step ashore without a word either of thanks or of recognition. Ransome pulled in the oars and sat staring after him as he plodded barefoot, still carrying the ashes, through the mud toward Aunt Phoebe and the distant Mission.

When he returned to the house, the servant whom he had not seen since he had appeared with the hurricane lantern was waiting on the balcony. The man was standing, looking out over the drowned city, turned away a little so that he did not see the boat approaching. He was a thin, ugly little man, very black, and now in the midst of the devastated landscape he was the only living thing, for even the birds and the sacred monkeys had deserted the flooded area as if they had divined that it was accursed by nature.

The servant did not move, and in the tranced immobility of the figure Ransome found something vaguely disturbing. Here was a man who had lost everything—his wife, his children, perhaps his father and his mother and even his grandparents (for the compound had been a whole village in which there were shrines to Kali and Shiva and Rama). This man created a kind of awe. He was, one might have said, a fragile monument of patience and endurance, tiny and ugly and childish against the menace of the darkening monsoon sky. This man was India, more than any of the others, more than Mr. Bannerjee, or the Major, or Raschid Ali Khan or even the Old Maharajah himself, the India which went on, breeding and breeding, indestructible, like those swarms of bees clinging to the marble eaves of the great palace. This was life, a principle, ripening from a starved childhood into a maturity in which there were only animal pleasures and superstitions scarcely different from those of the swarming, noisy, sacred monkeys.

For a time, as if enchanted, Ransome sat in the drifting boat, trying to discover what this man *was*—what was his need, his soul, his spirit, his essence. What significance could he himself have to that skinny, dark, motionless figure on the balcony, that figure to whom the British Empire meant nothing, whose imagination did not extend beyond the limits of the wrecked city, not even so far as the solitude of El-Kautara or the sacred mountain of Abana. He was not quite an animal, for he was made in human shape. What could it mean to him to be left in a second, utterly alone in a world which until a little time before had been solid and secure? Of what was he thinking now as he stood, still as the stubby statute of the Good Old Queen, looking out over the dead city? For him what was reality and what spirit? How was it possible to reach the spirit of that dark, half-real image?

And wearily there came to Ransome a slow impulse toward self-abnegation, rising up in him like that strange feeling he had had long ago as he sat against the mud-stained wall of a shattered house in Belgium. It was an odd desire, faintly sensuous in its implications, to lose himself— that self which was the Honorable Thomas Ransome, unhappy, at times drunken, egotistical, intelligent, disappointed, neurotic, despairing. It was a desire to merge himself—whatever there was of soul, of intelligence, of personality, known as Thomas Ransome—into the mixture of what was known as humanity, a desire as strong as that of thirst, to know this man standing there against the sky, and his brothers, whether black or white, yellow or brown, a desire to fathom the endless, inexplicable patience and resignation of all his kind. For a second he was aware, as if the low-hanging clouds had lifted suddenly to reveal the blazing sun they hid, of having had a glimpse of salvation and peace.

And then suddenly, eluding him, the sensation and the vision were gone.

At the same time, at the second the experience ceased, the black man on the balcony turned and looked toward him into the light which came from below the rim of clouds. For Ransome the trees about him were no longer luminous and glorified, but only the familiar banyans and peepul trees beneath whose branches he had sat so many times drinking the bad cocktails at Mr. Bannerjee's badminton parties. And the ugly black man was no longer some one very near to him, so near that he had been on the verge of discovering his secret, but simply Mr. Bannerjee's Gujerati servant, dirty, inefficient, groveling when abused by his master.

As the boat came again beneath the balcony, he called out to the man in Hindustani, "Where is Memsahib?"

The man answered him in Gujerati, "Memsahib sleeping" and made pantomimed sleep with a sudden gesture of singular beauty.

Ransome thought, "Let the child sleep. She probably hasn't slept for two days," and pantomiming his meaning, told the man to come into the boat.

The man at first refused, and only came reluctantly when Ransome ordered him abruptly.

In a mixture of pidgin tongues, he asked the man if he had nothing to bring with him, but the man replied, "No, Sahib, nothing" . . . nothing but the ragged bit of cloth he wore about his skinny waist between his skinny thighs.

They set out and on the way he tried with all the Gujerati he could muster to talk with the man, but the servant seemed either dazed or stupid. Nothing could be got from him save an occasional animal gesture of pantomime which meant nothing to Ransome.

At the Distillery the man stepped out and, falling on his knees pressed his forehead into the red mud in an exaggerated salaam.

Ransome asked, "Where will you go?" But the man did not understand and, aware that the sun was sinking, he turned away and took up the oars. The man waited as if out of respect until the boat was a hundred yards from the shore and then, turning, he set out across the vast muddy plain, straight away into the sulphurous yellow light that rimmed the sky beyond. Until the boat lost itself among the half-drowned trees, the crooked tiny black figure was still visible, growing smaller and smaller in the terrifying vastness of the Indian landscape.

He had passed his own house and the house of Raschid Ali Khan when the darkness came down suddenly. It was as if in a few moments the trees, the houses, the familiar landmarks melted into blackness, or as if the waters themselves had risen and enveloped everything. For a second, alarmed, he stopped rowing and thought, "I must not get lost. If she should waken and find herself alone in the house she might be frightened," and again, as he had done so many times during the war, he sought to take command of himself in a new way, to force his body to exert an extra sense to guide him straight to the house. There were no stars to steer by, and now suddenly no trees or houses, for even if he could have seen them the neam and peepul and banyan trees had been planted long ago without order or system. Calculating that the lag of Fern's one contrived and limping oar would pull him always toward the left, he set out once more, glancing over his shoulder in a vain effort to discover some evidence that he had not already lost his way.

The rain which just before sunset had stopped for a little while began again now, descending in ropes of water with such violence that it beat up a fine mist above the flood. For ten minutes he rowed with a terrifying feeling of blind helplessness, for the evocation of that sixth sense which long ago had been real, had now failed. Again and again he ran the little boat blindly among the branches of trees and then suddenly he became aware that, despite his efforts, it had taken a direction of its own and that the oars were making no impression any longer. He had blundered and now he was no longer in the backwaters, but in a part of the flood where the force of the river's rushing current made itself felt. For a second he thought, "Now I am lost. I will be swept away like all the others." He did not want to die and he struggled for a time until he

[361]

saw that rowing was of no avail, especially when he did not know whither he was bound and whether each stroke of the oars might not be bringing him nearer to death. So he ceased all effort presently and let himself drift, thinking quietly, "Well, if it is over, it is over and maybe it's better that way."

He could not tell, now in the darkness, whether the boat was drifting rapidly or merely swinging about in the eddies off the main current, but presently a cluster of leaves brushed his face and reaching out, he seized a branch and held fast. Now the worst was over. At least he could spend the night here, wet and miserable as he was, and with the coming of daylight he could discover where he was. Then he remembered the cord of Mr. Bannerjee's Bond Street dressing-gown, and groping he found it on the bottom of the boat and fastened one end to a stout branch of the tree. Now he might even sleep with safety in the midst of the murmurous threatening darkness.

For a long time he waited, wakeful despite the weariness of two days without sleep. He was hungry, and even in the damp heat he had begun to shiver. He thought again, "I must get back to her somehow." If she wakened she might be frightened in that strange house with its ancient evil legends and the spirit of old Mr. Bannerjee still haunting its dark corridors. And then slowly he began to experience a sensation which he had not known since the war, a feeling of the presence there all about him in the darkness among the rustling trees of all those dead who had vanished in the catastrophe. Long ago the same feeling terrified him far more than any shells or bullets; long ago that same feeling had crept over him slowly like the rising of icy water, against his will, defeating his intelligence and his reason. Long ago he had felt the invisible, intangible, presence of the thousands of those whose bodies lay shattered and torn above and in the fertile Flemish mud all about him. Then the terror chilled his blood and made the hair rise on his body; long ago the fear had been all the worse because it was beyond reason and his own boyish rejection of immortality. It was as if those unseen and unseeable spirits had stood there in the gray fog which hung above the mud, accusing him, saying, "We are not dead. There is no death."

But now there was no terror. Sitting alone in the little boat in all that blackness, he knew that the spirits were there, not born of his imagination as he had tried long ago to make himself believe, but real, possessing perhaps even a substance which could be neither seen nor felt with the poor senses he possessed. It was not terror which he experienced now, but a sense of peace and understanding.

How long he remained, shaking and exhausted, in the tugging boat he did not know, for in the blackness all sense of time seemed to vanish, but presently he became aware that a kind of light had entered the darkness, gradually more and more apparent, suffusing dimly the whole air and bringing a vague black form to the trees all about him. It was a light that came downward from the clouds, the reflection of some fire which had broken out again in the town. Slowly the light increased until at last only a little way off he was able to make out the complicated, richly carved phallic roof of the Shiva temple, and then quite near at hand all that was visible of the stubby cast-iron Queen Victoria. Only the head remained above the water and about the short thick neck there had collected a garland of grasses and rotting flowers brought down by the current of the river. Half-drowned, she had remained somehow, stubborn and undefeatable, on the central buttress of the shattered bridge.

As the rosy light increased he discovered against the sky not far away in a filigree of black the great fan of the ancient Java fig tree that stood near the badminton court, and knew that if he could reach the tree itself the rest would be easy. There was no use in attempting to propel the boat with the oars, so at last he untied the cord, and drawing it and himself from branch to branch clotted with rubbish, he made his way along the row of banyan trees which bordered the Racecourse Road. It was a slow business because the gilded canopy kept being caught by the branches. After what seemed hours he arrived beneath the tree and there, dripping with sweat, he waited for a moment to rest. The chill was gone now. Rowing the boat for the last hundred yards, he arrived quickly at the balcony of the dead house, and climbing over the rail he made the boat fast once more with the cord of Mr. Bannerjee's dressing-gown.

The house was still, more quiet even than the desolation outside, and for a moment he thought, "Perhaps she has gone away. Perhaps some one has come for her," and felt suddenly the sickness of disappointment. By the dim, reflected glow of the light outside he made his way slowly along the hallway until he came at last to the room where he had left her.

She had not gone away. She was still asleep beneath the netting on the bed, stretched out like a child with one arm thrown over her head, the short blonde hair curly and towsled in the damp.

Exhausted now and puzzled, he stood there for a long time, looking down at her in the dim light that came through the window. All at once, for some reason, she seemed very remote from him and no longer childish. In her very youth there was something which was ageless, which touched him profoundly, and in his own weariness, in his thirst and hunger, brought a lump into his throat. He experienced both shame and envy for the youth, the very youngness, which surrounded her like an aura, envy too for a kind of romance which he felt in her and which he had never known. For a fleeting moment he divined how wonderful it would be to have been young once as she was young, to have believed in the world as she believed in it. That was something he had never known and would never know now, because it was too late. But he was aware too of the tragedy which lay in her very youngness, of what lay before her, thinking how little she knew of the world, how little there was of truth between the reality and the tissue of that false world she had created out of her own imagination. What would happen to her when she passed from the one world into the other?

But the chills began to return, and going into Mr. Bannerjee's room he rummaged about in the dim light until he found a *dhoti*. After stripping himself and rubbing himself down with a bed cover, he put on the *dhoti* and returned to the room where Fern lay sleeping. At the same moment there was an explosion coming from a great distance which rocked the shattered wooden house. And then another and another. Bits of plaster fell from the ceiling about him, and he thought, "That would be Raschid and Harry Loder blowing up the wreckage." In the morning the flood would be gone.

On the hard bed beneath the netting the girl stirred but did not waken, and he thought, "How tired she must have been."

The fire in the town was burning itself out and the light was fading. With cushions he made himself a bed, and wrapping the *dhoti* about his head after the fashion of the millions who slept each night in the streets over all India, he lay down on the floor beside her, so that when she wakened she would not be afraid.

It did not occur to him that what he did, staying there all the night with her, might create a fresh scandal. That old world, that world of gossip and petty jealousies and ambitions, that world of the Club and the Boys, of Pukka Lil and the Simon tennis parties had been swept away, leaving in its place a world that would be for a time at least savage and primitive and desperate.

At the Mission Aunt Phoebe went about her work.

There was no boy now to help her, for in the early morning she had sent away the only boy who had returned to seek news of the Smileys. He had gone unwillingly and had not returned. And among the refugees she found no help. When she looked over her guests without passion now in the midst of disaster, she saw that Mrs. Hoggett-Egburry was not only an inebriate but a fool, and that Mrs. Simon was only another kind of fool. She would be useless in a crisis, only sobbing and wringing her hands (when she was not asleep) and talking of "her loss"—the loss, Aunt Phoebe thought sourly, of a husband and a daughter whom she had always bullied and made unhappy, to whom death itself must have come as a relief. Mrs. Bannerjee had never done any work and knew nothing about it, and merely sat chewing her *pan* with the indifferent calm of a *yogi*. To Aunt Phoebe, Mrs. Bannerjee was no beauty. To Aunt Phoebe she was simply a lazy woman without feelings. Miss Murgatroyd, when she was not bringing down upon her head the snubs and petty cruelties of Mrs. Bannerjee, fluttered about, making an effort to be useful; but she too was a fool, perhaps the biggest of the lot.

So Aunt Phoebe thought, "The best thing I can do is to keep them all out of the way." But they would not be kept out of the way in either the huge storeroom or the bedrooms. As if they were aware that security lay only in the presence of the old woman, they kept coming and going to and from the kitchen. Mrs. Hoggett-Egburry wanted aspirin and Mrs. Simon something to make her sleep.

Yet, despite all the irritations, the old lady was enjoying herself as she had not enjoyed herself since the days of prairie fires and tornadoes. The absence of news about the Smileys disturbed her, but not very profoundly, because she had faith, a peculiarly potent faith which believed not only that God would protect her nephew and his wife, but that if He failed to protect them, it would be because He had His own reasons. And because she was old and had lived all her life in simplicity close to the earth, she possessed at eighty-two a wisdom and a knowledge which none of the others, even the Hindus, were able to share. She knew that in the course of nature it would not matter very much what happened to the Smileys or to herself. The one thing that mattered was that they had lived honorably and that in death there could be no reproaches; such knowledge was wonderful for putting the mind at ease. It did seem to her a pity that if people must die, the Lord had not taken away the fools and the useless ones like Mrs. Hoggett-Egburry and Mrs Simon and the Bannerjees.

And she was at peace because her mind was occupied with a thousand details and because her hands were busy. No one knew better than herself the solace which work might bring. In all her life she had never had time either to think of herself or to "enjoy" grief. There had been moments since she came to Ranchipur when she had been idle, moments when she was threatened by a temptation to work mischief as she had done in letting out the poor comfortable old hyena, moments when she tormented Mrs. Simon deliberately by appearing on the verandah with her rocking chair and lemonade and palm leaf fan. The only flaw she had found in the life of Ranchipur was that there was, at moments, not enough to do. And now she was busy, with making an invoice of the storeroom to see how long the food there would hold out, with cooking and making certain that none of the refugees received more than his proper ration, with finding aspirin for Mrs. Hoggett-Egburry and brewing *neam* tea for Mrs. Simon's nerves.

She went about her work with the revolver Harry Loder had given her still strapped about her waist over her apron, partly because she did not know what to do with it and partly because it was exciting to think that it might be useful. She had not much faith in the necessity for it until late in the afternoon when she saw coming across the muddy fields the tall, thin, black figures of three Bhils. They came straight toward the house and in silence she watched their approach as she might have watched the approach of three redskins across the prairies of her childhood. She saw no use in alarming the others, and she determined first to discover what it was they wanted.

They had come down from the hills to plunder and appeared astonished when they found the door of a house they had supposed empty barred by an old woman with a revolver (which Aunt Phoebe took out of its holster as they drew near). She could not speak their language, but when they made signs that they wanted to come into the house and wanted something to eat, she in her turn made vigorous pantomimes showing them that they could not enter and that there was nothing to eat. They were black and menacing enough in appearance, with rags and goatskins for coverings and long, black, greasy hair which fell to their shoulders. They had no firearms but each of them carried a long spear.

For a moment they gibbered and chattered among themselves and they might have attempted to force their way in save that in the midst of their conference Mrs. Hoggett-Egburry came into the kitchen and, seeing them, uttered a shrill scream which attracted all the other refugees. The sight of Mrs. Hoggett-Egburry, wrapped like a mummy in sheets (for both Aunt Phoebe and Mrs. Smiley were small thin women and their clothes of no use to her) put them to rout. Sullenly they turned and walked through the red mud in the direction of the town.

Mrs. Hoggett-Egburry, threatening again to faint, cried for brandy, but there was none. Miss Murgatroyd and Mrs. Simon both began talking at once; Miss Murgatroyd predicting the direst horrors of rape and torture, and Mrs. Simon crying out, "What is going to happen to us now? I know what they're like . . . the Bhils. I know what they're like around the Mission. They've been waiting for years just to cut our throats." And then suddenly she thought of Fern and cried out, "Where is Fern? What have they done to her? Why hasn't she come back?"

Aunt Phoebe looked at her sourly and said, "Fern is all right. Don't you worry. From what I know about Fern, she's got a head on her shoulders."

Then in the doorway appeared a new sight, more strange and more exotic than the Bhils. It was Lady Esketh, with her white evening gown hitched about her waist, her arms covered with jewels, her legs spattered to the knees with red mud. With a dignity which was suddenly

[367]

comic, she said, "I am Lady Esketh," and then to Aunt Phoebe, "I suppose you are Aunt Phoebe. Tom Ransome told me to come straight to you."

"Yes," said Aunt Phoebe, feeling suddenly shy, "that's right. That was right. Come right in." Then remembering her manners, she said, "This is Mrs. Simon and Mrs. Hoggett-Egburry."

"How d'you do?" said Lady Esketh, at the same time pulling the tucked up dress from the rhinestone belt and letting it fall to the floor.

Upon Mrs. Hoggett-Egburry the effect of the introduction was far greater than any brandy could have been; she was meeting Lady Esketh at last, in spite of everything; she recovered herself at once and stood up as if in the presence of royalty. She was the first to find her tongue. She said, with her China-blue eyes wide open, "Didn't you meet them? Didn't they attack you?"

"Who?" asked Lady Esketh.

"The Bhils."

"What are Bills?"

"Those savages . . . black men with spears."

"Oh, them! Yes, I saw them."

Then Mrs. Simon spoke breathlessly, "Didn't they attack you . . . with all those jewels?"

"No. They didn't see me."

"What did your . . . I mean, what did you do?" Mrs. Hoggett-Egburry had very nearly stumbled. Under the stress of emotion she had slipped back across the years of officialdom and had very nearly said, "Your Ladyship."

"I didn't like their looks. I hid in a ditch till they went past."

"Oh," said Mrs. Hoggett-Egburry, "a *nullah*. How very clever of you!"

Aunt Phoebe knew suddenly that she was going to like the newcomer. She did not suffer fools gladly; she was always astonished by the number of people who reached middle-age still remaining fools. Clearly, Lady Esketh was no fool.

"You'd better have some dry clothes," said Aunt Phoebe.

"Yes, thanks. And some kind of a bath."

"There's a *chattee* . . . ' began Mrs. Hoggett-Egburry.

[368]

"There's a stone crock full of water and a dipper. I'll heat up some water," said Aunt Phoebe. "Come on with me."

Mrs. Hoggett-Egburry giggled, aware suddenly of her mummy-like attire. "We haven't any clothes, any of us," she said, "I was caught in my neglijay. It's drying now, but it's so hard to dry things in monsoon weather."

As for Mrs. Simon, she appeared to have become mute. She stood quite still, staring at Lady Esketh and the fortune in jewels she wore on one wrist. This was her dream of what a duchess should be. She forgot even the bodies of Mr. Simon and poor, stupid Hazel crushed beneath tons of stone and plaster. While she stared Lady Esketh began to unfasten the bracelets, saying, "What can I do with these?"

"Give them to me," said Aunt Phoebe. "I'll keep them in my stocking." Then a wicked gleam came into her eyes—that same look of devilment which Ransome had caught in her wrinkled face on the day the hyena drove Mrs. Hoggett-Egburry up the arbor. "I guess no matter what happens," she said, "they won't be looking under *my* skirts."

When she had gone, taking Lady Esketh with her, Mrs. Simon said, "What a way to talk! Now you can see!"

"In front of Lady Esketh, too!"

"How can she talk like that . . . when anything might happen?"

And then Mr. Bannerjee appeared in the doorway, his head covered with ashes, carrying his lacquer box. At sight of him both women screamed, and then recognizing him beneath the ashes, they turned their backs and occupied themselves with Mrs. Hoggett-Egburry's *peignoir*, which was nearly dry. Mr. Bannerjee in European clothes was bad enough. In a *dhoti*, covered with ashes, Mr. Bannerjee, the elegant, the cosmopolitan, looked like any filthy *sadhu*.

Almost at once he became a nuisance, for in an accession of orthodoxy he demanded a corner of the stove and a set of kitchen utensils where he might prepare food for himself and Mrs. Bannerjee uncontaminated by the hand of the untouchable Aunt Phoebe.

In the bathroom by the *chattee*, Aunt Phoebe and Lady Esketh began to understand each other. Aunt Phoebe brought cotton underwear (which Lady Esketh had not seen since the pinched days long ago when she had lived in a Florentine pension with a bankrupt father) and a dress of calico which she had never seen in all her life, a dress which was simply two pieces of cloth sewn together with sleeves by a Gujerati dressmaker who had squatted on the verandah floor while he made it.

Aunt Phoebe felt a sudden shyness, not because Lady Esketh was fashionable or because she was rich or because she was the god-daughter of a queen, but because she was called "Lady" Esketh. Aunt Phoebe had never called anyone "Lady" in her life, and in spite of a knowledge remote and somewhat vague, that there were such things as titles, it seemed to her that it was a silly thing to call anyone "Lady" Esketh or Lady Smith or Lady Jones. Her shyness was born of the unwillingness of her tongue to pronounce the word "Lady," so in all their conversations she simply addressed Lady Esketh as "you."

Almost at once Lady Esketh had asked, "Who are the two women in the kitchen?" And Aunt Phoebe had responded, "The one in sheets is Mrs. Hoggett-Egburry. She's the wife of the bank manager. The other is Mrs. Simon, the wife of the other missionary."

"The one who has a daughter called Fern?"

"Yes," said Aunt Phoebe. "The poor thing has lost her other daughter and her husband. They were killed."

"Oh, I'm sorry."

For a moment the unreal horror of the reality returned, making them both mute.

There was a long silence, and then Lady Esketh, who had quite shamelessly taken off all her clothes and was standing quite naked beside the *chattee*, said, "Have you heard of what has happened to the hospital?"

"No. Nobody knows anything. I sent one of the boys to find out, but he never came back."

"I don't know whether my own husband is alive or dead. He was ill . . . in the old Summer Palace."

Aunt Phoebe thought, "Poor thing" and then knew at once that her thought was merely conventional. Whatever happened to this strange woman standing there naked, dousing herself with cold water from the *chattee*, she would never be a poor thing. So she said, "I expect that tomorrow things will be better."

Then Aunt Phoebe left Lady Esketh with the clothes, and in a little while, dressed in the calico frock, she came in the kitchen and Aunt Phoebe thought, "It's wonderful what a difference there is in the way people wear clothes." In the calico dress which fitted her no better than it had fitted Mrs. Smiley, for whom it had been made, Lady Esketh somehow looked smart, or at least she looked what Aunt Phoebe supposed smartness to be, for it had never been a subject in which she had taken any great interest.

Lady Esketh said, "If there's anything I can do to help, you must tell me what it is. I'm not very clever, but I'd like to help. I don't care what."

Aunt Phoebe started to say that she could manage and that there wasn't any reason to spoil the looks of the lovely white hands with the lacquered nails, but before she could speak, Lady Esketh said, "I really mean it. You see, I want to be useful. I want to do something." And into her voice and into the blue eyes there came the shadow of something which Aunt Phoebe in her wisdom understood, something which astonished her. For a second she was silent and then she said, "Well, you might scrape the yams," but when she placed the basin and the yams and the knife before her, she saw that Lady Esketh had not the faintest idea of how to scrape yams, so she took the knife in her own work-worn hands and said, "See, like this."

Lady Esketh said, "I'm sorry, but I'm such a fool about things like that" and into her face came a look of childishness, almost of innocence, which Ransome had discovered in his drunkenness on the night of Mr. Bannerjee's party a little while before the earthquake.

Turning away to the stove, Aunt Phoebe thought, "That's it! That's what she wants." The yams would discolor her white hands and the water would crack the lovely nails, but that was what she wanted more than anything in all the world.

Together they got ready the dinner for Mrs. Hoggett-Egburry and Mrs. Simon and Miss Murgatroyd. On his end of the stove Mr. Bannerjee prepared a dish of rice and saffron. At last he had put aside his lacquered box.

It was Lady Esketh and Mrs. Simon who kept watch through the night, armed with Aunt Phoebe's revolver. A little after midnight reverberations of the distant explosions from the direction of Mount Abana rocked the house and brought the others into the candle-lighted kitchen where the two women sat with the door barricaded by chairs and tables. It was Aunt Phoebe who divined the cause of the explosions. Nothing else of importance occurred during the night. No Bhils appeared and the only sound from the muddy plain outside was the steady roar of monsoon rain and the howling of the jackals and the occasional maniacal laughter of a hyena.

As the night drew on the two women talked to each other. At first there had only been an exchange of occasional remarks, civil but uninteresting, for Mrs. Simon was still bedazzled and Lady Esketh found herself bored and unhappy. Miss Hodge had been one thing, but Mrs. Simon, she found was another. The groveling and snobbery of Miss Hodge she understood well enough; out of years of experience at bazaars and horticultural shows she knew all the necessary answers, the gracious word or two of formula that would make drab women like Miss Hodge and Mrs. Hoggett-Egburry glow with an inner happiness. But Mrs. Simon was different. In her American snobbery Lady Esketh detected a kind of formlessness; it was the manifestation of an individual rather than a whole caste, and so it puzzled her. The old answers which had satisfied Miss Hodge did not appear to satisfy Mrs. Simon. She divined that both women were commonplace and boring, but she discovered almost at once that their quality was different. Mrs. Simon had a chip on her shoulder; poor Miss Hodge was grateful for any kind word. Mrs. Simon wanted more than formulas. She demanded intimacy on an equal footing as the final price of a tolerable relationship.

For the first time in her life Lady Esketh felt ill-at-ease, thinking, "Perhaps, after all, our way is the best. At least you know where you stand." Mrs. Simon dared to ask her direct questions about her husband, about his illness, what she thought about Ranchipur and the Maharani and about Ransome. It was not only that she expected an answer; she expected the same intimate revelations which she herself produced with such breath-taking frankness and simplicity.

When she brought the name of Ransome into their desultory talk, obliquely rather like a crab dragging its prey sidewise, she hinted at an intimacy between him and Fern which made Edwina feel that he had deliberately deceived her about the depth of his relationship to the girl.

[372]

She talked to Lady Esketh with a curious detachment about her husband and her daughter who were dead, saying, "Tomorrow, somehow, we must bury them."

On the other side of the table, with the candle between them, Lady Esketh found that she was being shocked, something which she had not thought possible. The woman slowly became to her a little inhuman. It was as if nothing in the world, neither her dead husband and daughter, nor her living child existed except in relation to her own ego. As she listened it seemed to her that the woman almost believed that poor Hazel and the Reverend Mr. Simon had arranged to have themselves killed in order to spite her. And as she sat there, idly answering "yes" or "no" or "how terrible!" it occurred to her again how little, for all her experience, she really knew of what the world was like, how little she knew of its meannesses and crudeness and petty ambitions and jealousies. She had never known because when they came near her she had always turned away from them. Now, willy-nilly, these things of which she had been unaware were being forced on her by the hard-faced middle-aged woman seated on the opposite side of the table. Watching the missionary's wife, she experienced at the same time resentment and pity—resentment at Mrs. Simon's vulgarity and pity for her very smallness and for all the harshness she divined in a background and a childhood of which she knew nothing whatever.

Listening with only half her mind, the thought of Albert returned to her, and for a moment it seemed to her that he was less awful than she had believed. His faults, his vices, were at least great ones. The evil he had done was vast and far-reaching. In his selfishness, in his ambition, there was a kind of evil grandeur. And then forgetting Mrs. Simon altogether, she thought, "He is very likely dead . . . if not by the earthquake, from the illness. I shall never see him again and I am free." And then after a moment, "But what am I to do with my freedom? Where am I to go? What reason have I for living?"

The jackals were howling again, quite near, at the edge of the compound, and the absurd thought occurred to her that this adventure should be romantic and exciting in quality, but that for some reason she could not quite discover, it was not; it seemed only squalid and empty, the wrecked house, the strange assortment of commonplace people, even her feeling for Tom. She had never been afraid, even for a moment. For a little time she had been excited, but now the adventure had gone all flat and tasteless. The discomfort and drabness and boredom had outweighed whatever excitement there had been in it. Out of it all there remained only the Major, and very likely he was dead.

Then she was aware that the odd, common little woman opposite her was crying, not noisily and hysterically, but quietly, the tears rolling down the badly made-up cheeks. Very quietly she was talking, unaware even whether Lady Esketh was listening or not.

She was saying: "I could have been better to him . . . and kinder to him. Now I can't be . . . never again . . . because he's gone." Lady Esketh was aware that the face was no longer hard; it had turned flabby and the rice powder was streaked and blotched by the tears. She went on talking in a curious muffled voice, saying, "Sometimes I nagged him. I nagged Hazel, too, but that wasn't the same. I always meant to make it up to him somehow . . . and now it's too late. I made him do things he didn't want to do, and sometimes he used to get so tired. I didn't mean it that way. I meant to help him. He wasn't the kind of man who could help himself." She rubbed the smudged face with her handkerchief and said, "He was weak, but he was a good man. I wish you could have known him."

Watching the woman, Lady Esketh experienced a kind of cold horror at her sorrow, at the pitiful egotistical quality of her confession. She wanted to go away, to turn her back and talk to some one else. She was even afraid, for she divined the half-mad quality of the hysteria in Mrs. Simon. But there was no place to go and no one to talk to. She remembered suddenly, with a faint desire to laugh, that she had a duty imposed upon her; she was sitting there in a calico dress with a revolver in her lap, acting as sentinel. Outside there was nothing but that endless plain of red mud with its jackals and hyenas and perhaps wandering troops of those savages she had seen a little while before. All at once she was angry at Ransome for having sent her ahead instead of allowing her to remain behind with him. Then she thought, "But he didn't want me. He wanted to be alone with that girl. Probably it was his first chance. He has the girl. Why shouldn't I have my beautiful Doctor?"

Raschid and Ranjit Singh had worked quickly. There had been trouble with Raschid's own people, the Muslims, who found the burning of bodies against their faith. Because there were not many of them the old Maharani gave permission for the burial of all Muslim dead in a piece of ground near the Parsee Tower of Silence. The Tower itself was black now with the figures of gorged vultures, fluttering and preening their filthy wings, for the Parsees, too, had been allowed burial according to their faith so long as the bodies were carried at once to the Tower.

Beneath what remained of the *porte-cochère* at the Summer Palace they had built a pyre for Lord Esketh from shattered beams wrested out of the ruins, and as the little party advanced up the drive the coolies waited for Lady Esketh to set fire to the heap. On the top lay the body, wrapped now, like the bodies at the burning-ghats, in a shroud. Ransome had made certain of that because what remained of Lord Esketh was not a pretty sight. As they came nearer Edwina saw that the shroud was made of the pink sheets of crêpe-de-chine with which she always traveled. The great embroidered monogram, E. E., showed plainly on the sides. Grimly she thought, "He would have liked that—to be wrapped in the pink sheets from my bed."

The whole thing had a makeshift air, with no mourners save the coolies who stood about staring at the widow with an animal curiosity. In London, thought Edwina, there would have been a great funeral, with a service perhaps in St. Margaret's or St. George's, attended by all those who had profited from contact with the deceased during life, by all those who for the sake of a maggot-eaten, hypocritical society would have to go to keep up the pretense that the late Lord Esketh was, even in death an important, an honorable man and a pillar of the British system. They would sit in the pews, knowing in their hearts that he had been a madman and a criminal, but never by so much as a breath or a glance would they betray the knowledge to their neighbors, because each of them was in his own way up to the game which Esketh had played in life far more shrewdly and successfully than themselves. She saw suddenly that this giant hypocrisy was a kind of system, a major contribution by Anglo-Saxon society to the civilization of the West, a contribution peculiarly English. They all pretended not to see the vices, the abuses, the shortcomings of others, so that their own would not be discovered. So long as you played their game you could do as you pleased and get away with it. Even Albert had not minded how many lovers she had so long as the world did not know it. Beneath the surface there was layer upon layer of rotting corruption, only you ignored it or turned away your head. And when you didn't play the game and were honest they tore you to pieces the way they tore to pieces Byron and Oscar Wilde, Shelley and Hastings and so many others.

"That's how I got away with it for so long," she thought. "I couldn't have elsewhere—in any other country."

It was a strength born of a cynicism far more profound than anything ever conceived or devised by the clear-headed, cynical French. There would be eulogies and fantastic obituaries in all the newspapers in England, even in those which had fought him in life and hated him. And the Esketh press would have columns and black borders and pictures and tributes by men he had cheated and abused in life, who hated him as she and Bates hated him. Only they didn't even know yet that he was dead. There would be streamers about "Lord and Lady Esketh missing. Ranchipur disaster, etc." But they couldn't know yet. The men and women who worked for him wouldn't yet be able to rejoice in their hearts that he was dead. They could only hope.

For a second her lips crooked into a half-smile when she thought again, "What a biography Bates and I could write together!" And then she thought, "I have come here even now to keep up appearances, to keep the façade from crumbling," because in her heart she did not care what they did with that mass of putrefaction wrapped in her expensive pink sheets.

Ashes to ashes all right. When the heap was gone they would scrape up what was left and put it in a Huntley & Palmer biscuit-tin and send it back to that brother of his she had never been allowed to see because she was fashionable Edwina Esketh and he did not want her even to suspect the sordid commonplaceness of his lower middle-class origin.

While Mr. Smiley read on, she felt Ransome's hand reach out and take her own. It was a nice gesture, she thought, a symbol of that odd bitter understanding which had always existed between them. He was trying to give her sympathy and strength, not because Lord Esketh was dead and she was a widow (she knew he had no illusions about that), but for all the wasted years she had spent with him, for all the follies she had committed, for all the recklessness and hypocrisy of her life. And suddenly she saw that Tom had run away out of that old life long ago because he could not fit in, because he would not play the game of hypocrisy. He might be weak and neurotic, a drunkard and a defeatist, but he had honesty and he saw clearly. He had refused to play their nasty game.

Then Mr. Smiley was finished and Tom said, "Do you want to light the pyre? It's the usual thing here for the nearest relative." And dumbly she said, "Yes," and one of the coolies who stood expectantly by gave her a copy of the *Times of India* twisted into a torch which Tom lighted with his *briquet* and she thrust it into the pyre. The flames hesitated for a moment and then leaped up and up greedily toward the body wrapped in sheets of pale pink crêpe-de-chine.

For a little time she watched, fascinated, and then turning to Tom she asked, like a child, "May I go now?" and Mr. Smiley said, "There's nothing to be gained by staying."

She liked Mr. Smiley. She glanced at him quickly with a half-smile. There was something so simple and uncomplicated and sure about him.

"One of my boys," said Mr. Smiley, "will look after the ashes."

And so the great Lord Esketh was left alone with the coolies and the all-devouring, purifying fire.

Halfway through the bazaar they met Miss Hodge. She came running toward them, her pudgy face filled with a look of childish terror.

"Why did you leave me behind?" she cried. Then she took Lady Esketh's hand once more, and whimpering, she said, "I looked everywhere for you."

Ransome saw Edwina put her arm through that of Miss Hodge and heard her say, gently, "We didn't mean to leave you. We didn't think you would care to go."

Poor Miss Hodge's lips trembled as though she were going to cry, and then she smiled, happily, because she was walking arm in arm with her friend Lady Esketh as if they were two schoolgirls.

When they reached the hospital, Ransome and Mr. Smiley left them to go to the Maharani's tent. Miss MacDaid was waiting grimly, with fresh tasks—bathing patients and taking temperatures, carrying bedpans.

She said, abruptly, "I've fixed up a room for you and Miss Hodge and Fern Simon in the out-patient ward. It isn't very big and there are only Indian beds. You'd better clean it thoroughly before you try to sleep in it."

It was the airplane which precipitated the crisis. It came the next morning from the direction of Mount Abana, appearing suddenly, glistening in a moment of sunlight above the white temples which crowned the summit. People in the streets—coolies and sweeper women, soldiers and policemen, the hungry, the sick and dying—looked toward the sky and watched it approach. Some cried out; some were silent; but in the heart of each one was the thought, "The world outside has not forgotten us."

Quickly it arrived above the ruined city, circling twice before the flyer chose a millet-field beyond the Parsee's Tower of Silence as a landing-place. Then it roared lower and lower until at last the wheels of the undercarriage struck the red mud and sank deeper and deeper. For a moment in the suddenness of checked flight, the plane threatened to stand upon its nose, but quickly it recovered itself and settled down as the crowd, running painfully through the mud, arrived. The flyer was a Muslim. When he climbed out, he asked in Hindustani for Lord and Lady Esketh. He had, he said, been sent by Delhi to rescue them.

It was a clerk from the Revenue Office who answered him. The others were small, dark people, Untouchables and low-caste, who knew nothing of such great personages. He was a sallow little man, gossipy and self-important, who knew everything that happened in Ranchipur.

"The great sahib is dead," he said. "The mem-sahib is at the hospital, but the man you should see is Sahib Ransome." And he led the flyer to the *jobedar's* house in the Great Gate.

From the moment Gopal Rao came in, excited, to tell him that the plane had been sighted, Ransome knew why it had come . . . perhaps for news, but certainly to fetch Edwina. He had thought of horsemen, bullocks, even of messengers on elephants, but the coming of an airplane had not occurred to him. Even now the idea had no reality; it was as if some monstrous Wellsean invention of the future had appeared suddenly in the skies above the tent of an ancient Mahratta queen. In the *jobedar's* house, in the luxurious striped pavilion of the Maharani, he had, he saw suddenly, been living in the fifteenth century instead of the twentieth. And then when the trim Muslim flyer stood there before him, saying that he had come to fetch Lady Esketh, he suspected suddenly that Edwina would not return with him, and he remembered the Maharani's hostility and contempt and her hint that Lady Esketh must be gotten out as soon as possible because the old lady wanted her no longer in Ranchipur. If the old Maharani willed it, Edwina would have to go. As Regent she was an absolute despot. She could, if necessary, order Edwina to be trussed like a partridge and carried aboard the plane. He did not know why he thought Edwina would choose to stay behind in this pest hole of Ranchipur; it was no more than a feeling, a bit of instinct. Since she had come back from the Mission she seemed a little strange to him, withdrawn and almost hostile. Only in that moment when his hand touched hers as they stood beside the funeral pyre had there been a flash of the old sympathy and understanding.

So when he spoke to the flyer and told him that he would go at once to fetch Lady Esketh, his brow was furrowed by a deep frown. He gave orders that the man should have something to eat and drink and then set out for the hospital.

He found her, dressed now in the blue costume worn by student nurses, putting in order the room which she shared with Miss Hodge and Fern, and the sight of her sweeping beneath the crude cord-laced Indian bed filled him again with a desire to laugh. Miss Hodge was with her, puttering about.

Thinking that if he attacked abruptly he might win his point, he said, "An airplane has been sent for you. You can go as soon as you collect whatever you take with you."

She stood up and leaned the broom against the wall. "Who sent it?" she asked.

"The Viceroy, I suppose. A person of your importance can't get lost so easily."

"No, I suppose not. I don't know whether I want to go."

"You'd better. You're a fool to think of staying here."

Then Miss Hodge cried out hysterically, "You won't go. You won't leave me here alone!" and when Ransome looked at her he saw that she had been crying. Her eyes were red and swollen and she looked pudgier, madder, and uglier than she had ever looked.

Edwina turned and, speaking as if she were addressing a child, said, "No, I won't desert you. I'll take care of you." To Ransome she said, "I've got to have a little time to think it over."

"You're crazy to stay," he repeated. "You look like the devil already."

"Thanks. I know how I look. I saw my face this morning in the mirror. Why do you want to be rid of me?"

"You make more complications than you're worth."

"That's not very clear. What do you mean . . . him?"

"Perhaps other things, too."

"I'm not bothering him. I've scarcely seen him. He couldn't find me very attractive like this."

"There are other things, too."

"What?"

"The Maharani wants to get rid of you as soon as possible."

"Why?"

He gave a faint grin. "She doesn't like you."

"I know that."

"She always knows everything. She probably even knows why you want to stay."

"He's got nothing to do with it . . . at least not very much."

"You know she can order you to go."

For a moment she considered this. Then she said, "And if I refuse she could bundle me off. She couldn't put me in prison."

"I wouldn't be too sure. She's got absolute power now. She's been wanting it for years. She hates Europeans . . especially European women. She could say it was for your own safety. She's an extraordinary old lady." And he saw suddenly that he had taken the wrong track. Her face had grown stubborn, almost hard.

"I suppose even you think I'm useless."

"No. I think it would be better if you got back to your old life. That's where you belong. It's too late to change now, even if you wanted to."

"You are a bastard."

"You may even get cholera or typhus and die. They're even more deadly with Europeans."

"If I stay it'll be for reasons you don't understand."

"Perhaps."

They had quite forgotten Miss Hodge. She stood there, all ears, fascinated. Even in her madness she was aware that she had never before heard people talking like this, so bluntly, so bitterly. It was not at all like the conversations she had imagined between people in fashionable society. None of her heroines had ever used the word "bastard." The poor, pudgy face was a mask of bewilderment.

"Can't you put in a word for me with the Maharani?"

"I might."

"Go and see her. When you come back I'll have reached a decision. If she won't have me, I'll go." Then she put her hand on his arm and said, "But be square with me, Tom. I don't want to go back . . . I'm afraid to go back. I want to stay here." And into the blue eyes came that look of childishness, almost of innocence, which he had, in his drunkenness, seen there on the night of Mr. Bannerjee's dinner. "Fight for me, Tom . . . this once."

He knew what he should have said—that he knew why it was that she wanted to stay, that her reasons were muddled and sentimental, that she was behaving like the heroine of a cheap novel, and that he meant to ship her back at once into the cheap, bloody life where she belonged. But he had, he knew, neither the heart nor the right to say that to her, so gently he said, "I'll try. I swear it. But it's against all common sense."

"Thank you," she said, and kissed him suddenly on the cheek.

As he turned to go, Miss Hodge suddenly regained her speech, "Tell him," she said, with sudden excitement, "tell him now . . ."

"Tell him what?"

"About the Sikh soldier."

"What about the Sikh soldier?" asked Ransome.

"It's nothing," said Edwina. "I'll tell you when you come back. Go on now. Do what you promised."

"I don't promise anything," said Ransome. "Only remember that being the widow of the great Lord Esketh doesn't mean a damned thing now, least of all to the old lady."

He found the Maharani in the tent, and she received him not in the audience-hall with its carpets and paintings, but in her own chamber, where she sat on the floor alone with the old Princess of Bewanagar. She looked tired with great dark circles under the brilliant eyes, and she wore no jewels save two drops of diamonds in her ears. There was a fierceness in her aspect, a kind of grimness which he had seen only once or twice before in all the years he had known her, at moments when she had lost her temper and become suddenly a tigress.

She looked at him and said, "Well?"

"It's about Lady Esketh, Your Highness."

There was no need to tell her about the plane. As always, she knew everything, almost as soon as it happened. She knew about the plane, whence it had come, by whom it was sent, even that the flyer was a Muslim called Captain Yussef Baig. And she said, with a certain bitterness, "It came empty—no food, no bandages, no anæsthetics, nothing but two empty seats for that Englishman and his wife."

"It is returning with all those things, Your Highness. The Major and Miss MacDaid are making a list for the pilot."

"What is it about Lady Esketh?"

"She doesn't want to go. She wants to stay here."

The black eyes contracted a little, so that they seemed concentrated points of fire. "And why doesn't she want to go?"

He shrugged his shoulders. Then a faint grin came over the handsome, tired, old face and he divined that she knew that, too—how Edwina had looked at the Major that night at Mrs. Bannerjee's. Or perhaps she had noticed it even on that first night during the state dinner in the palace. There was so little that escaped her.

She said, "So that's it?"

"I don't think that's it, altogether." He knew now that his chances were better. The grin, the sudden human flash of humor. She was, he knew, above all else profoundly human.

"I don't want her here," she said. "She's a . . ." For a moment she hesitated and then said, "a slut."

Ransome did not deny this. Knowing what he knew, he understood that it was no use trying to change her belief.

"She's working at the hospital now," he said, "being very useful."

"What sort of work?"

"The hardest—the filthiest."

Again the faint shadow of humor and understanding came into the eyes. "I suppose Miss MacDaid saw to that. Well, any girl from the High School could be as useful."

He saw that she meant to yield nothing; but the look in the black eyes softened a little and an inspiration came to him. He knew how she had fought for the women of India to educate them, to make them free, to raise them from the dust. If he could make her see Edwina as a fellow woman. . . .

"She's really doing a man's work," he said, and suddenly added, "She hated her husband. She's glad he's dead. She's been through a good deal since she came here."

He saw that she was considering all this, but was unwilling to let him know that she was considering it. She asked, "Why do you want her to stay?" And he thought again, "She knows all that, too." But he said, "I don't want her to stay. I did my best to persuade her to leave."

"Then why are you asking me to yield?"

That, he knew, was a poser. For a moment he was silent. Then he said, "That is a very long story, Your Highness. It began a very long time ago. There's nothing between us now . . . nothing at all save old friendship. I suppose it's because of that and because she has a lot of character."

"Character!" the old lady snorted.

He did not give way. "Yes, Your Highness, character. Sometimes it's been used in the wrong way, but it's character just the same."

She liked that. He felt suddenly that by some miracle he would end even by making her like Edwina.

She said, "How does the Major feel about it?"

"I don't know. I only saw him for a moment. We talked about the supplies he needed."

She looked away from him thoughtfully and then said, "Ask the Major. If he agrees, I will let it pass. She can stay. But I won't be responsible for anything that happens to her. I will send a letter to the Viceroy saying so—that I could not force her to go."

"Then I can count on that?"

"Haven't I just told you?"

"Thank you, Your Highness."

He bowed and made as to leave, but she said, "I want to thank you, Ransome, for all you're doing. Raschid and Colonel Singh told me that you'd worked all night. When did you sleep?"

"Two days ago."

"Settle this and then go to bed. We need you and you look very tired."

"Thank you, Your Highness."

"Tell the Major I'm sending Mr. Bauer to help him. He's a nurse. He'll be of use."

"Very good, Your Highness."

Then he made an Indian bow, pressing his fingertips together, and left her, excited even in his weariness that he had won half the battle. In the anteroom he passed the Russian woman, bowed, and said, *"Bon jour,"* to her. He had never met her, but formality seemed idiotic in such times as these. She seemed agitated, and giving him a half-smile and a penetrating look out of her green cat's eyes, she went past him into the Maharani's chamber.

She was angry and disappointed that she had not been with the Maharani to hear what Ransome and Her Highness had been talking of. Now she would have to discover from the Maharani herself, drawing it out bit by bit, with subtle questions and hints, slowly and painfully, because the old fox would know what she was up to and make it as difficult as possible and perhaps never let her know at all.

The whole world had gone wrong for Maria Lishinskaia from the very moment she had seen the old Maharajah fall dead in Harry's arms. She had seen him only once since then and only for a second. She couldn't tell him now to come to her room, and there were times when her desire became so great that her whole body became feverish and her brain grew dizzy, when every sound, every smell, shattered her nerves—the beating of the rain on the triple-roofed tent, the horrible faint odor of death that drifted through the great Park from the town, the cries of jackals and hyenas and the distant isolated wailing that never stopped day or night. And they became, all these sounds, a part of her desire.

She had never suffered like this, never in Russia before she escaped, or afterward wandering through Germany, selling herself here and there for enough to eat and to keep her body clothed. It was, she told herself, this damned country, this hellish climate, this world of mad voluptuousness and cruelty with its lingams everywhere, in temples, in village huts, in palaces, by the dusty roadside. Wherever you turned it was always there before you, the lingam, symbol of creation, of *volupté* and strange desires and pleasures. Shiva, always Shiva, and Kali, the Destroyer.

When she pushed aside the curtains and came into the presence, the Maharani looked at her and said, "News?"

"No news."

The old lady opened her box of betel-nuts and said, casually, "I'm sending Harry Bauer to the hospital," and Maria Lishinskaia's heart stopped beating. "They can use him there. They are overwhelmed with work."

"Now," thought Maria Lishinskaia, "I will never see him. Or maybe it will be easier. Maybe I can go to him there."

The Maharani watched her and then said, "The old barracks and what's left of the Music School are filled with cholera patients. The Major can put him in charge of one of them. He knows about disinfectants and protecting himself. He'll be of great use."

The sallow face of Maria Lishinskaia turned a greenish white, and before her there rose the picture of her own town in the Ukraine long ago when people died like flies of cholera, dropping in the streets, in the shops, writhing, black in the face. She thought, "I never have luck. I have never had any luck. Even when I fight it is no good. There is nothing . . . nothing." And aloud she said, "If anything happens to him I will keel myself."

It was the first time that she had even hinted to Her Highness that she loved Harry Bauer.

"Nothing will happen to him. He is young. He is strong. He is vigorous." She chose her words carefully, knowing the image they would raise in the tormented mind of poor Maria Lishinskaia, knowing, too, that often enough it was the young and the strong who were stricken first by cholera.

The Russian woman felt suddenly that she was suffocating. The walls of the tent whirled about her. She managed to say, "May I go and lie down, Your Highness? I feel very faint."

"Of course." And she went away, blind with fear and desire, not knowing that she was being tortured again because the Maharani was in a bad humor. The old lady was furious now with herself, because she had yielded about Lady Esketh, because the sight of Ransome had made her weak. She liked men and she liked Ransome, and in her heart she hated all women, even those whom she had spent her life trying to help. She was old now. She could only pry and peep and watch the affairs of women like Lady Esketh and Maria Lishinskaia. It was all the worse because in her aging body the spirit was young.

At the hospital, the Major lay trying to sleep on a bed in the tiny room off the hall which served him as a private sanctum. He had been sent there by Miss MacDaid, who said to him, sharply, "You're behaving like a fool. Doctor Pindar and I can manage things for five or six hours. God saved your life once. He may not do it twice. You've got to have some rest."

For forty-eight hours he had not stopped working. There was the hospital itself and the old barracks, and the Music School with their cholera patients, and the disinfecting and guarding of wells, and conferences with Raschid and Ranjit Singh and the Maharani, and there had been what seemed an endless amount of operating by the feeble light of two candles. They could not use more than two because there was only a box or two left and no one knew when there would be more candles or any oil at all. But even all the operating had failed to save most of the patients from infections and gangrene.

He was beyond sleep now. His still bandaged head ached unmercifully and one worry after another chased through his tired brain. Now and then the figure of Lady Esketh appeared before his tired closed eyes, not as she had been on that night at the palace or at the

Bannerjee's dinner, but as he had seen her coming up the drive in Mrs. Smiley's calico dress, tired, bedraggled, and untidy, as she had looked at him defiantly in the hallway. The woman he had seen at the palace and at the Bannerjee's had possessed no power of stirring him. He had lived in Europe. He had had European women, not only whores, but women of position. It had always been easy enough, too easy for his fastidious taste. And never once had he slept with a European woman free from misgiving or without being shocked by something hard and callous in her, something which upset him and put his nerves on edge. Because love or even the counterfeit of love should not be like that, but something which had in it a gaiety and a voluptuous beauty such as Natara Devi had given it.

That was something European women never understood—that an Oriental, however male, had painfully acute nerves and sensibilities. A male Englishman was stupid and insensitive and sometimes bestial. Perhaps that was why English prostitutes were so shocking, that and because Christianity in the West had made of love even in marriage a shameful, dirty thing.

When he had shared the cup of tea with her in the Summer Palace after Miss Hodge had gone her flustered way she had behaved like a prostitute. Because in spite of all her fine speeches, he had been aware of what it was she wanted. He had known that he could have had her there on the sofa with her husband dying in the next room, and for a moment he had been tempted because it would have been easy. But he had not wanted her very much and two things held him back, one that she was an important European woman and might attach herself to him permanently, making a scandal because he had no desire to go on with the thing, and the other that he had known it was worth nothing; it would have been no more enjoyable than a bout with a Jermyn Street whore who liked her trade.

No, that woman in the Summer Palace, with the smooth, shining face, the elaborate make-up, and the Paris clothes had not interested him. She had been too perfect, too artificial for his warm, direct nature. He had known that there would have been no laughter in their love-making, no playfulness, but only a kind of vicious hunger that came over people who were taught that love-making was sin but could none the less save themselves from it. It was a subtle thing, that strange mixture of hypocrisy and hardness he had found in the West. It was as if their hatred of the very act gave them an inverted and vicious pleasure in it which frightened him and revolted him. It was something he would never know. Even vice and perversion in the East had not that terrifying quality of bitterness and corruption and shame.

The woman with the smooth hair and the jewels had left him unmoved, but the tired woman in Mrs. Smiley's old dress had roused his interest. The one in the calico dress looked infinitely older, but there was a quality of humanness about her. When she looked at him scornfully for a second, he had almost doubted that she was the same woman he had seen at the Bannerjee's. Perhaps, his tired brain thought, there was more in split personalities than the psychologists knew. Perhaps she was two women or three or more. Perhaps the shock of the disaster and of her husband's horrible death had set one of them free.

And since her coming to the hospital her behavior had been that of a woman who was a stranger to the woman who in the Summer Palace had put her hands behind her to keep him from seeing that they were trembling. Oh, he saw things like that. It was in his nature to see them, and training as a doctor and a surgeon had sharpened the talent. She should have divined that, for even the woman of the Summer Palace was not a stupid woman. This other one, since she came to the hospital, had scarcely noticed him at all. There was about her something dead, save in the moments when a certain fire came into the blue eyes; not dead, perhaps, but like something submerged, deadened for the moment. He felt a desire, partly scientific, to talk with her in order to discover what lay at the roots of the mystery, but with this woman he felt shy. The other one he had not feared at all, because he had felt contempt and even a little pity for her. He knew that she had been given the worst and most revolting of tasks by Miss MacDaid in the hope that she would not have the strength or will to go through with them, but she had accepted the tasks without complaint, although he was certain that last night when Miss MacDaid had handed her the dressings from a gangrenous wound, she had gone away for a moment in order to vomit. It was as if Miss MacDaid, in her hardness, had challenged her, and she had taken up the challenge with every handicap, with everything against her. Fern Simon, for whom Miss MacDaid also professed contempt, had gotten off much more easily.

Then he forgot her again and began to worry, thinking in despair how hard it was to help his own people at a time like this, because there seemed to be in them no will to fight. They gave up and died so easily without a struggle, perhaps because they were always undernourished and life meant little enough to them in any case. Perhaps they were like that in the West, in the horrible mill and mining towns which had shocked him and Miss MacDaid. And the cholera . . . it was hard enough to check when conditions were normal, but now with the dead about and the wells polluted and the mangoes ripe and being sold on the streets . . . they had to eat mangoes, for there was little else. The mangoes grew everywhere. They passed from hand to hand, half of them through the hands of men and women already polluted who would fall down in a little while, turn black, and die. You could not make every ignorant sweeper wash the mangoes in permanganate before he ate them. And there was typhoid, too, which would grow worse and worse, for already they were stealing water from the wells after nightfall and taking it from puddles in the street.

Then all at once he felt drowsy, and just as he was falling asleep to the sound of the beating rain he heard the sound of voices in the corridor—Ransome's and Miss MacDaid's. She was saying, "He's asleep and can't be disturbed."

"How long will he sleep?"

"I don't know. I certainly shan't disturb him till he wakes."

"I suppose you're right. He is the most valuable man."

Drowsily he rose and went to the door. When he opened it, he said, "I wasn't asleep yet. What is it?"

Miss MacDaid looked at Ransome furiously and gave an indignant snort. The nerves of everyone, even those of the old war-horse, Miss MacDaid, were beginning to give way.

Ransome told him what the Maharani had said about Lady Esketh staying in Ranchipur. "It's up to you," he said.

The Major, struggling with his drowsiness, did not answer at once, and Miss MacDaid said, "I can think of nothing more unwise than letting her stay."

[453]

The Major looked at her. "She's worked well, hasn't she? She's been a genuine help."

And the honest Miss MacDaid replied, "Yes, I must say she's worked hard and well, but that's not the point."

He was feeling confused. All at once he felt that he was going to sleep on his feet, standing there in the doorway. He was drowning in sleep. He said, "Let her stay. She can always leave when she's had enough." But it was the woman in Mrs. Smiley's calico dress he was thinking of. The other one he would have sent away at once.

Ransome found Edwina in her room. When he told her the news she said, "That's good. I wanted to stay. Now some one else can go in the extra seat. I'm going to send Bates in my place."

"There may be a row about that. . . . I mean about sending a servant when there are important people who will want to go."

"What sort of important people?"

"The Maharani will want to send a courier."

"That still leaves a place for Bates." The old arrogant look came into her face. "Anyway, it's my plane. It was sent for me. I shall send whom I like in it. Bates is ill. It isn't fair not to send him. He never wanted to come to India. He hated it."

He shrugged his shoulders.

"I don't care who goes in the extra place."

"You'd better send word to him at once. The man who brought the plane will want to pass the Surat marshes before dark."

"I don't know whom to send. I haven't any servant."

"I'll send for him. Are you certain he's willing to go?"

"Certain."

"Where's Fern?" he asked, suddenly.

"I don't know. She's been helping Miss MacDaid check up on supplies and making a list of things she needs." She looked up at him directly and asked, "It's all right now, isn't it? I mean between you and her."

"Yes."

"I thought it must be. You look different." Then abruptly she asked, "Why don't you marry her?"

[454]

"No, that's no good. Even after what's happened."

"That's what you need . . . a girl like that."

"She's too young. Anyway, you don't know anything about her."

She did not answer this. Instead she said, with a funny grimace, "It's too bad there's nobody for me. Too bad a woman can't marry a man much younger than herself." Then she told him to go, saying that she must be back at her work and that he must send for Bates.

"I suppose I should thank the old girl."

"Yes, it's the least you can do and she'd like it."

He went away, puzzled. He still could not make her out. He still could not imagine why she wanted to stay behind, unless it was some new and subtle game for bringing the Major to bed with her. She was, he knew, capable of anything, and she had had a vast amount of experience.

But the departure of the plane was far less simple than Ransome had imagined. He sent for Bates, and then went to see the Maharani, who chose to send Gopal Rao as her messenger, just at the moment when the young Mahratta was needed most in the organization Ransome had built up. And then Miss MacDaid had put a veto on the departure of Bates without a proper examination by Doctor Pindar, the Major's assistant.

"It's no use sending him unless we know his illness is harmless. They wouldn't let him land."

And then returning to the *jobedar's* rooms he discovered that the news that Lady Esketh was staying behind had traveled swiftly over the whole city. The first room was filled by a dozen men, all screaming at Gopal Rao and clamoring to be put aboard the plane and sent to Bombay. There were two Parsee bankers and a Pathan money-lender, the superintendent of the cotton mills and Chandra Lal, the richest merchant in Ranchipur. And among them was Mr. Bannerjee, who had turned up carrying the lacquered box with the ashes of his father. All of them save Mr. Bannerjee had to leave, they said, because of business. They all talked at once and mentioned sums so vast that there was not in all the world enough gold to cover their mythical transactions. Three of them in turn drew him aside into a corner on the pretense of giving him

[455]

confidential reasons for having to leave, but in each case the confidences proved only to be the offers of huge bribes. It was not business with Mr. Bannerjee; it was his father's ashes which must be got to the Ganges as soon as possible. When the bribes were refused, they were puzzled and hurt.

It was odd, Ransome thought wryly, that only the merchants and money-lenders and one religious maniac were so desperately anxious to leave. Money and religion, he thought, were likely to go hand in hand.

But it wasn't only money. It was fear too. There was terror in every face. In the face of the plump Mr. Bannerjee terror revealed the yellowish whites of his eyes. Ransome hated him now. He had hated him since the moment he had plumped officiously into the little pleasure-boat off his own balcony. He had contempt for the man's superstitious terror. Mr. Bannerjee was afraid of cholera, afraid of Ranchipur, of the rains, of Kali, of India itself. Suddenly Ransome yielded to his desire to terrify him even more. He found himself saying, rudely, "If you think you can escape Kali by leaving Ranchipur, you are mad. Kali, the Destroyer, is everywhere." And he had the satisfaction of seeing even a wilder look of terror come into the eyes of the one-time leader of Ranchipur's cosmopolitan set.

Then when they heard that Bates was to have the one seat left over, they began to mutter about favoritism, saying that this was India and Indians should have first chance. It was always the Europeans who got everything. The Indian was always pushed into the background. They muttered about revolt and gave him fierce looks of impotent anger, until Ransome, in exhaustion and half-hysterical rage, shouted, "Get out! All of you! Get out or I'll have the Sikhs throw you out! You're the last to want us to go. You fought Gandhi. You fought poor Jobnekar. If we went, then there would be revolution and you might lose a few rupees. Get out! All of you!"

Cowed, they went outside, but they did not go away. They remained mumbling and chattering to each other in the shelter of the Great Gateway.

While he had shouted at them, the Muslim pilot, descendant of Baber and Genghis Khan and Akbar, stood in the corner of the room, a cigarette hanging from his mouth beneath the jaunty little mustache.

There was a grin on his face, a grin that was immensely eloquent. When only Gopal Rao and the pilot and Ransome were left in the room, the pilot, still grinning, said, "When one Muslim shouts, ten Hindus tremble."

And Gopal Rao rose from the table, his eyes burning and black. The Muslim still grinned, but he said, "Except Mahrattas and maybe Sikhs and Rajputs."

Rao sat down again, but he said, "There have been times when one Mahratta war cry crumbled a whole empire."

"It is always there," thought Ransome, "just beneath the surface."

Gopal Rao said, "Anyway, they're only Bunyas, those dogs out there . . . Bunyas and Gujerati and Parsees."

The black eyes of the Muslim flyer narrowed to slits and he said, "Yes, the future rests with you and me, my friend."

But the Bunyas were not the only ones who tried to flee in terror from the stricken city. While they waited for Bates to arrive from the Mission, Colonel Ranjit Singh appeared with fresh stories. The citizens of Ranchipur City had begun to flee into the districts and the villages. What remained of his Sikhs had not only the wells to guard; they had to surround the city as well, because the Maharani would not have disease carried into the villages and the districts and down to the sea. It was enough that the city itself should be stricken. There was no need to decimate a whole state and carry disease beyond its borders into the rest of India. The panic had seized the whole city, sweeping over it like a flame. Whole families tried to migrate, with all their belongings. There had been rioting and seven men had been shot when they tried to break through and run for it.

"It was the Maharani's orders," he said, and added, grimly, "They are all dead. They'll make no more work for the Major at the hospital."

Ransome said nothing, but he had suddenly a bitter vision of Ranjit Singh's men making sure with an extra bullet that the rioters were dead. But life was cheap in India. Living millions sprang somehow from the dead millions, like fungus from rotten wood.

Food was on its way. Millet and wheat and rice were being brought in from the villages and the sea. Raschid had seen to that. The bullock carts came to within five miles of the city over the mired roads. There, at depots, they deposited the grain, where it was picked up again by coolies and bullock carts from the city. The Major had said that the pest hole must be kept isolated, and Raschid with his Mahratta police and Ranjit Singh with his Sikhs were carrying out his orders. It was the new India fighting against the old, the India which had taken the best from the West, battling the old swarming India which migrated in panic before famine and disease. It was a new idea for India—that the few must suffer for the good of many. It was a lesson that even the cowering, muttering merchants and the superstitious Mr. Bannerjee and the other merchants and the priests of all India would have to learn.

Then Colonel Ranjit Singh went away and a messenger appeared with a note from Miss MacDaid. They needed stimulants desperately at the hospital. She called upon him, she wrote, because he probably had the only brandy and whisky still available in Ranchipur. Could he send her what he had?

Quickly he wrote a note to John the Baptist in French, telling him to send everything in the cellar to Miss MacDaid. There were perhaps a couple of dozen bottles. Then he took a key from his pocket and gave it to the messenger along with the note, and sped him on his way. He saw him go not without regret. For four days he had had nothing to drink and now and then there had been moments when his whole body had cried out for a drink, just one small drink. Well, it was gone now, all of it, his good French brandy, to be poured down the throats of sweepers and low-caste Gujerati who would never know the joy, the peace, the blind contentment it could bring. They would only cough and choke when it burned their palates and, if they had strength enough, spit it out in protest.

Bates arrived when the afternoon was well along, carried on a shutter from the Mission by four coolies. He was feverish and dressed again in his valet's clothes. They looked a little more respectable now. Part of the delay had been caused by Aunt Phoebe, who insisted on cleaning them as far as was possible. He could not, she said, arrive in Bombay looking as if he had come from a pig-sty. Doctor Pindar examined him. He had pleurisy and he was feverish, but he could make the journey well wrapped in blankets. If they permitted him to land in Bombay they would no doubt place him in an isolation hospital until it was certain that he was not suffering from cholera or plague. Doctor Pindar had thought it foolish to send him away under the circumstances, but Bates was set on going and Lady Esketh kept insisting almost hysterically that he should go, and so little Doctor Pindar had yielded.

They were ready to leave now and set out for the plane in the millet field beyond the Tower of Silence—the pilot, Ransome, Bates and the doctor. Bringing up the end of the procession came the Parsees, the Bunyas, and Mr. Bannerjee with his father's ashes, all still hopeful, perhaps, that Bates would die on the way and that there would be a place in the plane for one of them. They still grumbled and muttered as they walked through the mud. On the shutter Bates lay feverish, scarcely seeing the ruined houses and the great heaps of ashes where the dead had been burned. He was going home, back to Manchester, to the semi-detached villa where his spinster sister would keep house for him. He was going to leave this bloody awful country forever. He was going home to greens and boiled mutton and the racing-sheets and cricket scores, to the corner pub and the *Evening News*. He did not think at all of Her Ladyship left behind in a desolate, pest-ridden city. Her Ladyship, he knew from long years of experience, was capable of looking out for herself, more capable even than His Lordship had ever been. And at the hospital she had leaned over him and said in a fierce whisper, "It's all right, Bates. I want you to go. Don't let them keep you here. I want you to go. I've Mr. Ransome to look out for me." Not that he cared a damn what happened to her with all her money and everything! Except that she was a sport in her way. Probably she never suspected that the old bastard had known all along about her lovers. Now she'd know when she opened the box and found the list written in the old bastard's handwriting. But she'd never know how much His Lordship paid for each name. She'd never know how much he, Bates, had made out of her and her love-affairs. He was lucky that she wanted to get him out of the way so she could have a free hand with this fellow Ransome walking there beside him. Anyway, Ransome was better than some of the others she'd had. He might be a cad, but at least he had the manners of a gentleman.

He was lucky because he was going to Paradise—back to Manchester

[459]

among decent, moral people who weren't rich and powerful. He closed his eyes and set his teeth against the jolting of the shutter. Each time the coolies took a step, a knife stabbed him in the chest.

But when they came to the field there was no hope of starting the plane. The pilot turned the motors, but the wheels were sunk deep in the mud; so Gopal Rao took charge and commandeered men out of the curious crowd which had gathered, and they dragged it as far as the metaled road which ran straight as an arrow toward where the great dam had once been. Then as they were about to start, a messenger came running up with a letter which he delivered to the pilot. It was from Lady Esketh, addressed to Lord Esketh's secretary in Bombay, telling him she meant to stay in Ranchipur and commending Bates to his care. There were also instructions to cable to the relatives of the two maids, Harris and Elsie—to Harris' brother in Nottingham and Elsie's sister in Putney. Their bodies had been burned like His Lordship's, but she would see to it that the ashes reached them as soon as possible, so that Harris and Elsie might sleep among their families at home.

Then the plane started, roaring up the straight, long road and shortly vanished into the low clouds that hung above the white temples of Mount Abana. The Bunyas, the Parsees, and Mr. Bannerjee, still carrying the ashes, looked after it until it disappeared and then turned back grumbling, toward the city, past the rim of black vultures on the Tower of Silence. There was no way now to escape, save by bullock cart and the bribery of the Sikh sentinels.

At the bazaar Ransome left the little procession to go to the hospital. He was exhausted now. Sleep dogged his eyes and as he walked he stumbled where there were no obstacles at all. But before he slept he had to see Fern, to discover if everything was going well with her, for in his tired brain there was born the obsession that he must care for her now until she could escape from this dying city and return to America and the easy, healthy life which was her birthright. In the two days since she had wakened him there on the floor of Mr. Bannerjee's bedroom he had managed somehow to think it all out. He knew now what had to be done. She would go home to America, and he would stay

[460]

behind here in Ranchipur, perhaps to die at last in the old yellow Georgian house covered with scarlet creepers.

On the doorstep he met the Major, restored by his few hours of sleep, and the dead Maharajah's nurse, setting out for the half-ruined Music School where Harry Bauer was to be put in charge of the sick who lay in long rows on the floor. And in the hallway he met Edwina and told her that the plane had gone, carrying Bates on the first step of his long journey homeward.

She seemed excited. There was a new light in the blue eyes, and she said, "Now I can tell you about Miss Hodge."

Wearily he asked, "What about Miss Hodge?"

"What she wanted me to tell you. She thinks she was raped by the Sikh who rescued her."

Anger thrust back the weariness which dragged at him. "Ridiculous! The old fool!"

"She's afraid she's going to have a baby." There was a twinkle in the blue eyes. "Sometimes she cried about it like a young girl. But most of the time she sits groaning to herself. I think on the whole she's pleased with the idea."

"Where is she now?"

"In there, holding a slop-pail for me."

Wearily he pressed his hand to his eyes, "Don't let her tell that story about everywhere. It could make trouble."

"I'll tell her it's to be a secret just between us two."

"That's right." After a moment he asked, "What are we going to do about her?"

"I'll take care of her. Don't worry about that. She'll do anything I say."

"She must be a nuisance."

"No, I get a lot of work out of her. And her stomach is stronger than mine. She holds the pail and soap while I go out to be sick." She took both of his hands and said, "This is a hell of a country. Everybody in it is potty, but I'm beginning to understand about it. I'm beginning to understand about Shiva and his little dingus. It's even got Miss Hodge."

Then she went back into the ward where Miss Hodge sat patiently with a silly grin on her face, holding the basin and soap and cotton towels.

He stood for a moment, bewildered, rocking on his feet. Edwina, the fragile, the porcelain, was becoming a war-horse like Miss MacDaid.

He found Fern in the room she shared with Edwina and Miss Hodge. She had just changed her blue cotton uniform and was running a brush through her short blonde hair before a broken bit of mirror she had found somewhere. At the sound of his footsteps at the doorway she turned, and then came quickly toward him, but when she neared the doorway she turned shy and blushed so that he had to put out his arms and hold her to him. For a long time they stood there in silence, her head on his shoulder. Then looking up at him she said, "You look awfully tired."

"I am. Let's sit down."

So together they sat on one of the rope beds. She still held one of his hands and asked, "What's the matter?"

"Nothing. Why?"

Then suddenly she couldn't tell him why—that she had felt a difference in him, as if he had withdrawn somehow to a distance, as if a shadow had come across the intimacy between them. In her simplicity she was aware of how complicated he was, and she could think of no words to make him understand.

He asked, smiling at her, "Are you all right?"

"Yes, I'm fine."

"Have you had some sleep?"

"Yes."

"Don't you think you'd better go back to the Mission?"

"No. . . . I'm perfectly happy." Her face brightened. "Even Miss Mac-Daid says I'm a help." Then she looked at him and saw that his eyes were closed. "You could sleep here," she said.

"No, I'll go back." But the world was swinging away from him. The walls of the room retreated, grew hazy, and then vanished. From a great distance he heard Fern's voice saying, "There. That's right. Now go to sleep." And then the voice was gone and the room, the city, everything, and there was only silence and oblivion and peace.

For a long time, until she knew that she must leave him and go to Miss MacDaid, she sat on the end of the bed, looking down on him, a little frightened because his sleep was so profound that it was as if he were dead. And her heart was sad because it seemed to her that he had in some way slipped away from her back into that world which had existed before the disaster, the world which had made her miserable with its cliques and snobbery and smallness and the complications which were beyond her understanding. This new world, even with its misery and horror, she liked much better because it was direct and simple and she could see and understand and get on with the business of living.

As she sat there one thing became clear to her—that she had above all else to save him, not from that old wretched world which one day was certain to return, nor even from people like Lady Esketh, but from himself. It was that perverse, puzzling self which was his enemy. For a little while, after the waking in Mr. Bannerjee's house, she had been able to drive it off. If she were to save him, she must drive it off again and again.

At last, afraid that Miss MacDaid would think her a slacker and send her back to the Mission and her mother, she left him.

She found Miss MacDaid in her office. The tyrant looked at her sharply and asked, "Have you had enough?"

But Fern was not to be terrified or bullied. Boldly she asked, "Enough of what?"

"Enough of scrubbing and filth and hard work?"

"No," said Fern. "I hadn't even thought about it."

"You're willing to go on?"

"Yes."

"And you know the risks?"

"Yes."

"That you may get cholera or typhus or typhoid?"

"Yes."

"You know you'll be able to go away one of these days to Bombay. You might as well go to the Mission and be safe till then."

"The Mission is the last place I want to go. I want to be of use. I'm going to stay till the end, till things are in order again."

She said this so stubbornly and with such a will that for a moment Miss MacDaid was reduced to silence, her worn leathery face filled with astonishment. She had thought this girl a silly adolescent fool; that she had been apparently wrong in her judgment upset her.

Abruptly she asked, "Why?"

But Fern was not caught. She would not say, "Because I will not go

[463]

away so long as Ransome stays here." She said, "I don't know why. I just want to stay." And in Miss MacDaid's mind an idea was born. Greedily she thought, "Maybe she will make a good recruit. Maybe she'll take to the work and stay on. Maybe she'll carry it on."

Aloud she said, "I've a job for you. Have you ever cleaned house?"

"Yes."

"Properly, I mean. Scrubbing in corners, disinfecting, seeing that everything is spotless."

"Yes," said Fern. It wasn't quite true. Her mother had always been a bad housekeeper. With a dozen Mission Bhils to work for her, house-cleaning had been as often as not no more than a lick and a promise. And she had taught her daughters nothing save that they must marry one of The Boys.

Miss MacDaid, thinking of Mrs. Simon, looked at her dubiously. "I mean hospital cleanliness."

"Yes, I could do it."

"I'm sending Harry Bauer to take over what's left of the Music School. You can superintend cleaning it up and keeping it clean. You'll have a half-dozen sweeper women—if they don't run away. Can you speak Gujerati?"

"A few words. I can learn. I can show them if they don't understand me."

"It's a pity you've never learned. You've lived here all your life."

Fern did not answer because there was no answer to make. She only had a quick vision of herself as she had been long ago, centuries ago, The Pearl of the Orient, reading cinema magazines and sulking. A slow flush crept over her face partly in rising anger at the flat-footed Miss MacDaid, partly in shame for herself.

"I'll go over there with you and get you started," said Miss MacDaid. "You'd better fetch whatever you have to take with you. You'll be staying there from now on." She looked sharply at the girl, "You understand, I'm showing great confidence in you?"

"Yes," said Fern, "I understand." But she wanted to cry out, "Let me stay here until he wakes and I can talk to him. I must bring him back. I must save him." But that, she knew, would be to Miss MacDaid the silliest of reasons.

Quickly she left Miss MacDaid and went to the room where Ransome lay asleep. He lay as she had left him, with one arm thrown over his head. His paleness shocked and frightened her. She thought, wildly, "I might never see him again. One of us might die." You could die like that of cholera, suddenly dropping on the street. Then she was ashamed of herself for being melodramatic, and set about collecting the few things she had to take with her—his shorts and tennis shirt, an extra student nurse's costume, a bit of candle, some damp matches, the toothbrush Miss MacDaid had given her, and the roll of gauze she had for bathing and disinfecting. Last of all she took down from the shelf over Lady Esketh's bed the piece of broken mirror which they had shared. Striking it sharply against the sill of the window, she broke it in two and took the smaller piece, thinking, "That will be enough for her."

The sound of breaking glass had no effect on Ransome. Wickedly she had hoped that the sound would waken him so that she might say good-by, but he still lay as if dead, breathing slowly and heavily. And she thought, "When he wakes she will be here instead of me"—Lady Esketh who would drag him back, back into his old self, remote from her and strange, into that distant world which she had never known, from which she was shut out.

She wanted to cry, but managed to check the tears and, bending down, she kissed him on the forehead. But the touch of her lips had no more effect than the breaking of the mirror; she had hoped, too, that the kiss might waken him.

So, gathering up her belongings, she left the room and went back to Miss MacDaid to say, "I am ready now."

Together they set out along the Great Tank. It was evening now, near to that moment when the darkness came down suddenly. Part of the wall of the ancient tank had fallen in, and beyond it, on the wide, shallow steps, low-caste women were gathering together their washing. The great bats from the dead city of El-Kautara had returned and were sweeping back and forth above the water. There was no longer any din from the Music School nor any lights before the cinema to confuse them. At that hour, in the quick twilight, everything was still, with the stillness of death.

As she walked beside Miss MacDaid, neither of them spoke. She had to hurry to keep up with the tireless stride of the Scotswoman. And then just as they neared the end of the tank, a terrifying thought came to her.

She had broken a mirror, and that would bring bad luck. Quickly she told herself that she had broken it deliberately and not by accident, and that therefore the curse would not hold, but just as quickly she thought, "That might make it worse, to have done it on purpose." And the bit of broken glass became an unbearable thing. It seemed to burn her hand. Slyly she slipped a little behind Miss MacDaid, and making sure that her companion was not looking, she threw the bit of mirror into the Tank. Somewhere she had heard it said, "You must throw the pieces into water."

In the stillness the mirror striking the water made a faint "plop" and quickly Miss MacDaid turned and asked, "What was that?"

"I don't know," said Fern. "Perhaps a fish."

For a couple of hours Ransome slept like a dead man. Then, troubled by fits of returning consciousness, he dreamt wildly, even struggling in his heavy sleep like a man in delirium. One part of his mind kept dragging at him, crying out, "Wake up! There is work to do! People are depending on you!" Another kept pulling him backward into the pit of oblivion where he had been immersed for a little time in peace and nothingness. And the struggle was confused by strange visions and nightmares of Shiva and his "dingus," of swarming things, of dead people, of pestilence and death. Once Esketh himself appeared wrapped in the "bloody cerements of the dead," only the cerements were the pink sheets of his wife with her monogram interwoven with the symbol of Shiva across the stomach of the dead man.

Then at last the conscious mind won the victory and he wakened, slowly, bewildered. It was dark, and outside the awful rain was coming down in torrents, and by the dim light of a stub of a candle he made out the figures of Miss Hodge and Edwina. Edwina had placed the candle near the piece of broken mirror and was doing something with her hair. Slowly he discovered that she was winding the ends of her short blonde hair about bits of the *Times of India* which lay beside her on the bed. As he lay, bathed in sweat, he watched her with his eyes half closed, fascinated by the precision and skill with which she went about the task. She would tear off a bit of paper, twist it into the proper shape, and then wind the blonde hair about it and fasten it with a hairpin. He thought: "Where on earth did she get hair pins? Perhaps from Miss MacDaid. She must then be on better terms with the old girl." And he thought, too, "It is not for me she is taking this trouble." With each new curl paper adjusted, her head, once so smooth and shiny and perfect, grew more and more grotesque, like the head of a charwoman on Saturday night. Very likely she had learned the trick long ago when she was poor, when even the price of metal hair-curlers had been a debatable item in the budget of her father. And then he thought suddenly, for the first time, that with Esketh dead, she must be one of the richest women in the world.

By the dim light of the candle stub he could make out the reflection of her face in the discolored mirror. It was weary and there were blue circles in the delicate skin beneath the blue eyes. She worked with extraordinary concentration, bending down a little so that she could obtain a full view of her head in the mirror.

Opposite her Miss Hodge sat on the edge of her bed, her hands folded in her lap, staring into space, with a happy expression of utter vacancy in her pudgy face. There was something peaceful, almost domestic, in the little scene. He thought, "It's better for poor Miss Hodge that she's gone potty. She's happy now." It was extraordinary that she could have forgotten so quickly and completely the existence of Miss Dirks at whose side she had spent her whole life. Drowsily, watching her out of the shadows, he thought, "Perhaps all those years she was oppressed. Perhaps during all those years she had to pretend that she was somebody else." You couldn't live near poor Miss Dirks with her granite face written over with Duty. You would have to be suppressed or run away. Perhaps all those years poor Miss Hodge had wanted another kind of life.

As he watched her her lips began to move and she began to talk, "So the Bishop said to me, 'My dear Miss Hodge. That must have been an extraordinary experience. And you made yourself a martyr. I've no doubt that you'll be decorated.' And he said, 'A second Florence Nightingale, that's what you are.' And I said, 'But what I did during the disaster was nothing compared to my friend Edwina Esketh. I held the slop-basin while she went outside to vomit.' Then the Duchess came up and said,

Vomit! Oh dear, that reminds me of when I was carrying Penelope—that's my youngest daughter.' And I said, 'I know about that! That time the Sikh attacked me . . . against my will, mind you, but afterwards I didn't mind so much.' And the Bishop said, 'My dear woman, what experiences you have had. Certainly I shall speak to the Archbishop, who no doubt will speak to the King about a decoration. Attacked by a Sikh! Think of that, Duchess!' And the Duchess said, 'Well, as I've always told the Duke, I'm one for taking everything in my stride.'"

Then Miss Hodge looked up and smiled at some figure she alone could see, and said, "Wasn't that wonderful of the Duchess, Sarah . . . putting me at my ease like that?"

Ransome listened, fascinated, but the monologue came to an end as Miss Hodge's voice fell into nothing. She looked down at her folded hands again, smiling her crazy smile, and Ransome thought, "Perhaps she doesn't know Miss Dirks is dead. Perhaps her mind won't accept the fact."

Edwina went on with the business of her curls, never even glancing over her shoulder at poor Miss Hodge. For a second Ransome thought, "Maybe I've gone potty, too. Maybe Miss Hodge isn't talking at all. Maybe I'm only imagining it. A drink is what I need. A drink will pull me together. That's why I slept so badly—because I needed a drink." You couldn't cut off alcohol just like that, sharply, especially when you'd been used to a bottle or more a day.

Then Edwina finished her task and as she turned, he swung himself upward in a single movement, and sat on the edge of the bed.

He said, "Well?"

And Edwina, as if there was nothing extraordinary about the appearance of her head, asked, "Do you want a drink? I know where it is. I could steal it for you."

"No." For a second his whole body cried out against his will. He began to tremble. Then he said, "No, one drink wouldn't be any good. It would only make it worse."

"Fern stole half the mirror. It's bad luck to break a mirror."

"Where is she?"

"Gone to the Music School to help that Swiss nurse."

[468]

"They shouldn't have sent her there. That's where the cholera is."

"She wanted to go. I must say your girl friend has guts."

"It's funny how many people have when there's need of guts." He indicated Miss Hodge with a nod of his head. "Did you hear all that?"

"Yes. She talks like that part of the time."

"Does she think Miss Dirks is still alive?"

Edwina nodded, but the name had penetrated the reverie into which Miss Hodge had fallen. Looking up, Miss Hodge said, "Miss Dirks! She's gone to the High School to look after the new books that came from home. She'll be back before long. You can always count on her." Then for the first time she recognized Ransome and said, "We were so sorry about the tea party on Friday, but we had to entertain Lady Esketh. You see, she's a great friend of mine. I couldn't well put her off like."

"That's all right. I understood," said Ransome. "We'll have it another time . . . next week, perhaps."

Then smiling, with the look of a hostess who had successfully re-arranged her engagements, Miss Hodge returned to her reverie.

"Have you got a comb?" Ransome asked Edwina. "I feel that my hair is standing on end."

"It is," said Edwina, and gave him the piece of broken comb that lay beside the mirror.

"The plane is coming back tomorrow or day after," he said as he regarded himself in the mirror. "You've made up your mind about staying on?" Through the speech he felt a sudden shock at his appearance. The dark eyes seemed twice their usual size. The face was yellow.

"I'm going to stay," she smiled. "I'm being a success. Even with Miss MacDaid. She loaned me her hairpins." Then she said, "Why does she hate me so much?"

"One reason is that she hates everything you represent. The other reason you might guess."

"I have, but I haven't bothered him. I haven't even seen him."

"Better not. He's the white-headed boy of the old girl." He put down the comb and set his jacket straight, as if he were going out to dinner. "Now I'll be off."

"Where are you going?"

"What time is it?"

"I don't know, exactly. About nine o'clock—not far off it."

"I'll go to the Maharani's pavilion and stop at the Music School on the way."

She was silent for a moment. Then she said, "I was too tired to sleep last night. I lay awake for a long time thinking, and an idea came to me."

"What?"

"That you and I might get married."

He grinned, "Well, that is an idea. It's occurred to me once or twice."

"I'm a very rich woman now."

"He might have left his money elsewhere."

"He didn't. I've got the will. It's at the Mission. I've got at least a couple of million pounds."

"So what?"

"So what! I don't know what in hell to do with it."

"I'll think over your offer."

"Well, funnier things could happen." She looked up at him. "I suppose you're wondering if I'd behave myself."

"The thought did occur to me. I suppose it's only natural."

"Well, I would. At least, I think I would."

"You could do worse than marry me."

"Oh, I know that. I've thought it all out."

Then he saw that she was regarding him too sharply. She was watching him. She wanted to find out about Fern.

"Anyway, we can decide when we're out of this mess. It isn't as if we were twenty and burning to climb into bed."

She smiled, a little sadly he thought. "No," she said, "it certainly isn't."

Then he went away, saying that he would see her when he found time to come to the hospital.

When he had gone she had to persuade Miss Hodge to undress and lie down on the bed, for Miss Hodge had become attached to the idea that she would sit up and wait for Miss Dirks to return from the High School.

"I always sit up for her. We always sit up for each other," she said.

[470]

"She'd understand your going to bed tonight after all the work you've done today. She'll be very cross with me if she finds I've let you stay up."

"All right," said Miss Hodge. "I wouldn't want her to be cross with you. She's terrible—Sarah—when she's cross." She began to take off the blue uniform. "She was cross with me on account of the tea party. Do you know what she called me?"

"No," said Edwina. "What?"

"A boot-licker. And it was all on account of you."

She was started now and she went on talking. She talked and talked, telling Edwina bits of her own history and the history of Sarah Dirks. After Edwina had extinguished the precious candle and lay on the hard bed, she went on talking in the darkness. The history wasn't very interesting, a mass of tiny details, of petty quarrels and incidents. But presently, in the darkness against the sound of the monsoon rain, Edwina heard her telling the story of what had happened at Heathedge School, long ago. She told it simply, the jealousy of other teachers, the gossip, the stories, the unhappiness, not even now, nearly thirty years afterward, understanding what it was that had happened or why they had been asked to leave. She had simply followed Miss Dirks, here to Ranchipur, to the ends of the earth.

And Edwina, too weary to fall asleep, found herself listening, as if it were a child instead of poor old crazy Miss Hodge who was talking, a child telling her not the story of the wickedness born of stifled, unnatural emotions in the breasts of a dozen middle-aged spinsters in a Non-Conformist school in England, but the story of some barbaric cruelty practised by children in a schoolyard.

She listened with a kind of wonder, and presently she heard Miss Hodge, in a child-like voice, asking, "Do you understand, Lady Esketh? What was it we did that was wrong? Why did they send us away? Sarah would never talk of it. She always said I wouldn't understand."

From the other bed Edwina answered, "Yes, I understand. Those other women were wicked. They persecuted you both. But it wasn't their fault. It was because their lives were so mean and small and they had been taught evil by people who professed to be Christian. You mustn't blame Miss Dirks. She was quite right in going away and coming out here."

"Oh, I'm sure Sarah was right. She always is. Only she is so dreadfully proud—too proud I sometimes think. When she comes in I'll talk to her about it all. I'm sure she wouldn't mind now."

"But you'd better go to sleep now," said Edwina. "And when she comes in I'll wake you and you can talk to her."

"You promise?"

"I promise."

Then she was still and Edwina presently heard the sound of her heavy breathing, but she herself lay awake, considering the story and the character of Miss Dirks, who had been created again in poor Miss Hodge's rambling narrative. For a little time she had risen from the dead, so that Edwina saw her almost as if she were alive, grim and dutiful and in her heart sentimental, shouldering the misery of others without any glory, without even a conscious sense of martyrdom, because that was the way she was born. She understood, too, the long exile and the homesickness for the green land of England, and the pride that was in Miss Dirks, forbidding her to fight back, and the meanness and perverted malice in that little group of Non-Conformist old maids at Heathedge School.

She felt a quick astonishment and pity for the bleak lives of the two old maids, and a wonder at their devotion, but most of all a wonder at how dreadful and cramped the lives of people could be. Herself, she had always been free, a child of light who had been given everything, above and aloof from the meager false teachings of priests and evangelists. They had never touched her because they had never had the power, but they had perverted the lives of poor Miss Hodge and Miss Dirks, and the lives of the poor barren virgins who had taught at Heathedge School, shunning men, never rolling in the shadow of a hedge on a moonlight night with some clerk or plow-boy, never being what God meant them to be—women to love and be loved.

"No," she thought, "even my own slut's life is more normal, is better than that. Even Shiva and his dingus is better than the chastity and barrenness of the Christian Church."

The story of poor Miss Hodge made her feel faintly sick. The only things was that it did not matter now to Miss Hodge. The poor, crazy old thing was happy, and somehow she must be kept happy, even if she herself had to care for her, to have her tagging around after her for the rest of her life. Miss Hodge had a little happiness coming to her, even if it was born of madness which had no reality.

As Ransome passed the little office of the Major the door was open and light shone out from it. Thinking he would say good-night to his friend, he thrust his head in the door; but once the Major had seen him he would not let him go. Considering that he had had scarcely any sleep and had been working without rest for days, he looked strong and well, with an air of satisfaction about him.

He said, "Sit down and talk to me for a moment."

So Ransome sat down, and the first thing the Major asked was, "Do you want a drink? Because if you do I can get it for you. It's your own stuff."

"No, thanks."

"You mustn't be a bloody fool about it. I know how you must feel to have it shut off like that, suddenly. You're shaking right now."

"I don't need it," said Ransome. "I don't want it."

"Very well," said the Major. "If you want it let me know."

"I will."

He was ashamed for the first time of his drinking, for it was only now, during the last twenty-four hours, that he had come to understand how bad it had been, that he had really been a drunkard and that the Major knew it and Miss MacDaid and perhaps even Raschid and the Smileys and even Fern. The knowledge made him ashamed because he saw that all along for months, perhaps ever since they had known him, they had been humoring him, as they might a child, because they were fond of him. They had been generous and kindly even at moments when he must have been a bore and quarrelsome. And he thought, "The only way I can stop is stop—suddenly like that. God or somebody has given me the chance. It's up to me to take it."

"Things are better," the Major said.

"How?"

"The organizing has worked. Everybody has done his job. Everybody has worked side by side now to the last of the Sikhs and policemen. I never thought it would happen."

"And the cholera?"

"That'll go on till it wears itself out. All we can do is fight, but that doesn't matter. It's the other thing that matters—the spirit." He clapped a hand on Ransome's shaking knee. "It's the spirit," he said, "the new spirit. It works! Do you realize, man, what we're going through? Do you realize that Muslim and Hindu, European and Mahratta and Sikh, Gujerati and Sweeper, have all been working together for the common good?"

"It's true," said Ransome. "I hadn't thought of it."

"It's because you're not an Indian. It's because you couldn't understand what's to be overcome. You can't imagine what a disaster like this would have been twenty-five years ago in Ranchipur. Then it would have been the Bannerjees and the Bunyas and the priests who would have won, defeating us. It's the old gentleman we have to thank first of all. He fought for fifty years, until he died."

He went on talking, a little wildly in his satisfaction. They had succeeded in sealing the wells. They had brought food from the districts. They had kept the terrified from escaping to spread cholera into the remote villages, perhaps even into the rest of India. There were already men working to restore the tracks of the railway, working even now in the monsoon rains by the light of great fires.

Then Miss MacDaid came in, and in her tired horse-like face he discovered the same light of victory. Moved profoundly at sight of her, he thought, "It's only fair that she should have such a reward."

This was her East which she loved, being born again. It was true. They had helped to prove it—no one could say again that Indians quarreled among themselves, that they had grown panicky and hopeless in the face of disaster. He felt suddenly that he must go away quickly, leaving the two of them alone, that there was something indecent about his presence, because he had done nothing at all. Yet the same joy brushed him closely, as it had for a moment two days before when he stood before the Maharani and the Major pressed his hand.

"But it's not over yet," the realistic Scotswoman said. "It's only just begun."

As Ransome rose to go the Major said, "Have you seen Lady Esketh?"

"Yes."

"Does she still want to stay?"

"Yes. She's determined to stay."

The Major was silent for a moment, looking at Ransome as if there was something he wanted to say but was not sure that their friendship was intimate enough to bear the strain. It was Miss MacDaid who plunged. "Why?" she asked. "I mean, really why."

For a second he hesitated, considering, and then said, "I really don't know." He might have a great many ideas, among them even the idea that she wanted to stay in the wild hope of having a love-affair with the Major himself. But he was no longer certain of that, even if he had dared to say it. "I don't know. She's a very extraordinary woman. Quite honestly, has she been useful?"

It was Miss MacDaid who answered him. "Yes," she said, "she has. She's not stupid."

"No, she's never been stupid."

Then he went away, out into the rain, feeling lonely and oddly envious of the two of them, left behind in their satisfaction in the Major's office.

Twice on his way to the Music School he was challenged by tall Sikhs guarding wells. Twice, as they recognized him, they presented arms as if he were an important functionary. Half-way along the Tank the faint hot breeze which sprang up as the rain stopped for a time, brought toward him from the ruined silhouette of the School, a faint, sweet, sickish odor, not the smell of death now, but the odor of cholera. It was a smell he had never known before, and now it seemed more horrible to him than the smell even of burning flesh; this new smell was the odor of life in death. Near the end of the Great Tank he came suddenly upon a troop of Sweepers. They were carrying out of the School the bodies of those who had died during the day and heaping them in the fitful moonlight on a great pyre near the Rama Temple. Turning away his head, he passed quickly through the cracked arch of the main entrance to the School.

It was dark inside, and the hallway which had once resounded to the clamor of a hundred drums and zithers and melodeons was silent, but there was still the horrible smell of cholera. Beyond the doorway the dead lay in rows on the floor, waiting to be carried out and burned. There were no longer any protests from priests or mullahs or relatives. It had

[475]

got beyond all that; bodies were burned now, willy-nilly, Parsees, Muslims, Hindus, Sweepers, all in one great heap.

As he walked along the main corridor toward the little theater where Jemnaz Singh, in his turban and *atchkan* of purple and candy pink and poison green, had once sung for him, he wondered that with all these dead and dying about, the Major and Miss MacDaid could feel triumphant, and then he understood that to them these bodies were nothing; it was the spirit of these people they were trying to save, for it was their spirits which made up the spirit of India and of all the East.

Then just before him he saw a faint light in a doorway, and turning, he came upon Harry Bauer. The ex-swimming-teacher had taken this little room for his own and contrived a hard bed from the school benches. He was dressed all in white, and as he turned toward the door the sight of him with his pale skin and blue eyes and blond hair gave Ransome a sudden shock. In the midst of all the misery and filth, among all the dark people, in the confusion and cruelty of India, he seemed, in the dim light of the candle, incredibly clean and young and pure. He thought, suddenly, "Like the victim made ready for the sacrifice."

"*Bon jour*," he said in his Swiss French. "*Entrez*."

Ransome had seen the nurse before, distantly, but had never spoken to him. The Swiss produced a miraculous packet of cigarettes and said, "Will you have one?"

Next to a drink, it was the thing Ransome had wanted most for days. He said, "You're lucky to have them."

"I've a lot of them. You can have a packet if you like." And from under the bed he produced a neat square box containing shaving-things, a toothbrush, a towel, a pack of soiled cards, textbooks on gymnastics, and a dozen packages of cheap cigarettes. He held the candle for Ransome to get a light. Then Ransome said, "Is there anything you want?"

Harry Bauer grinned. "Everything. There isn't anything."

"We'll do our best for you. The plane is supposed to be bringing supplies tomorrow."

"There isn't much you need or much you can do for cholera. . . ."

"No." Suddenly he was seized by a panic. He wanted to ask where Fern was, and did not dare. She might be stricken herself. She might be dead. He began to shake, ashamed that the Swiss should see him thus, hoping that he would not notice it. But Harry Bauer said, "Have you got a fever?"

"No. It's nothing."

"I can give you a gin and tonic. It's good for that sort of thing."

His whole body cried out, but he managed to say, "No, I'll be all right." And then, swiftly, "Where is Miss Simon?"

"She's down the hall, at the very end. She's in charge for the moment."

"I'll go and see her," said Ransome. "Thanks for the cigarettes and the offer of a drink."

"*Rien de tout,*" said Harry Bauer.

As Ransome walked along the hall he thought, "That Swiss knows how to take care of himself." Of them all, he seemed the best organized, with his cigarettes and gin and tonic and books and soiled playing-cards. He no longer appeared the poor victim arrayed for sacrifice, clean and antiseptic and immune, but a wise and sturdy peasant looking out for his own comfort.

Halfway down the hall, he stepped aside while coolies carried the body of a woman out of a classroom. The awful smell had got to him now, through every resistance. Suddenly he leaned against the wall and was sick. When he had recovered he reached the room at the end of the hall, where he found Fern sitting bolt upright on a bed made of benches. She looked white and tired, and at sight of him she began to cry, quite silently, the tears running down her face. Sitting down beside her he put his arm about her and drew her close to him.

"Go on," he said, "cry. It'll make you feel better."

"It's not because I'm afraid," she said. "It's because it's so awful. It's so awful because you can't do anything. They go on dying and dying. I don't mind the work or the smell; I don't mind anything but that. Honestly I don't. I'm not afraid."

He pressed her cheek against him, thinking, "No, I must never leave her—never." And said, "You're a swell kid. You shouldn't be here. You ought to go back to the Mission."

"No, I can't do that. I don't want to do that. I couldn't sit there doing nothing." She had stopped crying and lay now in his arms quite still, like a child. "I'll be all right now," she said. "Only I get so lonely sometimes. It's so good to have you back for a moment." Then she was silent, and

[477]

presently she said, in a low soft voice, "Don't leave me, Tom. Don't go away and leave me."

"I'll stay as long as I can, my dear."

"I don't mean that. I mean to go away from me in your spirit, the way you did last night."

He knew what she meant, and he divined what it cost her to speak the words, but he was silent.

"I can stand anything if you won't do that." She fumbled for words, for which she had no genius, and presently he helped her, saying, "I know what you mean. I won't leave you again."

"You promise?"

"I promise."

And then she knew that he had come back to her. He was with her as he had been that morning in the Bannerjee's house, as he had been until he said good-by to her at the Mission. She thought, "Now I can talk to him," and she sat up and asked, "Is Lady Esketh all right?"

"Yes. I just left her."

"I like her, you know. It's funny, but I like her."

"I knew you would."

Then the doorway was partly filled by the wan thin figure of Mr. Smiley. Behind him appeared the dark faces of a half-dozen Untouchable boys.

"Hello, Smiley!" said Ransome. "Come in."

"I brought Fern some help," he said. "I've got six of my boys with me. I'm going to leave them. You can use them, can't you?"

Fern stood up and an extraordinary change came over her. "Thanks, Mr. Smiley. We can use them. You know how filthy cholera is. Maybe they won't want to do what has to be done."

"They'll do it. They come of Sweeper families." Then he turned and said, "Come in," in English and the boys trooped awkwardly into the room. They stood staring, a little frightened, with great dark eyes. Mr. Smiley in Gujerati gave instructions to them.

"You're to do whatever the Memsahib asks you to do, no matter what. We have all got to work to clean up the city. I'm trusting you and Memsahib Smiley is trusting you."

One of the boys said, in English, "Yes, Mr. Smiley," and the five others nodded their heads.

"I'll come back tomorrow," said Mr. Smiley. To Fern and Ransome he said, "Good-night. I have to get a bag of rice from Raschid and go back to the Orphanage."

And he went quickly away. Almost like a phantom he seemed, so pale and thin and tired.

Then Ransome said, "I'll go now. I'll come back tomorrow when there's time."

He wanted to take her in his arms and kiss her good-by, but that was impossible with the six Sweeper boys standing there staring at them with their big frightened doe's eyes. So he pressed her hand and said in a low voice, "I won't go away again. I promise."

Outside they had lighted the pyre and in the light of the fire he discovered the straight spare figure and black beard of Colonel Ranjit Singh talking to the Sikh in charge. When he spoke to him Ranjit Singh said, "The worst is past." He looked at the cobalt sky and said, "It's cooler tonight. Maybe the bloody rain will stop for a time."

"I'm on my way to Her Highness. Are you going there?"

"Yes. We'll go together."

When the Colonel had made certain that the fire was well started he turned and said, "Come. Her Highness does not like to wait."

Then as they neared the Tank Ransome noticed a shadow slipping from one to another of the peepul trees that stood by the water. Watching, he saw the shadow turn into the figure of a woman dressed in European clothes.

"Look," he said softly. "Who is that?"

Ranjit Singh stopped, and turning looked after the figure of the woman. She slipped from tree to tree and as she neared the burning pyre she ran quickly across the open space and up the steps of the half-ruined School.

Ranjit Singh said, abruptly, "It's the Russian woman."

"Why should she be going into that pest-house?"

When Ranjit Singh answered there was the echo of grim mirth in his voice: "The nurse is there—His Highness' nurse—the Swiss."

"Oh!" So that was it, thought Ransome. Very likely every Indian in Ranchipur knew of it.

For a little time they walked in silence. Then Ransome said, "Better not speak of it to Her Highness."

"No. Surely not."

But Ransome had a sudden vision of Harry Bauer white and clean, standing in the middle of the candle-lit room. There was something corrupt about the figure of Maria Lishinskaia slipping from tree to tree, shadow to shadow, and in the last hysterical dash into the building by the light of the funeral pyre.

When Ransome had gone, Miss MacDaid and the Major set to work once more organizing supplies and making lists of stuff to be sent for in Bombay when the plane returned with Gopal Rao. And as they worked, the sense of victory faded and slowly fear and despair began to threaten them again, for now, for the first time since the disaster, there was time to succumb to these things. As they checked supplies they discovered that there was little of anything, and of some things, nothing at all. To treat each case of cholera, each case of typhoid, of the ever-present smallpox, was beyond human possibility.

"Doctor Pindar must have sleep," said the Major, suddenly. "He fainted this afternoon at the Music School."

There was no more sodium bicarbonate, no more calcium chloride, only a hundred or so permanganate pills (what were a hundred when they would be needed for a single patient in forty-eight hours?). No more Kaolin. No more aspirin. Not even any more chlorine compound for the infected wells. The plane would bring a supply of most of those things tomorrow but what the plane could bring would be nothing. And even if the supply was sufficient, there was only the Major and Miss MacDaid and Dr. Pindar to administer the palliatives.

"Tomorrow we shall have to teach Fern Simon, Lady Esketh, Mrs. Gupta, and Bauer how to give the necessary treatment. Miss Hodge won't be of any use."

These were small means of helping all those who were already stricken. The only hope was to sterilize and prevent, and for that Ransome and Raschid and Colonel Ranjit Singh were the ones. They themselves had no time.

The plague, luckily, had kept its distance. Since Esketh and the *syces* at the royal stables there were no new cases, perhaps, thought the Major, because the rats had been drowned out.

While they sat there, each bending over his paper, without looking at each other because they dared not risk it, terror began to take possession of them, not the fear and horror which had afflicted them in the midst of the disaster—that was a simple, primitive, natural fear—but a slow horror which Miss MacDaid had not known since the cholera year when poor Miss Eldridge, who came with her from Bombay, had died. This thing they were fighting was insidious and horrible, stronger than themselves, or their once splendid hospital, or the organization they had built up. It crept up behind your back; it attacked you from the side, from ambush. It struck everywhere.

Miss MacDaid said, suddenly, "Her Highness should have gone away in the plane."

"There was never any question of it. I suggested it and was turned down. It was the first time the old lady ever lost her temper with me. She said, 'These are my people. This is where I belong!' "

"Perhaps they'll send other planes with supplies—the Indian Government, I mean."

"Yes, I should think it likely. Raschid thinks the railroad will be passable in two or three days." The Major opened a drawer in his desk and thrust his pile of papers into it. "You'd better go and sleep for a time now. Whose turn is it to watch?"

"Lady Esketh's."

She looked away from him, but she heard him say, "I'll make a round before turning in, to make sure everything is all right."

She started to speak, and then, as if thinking better of it, was silent. Gathering up her papers, she rose and asked, "What time do you think the plane will return?"

"Not much before noon. They can't risk flying by night in monsoon weather."

"Have you seen Homer Smiley?"

"He came in a little after dark. Everything is all right at the Mission, except that Mrs. Hoggett-Egburry had hysterics when she heard that Lady Esketh's servant had a place in the plane and she, the wife of an Imperial

Bank manager, had been left behind. Smiley wants to send both her and Mrs. Simon to Bombay."

"It would be better for everybody."

He knew that the morsel of gossip had brought her relief, pushing away a little for an instant the sense of horror and fear. He felt as he knew she did—the terror of failure. The subject of Mrs. Hoggett-Egburry and Mrs. Simon was always comic to both of them.

"It's poor Aunt Phoebe who has to put up with them."

Miss MacDaid rose, gathered up her papers, and said, "I'll go now and wake Lady Esketh, so that Mrs. Gupta can get some rest. If anything comes up, don't hesitate to call me."

Miss MacDaid was happy again, not triumphant, as she had been for a moment there in the office with the Major and Ransome, but happy in a quiet way, because there was work to do, mountains of it, and because everything depended upon herself and the Major and because she left his little office knowing that she shared with him a kind of intimacy that neither of them gave to anyone else. Even poor fragile Natara Devi, dead now, the bells on her little red *tonga* silenced forever, had never possessed the Major as Miss MacDaid possessed him.

"Natara Devi," thought Miss MacDaid, primly and with satisfaction, "was never more than a body, a piece of flesh beautifully molded and colored, but a machine which gave him satisfaction." Natara Devi, she kept telling herself, had never known him at all. All the way down the dark corridor she kept telling herself that women like Natara Devi and Lady Esketh did not count. They were merely flesh and in them there was no spirit. They were only prostitutes. A wife would have been different. A wife might have known with him the kind of intimacy which she herself knew.

The more she kept telling herself these things the more she was able to stifle the terrifying envy of the poor dead Natara Devi; the more she was able to forget the awful bitter regret that she was not younger and beautiful like the dancing-girl or Lady Esketh.

And she thought, "Now that she has had to come out into the open without all her maids and beauty creams and fine clothes and jewels, he can see that she's just like any other woman. He can see that her good looks were made up out of pots and jars." And with a kind of mental cackle she thought, "He doesn't notice her now. Her goose is cooked."

But poor Miss MacDaid, for all her experience with suffering and disease and hardship, knew very little about what went on in the minds and hearts of men and women. She had never had time to read novels—she had not read more than three or four in all her life—but in a way she was by nature a romantic novelist, never seeing nor appraising the greater strangeness of reality; and so she conceived love in the same fashion as cinema producers, that it was an emotion possible only between people who were young and beautiful and served by camera men who understood their planes and profiles. As she walked along the corridor to waken Lady Esketh, she was able to convince herself that the Englishwoman was no longer a danger. A Lady Esketh with a pallid face and stringy hair and looking her age and more, dressed in a nurse's costume like any Untouchable girl, could not possibly attract a male like the Major. "No"—Miss MacDaid kept telling herself, the set of her jaw relaxing—"No, the slut is finished. She can't ruin him now."

She pushed open the door, and in the light that entered the window from the great pyre outside the Music School, she found Lady Esketh's bed, and bending over her, she shook her abruptly. Lady Esketh wakened almost at once and sat up on the edge of the bed.

"It's time to relieve Mrs. Gupta," she said. "I'll come myself to take your place at five." And then in the red glare she saw the curl papers that covered the head of Lady Esketh, and the sight of them was like the effect of a black stormcloud appearing above the horizon on a brilliant day.

"You'd better take those things off your hair," she said. "They might frighten the patients."

"Of course," said Lady Esketh, and began unwrapping the bits of paper. It took quite a long time to unfasten them all, but Miss MacDaid waited, grimly watching like a headmistress, a little alarmed as one by one they disappeared and left the blonde hair no longer lank and stringy, but curled into neat waves. The effect was even more alarming when Lady Esketh ran her fingers lightly through her hair and let it fall golden and shining in a kind of halo about the small pale face. It was as if she had taken ten years and cast them from her.

The sharp lines appeared again at the corners of Miss MacDaid's jaw and she said, sharply, "Come along now. Poor Mrs. Gupta has got to have some rest. She isn't very strong."

So Lady Esketh threw the coarse blue uniform about her and followed Miss MacDaid, still fastening the buttons that held it together as she went.

When Miss MacDaid took her to the main ward they found Mrs. Gupta, yellow and exhausted, keeping watch. After Miss MacDaid had sent her away, she led Lady Esketh from room to room filled with dead and dying.

It was miraculous how in the dim light from the wick and bowl of oil she carried, Miss MacDaid knew every patient, his or her history, and the state of the illness. Again and again Lady Esketh found herself staring at the big, leathery, plain face in a kind of wonder. The Scotswoman, she thought, must be a kind of witch, to keep all that knowledge in her head.

Here and there Miss MacDaid paused by the side of a bed to jot a note on a block of paper she carried. Twice at the bed of a patient who was groaning with misery she stopped to thrust a hypodermic needle into an arm or a thigh. Then they passed on, followed by the mute glances of a hundred dark eyes. Most of the sick were typhoid patients, some had black malaria, and nearly half of them were victims of the flood and earthquake with shattered limbs and fractured skulls and horrible internal injuries. So that she might leave minute instructions for those who kept watch while she had snatches of sleep, Miss MacDaid had numbers to all the patients, crude numbers marked with pencil on bits of cardboard or paper pinned to the cheap cotton *dhotis* and *saris*.

When they had returned to the main ward she said, "You must not fall asleep. You must go through the wards every fifteen minutes. It is important that they see you, so that they know they are not forgotten or abandoned. When they think that, they simply turn over and die." Then she gave Lady Esketh a paper on which were written five numbers. "If any of these wakes or cries out, you are to call me. Don't trouble the Major. If it's necessary, I'll wake him." And then she gave her another paper with four numbers written on it, "All of these are going to die," she said. "You must watch the beds because none of them will cry out. I have seen to it that they will not wake again. If they die you must call the porters to carry out the bodies. The others won't notice so much in the dark." Suddenly she looked sharply at Lady Esketh. "Have you ever seen a dead person? Do you know when they are dead?"

"I never saw one until I came here. I'm not sure if I would know."

For a moment Miss MacDaid was silent, then she said, "You'll know. There's something that tells you. The main thing is not to fall asleep and to call me if there's any trouble. I'm counting on you. It's more responsibility than I should give to any greenhorn, but there's nothing else to do. I've got to have some rest if I'm to keep going. I can't afford to break down. I'll come at five o'clock." She turned to leave, and then stopped to say, "Do you want Miss Hodge to help you?"

"No."

"Not even for company?"

"No. Let the poor old thing sleep."

"Good-night."

"Good-night."

When Miss MacDaid had gone, Lady Esketh sat down at the table with the oil and wick on it. It was empty save for a pitcher of boiled water covered by a filter paper, a glass, an alarm clock, a roll of cotton gauze, a block of paper with a pencil, and the two bits of paper with the numbers which Miss MacDaid had given her. She was awake now, and yet her mind felt numb and entranced. She read the numbers on the first paper—7, 114, 83, 28, 51. Those were the ones who were deathly ill but might be saved. If they cried out or wakened, she was to fetch Miss MacDaid. On the other were written the numbers—211, 72, 13, 96. Those were the ones who were to die, for whom there was no hope, who lay already stupefied by Miss MacDaid's needle, so that they should not moan or cry out and alarm the others. These she must watch, waiting for them to die, so that they might be carried out and their bodies burned.

"I must keep all this straight," she thought, "I must keep my head clear. I must not make any mistakes." To make certain she took up the pencil and at the top of the one list she wrote the word "dead" and at the top of the other the word "dying," and as she wrote, she thought, "That is how it must feel to be God."

Until three days ago she had never encountered death. Once or twice in her life death had crossed her path, but each time she had avoided it. There were the deaths of friends during the War, long ago, the boys and older men she had known, but all that had been far away and there were so many deaths then, and they happened so far away in the mud of Belgium or before Amiens or on the Chemin des Dames, that in the hysteria and numbness of war time they had had little reality. Their deaths had been little more than a telegram—"The War Office regrets . . ." like the refusal of an invitation. R.S.V.P. *Répondez s'il vous plaît. Répondez a la morte. Ecrive si vous pourrez gardere rendez-vous.* And there was her father dead suddenly of a stroke in Vienna. When they had asked her if she wished to see the corpse she had refused. What was dead was dead. What you loved was gone. What remained was only clay. And Albert. She had not seen him dead, but only as a bloated object mercifully concealed in her own pink silk sheets. He must have hated dying, if he knew it. Albert would never want to die. The animal in him would want to go on and on; that vast, bullying vitality would keep dragging him back from death. Even if he were drugged, the body would fight. He hadn't been like these poor Indians whose undernourished bodies put up no fight, who simply closed their eyes and died as if, willing it, they were only going to sleep.

Now for three days she had seen death all about her. She had seen the corpses drifting past the balcony where she stood with Tom Ransome, waiting for the flood to abate, and the body of that skinny Hindu hanging from the branches of a tree held only by his own poor cotton *dhoti*, and Albert's shapeless corpse wrapped in her sheets, and the bodies lying in the streets, some shattered and broken by the flood and others contorted and purple with the awful death by cholera. And she had seen not only the dead, but death itself, slipping in down the long untidy rooms to steal creature after creature away from the Major and Miss MacDaid.

The sight of so much death had made her numb, and she began to understand how it was that people like Miss MacDaid, who had seen hundreds and perhaps thousands of dying people, were no longer afraid of anything on this earth; and how it was that they could go on leading lives of their own, as if there was a part of them detached, as if at times they shut themselves away in a compartment which belonged to them alone. That was why Miss MacDaid, who was so brave and good, could still find a place in her heart for contempt and scorn and even hardness. If they had been soft—people like Miss MacDaid and the Major—they would have failed and been cast aside, broken and useless, long ago. She thought, with pride, "I too must have something of that in me. I've stood everything—filth and smells, misery and death. I am not even tired."

For there was, strangely enough, no weariness in her, now that she was awake, but only a kind of peace such as she had never felt before or even suspected, and a curious satisfaction—the satisfaction, she knew suddenly, for which she had been looking all her life. She had won their respect. She no longer vomited at the sight of a filthy bed or at the awful smell of gangrene. Unless she thought of it, she did not even notice the odor of burning flesh or the sickly-sweet smell of the cholera in the Music School which the damp lazy breeze sometimes carried in through the screened windows of the hospital. A shell had grown about her, quickly, in little more than seventy-two hours, protecting her as it protected Miss MacDaid and the Major. Nothing could touch her now, not even the disease and decay all about them. Miss MacDaid and the Major had been safe for so long, for so many years. Perhaps there was something, some mystical quality, which protected people like them—the nuns, the doctors, the nurses who fought epidemics and lived among lepers and in places stricken with typhus and cholera.

Then suddenly she remembered her duty, that she must make a round of the whole hospital once every fifteen minutes until Miss MacDaid came to relieve her. She glanced at the battered old alarm clock and saw that there was still four minutes to pass before she must go, carrying the enameled pitcher of cold water from bed to bed. And at the same time she was aware that she was being watched and her eyes met in the light from the fire outside the window those of a typhoid patient in the narrow bed nearest the table.

At first, because the figure in the bed was so small and thin, she thought the patient was a child. The eyes were enormous and black and ageless, but they were sunk in the head of the woman who looked old and shrunken. The dark skin, yellowed now by illness, was drawn like paper over the fine bones of the skull. For a second she stared fascinated by the delicacy of the face, and then, shuddering a little, it seemed to her that the face and head seemed dead. Without hair it would have been a bleached skull. It was the face of a woman who since she was born had never had enough to eat. She thought, "Death is coming for her. R.S.V.P. *Répondez s'il vous plaît.*" How many times, in that remote and immensely distant world of London, she had written those initials. . . .

Then she was aware that the purple lips were moving. She could not hear what the woman was trying to say, for no voice came from the lips, but only a dry whispering sound like the rustling of dead leaves. Then feebly a skinny hand, immensely old, stole up, shaking as if with palsy, to the purple lips in the gesture which all peasants and workmen make the world over to indicate hunger and thirst, and she thought, "The poor woman wants water," and rising quickly she lifted the filter paper from the pitcher and poured the glass on the table before her full to the brim.

At the bedside she had to lift the woman up with one hand while she held the glass with the other. The creature had no weight at all, not even the solid weight of a child. Through the sweat-dampened white cotton *sari* she could feel the burning heat of the fever. The woman drank greedily, and when she had drained the glass she lay back with her full weight on Lady Esketh's arm. Opening her eyes, she looked up at the Englishwoman and tried to smile. Even in her illness there was something deprecating and humble about the look in the eyes which made Lady Esketh want to cry suddenly, to say, "You must not look at me like that. I am your sister. We are both women. God made us both." But she could not, she knew, make the woman understand. All she could do was to smile at her. Again the sound of rustling leaves came from the woman's lips and she closed her eyes again and lay back on the damp pillow, in peace.

Lady Esketh thought, "The four minutes must have passed," and placing the glass back on the table, she lifted one of the stone jars to the edge of the table and held one of the enameled pitchers beneath it. The jar was heavy and it took all her strength to manage it, to tilt it gently so that she could control the flow of the water. She was struggling with the jar when she heard a voice say, "Wait. I'll do that for you," and turning, she saw the figure of the Major. He was beside her and one of his hands touched hers as he lifted the jar from her grasp. For a second she felt a dizzy sensation of happiness, and then, leaning against the table, she recovered herself and said, "Thank you. It is heavy."

For a moment she had trembled as she had trembled when Miss Hodge had gone away, leaving them alone in that dreary sitting-room in the old Summer Palace, but the feeling went away quickly, and quietly she moved a little away from him and stood very straight, as if she were no more than the poor, pimply Mrs. Gupta.

Then he said, smiling at her, "It must be time to make your first round. I'll go with you." He filled the other pitcher and picked them both up.

"No," she said. "Let me carry one of them. I'd like to."

He looked at her for a second and the shadow of a grin appeared on his face. She divined that it was not a grin of mockery, but of something simpler and warmer; it was almost as if he saw her as a child playing "hospital."

Angrily she said, "You needn't look like that."

He understood, because he did not even answer her. She said, "In any case you'll need these lists," and she handed him the papers with the numbers written on them by Miss MacDaid. Then she took one of the pitchers from him and they set out.

The sudden anger vanished and she followed him with docility as if she might have been Mrs. Gupta, practised, experienced, almost to the point of boredom. And he paid her no more attention than if she had been plain, kindly Mrs. Gupta. He went from bed to bed, stopping at each one while she filled the enameled cup that stood on the little shelf beside it. A few of the sick were asleep, and a dozen or more were delirious, but most of them lay with their great black eyes wide open, looking up patiently as she and the Major passed each bed.

At each of the beds on the list marked "dying" he stopped for a moment, to feel the pulse, to lay a hand on a burning head. But all the time he took no notice of her at all, save once when he said, as if in apology, "Laying a hand on their heads does no good except to give them courage. You see they know I am a Brahmin, and for centuries they have been made to step aside lest their shadow fall on us and pollute us."

Of the list marked "dead" three were still alive, but the fourth who had gangrenous wounds, lay still and rigid and she saw at once that there was no need to fill the cup at his side. He was a very black, skinny man and his eyes were half-closed as they had been during the coma produced by Miss MacDaid's merciful needle. It was odd how you knew, as if by some extra sense, that the man was dead. There was perhaps something in the peculiar tilt of the head, like a flower wilted on its stem, and, in the way the feet stuck up at a rigid angle beneath the soiled *dhoti*. She had known at once. Now she would always know.

Then she saw the Major place the crude lamp on the little shelf and bend down over the man from his great height. With one finger he pulled back an eyelid and snapped a nail against the yellow eyeball. There was no reaction at all, and turning to her, he said, "Go and tell the porter to carry him away."

When she returned with two sleepy Sweepers carrying a stretcher between them, they went on with the journey, past bed after bed, past pair after pair of dark eyes that were like the eyes of sick animals filled with weariness and a kind of dumb faith and trust. And when they had reached the end and were returning the Major stopped suddenly and said, "Listen!" and in the night stillness, above the faint moan which arose from a bed here and there, she heard the fine thread of music from a flute and the dull distant thumping of brown fingers on a drum.

The Major said, "That is a good sign."

"Yes?"

"It means that life is going on again."

When they returned to the table in the corner of the main ward, he said, "May I sit with you for a moment?"

"Of course, if you like, but you'd better get some sleep."

"I slept early in the evening. I couldn't sleep now. What I need is not sleep, but something to make me feel normal and human again. For three days I've been a machine."

She knew what he meant, and she was touched in the strangest way. For what he really said was, "I should like to talk for a little time— or just sit and not talk at all—with a woman—not a woman like Miss MacDaid or Mrs. Gupta but a woman like yourself." And again she thought of how he must have his life arranged in compartments.

[490]

He sat down on the end of the table, crossing one leg over the other, and smiled at her. Then in a low voice, so that he would not disturb the sick, he said, "I have to tell you that I think you've been a brick! It isn't easy, what you're doing, not for somebody who has never done it before."

"I'm not so wonderful," she said. "Two or three times I almost gave in and quit. But that's over now. I don't mind anything. I don't even get sick any more. It's funny how quickly you get used to things."

"We'll have nurses from Bombay before long—and some of our own Ranchipur women. Then you can quit and go away."

She thought, "No, I don't want to go away . . . ever. I want to stay! I want to stay!" And aloud, "I'll stay as long as I'm needed. . . . I mean as long as I'm of any use."

He was silent for a moment and then taking up the bottle of alcohol, he soaked a bit of cotton and carefully rubbed the finger which had touched the dead man. He looked tired and much thinner, but the weariness gave him a new beauty. He had a kind of maleness she had never before encountered—not the clumsy maleness of a European, nor even the cruel maleness of that boxer she had known long ago in another life, but a maleness that was finely drawn and delicate, like that of a coiled steel spring.

Without looking up, he went on swabbing his hands delicately and carefully with the alcohol, and said, "You are an astonishing woman." And when he did not go on, she could think of nothing better to say than, "English people are very often eccentric."

"I don't mean anything so banal as that." Then he looked at her and said, "Please don't think I'm being personal for any silly reason. It's so difficult for people to get together, to understand each other. Neither of us is a child."

"No."

"It has occurred to me that you are intelligent."

"Perhaps."

"I didn't think so."

She had a sudden image of herself as she had been that night at the palace beneath the bee-filled chandeliers, hurrying away in boredom to

[491]

throw herself into Tom's arms in that stuffy room belowstairs. Quietly she said, "There wasn't any reason for you to think so."

Suddenly he shook his head as if he would clear his mind of weariness.

"What I'm trying to say is difficult—especially to you. I know you have had plenty of experience."

"Yes, that's true."

"Do I seem naïf?"

"No." It occurred to her that he could never have been naïf, even as a child. But now he was making himself vulnerable. He was giving her, whole-heartedly, openly, his friendship and admiration. She might hurt him by trampling on it, by disillusioning him. The woman she had been that dreary afternoon in the Summer Palace would have hurt him, not in his intelligence, which was great, but in his human sensibility —the human sensibility which she was beginning to believe was so great a part of Indians. It was even in these poor, suffering, dying, low-caste people—a kind of sensibility which only the finest of Europeans ever had. She thought, "I'm beginning to know about India and Indians."

He was saying, "You remember that afternoon when you offered me tea at the old Summer Palace?" She looked away from him at the list marked "dead" and "dying," and he went on, "I found you attractive then and exciting. And I knew what you wanted. I knew I could have it for the taking. That's why I stayed and had a cup of tepid tea . . . because I was tempted. And you were trying all the time to make me believe that you were inexperienced and"—for a moment he hesitated— "and respectable, because you thought that was the best way to deceive me and get what you wanted."

She looked up quickly from the lists, filled with shame and a wild impulse to protest that what he was saying was not true, but almost at once she thought, "No, that would be a lie. That would spoil everything. That would bring back the woman who offered him the tepid tea—into this place. And she does not belong here. She has nothing to do with this." And she saw that he was holding up his hand as if to check her words.

"Wait," he was saying. "I don't think much of respectability. I think a great deal more of truth. I was tempted that afternoon to take what would have been very agreeable to take—once or twice. But I didn't

[492]

because of something I knew lay behind the flushed cheeks and trembling hands I saw. And I was right. I know now I was right. It was the difference between taking a counterfeit and waiting for the real coin. Do you see what I mean? If I had taken what you offered me then we should not have what we have found now. I would have thought you a cheap woman. I would have given you nothing but my body, which for a doctor and a surgeon is all too easy to give because it is only a machine and means nothing. But if I had done that then, nothing better could have happened. We would never have known each other at all."

She was looking again at the table with an odd turmoil of shame and triumph in her heart. No man had ever talked to her like this, and for a moment she experienced again that feeling of confusion and terror that had come to her in the nightmare after she had quarreled with Esketh—when wildly she had been searching in the jungle and across endless plains and through great cities for something—only what it was she did not know. Now, for a second, she knew what it was. Then the knowledge eluded her and she was lost again.

"Don't think I'm being complicated and latin," he was saying. "Only human relations are such strange things, and I like to have things straight. Most people go through life and die without ever *knowing* what life may be, and the glory that there can be in human relationship. But the glory only comes when one can rise above the pettiness of daily life. You see, that is the end of all religion. That is what all of them try to attain. That's what I meant when I said respectability was of no importance. Respectability is for the stupid, the weak, and the hypocritical."

He shifted his position, suddenly slipping off the table to lean against it, his arms folded on his big chest. "I wanted you to know what I felt . . . because I think so much of you that I believe it worth while to risk making an ass of myself. And now, whenever we meet, whenever we see each other, whenever we think of each other, we will know that we are friends, that we *know* each other. It is a great thing to *know* even one person in a lifetime." Then he unfolded his arms and took one of her hands in his. "Maybe you are mocking me in your heart."

"No . . . no."

"Maybe you are thinking me a cheap fortune-teller like the ones that

[493]

fill the bazaars. I can tell you that you have discovered a secret. You know what it is." Then he let her hand go free and said, "I must go now. Now I can sleep." One hand slipped about her shoulder. "It's time to make the rounds—ten minutes past the time, but that's my fault. Good-night."

In a whisper she answered his good-night and then he was gone. For a little time she sat quite still, bewildered, and then, remembering that the rounds had to be made, she rose and lifting one of the stone jars filled the two pitchers with the precious boiled water, and set out.

This time she scarcely saw the figures of the sick. Only at the beds of the dying did she stop for a moment, seeking some sign that there was still life in the worn bodies. Number 72 had died. When she held the lamp high above the bed, she was sure of it. Now she knew what death was like. There was not even a need to flick the eyeball with her finger nail as the Major had done. Quietly she went down the stairs and wakened the sleeping porters.

When they had gone away, she went to the window and looked out over the town. The huge fire with its burden of corpses had almost died away; it was only a great heap of embers now which gave out a white heat but very little light. The rain had stopped and an old moon had come up beyond the Great Tank, and between her and the old wooden palace there was a path of golden light, crossed back and forth, endlessly by the flight of the huge bats from the dead city of the Moghuls beneath the sacred mountain. The faint distant sound of the flute and the drums still came to her from the opposite side of the river.

The beauty and the cruelty of the scene went deep within her like the thrust of a knife cauterizing a wound. It was out of this he had been born!

As she watched, the black figures of the porters carrying the dead woman crept out across the ruined garden in the direction of the Music School to leave their burden there beside all the other dead who would be burned as soon as a fresh pyre was built.

The heat was dreadful and as she turned from the window she wiped the sweat from her face with a bit of cotton gauze and then sitting down again at the table, she poured herself a glass of water and drank it. She then took up the list marked "dead," and with her pencil she drew a line through two numbers 72 and 13, and again the feeling of being God returned to her for an instant.

She thought, "It is happening. The thing which brought me to India is working out. I must stay here until it is finished, even if I never see England again." If she were to go now, tomorrow, on one of the planes which would come out of the world beyond Mount Abana, what remained to her of life would be without meaning. It was here that she belonged, here in all this death and filth and misery and beauty. "Perhaps," she thought, "I have always belonged here."

Then there came to her again that faint sound like the whispering of dead leaves stirred by a breeze, and raising her eyes they met again the patient, doe-eyes of the dying woman in the bed. The purple lips moved, framing the Gujerati word for water. Again the skinny fingers appeared from beneath the *sari* and were thrust into the gaping mouth.

Quietly she rose and took up the glass pitcher. But immediately she put it down again with a faint quick sense of horror. She had given this woman to drink from the glass on the table instead of from the woman's own cup and afterward she had drunk from the same glass.

The whispering sound went on and, taking up one of the enameled pitchers, she crossed to the side of the bed, filled the woman's own cup with water and held it to her lips, thinking, "What is done is done!" wondering, too, if there was some way of disinfecting one's insides.

Then as she turned away from the bed she heard a groan from one of the beds at the far end of the ward, and following the sound she found an old man who had wakened out of Miss MacDaid's merciful sleep. His body shook with the convulsions of pain. Quickly she brought the light and looked at the number. It was number 83 on the list of "dying." She hurried away down the stairs to find Miss MacDaid.

When they returned, Miss MacDaid thrust the needle again into the skinny black thigh of the old man, and as she turned away she said, "He is finished. Transfer his number to the other list."

She said nothing to Miss MacDaid about the incident of the glass because she would not have the nurse think that she had been such an absent-minded fool. Now she experienced a faint sense of disgust but no longer any fear, for it seemed to her that what happened to her was no longer in her hands.

In the hunting-tent the Maharani sat cross-legged on a little dais with the old Princess of Bewanagar, facing the circle of men—Raschid Ali Khan, Colonel Ranjit Singh, Homer Smiley, Nil Kant Rao, and Ransome. One by one, the Muslim, the Sikh, the American, the Mahratta and the Englishman were telling her what they had to tell of the progress of the fight; and what each one had to say brought new courage and new life to the heart of the handsome old woman seated on the cushion of Benares brocade. She looked tired now and worn, but the old untamable beauty was still here, accentuated by the deep shadows from the flame of the wick burning in oil.

She had fought—all her life she had fought—against superstition and intrigue and prejudice. She had fought by the side of the dead Maharajah, without the strength which he found in his simplicity and faith. She had fought, too, for the love of fighting, doubting always in her heart that they would ever win the struggle for integrity and grace, and the salvation and rebirth of her own state and of all of India. She had never, like the old Maharajah, believed either in the goodness or strength of her people, or even in the ultimate victory. And she had fought, a little like the immensely old Dewan, without scruple, sometimes with cruelty, often with hatred, and always with the toughness and bravery of her own Mahratta people. She had hated Europeans as invaders, as vulgar and stupid and insensible, admitting despite her own unwillingness such things as the friendship of the great Viceroy and the sensibility and intelligence of men like Ransome, and the goodness of people like the Smileys. There had been times when she grew weary, and moments when she had been tempted to turn evil and bitter, like so many of the princes of India. There had even been a moment, one terrible moment, a little while before these men, sitting before her, had come into the tent, when she had been tempted to give up the battle and flee, to leave by airplane for the security of Bombay; perhaps of Europe. In her weariness, it had seemed to her that everything for which they had fought, her dead husband and herself, had been swept away forever. For a little time she had felt too old and too ill to begin the battle all over again.

But that terrible moment of temptation was gone now. As she had watched these men and listened to them, she felt shame that the moment of weakness had ever come to her. They were fine men and beautiful men, all perhaps save Mr. Smiley, who was a noble man but not very beautiful; and she knew a fine man when she saw one. And she could not doubt their devotion to her. What they gave her was not the devotion of lovers, but something beyond that, something which had less reason and was able to withstand greater tests. But she knew, too, that if the devotion had come from men less strong and beautiful, it would have pleased her less. The devotion was a thing apart, unimpeachable, shining and splendid, but she liked it the more because it came from men like the brawny Raschid, the lean, silken Ranjit Singh, the fierce Nil Kant Rao and the morbid, good-looking Ransome. It pleased her savage sense of beauty and splendor. A queen should be served by men like these.

They had worked for her and for India, without sleep and without complaint, in filth and misery and danger, a danger worse and more insidious than the danger of battle. The task had seemed impossible, yet victory was in sight. When she was gone they would be here to carry on the fight. They would be here to rebuild the schools, the bridges, the railroad, even the great dam itself. She would sell all her jewels and give her money to the state because the thing for which she and the dead Maharajah had worked was only emerging from the womb of Indian time, but it must go on and on, gaining force from the light and faith brought by such men as these. India, vast, cruel, rich India, was stirring and waking.

And as she sat there, she saw among the faces, that of a man who had died more than twenty years ago in the house where Ransome now lived. She saw him as she had seen him when she came down from her village, timid and proud, a child of thirteen, but already a woman, to marry the young Maharajah of Ranchipur. Now as an old woman she could still see the intelligent, kindly face, full of gentleness and a wisdom which was more like the wisdom of the East than of Europe in its calm and understanding. Yes, he was there, too, in this council of strong men who served and admired her; in the end it was because of him that they were all assembled here in the hunting-tent. It was because of him that the Maharajah had fought for so long to free his people and lift them up. It was because of him that she was seated here now, ruling wisely and with understanding and courage. He had loved her ancient, splendid India so much that in the end he had come back to die in Ranchipur in the evening in his garden at the hour when the cows came homeward beneath a trailing cloud of red dust, when the air smelled of jasmine and cow dung, smoke and spices, and the jackals came out of hiding to cry at the rising moon, and the flutes and tomtoms began in the villages. Long ago there had been many Britishers like him—John Lawrence, the scholar, the tutor who *knew* India. They were rarer now. Here and there you might find one.

The men were talking now among themselves and she did not trouble to listen, for their own business they knew far better than she could know it. Her thoughts drifted away to Europe, to the casinos and the great jewelers' shops and the state dinners, the expositions made to help commerce, the great hotels and watering-places. It seemed all at once a distant world, more distant than it had been long ago when as a young woman she had defied the Vedic law and crossed the Black Water. Then Europe had fascinated her as a glittering pageant might fascinate a child, but now, she knew, she was wearied of it. Long ago she had come to understand its greed, its falseness, and its tragic materialism, its desperate snatching at any small hope, its dictators and its degeneracy. Let it alone; soon enough it would destroy itself. Men like that Lord Esketh were destroying it. To save it was a more terrible task than to bring together in one pride and honor poor torn, divided India. For Europe was tired and the East was wakening refreshed and vigorous from a long sleep.

No, she would never go to Europe again. She would die without even visiting the spectacle another time. And she would not go away even to Poona or Ootacamund. She would stay behind, all through the terrible life-bringing monsoon, all through the winter when the red dust rose in clouds off the plains that stretched away on one side to the sea, on the other to the sacred mountain of Abana. There was much to be done, so much to be built up, so much to be left behind when she died, that others might have a foundation on which to build.

Then through the cloud of reverie she was aware that the curtains had been thrust aside at the far end of the tent and that the young Major had come in hurriedly. He advanced straight toward her and bending low, with his fingertips pressed together, he excused himself for being late by saying that he could not escape from the hospital.

She frowned at him in a pantomime of displeasure, as it was her duty as a queen to do, but the frown passed quickly when he smiled with a bold glance which told her that he knew the frown was false. With him she could never be bad-tempered because he was young and good-looking and affectionate. Her own sons were tragically dead, slain by the West, but the Major had in a way taken their place.

He brought her news of the epidemic, news which he made a little better than the fact because he understood that she was tired. Then he talked with the other men for a time, and when at last they went away, she asked him to stay behind, partly because his presence always cheered her and made her feel young, and partly because there were things which she wished to discuss with him and gossip which she wished to hear.

When the others had gone, she awakened her friend, the old Princess, who sat nodding, asleep bolt upright on her cushion, and said, "Go put yourself to bed, Sita."

When the old Princess had gone sleepily away, they talked together in Mahratta, which was her own language and his by adoption. She said, "There are a great many things to discuss—non-official things. First, before His Highness died he told me that you thought of marrying."

"Yes, Your Highness."

"Are you still of the same mind?"

"Yes, Your Highness."

"How old are you?"

"Thirty-six."

She grunted thoughtfully, and said, "If you are to breed strong children you must begin."

The Major grinned. "Age makes no difference so long as the stock is strong and one can still breed. Each one of us is but the receptacle of seed. We merely pass it on."

"Humph! Your science has a great many theories that any *Ryot* can disprove by example." She opened the gold-and-ruby box at her side and took out cardamon seeds to chew. "When things are more settled I'll send for the girl and her parents." She regarded him shrewdly. "It does not matter to you that she is only half Indian—that the other half is European . . . or American?"

"No, Your Highness. It is not the cross of races that makes the Eurasian a problem. It's the crossing of bad stock—the remittance man and the low-caste woman. His Highness told me about the girl."

Again she looked at him shrewdly. "You have no nonsense about a love match?"

"No, Your Highness . . . that is, within limits. I should want to know my wife before I married her. That is only fair to both of us."

"There is a good deal of nonsense in the West about love marriage. There is nothing more miserable than a marriage in which passion has been satisfied and is dead. She is a nice girl. If I had sons I would choose her for a wife for one of them."

"I am sure Your Highness is a good judge."

"And then there is the question of Ransome," she said. "He has worked well?"

"Yes, Your Highness, he could not have done his job better. It's not an easy one. He has scarcely slept."

"And his drinking?"

"So far as I know he has not had a drink for nearly four days."

"That proves nothing when whisky is so difficult to get."

"It is not difficult, Your Highness. He had brandy in his own cellar. He gave it all to the hospital. I myself offered him a drink and he refused it. I offered it to him whenever he wanted it and still he refused."

She considered the statement for a moment, sitting still and thoughtful as a Buddha in the yellow lamplight. Then she said, "I am fond of him. Something could be made of him."

"He is a defeatist, Your Highness, but a nice fellow. He is sick. I think he has always been sick."

"I should like to help him if I could. . . . There are times when he makes me think of His Highness' old tutor. He was dead before you were born, so you wouldn't know what he was like. He lived in a different age. I think it is the times which have made Ransome sick." She opened the gold box studded with rubies once more. "Do you think he would work for the state?"

"I don't know, Your Highness."

"It might help him. What is this story of his violating the Missionary's daughter?"

"I don't know, Your Highness. Knowing him, I cannot believe it. It is not in his nature."

Her black eyes narrowed a little and she said, "On the night of the Palace dinner, something happened between him and Lady Esketh."

"Yes, Your Highness."

"What did that mean?"

"Nothing, I should say."

"A pity. Pleasures such as that are barren."

"They are both unhappy. They are both sick."

"Why does she want to stay here? It makes no sense."

"I don't know, Your Highness, but I think she is trying to find something—there is no name for what she is trying to find—unless you call it reality—and that is a poor name."

"It is you who permitted her to stay. You admire her?"

"Yes, Your Highness."

She frowned with displeasure. "Why?"

For a moment he hesitated. Then he said, "Forgive me, Masaheb, but she has many of your qualities."

The frown deepened. "How?"

"She is without fear. There is a quality of indefeatability about her. She likes good-looking men. She has independence and character. For the past two days she was made sick twenty times a day by the hospital work, but she went on working. That is as good a test as I know. She does not deceive herself and she does not run away from things. Long ago, I think, she took a wrong path."

As he spoke, he watched her, shrewdly aware that the frown softened, that the fierce old lady was pleased. Shrewdly he knew, because he knew her so well, that deep inside her there was a silent chuckle of pleasure, because he understood her so well, because he had divined

[501]

qualities in her which she fancied she had managed to keep hidden from most others, because he dared to be bold with her, even at times scolding her.

"Was it because of her that you were late tonight?"

With a humility which he knew she divined as false, he said in a low voice, "Yes, Your Highness."

"Will this interfere with your marriage?"

"No, Your Highness, Lady Esketh was not made for breeding. Marriage is an affair of the state. It should be made for the good of the community."

"I am glad that you are not a fool. When will she go away?"

"That I cannot answer, Your Highness."

"She must go before the other one comes."

"Of course."

"I will leave that to you. Otherwise it will be very troublesome for everyone."

"I understand, Your Highness."

"And one more thing. I hear stories of an old lady who lives with the Smileys."

"Yes, Mrs. Smiley's aunt."

"It seems that she has done great work in spite of being old. She has cooked at the Orphanage and taken in refugees."

"She is an extraordinary woman."

"I should like to see her."

"I can send her to you, if you will fix the time."

"Tomorrow at three. What is her name?"

"Mrs. Bascomb. . . . Mrs. Phoebe Bascomb."

"Write that for me. I can't remember names like that."

He took out a bit of paper, wrote the name and gave it to her.

"Is the railway bridge passable?"

"Yes, they have laid planks over the rails."

"When you go out, tell the aide-de-camp to send His Highness' bullock carriage for her."

"She could come alone, Your Highness. She is very spry."

"No, I prefer to send the carriage. I will use it myself from now

[502]

on. The motion of elephants is bad for my digestion. And Miss Dirks
. . . they have not found her body?"

"No, Your Highness."

"Was it true that she was dying?"

"Yes, Your Highness."

The Maharani was silent for a moment. "She was a good woman.
I never understood her, but she was a good woman. We must erect
a monument to her when times are settled again. And the other one
. . . Miss Hodge?"

"She is quite mad, Your Highness."

"Where is she? Who is caring for her?"

"Lady Esketh."

"Lady Esketh!"

"Yes, the poor thing won't be separated from her."

She shook her head and made a clucking sound, very like the sounds
Aunt Phoebe made when moved or astonished. "The English are very
odd people . . . very unexpected."

"They are a sentimental people, Your Highness, and very ashamed
of it."

"We must arrange for Miss Hodge to have a pension."

She collected the boxes and belongings about her. "You had better
go now. You must need rest."

"Thank you."

Then she rose and went slowly out into another part of the tent.

While the serving-women undressed her and massaged her and
rubbed her face and head with scented oils, she asked the head woman,
"Where is the Russian? Has she returned yet?"

"No, Masaheb."

The Maharani was suddenly angry. She wanted to be read to, so
that she would be able for a little time to forget the misery of the
city. She wanted even to torture Maria Lishinskaia a little so that she
would be able to sleep. She thought, "I'll send Maria Lishinskaia away.
I'll give her a pension and send her back to Europe." The Russian
woman grew more and more tiresome with her hysterics and her ob-
sessions. There wasn't even much satisfaction any longer in tormenting
her. And she was the last bond which bound the old lady to the Europe

of casinos and gala dinners and jewelers' shops. She would send Maria Lishinskaia away, out of her life. Then she would be free of Europe. She would be Indian again, pure Indian, as she had been long ago as a young woman when she had thought she might learn things from Europe.

But there was no need to send away Maria Lishinskaia. She had already gone, of her own will, for she was already dead, hanging in the light of the dying moon by her own scarf from one of the iron hooks in the Great Gateway which the Sikhs used to support their lances. It was there that Ransome found her when he returned from the hunting-pavilion.

Part IV

Part IV

IN THE morning, a little before noon, not one plane appeared, but three, coming out of the steaming rain above the mist-hidden sacred mountain. And in them were bales and bundles of supplies and three nurses— one a Parsee woman, one an Anglo-Indian, and one a British nurse. Gopal Rao was with them, black-eyed, content, swaggering a little with importance because he had seen the Governor of the Bombay Presidency and told him the details of the disaster. He went at once to the Maharani to tell her that more supplies were being sent by plane and that as soon as the railroad was restored, food and more medical supplies would be rushed into the city. Colonel Ranjit Singh and Raschid Ali Khan, lean and grim as a falcon and more than ever like one of Baber's horsemen, were there. They had been as far as Mount Abana on the elephants and the news had come through that men were already at work on the other side of the mountain beyond the canyon. The restoration of railroad service was now only a matter of hours. Gopal Rao reported that the government of Bombay was sending the head of the Institute for Tropical Diseases and two trained workers the next day by plane. The news was all good and for a moment the light of victory came again into the weary faces of the Maharani, the Colonel, and Raschid Ali Khan.

Gopal Rao and Colonel Ranjit Singh went away, but Raschid Ali Khan as Police Minister stayed behind for the dreary business of the inquest into the suicide of Maria Lishinskaia. Ransome came for it, and the Major, and last of all Harry Bauer.

The Swiss no longer looked cool and fresh and clean as Ransome had seen him the night before. The white drill suit was crumpled and soiled and there was a dullness about him, as if the radiant health had been dimmed, as if a shadow had fallen upon him. On one side of his face there were two long scratches.

The Major testified that Maria Lishinskaia had undoubtedly died by her own hand. She had fastened one end of the scarf about her throat, attached it to the hook, and then kicked away the chair on which she had been standing. Undoubtedly she had meant to die, for the scarf had stretched and when she was found her dead feet were touching the ground. She could, he thought, have saved herself. When Ransome found her the body was still warm. She could not, the Major thought, have been dead for more than a few minutes. The *jobedar* had been asleep in his room and had heard nothing.

Then Ransome told of having seen her earlier in the evening while he was walking along the edge of the Great Tank with Colonel Ranjit Singh. He described how she had slipped from tree to tree, shadow to shadow until the final mad dash past the corpses into the pest-house of the Music School. Colonel Ranjit Singh had recognized her too and they had agreed to say nothing.

When it was Harry Bauer's turn he was secretive and difficult and told his story sullenly and grudgingly. Looking at the floor of the tent, he said in a low voice, "I did not know she was coming. She came to see me and talked for a time and went away."

But this did not satisfy Raschid. The Police Minister asked, "She was your mistress, wasn't she?"

"Yes."

"For how long?"

"For nearly two years. It began at Carlsbad. I never loved her, but here it was a convenience. I tried to stop it. She wanted to marry me. I never wanted to marry her. I am going to marry a girl from Vevey when I go home. I told her that, but it didn't do any good. She was always threatening to kill herself, but I didn't believe she would do it. She was a little crazy, I think. I would have broken it off, but she pestered me. She was always coming into my room. She even got into bed with me sometimes." He still stared at the floor, but his drooping shoulders shrugged, "What could I do? I am healthy and this is a hot country and one eats lots of spices. I said, 'Oh, all right. Why not?'"

"Is that all? Did you talk quietly?"

"Yes."

"Miss Simon said she came for you and heard you quarreling and the deceased shouting, 'I'll kill you and myself.'"

"Yes, that was true."

"You quarreled?"

"No. She attacked me."

"Is that how your face was scratched?"

"Yes."

"What did you quarrel about?"

He was silent for a moment, and then in a low voice he said, "She wanted me to sleep with her. She did awful things and said horrible things."

"Because you refused?"

"Yes. It was ugly and indecent. It wasn't the place for . . . that. With all those dead and dying around us. I didn't want to. I couldn't have done it. She was disgusting to me."

So that was it, thought Ransome. His Swiss respectability was offended.

"She was disgusting to me. I told her so. And then she tried to kill me. She came at me like a panther . . . and I hit her."

"Yes?"

"I think that was what did it. When I hit her, she stopped her screaming. She went into a corner of the room and covered her face with her hands."

"Did she say anything?"

"She was quiet for a long time and then she began to cry . . . not wildly or hysterically the way she usually did, but quietly. Afterward when she was gone and I was alone, that was the only thing that alarmed me. She was so quiet."

"What did she say?"

The smooth, handsome, stupid face looked puzzled for a moment. Then he said, "She talked in a very low voice. I don't know that I can remember exactly. I think she covered her face with her hands and then she said, 'What has happened to me? I am crazy.' Then she said, 'I am sorry I hit you. Forgive me. I cannot die if you do not forgive me.' And I said, 'It's all right. I forgive you, but I'm finished. I never want to see you again. You are horrible.' Then she took her hands from in front of her face and said, 'It's all right. You'll never see me again. I won't trouble you. I won't trouble anybody ever again, not even myself. I should have done it long ago—long ago—even before Leipsic and

Dresden.' Then she said, 'Good-by. I hope that some day that wonderful body which is the only thing you love will suffer as I have.'"

His voice grew lower and lower as he finished the story. He said, "All the time it was as if she were talking to herself. I never thought she'd do it. She was always saying she would kill herself, but she never did."

Even when he had finished he did not look at them. He said, "All I want is to go away in peace. I want to leave this place. I want to go back to Switzerland and marry and have peace. I should never have come here."

For a moment there was silence, and then Raschid asked, "Is there anyone to be notified, Your Highness? Had she any relatives or friends?"

"None that I know of. You might look among her papers. She always said that all her family and friends were lost or dead."

Raschid turned to the Swiss, "That's all. You may go now. As soon as there is a way of leaving, I will send you. Perhaps you can go on one of the returning planes."

"That's all I want," Harry Bauer repeated, dully. "To go away. To go home out of this cursed country." He was frightened now as an animal is frightened because his body was sick. On the way to the door of the tent he stumbled and nearly fell, and for a moment he stood clinging to the curtains of the doorway. Ransome's eye met that of the Major and a look of horror passed between them.

Then the Major whispered to him, "You had better go with him to make certain he gets as far as the Music School."

On the way from the hunting-tent to the Music School Ransome gave the Swiss his arm to keep him from falling, and as they reached the Great Tank Harry Bauer leaned suddenly against the wall and began to vomit, and then Ransome knew that it was finished with him. With the aid of a passing coolie, he got him as far as the School and into the room which the Swiss had arranged with the efficiency of a soldier. He was apathetic now and sat on the edge of the bed, staring before him while Ransome stripped off the white jacket and loosened the collar of the shirt. He did not speak for a while and then only with a great effort

Looking up at Ransome, with dilated, unseeing pupils, he said, haltingly in French, "I want to go back. I must go back. Send me away from this awful country." And then he began again to vomit terribly, the attack shaking his body from head to foot.

When he was quiet again Ransome said, "I'll go to fetch the doctor." In the hallway he met the Major. "I came as soon as I could," he said. "The old lady wanted to talk to me."

"Do you think there's any chance?"

"I should say not. At any rate, the planes brought stuff to treat him."

"Who is to take his place?"

"I don't know."

"I will."

"You're needed elsewhere."

"They can get on without me. Gopal Rao can do my job." He looked at the Major searchingly. "I want to do it."

"You know the danger?"

"Yes."

"The old lady won't like it."

"I want to do it. I must do it."

"I see. Very well, then. But go now and have a bath and throw away those clothes and wash your hands in alcohol. The Swiss was as clean as any man could be, but it didn't save him."

It had come to him in the moment when he stood supporting Harry Bauer at the edge of the Great Tank. By the vomiting he knew that it was all finished with Harry Bauer and that by tomorrow he would be dead; and his spirit, deadened again as it had been long ago by the presence of death all about him, accepted the fact of death coldly and without emotion. His arms supported the body of a man who was already dead, but who would live on for a few hours mercifully numbed and confused by the disease which destroyed him. He was one more out of the thousands, one more ant in the hill which God had wantonly kicked apart four days before—one more ant whose death would make little difference to anyone now that the Russian woman had hanged herself to the hook in the Great Gate. The fact of death would make little difference to anyone save the Swiss himself with his peasant selfish-

[511]

ness and materialism, with his plans for returning home, for marrying and breeding a family and acquiring property and leaving behind a son to carry on the common name of Bauer, to carry on the ego that had been Harry Bauer, the ego that was crushed out by the foot of God far away from the terraced vineyards above Vevey.

And if this were Tom Ransome instead of Harry Bauer who stood there, supported by a stranger, vomiting away his life by the edge of the Great Tank . . . just one more ant, a stranger ant from another colony, who had run away to escape, to lose himself in that vast ant heap of India. And so that was that. Today, tomorrow, or next day it might be Tom Ransome who was trampled carelessly out of existence. And suddenly by the edge of the tank, as Harry Bauer ceased vomiting and leaned against him in the crumpled soiled white clothes, retching painfully, he saw himself clearly perhaps for the first time and his spirit turned away revolted from what he saw of uselessness, of egotism, of selfishness, of cant. He knew then what it was he had to do. He had to destroy himself with all the past, with all the questionings and doubts and all the haze of useless thought which had paralyzed him since he was born. He must destroy that which was Tom Ransome; he must annihilate it, crushing the very ego into the red soil of Ranchipur. He must tear down and humiliate that muddled thinker, that liberal, that quixotic, self-questioning egotist. In this world in which he found himself, in that old tired world which he had left, there was no place for such men as Tom Ransome. One ounce of action was worth a ton of thought. Philosophy was a luxury for the weak—detachment the vice of the idle. He must destroy all that to emerge at last as simple, as naked, as the servant of Mr. Bannerjee standing there on the balcony in the fading light, looking out over the ruined city of Ranchipur.

This time the vision did not leave him, fading away into an obscurity where it was lost from faith or understanding. It stayed with him while he carried the dying Swiss into the Music School, while he undressed him and went in search of the Major.

And now while he stood by the *chattee*, pouring tepid water over his naked body, scrubbing himself sparingly with the precious bit of tired soap, the vision was still with him, and when he thought of the Major he knew that the Major must have seen something, some new look, in the eyes, and understood, and once again he experienced a warm surging wave of friendliness toward the Major and Raschid and the Smileys and even the old Maharani. He had been their friend but he had always been apart from them, separated by some vague barrier which left him isolated and turned the friendship sterile. Now it was different. He *knew* them. He divined what it was they were, in its very essence. He must cling to this new understanding; he must not let this vision escape as it had done so many times before. By his very bootstraps he must pull himself up, and once he was secure, he must turn his back forever on that old barren, querulous self.

When he had dressed again he went to find Fern, and discovered her in the office where timid Mr. Das, the director of the Music School, had once sat trying to keep his muddled accounts in European fashion; and when he came in the door he saw her in a new way, as if before she had existed in a shadow where she remained indistinct and endowed with qualities and a character built up out of the imagination which fed the ego of the old Tom Ransome. He saw in her what Aunt Phoebe, with her simplicity and age had seen long ago on the night when he brought Fern from his own house to the Smileys.

He said, "Harry Bauer is dying."

"I know."

"I've come to take his place."

For a second she regarded him in dismay. "No, you mustn't do that. You're too valuable."

"I'm not valuable at all. I have to do it."

Then he saw, with a quickening of life itself, that she was glad.

"It's all arranged," he said. "You'll have to show me the ropes. I want some alcohol first to wash my hands."

She gave him the alcohol and stood watching him.

She said, "There are fewer cases today. The Major thinks it may mean the epidemic is under control."

"And deaths——"

"As many as ever. Most of them die . . . nine out of ten." The tired young face had a kind of gravity in it which he had seen sometimes in the face of Aunt Phoebe. "Luckily they die quickly. It leaves place for the others."

Then suddenly he put his arms about her and hugged her close to him, passionately; this new Fern was somehow a woman and new to him and precious in a way no woman had ever been before.

He said, "It will be better working together."

In a voice so low that he could scarcely hear her, she said, "I'm frightened."

"It'll be all right now. I know it will be all right." It would be all right if he kept that vision, if he destroyed what he had been before. Then he would never "go away" again, leaving her alone and frightened.

She said, "You must not sleep in Harry Bauer's room."

He looked at her for a moment in silence and then said, "I'll make up a bed here in the office."

Then she smiled for the first time he had seen her smile since the earthquake, and said, "That is what I wanted. I want you near me. It'll be so much easier that way, if you're near me."

"Nobody will gossip now."

"It wouldn't matter much if they did." She pressed her face close to him and said, "I'm ashamed."

"Why?"

"Because I am happy."

For a moment he did not answer her, and then he said, "You mustn't be ashamed. It was meant to be like that, else the world wouldn't go on."

"We must make the rounds now. I'll show you what has to be done. Some of them will be dead."

At five o'clock Harry Bauer was dead. All through the afternoon Ransome came and went to and from the little room where the Swiss had installed himself so neatly, giving him the Kaolin solution and the chloride of sodium and calcium. That the Swiss should live became a kind of obsession with him. Harry Bauer had to recover and go back again to Switzerland and that life to which he had always belonged. Ransome even understood for a time the will to life which Miss MacDaid exerted over the ill and the dying. When he bent over the half-dead body of Bauer and wiped the froth away from the purple lips, he kept thinking, "You must live! You must not die!" But Harry Bauer only

[514]

lay still without response, save when now and then the agonizing cramps drew his legs up beneath his chin. The Major knew that there was never any chance because the cholera asked nothing better as a feeding-ground than a fresh, young, and healthy body from the West. A little before five, when Ransome came into the room, he was aware that a change had come over the Swiss. He lay very still with the head drawn back, the mouth open. There was no sign of breathing and no pulse, and he thought, "He is dead. Now he will never go home."

He went to fetch Fern who knew better than he the signs of death by cholera. Bending over him, she said, "It's no use." They went away, leaving the body until the Major came back; and a little after six he arrived and went with Ransome to Bauer's room. When Ransome touched the wrist there was still the heat of fever in it. The Major took the surer way; drawing back the sheet, he said, "Look!" The muscular body—the beautiful body which Maria Lishinskaia had said was the only thing in the world which Harry Bauer loved—was no longer white. The muscles were turning dark brown, so that they lay outlined like the muscles of an anatomist's chart against the gray of other tissues. Then as they stood there one leg moved slowly upward and then outward like the leg of a dancer in a ballet.

"But he moved," said Ransome.

"That is cholera," said the Major, drawing back the sheet. "You see, the body is only a machine. The spirit has fled, but the muscles go on working, like a fly-wheel that is running down."

At noon the Major sent a message to Aunt Phoebe to say that the bullock carriage was coming to take her to the Maharani. In his note he asked for no answer, and the assumption that the message was a command annoyed the old lady for a moment. Then when the messenger had left she was annoyed because such a visit would, she knew, kill four or five hours out of a day in which every minute was precious. When Bertha Smiley came in from the orphanage she told her the news and asked, "What do you suppose it means?"

"It means, I suppose, that she has heard about you and wants to see you. She is full of curiosity."

"I suppose I ought to dress up."

"Yes . . . of course."

"My new foulard?" suggested Aunt Phoebe. "With the collar of Battenberg lace."

"Yes and your corals."

"Do you suppose we'll get on?"

"I should think so. She'll either be very stiff and grand or . . ." She searched for a simile and found it—"or just like one of your old friends in Cedar Falls. There's nothing to be afraid of."

"I'm not afraid," said Aunt Phoebe, "only maybe I won't know how to behave."

"It's easy. I'll show you. Suppose you're the Maharani. I'll be you. Now I'll come in the door with my hands like this, and then I bow and say, 'Good-afternoon, Your Highness.' And then she'll talk. She likes to talk, so don't interrupt her too much. She'll probably ask you a lot of questions."

"I wish she'd given me more time to get ready."

"You'll be all right. She doesn't care much how you're dressed or if your hair is curled. All you must remember is to keep calling her, 'Your Highness.' She likes that."

"I'll remember." She started for the kitchen, but Bertha stopped her. "I can manage the noon meal. Homer's at the Orphanage. I can stay here till you go. Go and get yourself ready. In all the damp your foulard will need pressing."

Aunt Phoebe protested for a moment and then gave in, grumbling a little as she disappeared in the direction of her own room.

Now that the shock of the invitation had passed she began to feel a little excited, so excited that she even allowed that Bertha, with the help of one boy, could manage the lunch. Mrs. Simon and Mrs. Hoggett-Egburry were still with them, because neither of them was willing to sleep alone in Mrs. Hoggett-Egburry's bungalow. They were there during most of the day, putting the place in order, but they returned for their meals and slept in the storeroom at the Mission. While Aunt Phoebe took the foulard out of the eucalyptus chest, she thanked Heaven that they had made up their quarrel, whatever it had been about, and were again as thick as thieves. She did not mind the Mississippi laziness of Mrs. Simon or the Cockney sluttishness of Mrs. Hoggett-Egburry, but she did mind their foolishness and their mutual habit of talking all the time, whether they had anything to say or not. And she was contemptuous of them for their terror, for since the disaster and the epidemic neither of them would venture near an Indian. They had even proposed to Aunt Phoebe to send away the one Untouchable boy who helped her in the kitchen, saying that he would bring cholera from the city.

But Aunt Phoebe had only said, maliciously, "That wouldn't do any good. Europeans can carry cholera just as well . . . better, the Major says, because cholera likes fresh European blood. Europeans just die like flies of it."

In Aunt Phoebe's mind there was no need to take precautions beyond those of the simplest cleanliness. If you got cholera, you got it. Maybe the Lord intended it or maybe it just happened by accident but you couldn't do anything about it.

In the beginning the terror of Mrs. Hoggett-Egburry had been worse than that of Mrs. Simon, but gradually the infection had spread, until now both of them lived in a perpetual state of hysteria, heightened in the case of Mrs. Hoggett-Egburry by the brandy which she had found in her house untouched by the raiding Bhils.

Aunt Phoebe was running an iron over the foulard dress when she saw the two figures through the window coming back to the Mission for lunch along the road from the direction of the Distillery. It was raining again and both of them carried umbrellas and bags slung over their shoulders—bags, Aunt Phoebe knew, filled with Mrs. Hoggett-Egburry's magpie collection of bric-à-brac. For two days they had been carrying it from the bungalow into the Mission storeroom. One corner of the room was filled with brassware and cheap shawls and *saris,* inlaid taborets and embroidered cushions. The police had recovered the sewing-machine, the alarm clock and three brass trays, and the Bhils who took them were shut up now in a big barred room in the elephant *Philkana.* But the enlarged and tinted photograph of Mrs. Hoggett-Egburry in her prime was still missing.

Now, as Aunt Phoebe watched them, she discerned the figure of a coolie coming along the road toward them, and putting down her iron she waited to see what would happen. When the coolie came within twenty yards of the two burdened women, Mrs. Hoggett-Egburry and

Mrs. Simon took to the muddy fields, never stopping until they were fifty yards from the road. From that distance they called out to him in bad Hindustani not to come any nearer. The man gave them a single glance and continued on his way toward the town. And when he passed, they returned to the road on their way to the Mission.

Aunt Phoebe gave a chuckle and returned to pressing the damp wrinkles out of the foulard.

"Like a couple of orthodox Brahmins," she thought.

In a little while she heard them in the storeroom, talking together and unloading their cargo of treasure, and then through the window she saw coming up the Mission drive one of the Mahratta policemen.

He had come from Gopal Rao, bringing a note addressed to Mrs. Hoggett-Egburry. It was to say that Mr. Hoggett-Egburry had arranged for one of the planes to bring his wife to the safety of Bombay. There were two places in the plane besides that of the pilot. Mrs. Hoggett-Egburry could bring with her whom she liked. When she finished reading the note she sank into a kitchen chair and said, "Thank God! We're saved!"

"What? What is it?" Mrs. Simon asked. "How are we saved?"

"'Erbert has sent a plane for us. I knew he wouldn't abandon me."

"You can go. I can't . . . and leave Fern."

But Aunt Phoebe, who was taking no chances, came in just in time to hear what she said, and before Mrs. Hoggett-Egburry could answer she said, "Fern won't go. I'll look after her. You don't need to worry."

"I couldn't do that."

"It's the only thing to do. Suppose you got cholera and died here and left Fern an orphan. That would be nice, wouldn't it? With nobody at all to look after her."

Mrs. Hoggett-Egburry said, "She's right, Mary Lou. Think of it, especially now that she's going to be married. You must think of yourself as well as Fern."

"I'd have to think it over."

But Aunt Phoebe said, "You better get together what you're goin' to take with you. These planes'll have to get out of here before dark. Don't you worry. I understand Fern. Bertha and I can keep an eye on her."

"I'd have to see her before I left."

But Mrs. Hoggett-Egburry intervened tipsily, "And go to that pesthouse? I forbid you. You might bring infection along with you. They wouldn't let you land in Bombay. You can't do that. And think of it, Fern engaged, and such a good match, too. It's a time for common sense now."

"You'd better get your things together," repeated Aunt Phoebe, quietly.

"I'll think about it," said Mrs. Simon, and began to cry suddenly. "I've never flown before," she said.

"Neither have I," said Mrs. Hoggett-Egburry, "but I'd rather fly than die here like a rat in a hole. The Smileys can keep my brassware, can't you? It won't be any trouble."

"No," said Bertha Smiley.

"We'll take good care of it," said Aunt Phoebe.

"It's all so awful," said Mrs. Simon, still sobbing. "I don't see why Fern has to make everything worse by staying in that awful town. She never thought of anything but herself since she was born."

"Come along now," said Aunt Phoebe. "If you're ready by three o'clock you can go into town with me."

"We can't walk all that way," said Mrs. Hoggett-Egburry.

"You won't have to," said Aunt Phoebe. "The Maharani is sending her bullock carriage for me. You can ride with me." And then as if what she had said was no Parthian shot, but only a simple observation she left them.

When she had gone, Mrs. Hoggett-Egburry and Mrs. Simon, her tears suddenly dried, went into the storeroom to make ready for their flight. When the door was closed Mrs. Simon spoke the thought which was in both their minds: "How do you suppose she got invited to the Maharani's?"

There was no answer. Mrs. Hoggett-Egburry rolled her eyes and turned to select out of the heap of her belongings those things which she meant to take with her.

"I must say, nothing here makes sense. When I get to Bombay I'm going to make Herbert resign from the bank and take me back to England. A man with his talents can find a good place there. And if he can't we'll just go down and live quietly in Shropshire. I've got a lot of relatives there . . . county people, you know. I won't go on spending the best years of my life in a place like Ranchipur." She gave a tipsy snort of indignation. "Imagine! That old trout being sent for by the Maharani!"

For Mrs. Simon the preparations were simple enough, since everything she possessed in the world lay buried beneath the heap of stones which had once been her house. Between her and Mrs. Hoggett-Egburry there had been a reconciliation, and now that the first hysteria and terror were past, they got on a little better, partly because they had, in a sense, been forced into each other's arms, since no one in Ranchipur save the Smileys who fed them, took the least notice of them. But the reconciliation was not accompanied by a restoration of Mrs. Hoggett-Egburry's prestige. Mrs. Simon held the secret of her drinking over her like a club, and now that the secret was out, Mrs. Hoggett-Egburry no longer confined herself to drinking secretly and to getting drunk only in the evenings in the privacy of her own house. Now she drank when and where it suited her fancy. In a way it recompensed her for her loss of prestige. Now Mrs. Simon called her openly by her Christian name, and she, in turn, called Mrs. Simon "Mary Lou." And since Mrs. Simon had given it out as a fact that she was to be the mother-in-law of the brother of an earl, she was sure of her superiority. Yet in their hearts they hated each other, with the hatred of two females who have always disliked and distrusted each other.

While Mrs. Hoggett-Egburry sat unsteadily on a stool rummaging among all her bazaar finery, Mrs. Simon lay on the bed, weeping, and saying over and over again, "I can't go. I can't leave Fern. She's all I've got in the world." She was aware now, more than ever, of the loss of her husband and her daughter Hazel, for she felt an attack coming on with no audience, no one to be concerned over her, no one to comfort her and make soft speeches.

Mrs. Hoggett-Egburry went on selecting things out of the heap and placing them in piles on either side of the stool. There was a semblance of order, but no fact. She would place things now in one pile, now in the other, now back again in the general heap, until at last, in desperate confusion, she sat up, looked toward the bed, and said, "God-damn it, Mary Lou, lend me a hand with this stuff."

But Mrs. Simon only moaned and said, "Don't ask me to do anything now."

Then Mrs. Hoggett-Egburry sat up, looked at the bed again, and measuring her words with a deadly drunken accuracy, said, "You're alone, all right! You haven't got anybody. You'd better pack up and go back to Unity Point and all your old mammies, because if you ever think you're going to get Fern back again, you're crazy. That girl's got too much sense."

Mrs. Simon gave a low scream and covered her face with her hands as if she had been struck, but there was no audience. Mrs. Hoggett-Egburry simply turned her back and lost herself in the interminable confusion of her "sorting."

The bullock carriage was half an hour late in arriving, and until it appeared Aunt Phoebe, Mrs. Hoggett-Egburry and Mrs. Simon sat on stiff kitchen chairs, waiting, Mrs. Hoggett-Egburry surrounded by bundles and parcels containing her treasures. The two "friends" were not speaking to each other, and between them Aunt Phoebe sat in serene malice, aware that the confusion of one's enemies so complete was seldom delivered into one's hands in this world. Now and then Mrs. Simon sniffed and dabbed at her eyes with her handkerchief. She wore one of Mrs. Smiley's topees and one of Mrs. Hoggett-Egburry's pongee suits which she had borrowed before the latest insults. It was too large for her and gave her at once a mournful and a ridiculous appearance.

When the carriage at last arrived, drawn by the white Mysore bullocks with gilded horns, it was not at all what Aunt Phoebe had expected. Never having seen a royal bullock carriage, she had imagined it to be rather like the horse cabs which had met the trains in Cedar Falls, with ample room for both passengers and baggage. Instead, it turned out to be a kind of throne, mounted upon four wheels with a seat for the bullock-driver at the front. It was an ample throne but not ample enough to cope with the bottoms of the three ladies. If Mrs. Hoggett-Egburry and Mrs. Simon were to reach the plane in time there was nothing to be done except for all three to adjust themselves somehow. It ended with Aunt Phoebe sitting in the middle of the throne, her narrow seat wedged between the ample ones of the two other travelers. On top of them were heaped Mrs. Hoggett-Egburry's bundles and parcels.

The whole performance was regarded by the bullock-driver with distrust. Never before had he seen the royal carriage used as an omnibus, and being already late, he was fearful of the Maharani's anger. And he was bewildered, too, by the strange jargon which the ladies in turn and sometimes together directed at him. Meanwhile the rain descended in torrents so that by the time the three women were settled beneath the collapsible top of the carriage, all Aunt Phoebe's care in pressing her new foulard had come to naught.

But at last they were settled and the driver climbing up on the seat, poked the two disgruntled bullocks in the behind, and the party set off down the Mission drive.

The bullocks were luxurious animals, aware that their ancestors had been bred long ago in Mysore to draw the cannon of the Tippoo Sahib. They were fed and washed and their horns gilded afresh every morning and they were accustomed only to drawing the old Maharajah on his evening drives. Never before had they drawn a cargo so common as that composed of Aunt Phoebe, Mrs. Simon and Mrs. Hoggett-Egburry with all her parcels, and now they were being prodded by a driver who was terrified of delivering his passenger behind schedule at the tent of the Maharani. They broke into the trot for which they were famous, grunting and moaning as they moved along the metaled road. The gait was bumpy and uncomfortable, drawing the light carriage forward in a series of jerks which terrified Mrs. Simon and Mrs. Hoggett-Egburry. They were at last riding in a conveyance belonging to the Maharani, but they were doing so only on the sufferance of Aunt Phoebe and on their way out of Ranchipur perhaps forever.

The trotting accompanied by the terrifying moaning and grunting of the bullocks, continued as far as the railroad bridge, and then the bullocks were forced to go slowly lest one of the loose planks spring up and wreck the carriage. The river was a little lower now, but it still roared only a foot or two beneath the bridge. The sight of the rushing water made Mrs. Hoggett-Egburry dizzy and she closed her eyes and leaned back, thinking hazily, with Cockney common sense, "If I'm going to die, I might as well not see it coming on." Mrs. Simon closed her eyes and added her groans to the protesting noises made by the sulking bullocks. As for Aunt Phoebe, she sat bolt upright, clutching two of Mrs. Hoggett-Egburry's bundles, staring toward the city. For four days she had been devoured by a desire to see what had happened to the town and there had never been an instant free in which she might have satisfied her curiosity. The driver shouted imprecations at the bullocks, the loose planks jiggled and banged beneath the carriage, and at last they reached solid ground again. Opening her eyes, Mrs. Simon said, "Thank God!" and covered her face up to the eyes with an Indian scarf. At once Mrs. Hoggett-Egburry imitated her action.

By the roadside there were no bodies now, but here and there the bones of a donkey or a cow or a *pie* dog picked white and clean by the vultures. In the mud, among the ruins of the houses, the townspeople had built ramshackle shelters and as the carriage passed, faces peered out in wonder at the spectacle of the Maharajah's grunting bullocks with gilded horns drawing three Europeans buried beneath parcels, two of them apparently veiled like Muslim women. Here and there troops of coolies were at work clearing away the rubbish strewn among the ruins by the flood. Mrs. Hoggett-Egburry forgot her terror and stared tipsily at the sights about her, thinking dimly that all these details would make a wonderful story once Herbert had retired and they were home again in England.

They passed near the Music School where the coolies were burning a score of bodies, and at last came to the Great Gate where the three women, speaking bad Hindustani to the driver, whose only language was Mahratta, persuaded him to stop. But no sooner had the carriage ceased to move and the bullocks to grunt and groan, than Mrs. Simon began again to cry. The sight of the Music School and the burning of the bodies had upset her and filled her with a fresh surge of love and devotion for Fern, and now she insisted that before she left she must say good-by to her. But this time Mrs. Hoggett-Egburry was having no nonsense. She said, "If you go near that Music School, you can't go in the plane with me."

Then Gopal Rao appeared, a glint of amusement in his young Mahratta eyes, and began to take out the bundles which buried them. Mrs. Hoggett-Egburry and Mrs. Simon went on quarreling, a muffled quarrel conducted entirely through the scarfs which they held to their faces.

Mrs. Hoggett-Egburry said, "If you think I'm going to sit here inhaling cholera germs while you go off to see Fern in that pest-house, you're crazy." And with tipsy haughtiness she addressed Gopal Rao. "Boy," she said, "where is the plane?"

For a second anger flashed in the black eyes, but it died away quickly and Gopal Rao giggled, "It's in a field beyond the Parsee Tower."

"But how are we to get there?"

"I'm afraid you must walk." He was polite now, ironically, mockingly polite, his temper recovered, his Mahratta humor restored. With his Indian intuition he knew that these two middle-aged women were ridiculous and of no importance in the European scale of values. He was a Mahratta, a descendant of raiding warriors. Their bad manners could not touch him.

"I can't walk all that way," she said. "Look at my feet." And she exhibited a tiny foot shod with the highest and most frivolous of heels. She had dressed herself, it was clear, not for the escape, but for the arrival in Bombay.

"Madame," said Gopal Rao, "there is no other way. We cannot bring the plane here. A plane must have space to raise itself into the air."

"There is the bullock cart." But when she turned the bullock carriage was already moving off at top speed, the bullocks moaning and grunting more loudly than ever beneath the prods of a driver, goaded in his turn by terror of the Maharani. Aunt Phoebe was enjoying the scene and would have preferred to remain for a little time, but the driver carried her away willy-nilly to deliver her to the Maharani.

At the same moment two figures appeared in the gateway. They were Lady Esketh, dressed in a nurse's costume, and Miss Hodge. They were walking hand in hand like two schoolgirls. At sight of them Mrs. Hoggett-Egburry turned and said, "Good-afternoon, Lady Esketh."

Edwina said, "Good-afternoon."

Mrs. Simon, still hysterical, said, "Good-afternoon," and then Mrs. Hoggett-Egburry saw her chance. She said, "We're just going to Bombay by plane. I have an extra place. I could take you with me if you care to go."

Mrs. Simon's mouth opened and closed behind the scarf, but no sound came out. She was so astonished by the treachery of her friend that she could not speak. There was no need, for Lady Esketh said, "Thanks for the offer, but I'm staying here. I hope you have a pleasant trip," and then she and Miss Hodge went on their way.

Meanwhile Gopal Rao had burdened three coolies with the bundles and said, "We must go along now. The plane must leave to arrive in Bombay before dark. I will show you the way." And without further ado he led the way, followed by the three coolies carrying the bundles. For a moment the two women stood looking after the procession and then their terror of Ranchipur, of cholera, of death, claimed them again and as docile as two calves they turned and followed the little procession through the mud and the filth in the direction of the Tower of Silence, Mrs. Hoggett-Egburry wobbly on her high heels, her breasts and behind quivering and shaking with each step.

The Maharani, it appeared, was not astonished by the lateness of Aunt Phoebe's arrival. She came into the tent and upset all Bertha Smiley's instructions by coming forward and shaking hands with Aunt Phoebe. From somewhere the servants had produced a rocking-chair and the Maharani invited Aunt Phoebe to sit in it. Then she introduced the Princess of Bewanagar who also took Aunt Phoebe's hand. The Maharani herself did not sit on a cushion, but on an Empire chair salvaged from the Palace. The old Princess seated herself in a folding camp chair, and the Maharani said, "It is very good of you to come and see me. I have been wanting to know you for a long time, but my life here is so filled with things."

"Your Highness," said Aunt Phoebe, "it was very kind of Your Highness to send for me."

"They tell me you have done a great deal for my people during the disaster."

"I did what had to be done, Your Highness," said Aunt Phoebe, simply. "I'm very sorry to be late, but the driver was late and then there was those two women. I had to bring them into town."

"What two women?"

"Mrs. Hoggett-Egburry and Mrs. Simon."

The Maharani frowned. "Couldn't they walk?"

"Yes, Your Highness, but I wanted to make sure that they got off."

The frown relaxed into the ghost of a smile. "Mrs. Hoggett-Egburry," she said. "That's the bank manager's wife, isn't it?"

"Yes, Your Highness."

"And the other one is the missionary's wife."

"That's right, Your Highness."

"Yes, she's been to the Palace. I remember her."

Then there was a silence in which Aunt Phoebe, waiting nervously, began to rock herself gently.

A servant appeared bringing tea, and the Maharani said, "I am very grateful to you and the Smileys for all you have done."

The old Princess began pouring the tea, and with a teacup in her hand Aunt Phoebe began to feel a little more at home. She had seen the Maharani a half-dozen times in the distance, driving in the hot evenings in her Rolls-Royce, staring in front of her, seeing no one as she passed among her people, and to Aunt Phoebe she had always seemed remote and unreal and inhuman, like a goddess carved out of stone. Now she saw that the Maharani was real, made of flesh and blood; from the way she sat down carefully in the Empire chair it was evident that she even perhaps had a touch of sciatica.

"They are two very silly women," said Her Highness, suddenly.

Knowing whom the Maharani meant, Aunt Phoebe said, "Yes, Your Highness, women like that are only a nuisance in such times."

"Very common," said the Maharani. And then, unable to contain her curiosity any longer, she asked, "Why did you leave America to come here?"

"I wanted to see India, Your Highness, and once I got here I liked it."

"Do you still like it—even now?"

"Yes, Your Highness, even now. There's nothing to be afraid of at my age."

"How old are you?"

"I'll be eighty-two in September."

They were beginning to get on. Aunt Phoebe liked frankness and detested nonsense. The Maharani did not mince about. She asked direct questions.

[526]

"Tell me about yourself . . . about your life in America."

"I don't know what there is to tell, Your Highness."

"About your family and what kind of a house you lived in and what it was like when you were young."

Aunt Phoebe knew what it was she wanted. She wanted to know about America and people like herself exactly the way Aunt Phoebe had wanted to know about India and people like the Maharani. So she began to tell about Iowa and her girlhood and her parents and grandparents and described the farm and the fierce winters and summers that were as hot in good corn weather as Ranchipur during the monsoon rains. And as she talked, the nervousness left her, and as the Maharani went on asking questions, she saw that in this old lady, talking shyly while she gently rocked herself, there was wisdom and simplicity and dignity and humor and goodness and understanding, and that there was, too, impatience and even a little malice where the foolish and the vain were concerned. They began to understand each other and to "get on," and presently Aunt Phoebe forgot Bertha Smiley's instructions to use "Your Highness" with every sentence and sometimes merely said "You."

After a time the Maharani began to talk of her own youth and childhood and of the harshness of life in that distant, wild, dusty red plateau where she had been born and which she had not seen since she was a child of thirteen. She felt herself at ease with the old lady from the Middle West of America. She was neither obsequious nor presumptuous and it was clear that she had come simply for a cup of tea and a chat, wanting neither favors nor bringing an ax to grind. She was both comfortable and by her very age comforting. The Maharani, while Aunt Phoebe rocked and gossiped, felt toward her as Raschid felt and Ransome and the Major and poor dead Mr. Jobnekar. Sometimes the old Princess, chuckling, interrupted her friend the Maharani to say, "No, it was not like that," or, "You are wrong, Masaheb, it was the year of the great drought."

Aunt Phoebe, rocking and listening, would sometimes say, "Well, what an interesting story," or, "It doesn't seem possible." She felt presently that she might be outstaying her welcome and she began to feel worried about getting back to the Orphanage in order to give Bertha a little rest, but she kept reminding herself what Bertha had told her—that she must stay until the Maharani dismissed her.

It was nearly six o'clock when the Maharani rose at last, shook her hand, and said, "You must come again very soon. I'll send the bullock carriage for you."

"Thank you," said Aunt Phoebe. "I'd like to come. I've enjoyed my afternoon."

Then she shook hands with the plump old Princess and when they had gone, an A.D.C. led her to the bullock carriage and, climbing onto the throne, she set out for home behind the white Mysore bullocks with gilded horns thinking what an interesting letter she would have to write home to her sons. She could not imagine what people meant when they said Indians were different, and about her heart there was a sudden warmth because, even as old as she was, she had discovered two new friends. She had been very lucky of late with new friends—there was also Lady Esketh and Fern. She thought, "The next time I come in I must go to the hospital and call on them."

Since Lady Esketh had come to the hospital it was her first opportunity to leave it. When the new nurses arrived Miss MacDaid, meeting her in the corridor, had said, "You're looking seedy. You'd better go for some air." And so she had gone out, pleased to escape from the hospital if only into the desolation of the city. She had meant to go alone, for there were many things which she wished to consider in peace, but as she left, Miss Hodge came running to her in a panic, crying out, "Where are you going? You're not going to leave me?" so there was nothing for it but to take Miss Hodge with her, leading her by the hand as if she were a child.

It was not that poor Miss Hodge was a trouble—she was perfectly happy to walk in silence by her side—it was only that she wanted to be alone for a little while. For four days she had never been alone for a moment save in the still hours of the morning when she kept watch over more than two hundred ill and dying people. For the first time in her life she divined that privacy, which she had always taken for granted, was a great and precious luxury. To be alone in one's room seemed suddenly a kind of paradise. In her heart she did not like women, and sharing a room with a woman, even silly, harmless Miss Hodge, was for her an ordeal against which her instinct, her nerves, her whole being, cried out. Then in more reasonable moments while she sat in the ward, keeping watch, she thought, "There must be people in the world who in all their lives have never had a room to themselves. I suppose most people have to live like that." However that made it no easier for her. But she managed somehow to keep her temper when Fern Simon stole half the precious bit of mirror; she kept it even when Miss Hodge became tiresome, staring at her while she did her nails and her hair, following her even when she went outside to the temporary privy, standing patiently outside like a dog awaiting his master. She kept her temper lest she should give Miss MacDaid some reason for sending her away. But that made the loss of privacy no better, but only worse. Now that the three nurses had come, she was more frightened than ever of being dismissed. She could not go away now. She could not be where she could not see him, however casually, now and then during the day and the night. Sometimes he passed by her on the stairway or in the ward, taking no more notice of her than if she had been a chair or a table, but twice since he had talked to her by the light from the funeral pyre outside the windows, he had looked at her for a second, and in the meeting of their eyes she knew that he had forgotten nothing of what he had said. Each time her whole body had grown warm for a second and she had turned away in confusion, the whole room reeling about her; and for the rest of the day she had gone about the filthiest of tasks, unaware of her surroundings, moving in a kind of haze.

Now as she walked through the ruined streets into the Park of the Maharajah with Miss Hodge trotting happily at her side, she was filled with wonder at the thing which had happened to her—that at thirty-seven she was in love for the first time. That it happened after so much experience only increased the sense of wonder; despairing sometimes, she had believed that she would never find the thing for which she had been searching without knowing what it was. And now she knew.

It was different from anything she had ever experienced or imagined. It was, she thought, like some manifestation of nature, like the opening of a flower, petal by petal, before the warmth of the sun. It was as if inside her the spirit was growing, expanding, as if all her sensibilities were acutely aware of the process. As she walked her body no longer seemed to have weight; it was as if she floated over the muddy earth. She thought: "I am young. It is the first time I have ever been young." For long ago at seventeen she had been thrust into a harsh realistic world full of death and despair and the need for haste, a world in which there was no time or place for youth save to be slaughtered.

And it was extraordinary how different was this feeling she knew now, how little of the body there was in it, how little of curiosity or even desire, how little of that terrible boredom and thirst for satisfaction she had known in all her other adventures, even in that first one long ago with Tom Ransome. For the first time she was filled with a desire to discipline herself, to dominate and even to humiliate her body. Desire no longer seemed of importance; it was enough now to serve, enough that she might be near him forever as she was near him now, working, satisfied, made happy by a glance or a word. She remembered what he had said—that to a doctor and a surgeon the body was a machine, no more, no less. The senses brought both pleasure and pain, but that was not important. The important thing was that which lay above and beyond the body, without which no perfect ecstasy was possible.

Above the annoying chatter of Miss Hodge, dragging like a weight at her hand, a strange thought came to her—that this new knowledge, this new ecstasy was possible to her because in all her experience, in all her promiscuousness, her body had been no more than a machine which she had used in cold blood; and so the part that was herself had been saved. She had never slept with a man for whom she had not felt contempt, Ransome for his weakness and paralyzing self-questioning, Esketh because he had been a brute, André Simon, the boxer, because in spite of the pleasure his animalness gave her, she hated him for his stupidity. Now in this new world, the others scarcely existed any longer; she found it difficult to recall them, to remember their voices, the way they made love or even their appearances. The Major was the first man for whom she had respect. She wanted to be like him, to lose her own identity in his, to work as he worked, to make herself seem worthy of his respect. The weariness, the boredom, were gone now; they were, she believed, gone forever. She had escaped that terror which had haunted her during the past few years, of growing old and ugly and lecherous

[530]

like the women in distant Europe who haunted night clubs and watering-places and kept young men. Now she was free; she asked no more than the privilege of being near him, of working for him, of talking to him now and then.

And as she walked with Miss Hodge she saw nothing of the desolation of the ruined city nor felt the awful heat or the drenching rain that kept falling in sudden showers. She was aware only of a kind of rosy glow that seemed to fill all the sky.

She thought, "The thing is working out. That is why I came to India. . . . Something had to happen to me here."

Then she was aware of the bullock carriage and of the hubbub about it, and the figures of Gopal Rao and Mrs. Hoggett-Egburry and Mrs. Simon and Aunt Phoebe, the coolies, the multitude of bundles, and the complaining bullocks. They appeared dimly to her. She heard Mrs. Hoggett-Egburry addressing her and she was aware of answering, but stronger than anything in that moment was the sudden sense of the richness of life, of the comic quality of the scene beneath the arch of the Great Gateway. It was all exciting, now as if she were a child who was seeing the great world for the first time.

Then as they quickly passed the little group, she felt Miss Hodge tugging at her hand and saying, "Why, there's our bungalow. Let's go in and see if Sarah has come back."

So, moved a little by curiosity and indifferent to where she went, she pushed open the gate. On the way up the path Miss Hodge said, "I wanted you to see how nice we've fixed up the bungalow. You'd never believe it was in India. It's just like a house at home."

The door stood ajar and as she pushed it open Miss Hodge called out, "Sarah! Sarah!" and when there was no answer she said, "I can't understand it. She wouldn't go out leaving the door open."

And then Edwina saw that in Miss Hodge's crazy mind the flood had never touched the bungalow. She had returned to it expecting to find it exactly as it was before the disaster, the cushions, the doilies, the nostalgic photographs all in their places.

But the sitting-room was stained with mud. Some of the photographs had fallen from the wall and lay shattered on the floor. There was a sickly smell of mildew and drying mud. Once again Miss Hodge called,

"Sarah! Sarah!" and then from somewhere in the deep recesses of her mad brain knowledge and truth and sanity appeared for an instant. She let go of Edwina's hand and leaned against the door, a look of horror in her eyes.

Edwina said, "It'll be all right. We'll come around one of these days and put the place in order."

Miss Hodge didn't answer her. She only said in a low voice, "I know now. Sarah is dead. She is never coming back. I know now. She went out into the flood to see after the school books. Poor Sarah! Why didn't you tell me she was dead?" Then she slipped down the edge of the doorway to the floor in a faint.

Because the bungalow was opposite the Gateway where there were always sentinels, it had not been looted. Everything was as it had been when Miss Hodge had taken refuge on the roof, even the brandy bottle which Sarah Dirks had left on the table after she had tried to make Miss Hodge drunk so that she might escape and die. Now Edwina smelled the bottle and poured a glass of brandy between the lips of Miss Hodge. When at last she opened her eyes, the moment of sanity had mercifully gone.

Weakly she said, "Where am I?"

"You're in your own bungalow. We came to see what state it was in."

Miss Hodge sat up and said, "I'm sorry. I used to have fainting-fits like this when I was a girl." Then the odd shadow of a smile appeared at the corners of her fleshy mouth, a shadow of satisfaction even of complacency, "I suppose it's my condition that made me faint," she said. "Perhaps I'd better speak of it to the Major." A shadow crossed her face. "Do you think Sarah will understand that it wasn't really my fault?"

"Of course she'll understand. We'll have to go back to the hospital now." She wanted to take Miss Hodge away quickly. She was afraid that a terrible moment of sanity might return to her. It would be a pity, for she was very happy as she was.

As they passed the Music School, Edwina said, "I'm going in here for a moment. You wait for me here under this tree."

But Miss Hodge said, "Do let me come with you. I'd like to."

"It's a pest-house. It's full of cholera patients."

"I don't mind that. I'm not afraid. I'm very lucky."

"Do it to please me."

"All right," said Miss Hodge; "if you ask me that way." So she sat down on the edge of the wall surrounding the Great Tank, beneath a peepul tree, looking down at her hands, smiling peacefully.

Inside the unfamiliar hallway Edwina found herself alone save for the bodies of three men dead of cholera, wrapped in their *dhotis*, the legs drawn up part way to the chin. Near them there was a great pool of water where the rain had come through the damaged roof. For a second, sharply aware of the desolation of the scene, she stood still thinking, almost with jealousy: "This is more horrible than the hospital! Fern was sent here. It must have been because they trusted her more than me."

She had meant to speak to Fern, to give her a friendly "hello" in passing, but now she did not know how to find her in this strange, desolate place. A Sweeper passed carrying a brush and an iron pail. He looked at her curiously, and when she attempted to speak to him in English he only shook his head and passed her like a deaf mute, without changing his expression.

The smell was everywhere, the dreadful smell of cholera patients. She thought, "Fern might be in that room," but when she pushed open the door she saw in the dim rainy light only two rows of cholera patients lying on the floor of a long room. The awful stench flowed past her into the hallway and suddenly she was overcome by nausea and fear. Then as she turned to close the door she saw Ransome dimly coming down the corridor beyond the pool of water.

As he came nearer he recognized her and said, "What are you doing here?"

"I had an hour off. I dropped in to see Fern."

"She's asleep. Since the new nurse came it's easier for her. The Swiss is dead."

"Cholera?"

"Yes."

"Is that why you are here?"

"No. I've come to stay. I'm in charge here now—with Fern and the new nurse."

"I don't envy you."

[533]

"It isn't very pleasant. You oughtn't to come here and you oughtn't to stay. There are too many mysterious ways of getting cholera."

"What about yourself?"

"My luck always holds for this sort of thing. And I believe in disinfectant." He took her arm. "Come along. If you want to talk, let's go out into the air."

She went with him, thinking that somehow he had changed. How, she could not discover, but he was different, less cynical, less negative. "Perhaps," she thought, "it's only because he's sober now."

Outside he told her that he had asked for the job. He didn't suppose he'd have it for long, or that they would need her much longer at the hospital.

"The railroad will be open in a day or two and then they'll have experts. They won't need amateurs any longer."

"It's a pity. . . . I mean as far as we're concerned. It's very satisfactory to feel useful." He didn't answer her and she said, "I've got to be back at the hospital in ten minutes. Drop in and see me when you have time."

"The Major doesn't want us to go near the hospital. You should have better sense than to come here."

"I'll take a whole bath in alcohol when I return."

She went away to pick up Miss Hodge under the peepul tree, leaving him to go back into the stench. The coolies began carrying out the bodies to pile them on a freshly built pyre.

"Did you see Fern?" asked Miss Hodge.

"No; she was asleep."

"I always liked Mr. Ransome. He's so kind and polite. He invited Sarah and me to tea on Friday."

As they neared the hospital two figures went up the drive a little ahead of them. One was Mrs. Bannerjee and the other Miss Murgatroyd, no longer wearing the tired pale blue with the rosettes, but clad in a tennis dress. They disappeared into Miss MacDaid's little office closing the door behind them.

In their little room, Lady Esketh and Miss Hodge lay down on their Indian beds. In monsoon weather any effort was exhausting and the walk through the rain left them both limp and bereft of all vitality. Edwina's head ached with a slow, dull ache as if there was a weight inside it,.

pressing against her eyeballs. They lay there in silence, Miss Hodge so exhausted that for a little time she did not talk.

When Miss MacDaid came to summon Edwina, she said, "Mr. Bannerjee has cholera. He had meant to leave on one of the planes to take his father's ashes to Benares, but he fell down as he was leaving the house. He's in a coma now. There's probably no chance for him."

Edwina rose and, washing her face in tepid water, pressed her hands against her aching head, thinking, "Miss MacDaid has gone on year after year in this filthy climate. She must be strong as an ox." And at the same time, "Poor silly Mr. Bannerjee!" It seemed to her that one by one they were all dying, the whole population of Ranchipur.

It was worse than Ransome had believed possible. It was not the work he minded, but the stench and the filth of vomit and excrement which accompanied cholera, and the horrible grotesqueness of the death which seemed to go on long after the spirit had left the body. For a man less fastidious it would have been easier.

The new nurse was a help. She was a gaunt Ulster woman called Miss Cameron, and she was rather like Miss MacDaid. She settled efficiently and with quickness into the room where Harry Bauer had died, a half-hour after the body of the Swiss had been carried out, and she went about her work in a matter-of-fact way as if she had been born and spent her whole life in the midst of epidemics. And she brought with her a curious feeling of confidence. Where Fern and Harry Bauer had worked valiantly but without knowledge, she stepped in, organizing, planning, wasting neither time nor energy.

The first three hours Ransome spent with her while Fern slept. Then she dismissed him and told him to sleep for a time while she took Fern with her on the grim rounds. Until she came, the Music School had been only a place where cholera patients were isolated until they died, a kind of waiting-room for the funeral pyre which burned day and night near the western steps of the Great Tank. But now it was different—there were medicines and a nurse who knew how to administer them, so for some of those who lay in quiet misery in rows on the floor, there was hope. There were candles now, too, so that the rooms of the Music School were no longer in darkness. It was odd, thought Ransome, how much difference light made in the midst of disaster. The old Maharajah had said that light and fire were the most civilizing of all things discovered by man. It was for light that he had long ago constructed the tragic, broken barrage, light which might be carried even into the remote villages of the districts.

When he had eaten a little cold rice and curry, he lay on the bed made of the Music School benches, and almost at once he fell into a sleep which was not like sleep at all, but like a coma in which all sensibility, all nerves were utterly deadened.

And while he slept Fern made the rounds with Miss Cameron, learning about solutions of Kaolin and the saving chloride of calcium and sodium. The supply was small but it would last until the planes brought more, until the railroad was open again.

She was tired with the weariness which comes with lack of sleep and under-nourishment, but now the stench no longer troubled her; the groans she scarcely heard. It was in a way as if she had become a machine, driven by an inward strength and vitality which she had never known before. The sense of reserve force brought her a feeling of exhilaration almost of triumph. She thought, "I am tough and strong. There is nothing I cannot do." And she no longer thought of Blythe Summerfield, the Pearl of the Orient, with shame; all that was too far away now, as if the girl who had come languidly and sullenly down the stairway at her mother's farewell garden party had existed years ago instead of less than a week before. And she thought again how odd it was that the movement of life could not be measured by the hands of a clock, but by what happened to you. These last few days had been longer, fuller, more important than all the rest of her life taken together.

When they had made the rounds the big Ulster woman said, "You'd better go and rest now. I can take a long watch. I'm fresh. I'll wake your husband at midnight."

Her impulse was to say, "But he's not my husband!" She checked herself, thinking, "It's too much trouble to explain now. I am too tired." And besides, there was no explanation to be made. The new nurse had been over all that remained of the wrecked building; she knew now that she was sharing the room with Tom. And in any case it didn't matter very much.

She went back to the room which Mr. Das had once used as an office, and closing the door behind her she walked to the bed where Tom lay asleep. Quietly, so as not to waken him, she sat on the edge of it, looking down at him. She knew now what it was she wanted to do. She wanted to stay on in Ranchipur perhaps forever. Miss MacDaid could teach her everything. She could work among the villages and be friends with the Smileys and Miss MacDaid and the Major and Raschid Ali Khan. Then she would be some one in a world which was real as the world of Miss MacDaid and Miss Cameron was real. And she would have Tom with her. She could take care of him forever. And in her heart, wickedly, she was grateful to God for the disaster because it had changed all her life. Gently, almost shyly, she reached out and touched his hand, and for a moment she knew that same feeling of ecstasy that had come so late to Lady Esketh.

For a long time she sat thus, happily, unaware now of the smell of death which filled all the building, thinking of what Tom had said, "It was meant to be like this, else life would not go on." And presently she thought, "I must get some sleep or I shan't be able to work," and lying down on the floor beside the benches she fell asleep, thinking, "I am older than he is, really. In a way I've always been older, the way Aunt Phoebe is older. Perhaps women are always older."

In those few moments which he had alone, the Major found himself troubled by the thought of Lady Esketh. She troubled him more than he desired or had thought possible, and the feeling he had for her was a puzzling one, in which curiosity, pity, and physical attraction all played their parts. It was the first time that a woman had ever been to him more than a pleasant convenience, and why this was so he could not say save that he had never before encountered a woman so experienced, so honest, and so contradictory. She left his realistic mind perplexed and unsatisfied. And so he found himself thinking of her again and again, as he was falling asleep, on his journeys to and from the Maharani, and the Music School and about the city. It was, in a way, as if she were a kind of monstrosity which, in order to understand and to satisfy his inquiring mind, he must dissect.

He did not deceive himself. He found her attractive in a way he had found no other woman, yet there were moments when by a gesture, the turn of the head, or the expression in the eyes he found himself a little awed by her, by her sureness, by her very air of race and breeding. He admired her for the honesty, the disillusionment that was always there in the blue eyes, like a shadow of despair. He liked her because there were moments when she seemed to be utterly sceptical, believing in nothing, not even in the pleasures her own body must have brought her. Not many women and only a few men were like that. Because of these qualities, he knew that he had been able to talk to her in the way he had done there in the ward a little before daybreak. You could not talk like that even to Miss MacDaid, because at the core of Miss MacDaid there was a soft spot of sentimentality. He knew, too, because he was experienced in such things, that he could have her now as easily as he could have had her that late afternoon at the Summer Palace, only now the possessing of her would be an infinitely richer experience. Love he was inclined to regard scientifically, anatomically, and in his heart he knew that such an affair would be a richer experience than he had ever known before; but it was that very element—the quality of richness—which alarmed him. It was there that the element of the unpredictable, the undissectible made its appearance. In the West they called the thing love, making from it novels and romances and plays and poems and cinemas, few of them understanding that it was, when dissected, a mixture of chemicals, of glands, of instinct, of man's fear of loneliness and the compulsion upon him to breed as he ate and slept and breathed. It was all that, but something more as well, for there was the unpredictable element which one might call quantity X which could not be pinned down and analyzed, that element which had made its appearance at the moment he had looked up and seen her coming up the drive of the hospital, clad in one of Mrs. Smiley's calico dresses.

It was this unpredictable, unfamiliar element which put him on his guard. It might lead him into the most absurd follies; it might blind him to his knowledge that she was too old and too experienced, that her very position in that world of the West made any sort of lasting liaison impossible. It might blind him even to the fact of what he was and what he must go on being, until he died—a worker, a scientist, a man without emotions who must guard his body and keep it free, as a perfect machine, for the work he had to do in Ranchipur, in India, perhaps one day through all the East. That was why the Maharani had kept him behind to talk to him, to urge him to marry. In her wisdom she divined the danger, and she would fight to save him from folly when he could no longer save himself. In an odd fashion, his life did not belong to himself, any more than the Maharani's had ever belonged to her. There was a side of her which was for all the world like a dancing-girl. But she had remained a Queen, beyond folly, all her life.

But he asked himself, too, what was so easy to ask, what Edwina, he divined, had asked herself many times. "It is my life. I am alive but once. Why should I not do with it as I please? Why should I not have that satisfaction which fate has placed in my path? Why should I turn away and deny it?" But another voice answered, "And destroy yourself." In spite of her gallantry, in spite of her honesty, in spite even of the curious, childlike quality which he, like Ransome, had divined in her, there was something corrupt about her, something wrong and old, born more of blood that was too old than of experience.

And resistance was made the more difficult because he knew that it lay in his hands to keep and preserve for her the discovery she had made which in the end might save and even redeem her. If he turned away from her, if he sent her away back again into the world from which she had come, she was lost forever.

Then in the midst of his thoughts he would suddenly be tempted to laugh and standing outside himself, would think, "You are being a God-damned fool! A sentimentalist! An idiot! What has she to do with you or you with her? Forget it! You have other more important things. You are a man and not a calf-eyed young bull."

It was extraordinary how the unpredictable element could destroy his reason and common sense. It was that which seized upon him a little before midnight, that and not his own intelligence, which made him set the battered alarm clock to waken him a little before four in the morning, so that he might go and talk to her while she sat there at her table, waiting upon the dead and the dying. It was only to her that he could talk, as he had never talked to anyone, knowing that she would understand everything he said and much that he did not say. The ward with the typhoid patients was the only place where they might be alone, away from Miss MacDaid and crazy Miss Hodge, Mrs. Gupta, Dr. Pindar, and all the others, all the hundreds and thousands who were always coming to him, looking to him for help. That hour they had spent together had been the most precious hour of all his life, not because she was beautiful or desirable but because they had understood each other, because for a little while human loneliness had ceased to exist. She had asked nothing of him and he nothing of her. For a little time they had shared a single spirit.

At three o'clock, little Dr. Pindar came to wake Edwina. It had stopped raining and the night was still, the air washed clear, no breeze stirring the leaves of the burgeoning trees. She wakened slowly, woolly-headed from the medicine she had taken to stop the ache at the back of her eyes. The ache was still there and her body felt hot, not with the damp heat of the monsoon, but with a dry burning heat which came from inside herself. For a moment she did not know where she was; it was not until her mind had focused itself on the absurd figure of the little doctor standing there holding a candle stub that she remembered.

Wearily she rose and lighted her own stub of candle from his.

"Go along to bed, Doctor. I'll be there in a moment."

He gave her the lists, and as she glanced at them she thought, "There are fewer tonight." There were only two on the list of those who were hopeless, and three on the dangerous list. Nearly all the gangrene patients were dead now.

"Miss MacDaid will relieve you at six," he said, and went away.

The ward was unchanged save that here and there against the wall candles burned to give the patients cheer and courage. The air was so still that the tiny flames burned without a flicker as if in a vacuum. Taking up the pencil, she wrote again on one of the lists "dead" and on the other "dying." Tonight it was more than ever necessary that she did not make a mistake. She looked up from the table at the bed nearest her. The woman who had asked her mutely for water was no longer there. The bed was empty. She thought, "That is the first empty bed. Things must be better now." And then she realized that the bed was empty only because so many patients had died and been carried away.

When she lifted the stone jar to empty the cool water into the pitchers she staggered and let it fall. Luckily it fell upright so that only a little of the precious boiled water was spilled over her feet. But she was frightened, childishly, by her clumsiness, and afraid lest Miss MacDaid might appear suddenly and discover the accident.

At a second try she succeeded in lifting the jar to the edge of the table and from that support she filled one of the pitchers and set out to replenish the enameled cups on the little shelves. But as she moved she was aware of the aching of her body; the pitcher dragged at her arm, pulling the joints at the elbow, the shoulder, the wrist. Terror suddenly struck her, not terror of death or illness, but a fear that she might not be able to go on working, that she might fail him and give Miss MacDaid an excuse for sending her away.

She thought wildly, "I will not be ill. I will conquer it by force of will. I will not admit it." And the memory of the folly she had committed two nights ago when she had drunk from the same cup as the woman who died, returned to her. "Only it couldn't be that," she thought. "Typhoid couldn't come on so quickly as that." It must only be weariness seizing her now that the excitement had gone. "I've been living on nerves and false energy for days."

She made the rounds, dragging one foot after the other, and when she returned to the table the awful still heat seemed intolerable. It was as if her body were a furnace; her skin was dry and she thought, wildly, "I'll take some aspirin. That will make me sweat," and she took three of the precious tablets kept in the drawer of the table, and thought again, "I will not be ill. I've never been ill in all my life. I am not ill. It is all imagination." And for a little time she felt miraculously better.

Then the hands of the cheap alarm clock began to fascinate her. She watched them moving, slowly, inexorably, jumping slightly each time a minute passed, bringing her nearer to the time when she must again drag the awful weight of the pitcher from bed to bed. She thought, "Perhaps he will come in again and help me. If only he would come tonight. If only I could see him sitting there on the table it would give me strength. Then I could forget the God-damned thing." And she began to cry suddenly, not out of self-pity but out of rage because this body, this machine, had betrayed her. She looked away from the awful hypnotizing clock with its metal hands moving slowly round the stained ugly face. There was no way of stopping it. Framed in the window there was a distant view of the Great Tank with a path of golden light from the waning moon. The sight of the water made her feel less stifled, and suddenly she found herself saying over and over again, "Dear God, do bring him here tonight, dear God, do make him come to me," for it seemed to her suddenly that if she did not see him, she would be lost. It was odd how weak she felt, how little self-sufficient. She knew suddenly for the first time in all her life how profound and devastating loneliness might be.

Dimly she heard a faint groan, and rising she went from bed to bed, until at length she came to one in which lay a girl who was too weak to reach out for her cup of water. Bending over her, Edwina lifted the girl up and held the cup to her lips. When she had finished drinking, she lay back again very still, and as Edwina turned away from her she saw the Major standing at the end of the bed, smiling at her in the soft candle-light.

He said, "I couldn't sleep. I thought I'd come in and talk to you."

Even in her weariness she knew that he was lying. She knew all at once with a wave of returning vitality that he had come because he needed to see her as she had needed to see him, and she thought, "I mustn't let him know that I am ill." So she smiled at him and said, simply, "I'm glad."

They went to the end of the room where he sat on the table as he had done two nights ago.

"You're not tired?" he asked.

"No."

"It's the only time when we can be alone. It wasn't true what I said. The alarm clock wakened me. I set it to wake me."

"You shouldn't have done it. You get little enough rest."

"There are all sorts of rest. This is better than sleep. . . . What I said the other night was true."

"I've been happy since then."

She no longer felt ill. The terrible heat seemed miraculously to abate. Her bones no longer ached. It was true—what she had thought—that if he came to her, she wouldn't be ill any longer. She looked up at him without shame or shyness, watching the face that seemed to her now to encompass the beauty of the earth. It was a tired face, much thinner than it had been on the night she saw him first at the Palace, but the thinness gave it a new beauty. The gray eyes were smiling, and the full sensuous

[542]

lips curved a little at the corners of his mouth. She thought, "I am happy. I have never known what happiness was before. I shall never want more than this."

"You can have more rest now," he said. "There are two doctors and three more nurses coming tomorrow. You had better go back to the Mission."

Desperately she said, "But I want to stay here. I must work. I must go on working."

"You could still work. You could come here in the mornings. You'd be more comfortable there. You could have a room of your own."

"It wouldn't do any good. I couldn't send away Miss Hodge."

At the flame of the candle he lighted one of the precious cigarettes from the supply which Harry Bauer had kept in the box beneath his bed. For a moment he looked at the flame of the candle. Then he gave it to her and lighted another for himself.

"You see," he said, "I don't want anything to happen to you. I'm selfish. I want you to be safe."

The unpredictable element had returned. Deep in the recesses of his complicated mind a small voice was saying, "You should never have come here," but against the other voices which cried out, "Take this pleasure. Only evil comes of casting away what the gods have given into your hands," it went unheard. This woman was the other half of himself.

She held the cigarette in her hands, away from her lips because she could not bear the taste of it. She thought, "I mustn't let him notice. I must let it burn itself out." Aloud she said, "What is to happen to us? What is there to do?"

"We need not worry about that. It was meant to be so. It is out of our hands."

She wanted to cry out, "It is too late," but she kept silent because she had to crush back the tears of happiness and weakness.

"It doesn't matter," she thought. "Nothing matters."

In the distance, from across the Great Tank, came the sound of drums, the male and the female drum, played by devout hands, and then slowly the music of a flute joined the sound of the drums, and looking away from him, she saw that the path of moonlight on the surface of the Tank was dimmed by the first faint glow of morning.

[543]

He too was listening. Presently he said, "It is the Temple of Vishnu welcoming another dawn." Then he reached out and took her hand, and her heart cried out, "Thank you, God. Thank you for the beauty of the dawn, of life, of everything," and for a moment she felt that she was fainting. When she looked at him she saw that the smile had gone out of the gray-blue eyes and there was fear in the face she loved so much.

He said, "You are ill. You have fever."

"No."

"You shouldn't be here."

"I'm only tired, that's all."

"Being tired doesn't give you a fever like that. I'll keep watch. You must go to bed."

"No. It's nothing. Really, it's nothing."

He had grown strangely excited. He stood up, still holding her hand. "You must do as I say. Nothing must happen to you now."

"Nothing will happen to me. I'm strong as an ox and I've always been lucky."

He did not answer her. He only bent down from his great height and lifted her from the chair. "I'm going to take you to your bed."

She didn't resist. She didn't struggle any longer. She felt his arms about her and let her head rest on his shoulder. She heard the beating of the strong heart and presently the touch of his lips on her hair. He was carrying her out of the room, down the stairs, along the corridor to the little room she shared with Miss Hodge. It was a short journey but she wanted it to go on forever while she lay there in his arms, his heart beating against her ear. And her spirit and her tired brain cried out, "Thank you, God. Thank you, God. Now nothing matters. Now I have found it. Now I know."

In the little room he laid her gently on the hard bench and loosened the buttons of the cheap blue nurse's uniform. Then he said, "I'll go and waken Miss MacDaid. It will only mean an hour more for her."

"Come back. Don't stay away."

"No, I'll come right back."

Then he went away, and as she lay back on the bed she began to shiver. Her whole body trembled so violently that the bed shook and the cording creaked. In the bed on the opposite side of the room, Miss Hodge stirred, groaned in her sleep, but mercifully did not waken.

Miss MacDaid, aware that her shoulder was being gently shaken, opened her eyes in the first thin light of morning and saw the Major standing over her.

"Yes," she said at once out of long habit. "What is it?"

"Lady Esketh is ill. I've sent her to bed."

She sat up, gathering the cotton sheet modestly up to her throat. She had never been beautiful, but now in the early morning light, her eyes swollen with sleep, the strong, tired face sagging with unsatisfied weariness, there was something frightening in her ugliness. Duty bade her ask, "What is it?"

"I don't know yet. Fever . . . high fever. Malaria, I should think, or probably typhoid."

Vanity struck through Miss MacDaid's sense of duty and she said, "Go back to her. I'll come as soon as I'm dressed."

She did not trouble to light a candle. By the rising light of the dawn she dressed herself and washed her face in tepid water and plastered down her thin hair. Hazily she felt a sense of satisfaction that Lady Esketh was beaten. She had resisted hard work and filth and every sort of disgusting task, but in the end she was not tough enough. She had been brought down by millions of tiny microbes. Miss MacDaid thought, "Now she'll be out of the running. When she recovers there will be an excuse to send her to Bombay, and once there she will be near the West again and forget all those crazy ideas about staying here forever." Abstractly she admired the woman for the fashion in which she had taken up the challenge of work, but in a less objective way she hated her as she had never hated anyone, not even poor Natara Devi, whom she had never seen except distantly when she drove out in her little red *tonga*. Because Natara Devi had never been a menace. Natara Devi had never been anything more than a beautiful body.

For she was afraid again of Lady Esketh. Twice in the last two days she had seen a glance pass between her and the Major, a glance which lasted no longer than the fraction of a second, but was terrible to her because in it she had divined a kind of intimacy which she herself had never shared. In the glance she had perceived the shadow of something for which she herself had been searching all her life; and for a second she had felt herself transformed from a good, hard-working woman of strong character and principles into a demon, a witch, a potential murderess; and each time the experience had left her shaken and ill and a little terrified. "Why should she have him?" her old virgin's heart cried out in bitterness. "Why should she ruin him . . . she of all people to whom God gave everything." For a second she thought in anguish, "No, I will kill her first. It will never happen. I would be right in God's eyes if I killed her."

And then, with returning sanity, she had seen how near to madness she had come, how terrible could be the animal revolt and violence of the organism in which dwelt the thing that was Miss MacDaid; and plunging into work, she had tried to forget both Lady Esketh and the Major, thinking, "Neither of them is of importance; neither of them matters," but at once the voice of her wisdom denied her, saying, "They are both important because they are among the blessed. Wherever they go, whatever they do, it will matter to you and to all the others about them. There will always be people to love and admire them. All your work, all your devotion, has not given you that right, that power. They have it because they were born with it." But it was unfair, her heart cried out. And then in moments more calm, she thought, "Perhaps there is something in the nonsense of reincarnation or why should some people be born with everything and others be given so little?" Then she would suddenly, in the midst of her work, find herself thinking of them in a new and different way, as if they were god and goddess and herself but a savage, regarding the spectacle with awe, and with a strange humbleness she would find herself admiring Lady Esketh with a kind of maternal envy. And then there were moments of half-wakefulness on the verge of sleep when she seemed to identify herself with Lady Esketh and experience the delights of being among the blessed.

But now in the gray light she felt only sullen and rebellious and filled with contempt, thinking, "She can't be so ill that she couldn't finish out her watch. If it had been me, I should have stayed at my post. I've done it before, many times. There must be softness in her." Or perhaps it was the Major who had ordered her to go to bed. Who could tell what had happened between them when they were alone? How had he known she was ill? How had he come to be in the ward at an hour when he was supposed to be snatching a little rest?

She clapped her hands for a porter and told him to bring her tea, and then she went to the table in the ward where Edwina and the Major had been a little while before. Then she found the two papers with the numbers on them and discovered the words "dead" and "dying" which Lady Esketh had written on them so that she would not become confused. The porter brought her tea presently, and while she sat drinking it her eyes never left the two papers. Presently when she had finished her tea and before she made her first round of the hospital, she took a pencil from the pocket in the immaculate bosom of her shirtwaist and wrote at the end of the list marked "dying" the notation, "Lady Esketh, wife of the first Baron Esketh." Then she took the paper and held it in the flame of the dying candle until nothing remained but ashes. The witch-like expression left her eyes. She took up the heavy stone jar of water in her strong, capable, kindly hands, filled the two pitchers and set out on her rounds. At bed No. 7 she halted, a little astonished because the old man who lay in it, listed not among the dead, but only among the dying had slipped away, unnoticed. He lay with his head on one side, peacefully, his mouth open a little way like a sleeper who snored. But he was dead. She knew the look of death. No one could know it better. His death meant nothing to her—it was only one more of the swarming millions who were, she knew in her heart, better off dead—but the fact that he had been on the list she burned she took as an omen.

Three planes came that day from beyond Mount Abana, bearing Colonel Moti from the Institute of Tropical Diseases and two trained workers, and new supplies of permanganates and chlorides and all the other medicines which were needed so desperately. The Colonel was a thin, wiry man of forty, with fierce black eyes, intense, capable, fierce and radical, a Sikh who had been accused of communism and even of being an anarchist; but India and the East could not do without him, for he knew more of tropical diseases and their prevention than any man in the world. He was a cynic, too, who spent his life fighting disease, searching for serums to prevent death, wondering all the while whether it was not better to let men die. He was an old friend of the Major and together they went at once to the tent of the Maharani to hold a conference with Raschid Ali Khan and Col. Ranjit Singh, whose Sikhs would be needed to enforce the measures that were to stamp out the cholera and typhoid.

A little after two o'clock, without lunch, Colonel Moti and his assistants, a young Bengali and a Malabari from Trivandrum, were at work, each in a different part of the ruined city. With each of them went a meager detachment of Sikhs and a troup of sweepers, and in a little while ditches were opened to carry off the stagnant water, wrecked houses were set alight, and for a time it was as if the fire had broken out again. In the burned central market, where market gardeners had returned to set up their stands of mangoes and melons, limes and guavas and radishes, everything was sprayed or dipped in permanganate. Well after well was disinfected with chloride. And wherever the little bands of workers appeared there were wails and outcries at the sight of property destroyed and superstitions ignored or violated. Everywhere there were clusters of Hindus muttering together, threatening mutiny, but of these neither Colonel Moti nor his assistants took any notice. He had orders from the Maharani to do as he wished, and the lean Sikhs who surrounded him with bayonets drawn asked nothing better than the prospect of violence and perhaps death.

A kind of God-like frenzy took possession of the Colonel himself. Now, for the first time, he found an utterly free hand to destroy, to annihilate refuges for rats and mosquitoes and fleas, to tear down and burn filthy houses, to destroy the microbes which clung to the fruits and vegetables and sweetmeats. Behind his frenzy lay a vague knowledge that he was destroying, too, as if symbolically, the old ignorance, the superstitions, the decayed faith which had inclosed his people for so many thousands of years. He hated worst of all, worse than the rats, the fleas and the microbes, the Brahmin priests, and whenever one of them approached him and his circle to protest, he spat at them and bade them in fierce Hindustani to be gone. For thirty years he had cherished a suppressed desire to destroy an old world, that a new one might be born. And now he had his chance and he enjoyed it fiercely.

[548]

It was thus that the second fire began and swept Ranchipur City. He fired the ruins of the bazaar in a dozen places and in a little while the whole wrecked area was a blazing furnace. From there the unmanageable flames spread to the ruins of the old Summer Palace and the wrecked cinema and, fanned by the monsoon winds, to the old wooden palace, consuming it with all its dark history of tyranny and poison and garrotings. It spread as far as the river, sparing only the hospital which stood in its own wide grounds, and the Music School which lay beyond the Great Tank.

By six o'clock little was left of the wrecked city but heaps of glowing ashes, and here and there on the outskirts, where a few wrecked houses and sheds remained, the Colonel, drenched by rain and sweat, still worked furiously, covering things with oil and setting them alight. The Girls' High School with the precious books Miss Dirks had gone to save, and the bungalow of Miss Dirks and Miss Hodge, with all its cushions and photographs and lace and the precious East Indian china, went up in flames.

From the doorway of the striped hunting-tent on the hill by the Great Palace, the old Maharani watched the destruction, a little terrified at first, but as she began to divine the purpose of all the destruction, satisfied and grateful to the fanatic Colonel Moti. She saw that the utter destruction of the city was a blessing and one which she herself would never have had the courage to order, because daily she was still dragged back by old traditions, old customs, even old superstitions that still lived in her blood. While she sat there by the old Princess of Bewanagar, she understood slowly that even the earthquake and the flood had, in their way, been a blessing. The old Maharajah had fought slowly, compromising always out of necessity with the vast imponderable past. Now all that was swept away and a new city would rise from earth that was purged and clean, a new city in which there would be temples built of concrete and steel, where there would be no Untouchable quarter and none of the dark hovels where cholera and plague and typhus lurked eternally, only waiting to strike out with the venomous swiftness of the thrust of the Russell's Viper. And when the dam was rebuilt at the Reservoir, the wells in the city from which infection spread would be closed forever and there would be only the fresh clean water of the hills.

The spectacle of destruction brought a kind of wild pure satisfaction to her heart. It was thus her Mahratta people had destroyed cities and villages in their wild raids. That was why Bengalis frightened their children by saying, "If you are not good the Mahrattas will get you."

A little after the swift darkness had come down Colonel Moti came to her tent to make a formal and hollow apology for having, by mistake, burned the city. She received him with severity, but after a little time she let him know that she understood the falseness of his apologies, and presently that she was pleased he had destroyed what remained of the city "by mistake." She liked him for his ruthlessness and the magnificence of the idea which lay behind it, and in his turn he liked her for the light in her black eyes which grew and grew while he talked to her.

When the Major came in a little after nine o'clock he found the two of them seated on the floor of the tent, bending over a sheet of blank rice paper on which Colonel Moti was drawing the plans of a new city that was to be built of bricks and concrete reinforced with steel in the American fashion, like Raschid's house and the night school for the low-caste boys which had withstood the earthquake, the flood and the fire. There would be a system of drainage that would leave no refuge for the insidious anopheles, the worst of all the enemies, the Colonel said, because malaria went on and on, seldom killing, but sapping the vitality of a whole great people.

His black eyes glittered with the enthusiasm of his dreams. "We will build a new city like none that exists or has ever existed in India—a city which can withstand the siege of disease. And you will find in a generation or two that its people are a new people, a new kind of Indian. The Americans have done it in awful places like Cuba and Panama and the Philippines. You will see!"

While the city still burned below the tent where they sat, the Maharani kindled slowly to his enthusiasm, so that all the weariness and disillusionment left her and she wanted to live on and on forever to carry out the dream of this destructive madman. It would take much money and she would have to fight the orthodox Hindus and even the old Dewan with his traditional antiquated ideas, but Raschid would be on her side and the Major and the little Smileys working away without trouble or fuss.

And while he watched and listened, the Major too caught the enthusiasm so that he forgot for a time the despair which had touched him on his way to the tent. For a little time he forgot everything, even that Edwina was very likely dying. Again, for a little time, he became the fanatic, impersonal and inhuman, concerned only with politics and with science, which he had been before the flood and the earthquake.

For as he rode his bicycle in the darkness, slowly following the line of the metalled road from the Mission by the reflected light of the burning city, he knew suddenly that there was no hope for her. Why he believed this he could not say, and he made no attempt to analyze the feeling. It was simply that he seemed to know it, as if the trees along the road had told him, and as if the wrecked houses and the spirits of the dead had spoken. Throughout the day he had wrestled with the angels of the spirit, now winning, now losing, but always divided and confused in his mind. Most of the day she had slept, quietly as a child, the fever consuming her. A half-dozen times he went into the little room where pudgy Miss Hodge sat on a stiff uncomfortable chair, staring for hours on end at the figure on the bed.

Once when Miss Hodge looked up as he came in, he thought wickedly, "Why could it not have been her they attacked. It would be better if she died." God, it seemed to him, was always bungling things. He had bungled it over Edwina and poor Mr. Jobnekar and Miss Dirks, taking them and leaving Miss Hodge and the merchants and Brahmin priests. If he or Moti could be God for a little time, either of them could do a better job.

At four o'clock when he went in to see her, she was awake, her eyes dull with fever, her cheeks burning. The faint pinkish spots had begun to appear, so that he knew now what the illness was. At sight of them he thought, "She must have been ill for two or three days. She must have caught the infection even before the earthquake happened." She had perhaps brought it with her from the north across the burning dusty plains. When she saw him, she smiled and said, "I was waiting for you," and held out her hand. He took it and sat on the edge of the bed. Neither of them took any notice of poor Miss Hodge, who rose from her chair and began fluttering about the room, changing the position of the water-pitcher, giving the bed cover a tug and a pat. The Major did not even see

[551]

her. The poor, crazy thing did not matter. No one mattered now. Nothing save that she should recover.

She said, "I know now what it came from. It was that glass."

"What glass?"

Then she told how she had, without thinking, given the woman dying of typhoid water from the pitcher on the table and how afterward she herself had drunk from the same glass. "It was that first night you came to help me. What you said made me so happy that afterward I forgot everything."

He tried to reassure her, telling her that the infection must have occurred long before, but she clung tenaciously to the idea, thinking to herself, "It was right. It was just that it should have happened like that . . . that I should at last be betrayed by my own happiness."

He asked, "Did you have a typhoid inoculation before coming out here?"

"No," she said. "To satisfy my husband I pretended that I had it, but I didn't bother. It was such a nuisance and I never really believe in those things."

His scientific mind was shocked. He said, "That was very wicked of you . . . and very stupid."

"I always thought that if one thing didn't get you another would in the end."

He didn't answer her. He only pressed her hand a little more tightly. It was wicked of her and it was stupid of her to believe all that fatalistic nonsense. Yet he loved her because she was like that, because of her reck-lessness, because she was a gambler who did not whine when she lost. That was the odd thing about it all, that in the end he had been caught by a woman who was everything of which he disapproved.

He said, "You should have told Miss MacDaid at once. You didn't get the infection from the glass. Perhaps it made it more acute."

"I didn't tell her because I was ashamed of doing such a stupid thing. And I was afraid she would send me away. And after the way you talked to me, I couldn't go away and not see you again."

She turned toward the narrow window and said, "What has happened? What is burning?"

"The whole town. It's on fire all over again."

"It's a little bit like hell, this place."

"The burning of the town is probably a good thing."

After a long time she turned to him again. "How long will I be ill?"

"I don't know. It depends on how much of a fight you put up. Typhoid is a long business."

For a moment she was thoughtful. Then she said, "I'm being a nuisance here."

"No."

"Wouldn't it be better if they took me to the Mission?"

"Perhaps . . . only there's no one there to care for you properly."

Again she was silent, thinking. Then she said, "Miss Hodge could go .vith me. She could do all the nasty work. She doesn't seem to mind it."

And Miss Hodge, who had been listening, said, "Yes, let me. I would love it."

"It's so dreary here," said Edwina. "It isn't as if I were of any use."

"I'd have to ask Aunt Phoebe. The burden will fall on her."

"I shouldn't be much of a burden. I'll be a very good patient. You could explain to Miss Hodge what had to be done."

It was a nonsensical idea. Even with all the work, it was easier to care for her here at the hospital. At the Mission, it would be more difficult for him to see her. He would have to take time from his rest to cover the three miles on a bicycle. But on the other hand he wanted her to be happy. He wanted her to get well again. It would be a pity for her to die, now when she had just begun to live.

She said again, "I would be so much happier there."

"I'll go and see Aunt Phoebe and ask her." He enveloped her small perfect hand in both his. "I'll go now, at once. You had better go back to sleep now. That's the best thing. The more sleep you have the better."

"Thanks, my dear."

She closed her eyes and lay still, and presently, when he thought she was asleep, he freed his hand gently and rose to go. She opened her eyes and said, "I would like to see Tom Ransome."

"No. You'd better not. He shouldn't come here from the Music School. It's too dangerous."

"All right."

"I'll go now."

She closed her eyes again, and when he had gone away Miss Hodge came and sat beside her.

It was the first time in all her life she had really been ill, and even in her weariness her whole body and spirit revolted. The still heat lay like a blanket over the hospital, and slowly the flames of the burning ruins filled the air with smoke. The fever came and went in waves of violence. There was no ice, not even water which was cool. Sometimes she drifted away into a blur of numbness and misery, and when her mind became clear again she thought, "Purgatory must be like this." Heat, heat, heat everywhere, but never enough of it to kill. Then the drugs brought on an attack of sweating and the bed and the coarse nightdress became soaked and Miss Hodge went to fetch fresh ones, and when she returned a chill began which shook Edwina's body with terrifying violence, and when it had passed she lay still again while the fever crept slowly back.

It did not occur to her that she might die, for death had never existed in her mind in relation to herself. Death might take those all about her, but herself it would pass by. Dimly she knew that her illness was a long affair, that it might go on for weeks and even months, but that seemed no longer to be of any importance. Only one thing existed in her dim brain and that was the determination not to sleep, lest while she was sleeping he might return and sit by her without her knowing it. She dared not to sleep lest a few minutes of happiness escape her.

The Major had to go the long way about on account of the fire which made the streets beyond the Tank impassable, and on the far side of the Central Market he had to dismount from the porter's bicycle and walk through the red mud of the fields until he came to the railroad bridge.

As he walked he knew that the fire was no accident. He was certain that Colonel Moti had arranged it deliberately, and it struck him as odd that a man capable of such self-discipline in science should at the same time be so utterly lawless in relation to society. He had not seen the fiery Sikh doctor for more than two years and he was aware that there was something dangerous about the man, some quality, too, that was exciting. In the moment or two they had spent together after Moti arrived he had felt the fire which lay behind the black eyes of his fellow scientist. In that brief interview, consisting of little more than a greeting and a few questions about the epidemic and the ways of fighting it, the Major had felt a vague sense of shame, as if he had been a slacker and had let down Moti since they last met. Now, examining himself, he saw that he shared Moti's passion for India, but he was less political-minded and above all else less ruthless. In Moti there was a kind of desperate necessity to act, a sense of life being too short for all that had to be done. There was about him the quality of a fanatic.

As he rode the porter's bicycle along the Distillery Road in the rain, he kept seeing the face of his friend—the hard mouth, the bony forehead, the hairiness that marked him as a Sikh even though he shaved three times a day, but above all the black eyes burning with impatience and intolerance for the folly and weakness of his fellow men. Moti would never have suffered such weakness as that of which he himself was now guilty. For Moti women did not exist at all, even as machines for sensual pleasure. All his energy, all his creative force, was gathered and concentrated into the fine pin point of blue flame which was like the obligation of the bloody Kali—the necessity of destroying the old that something finer and better might be created in its place. In Moti there was no unpredictable element. Moti would never commit the folly of which he himself was guilty.

Yet he could not find it in his heart to envy his friend. For a time when he thought of the brief moments of satisfaction he himself had known in the last two or three days, moments when loneliness no longer existed, when the ego died and with it all passion, all fanaticism, he felt a kind of pity that the life of Moti should be so meager.

He found Aunt Phoebe and Homer Smiley in the kitchen, feeding a small black child which Smiley had found wandering about, starved and terrified, on the outskirts of the burning ruins, one of the Daji caste whose parents and brothers and sisters had all disappeared. The child ate like a small animal, never looking up save obliquely, as if she expected a blow.

They were astonished to see him. He told them of Edwina's illness, and then, almost shyly, he repeated to them her wish to come to the Mission.

Homer Smiley said, "But she is better off at the hospital. There is so little here to make her comfortable."

[555]

"Miss Hodge will come with her. She is quite mad but harmless, and she can be useful. Her devotion makes her useful."

Aunt Phoebe, putting more rice in the plate of the hungry child, said, "I shouldn't mind. It might not be comfortable for her, but if she wants to come we can arrange it. I could put her in my room and sleep in the storeroom, now the others have gone."

"It isn't that we don't want her," said Homer Smiley. "I was thinking about what was best for her. You see what I mean?"

The Major was silent for a moment. Then he said, "Yes, of course, I see. When I first thought of it, I said the same thing, but I'm not sure that I was right. It isn't as if she were an ordinary patient. It isn't just a question of medical treatment. You see, she wants to come here because she'd feel happier here, and in her case happiness is of great importance."

"It's up to you, Major."

"Then I'll send her along as soon as I can arrange for it. Thank you. I know I'm asking a great deal, but I knew you would understand."

The child finished eating suddenly, as if she could not possibly stuff one more grain of rice into her big ugly mouth. Surprisingly, she put her two skinny hands together and salaamed.

Homer Smiley said, "I've got to leave you and get back to the Orphanage now. We'll have a lot more people to shelter after this fire."

He went away, taking the child with him, pushing his bicycle while she trudged along beside him. The Major watched them until they finally disappeared into the rain beyond the circle of dim light from the doorway. When he turned, Aunt Phoebe said, "I will take care of her myself. It's better now at the Orphanage. There's not so much work to do. And I like her."

They had a cup of tea, chatting together, for the first time since the disaster, of small homely things, and presently with reluctance, he rose and bade her good-by until tomorrow. As he left she said, suddenly, "You mustn't worry. I'll take good care of her. I know about typhoid. We had an epidemic in Cedar Falls in 'ninety-eight. Two of my brothers and a nephew were down with it at the same time."

He rode away refreshed and calmed by the few minutes in the company of Aunt Phoebe. Her serenity interested him because it was born not out of the resignation of the East, but of the action of the West. She had

[556]

at last achieved serenity, not like Bannerjee's father, out of negation and contemplation, but out of an activity which was objective and selfless. It was odd but true that there could be no peace or wisdom so long as the ego existed. One had to live like Aunt Phoebe to the full extent of one's powers during long waking hours, or to deny, like old Mr. Bannerjee, the existence of everything physical and material. Of the two approaches to peace, it seemed to him that Aunt Phoebe's was the wiser. Certainly it was the more human.

Presently he thought, "We could go away into some other place—to Malaysia or Indo-China or even China, and begin all over again. I could be useful. I could go on with my work and she would have peace," but immediately he knew that this was all nonsense, like the nonsense of Western novels and cinemas. He could never run away without destroying himself, and her as well. He could never leave this cruel, magnificent India because it was a part of his blood. All Cambridge, all the Medical School, all the new ideas, even the women he had slept with in the West, had not changed him. He was not of the West. He belonged here in this vast country of burning droughts and sudden terrible floods, of famine and earthquakes, of temples and jungles which pressed in close to the gates of the great cities. And remembering the nostalgia of all those years spent in the West, he could not imagine ever again leaving India.

In the reflected light from the burning town, a jackal ran delicately across the road just in front of him, and then the leaves of the Java fig trees whispering in the rain began to say, "She will die. She will die." The whispering he divined with sudden fear, was only the manifestation of some voice within himself, of some wisdom as old as India which knew that she must die because it had been so planned, because that was her destiny and his. He had known from the very beginning, from the moment he first saw her beneath the glittering, bee-filled chandelier at the Palace, that it was wrong. He understood now why, after the first glance when he found her exciting, serene and a little vicious, he had turned away quickly and avoided looking at her for the rest of the evening. It was wrong; it should never have been. But this knowledge did not deaden the pain and the desire which now had become physical again.

But the trees overhead kept whispering, "She will die. She will die. She will die!"

As he neared the railway bridge more knowledge came to him out of the depths of his own soul. He knew that she would die because she was too tired to make the effort to go on living. He had felt it while he sat on the edge of the bed talking to her. That was why she had asked to see Ransome. She was like those poor half-starved low-caste people who made no effort to live because it was easier to die.

In the morning the first train came through the gorge, tottering cautiously along the hastily rebuilt track. It brought food and supplies and more nurses and doctors, and on it was the old Dewan, somehow still immaculate with his white beard and his costume of fine, sheer, Bengali linen. He was accompanied now only by a son, a nephew, and a grandson, and he was welcomed by his old enemy-in-council Raschid Ali Khan, worn haggard by seventy-two hours of work. The two went at once to the Maharani's tent.

The old lady greeted him with mingled pleasure and apprehension. She was glad that he had come down from the hills to return in the midst of the awful heat of the monsoon, because his shrewdness and wisdom were of immense value, but she was sorry, too, because she knew that he would begin at once to talk of money and the cost of things, and to place a check on all her impatience to rebuild the city of Ranchipur before she died. For she had been utterly seduced by the ruthlessness and enthusiasm of Colonel Moti while they sat together making crude plans for the new city. The Dewan was an old Indian, the finest of old India, which looked backward to the sources of Indian faith and culture. In his immaculate white linen, he would sit obstinate and wily in every council, blocking every attempt at innovations from the West. He wanted India to belong to Herself, to return as he himself had done, to the sources of her great power. And Colonel Moti was the new Indian, eager to take what of good the West had to offer, eager to destroy the old, utterly, willy-nilly, good and bad together in order to make a fresh start. Her own feeling was simpler than that of either of them because it was feminine, intuitive, and impatient. She wanted a new Ranchipur to spring into being tomorrow, a city which would be a shining model to all India, and above all to the Europeans who said that India could not solve her own problem. She had immense pride which must be vindicated, and a recklessness that came to her in her very blood.

The bearded old man was shocked by the spectacle of the city, reduced now in the second great conflagration to a smoking heap of ashes. The temples were blackened, the evil wooden palace destroyed, the ancient landmarks which meant so much to his spirit were gone. All that remained were ugly modern buildings, built from Western plans, rising triumphant above the smoldering ruins of ancient India—the Night School for Untouchable Boys, the house of his enemy Raschid Ali Khan, the Engineering School, the plain, unornamented, efficient hospital. The rest was gone.

When he asked how it came about that the destruction was so complete the Maharani explained to him about the second fire, which, she said, had occurred by accident and was spread by the monsoon wind. But she saw at once that the old man was not deceived; his black, gimlet eyes contracted a little at the mention of Colonel Moti's name, and she saw him tremble ever so slightly. Moti, more than the British, was his enemy and the enemy of India. He had always been able to manage the British by cajoling and wiliness; he had found them stupid, stubborn, and tenacious, but easily tricked if one went slowly enough.

For more than sixty years he had worked in his own way, in the ancient Indian way, to lead them gently, as he had led Lord Esketh into a trap that night at the Palace, unknowingly, step by step, to their own ruin— while he saved everything that he loved of India herself. And the plan had succeeded. Given another century of life he would see India free and intact, an India of tradition and dignity and honor. The British would destroy themselves; they would in the end be swallowed up as India had always swallowed invaders. And now Moti and men like him, hotheads and fools, had risen to destroy all that he and true Indians like himself had worked so patiently and slowly to accomplish. It was Moti and the radicals who were his enemies and the enemies of India herself far more than the British. The British had been content to regard India as an investment, the richest investment the world had ever known; the spirit and soul of India they had left intact, not troubling themselves about it. But Moti and the hotheads meant to destroy the soul of India as Moti had destroyed the ruins of Ranchipur City.

The Maharani, watching the old man, knew what he was thinking.

[559]

She had come to understand years ago his wily plans and his success; sometimes she had even helped him, but never once had either of them shown by the faintest sign that he or she knew what lay in the mind of the other. Now she thought, "He is very old, perhaps ninety, which for an Indian is older than Brahma. He cannot live much longer. Coming back in the heat to fight Raschid and Moti and me will kill him. It is a pity. He was a good fighter, only he is blind."

She knew it now. She knew since she had talked with Moti. In the end the absolute power was hers. She could even dismiss him if he became troublesome. At last she was what she had longed all her life to be—an all-powerful Mahratta Queen. She thought, "But he will die. I will not need to dismiss him." The heat and the shock of the destruction of old Ranchipur would dismiss him for her. She knew, too, that in the end Moti and his hotheads meant to destroy her and all the other princes from the powerful Nizam and the rich Baroda to the meanest proprietary princeling. But before that she could accomplish much that the hotheads would find difficult to accomplish once they came to power, because her power was absolute within the borders of Ranchipur, a power which they could never possess. And suddenly she remembered the name which the Major said Ransome had given her—"The Last Queen."

The old Dewan made no protestations against Moti. Save for the second in which he trembled and the black eyes narrowed, he gave no sign that he did not approve of what had been done, even of the fantastic plan for a new city. It was not by fighting openly that he achieved his ends; he would work silently in his silky fashion, blocking every plan, every change, every scheme until at last it was slain as so many things were slain in India by weariness and inertia.

He went away presently to poke in the ashes of his own house, saying that he would return again in the cool of the evening. The Maharani ordered a tent to be put up for him near her own, where she might be kept informed by her own spies of his goings and comings, of what he said, even perhaps of what he thought. She knew, too, that no matter what precaution she might take, he would know when she saw Moti and Raschid Ali Khan and what they said. She had need of him for one thing—to sell the jewels. No one in the world could wring so good a price for them from the markets of the West. Cocottes would buy them and the rich, vulgar wives of *arrivistes* and speculators fattening upon the decay of western civilization. They would find their way back into the shops of the Place Vendôme and Bond Street and Fifth Avenue. But she was an old woman now and the passion for jewels was dead; it was not even of great importance what became of them. What mattered was that there would be millions of rupees to rebuild Ranchipur, to make of the city, the villages, the districts a model laboratory which might serve all the rest of India and the East.

For that she needed young men, strong men, clever men like Raschid and the Major and Colonel Moti. And she did not forget what Homer Smiley had already done and what he might still do, and that there was a place too for Ransome in her scheme of things. When the Dewan had gone she sent for both of them, ignoring the Major's warning against Ransome coming to her directly from the pest-house of the Music School; and when they arrived she proposed that Mr. Smiley quit the Mission and accept the post of Minister of Public Welfare, and that Ransome work with him. It was a post which had never before existed; it was Colonel Moti who suggested its necessity and importance, and he knew Mr. Smiley and his record and proposed him as the one man in Ranchipur, perhaps in all of India, for the job. She would have to find a new leader to take the place of poor Mr. Jobnekar, but that was not difficult now, not as it had been long ago when the Sweepers were confined to their own quarters and kept at the level of animals. They were clever people and they profited quickly by the advantages of education. And she had still to find a woman to replace poor Miss Dirks, to take over the education of the women; but that was easier now than it had been twenty-five years earlier, infinitely easier. There were Indian women, trained and capable and energetic, women like Mrs. Naidu, the friend of hotheaded Colonel Moti.

When she was alone again, the old Maharani sent for Gopal Rao and told him that he was to be her secretary and work with her. He suited her perfectly; he was good-looking and young and clever, and he had the same toughness and humor that was in her own Mahratta blood. He was to find some one at once, that very day, to take his place so that he might return to her to work. Dismissing him, she returned to her own apartment in the tent, feeling young again and strong as a tigress. The old

Dewan no longer troubled her. Surrounded by her phalanx of young men, she could defeat him. She would have their force behind her and in wiliness, she thought, chuckling, she was a match for him. If she was to be "The Last Queen" she would be a great one, to be remembered forever in the history of Ranchipur and of India.

When Mr. Smiley left the Maharani, he hurried on foot, burdened with the medicines and supplies delivered to him by Colonel Moti's assistant, directly to the Mission, where he overtook, on the drive a procession consisting of Lady Esketh borne on a litter by four coolies, with Miss Hodge plodding along beside, holding an umbrella over the sick woman. As he greeted them Lady Esketh opened her eyes and said, "It was very good of you to let me come to the Mission," and Mr. Smiley assured her that it was no trouble at all and that she would be much happier than she would have been at the hospital. Then she closed her eyes wearily again and gave herself up to the motion of the conveyance. Her bones ached and her head throbbed with fever, and she kept drifting into an unconsciousness which was not like sleep, but nearer to death.

As Mr. Smiley walked beside the procession, his heart sang in his worn body. Now he would be free of all the pettiness, the mean economy, the backbiting of the Mission Board and people like Mrs. Simon. Now her tiresome letters, her intrigues, would no longer matter. He could go on with his work, aided instead of hindered; he would have the wealth of Ranchipur behind him. It was the one gift from Heaven that he would have asked.

And he was happy, too, for other reasons; because of the pleasure it would give his wife and Aunt Phoebe and because he would have Ransome to work with him. Now he could help Ransome as for years he had been helping the low-caste people. As the two of them sat together with the Maharani while she told them her plan, he had believed that Ransome would refuse the task as he had always refused everything. But he had accepted quickly, with a decision which startled Mr. Smiley.

And when they left the tent together and turned in the direction of the Music School Ransome had said to him, "I hope you didn't mind my accepting." And Mr. Smiley had answered, "Why should I, my dear fellow?"

"I've never done anything to merit confidence. There are probably a dozen other fellows you'd prefer to have work with you."

"No, I can't think of one I'd rather have."

Then they had walked for a long time in silence, and as they came to the Great Tank where their ways parted, Ransome had said, suddenly, "Fern Simon is going to stay here. She wants to be a nurse. She's got some idea in her head about working in the districts."

"I'm glad," said Mr. Smiley. "She's a nice girl."

"There are one or two things I'd like to tell you and then we won't have to mention them again."

They stopped at the top of the wide shallow steps leading down to the water. For a moment Ransome looked away from him down at a woman pounding soiled linen on the rocks below. Mr. Smiley divined that he was making a great effort. Twice he swallowed hard before speaking, then he said, "I think I understand now what you and the Major and Raschid and the old girl are after. I didn't understand before—not fully. I want to help."

"Good," said Mr. Smiley, feeling something of Ransome's embarrassment. "That's fine."

"And there's another thing."

"Yes."

"Fern and I want to be married."

"Well," said Mr. Smiley, "I must say that's a surprise. It's fine; that is, I'm glad to hear it. Congratulations. My, what a surprise that will be to my wife and Aunt Phoebe!"

Ransome didn't say that he thought the news would be no great surprise to Aunt Phoebe. He said, "I'm not sure that it's the right thing. I wanted to talk to some one about it and I thought you were the best person. It isn't as if I were a young man. I'm years older than Fern."

"If you care for each other, that's not important."

"I know my own mind," said Ransome, "but it seems that I'm getting all the advantages."

"Fern is a mighty fine girl. She has the makings of a good woman."

"There's something else I have to say—it's really a confession."

"Yes?"

"It's that Fern and I have lived together already."

Mr. Smiley gave him a sudden glance of astonishment. He was not shocked, but he felt suddenly upset by his own innocence and lack of experience before a man like Ransome, who must know so much about women. The expression of astonishment changed to one of perplexity. The thin, homely face grew pink, and weakly he said, "I didn't know that. . . ." Then he coughed apologetically and added, "But of course I couldn't. How could I?" For a second he had an odd feeling that it was himself who had sinned and was in the wrong, because he knew nothing more exciting than the comfortable, homely love of Bertha Smiley. A look of wistfulness came into the eyes behind the spectacles.

"I'm not making excuses for myself," said Ransome. "I think Fern wanted it as much as I did. And it happened in an odd way . . . almost, you might say, an inevitable way. I don't think either of us could have done anything about it."

"I shouldn't think of setting myself up as a judge," said Mr. Smiley. "I've had too little experience in such matters. But if you get married, it's all right and no harm done to anyone."

"Sometimes, under such circumstances, marriage is a greater wrong than the original sin."

A smile crossed the wrinkled face of the missionary. Ransome was being complicated again, seeing too many sides of the question. Mr. Smiley said, "I don't think it's as complicated as that. There's a good deal in letting things work themselves out." The emotion which Mr. Smiley now felt was a little like that of an elderly aunt pleased at the news that two young people were in love. He loved Ransome and he liked Fern and wanted to help her to escape from all the unhappiness she had known, and he wanted to keep them both near him, and if they married they would go to live in Ransome's big yellow house and come to lunch on Saturdays with Raschid and the Major and Miss MacDaid and the other friends. He felt, wistfully, that the marriage would make life much pleasanter in Ranchipur.

"Can you marry us?" asked Ransome.

"Of course. You could be married at the Mission."

"Perhaps we'd better be married as quickly as possible." He started to say, "because we didn't take any precautions," but he checked himself, thinking that this would be beyond the understanding of Mr. Smiley.

"Yes, perhaps it would be better."

"We'll be through at the Music School in a day or two. They won't need amateurs any longer. Then we could be married."

"Whenever you say," said Mr. Smiley. He took Ransome's lean hand and said, "I'm glad. I think it's fine news." Then he smiled and said. "I've only one piece of advice."

"Yes?"

"Don't let Mrs. Simon set foot in the house."

Ransome laughed and said, "No danger."

"May I tell Mrs. Smiley and Aunt Phoebe?"

"Of course. They ought to know, considering that in a way they were in on the whole thing." After a second, he added, "Only I don't want you to think it happened the night I brought her to the Mission. I wasn't deceiving you then. It happened afterward during the flood—the night I got lost in the little boat. It happened in Bannerjee's house."

"I see," said Mr. Smiley, and again there was a note of wistfulness in his voice.

"I must go now," said Ransome. "We're still short-handed. Tomorrow the train is bringing more people to help—trained people."

Mr. Smiley patted his back in a suppressed friendly way and set out on his way to the Mission, and as Ransome turned toward the Music School, he thought, "How odd it is that, although I thought of Smiley as my friend, I never really knew him at all." It was as if before, despite all the apparent friendliness, despite the closeness of their association, despite the gay Saturday lunches, there had been a wall separating the two of them. It was different now, too, with Raschid and the Major and most of all with Fern. Some demon had gone out of him. Something, perhaps it was simplicity, born of the death and the filth and the misery, had come to take the demon's place. The world and even the familiar peepul trees and the Great Tank and the heat and the rain were different and new to him. His body was weary and cried out for a drink, but in his spirit there was no desire now to create out of brandy a false world that was better than the real one. The world about, tragic as it was, remained a good world. It had not seemed like this to him— shining and full of adventure—since he was a little boy setting out to visit his grandmother in Ohio.

Then as he walked along the wall of the Tank he saw Miss Murgatroyd coming toward him and he was tempted to turn toward the hospital so that he might avoid her, but she had seen him and so it was too late, for Miss Murgatroyd was too uncivilized to aid one in such a deception. She came toward him with the old hysterical eagerness, holding out her hand. She said, "I'm *so* glad to see you, Mr. Ransome, after all our adventures. I hear you've been doing valiant duty at the hospital."

"Yes," he said, forcing himself. "I've been working." Somehow she made the horrors of the hospital and the Music School seem fantastic and false. "Where have you been?" he asked.

"With poor Mrs. Bannerjee," and added, eagerly, "You heard about Mr. Bannerjee?"

"I only just heard that he was dead."

"He only lasted a few hours."

"And Mrs. Bannerjee?"

"She's all right. She's going away—back to Calcutta to live."

"And the old gentleman's ashes?"

For a moment Miss Murgatroyd hesitated. Then she giggled, "Mrs. Bannerjee threw them into the Ranchipur River after dark. She said that was good enough for the old humbug. She says now she won't have to be bored any longer in a dull place like Ranchipur. Calcutta is much more gay and exciting."

So that was it. There had been nothing splendid and icy about Mrs. Bannerjee. She had merely been dull. There had been no mysterious depths, but only the empty abyss of boredom. All the glamour, all the attraction, he had created out of his own boredom and restlessness and desire in a desperate effort to make the world about him an interesting place.

He said, "And what do you mean to do?"

She sighed, "Stay here on the job, I suppose. But it will be awfully boring without the Bannerjees' parties. There won't be any life at all."

She giggled again hysterically, but there was a catch in her voice and he thought, "Poor thing won't have anything now. She won't have Mrs. Bannerjee to torment her." She knew it and she was giggling to keep from crying. She was trying to make the Bannerjees seem ridiculous because she wanted to amuse and ingratiate herself. It was the beaten puppy again wagging its tail.

He said, "I must get back to my job now. When things are settled again we must have some more parties somehow. Perhaps we can organize a badminton club."

The muddy, pimply face of Miss Murgatroyd suddenly flushed with pleasure. "That would be wonderful," she said, and then, coyly shaking her finger at him, "I won't let you forget about it."

"No, you mustn't," and Ransome thought, grimly, "I'm sure you won't."

As he turned to go, she asked, "How is Lady Esketh?"

"She's ill."

"Yes, I heard that. Remember me to her when you see her. She was so sporting all through the flood." And in a gesture of tribute to that mythical progenitor, the Madras magistrate, she added, "You can always count on the English in a crisis."

Then she was gone and he went on toward the School, the old feeling of nausea at the pit of his stomach.

At the Mission, Mr. Smiley had to keep his news to himself until Aunt Phoebe had settled Lady Esketh into her own room on a bed placed near the window where there would be a current of air and where, while she was awake, she might look out into the hanging garden of Aunt Phoebe's petunias and orchids. When Aunt Phoebe, aided by Miss Hodge, had given her a bath of cool water from the *chattee*, she looked out of the window and said, "It is much pleasanter here. I don't feel so stifled." And then fell asleep almost at once.

When Aunt Phoebe returned to the kitchen, leaving Miss Hodge to keep watch, Mr. Smiley, bursting by now, said, "Well, I've some news for you."

"Good news?" she asked, doubtfully.

"I'm an Excellency now. I'm a Minister. His Excellency, Homer Smiley!"

She looked at him as if he had made a bad joke. "What in Heaven's name are you talking about? You've always been a minister ever since I've known you."

"Not that kind of Minister. I'm not even a missionary any more."

"If you aren't a missionary, then what are you? You talk like Mrs. Simon."

"I'm Minister of Public Welfare. The Maharani has just told me so." And then he explained all that this meant, and Aunt Phoebe, impressed, sat down and gave him an attention and a respect she had never given before to a man whom she had always regarded as one of her own children.

"And that's not all," he said, "Ransome has been made Assistant Minister"; and when that had sunk in he said, "And there's still more. Ransome and Fern are going to be married."

It seemed that this bit of news impressed her most. She said, "I'm glad of that. It's all right now, but I was worried."

"What's all right?"

"Nothing," said Aunt Phoebe, with an air of triumph. "It's a secret only I know about."

Heroically Mr. Smiley kept silent. "Let her have her fun," he thought, "Let her think she's the only one who knows."

"And now," said Aunt Phoebe, "you'd better run along to the Orphanage and tell Bertha." She chuckled, "That damned Missionary Board can't bother you any more."

"Now I'll have all the money I want for schools and libraries and laboratories. Ransome and I together can accomplish miracles."

"It's going to be all right with Ransome now. What he needed was a regular woman and some home life. He was the loneliest man I ever knew. And it'll be good for Fern, too. I guess they both must have got a little common sense. I'll bet he won't even drink any more. When are they going to be married?"

"Tomorrow, perhaps, or the day after."

While he gathered up his burden of supplies, she was silent. As he left, she said, "I can't help thinking what a lot has gone on these past few days." And with that under-statement she returned calmly to the business of preparing supper and the broth the Major had prescribed for Lady Esketh. And as she worked, she thought, "It's terrible what has happened to that poor woman in a few days. Miss MacDaid must have worked her to the bone." For it seemed to her that Lady Esketh was a different person from the one who had hid in the ditch while the Bhils passed on their way to loot Mrs. Hoggett-Egburry's bungalow, different too from the woman who had stood shamelessly naked by the *chattee* pouring cold water on herself. She was thin as a rail and there didn't seem to be any spunk left in her. She poked the fire in the Indian stove and thought, "There'll be white flour by the train tomorrow and then we can have some decent bread."

Two days passed, and there was no longer anything for Fern and Ransome to do at the Music School. Their work was finished with the arrival of more doctors and more nurses and they were sent away to the hospital, Fern to help Miss MacDaid with the supplies, and Ransome to do whatever there was to be done. When Miss MacDaid saw the girl, she said at once, "The first thing for you to do is to go to bed and sleep . . . sleep until you wake up. Then you'll be of some use. You're no good for anything the way you are."

At the moment she left the Music School, the accumulated weariness descended on her like a cloud. Now that it was over, fatigue dragged at her eyelids and weighted her aching back. She was so tired that as she walked beside Ransome along the Tank toward the hospital she could not speak; but behind the veil of exhaustion there was a dull sense of happiness because it was over now and she had not been whipped. And when Miss MacDaid brusquely said, "You did a good job for a girl who didn't know anything," she burst into tears, sobbing helplessly until at last Miss MacDaid gave her an injection to quiet her and make her sleep. The veteran knew what such fatigue could be; she knew, too, that it was worse when one was young. At fifty she herself bore it more easily than she had done long ago in that other epidemic which had carried off poor Miss Eldridge.

As for Ransome, he collapsed on a chair in the Major's office, his long legs sticking out in front of him, his head resting against the back of the chair. For a moment or two he closed his eyes. Then he heard the Major saying, "You look finished."

"I'm not, but I could do with a spot of sleep."

"I was coming to see you. It's about Lady Esketh. She wants you to come to the Mission. I didn't tell you before. I thought it was too dangerous for you to go straight to her from the Music School. If you could manage it, I'd like to have you go with me to the Mission as soon as you can get yourself cleaned up."

The Major's voice sounded odd and for a moment he thought, "It is only because I'm so tired that it sounds that way." Then as he sat up in the chair and looked at his friend, seeing him for the first time since he came into the room, he understood that the illusion was not born of his own weariness. The voice of the Major was tired and he spoke with a kind of gentleness which was unlike him. And in the eyes there was a look of misery and defeat. It was not only that he looked thin and worn. It was as if a light—that light which seemed always to be shining inside him giving strength to all those about him—had been dimmed or extinguished. Until now he had always been radiant and confident and sure, as if he had been set aside by the gods as one beyond human frailty and unhappiness.

For himself, he was haunted by the vision of his own bed—the great comfortable old bed which John the Baptist no doubt had in readiness, a bed into which he might sink, swallowed up in oblivion and peace for the first time in days, in one sense for the first time in all his life. And he did not want to see Edwina. He was a little afraid of her mockery and hardness and sense of reality.

So he asked, "Is it absolutely necessary to go now?"

The Major looked at the papers in front of him for a moment and then said, "Yes, I think it is. We can go out to the Mission the short way on bicycles. The Racecourse-bridge is mended."

Wearily Ransome said, "Okay," and then asked, "How is she?"

"Not too well."

"What does that mean?"

The Major answered him in a low voice, as if he were speaking to himself. "It means just that."

Dully Ransome thought, "It can't be true. Edwina couldn't be dying. Not Edwina, of all people." Then suddenly, looking at the Major, he understood everything, the whole complex story.

It had happened . . . the thing he was afraid of. It had happened in spite of everything. He understood now the misery in the gray-blue eyes of his friend, the misery of a man who had saved so many lives and felt

[570]

himself powerless to save this one, the most important of all. He had been caught, after all, like any other man. The gods hadn't given him a special dispensation. They had only been malicious, saving him to be caught at last by Edwina, Edwina, of all people.

All at once he experienced a great wave of wonder and of tenderness, and to let the Major know that he understood he rose and, crossing the room, placed one hand on his shoulder and said, "She's an extraordinary woman. She won't die. She can't die. She's indestructible. She won't die, because she doesn't want to."

Without looking at him, the Major said, "I'm afraid that she does. That's the trouble. She isn't putting up any fight."

What had happened to her? What could have changed her so profoundly—the Edwina he had known for so long with all her toughness and perversity. Edwina would fight to cheat death, out of perversity alone.

The Major rose and said, "We'd better be off. Take a shower and wash your hands with alcohol. I'll take Miss MacDaid's bicycle and you can take the porter's."

All the way to the Mission they rode in silence, past the stubby statue of Queen Victoria, standing there unshaken by the whole disaster, past the drowned Zoölogical Gardens, past the Bannerjees' house, empty now save for the figure of the thin black man whom Ransome had rescued from the balcony, past Ransome's own house and the house of Raschid Ali Khan, where four of the seven children were playing beneath the big banyan tree.

Aunt Phoebe met them saying, "She's awake. I tried to make her sleep, but she said she wouldn't until you came. She seems brighter."

"Her temperature?" asked the Major.

"The same. It hasn't gone down."

"It can't stay like that." Then he turned to Ransome and said, "You go in and see her first. She's been waiting for you."

She was sitting propped up in Aunt Phoebe's bed, with the metal dispatch-case which Bates had saved, on her knees. She looked very thin and the only color in her face were the patches of red on each cheek made by the fever. She wore one of Bertha Smiley's cheap cotton nightgowns and along the parting of her hair there was a streak that was darker than the rest. In the heat it hung straight and limp, close to her face. Her appearance shocked him and he thought, "I must not let her see how I feel," so with an imbecilic false cheerfulness he said, "Well, you have got yourself into a pretty mess."

At the sound of his voice Miss Hodge sprang out of her chair and came to greet him, saying, "I'm so glad you've come, Mr. Ransome. We've both been waiting for you for days. Here, take my chair by the bed."

Edwina said, "Remember, Miss Hodge, you were going to help Aunt Phoebe while Mr. Ransome was here."

"That's right! That's right!" said Miss Hodge, brightly. "I'm so forgetful lately. Our invalid is much better today, Mr. Ransome. She'll be up and about by the time Miss Dirks comes back."

Then like a flustered hen she went out, closing the door behind her. Ransome crossed the room and sat by the bed. He reached out and took Edwina's hand and said, "I've been wanting to see you for days."

"You look tired. Was it pretty awful at the Music School?"

"Pretty awful."

"How's it getting on with Fern?"

"Okay. We're going to be married."

"Aunt Phoebe told me that . . . said it was a great secret." She sighed, "You're a lucky bastard."

"Yes. I think I am. But it took a long time for the luck to change."

"To have a pretty girl fall in love with you at your age."

He thought, "It will amuse her if I tell her the whole story. It may cheer her up." So he said, grinning, "It was a fantastic courtship. I can tell you now. You played a part in it. Without ever knowing it, you saved Fern from being ravished."

A look of interest came into the tired eyes. "How?" she asked.

So he told her how he, on that first night, had come home from the hurried and savorless embrace in the Elinor Glyn room with the panther skin on the floor to find Fern waiting for him, determined to spend the night in his bed. And he told her how he had been tempted and how, because of his satiation and disgust, he resisted with very little effort and induced Fern to go to the Smileys' for the night. As she listened, she frowned and once, as if she were thinking of herself and did not hear him, she said, "We were a couple of bloody fools!" When he had finished, she said, "Something happened the night you were left alone with her at the Bannerjees' house. What was it?" and he told her that part of the story as well, feeling a little shy, but believing that now she would understand and see it as he had seen it. He said, "The most unlikely things can happen here. It was the very last thing I ever thought would happen to a sonofabitch like me."

The story did not appear to cheer her. Indeed, it seemed to him that she had scarcely listened to it. He remembered how once, only a night or two before the earthquake, he had thought drunkenly that it would make her laugh to know that by her own abandoned perversity she had saved the virginity of a woman she had never seen. Now he saw that the story wasn't like that, at all. It wasn't funny. This Edwina lying here in the bed beside him didn't think it funny. It had become something different, like lead transmuted into gold, because something had happened to both of them. It must be, he thought, that they had become human, and he saw now that as far back as he could remember there had been an inhuman quality about them both.

Suddenly, looking away from him, she said, "I've got something to tell you, too. It's a kind of confession. Don't mind if I don't look at you while I tell it. It makes me feel such a bloody fool."

He divined what was coming, and he said, "Tell it in your own way, my dear."

"It's so silly, Tom, to reach my age, to be such a slut all my life and look as I do now and then to fall in love for the first time. I feel such a fool. . . ."

"I suspected what happened."

"It's so idiotic to feel the way I do. There's something ridiculous and shameful . . . that it should mean so much to me just to have him come and sit in that chair for five minutes. It means more to me than everything that happened to me before. . . ."

He said nothing, but pressed her hand gently, thinking, "It's because you look as you do . . . with no color in your face, in a cheap nightgown with the dye coming out of your hair. It's because of all that he loves you. You're more beautiful now than you were before." For that quality of innocence and childishness was very clear now, no longer obscured behind a façade of falseness and disillusionment. The emaciation revealed the fineness of the bones in her face. There was about it now the delicacy of decadence and overbreeding. The blue eyes seemed enormous. Again he thought, as he had thought that night in the midst of Mr. Bannerjee's awful dinner, "Shining and free . . . and now she is no longer free."

She was talking again, slowly, almost with effort, as if she were very tired. "It makes you have the oddest ideas . . . almost as if you felt religious. I have a feeling that it was all meant to be . . . the strangest feeling that it began long ago when I was a child, and it had to go through to the very end. I *had* to come to India. I *had* to stay in Ranchipur. Even the earthquake was a part of it." She looked at him for the first time since she had begun to talk. "But it's a very satisfactory feeling . . . a kind of completeness, as if I had lived my life and what happened afterward would never matter very much. It's the way a painter must feel when he's completed a picture which satisfies him." She pressed his hand and then said, "I had to tell some one . . . and we always understood each other from the very beginning. We always understood each other, but neither of us could help the other out of the ditch. It had to be some one else."

"Yes, I think we've always understood each other too damned well." He stood up, still holding her hand, and said, "I'll go now and come back later. Now that I'm no longer at the Music School I can come and go as I like."

Quickly, almost as if she were frightened by the idea of his going, she said, "Don't go. I'm not tired. What are you going to do?"

"I'm going to stay on here in Ranchipur, perhaps forever."

"Will Fern like that? She's awfully young."

"It's her own idea. She wants to be a nurse."

"Is Miss MacDaid pleased?"

"I suppose so. It's a little difficult to tell when Miss MacDaid is pleased or when she isn't."

"The old trout did her best to fix me." Again she smiled and added, "I don't blame her. She was quite right."

Then he told her about his new job and she said again, "You're full

[574]

of luck. The old Maharani must be a wonderful old lady. It's a pity she disliked me. She never gave me a chance."

"The impression you made that first night wasn't exactly what one would call endearing. I doubt if she dislikes you specially. She doesn't like any women except one or two over seventy. She always asks after you."

"I really wanted to talk business. Can you open that box for me?"

He opened it and she took out a few papers and then a small box which she opened. Inside the box there was a ring consisting of a single enormous sapphire mounted in platinum. "I don't suppose you have any ring for Fern. Give her this one. I'd like you both to have it."

"That's sweet of you, my dear. It's what you might call a rich gift."

"Does she like sapphires?"

"I don't know. I don't suppose she knows one jewel from another."

"I wish she'd come and see me. I'd like to talk to her."

"I'll tell her. I'm sure she'd like to come."

"I've never had any sort of will, even for my own settlement. That's what I wanted to talk to you about. Now that I've got all this money, I suppose I should do something about it."

"You needn't do it now. You can wait till you're well again."

She smiled. "No. I've made up my mind to alter my character. I've always been careless about things that bored me. I wouldn't be ill now if I'd taken the trouble to have a typhoid inoculation. I've always hated the details and shoved them off on some one else." She leaned back on the pillow as if the long speech had wearied her, and he asked, "What do you want to do?"

Without attempting to sit up, she answered him. "I'd like to make provision to dispose of some of the money if anything should happen to me. I couldn't possibly dispose of it all. There's so much I couldn't think up places to leave it. I don't know anything about the legal side, but if I wrote down two or three bequests and signed the paper and had it witnessed, I should think it would hold good . . . especially in the circumstances."

"I'm not a solicitor. Raschid is a lawyer. Probably he'd know." He took her hand. "But the whole thing is a lot of nonsense. There's no hurry about it."

She ignored the remark, saying, "Could you write it out for me if I told you what I wanted?"

"Yes."

"I can't think what's become of Elsworth . . . that's Albert's secretary. I don't see why I haven't heard from him. He's in Bombay."

"He was responsible for sending the plane. I suppose he's been busy. All hell must have broken loose for him when the news of Esketh's death reached England. The news would upset a lot of people . . . newspapers, companies, shareholders—things like that."

She looked out of the window for a time in silence. "It's funny," she said, presently, "that Albert matters so much. He was really so unimportant."

"I think you'd better tell me now what it is you want, and then, while the Major is having a look at you, I'll write it down in the best legal fashion. You've talked enough, I should think."

"There's Miss Hodge," she said. "I'd like to make sure she's safe and well cared for for the rest of her life. The poor old thing has had an awful life. I'd like to leave her twenty or thirty thousand pounds."

He took a pencil stub from his pocket and a paper on which was written a report of the actual supplies at the Music School. "Twenty thousand pounds is a great deal of money . . . more than enough to care for her. Besides, Miss Dirks left everything she had to her. She told me so. And she'll have a pension from the Maharani."

"Don't be tiresome, Tom. It's my money and there's such a lot of it."

So thinking it was better not to argue, he wrote on the back of the paper, "Miss Hodge, Twenty Thousand."

"I suppose when life becomes civilized again the poor thing will have to have some sort of nurse or guardian. It would be too awful to shut her up." For a time she was thoughtful, and presently she said, "Why couldn't you apply to be her guardian? She says she can't go to England until Miss Dirks comes back, and I don't suppose it would be any good for her to go home now, anyway. She says there's hardly anybody left there except some cousins who wouldn't want to be burdened with her. The truth is that if she was sent back there she'd very likely be shut up. Out here nobody will take any notice of her. And some day she'll *know* that Miss Dirks is dead."

"Yes, all that could be arranged."

"And I'd like to leave a hundred thousand pounds to the hospital as a kind of endowment fund to do with as they like."

"Yes."

"And fifty thousand pounds to the Smileys." She looked at him. "Do you think that is enough?"

"I should think so. Money doesn't mean very much to them one way or another. They won't spend it on themselves."

"And I've an old aunt, and a young cousin in the navy I haven't seen for two years. I'd like to leave them each fifty thousand. Their names are Lady Sylvia Welldon and Lieutenant Arthur Welldon. She lives in a house called Parmely Vicarage near Salisbury. That address will do for both."

Closing her eyes, she turned away from him and said, "It's funny, sitting here like God, changing people's lives just because a long time ago when I was poor I gave in and married Albert." She sighed, "I've given away a fortune already and I haven't even disposed of a fraction of what there is. It must be tiresome to be so very rich. I'd never thought about it before. For a long time now I've always had what I wanted just for the asking. I'd like to leave you fifty thousand or so if you want it . . . as much as you like." She laughed. "Name your figure, Tom. Not many men have such a chance . . . and Albert would hate it so to think all that money for which he cheated and stole to raise himself in the world was going to a gentleman. He wanted so much to be a gentleman, but you couldn't make a silk purse from a sow's ear."

"I've got plenty for myself. My grandmother saw to that. Anyway, if I'm drawing up the will it wouldn't be legal for me to be in it." Then an idea came to him and he said, "But so long as you're scattering it about, you could leave it to the Ranchipur Ministry of Public Welfare. Then Smiley and I would have the use of it."

"Good. Put down a hundred thousand for that. If you want more, say so."

"No, I think that will do."

She sat up again and said, "That's all I can think of now. I'm too tired to think any more and my head aches like the devil. They can do what they like with the rest. Albert has a brother he never let me see.

He lives in a villa in the Liverpool suburbs. It would be fun to see how a windfall of a million pounds would change his life. I suppose there'd be no end of people fighting over the money."

He stood up and thrust the paper into his pocket. "I'll go and write it out. Forget it now and try to rest." He took the tin box off her knees, and bending over he held her up with one arm while he laid the pillows flat again. She seemed to weigh nothing at all, and as she lay down she said, "That box is full of jewelry. You might as well give it to Fern."

"Don't talk nonsense."

"I'm not. Has your brother an heir?"

"No."

"Well, if you and Fern have children, your son might be Earl of Nolham. He'd have a wife and some day she might like the magnificent jewels left her by an English trollope called Lady Esketh who died in Ranchipur during the great disaster of 1936. She'd always have a story to tell about them. It would help when she had to make conversation at boring dinners. We're such snobs at home. We like stories like that." She sighed and added, "Don't argue with me. I'm too tired. Put that in the will, too . . . that the jewels are to go to Fern." She opened her eyes, smiled, and looked up at him. "I suppose," she said, "this is the way it feels to repent and get religion. . . ." Her voice grew weaker. . . . "Giving away my worldly goods." In a whisper she said, "Anyway, it's a nice feeling."

Then he went out of the room, and as he entered the kitchen the Major rose quickly and looked at him with an expression of anxiety, as if he, the physician, were seeking reassurance from Ransome.

Ransome said, "I think the visit did her good. She wants me to draw up a kind of will for her. I told her it was nonsense, but she seemed set on it and I don't suppose it will do any good to cross her. She doesn't seem as ill as I thought she would be."

But it wasn't, he knew, the actual illness. It was the apathy he felt in her, the strange certainty she seemed to have that it was all finished; and her willingness, almost her eagerness, to accept the fact. The Major had believed that the visit would help her. He had been brought by the Major as if he were some miraculous medicine, which might help where all else had failed. This man, his friend, loved her; you could not look at him and doubt it. From the beginning he, Ransome, had been afraid of what might happen between the two of them, and half-heartedly he had tried to prevent it. And now it had happened; only what happened wasn't at all what he had feared; in a way it was worse. He had been afraid that she would seduce and fascinate the Major and then when she had had enough, she would run away, back to England and the cynical security of her own world. But it hadn't happened like that. He saw suddenly that there was no solution, no way out, and he understood that she knew it better than any of them. In a decent climate, in a less savage world, the strength and vitality of her own healthy body might have carried her through against her own will, but here in India everything was ranged against that machine which was called the body.

The Major knew all that. It was written in the suffering gray-blue eyes. Ransome knew now why the Major had said, "That's the trouble. She isn't putting up any fight." For the first time death touched Ransome as a reality. The abstract quality of death during the war and during the earthquake had meant nothing. The death of that shadowy unhappy mother had been of no importance, nor that of his own father whom he had disliked. Even the death of his grandmother had never brought its reality close to him, for although he had loved her, she was already an old woman and death had been as natural as going to sleep. Now he saw it clearly. Edwina was dying and no one could help her, no one could save her. "It is a waste," he thought, "so terrible a waste." Yet he understood why it was that she was dying. A month ago he might have been in the same place.

Aunt Phoebe went to the cupboard and returned with ink and pen and letter paper on which was printed AMERICAN MISSION. EDUCATIONAL BRANCH. RANCHIPUR STATE. and he seated himself and went to work, trying desperately to remember the legal phraseology of the wills of his father and his grandmother . . . *I do devise and bequeath.* . . . It sounded silly, but almost all legal phraseology sounded silly and archaic and confused.

Aunt Phoebe, as she passed him, said, in a low voice with exaggerated casualness, "I wouldn't have believed it possible."

He knew what she meant. It touched him that there still remained in the spare, hard-worked old body such a capacity for wonder and romance, and then he saw that this was part of her strength, one of the reasons why she had never grown old, why she was forever young. The wonder and delight were something neither he nor Edwina had ever known. It was perhaps given only to a chosen few. It might perhaps be learned. He might even now be approaching a comprehension of it.

Aunt Phoebe, mixing bread now at the far end of the kitchen table, said, "I'm eighty-two years old and I'm still finding out things."

From her corner where she sat peeling yams, Miss Hodge said, suddenly, "She's so nice. Lady Esketh. She's such a lady."

As the Major came through the door, Edwina opened her eyes and smiled at him. Briefly, almost stiffly, he asked her a few questions. He was being professional as he had been that afternoon at the Palace when she had done her best to change him into a lover. He said, "You're much better today," although it was a lie and "You have the most extraordinary vitality."

"I've always been tough as nails."

"We expect an ice-machine tomorrow. That'll make a great difference."

"I'd like to feel ice again. I'd like to sleep on ice. I feel as if I could never again be cold enough to suit me."

The stiffness seemed to grow upon him. It was as if the man who had talked to her in the early morning while she sat keeping watch in the ward, had withdrawn, leaving a stranger in his place. While he sat there talking to her, he was fighting the growing terror inside him, not now a terror of her dying, but a terror which was worse. It was a kind of terror he had never before experienced even dimly, but he recognized what it was as if it had been an old and recurring sickness, and the recognition terrified him the more. He kept thinking, "I must keep a tight hold on myself. If I let go, I will go to pieces. I shall weep and howl and behave like that ass Bannerjee. I'm not like that. I'm the new kind of Indian. I'm not like that. I won't let it claim me." He dug the nails into the palms of his hands. His whole strong body began to tremble. It was as if it cried out for relief, to be allowed to roll on the floor, to moan and cry, to beat its breast and tear its hair, to roll in the dust and cover its head with ashes and cow dung.

Wildly he thought, "It has never happened before. I did not know it was there hiding away" ... that awful treacherous emotional thing which had so many times wrecked India, which had begot so much cruelty and so much masochism, so much defeat and despair. The nails dug deeper into the palms and he thought, "I cannot betray them ... not I of all Indians. Not I who have proven that there is no such thing. I cannot betray myself. If I am betrayed once, I am lost. Then it will not matter what happens. I will be like Bannerjee and all the others who howl hysterically." Inwardly he cursed his race and his Brahmin caste, his heritage and the horrible cruel climate which turned men neurotic and unstable. He cursed the very soul of India.

And fearing himself he began to speak again, not emotionally but in a flat, dead, matter-of-fact voice which seemed to come not from that treacherous, hostile machine, his own body, but from a great distance. Through the mechanism of that weak and terrified body he heard *himself*, whatever it was that was the essence of him, saying, flatly, as if he were only planning a trip to Bombay or Delhi, "You are past the worst now. I have it all planned. When you are well again we will go away together. I've thought it all out. We shall go further east ... to the Malay states or to some part of India where nobody knows us (only there was no part of India where they were not known), and we shall have a new life. I will go on with my work. We will build up a new world. Yes, it will be satisfactory and not too difficult."

Then he felt the touch of her hand on his. He heard her saying, "Yes, that will be fine. That will be wonderful," and the treacherous body began again to shake, striving to throw itself on the floor, to cast away honor or courage, defiance and strength, in one wild gesture of despair and defeat.

He heard her asking, "What is it, my dear? Are you ill? Why are you trembling so?" And shame swept over him, shame for himself, for the finely bred Brahmin machine that was his body. He could never tell her what it was that made him tremble. He dared never let her even suspect ... she of all people, who had gone through a furnace of torment, who was dying now, without one hint of complaint. In that moment he hated all India, and most of all the body which was betraying him.

Again he heard the distant flat voice coming from a great distance, saying: "It is nothing at all. No more than physical tiredness. It will go away. Everything will be all right." But the thing did not go away; it clung to his spirit as a vicious panther clung by its claws to the naked flesh of its victim. It came out of his past, out of the past of his parents and grandparents and their remote ancestors. It was something she would never be able to understand; not even Ransome, his friend, would understand it, nor Raschid, who wasn't Indian, but burly Arab-Turk, not even the old Maharani with her wild, proud Mahratta blood. It was more ancient, more corrupt than anything in their blood. Beside himself, they were newcomers to India.

He heard the distant voice saying, "You mustn't talk any more. You'll tire yourself," and then the door opened and Ransome came in with the paper and pen and ink, and after him Aunt Phoebe, dusting the flour off her hands, and again his spirit cried out against the treacherous body, "Not now! O God! O Rama! O Vishnu! Not now! Not before them! They believe in me! Not before them!" And in the depths of his spirit he heard again the awful terrified howling of the dead Mr. Bannerjee.

He heard Ransome saying, "Well, my dear, I've done the best job I could. I've brought Aunt Phoebe to witness it. The Major can be the other witness. I'm afraid Miss Hodge wouldn't be recognized as a legal witness."

There was a note of weariness and falseness in Ransome's voice, but the very timbre of it illuminated in a sudden flash the Major's understanding. His friend Ransome was suffering, too; he was exhausted; he was near to defeat, but something in him made him carry on, pretending to believe what he could not believe, fighting somehow to the very end. The despair which had corroded Ransome was less terrible than this abysmal terror and despair that threatened to engulf himself. And the spectacle of Ransome's casualness, as if nothing tragic was happening, as if he were merely asking Edwina to sign her name to something of no importance whatever, brought to his spirit a sudden strength. He rose and turned away from them, pretending to look out of the window, but

He covered his face with his hands and pressed his fingers against his temples until the pain brought him relief.

He was still shaking when Ransome seated himself to read the will, asking at the end, "Is that satisfactory?"

"Yes. I wouldn't know in any case."

Then Ransome held the will while she signed it, and when she had finished he gave the pen to Aunt Phoebe and then to the Major. The signature of Aunt Phoebe was scratchy but firm. The Major's was uncertain and trembling, like that of an old man.

Then Edwina said to the Major, "When will you be coming back?"

"This evening again . . . after dark." The treacherous body was not yet subdued, and he spoke in a choked voice, with difficulty.

Edwina said, "I'd like to speak to Tom for a moment alone."

The Major turned to Ransome and said, "I'll wait for you. We'll ride back together." For he was afraid again, this time of the wide red flat plain, of the roaring river, of the banyans and Java fig trees that lined the road, of the ruined temples. They would drag him back into the abyss of time, back into that nightmarish world in which Mr. Bannerjee had passed the whole of his terrified existence. For the moment, until he became himself again, he had to stay close to Ransome. He had to shake off the hysteria before he again encountered the hard Scottish eye of Miss MacDaid, who knew the East and India better than any of them. She would look at him, and later in the evening she would say, in contempt, "So you too have turned Hindu . . . you of all people!" And now that she had resumed her afternoon exercise she would want to bicycle back.

Aunt Phoebe followed him out of the room, and when Edwina and Ransome were alone, Edwina looked at him and said, "What is the matter with him?"

"He's tired. He has right to be. Otherwise I noticed no difference."

"It's more than that."

He shrugged his shoulders, pretending not to understand, and she asked, "You don't think he might do something violent?"

"No. He's not that kind." Yet his heart, his instinct, denied his words. He did not know. It seemed to him that the man who had just left the room was a man he did not know at all.

"Will you help him all you can?"

[583]

"I'll help him as much as I can." But it wouldn't be easy. He was aware lately that the Major had been slipping away from him. He thought, "Perhaps in grief and emotion the difference comes out. Perhaps there is something Indian in him which can never accept or understand the European in me." But that way, he knew, lay nonsense . . . the nonsense of the mystics, and of the doggerel, "East is East," of all Kipling who knew only the India of cantonments and clubs and provincial newspapers.

Edwina was saying, "I've thought of another thing. I'd like to leave some money for something that would help the East and the West to understand each other. I don't know how to work it out. Could you think it over? I don't know how it's to be done. I'm too tired to think it out."

Bitterly Ransome answered her. "There's only one way, and that's to leave a fund for rat poison . . . to destroy ignorance and prejudice and greed and provinciality. It dies hard. . . . You'd have to kill off people like the Boys and the old Dewan, the merchants and the Lord Eskeths, the bank managers, the priests and people like Pukka Lil and Mrs. Simon and the old General."

She smiled. "Even that might be done if we went about it cleverly enough. I've never had many prejudices, myself. I suppose middle-class society would call that depraved, but I've an idea that God might list it under the head of Virtue."

She turned away from him to look out of the window, and in a moment she said, "Look!" and following her gaze, he saw the carriage of the Maharani drawn by the white bullocks with gilded horns, coming up the Mission drive.

"Aren't they pretty?" she said.

"It's the Maharani, probably come to ask after you."

"Thank her for me."

"I will."

He stood up and said, "It's all right now. You're going to get well . . . in spite of everything."

She turned back to him, regarding him for a moment with the blue eyes which looked so enormous in the thin pale face. Then she said, "And if I get well . . . so what."

Then he knew for certain that she understood more than any of them that there was no way out.

But he said, "I wouldn't worry about that. Let things take care of themselves."

"That's what I've always done," she said, "and now look at the God-damned thing."

As he turned away from her he became aware of the presence of Miss Hodge in the partly open doorway, and he said, "Come in, Miss Hodge. I'm going away now."

He left them there, Miss Hodge sitting by the bed, Edwina, her back toward the door, her eyes closed. Miss Hodge was telling her about the conversation she had just had with the Bishop and Lady So-and-so.

The Maharani did not get down from her carriage. She had come, she said, for two things—to ask after the health of Lady Esketh and to ask Aunt Phoebe if she would come again to tea on the following day. They all stood by the carriage while the bullocks groaned and snorted with indignation. Then the Maharani said, "I should like to speak to the Major for a moment," and the others withdrew to a little distance while the Major stepped nearer to the carriage.

She leaned down toward him and said, "I've had an answer from the parents of the girl. She's in Poona. They're bringing her here as soon as the rains stop."

"Very good, Your Highness."

"She's very pretty and intelligent and charming and educated."

"I'm sure she is, Your Highness."

"I think you'll find her a good wife. What you need, Major, is a home and some children."

Then abruptly she bowed to the others and bade them good-by and ordered the driver to be off. He prodded the bullocks. They began again their snorting complaints and set off down the drive at a quick trot. For a moment the Major stood looking after them. His body was no longer trembling. The spirit had won. He was quiet now. He behaved like Ransome and Edwina. Strength flowed through him and self-respect. He turned to Ransome and in an even, calm voice said, "Shall we go?" He had conquered the old terror, the old fears, the ancient claims of his ancestors. He knew suddenly that they would never return again to claim him.

"Wait a moment," said Ransome. "I want to see what's coming up the drive."

He pointed toward two Mahratta policemen who were advancing toward them, carrying a heavy flat object between them. As they came nearer Ransome divined that the object was a large picture framed in teakwood. As the policemen came up to them, one of them placed his end of the burden on the ground, while the other lifted it to an upright position, supporting it with one hand and regarding it at the same time with the air of a connoisseur displaying a masterpiece.

It was the enlarged and tinted photograph of Mrs. Hoggett-Egburry taken in her prime while playing in "Puss-in-Boots" . . . a large blonde, voluptuous picture well calculated to rouse the passion of dark-skinned savages like the Bhils. The glass was missing and the picture was stained her and there by water and grease and smoke.

One of the policemen spoke rapidly in Mahratta to the Major, who turned when he had finished and translated his story. The picture had been discovered by policemen searching for loot in one of the ruined mosques of the dead city of El-Kautara. There where no images had ever been permitted, where no woman had ever penetrated, the savage Bhils had set up the enlarged photograph of Pukka Lil as a goddess, and were worshiping her when the policemen broke in.

For Ransome the strain of the last hour was suddenly broken and he felt a wild impulse toward laughter—mad, soul-tearing laughter, soul satisfying, mocking, belly laughter over Pukka Lil and the Bhils, the General, India, the West, the dictators, the great bankers and politicians, over the whole idiotic human race, but most of all over himself.

Both policemen now stood, gazing like moon calves at the enlarged photograph, their terrier pugnacity wilted in their admiration for the blonde and buxom beauty of the bank manager's wife. Pretending to wipe the perspiration from his face, Ransome managed to hide behind the piece of surgical gauze which served him as a handkerchief until mercifully Aunt Phoebe said, "Tell them to take it into the storeroom with Mrs. Hoggett-Egburry's other things. I have to sleep there but I guess I can stand it."

At the gate of his own house he said, "I'm stopping here. I'll send the bike back with my boy. I'm going to get some sleep."

The Major stopped, too, took his hand, and said, "Thanks." The gray-blue eyes searched Ransome's face for a moment and he made as if to speak. Then quickly he looked away and said, "See you in the morning. Have a good sleep. You deserve it." And abruptly he pedaled away down the wet, shining road.

Ransome, troubled by the sudden change in his friend, stood looking after him until he had disappeared round the turn by the Bannerjees' house. The Major had meant to say something . . . something which at that moment might perhaps have explained a great deal which Ransome had not understood before, something which might have made their friendship closer and more profound. What it was he could not imagine, but his instinct told him that for a second they had come very near to each other, nearer than they had ever been before, and that if he himself had been an Indian the Major would not have checked himself. He wanted to leap on the porter's bicycle to ride after the Major and call out, "What was it you meant to say? Don't be afraid. Man is a lonely shut-in creature. Speak! Say what you must say to some one!" But he remained standing there beneath the great banyan tree because all his life he had been taught that such an action would be sentimental and even ridiculous. It was the sort of thing that one didn't do, and so he remained there as if paralyzed.

As the rain began again he turned and entered his own compound. He had not seen his house for more than a week, not since the flood abated, and now it looked strange to him, a little, he thought, because the man who entered the gate now was not the same one who had gone off drunkenly through the sulphur-yellow twilight to dine at Mr. Banner-jee's. But it was different, too, for physical reasons; the garden house lay shattered all about the old Buick which John the Baptist had covered with a piece of tarpaulin salvaged from somewhere, and part of the roof of the house had fallen in. But it was the trees and plants and vines which made the greatest difference. The leaves of the trees were a deep brilliant green and the flower-beds had become jungles where marigold and holly-hock, hibiscus and nasturtium, fuchsia and calendula ran riot. On the house and the walls of the compound the jasmine, the bignonia, the bou-gainvillæa, the convolvulus and the scarlet creeper had sent out greedy tendrils which spread everywhere, climbing across windows and doors, stifling the waterspouts, hiding the cornices and climbing across the low sloping roof.

He stopped for a moment, moved and filled with wonder as he always was by the miracle which the rains accomplished. While he stood there the lean, shining black figure of John the Baptist appeared in the shaken porte-cochère and came toward him to take the bicycle.

Ransome said, "Are you all right? Have you had enough to eat?" and in his soft Pondicherry French John the Baptist said, "Yes, I'm all right, Saheb. I am glad the Saheb has come back."

"I've come back to sleep. Is my bed ready?"

"Yes, Saheb, your bed has always been kept ready."

For a second Ransome thought the boy regarded him stiffly and with curiosity, almost as if he were a stranger. Then John the Baptist looked away quickly, as he had done that night when Ransome caught his eyes in the mirror.

"Will Saheb eat?" asked John the Baptist.

"Not now. I only want to sleep."

"Very good, Saheb."

"And you must send for the gardener tomorrow to come and cut away the vines. They're shutting out all the light and the air."

"The gardener is dead, Saheb."

For a second he was overcome again by a sickening weariness. He said, "Very well. Find another."

"Yes, Saheb."

Then he went into his own room and took off his clothes and went out again to stand in the compound with the warm rain beating against his naked body. At last when he felt clean again he returned to the room and threw himself onto the bed, to fall almost at once into a clean sound sleep, the first he had known for what seemed to him half his life.

At the end of the week the abnormal volume of the rains diminished little. Showers fell every half-hour, brief and sudden showers during which the water fell in torrents, but no longer did the rain continue day and night unbroken, flooding the fields and swelling the river. Between the showers there were moments when the sun appeared, no longer the dusty, brazen, red sun of the dry season, but a sun which raised the steam from the metaled roads and stone courtyards, so that all the countryside was like one vast steam bath. Through all the heat the fanatic-eyed Colonel Moti and his two assistants worked like demons, disinfecting, destroying, clearing away, and at the end of ten days the Colonel, arrogant, satisfied, triumphant, reported to the Maharani and her Council that he and his assistants had defied and vanquished the evil power of India herself; there was no longer any danger of a fresh outbreak if those in authority followed the instructions left by him. Before he left he told the Maharani and the Council that when the definite plans for the new city were made, it was their duty to call upon him for directions. Then he went away, defiant, burning with the passion of his purpose, as wiry, as fiery-eyed as ever, untouched either by disease or by the dreadful heat or the unceasing work.

The struggle of the Maharani and the old Dewan came to naught, for the morning after the Council meeting the old man, desiccated by the heat, corroded by his hatred and contempt for Colonel Moti, failed to waken. His son said that he was ninety-two years old, but no one really knew. They only knew that he was the last of his kind.

Two days later Lady Esketh died in the room at the American Mission. She died in the state of coma into which she had fallen a little while after Ransome and the Major had left her. In the days that followed, Fern had come three times to see her, but the visits were useless; once she was delirious, and on the other two occasions she was unconscious. A little time before she died she regained her senses again and the Major came and sat by her, holding tightly to her hand. She smiled at him, but she was too weak to speak, and while he sat beside her he talked to her as he had talked on the morning he found her alone in the ward, comforting her, easing her weariness, enveloping her in the great warmth of his spirit. It was like having him again pick her up and carry her away. He no longer pleaded with her to live nor did he try to deceive her into believing that she was not going to die. He knew now what it was that she desired, and he understood why she desired it, and in his own loneliness he knew that she was wiser than himself. His own flesh left him in peace now and the hysterical terror did not return, and during that moment of light in all the darkness which engulfed her, she knew that he was safe again, as safe as if she had never come into his life to bring ruin and hopelessness with her. A little while before she slipped back again into the darkness she managed to press his hand and whisper, "Don't send Miss Hodge away. I told her I would make you promise." He promised, and then for a moment bent over her and laid his face against hers, but she slipped away from him again back into the darkness.

Miss Hodge and Aunt Phoebe were with her when she died. Aunt Phoebe, who had sat by so many deathbeds, felt her hands turning cold and sent the Sweeper boy on his bicycle to fetch Ransome and the Major, but when they arrived she was already dead and they found Aunt Phoebe trying to calm Miss Hodge, who had thrown herself across the bed and was weeping hysterically.

The poor old thing had never before witnessed death. For her Miss Dirks had gone away on some long trip connected with the business of the school; perhaps she would never be dead. But she had seen her friend Lady Esketh die; she had felt the hands turning cold . . . Lady Esketh, her great friend whom she talked about so much to the Bishops and the aristocracy. Now she screamed, terrified and shaken, calling upon Lady Esketh not to go away leaving her behind, alone, with not a friend in the world. There was no means of quieting her until Ransome said, "You are not alone. I am your friend and Aunt Phoebe and the Major. None of us will leave you until Miss Dirks comes back."

She looked up at them then in a dazed way, still sobbing, her pudgy face swollen, and Ransome said, "Lady Esketh asked me to look after you, and Miss Dirks, too. I promised them both. You can live in my house if you like."

For a moment the disordered mind groped to understand the miracle which had happened . . . that she should be invited to live in the house of a man of the world like Ransome. The sobbing stopped and she said, timidly, "Would it be proper?"

Ransome patted her shoulder and said, "That doesn't matter. Of course it is." And then, quite sanely, she said, "Thank you. That's very kind of you. I'll come with you."

When he left the Mission she went with him back to his own house, where John the Baptist prepared a room for her on the first floor. She began to cry again, saying, "You're so good to me. I've been through so much. I didn't know people could be so good. When Sarah comes back she'll thank you properly. I'm so bad at such things."

Then she seemed happy, and that night she had dinner with him, telling him eagerly about the Bishops and the aristocracy. She had, it appeared, forgotten entirely the rape and the ensuing pregnancy.

But a little after ten o'clock John the Baptist appeared in Ransome's bedroom to say that the strange Memsaheb was going away again. He stopped her on the drive. She told him that she was going to Lady Esketh, who wouldn't know what to do without her. Gently, patiently, he persuaded her that Lady Esketh was dead and that there was nothing more to be done for her.

At the end of the week Aunt Phoebe and the Smileys gave the first of their Saturday lunch parties since the disaster. Confidentially Aunt Phoebe said to Ransome, "I don't suppose it will be as gay as the old parties were, but I'm a great believer in habit and routine. There's nothing so good for making you forget things as carrying on in the same old rut."

So about twelve o'clock there gathered about the long table in the Smileys' kitchen the old members of the Saturday Lunch Club. Poor Mr. Jobnekar was gone forever, but in his place there were two new members —Fern and Miss Hodge. For Miss Hodge was one of them now. She had a whole committee of guardians—Ransome and Aunt Phoebe, the Smileys and Fern, the Major and Raschid Ali Khan and even Miss MacDaid. She had, it seemed, forgotten the unfortunate episode with the Sikh and the ensuing worries; she spoke less of Miss Dirks and she seemed to have reconciled herself to the death of Lady Esketh. She moved between Ransome's house and the Mission, sometimes straying as far as the hospital, wandering along the road holding conversations with imaginary people. In Europe this behavior would have aroused mockery and perhaps even resentment, but in Ranchipur everybody knew about her and no one took the least notice. She forgot the tragedies of Miss Dirks and Lady

Esketh perhaps because she had a childlike mind, but also she was pleased now and satisfied and free. Poor Miss Hodge who for twenty-five years had wanted to go about and know interesting people, found in her madness a kind of prestige which life had always denied her.

Ransome and Homer Smiley came directly to lunch from the Orphanage, where the Ministry of Public Welfare had already set up a temporary office from which they distributed rice and *gram* and millet and set about a survey of contaminated wells. Miss MacDaid for the sake of exercise came on a bicycle instead of a *tonga*, accompanied by Fern.

On the way out from town, while they pedaled along side by side, Miss MacDaid conducted an examination of Fern, shouting at her whenever the bicycles drew a little apart. She began by calling out, "You're absolutely sure you want to be a nurse?"

"Yes, I'm sure."

"What makes you think so?"

Then for a time Fern pedaled in silence and at last she said, "Well, I do. I could give you a lot of reasons, but they'd all add up to the same thing. I want to stay here and I want to be a nurse."

"I always heard that you said you hated Ranchipur and talked against it."

Fern blushed. "I did, I guess, but it was different then." Her bicycle ran into a hole in the road, and to right herself she described a large arc which took her far away from Miss MacDaid.

"Well, it's worse now than it was before," shouted Miss MacDaid.

"No," Fern called back over her shoulder. "It's different now. I want to live and work here in Ranchipur and I don't know anything. I've never been educated properly. I think learning to be a nurse is the best way to make myself of some use."

Then until they reached Distillery Corner Miss MacDaid pedaled in silence, ruminating upon the strangeness of people and of Fern Simon in particular. She thought she knew why the girl had changed in such an extraordinary fashion, but her common sense told her that such a reason for change was not to be trusted. Love, Miss MacDaid supposed, was all right in its place, but a girl shouldn't let it dominate the whole of her life. You couldn't depend on it. After the first transports, everything depended upon how much wear and tear you could endure without changing your mind and breaking up. And in Ranchipur there was plenty of wear and tear, what with the vile climate and Hindu intrigues and shiftlessness and gossip and one thing and another. Besides the girl was much too pretty to be a good nurse. A nurse should never be too pretty; it made other women hostile and upset men patients. "A good nurse," thought Miss MacDaid, pedaling rapidly, "ought to look like an old Shire mare, the way I do."

"I want you to be sure in your own mind," she called across to Fern.

"I *am* sure."

She felt shy with Miss MacDaid—Miss MacDaid, who could be so gentle in dressing a wound, could be rough and agonizing in dealing with human frailty. But even if Fern had not been shy, she could not have told the reasons why she was so sure; she could not tell Miss MacDaid that she had changed not because she was in love with Tom, but because since that first night when he had taken her back and deposited her at the Smileys' she had been discovering many things, among them something known as common sense. She couldn't, for fear that Miss MacDaid would think her potty, tell the old war horse that since that night everything in the world had changed for her because something had been happening inside herself. She couldn't explain to Miss MacDaid that all the silliness, the sloppiness, the nonsense, had gone out of her forever in the misery she had seen in the hospital and at the Music School, or that the Ranchipur where she and Miss MacDaid were now cycling, was an utterly different Ranchipur from the one in which she had spent nearly the whole of her life. It wasn't the earthquake and the flood which had changed her, but something inside herself and something she had found in Tom and the Smileys and Aunt Phoebe and Miss MacDaid herself, and even in poor Lady Esketh—an honesty, a simplicity, a friendliness. Miss MacDaid would certainly think her crazy if she were to say that the very stones of the road, the leaves on the trees, the houses, the bullock carts, were new to her and charged with excitement and interest. It was exciting now to be pedaling along the Racecourse road, exciting to be talking to Miss MacDaid, exciting to think that in a few minutes she would see Tom and have him grin at her and press her hand beneath the table. It wasn't necessary to invent a character known as Blythe Summerfield, "The Pearl of the Orient." She even minded less the death of her father and poor Hazel. That was something which seemed to have happened years and years ago in another life.

Beside her, Miss MacDaid's stout legs pedaled faster and faster as her matter-of-fact brain worked faster and faster. She had now reached that stage where she was selling Fern to herself, because she wanted so much against her own common sense and experience to believe in the girl. She wanted desperately some one to carry on at the hospital when she herself became tired and old, some one who was young and strong as an ox, as she herself had always been, and Fern, if her strength and stubbornness held out, might be just the one. Certainly the girl was healthy to have gone through what she had been through and still look fresh, with color in her cheeks. Miss MacDaid tried to find reasons against Fern's plan, but always she found herself brought up sharply before one fact . . . that at the hospital and in the shambles of the Music School the girl had taken on and carried through without complaint a task which would have floored many a trained and veteran nurse. Talking to herself, she said: "You can't deny that. The girl has guts."

For the heart of Miss MacDaid was happy again, even when she looked at the gray suffering face of the Major; he would, she knew, one day recover from his suffering. There was no time now for suffering. Work would cure him, work would cauterize the wounds. In her flat-footed honesty she did not pretend to regret the death of Lady Esketh but regarded it rather as an intercession on the part of the gods; in a way it had been Lady Esketh's own fault, the result of her shallow life with its vanity and luxury and idleness and folly. If she had troubled to have had a typhoid inoculation she would not now be dead; but all things considered, for the good of the hospital and their work and the Major himself and the thousands who depended upon him, perhaps even for Lady Esketh herself, it was better that she was dead. Only one thing troubled her conscience, and that was the memory of having written down the name of Lady Esketh on the list of dying before she burned it.

"But that kind of thing," she kept telling herself, "is pure nonsense. That couldn't have had anything to do with it." Nevertheless the memory filled her with shame . . . that she, Miss MacDaid, the head of the Ranchipur Hospital, could sink to the level of indulging in witchcraft and hocus-pocus. But sometimes, in the night, she wondered about it; perhaps there was some sinister power in such goings-on which science had not yet explained.

The party, as Aunt Phoebe had foreseen, was not gay; it was friendly and it recaptured a little of that spirit of unity which had kept the little group together for so many years. None of them, save Miss Hodge, was able to shake off the presence of Edwina and poor Miss Dirks, Mr. Jobnekar and his family, Elmer and Hazel Simon, and all the others.

They were all there somehow, all the dead, in the Smiley's big cool kitchen, even when for a little time the group, talking of the plans for the new city, grew enthusiastic, and the old fire appeared for an instant in the eyes of the Major. They would always be there, for they were a part of the change, but their presence would grow a little less real with each week, each month, each year, because, as Aunt Phoebe said, the dead were gone and the living had such a poor time of it that there would be plenty to do besides mope.

At four o'clock the Major and Miss MacDaid rose to return to the hospital, Miss MacDaid with something of the old flustered, happy look in her eyes which had been there before Edwina came to Ranchipur. The Major belonged to her again, at least for a little time, and since that sudden mystical vision on the night she thought him dead, she possessed him in a new and more satisfactory way.

As Ransome and Homer Smiley left to return to the office of the Ministry of Public Welfare they encountered at the very doorway the figure of a plump little man with a pot belly, the pallid skin of the Englishman who has been too long in India, and the pomposity of an Eastern bank manager. It was Mr. Hoggett-Egburry who had come, he said, to thank the Smileys for all their kindness to his wife and to recover the magpie collection of bric-à-brac which she had left in Aunt Phoebe's care. Mrs. Hoggett-Egburry was, he said, well enough, but a little tired and very upset by all the sufferings she had been through. He was sending her back to England to her own people on a holiday. As he told this bit of news a sigh escaped him, the faintest ghost of a sigh, but one charged with relief, for he knew as well as the others that she would never return to India. It wasn't the first time such a thing had happened. She would go home and be lost at once in the swamp of mediocrity, in a whole society of people like herself who had been pinched and blanched and made bilious by the awfulness of India.

Ransome thought, "Anyway she's better off than most. She drinks, and when she's drunk she can still think she's important."

[595]

As Mr. Hoggett-Egburry entered the house, Ransome said to Homer Smiley, "I shall miss Pukka Lil. She'll leave a hole. Every Indian state should have at least one Pukka Lil. It's part of the scenery like the snakes and the temples."

Homer Smiley grinned, "I shouldn't worry," he said. "There'll be another along at any minute. There's probably one on tomorrow's train."

At sundown Ransome sat on his verandah on the side of the house overlooking the racecourse and the flat red muddy plain that extended as far as Mount Abana and the dead Moghul city of El-Kautara. There was no more brandy and whisky in Ranchipur, but there was gin brought in one of the first trains by Mr. Bottlewallah, an enterprising Parsee merchant, and so he drank gin and tonic water which he did not like but was the only thing available.

At the gateway beneath the great banyan John the Baptist squatted with two friends, making music with a flute and two drums. Beyond, across the flat expanse of the racecourse, a long procession of cows and water buffaloes moved toward the sunset, goaded from the rear by a black little urchin who carried a long bamboo pole. It was the hour of all the day which Ransome loved best, when the scent of jasmine came out strongly from the vine which covered half the house, to mingle with the odor of wood and cow dung smoke and spices. The rain had stopped for a time and the sun, setting, had turned the scudding clouds overhead a magnificent red and gold. Across the red plain violet light lay flatly like a fog, blurring the silhouettes of the returning cattle.

He was tired now by the long day of work in steam-bath heat, by the clamoring and quarreling of the swarming hordes at the storehouse, but most of all by the accumulated weariness of days. He thought, sipping comfortably his gin and tonic, "Fern will be along presently."

But it was the thought of Edwina which kept returning to him. All the way home from the Orphanage he had thought of her, wondering at her story and the odd destiny that finished her off in a place like Ranchipur. Now he thought, suddenly, "It's a pity she couldn't have come to the Saturday party. She would have liked it so much." And he saw with astonishment how well she would have fitted in with the others. She had belonged to them always, but the discovery of the fact had come too late.

The rest of her life had all been wasted. The thought threw a new light upon her curious, perverse character.

Then as he lighted a cigar he saw coming down the road from the direction of the town the bullock carriage of the Maharani. It was moving at a quick trot, the gait which the old lady liked and the bullocks detested, but as the carriage approached his own house the driver checked the bullocks to a walk, and as they passed his own gateway two heads were thrust out from beneath the gilded leather hood and looked toward his house. At sight of him seated on the veranda they were withdrawn again quickly but not before he had recognized one of them as the Maharani and the other as Aunt Phoebe. Chuckling, he thought, "The last Queen and the last democrat riding out together," and there swept over him a profound wave of love for this preposterous and beautiful and terrible country, this India where tragedy and farce lay so near to each other just beneath the surface of life.

In the gateway John the Baptist and his friends, recovering from the salaams into which they had thrown themselves at sight of the royal bullocks, resumed their music, the sound drifting over the plain to lose itself in the growing violet light. For a long time he sat with his eyes closed, listening lazily with half his mind, thinking of nothing in particular, but filled with wonder at the intricacy and the improbable beauty and cruelty of man's existence. Beyond the racecourse there rose suddenly at the moment the sun slipped below the horizon, the long-drawn, solitary cry of a jackal and his whole body contracted for a second because the sound was so like that of the wails which had risen from the dying city as the flood swept down upon it. Then another jackal howled, and another, and suddenly, swiftly, the darkness came down as if a black curtain had fallen, and between the wildly drifting clouds the stars came out, glittering in the clean-washed air like the diamonds of the Maharani. In the gateway beneath the ancient banyan the black figures of John the Baptist and his friends dissolved into the darkness, but the music of the flute and drums went on and on in the hot damp stillness.

THE END

Begun in Cooch Behar, January, 1933
Completed in New York, July, 1937